JANE KAMENSKY AND JILL LEPORE

Blindspot

A NOVEL

SPIEGEL & GRAU

TRADE PAPERBACKS

NEW YORK

2009 Spiegel & Grau Trade Paperback Edition

Published in the United States by Spiegel & Grau, an imprint of
The Random House Publishing Group, a division of Random House, Inc., New York.

SPIEGEL & GRAU and Design is a registered trademark of Random House, Inc.

RANDOM HOUSE READER'S CIRCLE & Design is a registered trademark of
Random House, Inc.

Originally published in hardcover in the United States by Spiegel & Grau, an imprint of
The Random House Publishing Group, a division of Random House, Inc., in 2008.

Map on pages 510–11 courtesy of the Library of Congress, Geography and Map Division.

Library of Congress Cataloging-in-Publication Data
Kamensky, Jane.
Blindspot / Jane Kamensky and Jill Lepore.
p. cm.
ISBN 978-0-385-52620-3
1. Painters—Fiction. 2. Exiles—Fiction. 3. Scots—New York—Fiction. 4. Scots—
United States—History—18th century—Fiction. I. Lepore, Jill. II. Title.
PS3611.A466B57 2008
813'.6—dc22   2008003111

Printed in the United States of America

www.randomhousereaderscircle.com

2 4 6 8 9 7 5 3 1

Book design by Caroline Cunningham

To our husbands

One thing, kind Sir, of you I crave,
Tis that which you can never have,
Nor ever had in ages past,
Nor ever will while time shall last;
Yet if you love me, as you say,
You'll give it me without delay.

Public practice of any art,
and staring in men's faces,
is very indelicate in a female.
—SAMUEL JOHNSON
(1709–1784)

A painter must paint.
—STEWART JAMESON
(B. 1735–)

FROM THE *EDINBURGH EVENING COURANT*,
APRIL 15, 1764.

ESCAPED

*T*he fifth day this month, from the Sheriff of
the City of Edinburgh, one Stewart Jameson,
face-painter and libertine, on pain of being confined
for debt. He is an able-bodied man of near thirty
years, over six feet tall, has black hair, and blue eyes.
He is likely to style himself a gentleman. Had on,
when last seen, a brown coat, a fawn-colored waistcoat, an old red great coat, a cocked hat, and sundry
other clothes. He may be in company with a Negro
man of about five-and-twenty years of age, who lately
ran away from his master, the Earl of Berkeley. This
Negro, whose name is Fortune, is very dark, stands five
foot nine inches, and is a thin, lathey-made fellow.
Had on, when he went away, a white shirt, a cloth
waistcoat with worsted lace on it, leather breeches,
light blue stockings, and silver buckles. Speaks good
English, and can read and write. He may try to pass
for a doctor. Both men are very much addicted to card
playing and horse racing. The pair may attempt to
ship for the colonies. Whoever takes up one or both,
and secures them, that they may be brought to the said
Sheriff, shall have the cost of their passage returned,
plus a reward of eight pounds for Jameson, four for
the other, promised by R. McGREEVY & Brothers,
Merchants.

N.B. All masters of vessels and others are forbid to
entertain, conceal, or carry off said fugitives.

A PAINTER'S EYE

The Life, Art, and Adventures

of Stewart Jameson

CHAPTER I

In Which the Author's Forbearance
Is Amply Demonstrated

Had Columbus my gut, the world would be a smaller place. And maybe the better for it. O brave new world: wild, rebellious, mysterious, and strange. And distant. God above, who knew it could be so bloody far?

Now begins a gentleman's exile, and, with it, my tale.

You may wonder, dear Reader, dear, unfathomable Reader, why I have undertaken this voyage, why a man of parts, of fine parts, I may say, and education, better than most, would hazard a crossing and that, in April, the most treacherous of months—showers sweet turn to tempests bitter—and, worse, on a galleon with no berth for a gentleman but a bunk not fit for a dog, not even my mastiff, Gulliver—and I, though six foot tall, his Lilliputian—who, despite my best efforts, splays himself, fleas and all, atop my moth-ridden blanket, with me huddled under it, as if I were a city and he a great army, equipped with cauldrons of drool, besieging me.

While you wonder why I wander, know this: run I must.

Aye, I would have stayed home if I could. If I could. Instead, each day the winds blow me farther from the dales and vales of Jamesons past, clan of clans, men among men, though, truth be told—and here, dear Reader, it will be told, and without ornament—our tartan is sold by the yard at Covent Garden to every shaver, ever striver, every waster with twopence in his pocket and a plan to marry a merry widow with ten thousand a year and an estate in Derbyshire, with horses, comely, and tenants, timely in their rents. Had I ever come across such a lady—let us call her the Widow Bountiful—I would have wooed her with sighs enough to heat a stone-cold bed-chamber in the dead of winter. Perhaps she waits for me, my Widow B., somewhere on the other side of this wretched sea. Hark, she pants for me. Or, no, 'tis only Gulliver, giant cur.

As a man of both sense and sincerity, I admit, freely, and with that same unsparing candor which you must henceforth expect of me, that I leave behind little but debt. Twould be an even greater sorrow to leave Edinburgh, that nursery of enlightened genius, did not each degree of longitude stretch the distance betwixt me and my creditors, to whom I owe so much gold, and so little gratitude, the brothers McGreevy, with their Monday duns, Tuesday threats, and Wednesday bludgeons. Suffice to say: I sailed on a Thursday, a day too late, with the scars to show for it. Departed, the *Sea-Serpent*, April 5, 1764.

Sterner men on stouter ships have crossed this vast and furious ocean, training their hopeful gaze upon the horizon; I, ever squeamish, scan only the depths and see naught but gloom. I would blind myself—and spare you the sight—but I find, as ever, that I cannot close my painter's eye. Here the blue sloshes into green, and there, gray, and just here, as I lean over the gunwales, lo but the ocean becomes a rainbow of muck, a palette of putrefaction. The lurching, the To and the Fro, are my twin tormentors; and the sea, my sewer and my jailer.

Wheel of Fortune, pray, turn: let some young Bluebeard take the *Sea-Serpent* as his prize. Let his pirates throw me overboard. Let them haul me 'neath the keel and drown me. Sweet Jesus, just get me off this ship.

Captain Pumble, a bulge-eyed, blotchy frog of a man, hops about the deck, uncloaked, even against the fearsome wind, as I, shivering, lean over the rails once again. He tells me that Boston will be temperate by the time we dock.

"Yar, 'twill be blooming in the city," croaks he, clapping me on the back, as jolly as if we were sat in a tavern, instead of steering through a storm. "Ladies walking about without shawls. And a dandy, and a Scots gent, no less, will be most welcome by the lasses. Or is it the gents you favor, Jameson?"

Between you and me, Reader: this Pumble has not entirely earned my affection.

"At the moment, Captain," I manage to reply. "I favor deep pockets. Deep pockets, and solid ground."

It is customary, at this point in a narrative of a gentleman's adventures in the world, be he knave or rogue, to offer a pedigree. So be it.

The brown hound that whelped my Gulliver belonged to a butcher who cut meat for the Laird of Firth, a corpulent and stingy man—for I find that podginess and parsimony generally travel together—who claimed that his mastiffs were descended from the kennel of the Kubla Khan, brought West by Marco Polo, and on down, across the generations, to the court of Henry VIII and his bloody Mary, and thence to Scotland. In Firth, the Laird fed his dogs better than most gentlemen feed their valets. But the old miser—too cheap to pay for the meat—instead gave the butcher his best bitch, her belly swollen with pups who, once weaned, nearly ate the butcher out of his shop. Cheated and bested, he returned the litter to the Laird. Twas then came I to town, to paint a portrait of the Laird and his favorite dog, a beast as big as himself, with teeth a sailor might scrimshaw. The subject would have defeated even my friend Gainsborough. My portrait, a study in Venetian red, caught the Laird's greed in his ruddy cheeks, his bleary eyes, his dog's great maw. Alas, rarely does a man love his true self. Seeing his and his mascot's likeness so well captured displeased this gentleman, who refused to pay the balance of my fee, instead tendering a black-and-white pup, the runt of the litter, though as tall at the withers as a lad of ten. And so was I saddled with Gulliver, sired by gullibility, son of a butcher's bitch.

A devil's bargain, you might think, Reader: 'twas either the cur, or naught. Would you deny me the dog's company? Surely my exile would be even lonelier had I forfeited my fee. And be forewarned: I have made worse bargains.

CHAPTER 2

In Which Our Author Secures a Situation in a City on a Hill

As Pumble navigated the *Sea-Serpent* through the harbor—I craving land more than poor, scurvy Magellan ever did, and Gulliver, galumphing about deck, in a frenzy of anticipation—we sailed past a chain of small islands, perfect refuges for pirates.

"Are you quite sure we won't run aground, Captain?" I ventured, for, though the day was clear and the water calm, we tacked perilous close to the isles.

"I could put you at the helm, if you like, Jameson. Got the sea in your blood, eh?" he smirked. But then he softened, slightly. "No, you sorry Scot. Rest easy. I won't smash her to bits. Though this shallow harbor has wrecked many a ship, I don't mind saying."

"Shallow, Captain?" I asked nervously.

"Yar, she's deep enough for the *Sea-Serpent*, but New York, where I'm bound, has deeper. Which is why that city builds banking houses, while this here Boston builds churches." He nodded toward the town—cut against the sky, as if in silhouette—and pointed out the North Church, with its proud wooden spire, the tallest among a thicket of steeples. Prim, pious, and provincial. Trim, trim, and tidy, all.

"Ah, well then," I answered, brightening. "Tis proved: a merchant measures his prospects by a port's fathoms and not by its people's piety, just as a whore measures a man's parts by the bulge of his purse and not of his breeches."

Pumble rewarded me with no more than a mincing smile.

Mark me, dear Reader: bidding my captain farewell will not break my heart.

Closer to shore, I spied people bustling about—along streets riddled with ruts and gutters of mud and manure whose stench reached us even before we docked—everyone hurrying, but at a trot and not a gallop. Here is no London, where men race as foxes chased by hounds. Here is a place where, pray God, I can stand still.

I put on my hat, left my bags on board, and stepped ashore. Stumbling about the dock, my spirits soon improved, and my gut seemed to slow and finally halt its orbit round my middle. Along what is called the Long Wharf, I found a tavern, the Blue Herring, and I quaffed. Say I: there is fine beer here, brewed, I am told, by a man named Adams, in barrels built of the pine woods of New Hampshire. Steadied, fortified, I took a brief tour of the waterfront, and report, also, this: if there is nothing elevated and fine in the town of Boston, there is little to be found that is particularly unpleasant, save the restraint of the townspeople, who stare at strangers—even at a tall, brass-buttoned Scottish gentleman, and likelier than most—with a coldness that runs to cruelty.

I next made my way west along King Street, cluttered with shops, though whether this ambitious avenue is a credit to our third George in this, the fifth year of his reign, I could not claim. The trade seemed lackluster at best. Along a street called Corn-hill, I saw an utter desolation: the ruins of dwelling-houses, stores, and shops, burned in a fire that looked to have raged some winters ago, in a city too straitened to rebuild.

Just in front of a brick building called the Town House, which sits in the very middle of King Street, I found a spindle-shanked boy, no more than ten, peddling salted cod wrapped in old newspaper.

"I'm afraid I can't stomach the fish, lad," I said to him. "But be so good as to tell me where I might find fresher news than what's printed in your wrappers."

He directed me up an alley dubbed Crooked Lane—though all the streets here would equally well bear that name—to a dark, cluttered print shop whose stink made my eyes to tear ere I crossed the threshold. (My father had once wanted to apprentice me to an engraver, Reader, but I forswore the trade just as soon as I learned that every printer washes his plates in his own water. I would not toil in a piss-house.)

Behind the counter, tinkering with types, stood a man of about my own age, wise-eyed and wigless, his face as flat and round as the moon, his ginger hair tied back. From this gentleman, Mr. Benjamin Edes, I purchased a deck of cards, a map, and, for five shillings, a rather windy history of the town, written by one Thomas Newcombe, wherein I have since read that Boston's founder, a proper Puritan named John Winthrop, proclaimed to his followers in 1630, as they neared shore: "We shall be as a City upon a Hill, the eyes of all people are upon us; so that if we shall deal falsely with our God, we shall be made a story and a byword through the world."

Now, careful Reader, I ask you this: From such a lofty start, can any city do less than fall? 'Tis a small port, and charming enough. But it does not content itself with its smallness, its slack bustle, its less-than-profound harbor. Nay, 'twould be Jerusalem. Here is a town that, by pretending to be more than it is, makes itself less. I had rather not draw an overhasty conclusion. But I have to wonder whether this is what hobbles Boston: its oversized ambition. The very opposite of what hobbles me.

While the printer tallied my items in his ledger, I picked up a copy of his twice-weekly newspaper, the *Boston Gazette*, and flipped to its back pages, filled with advertisements: "A fine Negro Male Child to be given away. It has been kept remote from the Small-Pox." "To be SOLD: The very Best Vinegar for Pickles." "RAN AWAY from his Master: A stout Irish servant."

"Are you looking for something else, sir?" Edes asked.

"Aye. My bearings."

"Just landed, I take it? If you don't mind my saying, sir, you're still a bit green about the gills."

"Green's an improvement, I assure you," was my smiling reply. "Aye, I'm just in, from Edinburgh."

"It's as well you ain't come from London, sir, else you'd bring bad tidings, sure."

I gave him a puzzled expression.

"You wouldn't have heard, sir, if you've been at sea these last two months. Parliament voted as you set sail, and the news washed up on our shores the day before you did. I'm just now setting the type to put it in Thursday's edition. Bastards mean to tax us to pay for their war, what's ended not a twelvemonth ago, with the French and the Indians. Tax our sugar, they will. Worse: we ain't allowed to pay with our own paper money. Coin of the realm, it has to be. I ask you, sir, who has hard money in these hard times? And mind, they promise, next, to tax with stamps our every piece of paper!"

"I'm sorry to hear it," I offered, and sincerely. I liked this plainspoken printer, and admired his argument, for the town looked poor enough already.

"Not so sorry as you'll be when the shops start closing, for ain't we struggling, after seven years of war? But I suppose I needn't tell a Scotsman about English wars and English taxes."

"Aye, that you don't," I agreed. "My grandfather fell at Culloden. But I trust you colonials will protest these measures. For as I always say, an empty stomach has a loud mouth."

"Ain't heard that one afore, sir, and 'tis true enough," he said, flashing a smile. "But we won't be laughing when the King sends over his redcoats, those lobsterbacked sons of bitches! Their fingers will be in our purses soon enough. There's only so much a free people will bear, I tell you, and only so far the hand of tyranny can stretch, ere its reach exceeds its grasp."

I shook my head, and pushed back my hat.

"Edes, your metaphors alarm me. Many's the hand I would welcome in my pocket," I said with a wink. "But not the hand of tyranny."

Now did the printer laugh, easy, warm, and unrestrained.

"Say, Edes, do you get any Scottish papers here?"

"Indeed, sir. When traveling gentlemen bring them by. You'll have no trouble hearing news from home. Old news, mind, but news just the same."

Reader, this news of news is good and bad. Maybe I haven't fled far enough.

"Let me know when the next batch comes in, will you?"

"Certainly, sir. But where will I find you?"

"Aye, where? A fine question. Do you know of any lodgings?"

"I do, sir. I do at that. Old Ayers, the cooper, is looking to rent, though I don't know what he'd make of your small horse here." He nudged Gulliver's slobbering snout off the counter. "Would you be needing a stable for this beast, then?"

"Better a barracks," I countered.

"I can see he's as fierce as a foot soldier and sharper than a bayonet," Edes agreed, with counterfeit gravity. "But still, I fancy Ayers's house might suit you."

He directed my attention to the following advertisement, in the paper at hand:

> *TO BE LET* on reasonable Terms by Elnathan Ayers, a commodious well-finished Brick Dwelling House on Queen Street, having six Fine Rooms in it, with a large Pantry, a Plank Cellar sixty Feet long, a good Paved Yard, a choice Well of Water, and a Cistern that holds ten Hogsheads of Rain. Very convenient & suitable to carry on Business. Also a Tenement, attached, with Two Rooms. Any Person who can give good Security for the Payment of the Rent may apply to the Printer hereof, and know further.

"This may well fit my needs," I said, cheerfully, for I was delighted at the description. "Where might I find Mr. Ayers?"

I will spare you, patient Reader, whose patience I endeavor not to try, a tedious recounting of my interview with Ayers, the ease with which I convinced him to waive his request for security—and quieted his fear of my four-footed companion—the miscellany of annoyances I encountered in arranging for my baggage to be removed from the pier—and the savor of my first meal on this side of that wide water: a plate of green peas, a rasher of bacon, and more beer—which, I happily report, did not revolt at digestion. Instead, know only this: we had landed just after dawn; by dusk I was settled in my new lodgings at Queen Street, having agreed to keep on two servants housed in the tenement—a man and his wife, by the name of Goddard—employed by the previous occupant.

And lo, I am, here in America, a new man. In the great ledger that is life, I have so far tallied more than my share of misfortunes, but for my talent with the brush, a gift for which I cannot claim much, except that I have seized it. Tis a small canvas, this Boston, but I will grace it with my art. The past be damned: a stranger can make the world anew. If Fate favors me, I may even find my Fortune before the McGreevys find me.

And yet: What else does a portrait painter require to establish his reputation? Before entertaining sitters, he must have an apprentice, an assistant of some promise—but not, mind, too much—and eager to please. On this, my second day in a town that will ever fall short of its ambition but which, I hope, will realize mine, I retraced my steps to Edes's shop, this time to place my own advertisement in his *Gazette*, of June 4, 1764, *viz.*:

> Stewart Jameson, Portrait Painter, Has lately arrived from Edinburgh, and Takes this Opportunity to ac- quaint the Public of this City, that he is removed to Queen Street, near Mr. Cabot, Chemist. He conducts Face-painting, and hath at present by him, a large Col- lection of Gentlemen and Ladies Pictures, which may be seen at his House.

> *N.B.* Wanted, A Likely Lad, from fourteen to nine- teen Years of Age, of a promising Genius, to wait as an Apprentice to Mr. Jameson. Inquire of the Painter.

From the *Boston Gazette*, Thursday, June 7, 1764.

LONDON.

As Readers in New-England have a particular interest in the resolutions recently debated in Parliament, the printer takes the liberty of excerpting, below, a report received from a ship just arrived from London.

— B. T. Edes.

Extracts from the Votes of the House of Commons on March 10, 1764.

Resolutions from the Committee charged to consider further Ways and Means for raising the revenue to His Majesty, in consideration of the cost of the recent War in America, which has doubled Britain's debt, so that more than half the kingdom's annual revenues are now devoted to paying interest on the balance, *viz.*:

Resolved, That a further duty be laid upon all Sugars imported into any British colony or plantation in America.

Resolved, That none of His Majesty's colonies or plantations in America shall be allowed, after the 8th of October 1764, to print, issue, publish, or use any of its own paper bills of credit as legal tender, or in payment of any bargains, contracts, debts, dues, or demands whatsoever, as such colonial paper money is prejudicial to the trade and commerce of His Majesty's subjects.

Resolved, That all the said duties shall be paid, in hard coin, into the receipt of His Majesty's Exchequer, and there reserved, to be disposed of by Parliament, toward defraying the necessary expenses of defending and protecting the British possessions in America.

Resolved, That it may be proper to charge certain Stamp duties in the said colonies and plantations.

Letter I.

To Miss Elizabeth Partridge
Delancey Street
New York City

June the 24th, 1764

To my ever kind Elizabeth,

How glorious to write those words again, though it will shock you to see my once-familiar hand. Companion of my youth, now as lost to me as my own innocence! I once lived from fortnight to fortnight, awaiting the next link in the chain of ink upon paper that bound us one to the other, closer kin than sisters. It has been three years, two months, and eighteen days since I broke that chain, sundered it utterly, without warning. Not a letter, not a word.

What can you have made of my silence? Surely you think me dead, a kinder ending than the gossips here in Boston must have given my tale. You did well to mourn me, for the girl you knew *is* lost to this world. But do not bury me quite yet, dear Elizabeth. Rather I entreat you to hear my heart's secrets, keep them close, and nurse with me a faint, nay, blasphemous hope for my second birth.

You will deem me coy, I fear. But pray, do not judge me harshly for practicing now the girlish indirection we disdained in our younger years. A woman's life, as I have been forced to learn, is far stranger, crueler, and more tangled than the plots of those sentimental novels we once read. Perhaps your own world still resembles those fictions, and your virtue, like Pamela's, has been rewarded at last. I cannot say the same.

You have grown, I suppose, into a well-married gentlewoman, a babe even now playing in your flower garden. You will be happy, and pleased with your life, and you may fault me for revealing too little, too late. Trust that it would be worse, far worse, to tell you too much, too soon.

To know me now you must first revise the miniature portrait I painted for you when we parted. There you see a younger me, still a girl, in a fine, chaste gown of azure satin, my auburn curls carefully piled atop my head by the doting maidservant who tried, in vain, to take the place of my poor mother. From your mind's eye, if not from that portrait's velvet envelope, you must rub that picture out. Long since, my locks have been clipped as short and crudely as any lamb's, by shearers whose only thought is to deny vermin room to secret themselves. Barely female, and scarcely human, I wear a shapeless suit of rough muslin, parti-colored as if for a prisoner within the walls of Newgate, cloth woven by my own work-roughened hands, no woman's hands, much less a lady's. Certainly not Fanny Easton's. "Weston" was the name I gave them, and am known by no other.

Do you imagine me seated in a turkey-work chair before the polished mahogany table in my father's book-filled study as I pen these lines? That sketch, too, you must erase. I sit on a bench of rude planking before a pine table heaped with rags. The quill that speaks here, the sheets I write upon, even the time I borrow to tell you my tale: I have purloined them all.

Oh, that I had the palette to limn the scene for you, my dearest, my only friend! I live now on Tremont Street, three blocks and a world away from my father's merchant palace on Hanover. I pray that nothing you have experienced will allow you to picture this place. You must never have had occasion to notice the building, though 'tis one of the largest in this town, for 'twas designed to house the swelling ranks of the poor. More than a hundred and fifty of us, women and children, toil here—oh, so wretchedly do we toil!—in the threadmill, at the looms and wheels, in the bleach yard, and in the dye room, worked to the bone.

Townsmen in love with the idea of their own benevolence call this the Manufactory House. Witness the ennobling effects of industry! See the fruits of busy hands! I, who have earned my coarse bread here for more than two years, know better. This is a workhouse. Every day save Sunday (when I am made to praise my rescuers), I labor every minute there is light. I pick rags and untangle old rope; I spin thread and twine; I weave tick and diaper and handkerchief, using checks and stripes that cannot mask the crudeness of the cloth. The hours of darkness I pass on a dirty straw pallet beneath rough sheeting. How I curse these long summer days, wondering at the vicious calculus that weighs June's endless toil against January's endless night! Yes, I have a roof over my head, and enough thin gruel to keep me working, if less than alive. And there were months—long, cold months—when I knew neither. But no matter how often my keepers remind me that gratitude must answer generosity, I refuse to call myself fortunate. Lizzie, you must forget what we learned of charity from the ladies of King's Chapel. Poverty wants means, not morals.

The virtuous—I no longer count myself among them—would tell you otherwise. They need our salvation, for it confirms their own. Last week my father himself paraded through these very doors, dressed in ivory ruffles and pale green baize that matched his eyes, flanked by several of his fellow Overseers of the Poor, come on a mission to inspect their charges. In a room filled with sixty whirring wheels, and as many stooped and desperate women, he watched me spin. From not ten feet away, I stared back at him, refusing to lower my gaze before my betters. And then he turned to converse with one of his partners in this venture, his neighbor—though never his friend—Hiram Usher. While the two of them bent close to talk over the noise, I plundered his bag of this letter book, fresh from Mr. Edes's shop, along with an old *Gazette*, filled with news of men growing sour over sugar, as if there weren't enough bitterness in this world already. Father did not, could not see me, there among the hungry and the ragged. He cannot allow himself to recognize what he allowed me to become.

But Edward Easton is a good man! you will protest. And the world agrees with you. He is so far advanced in rank, even from when you knew him, Lizzie, that he now sits on this colony's highest court. He prospers, certainly. I cannot puzzle how he has managed it, but my fall has not checked his rise.

And how did I fall, you will ask? Far, and fast. Oh, Lizzie, must I retrace for you the course of my decline? Am I to play Moll Flanders—

nay, even Fanny Hill—to your Pamela? If it secures your sympathy, surely I must.

My first sorrow you know only too well: when I was twelve, with so many men away at war and so many soldiers bringing smallpox to the city, Mother died, claimed by that dread epidemic that also took my little brother and only sister. How sad and silent our household became! Just one brother left to me, sweet Daniel, then but fourteen, and already as distracted by grief as I was.

A captain of trade, Father knew not how to pilot a motherless girl across the shoals of womanhood. First he thought to buy me a companion. He settled on a young Negro girl, just four years my senior. But no servant can be a friend. In my heart, I remained alone. And though Father's loneliness was no less terrible, we could not find each other.

Unable to bear the sight of my mother's face copied in mine, he sent me to board at a dame school filled with silly girls—with you, the only pearl—to study French and violin, religion, just enough of history to recite the deeds of great men for good enough husbands, and a smidgen of geography, for what do girls need to know of the wide world?

I tell you, Lizzie, I have seen at once too much of that world, and too little. When our schoolmistress's carping tongue said my hands would best a needle fit, she meant crewelwork, not the cruel work heaped upon me here. She taught us embroidery, but my efforts could not match those of the better seven-year-olds. Perhaps my sampler still hangs on the wall in Father's library:

> *This needlework of mine can tell*
> *That I a child was learned well*
> *And by my elders I was taught*
> *Not to spend my time for naught.*

Fanny Easton, in the 12th year of her Age, 1756

The verse was clumsier even than my stitches. My talents, or at least my inclinations, lay elsewhere.

Do you remember how I longed for paint, even then? Not a needle but a brush! I detested the little boxes that gridded our cross-stitched samplers. I hungered for line, sinuous, elegant line, more real than life. I thirsted for color: lapis blues and carnelian reds and malachite greens like the damask dress in my mother's portrait, luminous corals like her blush. I yearned to improve on mere nature, to fashion man and woman in my own image, to be the God of a little canvas Eden. Better, I think now, that someone had thrashed this fancy out of me.

Instead, Father honored my wishes—indulged my *whim*, as he saw it—the year we turned fifteen, the year our school days ended, the year Daniel left for Harvard. Your papa spirited you away to New York, there to enhance his fortune. And mine, in a vain attempt to compensate my losses and distract me from my solitude, bought me the bauble I craved above all others: a painting master, Mr. Tobias Cummings, late of London, by way of the finest drawing rooms of Charleston and Philadelphia. Or so he said.

I will not repeat now what I wrote to you then, and endlessly, in one letter after another: how dashing—how *worldly*—Mr. Cummings (I dared not call him Tobias, not yet) seemed to a motherless girl who had scarcely ventured beyond Boston. He trailed letters of introduction from gentlemen on two continents, along with a stack of his own canvases, likenesses of men I wished to know and women I dreamed of becoming.

Was he a great painter? I suppose not. But Tobias brought color back to my gray, cold world. He taught me everything I would know of Art, and more than I ought to have learned of men. To both subjects, I took quickly. When I sent you my sketches, you feared that my abilities in life-drawing exceeded the bounds of maidenly accomplishment. You were right to worry. But 'twas too late for me to listen. So my letters to you stopped. And then, not long after, my monthlies did.

My father and the sham doctor whose silence he bought said my babe was stillborn. But they did not let me see its lifeless little form. Nor could they. For I heard her cries, I swear it. I wake at night, hearing her still. A daughter, I am sure, for I dreamed her all those long months I carried in secret. When I fled Father's house to search for her, I discovered what awaits a fallen woman on the streets of pious Boston, no matter how gentle her birth. Let me assure you: the Manufactory House is the best of it.

I have toiled here now for near two and a half years, each new day as drab and ugly as the one before it. But I shall not tarry here much longer. Before I began this letter, I chanced to spy in Edes's *Gazette* an advertisement that may save my life, though my dignity, my honor, my virtue, lie beyond rescue. For what manner of situation am I fit? You must wonder at the very thought. A wet-nurse, perhaps? Alas, for all I wandered, and all I searched, I never found my babe, and my milk dried up long ago. And what lady would take me as a servant, or a seamstress, or a tutor for her own tender innocents? Though Father cannot see me, too many in this hypocritical town must yet know my tale, if, no longer, my face.

But not Mr. Stewart Jameson, a stranger. I shall paste his advertisement on the back of this letter. Read it, and try to conjure the mixture of hope and desperation it stirs within me. No one will ever marry me, of that much I am sure. But I spy within those few lines of type the news of a man who may yet take my hand.

If I am to gain this situation, I must make this Jameson see my talent but not my sex, my artist's touch but not my woman's form. If I can but persuade him, I would turn my talent into capital, and that capital into liberty. But first, I must turn myself into someone else. Fanny *shall* die, and herewith gives you permission to grieve her loss, once again.

Then you must dry your tears, dear Lizzie. Expect a letter soon from a boy of a promising genius, not yet known to you, whose hand, and heart, you will nonetheless find familiar. In the meantime, please accept the kindest love of a most affectionate friend, whom once you knew as,

Frances Easton.

BOSTON.

*A*t a meeting of the Massachusetts General Assembly held Tuesday, June 26, at the Town House, Speaker of the Assembly, the Honorable Samuel Bradstreet, Esquire, spoke in opposition to the Sugar Act, recently passed by Parliament, and the proposed Currency Act, as well as rumors of a Stamp Act to follow. "These are not duties but taxes, which we humbly apprehend ought not to be laid without the Representatives of the People affected by them," Mr. Bradstreet declared in a rousing statement delivered before the Assembly, to a universal cry of "Huzzah!"

It is rumored that Governor Bernard has sent to London for ships of war and regiments of foot to enforce Parliament's new duties. It can only be hoped that such rank perfidy is but a false report.

The PRINTER has been asked to make the following announcement:

Hiram Usher, Esquire, Member of the Governor's Council, invites all the merchants of this town to meet at Faneuil Hall on Monday next, at eight o'clock in the evening, to discuss measures by which we may wean ourselves of our ruinous dependence on British imports.

CHAPTER 3

In Which Promise Arrives, and
Promises Are Made

A sitter, a sitter, my kingdom for a sitter! I have stocked my painting
room with pigments and spirits and oils, purchased dear, on account, from the apothecary whose shop is but two doors down. Yet, in near a month on these shores, all the Art I have undertaken hardly merits the name: I have painted a wooden shop sign, no more than crude line work: the words STEWART JAMESON, FACE-PAINTER above a head-and-shoulders of a bewigged gentleman in a velvet cloak. The painter's arms now hang outside my door, like a lure tied to a hook, dangling in so much still water. Have I crossed an ocean to sit by a pond? Reader, I am no angler; I am a painter. And mark me: a painter must paint. How dearly I wish that you, Sir—or perchance, Madam—were here with me this very instant, sitting for your portrait. Then we could truly take each other's measure. But no. There you perch, in your easy chair, reading by candlelight, while I, at my desk, scribble alone.

Pray, do not think me idle, for I would not write the day away, with no better company than Enoch Goddard, the grubbling rumbud who came with the place, and his slip-slop wife. And so: I must leave my lodgings, and do. Here is my daily docket: At dawn I ply the wharves, practicing the art of gossipation. At eleven I visit a coffeehouse, each day in a different quarter of town: the Crown, on King Street; the British, here on Queen; the Duke's, on Marlborough. Sip, chat. Sip, chat. From noon till two I walk the hall 'neath the Town House, which these Bostonians call their Exchange—though, truly, 'tis a far cry from London's Royal Exchange, where stockjobbers from the four corners of the globe make their deals amidst a great din and shuffle. I trade words with any dexterous exchange artist who will meet my eye. Of an evening I cast my net at the Blue Herring, before a flagon of beer, while I play at cards with any who happen by. Whist is my game, although I am scarce a sharp.

Yesterday, I stopped in at Edes's shop.

"I've got what you've been waiting for, Jameson," the printer said, narrowing his eyes, and handing me a copy of the *Edinburgh Evening Courant*. He watched me carefully as, with dread, I read the lines to which he directed my attention:

> ESCAPED . . . *one Stewart Jameson, face-painter and libertine, on pain of being confined for debt . . .*

So soon, dear Reader? Am I to be exposed so soon?

"Not the way any man hopes to see his name in print," I ventured, with rue, and truth enough.

"No, I expect not." His tone was grim, but I caught a glimmer of sympathy in his countenance.

"Edes, has anyone else seen this?"

"No. Not yet." There was nothing for it but to plead with the man.

"Sir: my reputation, my livelihood, even my liberty, lie in your hands. What will you do?"

"Well, for one thing, Jameson, I won't be extending you any more credit." He pulled out his account book, and flipped through the pages. "Let's see. I've run your ad for an apprentice for three weeks straight. Plus the cards, the map, and Newcombe's *History*, that's fourteen shillings. I'd like it now, in hard coin."

"Fair enough. Though, just at the moment"—I tried to offer a small laugh—"I'm afraid I'm a bit short. Might I do a piece of work for you instead?"

"Ah, the swindling begins." He shook his head. "What will you wheedle out of me next? No. I'm not so vain as to fancy a picture of myself, especially one painted by a charlatan."

I bridled at this, Reader. But I let it pass.

"No, no, of course. Though you'd make a fine subject," I hastened to reply. "But I find the woodcut that adorns your masthead a little . . . clumsy."

"The coastline, with the islands in the harbor? What's wrong with it?"

Good. I had hit upon a sore subject, and right he was to worry about it, for the man's masthead was monstrous.

"If you'll excuse my saying so, Edes, it looks more like a spinster's stockings drooping from a clothesline. Who the deuce carved it for you?"

"A fellow by the name of Revere. Lives in the North End. Charges a fortune."

"The silversmith? If I were you, Edes, I might let the man crimp my spoons, but I wouldn't let him near my newspaper."

He looked half convinced of this much already. I pressed on. "I promise you, I could make you a glorious masthead . . . better, finer, truer to your noble political sentiments. The masthead your virtuous paper deserves."

"Flattery and a debtor's promises I don't need, but if you get this masterpiece to me in a week's time, we'll call it even. Except, if it's shite, Jameson, I'll be wanting two quid."

I breathed a sigh of relief, and shook my head, my thoughts turning, for a moment, upon the swiftness with which I, who was once the toast of London, have been reduced to sign-painter and woodcut carver. Am I next to take up painting houses?

"It won't be shite, Edes," I assured him, and sincerely. Reader, pray, believe me: I am many things, but I am no charlatan.

Only as we shook hands to seal the deal did I notice that the printer still looked troubled.

"I've got more bad news for you, Jameson."

My heart sank.

"What? Will you publish my ruin regardless? Dear God, man. Please . . ."

If he were to warn his countrymen about my debts, I could hardly conduct my business here. And where to next? Reader, know this: I will not board another boat.

"A waste of ink, if you ask me," Edes answered. "But the *Courant*'s printer has sent out a notice asking American pressmen to publish your escape ad."

I could scarce hide my astonishment.

"Impossible," I stammered. "Why hunt me here? How could my creditors think to recover their money at so great a distance?"

Edes shrugged. "Impossible, no. But unusual, I grant you. It seems these McGreevys will cover the cost of printing."

"Goddamn their greasy greedy paws," I muttered.

Edes nodded—I fancied he shared my dim view of lenders—but then he demanded, "Tell me something, Jameson. Where is this black man, Fortune? Is he dangerous?"

I met his stare. "Surely you, above all men, realize: not everything you read in the paper is true."

He raised an eyebrow, but pressed me no more.

"But I must know, Edes, I must know: Do you mean to publish my ruin, or not?"

He looked me over, as if he were a judge delivering a sentence from the bench. At last, he sighed.

"God knows there are enough debtors in this town already. One more can hardly spoil the barrel. No, I won't do it."

Here, at last, is a piece of luck: I have happened upon a generous man.

"Thank you, Edes," I said, with a solemn bow. "Though for your discretion, I know not how I can ever repay you, much less my creditors."

His face grew puzzled.

"That's what I don't understand. Never have I seen a banker reach across the ocean to recover a debt, except in cases of staggering sums. Just how much do you owe?"

I groaned. "Two thousand quid."

"Ah. A king's ransom, then. Nigh on a decade's earnings for you or me, I hazard. Still, 'tis a strange affair, a strange affair. What can these McGreevys do? I've made inquiries: they have no American agents. They can scarcely pursue you here. 'Twould cost more than it recovers."

"Just so, Edes. Such is what I had supposed, which is why I crossed the ocean in the first place. But then: Why ask you to clutter your pages with a notice of my flight?"

The printer pursed his lips. "No banker would spend money for so little prospect of a return. Seems to me someone else must have put them up to it. Someone who means to make sure you know you can never go back, lest they clap you in irons."

I slammed a fist on the counter, near tipping a pot of ink.

"Zounds! I knew that much already!"

Edes put a hand on my shoulder.

"Steady, man."

"Sorry, Edes," I offered, as I righted the inkpot. "It's just—"

"I know," he said, amiably. "Damn them and their greasy, greedy paws."

"Exactly," I smiled, calmed and buoyed by his kindness.

"But if you don't mind my asking, Jameson," Edes continued, "who the devil hates you so much? What did you do, debauch the daughter of a Member of Parliament? Paint an unflattering portrait of some nobleman's prized mare?"

"No. Fucked the horse, painted the girl." I winked, putting on my hat. "Very pretty horse. But that's a tail for another time. Just now, I've got a masthead to design."

As I made to leave the shop, Edes called out to me.

"Listen, you horse-buggerer. I like you, but I've been wrong about people before. I won't print the ad—for now. But I warn you, if you turn out a blackguard, I'll make sure every man, woman, and child in this town knows it."

Suffice to say: I am trapped, dear Reader, even in my exile. Trapped in a town near as strapped as I am.

All over Boston, there is but a single subject of conversation: the tyranny of taxation. Far and wide, 'tis agreed that Samuel Bradstreet, the Speaker of the Assembly, argues eloquent. "The Torch of Liberty," or so he's dubbed. And here's his nub: How can the King ask the colonists to pay in taxes for a war they have already bought, and dear, with the blood of their sons? How can Parliament levy taxes against a people who have not a single representative in that body, so bloody far—three thousand miles of ocean—away?

"No taxation without representation!" Bradstreet hollers. Tis an apt slogan, mind, but a trifle obscure. A little too Latinate, is it not? Were I to meet this Bradstreet, I might suggest sending Parliament a starker message: Pay your own goddamned debts.

Aye, and I would pay mine. If I could, Reader. If I could.

Liberty is property, these colonials say, and property, liberty. Tis a truth a debtor knows better than most. But their argument does not end there. Alas, they do go on. And on. Just this morning I read a speech in Edes's *Gazette* wherein one Hiram Usher, a member of the Governor's Council, writes, "If taxes are charged upon us without representation, are we not reduced from free men to slaves?" Reader, a reminder: the flourishing portion of this colony's economy is the traffic in Africans. Might you and I not agree, then, that these patriots look one way and row another, as the saying goes? Ably do they see the shackles Parliament fastens about them, but to the fetters they clasp upon others, they are strangely blind.

Truly, I sympathize with the distractions of the day. I do. But I would rather these colonials find within their Politics some room for Art, and have their likenesses taken and—while I'm wishing—paid for in hard coin. For in my view, no people can be truly free who would not see themselves clear.

Happily, today marks a beginning to my business, of sorts. This morning, as I sat in the sunlight of my comfortable kitchen, its windows opening onto the dawn quiet of Queen Street, so unlike the relentless commotion of Edinburgh's Great—how much greater!—Queen Street, there came, before the breakfast was cleared, a knock at the front door, and Gulliver's answering yelp.

Mrs. Goddard shambled to the hall, and returned to grumble, "Master, there's a boy 'ere, wishing to speak with you, sir."

Letter II.

July the 2nd, 1764

To my dearest and only friend,

I have done it, Lizzie! I write from a proper table, with my own quill and ink, having practiced the arts of deception well enough to ensconce myself—my new self—in the attic garret of this trim brick house on Queen Street. Tis a modest enough place, yet as different from my last abode as a portrait by Joshua Reynolds is from a Cheapside print.

"Francis Weston, sir, pursuant to your notice in the *Gazette*," I said to Mr. Jameson.

I promise you that my heart pounded loudly enough for you to hear it in New York, drowned out only by my faltering voice, cracking like the shaky tenor of a sixteen-year-old boy, which is precisely what told him I was. Then I asked him to train his painter's eye upon my drawings.

* * *

This lad, and a slip of a one, stands no taller than my chin. He's a filthy thing, more like a chimney sweep than a painter's apprentice—thin enough to slide down any flue. He reeked of lye and wood smoke. A poor boy, meager and pale, with a much-bitten, crusty scalp, all but shaved. A desperate boy, as I could see in his brown eyes, shuttered with lashes long—haunting eyes, weary beyond measure. He wore clothes that would have fit two of him: loose trousers secured with a rope, and a moth-eaten jacket I took to be his father's. He held in one hand a cap and in the other a wool satchel, stitched together with cotton, a handiwork I noted as he placed the thing on the table, after we crossed the hall to the parlor.

He opened the bag. Why must I see his sketches? I need a lad of promise, one who will do my bidding, not one who pretends to Art. What matter his dreary drawings? Might I not be spared the clumsy courtesy of false praise? "Aye, what a fine eye for line, you have, Weston" (for that is the lad's name). "My, what an astonishing likeness of your sainted mother."

But. But. As he opened the bag, with his small, roughened hands, out came half a dozen likenesses, such as Hogarth himself might have made. Sweet Jesus. Charcoal on coarse paper. But the faces: young girls, rosy but knowing, and old men, wistful, and more than one of the same polished young gentleman, smiling with a kind of Lovelacian lovelessness that I cannot even describe. Surpassing work. My head near reeled at the sight, and I had to struggle to hide my joy. That I must have him, I know. But it will require a patch of deceit to secure him, for Reader, as you by now know all too well, I have aught to pay him, and not a sitter in sight.

❋   ❋   ❋

This Jameson is no Tobias Cummings, Lizzie. Of that I am sure, though it may be for worse as well as better. He is older, for one—I'd guess thirty, though you, a keener judge of men than I, might give him a year or two less. His form is well proportioned, for he stands just over six foot, and weighs, I would hazard, near thirteen stone: neither lean nor stout; long-limbed, but not lanky. From his size alone you would picture him imposing. And 'tis true, he is too big for his small rooms. Yet he moves with an unstudied grace, a natural man and no courtier.

Neither is he a man of fashion. His linens—for he met me in his shirtsleeves, in the artist's manner—are of a fine weave, far better than anything I worked in my late, doleful employments. But they shine with wear, and have been mended often, and not subtly, perhaps even by a man's unskilled hand. His lace, intricate Irish lace, has grown tatty and brown with age, which gave me to suspect he had been wealthy, and not very long ago. He speaks with a thick Scottish burr, the deep round timbre of the cello. With every word, his voice betrays a mix of kindness and caution.

He greeted me without a wig. His hair, no longer than the nape of his neck, falls in waves dark as pitch; his eyes are the blue of melancholy, creased with care and not a little laughter. Of how those eyes see, and the Art they trigger his hands to produce, I can tell you nothing. For I saw none of the work he described in his advertisement, and no more than a glimpse of the painting room, on the house's second story, just above the kitchen. Nor is it a master's place, I suppose, to captivate his apprentice. Of my own artistry he seemed quite skeptical. I have long since sworn off guessing what lies in the black hearts of even the best of men. But I suppose my work left him cold.

✳ ✳ ✳

Yｏu know nothing of composition, to be sure, lad," I said, frowning. "And your notion of perspective is no better than a schoolgirl's."

His face fell. Mine brightened. Of his prodigious talent, he seems to have no idea at all. So much the better.

"Still," I added, as if mulling it over, "I may be able to use such a one as you, young Weston."

"Thank you, sir," he said, looking toward the floor, but not before I could see that his eyes had grown moist. I would not have a *prima donna*, but neither do I need slavish gratitude. I hastened to turn our conversation to the business of the matter.

"But why have you come alone, lad?" I asked. "Where is your father?"

"My father?"

"Aye, of course, your father. I will need to speak with him."

"I am an orphan, sir," he answered, quietly. "I have none to answer for me, but, please, sir, I will work hard."

"Holy Moses in the bullrushes!" I blustered, though I was scarcely surprised to learn that a waif such as this had not a penny in his pocket. "Then who will pay me to take you on, young snipe? Am I to apply to the Overseers of the Poor?"

"No, sir. I have charge of myself," he said, biting his lip and clutching his satchel ever tighter. "I have no money, but I can earn my keep; I promise you, I am no stranger to a long day's labor."

"A blind man can see that, my lad. Your hands," said I, taking hold of them, "are coarser than a grinding stone."

He pulled away, as if my touch were a vile thing. What he has endured on the streets of this city, I had rather not ponder.

"Well, you shall have a place here," I declared, turning my face from him, unable to stifle a sigh at the sorrow of those calloused hands, and the tale they told. "Your pay will be your lodging, and mine will be your labor."

"Sir, you won't regret it, sir—"

I turned back to him, my tone now stern and swift.

"Enough. I have my own business this morning." Among other things, I will have to draw up papers, and buy this poor lad some clothes. "Come back this afternoon, that we may agree to terms."

With that, I led him to the door, and shut it behind him.

Astonished Reader, who could have thought, in this town on the edge of the world, to find such raw genius? Mastering this apprentice will be a delicate task. But by my hand, and his, I might yet be saved from debtor's prison. And one day, one day, I may even find my Fortune, and end this exile.

ARTICLES OF AGREEMENT indented and agreed upon the second day of July in the fifth year of the Reign of His Majesty King George the Third and in the year of our Lord one thousand seven hundred and sixty-four, between Stewart Jameson late of Edinburgh on the one part, and Francis Weston of the Town of Boston on the other part.

The said Stewart Jameson doth hereby covenant, promise, and agree to teach and instruct the said Francis Weston in the Arts and Mystery of Painting in general and particularly in the several Methods of grinding colors, mixing oils, and painting faces according to the best and utmost of his skill and knowledge, and likewise to provide for his said Apprentice Meat, Drink, Washing, Lodging, and Apparel during the term of five years.

The said Francis Weston doth hereby covenant, promise, and agree to and with the said Stewart Jameson that he shall well and diligently perform and execute all his lawful and reasonable commands and orders and behave himself toward the said Stewart Jameson in all things faithfully and diligently, these duties to include keeping accounts, mixing paints, and other tasks befitting an apprentice, and shall not nor will at any time or times during the said Term absent himself or depart from the business of the said Stewart Jameson nor shall embezzle, purloin, waste, spoil, make away with, lose, or unlawfully keep or detain any of the Money, Books, Manuscripts, Papers, Paints, Powders, Oils, Spirits, Brushes, Canvases, Goods, Effects, or Things belonging to any Person or Persons whomsoever without the consent of the said Stewart Jameson. The said Francis Weston further agrees that at cards, dice, or any unlawful games he shall not play, taverns or alehouses he shall not haunt or frequent, fornication he shall not commit, and matrimony he shall not contract.

And the said Stewart Jameson will at his own proper cost and charges provide for and allow to the said Francis Weston competent and sufficient clothing, apparel, and washing and also necessary and proper physic, remedies, medicines, and advice of Physician, Surgeon, and apothecary in case of sickness or accidents happening to the said Francis Weston and also during the time of such sickness or his recovery from accidents good and sufficient Meat, Drink, and Lodging.

In Witness whereof the said Parties to these presents have hereunto set their hands and seals the day and year first above written.

Sealed in the presence of

STEWART JAMESON
FRANCIS WESTON
BENJAMIN EDES
ENOCH GODDARD By his Mark X

BOSTON.

*O*n Tuesday, near threescore of the leading merchants of this town pledged their honor and their fortunes to a boycott of all goods imported from England—though some of our most *East*ward-facing factors have yet to sense the wisdom of this course.

On Thursday next, the Assembly will discuss the penury to which this colony will be reduced under Parliament's Currency Act. The said Act, which takes effect on the eighth of October, forbids His Majesty's colonies in America from issuing paper money, and requires the payment of all taxes, including the tax on Sugar, and the rumored Stamp Tax, in hard coin. On a motion from the Floor, members of the Assembly are also expected to vote their endorsement of the Petition to the King drafted by Samuel Bradstreet, Esquire, *viz.*:

The Rights of the British Colonies Demonstrated, in Opposition to the Tyranny of Taxation without Representation.

N.B. Mr. Bradstreet's statement will be sold at B. T. Edes's shop, printed, stitched, and bound, for five shillings. By way of inducements to purchasers, an excerpt is offered, below:

The liberties of freeborn Englishmen are spoken of as their best birthrights. But can there be any liberty where property is taken away without consent? Can it with any color of truth, justice, or equity be affirmed that the colonies are represented in Parliament? Has this whole continent of near three thousand miles in length the election of one Member of the House of Commons?

The imposition of taxes in the colonies is absolutely irreconcilable with the rights of the colonists as British subjects and as men. I say as men, for in a state of nature no man can take my property from me without my consent: if he does, he deprives me of my liberty and makes me a slave.

We all think ourselves happy under Great Britain. We love, esteem, and reverence our Mother Country, and adore our King. And could the choice of independency be offered the colonies or subjection to Great Britain upon any terms above absolute slavery, I am convinced they would accept the latter. British America will never prove undutiful till driven to it as the last fatal resort against an oppression that will make the weakest strong and the wisest mad.

Letter III.

July the 12th, 1764

Elizabeth, kind-hearted friend,

Your letter arrived today, a fact no less remarkable for having been so earnestly wished. Mr. Jameson seemed at once bemused and flummoxed when he handed me the envelope.

"Weston!" he boomed from the parlor. "Come at once!" (This, his favorite phrase.) I found him just sitting down to a game of cards with the printer, Edes, who has become his fast friend, regularly lending him papers from all over the colonies, for my master has an insatiable thirst for news. Jameson's great slobbering beast, Gulliver, slept at his feet.

"Mr. Edes brings a letter from New York, addressed to you in my care, written on good paper, and in a fine hand. A feminine hand, unless my painter's eye deceives me, lad, as I can assure you it never does, not for a moment."

I recognized your red seal at once, dearest Lizzie, and made to grab the envelope. But Jameson pulled it back and pressed it to his chest.

"A rich admirer from the nether ports, is it?" he mocked. "There are deep harbors there, I hear," he said, winking at Edes. "You're a sly one, Weston. I'm glad to see you've gained a few pounds since you crawled to my door, lad, but I still wouldn't have guessed you had the stuffing, nor the starch, to brave a courtship."

So you are become my *inamorata*! Tis a good thing an apprentice is expected to lower his gaze, for had I stared at my crude leather shoes for even a moment less, I must have been caught smiling. I tell you, Lizzie, my master barely looks at me. Have you ever noticed how little you regard your own servants? If I were to ask you, could you tell me the color of your dressing-maid's eyes?

Only when I brought your letter up to my garret to read did I fully realize my good fortune in finding you still ensconced in the comfortable home of your father. Had you married, or moved, he might well have read my letter, and learned my secrets. Your father is a good man, Lizzie. But Nicholas Partridge must still trade news with Edward Easton. And oh, I cannot lose this place! I have written myself a new beginning, and I lack the mettle to conjure yet another. Death on the streets awaits me if I am thrown from this house.

You cannot compass such risks, I know. Yet how pained you sound at your own plight. A spinster aunt, you dare to call yourself at barely one-and-twenty. Can you truly deem it ill luck to dwell secure, 'neath that kind man's wise governance, under the name he gave you at birth, in possession of both your porcelain skin and your maidenhead, Elizabeth?

"*Still*," you call your life. Do you rue that stillness, or savor it? Your reaction to my own strange circumstances leaves me unsure what your heart speaks. For you seem at once to chide and to envy me. I am amazed to hear from you the tale my father passed to yours to account for my long absence from Hanover Street. A distant aunt with a mysterious ailment, a tour of Roman antiquities, years spent holding that old woman's papery hand while contemplating the fate of ruined republics: Lizzie, this is the stuff of *novels*. I speak to you of life.

The mechanics of my disguise excite your curiosity. Were I to serve your tea, in your very own parlor, you would not recognize me. Indeed, when first I passed before the looking glass in Jameson's painting room—the first mirror I have seen in three years—I scarcely knew myself. I will never be much of a man, Lizzie, but I make a convincing boy. I was but a skinny girl when you knew me, nor, as the years passed, did I ever grow into a figure worthy of Rubens, not even when I was with child. After that, hunger made me narrower still, a subject more fit for El Greco. No, there is little enough of womanliness left in me, except for my breasts, which would betray me if I did not bind them. I wrap them, tightly, with strips of linen, before I dress in the outfit my master has bought for me: oznabrig trousers; a muslin shirt, clean if rough; a coarse waistcoat; and a woolen topcoat. Clothes for laboring, not for sitting still.

Mr. Jameson keeps me hard at work, day and night, doing everything expected of an apprentice, and much else besides. Dash it, Lizzie, no sooner had he secured my labor than he turned out the couple who served this house, an ill-kempt matron by the name of Goddard and her drunken husband. (*His* close scrutiny I feared, I must tell you.) Of his decision to dismiss them, Jameson gave them little notice and me less account.

"Cut your coat according to your cloth, lad," was his only answer to my inquiry. By which I take him to mean that a painter who has yet to secure a commission, nor pay this month's rent, can scarcely afford a staff of three. Tis among my duties to reckon his accounts, hacking my way through the thickets of bookkeeping with as little skill as I once brought to my needlework. But I know the value of naught.

There is art enough in keeping this household afloat, but whether great Art and its attendant rewards will ever emerge from his painting room I cannot say. This much I have discovered: in the attic storage room, opposite my garret chamber, a stash of a dozen canvases, wrapped, rolled, and tied. While my master slept, I unfurled a few, by candlelight, and gazed upon portraits of a quality I have never seen: lush, vibrant, penetrating, altogether animated. Why has a man of such talent landed here, of all places, so impoverished and alone? No wife, unless he has left one, no money unless he hides it better than his paintings. Is he a scoundrel?

Whatever manner of man is my master, I am not merely his apprentice, jacketed even in shirtsleeve weather, the better to disguise my true form, but a three-headed monster: painter, cook, and serving boy in one pretended body. Mrs. Goddard still comes, three days a week, to do the laundry, bake the bread, butcher the meat, lard the pantry, mend the linens, sweep the hearths, scour the floors, and fill the wood-box. Or such is what she's paid to do. But she performs her chores indifferently, and the work piles up. Jameson must have his fires tended and his meals served, his colors ground and mixed and his canvases stretched, his brushes sorted and his leads sharpened.

And of course, we need water. A hundred times a day, it seems, I run to the cistern in the yard to fetch it. Three flights down from my garret to the well, and then into the kitchen with two heavy pails full, and then up one more story to bring a pitcher to Jameson's bed-chamber in time for the master's toilet, then back down for another jug to boil the sizing that primes our canvases. Sometimes I think my arms will break beneath the weight of it—though I can ill afford to show the weakness of our sex.

I am fortunate that Mr. Jameson is not especially demanding about either his housekeeping or his meals. But if he slights his palate, he could not be more particular about his palette. In the painting room he becomes a grand stage master, giving directions with great exact-ness. The easel shall be so far from the window and no farther, set at a slant to catch the light, and moved every hour like the shadow on a sundial. His brushes must be arranged, always, in the same order, thickest to finest, and stiffest to softest within those gradations. The table next the easel must always have a jug of water, a flask of turpen-tine, a dry rag, and a moist one, but not too wet.

"Weston, there are three laws by which I govern my realm," he says, spreading his long arms wide to trace the limits of a domain not twelve feet by twenty. "One, never work in this room but that you crack the window, even in the deepest cold, lest we expire from the fumes. Two, always keep a wet blanket by the fire, for I will not have you burn Ayers's house down."

And then, silence.

"But you said there were three laws, sir," I said, making a show of counting his edicts upon my fingers.

"Dammit, lad. I am an artist, not a keeper of accounts. Two rules then. Now put your nose back to the grindstone."

And this is not merely one of Jameson's many proverbs, for truly, I am chained to the grindstone, as surely as any mill-horse. Hour upon hour, you would find me with a stone muller in my hand, mashing chunks of pigment into mineral oil. So finely must the powders be ground—about this, too, he is most particular—that I can work no more than a couple of teaspoons at a time.

"Too coarse!" he has told me, more than once, after smearing my paint upon glass to test it before the window. "Back to the grind-stone, lad."

But toil is not enough to keep my hard-won place here. I must find my master some custom, and fast, for plainly he chafes at idleness. He tries to busy himself with the newspapers Edes brings him, from all around these colonies: another expense. Will reading pay the rent? While he pores over paper, I traverse the town on his errands, walking from the Neck to the hills, across the Common, along the ropewalks, anywhere I choose, unknown even by those who once knew me.

My reward for this service is a city I daresay you have never seen, much less heard, a noonday world of hawkers and servants and slaves, their jibs and ahoys composing an intricate fugue. Safe in my disguise, I delight in the hurly-burly of it all, wending my way through the streets, in and out of shops and taverns and coffeehouses, through the markets and down to the docks and no one, not a soul, stares. What joy to be invisible! If I am little better than Jameson's slave, never, never, dear Elizabeth, have I known such liberty.

Is this freedom worth the price I paid for it? We were not bred for independence, you and I, shut away in our father's drawing rooms till we could be handed off to the bed-chambers of our husbands. Long ago, I fled that Algerine purdah, all anger and hurt and heedless pride. My father could not believe I would refuse Tobias.

"I will not be that man's wife," I told him.

"Then you will have to find a position in a family, someplace far from here," he insisted.

"I would rather be a whore than a governess," I told him, full reckless.

"You are halfway there already, Fanny, are you not?" he sneered. "The weather is fine, but let us see if you feel the same way when the cold sets in. There lies the door, and I shall not bar you from it. But remember: it swings only one way."

I did not leave then. But when I did, I fell so far and so fast that I can never turn back. Nor would I want to. Do you think me liberty-mad, Lizzie? That disease infects this whole town, if you believe what my father writes in Edes's paper, where he calls himself the Mast of Fidelity, though his authorship is an open secret. And even were it better concealed, I should recognize his voice clearly enough.

"Fanny," he told me, the night I at last packed my bag, "if you leave, I shall not welcome you back, for you will have dishonored your father. Do you know, this colony once hanged violators of the Fifth Commandment, as the Bible demands? We live in more enlightened times. But I will not shelter a rebel. I am the governor of this house, and I will accept no less than your entire deference to my authority. I give as much to my King, who rules this great empire as surely as the Almighty rules over us all."

I suppose I did dishonor my father, my God, and my King, Lizzie. I fled. But I *have* found shelter, and I mean to earn my keep here.

"What price does Boston place upon genius, Weston?" my master asked me.

"I have heard it said that the late Mr. Smibert—"

"Who the deuce is this Smibert?"

"A renowned face-painter, sir. From Scotland. You must have heard of him."

"John Smibert? Renowned? Aye, he was an Edinburgh man, Weston, though no genius, from aught I've seen of his work."

"Well, he commanded quite a price here, sir. Fifty pounds for a half-length, I believe. In your situation, sir, being new to these parts, might you . . . consider asking twenty-five?"

"I remind you," he thundered, for he is given to sudden outbursts of temper, "you are not in my situation, but rather in my employ. You might try governing your tongue accordingly."

"Yes, sir."

"Twenty-five quid, my arse," he muttered to himself as I left the room. "What am I, half a Smibert? A shitten *Smib*?"

Nonetheless, his notice in the *Gazette* now sets his price per sitter at twenty-five pounds, hard coin. Alas, it has hardly increased the traffic to Queen Street. So he sends me to drum up trade. In my little sack I carry his letters of introduction, to deliver to our most eminent families, households whose daughters were once our schoolmates and whose sons would fain have been our beaux, families with enough vanity coursing through their papered hallways to want portraits for the ages, so long as they may be paid for with paper money.

Two days ago Mr. Jameson asked me to convey a letter to the Ushers' house on Hanover. Yes, Lizzie, just across the street from Father's. I could think of nothing, almost nothing, that I wanted less than for Francis

Weston to stride past Fanny Easton's parlor window. But how could I refuse?

Where once I was admitted to the best parlor, I was directed belowstairs, and just as well. Had I entered by the hall, I might have run into the fair Miss Margaret Usher. And she might have developed eyes for more than her buttons and beaux, and spy something familiar about me. Instead, I explained my purpose to a soot-black footman tricked out in red livery. Pompey proffered a silver tray, and invited me to leave my master's card to await his master's eyes. I endured his cold gaze. For he gave me to understand there may be a commission in it: Usher's loutish elder son—I know you will remember Mordecai, with his Roman nose and roaming hands—has put aside thoughts of the ministry, and means to set himself up as an East India merchant. This change of costume, if not of morals, he means to celebrate with a picture, made with paints, ground to dust, by the tired hands of this,

Fanny Easton.

FROM THE *BOSTON GAZETTE*, MONDAY, JULY 16, 1764.

As readers of this paper may be curious about the Gazette's *new masthead, the printer takes this occasion to compliment the engraver's bold depiction of an eagle, broken free of her cage and soaring over Boston, a fitting celebration of this town's struggle for liberty.*

—B. T. EDES.

BOSTON.

To the Editor:

When I read in your pages of the speeches of the Torch of Liberty, I know not whether to laugh or to cry, sir. Does this flickering candle mean for us to disobey Parliament, and refuse to pay our taxes? Are we next to cast off the bonds of empire, and rule ourselves? Britain is our affectionate parent, to whom we owe every tender regard, and everlasting gratitude for our prosperity and protection. Will the overzealous passion for liberty compel children to question the word of their fathers? To gainsay legislative authority is to upturn the rule of law and to sap the very foundation of our government, whose sovereignty rests with the King in Parliament. *Democracy* can lead only to tyranny, disorder, and anarchy. We must render to our rulers their dues, and our duties. We must give tribute, to whom tribute is due; custom, to whom custom; fear, to whom fear; honor, to whom honor. The Almighty has ordained our beloved King, whose ministers may thus be properly styled the ministers of God. We owe them reverence, deference, and submission. In short, it falls to us to pay some price for the sweetness in our lives, and to pay it in hard coin. This, sir, is nothing more than the cost of our English liberties.

—THE MAST OF FIDELITY.

*R*AN *away about the 20th of this month,* from the Hon. Charles Woodward, Esquire, of Williamsburg, a very black *Negroe* Man named *FORTUNE*, of a middle Stature, about five-and-twenty years of age; has been well whipped, which his Back will show. Speaks very good English, and a little French and Spanish. He is a cunning, subtle Fellow, and pretends to be a Doctor; he can read and write, and probably has got a Pass forged. He went away with Irons on his Legs, a Kersey Waistcoat, and a Cotton Pair of Breeches, laced on the Sides for Conveniency of putting them on over his Irons; he has robbed me, in Cash, Household Linen, and other Goods to a considerable Value. This being the second Trip he has made since I bought him, not three weeks ago, he is branded with an **R** on his right hand. I desire he may receive such Correction as the Law directs. And I take this Opportunity to give public Notice, That I shall always be willing to reward any Person, according to his Trouble, that shall take up and bring home any *Negroe* belonging to me found abroad. Whoever apprehends and returns said *Fortune* shall have Ten Pounds *Virginia* Currency to be paid as a Reward, by

—*CHARLES WOODWARD, ESQUIRE*

N.B. It is strongly suspected that the said *Negroe* has gone out in the *William & Mary*, Capt. Peter Dirk, Commander, bound for *Philadelphia*. If he is found at so great a distance, the Reward for his return, above, will be doubled.

CHAPTER 4

Wherein Our Author Undertakes a Likeness of His Lad

Can it be? Does my Fortune endure?

I have read in a Virginia paper news I can scarce fathom.

Reader, my apologies. I pledged to tell you the truth, and without ornament. But heretofore, I have told you nothing of Fortune, my misnamed, unfortunate friend, lost to me. Lost *by* me. Tis too much sorrow, too much useless, wasted sorrow. I cannot bear to line my pages with it, much less to inflict it on you. Pray, forgive me.

And surely the Fortune advertised in the *Richmond Examiner* cannot be the man I once knew. Tis a common enough name for a slave. Still, pieces of the description suit him: "of a middle Stature, about five-and-twenty years of age." True, though vague enough. "Pretends to be a Doctor"? No pretense about it. "Cunning"? Altogether. The rest, I can hardly stand to read. Shackled, whipped, branded. Please, dear God. Let him be spared a fate he would surely deem worse than death. What can I do? Write to this fiend, Woodward? What would I say to such a man, much less offer him? Still, write I must, and have done, *viz.*:

Dear Mr. Woodward:

    Pursuant to your recent notice for a runaway named FORTUNE, I should like to inquire whether he answers to the name of Ignatius Alexander. If so, he is a man for whom I have long been searching, and on whom I have a prior claim. If you discover his whereabouts, I will gladly travel any distance to recover him and will amply compensate you, for he is of great value to me. Furthermore, I entreat you, Sir, to spare him any further ill usage.

                        Sincerely,
                        Stewart Jameson

I should be amazed if I were ever to receive a reply. Is there nothing more I can do? Take a stage to Virginia? And what then: Trudge through swamps, calling his name? I would do as well to search for a pig's bristle in a hundred haystacks. And if this Fortune *were* Alexander, even so far away, and fleeing slave-patrols, he would have far better success finding me than I would him. Why else have I advertised myself up and down the Atlantic?

"Are you mad, Jameson? Are you not hunted? Do you *wish* your creditors to find you?" Edes asked, astonished, when I requested him to post a notice to printers in neighboring colonies.

"Do I look a clod-pate, Edes? I will tell you naught but that a friend needs to find me. And I have disguised myself: *James Stuart and Sons, Joiners.*"

"A damned flimsy disguise," the printer scoffed, and right he was, too. But I have no choice.

Still, to sit here, doing nothing. Tis an agony.

God above, what would Alexander counsel?

Stay put, Jamie, you great sot.

This time, for once, I ought to listen to him. And so: I will stay put. For now. Not least because this Fortune cannot possibly be mine. Tis inconceivable.

Meanwhile, what?

A painter must paint.

F orty days in the desert! Are we to be plagued with still more sun?" I grumbled as my apprentice and I sat to breakfast in the kitchen this morning. Under the table, Gulliver gnawed at a bone left over from last night's supper.

"I'm afraid so, sir," answered the lad, between greedy spoonfuls of porridge. Suffice to say: the appetite of my apprentice rivals that of my dog. "But how does the sun plague you, sir?"

"A fair question, my lad. Where to begin?" I leaned back in my chair, and rubbed my chin. "You may be surprised to hear it, Weston, but I have made more than a few blunders in my life."

"What sorts of blunders, sir?"

"Every sort, lad. Indeed, were I a brooding man, the study of my errors would keep me awake at night, like so many raps at the door of my bed-chamber. Tap, tap, tap. But as it happens, I am *not* a brooding man, even when I am exceedingly discontent—the time, I find, when most men fall into the dissipation of ungoverned and, in my opinion, ill-advised contemplation."

Weston took advantage of this brief pause in my disquisition, wherein I was merely catching my breath, to stand up and walk to the hearth. The belly has no ears, as the saying goes. The lad was making an effort to listen, but 'twas an effort, I could tell, and by now he knew me well enough to know that my answer might take a while. He grasped the ladle resting on the edge of the pot sitting on a trivet by the fire.

"Excuse me, sir. I am all anticipation. But, pray, would you like more porridge?"

"Why Weston, you begin to mock me. This *is* a good sign."

"Might I finish it then, sir?"

"The oats? Christ on toast, lad. Aye."

"Thank you, sir. Are we getting to the sun soon, sir?"

"All in good time," I smiled. "But sooner if you would stop interrupting me. Fill your trencher, you mutton-headed glutton, and sit back down before I lose my thread. Scrape my bowl, too, if you want, lad, for the sound of Gulliver sucking on marrow has turned my stomach."

At last he sat, and I resumed.

"You see, Weston, not long ago, in Edinburgh, I shared lodgings with a learned gentleman, a scholar and a doctor by the name of Alexander, who worried every night, as Gulliver worries a bone—"

"Were you and this doctor at university together, sir?"

"No, lad. My schooling, such as it is, has been of a more practical sort. He sat for me, is how I met him." By God, I pinned him good. "I suppose I could show you the canvas, lad," I said with a shrug. "For I liked it well enough to copy it, and I dragged it across the godforsaken ocean. It's upstairs, somewhere . . ."

"I'd like that, sir. Very much. But the doctor: What was it that worried him?"

"Everything, lad. He couldn't rest until he had puzzled out the order of the bloody universe. And sometimes, by God, he seemed to be closing in on the solution. But for all his ponderous pondering, he woke worse than he began. I ask you now what I then asked him: 'What good does it do a man to lie between his sheets, fretting?' "

"I don't—"

"Weston, 'twas a *rhetorical* question. I don't need your answer."

He nodded, scraping another spoonful from his bowl.

"And so. Again: I asked the good doctor, 'What good comes of your nocturnal fussing?' and he answered, 'I am developing my faculties for the study of cause and consequence, and there are not enough hours in the day for such prodigious cogitation.' "

I laughed, heartily, but Weston was silent.

"It does not amuse you, lad? My friend's answer was so much rot, bunk, and claptrap, was it not? He was brilliant, mind. But that he would make bid to cover his insomnia with the grandiosity of genius? 'Tis too rich, Weston. But maybe only if you know the doctor," I sighed, disappointed. To have a joke fall so flat after so elaborate a setup, 'tis a pity.

"Well, lad, to return to the question: as for lying awake at night, I will have none of it; my thoughts are not an unruly mob, running riot over my slumber! They are my loyal subjects, and I their monarch; when I command 'Silence!' they obey. They do not file petitions and appeals, like you rebellious Americans; they do not *remonstrate*. And, surely, surely, there are better things for a man to do between his sheets than worry and, failing the doing of those better things, or just the One Thing, or, better still, *after doing it*, he might as well sleep."

I gave Weston a wink. He answered it with a blush. An improvement over a blank stare, but a modest one.

"Sir," he said, "are we getting to the sun soon?"

"The sun? Ach, aye, of course. I had nearly forgotten. As I said, Weston, I am not a brooding man, but I have always believed that, had I a mind for musing, I would be better served by making note, by day, of the few happy circumstances into which I have stumbled, rather than regretting my blunders, awake abed at night. In short: I had rather tally my assets than count my debts."

"Do I take it that the sun, sir, figures into your accounting somehow?"

"Patience, Weston. I'll get there. Alas, lad, 'tis not always so clear which is credit and which is debt. Take these lodgings. They seem an asset, sure: for two of the windows of my painting room take in the blistering brightness of forenoon while the other two let in the shimmer of afternoon and the soft glow of evening. No painter could ask for better exposure. Yet, in truth, I can but half count this advantage. For every day, every ray of this exquisite, precious summer sunshine—twelve long hours of it—spills onto the floor unused, squandered, like so much wasted seed. I might as well move to the cellar, and live in darkness: I have no one to paint. And so, to answer your question: thus, Weston, thus does the sun plague me. Your Boston is a lonely place."

He was too busy swallowing to speak. I eyed him carefully, and considered. Something seemed different.

"You look a trifle less the foundling today, Weston," I ventured.

"Sir?" he asked, putting down his spoon and wiping his mouth with his sleeve.

"Well, lad, you can hardly deny that you were half starved, and fully flea-bitten, when you crawled to my door three weeks ago. I've a notion you must have worms, for how such a mite as you can shovel in such a quantity of victuals, I know not. But I find you are much improved. It's not just that your hair begins to grow—and mind, I do not miss your bald pate."

I reached across the table to tousle his bristles.

He blushed again. Better and better.

"You've also put on a fair bit of flesh, and a decent color rises in your face. Aye, the work must suit you, lad."

"I am most grateful for my position, sir," he stammered. "I—"

"You mistake my meaning, Weston," I interrupted. "I wasn't prompting you for an expression of gratitude, though God knows I deserve it, and you offer it infrequently enough."

I pushed back my chair, and stood up, seized with the clarity of my decision.

"Finish your porridge, lad, and clean your face with soap and water, for once. And none of your dawdling. We have a canvas to prepare."

Letter IV.

July the 20th, 1764

Dearest Lizzie,

My thoughts are ever with you, my sweet friend, on these long summer days, as I marvel at the different paths our lives have taken. I rise with the sun, like some farmer's daughter—I who was raised in a room surrounded by thick velvet curtains that would shut out the day, so that I might lay abed, in a cloud of softest goose-down and fine white lawn, till I felt moved to ring the cook's boy for my chocolate, and the chambermaid to carry out my slops and choose for me a dress that matched my mood. So many trifles had I to attend to that I rarely left my bedchamber ere noon.

Are these your days still? They are no longer mine, and haven't been, not for ages. Before I ended up at the Manufactory House, there were nights when I slept on cobblestones, with no more shelter than a shop awning. And there were other nights—oh Lizzie, dare I tell you?—that I paid an impossible price for the great luxury of having a roof over my head. These last weeks, I have lain in what counts, by contrast, as a palace: on a pallet of straw and ticking, upon a narrow pine bedstead, in my tiny room, tucked 'neath the eaves, high above Queen Street. My own Versailles. As soon as the sun opens one bloody eye for his first peek over the horizon, the garret becomes a riot of light. I dress quickly, with no foolish choices to distract me. And then, aching with a hunger I have never known—for in my years of privation I disguised that gnawing need, even from myself—I make my way to the kitchen to make the tea and heat the porridge. Barely can I wait for the boil before I shovel it into my mouth. *A trencherman*, my father would call me, if he should see what I have become.

To see what I have become: truly, 'tis a puzzle, even to me. Let me test you with a riddle this bright summer morning.

> *A glass is something I need not,*
> *To daily see my face played out.*
> *My own good fortune I can spy,*
> *And so might any who pass by,*
> *A layer thicker every day,*
> *Soon my beginning's brushed away.*

Have you guessed it, dear friend? At last I am become at least one thing I was raised to be: the subject of a portrait.

❋   ❋   ❋

Kind Reader, pray, believe me: I know how to pin a man. Others look; I see. That I am an excellent face-painter, I claim, readily and unabashedly, for, although I am often called upon to employ false modesty as a tool of my trade, I strive to avoid it in my private affairs. Indeed, I have little use for humility with anyone of my intimate acquaintance and least of all with you. But it occurs to me that, up to this point in my narrative, you lack any evidence of my Art, and, in such straits, are left to measure my word against my pride. I would not ask any man to attempt such a calculation. Tis too hard a problem even for Pythagoras.

Bearing your entire ignorance of my genius in mind, it had been my intention to give you, instead, a picture by which to measure my mettle, an easier reckoning. I had hoped my first portrait would set you—and, indeed, all of Boston—astir. Alas, as no ladies and gentlemen have stepped forward to pose, I am left to train my sights upon Weston.

"Take a seat, lad. And turn three-quarters left," I commanded, pointing to a stool I had placed before a drape the color of burnt umber.

"Me, sir?"

"Mary and Joseph in a coach-and-four! Who else can I mean? We are just the two of us here. What, would you have me paint the dog?"

"But surely I am no fit subject, sir, and we must ready for Mr. Usher," he protested, all astonishment.

"Weston, sit. This gentleman you've promised to usher here is not coming till tomorrow. You are right, 'tis a Hobson's choice, between no fit subject, and no subject at all. But my easel stands ready; the canvas is wet; my brush grows stiff; the goddamned sun shines. It kills me not to paint. Would you have me expire? Trust me, lad: you are fit enough."

He was fit, of course, and more. Truly, the lad has an uncanny beauty.

"My cloak, sir, would you have me fetch it?"

"Nay, I want you like this, in shirtsleeves and waistcoat, a humble apprentice. Be who you are; wear what you wear. Again: sit."

He sat. I adjusted his pose.

"We need to set you to work."

He started to rise.

"Nay, dammit. Don't pop up like a jack-in-a-box, lad. What I mean is, we must set you up *as if* you were at work. I would not show the world my apprentice *idling*!"

I glanced around the room, pulled over a crude workbench, waist-high, and placed it to one side of my subject. I moved Weston's right elbow onto the bench. He flinched as I grasped his arm, but let me pose it where I would. I set upon the table a bottle of mineral oil, a jar of turpentine, a marble pestle and mortar, and a clutch of brushes.

"Good, good," I muttered. "Color, texture, form, light . . ."

"Sir?" Weston asked.

"'Tis meant as a sampler, lad, like a schoolgirl's embroidery. Do you see how each object offers a different chance to display a painter's skills?"

He looked, thoughtfully, slowly, from one object to the next, and nodded. Abruptly, he broke his pose to walk to the other side of the room. He returned with a crumpled white cotton rag, and placed it, just so, 'next the brushes.

"Excellent, Weston. Another stitch in the sampler. Now, sit, and take the jar in your left hand, as if you had been just about to clean the brushes."

He soon settled. I expected him to be restless and awkward—shrinking from my attention—and accordingly trotted out the tricks of my trade—silly stories and broad jests—the sort of piffle that softens my sitters into so much clay in my hands.

But not Weston. I found, as one hour passed, and then another, that he hardened, as if my gaze were the fire of a kiln. He was poised. More than poised: he was steady and unflustered. Imperturbable. Adamantine.

"Are you made of flint, lad? I have played my very best Falstaff, and yet you look pained. Am I such poor company? What is the secret, Weston?"

"The secret, sir?" he asked, his impassive face suddenly dissolving into a picture of fear. Reader, do I inspire terror where I look for mirth? Have I lost my touch?

"Aye, the secret, lad," I said, stepping out from behind the easel to place a reassuring hand upon his shoulder, and take a closer look at his eyes. "The secret every sitter must disclose to every good painter: What does it take to make you laugh?"

✳ ✳ ✳

How many portraits grace our fathers' fine homes, Lizzie? I'd guess perhaps a dozen between our two families: each of our parents at the time of their marriages, a grandfather or two, brothers captured upon their commencements from Harvard, our fathers' likenesses taken again in later years. I have seen many paintings of faces in my day. Yet never have I sat for a painter. I assure you: 'tis a strange experience, more like a dance than aught else, and just as riddled with coquetry.

Jameson smiles, an honest smile, while he paints, and 'tis clear that the making of Art settles his restless spirit. His countenance, his entire self, radiates the joy of the work. And he prattles, without pause. He gossips—more than any girl—about our household affairs, our straightened coffers; he natters on about his work, his friends, his rivals. He tests *bon mots* he is certain will amuse the gentry.

"When it gets right down to the bottom of it, lad," he says with a wink, "a painter must have one sitter ere he would have another."

You will hear more sound in it than sense, and, 'tis true, my master is given to flummery. But if I understand his meaning, he would make this canvas of me his calling card. I hazard it cannot fail to bring him custom. A schoolgirl's sampler, he called it, but I have seen it, and 'tis a far loftier Art.

Yet just when I think I begin to comprehend this Stewart Jameson, and he to understand this Francis Weston, he catches me short. For all his talk, what does he tell me about himself? He regales me with stories of his sea-sickened journey to our quaint shores. But when I ask what ill wind brought him here, he tacks to another tale. You are right to ask me, Lizzie, what I really know about my master. And surely the answer must be, very little indeed.

And what can he make of me? He stares at me, over the top of his easel, and seems discomfited by what he sees. And then he tells me, in so many words, that I am once again a failure. This daughter who would not obey her father, this woman who could not keep a lover, this mother who did not protect her babe, this servant who knows not how to answer her master: How many times must I disappoint, and in how many ways? To this litany, you must now add another, for my face, Jameson tells me, will not come to life upon canvas.

"What does it take to make you laugh, Weston?"

"Laugh, sir?"

"Laughter, lad," he said, his face filling with the imminence of his own. "Mayhap you have heard it: the sound that rises up from the belly, to the lungs and thence the throat, and escapes at last through a *smiling mouth*? It happens, betimes—have you never seen it?—it spouts out, when a man is happy."

I could not help myself. I broke into a fit of giggles. For the first time in months, nay in *years*, three long years, Lizzie, my heart felt light.

"Aye, lad, that's the stuff," he smiled at me, exceedingly pleased. "For a moment, I worried that someone had stolen your happiness from you."

"Would you paint me laughing, then, sir?" I asked, recomposing my features as if for the looking glass.

"What manner of hack do you take me for, Weston?" he cried, his dander rising once again. "Would you have me paint a court jester? Some crude Italian *caricatura*, or a medieval grotesque? Nay, I would not 'paint you laughing.' But I would paint *you*, which means I need to trick that carefully concealed spirit of yours itself into matter. I have learned a secret, though: you laugh at laughter. Aye, lad. Let us begin again."

✳   ✳   ✳

I chose the props well, though Weston's rag was the best of them, itself a little essay: soft but nubby, white but splotched, smooth but crumpled.

"Do you see, lad, how many pigments it takes to make a convincing white?" I asked, motioning him to come around the easel. "Here, where the light falls, I've used lead, for its white is the truest. Be careful when you grind it, mind. At the leadworks in Wapping, the men who walk the horses round the millstones seldom survive a dozen years in the business, and their horses fare even worse."

"And for the shadows in the folds, sir?" His eyes were fixed upon the canvas.

"Do you care nothing for the poor poisoned ponies, lad? Heartless little snipe. Aye, chalk scumbled with a wee bit of ivory black; it'll do for the folds."

Weston nodded, still staring.

"Dammit, lad, would you stand here all day? Glue your bottom to that chair. A sitter must sit."

The room's light was unrivaled, the colors a study of shade. The drape the color of coffee, the waistcoat the color of mud, both in contrast to the mixed whites of the rag and the linen shirt, against which, on the table, the rich, deep hues of paint left on the tips of the brushes staged a quiet rebellion of pigment. The polished marble of the mortar and pestle and the bottle of oil provided surface for reflection. I could not have asked for a better opportunity to employ my brush to its best effect.

I studied Weston's features, their delicacy of line, their softness; his long-lashed eyes. I began by shadowing his countenance almost into chiaroscuro, to dwell upon hollows and angles and eyes full of want, a ragpicker's eyes.

"Mark me well, lad, for I'll tell you this only once," I mused, as I built up the color upon his cheeks. "Here is my recipe for human flesh."

He wrinkled his nose.

"Painting it, lad, not cooking it! What, do you think me a cannibal? Where was I? Aye, my recipe for flesh—that is, flesh of the color of yours and mine. For 'twould take a boxful of pigments to capture all the skins of this wide world. But I digress. Mix lead white and yellow ocher in near equal measure, less of lake red, and a few flakes of burnt sienna. For the ruddy-faced—if you were to paint Mrs. Goddard, say—replace the lake with vermillion. For a rich man's wife—they work little enough out of doors—use more lead."

"And for the parts of face in shadow, sir?"

"Umber, Weston. Never take umbrage at umber."

He rolled his eyes. "Is that all, sir?"

"Aye, lad, that's bloody well all. Is it not enough for you, to learn one mystery of the guild today? And mind, my secrets are not to travel beyond these walls."

Twas, of course, a foolproof recipe. Yet as I stepped back and considered the results upon the canvas, it seemed as if it had all gone awry. My painted apprentice looked too old, too wise.

I whistled for the dog.

"We need Gulliver resting his skunk-striped snout upon your knee, lad. Every child's portrait wants a pet."

"I am not a tot, sir," he protested.

"Nay, Weston, but you are a stripling. And, by the conventions of portraiture, you need either a pet or a pair of kid gloves. You are haughty, lad, 'tis true, but I'm afraid you're not quite enough of an aristocrat to carry off the gloves."

Gulliver padded over, and held the pose long enough for me to block his outline, after which he went back to sleep by the window. I know his mangy muzzle well enough to paint him in at my leisure.

Weston's face would not be so easy. If Nature has formed this boy well, Fate has not treated him equally. I decided to capture the contrast. I would set his delicate features against his drab costume. And where I saw in him a worldliness of my own invention, the dog would remind me that he is but a child.

The work grown so demanding, and far more ambitious than I had intended, I found I needed to concentrate less on leading the conversation.

"Who taught you to paint, lad?" I asked. I would have him talk, so that I might be quiet, and better attend to the picture.

"A servant, sir."

"A servant taught you to paint? You surprise me. Whose servant?"

"My father's—"

"Your father's servant? Your father had a servant?"

"No. No, sir. My father's master's servant—"

"Your father's master's servant? What, a footman?"

"No, sir. My father's master's son's—"

"Are you next to recite Genesis to me, lad? There's a son? And who the deuce did he beget?"

"My father's master's son's—"

"Spit it out, lad!"

"—tutor, sir."

"Your father's master's son's tutor?"

"Yes, sir."

"Your father's master's son's tutor taught you to paint?"

"Yes, sir."

"I'm afraid you've left me reeling, lad. Have we not come full circle? Was not your father's master your master, too?"

"Sir?"

"Was not your father's master *your* master?"

"Oh. Yes. Yes. He was."

"Ah. So you had another master before me. Before or after your father died?"

"After my father . . . ? No, both, sir."

"Both?"

"Both before and after my father died. His master was my master."

"Tell me about him."

"About who, sir? My father? His master? The son? His tutor?"

"Zounds, lad! About your blasted father's master's son's tutor, who taught you to paint! Or about your master's son's father, if you've a mind. Or better still, about your father, if you have more to say on the subject. Would it pain you to be a little more long-winded? There is no clause in our agreement that stipulates you can't utter more than four words at once, is there?"

"No, sir," he answered. And then fell silent once again.

"Damn you and all your relations, Francis Weston!" I hollered, exasperated. "String together a story for me! Lie if you must, but I beg you, truly, I beg you, lad, speak in paragraphs, for once! My throat's grown hoarse with trying to amuse you."

"But 'tis not my place, sir," he said, so quiet I could barely hear him.

I put down my brush and palette. I walked across the room and bent before him, so that I could look him level in the eye. I sat on my heels and rested my hands on his knees, pressing the tips of my fingers into his thighs to steady myself. Reader, I confess it: before this moment I had not fully reckoned the depths of my loneliness. Twas but a fatherly touch, but 'twas as close as I have been to anyone in months.

"Weston," I said, as softly as I could, "whatever happened between you and your confounded master, know this: I am not a cannibal. I am not an ogre. I will not whip you if you drop a tray of oils, or kick you out on the street to starve if you but spill fresh paint on a finished canvas. I will yell, lad. I will yell plenty. Aye, and I will curse. I am the first to admit: I am a poor governor of my temper. But I won't strangle you. And I can't have my bluster be the only sound in this lonely house. Speak up," I said, straightening myself. "Consider it part of your apprenticeship in the Arts and Mystery of Painting Faces. Lesson One: Laugh once in a while, for God's sake. Lesson Two: Learn to put people at their ease. My method is to play the fool. You will have to discover yours."

⁕ ⁕ ⁕

Lizzie, am I man enough to be a face-painter? Jameson begged me to entertain him. What could I tell him but that I would reveal myself too much? A tale from my girl—no, my *boy*hood? Do you see my dilemma? My lies tie my tongue as tightly as they bind my breasts. I can barely keep my pronouns straight. Every minute, I am in danger of betraying myself, in a thousand ways, in word and deed. Imagine: I still begin every bow with a curtsy! And that is the least of it. When he touches me, in passing, as a master often has occasion to do, I know not how to respond. The lady in me cries, "Avaunt, unhand me, sir!" The woman in me warms 'neath his beautiful hands. But what, pray, is the boy supposed to do? Silence has seemed the prudent course. It fits my station, and reins in my passions. But my master begged me to regale him, and 'tis my duty to do his bidding.

"Sir," I offered at last, "I have, then, a riddle."

He groaned.

"Sir?"

"I'm sorry, lad, but I hate riddles. I can never fathom them."

"Oh. Never mind, then."

"Nay, go ahead," he sighed. "If you've nothing better. Show me how much cleverness you boast, and I'll show you what little I own. For that is the point of riddles, is it not? But first, lad, lower your chin again. Aye. Stop. Just so."

"I'm sure you'll solve this puzzle, sir. I learned it as a very little . . . boy, sir."

Oh, Lizzie, do you see what I mean? In two sentences, I nearly revealed myself! How am I to survive a paragraph?

"Are you listening, sir?" I inquired. He was working so intently—his face flushed with effort—that I could scarce believe he heard me.

"I am listening, Weston, and pray, continue, for this riddling improves your countenance greatly. You look at last a little less the statue, lad."

"Well, then, here it is, sir:

> "I never in my life beheld
> A garden, field or river clear,
> Yet neither garden, spring nor field,
> Can flourish if I am not there.
>
> "Round as an apple to the sight,
> And in all nations known to roam,
> I fly as quick as thought or light,
> Yet never stir a foot from home."

Again he groaned. "Adam on Eve in the Garden of Eden!" he cursed. "I hate this."

But he looked delighted.

I smiled at my discovery: it amuses him to be teased. Have I found my method? Perhaps I'm man enough for face-painting after all.

"God above, you're smiling again," he laughed. "Wait! That's it. 'God above.' God! Is it?"

"Does God not see gardens, fields, and rivers, sir? Does God not see all?"

"Are we to embark on a theological debate, lad? Tis one of the few things I hate more than a riddle, and I won't indulge you there. Come now. Am I right, or no?"

"No."

"Shite."

"Sir? No, sir, not that, either. True, 'shite' does make a garden grow, but it's usually not round as an apple, sir."

"Nay, Weston," he answered merrily. "That was an expletive, not an answer to your shitten riddle."

"Do you give up, sir?"

"Give me a clue, goddammit."

"Certainly, sir. Twas the subject of this morning's fascinating and most engrossing lecture, sir. At breakfast?"

"Ach." Another groan. "Son of a bitch."

"Well, you're half right, sir. Or at least a quarter. Not the son but the sun, sir."

※ ※ ※

I hazard you will be as surprised as I was to discover it, dear Reader, but my apprentice is a bit of a wit, and more of a flirt. He tests me with riddles, of the stupid sort with which my brother Colin used to cudgel me. Colin's quizzes always annoyed me—aye, and greatly, like everything else he did. Weston's amuse me. Tis confounding, is it not? Yet I owe it to myself, and more to my apprentice, to remember that I am not his brother, but his master.

"Here's another, sir, if you've a mind," he ventured, taking my half smile as permission.

"I've a *mind*, Weston, to paint you as a court jester, after all. But, pray, go ahead."

"I warn you, sir, this one is tricky. I fear you'll need a clue, so I'll give that to you first: it can only be said by a woman to a man."

"Ach. You've already lost me, lad."

"The riddle, sir. Tis said by a woman to a man."

"Fine. I'll exert myself to picture you in a skirt."

At that, the boy drew in his breath, sharply. After a pause, he recited:

> "One thing, kind Sir, of you I crave,
> Tis that which you can never have,
> Nor ever had in ages past,
> Nor ever will while time shall last;

Yet if you love me, as you say,
You'll give it me without delay."

"Sweet Jesus. A fuck, Weston?"

He offered a coy smile. "Is that an expletive, sir, or a guess?"

(Do you see, dear Reader? Am I wrong? Is he not trifling with me?)

I could not help but grin. "A guess, Weston."

"No, sir. Not that."

"Good, because that puts too sad a cast on it, if she had told him a rogering were 'that which you can never have.' A bit cold, isn't she?"

"True, sir. But she was, sir, prepared to have him give it to her without delay."

"Aye, Weston. Twas her panting for it that occasioned my guess."

"I sensed that, sir. But, alas, no, sir, 'tis not a . . . fuck. Have you another guess?"

I sighed and set down my brush on the lip of the easel. Aye, I have another guess, for I'm not as great a fool as I pretend, but I won't give it to my apprentice, just as I never gave that satisfaction to my brother, the bastard. All at once, I found I had grown weary of my canvas. My chatter, and my sitter's, barely covered my rising agitation. O Reader, dear Reader: Was it not time to stop?

"Nay, Weston." I took a rag from my pocket, and began wiping my hands. "I give up."

"Truly?" He seemed disappointed.

"Truly."

"You give up too easily, sir."

"You're not the first to tell me that, lad, and I doubt that you'll be the last," I answered irritably, wiping my brow, for the room had grown terrible hot. Good God, what manner of sitting is this, in which the sitter reveals the painter?

"A husband, sir," he continued. "The answer to the riddle. He can never have one, sir, nor has ever any man had any husband in ages past, but he can give one to her: himself."

"Very sly, lad. Aye, very cunning," I answered, absently, as I gave the canvas a painful inspection.

Reader, 'tis a mercy you cannot see it but must again take my word for it: this portrait is a disaster. I have entirely failed to capture him. I can only hope that my young apprentice, too clever by half, and more beautiful than I would wish him to be, still lacks the discernment to see as much.

"I find myself in need of a drink," I said, and true enough. "Come, Gulliver."

The boy held his pose.

"But are we . . . done, sir?"

"Not done, lad. No. But through for the day. I can't paint another stroke."

He unfolded himself from the chair.

"Aye, come here, lad, you might as well take a look. I can scarcely hide it from you."

✳   ✳   ✳

Oh, Lizzie, when I saw my face played back at me upon canvas I found my tongue was tied all over again.

"Sir, 'tis—"

"Goddammit, I don't want to hear it! Not a word. Not until it's finished. If anyone comes for me, I'll be at the Blue Herring. Clean up, will you, lad?"

And with that, he put his rag on the table next to mine, and stormed out the door, leaving me to my chores.

There was, as ever, much work to do. But I could not take my eyes off the canvas. I cannot think you would spy your long-ago friend in it, nor can I begin to name what I see there. Is it the portrait, or the subject that remains unfinished? I cannot puzzle it, Lizzie, much less discern what made my master lose his laughter in the course of painting the boy who once was,

Fanny Easton.

CHAPTER 5

Of an Aspiring Young Graduate

W hat did you study at this University of Cambridge, sir?" I asked Mr. Mordecai Usher, as he stood before a curry-colored cloth in my painting room, on the south side of the house's creaked and sloping second story, where the gauzy morning light lifted his face from the shadows.

"Why Jameson, what every Harvard man must: by day, the revelations of Scripture; by night, the arts of pleasure!" he declaimed.

Weston, who crouched before my sitter, polishing the buttons on Usher's plum-colored waistcoat, coughed, barely covering a laugh. (*Now* he laughs. I give the lad an inch and he takes a yard.) The mouth of a fool is his ruin, as the saying goes, but this fool Usher is a fidgeter, too, and I would fain keep him talking, his drivel a meager price to pay for a measure of stillness.

"Please, sir, if you could keep your hands at your side. Aye, much better. Thank you. I take it you are quite a seducer, then?"

And he spoke, for three-quarters of an hour, of his conquests. O, the ladies of Cambridge are not safe from him! O, how the college's scullery maids raise their skirts and the merry professors' wives loosen their stays when he nears!

Flimflam. Haggling with whores has been all his lechery, more like.

He might be handsome, I grant, with his luminous pale skin and fine stature—narrow-shouldered and straight-backed—were it not for the dullness of his wit, and the vacant cloudiness in his hazel eyes. *This* is a scholar? How shall I capture the emptiness of those eyes, without hinting at an oceanic vastness that casual spectators might mistake for profundity? Truly, they lack even the gloss of his cloak's poorly shined buttons.

"Weston, once more, and with more polish!"

Damn the lad, can he not complete even the meanest task? I confess I enjoy his company, but both of us bridle in our roles. I am no more fit to play his imperious master than he my obsequious apprentice.

As we readied for this Usher, I had taken the opportunity to instruct my student in how I should like to have my palette arranged.

"Mark me, Weston, for I would teach you another mystery of my Art," I announced. "Every painter culls his colors, to paint the world as he sees it. You may think me a melancholy sort, lad, for I like to keep blue—I favor Sander's blue—always at the ready, on the outer rim of the palette, next the hole where rests my thumb. Then the others work outward, as the fingers of my hand: white, yellow, vermillion, lake red, burnt umber, and last, ivory black."

"Six fingers, sir?" he asked, screwing up his brow in feigned puzzlement.

"Dammit lad, 'tis but a metaphor. Like the planets, then."

"Six planets? Tis not a very big universe you come from. And may I take it your sun is blue, sir?"

"Who are you, Isaac bloody Newton? You may know a pinch of astronomy, lad, but the moon will be blue before you learn your place."

Or before I learn mine. For I laughed. I could not help it. And then I broke off the lesson, and sent him to Cabot's to buy fish oil for varnish. I arranged the colors myself.

Dear Reader, anticipating that you, like me, have had too much of my taunting apprentice, I would tell you more of my sitter. Mordecai Usher is a middling young gentleman who has spurned the ministry in favor of becoming a merchant, a preference for which neither you nor I can fault him. A life of preaching, especially here in this New-England, is little better than a life of begging. To Madras he will soon sail—halfway around the world, and even hotter than here—to accept a position with the East India Company. This portrait, a bust of head and shoulders only (he proves his merchant's mettle by dickering over the price of a half-length), is but a parting gift—a sop—to his grieving parents, left behind in a manse on Hanover Street. May they have sons of greater merit and less venality yet remaining under their roof.

"You are richly napped, sir," I observed, for he wore a luxurious, billowing silk damask banyan over his satin waistcoat. The fop even capped his head with a velvet turban. "Do you not share your father's politics, then?"

"My father? What do you know of the man?"

"Excuse me if I am in error, sir, but I thought I had read in the paper that Councilor Usher leads this town's merchants in urging a boycott of British manufactures. Surely your Indian gown is not the work of Boston weavers?"

"Heavens, no." He smirked, fingering the ample cuff of his sleeve. "You can't get cloth of this quality from my father's Manufactory House. If you had ever felt that homespun against your hide, you would not ask such a ridiculous question."

"Is it a cloth merchant you intend to become in India, sir?"

"Of course, Jameson. The empire affords ever greater opportunities for business—and for pleasure," he snickered.

"After you sail to Madras, sir, who then will be your parents' comfort? Have you brothers and sisters?"

"My older sister is married, and lives in Newport, and my younger brother, Elias, is yet at college, where his exploits, I dare say, do not begin to rival my own," he answered, and continued—but just here, he changed his tone. "My younger sister remains a dear companion, nay a nurse, for my mother, who ails, greatly."

Now, at last, he seemed to settle. I would hear no more of his counterfeit conquests. Better to draw out this new thread.

"Might your younger sister grace my canvas one day, sir?"

Of her beauty, her accomplishments, her talent at the pianoforte, he spoke, gushingly. If but half of what he boasted were true, I would do well to meet this Miss Margaret Usher. With her father a merchant and a member of the Governor's Council, she has two thousand pounds if she has a penny. To repay the McGreevys I had in mind a widow's dower, 'tis true, but a maiden's portion would surely do. I would be glad to marry, and soon.

Reader, know: I could have had a wife long since, had I not proved particularly choosy. For years, long, lonely years, pretty maidens have paraded themselves before me, taking their turns about parlors, sitting for portraits, tripping about on ballroom floors—very many of them charming, fashionable, felicitous, delicious—and yet each and every one of them, finally, frivolous. They speak only of surfaces, as if they live in an endless childhood. By turns silly and prim, they want for passion. Excuse me, Madam, for I do not mean to offend your sex. But I speak as I find.

And lo, here is my dilemma. We painters are reputed libertines, and, in my case, at least, the charge is not entirely unjust. Unlike this cobsham, Usher, I have tasted many pleasures in my life; indeed, I have hardly discriminated insofar as the taking and giving of such pleasures is concerned. But I am sure you must agree, Sir, that such promiscuity better becomes a youth of twenty than a gentleman of thirty. Thus I have promised myself that here, in this America, I will be a new man: I will offer my caresses only where Fortune leads me, and marry for money, or where true affection takes them, and marry for love. But I will trifle with no one.

And who do I wish to caress? In short, and on the whole—if I may be so indelicate as to mention it—while I have enjoyed, as I say, diverse pleasures, I find I prefer the *touch* of women but the *conversation* of men. 'Tis a quandary, is it not? With every young lady and gentleman I fancy, I find myself reduced before long to the same straightened circumstance: her mind bores me; his body sates me only so far.

"Weston! Cease!"

My insolent apprentice having returned from his errand, he labored, in vain, to straighten Usher's waistcoat where it met his lace ruffles. Can he not keep out of my line of sight?

"Mr. Usher needs no more of your fussing, lad. He is hot enough in this weather without your breath forever against him. Run to the joiner near Belcher's Wharf, to see about those gilt frames. I'll pay a quid and sixpence, and no more, on account. Bid him deliver them by Friday next. Bring the cur; he grows restless. Make haste."

"But I've just got back, sir!"

"And you shall have to go out again."

"Yes, sir, milord, *sir*," he huffed.

What sin have I committed that I have been saddled with this surly genius, underfoot, over my shoulder, flitting about me, always? Of critics of my Art there are in this world quite enough without one so close to hand, chafing at his station. There will come a time when I will sever myself from this apprentice, or he from me, dear Reader, and I doubt it will be so long as five years hence. Even as the lad prepared to leave on his errand, he paused to stare at my canvas, his lively eyes a contrast to the blank ones into which I had gazed all morning.

"Would you critique the likeness, then, Weston?" I asked, rounding on him. "Or do you await a lesson? For I have no more time to lecture today."

"No, sir," he answered, softly. "It's just, it's just—"

"*What?*"

"The brow, sir," he pointed. "Should it not be in shadow, just there?"

Surely this is not to be endured. "To the wharf, Weston," I commanded, through clenched teeth. "*At once.*"

The lad and the dog finally gone, I spent another hour with Usher, before he and I alike were too weary—and sweaty—to continue. The air itself seemed to pant, blowing a humid breeze through the windows. At midday, Weston returned, bringing bread and cheese and beer. After dinner, I returned to the canvas while the light remained.

He was right about the brow, dammit. This, to you, dear Reader, I can admit, if not to the lad, for I will not stand corrected by my own apprentice. The cart cannot pull the horse. I fixed the brow. Usher should be pleased: the portrait is more than passing fair, although not half as haunting as *The Serving Boy*.

And hear this good news, Reader: neither you nor I need to endure another sitting with this prattler. Weston can finish the backdrop, and undertake the varnish. When the picture is dry and framed, I will myself deliver it, and meet the sister.

BOSTON.

*W*hen taxes and duties are laid upon us for imported sugars, we must, like honest and prudent Men, endeavor to do without those goods. While our merchants sign pledges foreswearing importation, and our legislators draft remonstrances to send to Parliament, His Majesty's men-of-war are anchored offshore, carrying near 900 troops ready to enforce the King's taxes. Let the humble artisans of this town make and build and do, that we may lard our pantries, fill our linen chests, and stock our cellars with the fruits of our own manufacture, and never buy another imported item.

To this end, the Printer has collected and written a few plain Instructions, for domestic Manufacture, which will appear in my pages over the next several issues, in anticipation of the institution of new duties on October the eighth.

* *Instructions for the Proper Fermentation of Grapes for Wine*
* *How to Manage the Distilling of Rye, or other Grain, superior to common Rum*
* *Concerning the Notable Attributes of Sugar Made from the Juice of Beets, preferable to that of Cane*
* *The Art of keeping Bees, revealed.*

—B. T. Edes.

Letter V.

August the 8th, 1764

Dearest Elizabeth,

Another letter from you, sooner than I dared hope. Every pen-stroke shows your polish, every sentence your poise. You speak of dancing masters and balls, sewing parties and carriage rides, new gowns and old money. My mind's eye sees you wrapped in satin and bathed in candlelight, perched before your spinet, like some gentle-woman in the pages of a conduct manual. I should envy your composure and the conditions that nourish it: your father's watchful eye and good guidance and yes, his warm home and ample purse. But I feel little surer of this than I do of aught else. Forgive me the ramblings of a disordered heart set down on a sweltering afternoon. I am a muddle of feeling and a puddle of sweat, the very opposite of your cool, dry humor.

Shall I blame the infernal heat of these garret rooms for my confusion? I tell you, I cannot make out the road that lies before me, nor is the path that led me here much clearer. Fanny endured such harsh lessons, so young. Yet *Francis* will not be made to hear them. So cruelly tutored in the world of men, have I learned *nothing*? I cannot judge the specimen of humanity upon whom the balance of my life pivots. Whether this Jameson pilots our ship toward fame or ruin, I dare not guess.

On paper, our situation can only be called grave. The balance in the household accounts has long since dipped below zero. We live on ink and air, like everyone else in this straitened town. The gossips in the coffeehouses say that the Exchequer shall soon prohibit the colony from issuing its own paper money. Shopkeepers take their pay in trade—in rum or molasses, muslin or dimity—while their patrons hoard what little gold and silver they have on hand.

And what, you ask, do we offer in barter? Jameson utters promises. Daily I scatter his orders about town, to the framer, the gilder, the grocer, the tailor, the chandler, the bookseller, the goldsmith—even the wigmaker. ("We need props, lad. Why, the Ushers of this world put even the meanest of their servants 'neath a periwig," he says, justifying the outlandish sum he has pledged for an imported wig of fine white curls. "Surely our sitters don't wish to have their scalps seen. Mind, not all of them, my lad, can boast your rising crop of chestnut ringlets," he says, tousling my hair as he would pet his dog.)

For the most part, the shopkeepers credit Jameson's signature as blindly as they do my boyish face. How long they will continue to place their trust in either is anyone's guess. And when they demand hard money, as surely they should, what can we tender? When the sailmaker who supplies our canvas questioned the prospects of payment, Jameson offered him a portrait in exchange. The idea plainly tickled Mr. Lambert, who will bring his family to sit for us tomorrow. Are we next to paint the fishmonger?

I am at pains to make Jameson see the marrow of our situation. But he answers my earnest pleas with fantastical schemes. We must open a drawing school. (What pupils to pay the cost of firewood?) We might convert the two street-level rooms vacated by the Goddards into a color shop, and paint merrily on the proceeds. (What money to *buy* the pigments and oils and prints he means to sell?) We should paint the politicians of this town, hawking Boston-made portraits as domestic manufactures. ("But you are from Edinburgh, sir," I remind him. "Aye, lad," he winks, "but we're painting *here*.")

Yet the starry-eyed dreamer holding the empty purse becomes a clear-eyed realist when he takes up his brush. This evening, in the waning summer light, the two of us stood before his easel together, as he inspected my application of varnish to Mordecai Usher's portrait. How this work floods the senses! The colors fill the eye, and the soft mottled textures my master created with his brush made me want to touch the canvas. My finger was nearly upon the striped velvet of Usher's turban before Jameson caught it in his hand, an artist's hand, soft and knowing, yet full of sinew.

"Ach, lad, you forget yourself." He smiled at my mistake. "'Tis but an illusion—the work of that dab of white, just there—and still wet. Did you not apply the varnish yourself? Aye, when I've trained your eye better, you won't be so easily fooled."

"But he looks as if he breathes, sir."

"Thank you, lad. 'It hath been thought a vast Commendation of a Painter to say his Figures *seem to breathe*,' Fielding once said, 'but surely, 'tis a much greater and nobler Applause, to say that they *appear to think*.' With this blockhead, I fancy I fell short."

I tell you Lizzie, there is something wondrous *sly* in Jameson's brush. Most face-painters traffic in flattery, showing sitters the prettiest versions of themselves, the people they wish they were. Our own Smibert: his women always had the dew of youth, his men, the valor of generals.

Jameson looks deeper. He paints what he sees, and then dares a sitter to see himself the same. Truly, he counterfeits the soul. His Mordecai Usher at first appears to flatter its subject, imparting measures of soul and sense the Almighty Creator withheld from the original. He wraps the pretended India nabob in a rich cloak, and sets his thin fingers upon a ledger crammed with fat sums. But the painter lets Usher's mouth betray him as the puppy he is. Were I the merchant's London factor, I might check those accounts twice.

But my master hasn't yet pinned his apprentice. He continues to fuss with *The Serving Boy*, making his Weston appear eager, desperate, and above all, innocent. So beautifully realized is this vision that it half convinces me. But surely, if there is one trait Fanny Easton lacks, it is innocence.

In your last letter, Lizzie, you asked why I would not marry the man who stole my innocence. How could I pledge myself to a man who had broken his promise even before he uttered it?

Hannah, my father called the slave girl he took on soon after my own dear sister Lydia died. She came from the Finleys' house, where she had lived since birth, and 'twas rumored she bore an uncanny resemblance to her master. Whatever her mother's history, she soon captured my father's sympathy. He spared her work whenever she asked, which was often enough. My gentle brother Daniel took it upon himself to tutor her. "A noble experiment," he called her learning. Noble? Certainly Hannah grew refined—and arrogant, willful, unyielding. And soon she set her cap for my Tobias.

I can hardly bear to sketch the scene, Lizzie. My babe had quickened; I could deny my condition no longer. I told Tobias, and he trembled at the news—with love, I thought, though fear was a likelier cause. Next I told my father, who filled with wounded rage to learn that his prize had been spoiled, for he had meant to use me to make a dynastic alliance. But his anger soon yielded to the merchant's cold reckoning, for Edward Easton, unlike Stewart Jameson, is a man who knows how to keep accounts. He devised a settlement that warmly encouraged Tobias to honor his promise—unspoken, yet plainly written on my belly. We would marry and remove to New Hampshire, where the Eastons hold a large grant. Twas signed and sealed.

And then I caught them, Tobias and Hannah, together in my father's library, in a posture of unmistakable intimacy. Oh, there was nothing indecorous about the scene—no ripped bodice, no flesh revealed, no hair awry, no maidenly blush upon her cheek. But from their voices alone, I knew her to be his lover.

My fury was terrifying, operatic—and pathetic. I tore my hair. I threw plates. I sliced Tobias's canvases to ribbons, and then brandished the knife at him. He fled, I know not where. Desperate to quiet me, my father sent Hannah away, to one of his island plantations. I gloried in that cruel victory. But the more I learned of a woman's life, the more I regretted the fate to which I had consigned poor Hannah. The specter of her suffering came to haunt me. She must long since have been worked to death, raising cane to sweeten my tea.

Bitter words these must sound to you, kind Elizabeth. Bitter life, I must reply. And there is the answer to my question: she envies you your soft surround after all, does this hardened,

Fanny Easton.

CHAPTER 6

Of Means and Manners

At nine o'clock this morning, Mr. and Mrs. Hugh Lambert, with children three, arrived at Queen Street, escorted by a yipping, leaping canine entourage, a pack of furred dervishes. Spaniels, four of them. Gulliver hurled himself at the door, at the risk of cracking his skull, though whether such an injury would wound his wit, I will not hazard to guess. Every day do I discover another useless talent of my worse than worthless dog: were I a marauder attempting entry to a walled city, he would do fine service as my battering ram.

"Weston! Come at once!" I hollered over the barking. From the painting-room window, I looked out on the street, below, where the Lamberts were tumbling out of their coach-and-four, its door painted with what I suppose passes, here in the provinces, for a coat of arms. Suffice to say: the family was ill matched to its equipage.

Lest you suppose I mock these Lamberts, I should explain, dear Reader, that from birth, I had not a gentleman's advantage. From my father, a dyer in Leith, I learned to mix colors. At thirteen, I was apprenticed to a plasterer in Edinburgh, on the High Street. I sculpted ceilings in stucco, and painted murals of nymphs in clouds. If my work failed to rival Michelangelo's, it had merit enough, and taught me well the tools of the trade. At twenty, I traveled to London to work as a coach painter, decorating the gilded carriages of gentlemen who would parade through the streets in a work of Art. For them I limned birds in flight, flowers in bloom, and Romans in battle. Preposterous pomp.

Reader, there are in this world two kinds of Arts: Mechanical and Fine. Let the latter be mine. I would paint before an easel. I joined the guild of Painter-Stainers, and hired myself out to a print seller on Drury Lane, copying portraits of lords and ladies. In the evenings, in my rooms in Covent Garden, I studied the works of the Old Masters, reproduced in borrowed books. A coach painter's three shillings a day is hardly enough to live on in the great metropolis, but I found I could paint faces for ten times that sum (or something like that, for I have always found the conversion of shillings into pounds a cumbersome calculation). After three more years of careful toil, I had done well, maybe better, and my friend Joshua Reynolds urged me to take up the artist's grandest subjects: the Death of Seneca, the Dilemma of Hercules, the Journey of the Magi. Call me feckless, sir—God knows, I have called myself worse—but I found I had no taste for either the loftiness of allegory or the heroism of history. I make my study, instead, of the humble particularities of the human face.

I bade Reynolds good-bye, and retreated to Edinburgh, to take up the modest but steady work of a London-trained portrait-painter. Thus did I climb the painter's ladder, rung by rung. So high, and no higher.

From this schooling I learned one lesson above all: I can spot the work of a hack. Such was the Lamberts' coach-door emblem, painted hastily, by a child or an oaf. (Before my visitors departed, I inspected it closely, and found this signature: *T. Cummings*.) It seemed to depict—could it be?—three blue fish? What, does this Lambert descend from seamen? Or from cod? No, 'tis surely this: Lambert belongs to the artisans' society that meets at the Blue Herring.

When Weston entered the room, I placed my hands on his slight shoulders, pulled him to stand before the pane, and pointed out the window.

"Observe yon Lamberts, Weston, and tell me: By the king's whiskers, who the deuce asked them to bring the contents of their kennel?"

"Not I, sir," answered he, stepping away, his face strangely flushed. "Had they not told you of this?"

"Surely not, lad, else I would not be standing here, as gape-mouthed as you. And had I known, I would have demanded a bit more lucre. What think you," I winked, "a shilling a snout?"

Weston smiled, no doubt relieved that I could scarcely blame him for the Lamberts' dogs.

"Sixpence a paw, sir," he replied, his smile widening. "And a tax on every tail."

"A fine idea, my young accountant. I'm sure Parliament would approve of our dunning these colonials, every chance we get."

He laughed, a sweet laugh. I would hear more of that sound.

"Your talk of tails and taxes brings to mind a sugary tale, lad. Did you ever hear of Mary Hamilton, of Somerset? Fielding dubbed her *The Female Husband*, in a book of that title, a delectable read, if you would ever catch up with your chores long enough to find the leisure. She put on her brother's periwig and pants and passed for a man—for years, mind, and even *married* some unfortunate girl—having found that she could convince one and every person she met of her masculine sex merely by talking, all the day long, of the price of sugar!"

I roared with laughter, though Weston was not nearly as amused as I had hoped.

"But what happened to her, sir?" he asked, concerned.

"And here I thought you were heartless, lad. To the wife?" I answered, absently, as I looked out the window again.

"No, to the female husband, sir."

"I believe she was tried at Quarter Sessions and whipped at Taunton Castle, four Sundays straight. Twas no more than she deserved for such a cruel and callous deceit, don't you think?"

"But she must have had a reason, sir."

"Maybe so, lad. Maybe so. But I have little patience with dissembling. I would look at a man, and see him, and not his disguise. Be who you are; wear what you wear. Take these Lamberts," I said, pointing. "Can they not be read as clear as the ink in Edes's paper? Are they not as plain as print?"

On the sidewalk, Mrs. Lambert wiped her children's begrimed faces with a handkerchief so gray that Gulliver would have turned up his muzzle at it. She is a squat but copious woman, and her offspring don't lack for nourishment. Her husband, as affable a fellow as ever I had dealt with, treated his curs with tiny morsels of meat drawn from a waistcoat pocket. A tall man, he is as lanky as his wife is stout. The two barely traded a glance yet any fool could see that between them lay an entire tenderness of sentiment and affection, blanketing the whole of their brood.

"Hark, hark the dogs do bark!" I sang, clapping Weston on the back, as we together walked to the door. "Here have arrived on our threshold lean Jack Sprat and his fat wife. Lo, I have crossed an ocean to illustrate nursery rhymes!"

We passed a pleasant day, and I hope I have not seen the last of the Lamberts, for they are good honest people, of tart and ready opinions. But henceforth, I expect to paint gentlemen in ruffles. This afternoon, I delivered the likeness of young Usher. With the wrapped portrait under my arm, I walked the short distance to Hanover Street, where many of the town's leading merchants have shoehorned stately homes between dry goods shops, ironmongers, and wheelwrights. The Ushers' three-story pile was painted robin's-egg blue and trimmed in a white that positively glows, even in strong daylight: a fortune spent upon powdered lead.

A liveried Negro man named Pompey answered the door and told me the family was taking tea in the parlor. These New-England Africans wear silver buckled belts, and not iron chains, though surely their bondage is only differently wretched. If few in number—hundreds in a city of thousands—near all the blacks in Boston are slaves, and ever will be. They labor as footmen, laundresses, porters, and journeymen. They people houses, streets, and shops. They toil on the docks. A gentleman can scarce get the water for his tea but that his bondsman carries it from the pump, and his black maid serves it upon a silver tray.

The elder Usher, called Hiram, speaks loudly in the Governor's Council on behalf of the colonists' liberties—By taxing us, Parliament would make us slaves!—but 'tis Councilor Usher who is the slaver. Six and ten swift sloops has he, to ply his inhuman trade, from Guinea to the West Indies to Boston and back again, a triangle of profit, perfidy, and pain.

Tis a geometry I know well, Reader, for my scurvy brother, Colin, ran away to sea to become a cabin boy, and climbed the rigging to become a captain of one of those ships, only to trade his officer's epaulettes for a vicar's vestments, and to devote his life to exposing the evils of the traffic on which he had built his bloodstained fortune. Suffice to say, sir: just so soon as my brother entered the church did I leave it.

When I arrived at the Ushers' house, Mordecai was absent, visiting his younger brother, Elias, at Cambridge. But in the parlor I found his mother, reading, and his sister, at her embroidery. I placed the picture on the mantel, and removed the sheet with a practiced flourish.

"My goodness, Jameson, here is a fine portrait, more like my son than I could have hoped for," said Mrs. Usher, upon the unveiling. She is a learned woman, and a discerning one, for her comment was laced with irony. She smiled at me, though weakly, for she is miserably ill. A cancer of the breast, and she has not long to live. I pitied her decline, and envied her husband the life he must have had with this penetrating lady, no mere ornament but a true companion.

"I would be glad to have the chance to limn your own exquisite and most delicate features, madam," I replied, bowing once again, "though I could scarcely capture your beauty."

"Enough flattery, Jameson," answered the lady. "For we are neighbors, are we not? Queen Street is but two blocks from here. And between neighbors there must be no flummery. That I was once fair, I, admit, for I have little use for girlish modesty. But I am now a gaunt, pale, sickly thing, and no fit subject for any man's brush. Yet, I do wish you might paint my Elias."

How I am silenced by a candid woman. For a moment I could not reply. She spoke of this Elias with great fondness; indeed, she was nearly overborne by sentiment, and I gathered he might prove a worthier man than Mordecai. The younger brother's the better gentleman, as the saying goes.

"I would be honored to paint your Elias, madam," I answered softly.

Mrs. Usher's merits gave me high hopes for the daughter, Margaret, who catered to her mother with a pleasing tenderness. Miss Usher is beautiful, certain, and I found my eyes lingered over her form, and its promise of many, aye, so many, pleasures—whose pondering I will leave off, virtuous Reader, in consideration of your modesty and, equally, hers, although, I confess, I myself am not a little distracted by my unspent desires.

While her mother remained in the parlor, the girl found favor with me, through her solicitude for a dying parent. Yet all too soon, her mother retired, and then how the daughter brightened, her muted palette gone garish. Her frivolity sprang out like clothes packed too tightly in a trunk whose lid has popped opened. She leaned toward me, and giggled about nonsense. We walked a turn about the room, pausing to admire a sample of the girl's fine needlework; a stupendously gaudy scene of duck-hunting, rendered in shells; and a locked mahogany cabinet, baroquely ornamented—edged in ormolu and inlaid with mother-of-pearl—and in which her father keeps his curios from the African trade.

We spent near half an hour, head-to-head, and though I would wish it otherwise, there is no answer for it: she bored me. If Margaret Usher possesses the beauty her mother once had, she boasts all the wit of her brother, Mordecai—a meager portion, to be sure, though her marriage portion is doubtless ample. Is this all I am to hope for as a partner in life? A maid who can speak of nothing but ribbons and lace? Which would be the harder yoke to bear: loneliness and poverty, or marriage to a woman who could not begin to understand my Art and who would never, ever be my better part?

"Come, Jameson, into my study," called Councilor Usher, curtly, from the hall, rescuing me from Margaret's poppycock about taffetas and tippets. This Usher is a small, taut, wiry man, secure in his status if not in his stature. I towered over him. He bade me sit, while he stood before his desk, in a dark room, appointed with what looked to me, from a glance at the shelves, to be an indifferent library, grouped by naught but the color of the bindings.

"I am glad to have you in town," he began. He spoke at a clip-clop, and without the least pretense of kindness. "I may have a piece of business for you."

"And the balance of the fee for your son's portrait, sir . . . ?"

"All in good time. No, I mean, another piece of business."

"Does it pertain to your project, sir, for domestic manufacture?"

"In a way, Jameson. In a way."

"I have read some of your thoughts on the matter, sir. Is your suit homespun, then?" I asked—a bit wryly, I admit—for he wore a trim burgundy poplin, with oversized gold buttons, an attire no less foppish and fashionable than his son's rather more outlandish costume.

"Of course not. Our dye works can't produce rich clarets such as this," he answered, fingering his lapel. "*Yet*. But see my handkerchief? Look here." He pointed to a small piece of nubby cloth, about the color and size of a dormouse, peeking shyly from his jacket pocket. "I wear my homespun with pride, and I will urge the men of Massachusetts to do the same when the Assembly meets next week to consider these duties Parliament lays upon us. Homespun! Home Brew! Home Rule!"

The Shroud of Turin in Boston burlap! What was he on about?

"Sir?"

"My motto, Jameson. Every movement needs a motto."

"Of course, sir." (How about: Half-baked! Half-assed! Half-cocked!) "And will you succeed? Are many in town of like mind?"

"More than half Boston's merchants have agreed to boycott British goods. A goodly number, but there are yet laggards. Some of the richest traders in town would rest their heads in Mother England's lap."

O, Reader, in this season of solitude, I would fain lay my head in a lady's lap, but mayhap not the lap of Mother England.

"Tories, sir?"

"Of the rankest kind, Jameson. For them the sun rises and sets in London. And they will scuttle our boycott if we can't persuade them to join us."

"And the Assemblymen, sir? Will they support you?"

"Whether the Crown's debt justifies these taxes and the sending of troops is sure to be a matter of heated debate under the Town House roof next week. Many feathers will be ruffled," he said, now slowing his speech, raising an eyebrow, and fingering a single red button upon his waistcoat. "Fine feathers. Cock's combs, if you take my meaning."

Dear God, what erumpent gibberish is this? What the deuce does the button signify? And Reader, what coxcombs?

Usher realized my confusion soon enough.

"What I mean, Jameson, is that I believe there are a number of gentlemen whose pictures you might soon take. If you mind my advice, the Governor himself may, in due course, agree to sit for you."

"Sir, I am honored that you find my talent worthy," I replied, accepting his offer of what I assumed to be a glass of port, but which tasted more like bilge. (Reader, this home brew is a bitter cup.)

"No doubt, Jameson. That is a fine portrait of my son," he said, nodding in the direction of the parlor. "And did you not fancy my lovely daughter?"

Is he now to pimp his own child? The devil has more dignity.

"She's delightful, sir."

"Delightful. And well endowed, I assure you."

"A happy union of beauty and fortune, then, sir."

"Well said. And tell me, how does your own business fare, Jameson? Have you found it profitable?"

"No man takes up Art for profit, sir."

"Perhaps, but no man paints for very long without it. We could help each other. There is at present no other London-trained artist here in Boston, not since Smibert died. If you make yourself useful to me, I could make you a success."

"Useful how, sir?" I asked, somewhat fearful of the answer.

Here Usher drew himself up to his full, bantam height, and spoke as if upon a stage, a speech apparently well rehearsed.

"Within the bristles of your brush, Jameson, nests the reputation of our gentry, and at a time when we celebrate our fledgling New-England associations, the better to fly against the tyranny of a distant and unfeeling old England."

"Thank you, sir," said I, dumbfounded at the aviary convolutions of his attempted eloquence. And now I had to wonder, how had his wife borne him all these years? "But I fear I would never be able to repay your patronage." I would not place myself in this man's debt for all the sheep in Scotland.

"Ah, but you will repay me, Jameson," he answered, turning impatient. "And sooner than you think. I have one commission lined up for you already: Sarah Bradstreet, my kinswoman as well as my near neighbor, desires a pair of portraits, herself and her husband on pendant canvases, to mark the thirtieth anniversary of their marriage. In Mrs. Bradstreet you will glimpse what my Lucy—who is her older sister—once was."

"Mr. Bradstreet is the Torch of Liberty, is he not, sir? I'd be honored to make his acquaintance."

"Then you shall meet him tomorrow evening, at the Red Hen Club."

"The Red Hen, sir?" I wondered if this might be the source of Usher's bird-witted metaphors. "I've not heard of it. Is it a secret fellowship, sir?"

"Just turn up at the tavern on Water Street, by the sign of the plow. Bradstreet is sure to be there."

"Again, sir, thank you, but—"

"Damn it, Jameson, I've got some letters to write now."

"And my fee, sir?"

"I'll give it to you at the Hens' tomorrow night." He eyed me gravely. "And you will dine here next week. My wife tells me you have a penetrating eye. You will tell me what you make of the cast of Bradstreet's mind, for 'tis a matter of much speculation."

From the *Boston Gazette*, Thursday, August 9, 1764.

BOSTON.

*Y*esterday at ten o'clock in the forenoon, the Twenty-fourth Regiment of Foot of His Majesty's Army rowed in longboats to the Long Wharf and marched up King Street to the Town House, where it secured two cannons at the west end of the building, facing the town. Acting on the Governor's orders, the regiment's officers commandeered the Town House for their quarters, while the grenadiers pitched camp on the Common. Like an animal that eats its young, thus does a King turn upon his People.

To the Printer:

A Modest Proposal, in the spirit of Mr. Jonathan SWIFT, for Preventing the Poor of this Town from Being a Burden to Their Country, and for Making Them Beneficial to the Public.

It is a melancholy object to those who walk through this great town to see the streets crowded with beggars importuning every passerby for alms. Whoever could find out a fair, cheap, and easy method of making these poor people into sound, useful members of the Commonwealth would deserve to have his statue erected as a preserver of the nation. Having turned my thoughts for many years upon this important subject, I now therefore humbly propose a solution, which I hope will not be liable to the least objection.

We need not fewer beggars, but more. Let us enact a boycott that will deprive the shopkeepers of their trade, and thus turn our artisans into indigents. Were we to herd these beggars into a grim house called a *Manufactory*, we might employ them to make clothes for the elevated merchants of this town, that they could afford to abstain from wearing foreign finery. And if these poor unfortunates starve at their spindles? Let us bring in slaves to turn their wheels.

In sum:

Boycotts make beggars,
Beggars weave linen,
Linen clothes merchants,
Merchants pledge boycotts,
Boycotts make beggars.

I profess, in the sincerity of my heart, that I have not the least personal interest in endeavoring to promote this necessary work, having no other motive than the public good of my country, by providing a perfect plan, in which none benefits but,

—MR. HOMESPUN USURER.

Letter VI.

August the 11th, 1764

Elizabeth, forgive me, darling!

I wrote you Wednesday in the pitiless heat of midday, full of passion and poison, and sent off my letter before I recovered my cooler humor. Now 'tis Saturday, near dawn and sultry still, and I find myself full of rum and laughter. Yes *rum*, Lizzie. For the first time in my life, I am quite utterly, merrily drunk, drunk as a lord, drunk as a sailor, drunk (dare I say) as a serving boy. Nearly drunk enough to forget my disguise. The chambers were packed tight, and as the temperature rose with the talk, I felt desperate to remove my jacket. I was lucky that each time, I remembered what lay beneath it. For I have passed the evening waiting upon Mr. Jameson at the Red Hen Club, a drone within a hidden hive of men. Tis not a pretty place, I assure you.

Now you best forgive me my cups, toothsome wench, that I may tell you a merry tale! (Thus do these clubmen speak of the fairer sex, when out of our hearing.) My excuses, should you ask, are two: The room grew so thick with tobacco smoke that I became quite parched. You would not have me thirst, would you, friend? And the punch was so delicious, livened by a hothouse full of oranges and a cane field's worth of sugar, taxed so dear. Brave, busy planters, giving their lives to sweeten mine, if but for a moment! I drank boldly, freely—deeply enough to earn a clout from my master, who seemed rather to enjoy bestowing the soft blow upon my ear, as the evening drew to a close on the edge of morning.

But I have got ahead of myself, telling you the denouement before the prologue. Forgive me! I begin again.

"Know ye what signifies the Hen, boy?"

You will not, Lizzie, any better than I did. I shook my head when the clubman queried me gruffly, clapping a heavy paw upon my back just below my bindings. Mr. Mason it was, the brawny barber and town coroner, a lumbering man who stands as tall as my master, and must weigh half again as much.

"Tis an august assembly, and I its grand master," he told me, proudly pointing to the sumptuously embroidered patch upon his fringed tricorn.

The gentlemen of the Red Hen, the Right Worshipful Master Mason went on to explain, take their name from a fable. As he told it, the bigger animals in this fairy-tale barnyard idled their days away, leaving the littlest red pullet to plant and water and weed their crops, refusing her every entreaty for help. But when they wanted to share the fruits of her labor, the plucky young chick told them she should reap as she had sown: by and for herself alone.

"Tis a sort of . . . *agricultural* society then?" I asked, more confused than I had been before his account began.

My question sent Mason into a paroxysm of laughter.

"Dunderheaded catch-fart! You've the sense of a woman!" he sputtered. "Tis a gentleman's society—a private club, for we elect our fellows. No rabble will you find here, and no wenches! Freed from the tyranny of our brabbling wives, we smoke a pipe, drink a health, and sing a bawdy song or two. Of an evening, we philosophize, debating religion, or news, or scandal."

"Is it a political society, then, sir?"

"Nay, we Hens like a party, but we are no partisans. All opinions are welcome here. Still, I suppose some might call us a *colonial* society, since we toast our King from so great a distance. Though whether we play Parliament's cock or pullet, I can never remember."

No sooner had Mason delivered this cryptic remark than he called the gents to supper, amplifying his deep voice with a pewter speaker's trumpet until it deafened. As the Hensmen gathered at table, we serving boys scuttled to and from the kitchen, bearing trays heaped with joints and gravies that made my mouth water. (Unable to answer my hunger, I continued to slake my thirst.)

Twas Hiram Usher whose invitation brought us here. ("I must collect my fee, Weston," Mr. Jameson had explained, "and we may as well sup on someone else's shilling.") The Councilor steered my master to a seat between Samuel and William Bradstreet. Oh yes, Lizzie, I *did* gasp when I saw the Bradstreets—not so much Samuel, the father. For he has near threescore years upon him now, and his eyes have dimmed with age. He sports a pair of silver spectacles that make him look more the schoolmaster than the Indies merchant. Yet you would spy great wealth written upon his person. His silk jacket is intricately threaded; his linens are immaculate; the buckles at his knees fairly gleam. Unlike many who display themselves in similar costumes, Bradstreet does not appear to have grown unkind with lucre and power. And his mind seems as sharp as ever it was, judging from the animation of his talk. Though his hearing is not as keen as it might be.

"*Colin* Jameson?" I heard Bradstreet shout, cupping his ear, when the two men were introduced.

"I'm afraid not, sir," answered my master, raising his voice so the venerable man might hear him better. "*Stewart* Jameson, sir," he corrected. "But the Reverend Jameson is my brother, even if he might hesitate to own the connection."

At this, Bradstreet appeared delighted, and, taking my master's hand, pumped it with enthusiasm.

"Capital, Jameson. Capital!"

From that moment on the two of them set mouth to ear, spurning all other company, and chattering as if their acquaintance stretched back years rather than minutes. Who my master's famous brother is, I had not yet found out, for my efforts to eavesdrop came to naught amidst the din. But to Bradstreet at least, his name was gold.

Twas not Samuel's rheumy gaze that threatened me, but that of his hawk-eyed son. I fumbled my trencher when I saw William Bradstreet, but he offered not so much as a glance in my direction; instead, he kept one eye upon his "*honestus pater*"—as he called his father—and the other on Councilor Usher.

Billy Bradstreet was always such a callow boy, with more gold than wit. Rash and selfish, he lacked the judicious temperament that advances men in fortune. Yet he was bound for eminence by the same fabric of wealth and connections that destined us for each other—at least as my father saw it. We were neighbors, then, of like age, equal station, and opposite sex, a fortune now triply reversed. If I can no longer be seen as a female prize, William's gay youth has likewise slipped away. He is fretful and feverish, his skin stretched taught across a visage puffed with pride and shrunken with envy. How eager he seemed to separate Jameson from his father. He could not rest till he had regaled my poor master with the entirety of his *curriculum vitae*: a tale winding from pious youth through first literary honors next door in Cambridge and two years reading law at the Inns of Court in London, every book a maiden waiting to be penetrated by his hermeneutical mind, every library a seraglio reserved to him alone. And what had he discovered 'neath the Bodleian's bodice? That the King's rule is law. Thus has Billy become the Deputy Attorney General.

"*Honorium Rex, regulam lex*," he thundered, his Latin thickening with each bumper of punch.

"I ask you, Jameson," he continued, probing my master's chest with his finger, "am I not as zealous as any missionary? And I am a successful one, too. For I represent the righteous, and together we teach the criminal to kneel before the throne of almighty justice."

Dear God, Lizzie. Had I married him, as my father once plotted, what should my life be now? *That* missionary position I cannot imagine. Oh, the confinement of it! To be so cosseted and so shackled by turns: 'twould be a slave's lot.

As the heathen wriggles under the Jesuit's grasp, so valiantly did my Jameson try to free himself from windy William.

"You are indeed a zealot, sir," I heard my master agree, mischievously.

As I grow into my own manhood, Lizzie, I come to judge my fellows more keenly. And this I know for certain: for all his faults, surely my master is the better man. A glance gave me to wonder whether Samuel Bradstreet might not think the same.

By eleven o'clock the clubmen—perhaps two dozen of them—decided they had sufficiently stuffed their bellies even if they had yet to drink their fill. One by one, they pushed back from the table, each offering a satirical toast.

"To the beggars!" proposed one Hensman. "For without their rags to give us paper, what should we use for money? At least till the King and his soldiers shut down our presses!"

"Forget the rags," Hiram Usher thundered. "To fine imported cloth! For without the fruits of Liverpool's looms, we could not bankrupt ourselves nearly so fast."

"To our creditors," Jameson offered, getting into the topsy-turvy spirit of the thing. "For without them we would all be lords of our own purses, and masters of our own destinies."

"To the Red Hens, true Englishmen, who will not be made debtors of Parliament," said a man whom I recognized as Thomas Newcombe, the kindhearted doctor who had tended my family in the darkest of our days. He raised his tankard and continued in full earnest. "And to Samuel Bradstreet, the Torch of Liberty, whose brave beacon lights our way."

"Hear, hear," said Samuel Bradstreet, pleased at the praise heaped upon his name. "Hear, hear, Thomas. And to History, which reminds us that no free people have ever submitted themselves to slavery without a fight."

No toasts following Bradstreet's, we cleared the plates and picked at the bones. Soon Mason signaled the evening's next entertainment by placing upon the table top a glass chicken, scarlet as the bloodiest dawn, some two feet high and decked with a tiny felted tricorn, a miniature of the grand master's cap. With seeming reverence, the Hensmen lit their pipes and prepared to begin the night's disputation.

Mason, his hat askew and his chin bespattered, gaveled the brethren to order.

"Deviled eggs of the Red Hen," he slurred. "'Tis time to bedevil our minds!"

He then solemnly declaimed: "RESOLVED, that our slaves, who should reap what they sow, must be henceforth and forever freed, this by the law of the Hen."

He was met by a silence more sullen than drunken. Throats cleared, eyes lowered, the odd fart escaped its breeches. But no one, not a soul, cheered or chuckled.

Then the elder Bradstreet rose to his feet, somewhat unsteadily, and began to speak, affirmatively—his tone more grave than the occasion encouraged—offering in defense of the motion some lines from Justice Sewall's ancient treatise, *The Selling of Joseph*, printed in Boston decades ago, as this cruel century began. Jameson nodded in agreement, but many others had trouble keeping themselves vertical. Still the punch swirled round and round.

Looking more hawk than hen, Hiram Usher issued the rebuttal.

"Good Hensman. Brother. I challenge you," he said, pointing a finger at Bradstreet. "Have ye no precedent more *recent* to support your outlandish position this evening? For we are modern men, no *Puritans* at risk of entertaining Satan. Remember that Sewall would have us hang our witches *and* free our Negroes, eh, would he not?" Usher barely suppressed a smile at his own wit.

Bradstreet countered, seething.

"You will recall, Councilor, that Justice Sewall had the grace to apologize when he came to understand he had committed great wrongs." The room fell into an awkward silence as he continued between clenched teeth. "Were you a true Christian, Hiram, I might give you the Reverend Whitefield's *Letters* on the topic, or Coleman's *Testimony Against the Antichristian Practice of Making Slaves of Men*, or better still, Reverend Colin Jameson's *Religious and Moral Considerations upon Philosophical Reflections on the Keeping of Negroes*, just printed in Edinburgh."

So here lies the source of this Colin's fame, Lizzie. Yet at the mention of his brother, my master looked miserable.

"But I will not waste Reverend Jameson's words on you, Hiram."

"Ach, there are enough of them," my Jameson muttered.

"For long and well as these good men argue against you, Hiram, *your* consideration shall never extend past your own empty heart and bulging pockets."

Usher flushed with rage, and stood to remove himself from the circle of fellowship. I feared I would soon see his hands round Bradstreet's neck. But then the son intervened, his face drawn smooth with false laughter.

"Fellow good white eggs of yon good hen," William began, rising to his feet, and rapping upon the floor with his cane. "Like every dutiful Christian, I must, of course, support my father. But please allow me, if you will, to offer an *amendment* to his position." (You must picture,

Lizzie, an unctuous low bow inserted just here.) "To bolster my case I shall call on Mr. Burke, rather than upon good Judge Sewall and that mad Quaker, Woolman. But you will find, curiously enough, that the argument is much the same. I submit: to free our slaves is the merest beginning to the new millennium my father so fearlessly envisions. Let us also release our Indians from their bondage to our liquors, our wives from the yokes of marriage, our children from the shackles of their parentage, our dogs from the leashes of their masters—yea, let us sever these fair *colonies* from the silken web of empire!"

By the time he played out the jest, William had spent himself. But breathless as he was, he knew his triumph, and bowed deeply before the Hensmen, grown merry again.

All but for two. As Mason called for toasts to conclude the program, my own Jameson and the elder Bradstreet looked as if they knew not whether to shout or weep.

William drank the first health.

"To the African's blush, may it be as rosy as her lips," he offered, "and to the painter's brush, may it be as long as his yard." With a look of barely veiled contempt, he raised his chin toward Jameson.

"To the King's body, and its lasting health!" cried another.

"To the factor's crammed warehouse, and his ill-gotten wealth!"

"Yea, and to the slaver's full hold, and his profitable stealth!" drank a third, nodding in Usher's direction.

At that, Samuel Bradstreet could take no more. He stood, his face red, and nudged his spectacles higher on his nose, the better to stare at—no, through, his brother-in-law.

"To the mercy of God, who sits in judgment above. May He damn you all to hell!" he sputtered, upsetting his chair as he stormed out into the fast-waning night. My Jameson stumbled after him, followed by his tipsy apprentice. We soon lost sight of Bradstreet in the darkness.

Whether 'twas the suddenness of our movement, or the coolness of the night air, I cannot say, but no sooner had we reached the street than the full force of the liquor hit me. A block toward Queen Street and I began to reel in earnest. I leaned against a hitching post, uncertain how to hazard another step.

"Weston? You all right, there, lad?" Jameson asked.

"Yesssir. I'm fine, sssir. Only . . . my head. Or is it my legs? The cobblestones seem so . . . bumpy. Why are they so bumpy, sssir?"

"Holy water into wine, lad!" he cursed, laughing, as he took a step toward me. "Have you forgotten the terms of your indenture? You signed on as a teetotaler for five long years."

"I'm sorry, sssir."

"Just how much punch did you drink, you little saucebox?"

"Only what the gen'lmen left in their glasses, sssir. Or is it, what the Hens left in the trough?"

He stood before me, 'neath the light of the stars, and bent low to give my face a careful inspection. "Sweet Jesus, Weston," he sighed, as he looked into my eyes. For a flicker of a moment—a brief, drunken moment—I thought he might kiss me.

"Ach, lad," he said, chucking me on the chin. He bent to lift me at the waist, threw me over his shoulder—as a sailor might hoist his duffel—and set off toward Queen Street. My top half flopped down his back, while he steadied his load with a hand pressed to my bottom. "I'll get you back to the coop, easy enough. But I warn you, your cock won't be crowing in the morning."

"My cock, sssir?"

"Weston," he said gravely, slowing to a halt. "Let your master give you a lesson in the Art and Mysteries of manhood. If drinking at the trough of the Hens has led you to forget your cock, you must pledge to sobriety till the end of your days."

"I promise, sssir. I ssswear it."

So, pledged the punch-drunk cockless boy that was this,

Fanny Easton.

BOSTON.

A *special meeting of the General Assembly* is to be held on Saturday, at the College in Cambridge, while His Majesty's officers occupy the Town House and troops assemble on the Common to parade before the Governor.

Assemblymen will be asked to entertain the following Bill, brought to the floor by the Speaker, Samuel Bradstreet, Esquire, *viz.*:

An Act for the Abolition of the Slave Trade.

Mr. Thaddeus Mason to bring a second bill, *viz.*:

An Act for the Construction of an Asylum for the Insane, in the City of Boston.

N.B. We hear that in this City well-disposed Gentlemen and their Ladies are making haste to the painting room, on Queen Street, of Stewart Jameson, Esquire, late of Edinburgh, a Face-Painter of Renown, Experience, and Genius.

CHAPTER 7

In Which Is Heard
Not a Little Clucking

I f you have hazarded time in the metropolis—that is to say, in London, and not in this backward backwoods—you may have walked past the grand home at Barn Elms, where the Kit-Cat Club meets in winter. "Ah!" you will have sighed, as you passed its blue door, "would that I had an invitation to dine therein!" And well you might, for I can report, having penetrated the place not three years ago, in the company of the Earl of Berkeley, an ignoble nobleman, that within those doors I rubbed elbows with dukes before a table laid with roasted beef and mutton and fowl on platters, heaping, next bowls of punch as deep as any well. Cast your eyes over this feast, let your mouth water, and now put aside the savoring of those delicacies and turn to look upward, along the pub's walls. There, in frames of gilt, hang forty-eight portraits of the club's long-standing members—cocksure, the lot of them—painted decades ago by Godfrey Kneller (a Hanoverian hack, but there can be no denying he had a head for business). These likenesses, Kneller's "kit-cats," for so they are called, are but two foot by three foot small, to fit within the foreshortened space between wainscot and crown molding. Thus do the Kit-Catters dine 'neath a gallery of portraits, each to be toasted every evening, till every man, with forty-eight swallows, has drunk himself under the table.

I'll not deny that I stroke my fancy by counting myself a wit, but mark me: I am no Johnson. Nevertheless, I have, in this brief dissertation, given you the etymology of the term *kit-cat*, for since Kneller did his work, decades ago, all portraits of such a size go by that club's name—and it were just as well it had not another, as I have heard the club had once been called the Dim-Wit, and I'm relieved that some right-thinking soul saw fit to change it, else I'd be now painting dim-wits for my dinner.

Reader, I would forgive you if you were to say, "This is all well and good, so far as it goes, Jameson, but I had picked up your book with a mind to read a history of your adventures, and not a dictionary of the English language. Who gives a fig for Kneller's kit-cats?" For having plucked my book from a shelf, accept my eternal thanks and, as for figs, please be assured that these too I have, and ready to hand: for, lo, here, in Boston, this less-than-London, have I become a lesser Kneller.

It happened thus: two days after I dined at the Red Hen, the lodge-master, Thaddeus Mason, a bear of a man, came to Queen Street and delivered unto me a sealed commission, to paint kit-cats of the Hensmen. Thirty-two portraits! At twenty-five pounds a head!

"Matthew, Mark, Luke, and John hitched to the grindstone!" I said to the lad. "There's so much to be done, and so fast. I feel like the farmer in the old joke about the hireling, the two chickens, and the donkey."

"How is that, sir?" he replied, theatrically perplexed, for I give him this: he has mastered the art of setting up my punch lines.

"Well, the barn's afire, you see, and the farmer and his man are trying to save their stock, never mind their seed."

Here Weston wrinkled his nose, as he always does at my riper puns.

"Nay, do not scorn me, lad," I smiled. "'Tis a moral story, and mark it well, for it holds a lesson you have yet to learn. Picture the scene I would paint: 'Tis August, blistering, like this one, but parched. Lightning strikes, and the farmer's hayloft goes up like tinder. Panic overspreads the animal kingdom. Cock-a-doodle-doo! the rooster crows at the flash of flames. Hee-haw, hee-haw, the donkey brays in terror. Cluck, cluck, the hens do squawk."

"More hens, sir?"

"Aye, lad. We need the hens. Let me finish, will you? The farmer and the hireling race toward the barn, to rescue the animals. 'What mercy there are two of us!' shouts the farmer to his man. 'I'll grab my cock and pullet while you look after my ass!' "

Weston groaned and blushed. I, who am ever my own best audience, suffered a rolling-fit of laughter.

Tolerant Reader, do not despair. I have since collected myself, and have sworn off such broad jests. At least for the remainder of this chapter.

But, truly: my painting room is like a house afire. Weston and I will be flat out for weeks, mayhap, for months. Since the club voted to secure my services, all its wives have come a-calling: the pock-faced and the smooth, the fair and the dark, in singles and in pairs. The tide of my trade has turned. The gentry wash up on my doorstep like so much flotsam. "Might I have a miniature of your kit-cat of my husband, Jameson?" (This, ten pounds for a scant three hours of Weston's time, a tidy sum, well worth the interruption of his study of still life, which subject he cannot bear, at any cost.) "My husband speaks so highly of your genius. Would you have time to paint me, as well, with my two little sons?" (Twenty-five quid for you, madam, a fiver a piece for your demi-galoots.) Not only this. Gentlemen not yet elected to the brood, but eager to nest, send their notes, as if a canvas of mine were a kind of ticket to gain entry to the Hen house:

> *My Dear Mr. Jameson,*
>
> *It having come to my obsequious attention that you take pictures of gentlemen who belong to secret clubs which I am panting to join, I hope to employ you to paint me, at your earliest convenience, but no later than yesterday. With all due regards, and with promise of paying as much as you might possibly require, and very likely even more, in chicken feed or silver coin, I remain,*
>
> —*Cornelius Suckbottom.*

Dear Reader, know this: I should like to dwell on my triumphs, and to caress my successes, pleasures with which I am afforded infrequently enough. And yet, even now, as the till fills, a gloomy figure casts a shadow over my canvas. My apprentice—this tender genius, this Prodigal artist, my right, my better hand, my straight man: I begin to regret him. He distracts me; he disconcerts me.

"Our accounts are at last in the black, sir," he offered, leading I knew not where.

"Aye, and we'd have twice as many farthings, had you not set my price at half a Smibert, lad."

"Yes. Well. I was wondering, sir. After we pay the landlord, and your creditors in town, might we have enough to again hire a regular housekeeper?"

Ah. He is keen to spare himself the labor Mrs. Goddard fails to manage.

"Reckon not your Hens before they are hatched, Weston," I cautioned him, for we have not yet counted our loot, a motley pile of copper and silver, the odd flash of gold, and a mountain of dubious paper. But as for wanting a housekeeper better than our Mrs. Grub-grime, who can blame him? Though I blamed him for a good deal else, including the disappearance, last week, of a tin of precious painter's lead. What use could Mrs. Goddard have for pigments? I could think of no other explanation than that my apprentice is a purloiner. But, Reader, I have anticipated myself. Let me relish my good fortune before cataloguing my bad.

Tis a strange feeling, to be flush, and not as hot as I remember. Mind you, I embrace Prosperity, though gingerly, for she is a fickle mistress, and no doubt will soon cast me out of her bed. Indeed, I find that I lose near as fast as I gain, for I must feather my nest to suit these preening Hens. Props, they would busy their portraits with props! I have dispatched Weston to Edes's to buy books bound in leather and edged in gilt, that the gentlemen may make at least a show of learning; and to the mantua maker's, that we might stock the closet in our painting room with dresses and shawls to wrap their ladies in borrowed loveliness. Let Boston wear its pretended virtue on its sleeve. I will soften its flaws, and cover its pocks, for a price.

But, first, let me make good my debt to you, kind Reader. I have implored your patience, with regard to my friend Alexander. Pray, put up your feet, for this may take a while. I must begin by telling you why the Earl of Berkeley is a man of unredeemable character.

One blustery winter evening in London in the year 1738, the Earl, when he had yet the excuse of youth for his impetuousness, dined at the Kit-Cat Club. While warming himself by the fire, he entered the evening's disputation, a heated debate, more farce than philosophy, on the nature of the color of men. One headstrong young gentleman, the Duke of Cornwall, argued that black and white were mere coatings of an identical inside; the Earl maintained the opposite, that black men are sinister and savage, through and through, and whites, enlightened, even unto their entrails.

As the evening progressed, so, too, did the gentlemen's bleariness, and, equally, their incaution. Ere the night was through, they had sealed an outrageous bet, the Earl staking no less than five thousand pounds— a fortune!—that even if he raised a black bairn from infancy, and supplied him with the best English education, he would merely coat a black soul with white, so that the blanched Negro would be yet savage at the age of five-and-twenty. The Duke wagered on the subject of this experiment growing to a civilized man, indistinguishable, except for his skin, from an English gentleman.

The very next day the Earl bought a babe off a slave ship, direct from Guinea. He named the infant Fortune—for this was the vicious nature of this nobleman's wit—and, as he had sworn to do, sent to him to the best wet-nurse for three counties round. When the lad reached the age of six, Berkeley enrolled him at the grammar school in the market town of Lowth. Ten years later, the boy was sent to the university, at Oxford, where he proved a surpassing scholar. He changed his name to Ignatius Alexander, rechristening himself in honor of a beloved tutor. By his diligence and his brilliance, he treasured up a staggering fund of learning. He was next sent to study physic in Edinburgh, where the dons commissioned me to paint his portrait, after which we became more intimately acquainted. For three years we shared lodgings in a ragged boardinghouse behind St. Giles. He was, I assure you, the finest friend I have ever had.

In 1763, Alexander, having achieved the age of five-and-twenty, was inspected by the Earl and the Duke together, before the entire faculty at the University of Edinburgh. To the aging noblemen's astonishment—

for they had never followed his progress, nor ever once visited him—he bested them both, on every subject.

"He is either a prodigy or a freak," maintained the Earl. "Or else he is a parrot, and no more. A trained orangoutang could do as much. In any event, he is unnatural, and we must start again, with a fresh one." But the faculty, arbitrating the case, ruled in the Duke's favor, without the least hesitation. The Earl, grumbling all the while, paid the Duke his five thousand pounds. But such was Berkeley's hatred for the ingenious subject of his experiment—and indeed, such was his eagerness to punish Alexander and, by the same means, to partly compensate himself for his losses—that he summarily announced his intention to auction his property to the highest bidder, the very next morning.

Suffice to say, Reader: there are catastrophes in this miserable wreck of a world that even I cannot laugh away. On the day of Alexander's fateful examination, I stood in the back of the lecture hall, overcome with rage. While Berkeley and Cornwall argued onstage, their heads bobbing amidst a sea of black-gowned scholars, Alexander quietly made for the door. "I must away, this instant," he whispered to me. "I shall hide myself at the Lion's Head Inn, in Haddington."

"Sander, you cannot mean to turn fugitive," I insisted. "I'll pay Berkeley's price."

"No, friend. Do *nothing*. Go home, and stay put. I will devise a solution."

Had I listened to him then, I would have spared us both a world of misery. But soon after Alexander fled from the room, undetected, I pressed myself upon Berkeley.

"You cannot mean to set the doctor on the auction block," I shouted.

"I do, and I shall, Jameson. Would you like to watch? The bidding begins at nine. I expect your most beloved *friend* will fetch a high price. So handsome and refined a Negro gentleman—mind you, a poet and a physician, too . . ."

I suppose I should mention that Berkeley hated me. I had not fucked his horse, but I had once, years before, rather trifled with his daughter, Catherine Thistlethwaite, Duchess of Hampton, an alluring woman, but a bitter, vain, and spiteful one. In her own clutching and vicious way, she loved me; she wished to keep me as she might keep a pet. Tis a common enough exchange between a young artist and a married woman—I would be her lover; she my patron—but I would not ply my brush for clothes, rent, and pocket money. I was just twenty when I painted her, and eager to oblige every sudden sally of lust. But I would not scruple to barter my very self. I would not. I regretted the attachment almost as soon as I had formed it—though not, as it turned out, quite soon enough—and broke with her. Rejection, *by a commoner,* no less, aroused her insatiable appetite for vengeance. "I will not rest, Stewart Jameson," she seethed, "till your heart bleeds."

O Reader, whether Sir, or Madam, you must agree: women say a good deal in the heat of passion, of which gentlemen commonly take little note. This was my error. Had I remembered the Duchess's words as I spoke to her father in the lecture hall—had I even recalled that Berkeley *was* her father—I might have deduced that he meant to use my love for Alexander to make good his daughter's vow, which had become his own. Alas, I did not remember; I did not deduce.

"Berkeley, how much can I give you to take Alexander off the table?"

The Earl laughed. "Jameson, you cannot possibly offer me sufficient inducement. I do so love auctions—such giddy spectacles, don't you agree? But if you were to bring me, say, two thousand pounds, before morning, I might find such a treasure, shall we say, hard to refuse."

What could I do? I went first to my brother, certain that his anti-slavery zeal would move him to raise the funds—or, at the very least, encourage him to act as my surety on a loan. But he refused. I next pleaded with bankers, but found none willing to extend me such a sum. At last, desperate, I approached the infamous, unscrupulous brothers McGreevy. They loaned me the money, demanding as collateral everything I owned. Every canvas, every brush. And, the McGreevys insisted, when they learned I would use the money to purchase a slave, even Alexander himself. Their impossible terms: the money or my life, due in a fortnight. With interest.

By nightfall, I had paid the Earl, and Alexander's papers of manumission had been drawn, signed, and sealed.

Had I been then the skeptic I am now, I might have expected what followed: Berkeley betrayed me. Thinking to be received with joy, I rode to the Lion's Head to deliver the papers to my friend. Instead, I led the Earl's man-hunters straight to their prey. Barely had I entered the Lion's mouth when they were upon me, clouting me with clubs. The world turned to black. I awoke on the floor, hours later, bleeding and beaten, and no sign of Alexander, nor of his papers. The auction had long since ended.

"You can look for your property in Jamaica," Berkeley said, laughing, when I confronted him. "Or was it Georgia? I'm so sorry, but I'm afraid I can't recall where the winning bidder said he planned to ship your friend. Somewhere in those barbarous colonies—perhaps my daughter might remember where. Yes, yes. Why don't you ask the Duchess, Jameson?"

The doctor, no doubt, had told me to stay put precisely in order to avoid this sequence of events. But I failed him.

Within a week, the McGreevys closed in on me, seizing all of my possessions, and demanding Alexander. I fled, thinking both to escape my creditors and to search for my friend, however unlikely my chances of success at either. Where the doctor is now, I know not, though I pray he is alive—and by alive, I mean, *free*, for slavery is death. Tis near a month since I wrote to Virginia, and near three since I arrived upon these far shores. O, I have stayed put. I have idled, thinking Sander might more readily discover me than I, him. But I cannot abide it any longer. Come the first of September, one way or another, I'll hire a horse, or board some sodding stagecoach, and ride off into the American wilderness to find him.

FROM THE *BOSTON GAZETTE*, THURSDAY, AUGUST 23, 1764.

To the Editor:

Your recent announcement of the renowned genius of a face-painter new to town, of unknown history, occasions these observations. There will always be a few Portrait Painters in every Country, who will succeed for a Time; but, don't let them imagine that they owe their Encouragement to their own particular Merit, or to the general good Taste of the Nation; no, no, 'tis to the Vanity and Self-love of their Sitters that they are chiefly obliged; Passions which must ever be gratified, and the Owners of them are ever ready to open their Purses to the irresistible Flattery of Portrait Painting. Tis to this, and this alone, that any such face-painter owes his dubious reputation.

—A WISE BARRISTER.

Letter VII.

August the 23rd, 1764

Dearest Lizzie,

I am sorry to have so long delayed my answer to your last, anxious letter, especially since I mean to offer you reassurance. But how frantic these paint-spattered days! I am grateful to steal a moment—and the strength—to write to you, even if my hand cramps with the effort. As I sit here, at dusk, my eyes growing heavy, my small mattress beckoning me, I find I can scarcely pinch the quill. Forgive the quaver in my lines. I have earned my crookedness. At long last, my apprenticeship has progressed far enough that my master allows me to paint beside him.

This morning, when I went belowstairs just after sunup—for our days begin at dawn—I found Mr. Jameson once again gazing upon *The Serving Boy*, which he had lately moved from the painting room to the parlor, where it hangs, unframed, unvarnished, unfinished.

"Hadn't we better get started, sir?"

"Aye, Weston. The Hens rise at cock's crow. But there's a lesson for you in this canvas, too, if only I could puzzle it."

"Is it something about the composition, sir?"

"That's not it. It's the likeness."

"The likeness, sir?" I asked, not a little worried.

"Aye, lad. It misses its mark. I've overshot a target before, mind. But here the distance between the original and the copy widens. Goddammit, it grows less like you every day."

"It must be the light in the parlor, sir. Can we not take breakfast upstairs? You hadn't finished with yesterday's lecture on greens . . ."

Once we had settled in the painting room, I began to mix the colors for Amos Quincy's linens, taking Jameson's direction, to impart just the right degree of brilliance, frill, and starch to the Attorney General's lace cravat, which he had tied loose over a billowing, ruffled shirt. Twas for me no easy feat, setting white upon white. My master stood beside the window, a small piece of ivory in one hand and his finest brush in the other, expertly knocking off a miniature for Mrs. Quincy.

I know, Lizzie, that you question the honor of the man under whose roof I have found shelter. But I cannot think I can have anything to fear from my master. Every day he inhabits his promise to teach me the mysteries of his Art. Indeed, 'tis lesson enough to watch him. He delights in his work as a child might, his entire countenance a study in concentration. This morning, when his hair fell across his brow, he pushed it away, absently, with the end of his brush, and stroked the cleft of his chin, smearing his face with paint, too intent on his work even to notice what he had done.

"Would you paint yourself, then, sir?" I teased.

He looked up, confused, as if awakened from a dream.

"Come again, Weston? I assure you, there is nothing I would enjoy painting less than a self-portrait."

"You'd be a beautiful subject, sir," I ventured, for 'tis true enough. "But all the same, that's not what I meant."

"You have a fine eye, lad, so you must know you're talking shite," he said, shaking his head. "Been at the punch again, have you?" But he could not hide the color that came to his cheeks. Can I paint that color for you, Lizzie? I don't think I've progressed far enough in my studies to capture such manly beauty.

I walked toward him, pulling a clean rag from my pocket.

"What I meant, sir, is that you've striped yourself." I wiped his brow, his cheek, his chin. For a moment, he covered my hand with his, and held it.

"That'll do, lad," he said quietly, taking my hand from his face. I stepped away, tucked the rag back in my pocket, and we resumed our work in an awkward silence. Perhaps, Lizzie, my master has more to fear from me than I do from him.

At ten the day's first sitter arrived, a game young Hen named Samuel Clough. Using a primed canvas I had set upon the big easel, Jameson worked up Clough's face to a fair likeness, blocking the regions of his clothing with charcoal and a wash of brun rouge. I stood before my own smaller easel, polishing the draperies upon Joseph Wilkins, another of yesterday's sitters, and listening as my master snared Clough with his practiced patter, which he had resumed easily enough after I dared to touch him.

Two hours later Mr. Clough took his leave. After a quick break for supper—small beer and a mutton potage I had left to simmer over the hearth—the change-up was on: Hensman John Griggs into the chair and onto Jameson's easel, still-wet Samuel Clough to mine, and patient Joseph Wilkins content to lean decorously against the wall, where his likeness could converse with Quincy's.

Griggs, a tooth-puller, has surely found the proper calling, for he is a talker, and requires a rapt audience. My master could scarce stand the rival.

"Good sir," Jameson implored him at long last, "I am all ears, I promise you, for there is so much left to learn of the art of extraction. But while I am sure your own teeth are peerless, I can hardly paint you with your mouth open."

Twas little use. "That reminds me of a patient," Griggs responded, and continued much as before. The bell atop the Old Brick Church had rung three before Jameson declared the sitting at an end.

"Ach, poor Weston," he sighed after Griggs left, when he saw me stretching the fingers and worrying the knuckles of my painting hand. "I should think a lad of your age might be well used to a cramp in the hand that holds his brush."

I wondered for a moment—for of course I am not a lad, of any age—and then blushed when I took his meaning, winning his customary wink when he saw that the joke had reached its target. But I begin to see the face of tragedy behind his mask of comedy. He is altogether at his ease while making cock-and-pullet jokes but my touch upon his brow unsettles him entirely. Is not his ribaldry a way to keep his distance, rather than a means of closing it? His humor is a tool, not unlike the mahlstick painters use to keep at arm's length from a wet canvas while working on the details. Barely had this thought occurred to me when he proved the point again.

"Fear not, lad. I know a way to relieve your aches," he said, merrily. "Let us break off work to deliver the Lamberts' portrait. But I wonder: Have we the ratio needed to accomplish the task?"

"Sir?" I asked.

"Truly, lad, your cart leads your horse if you have you learned colors but not sums. Did your father's master's son not have a bloody tutor for maths? And what poor contract have I signed, that asks me to be at once a painting master and a teacher of ciphers? What requires five times two, plus four times four? Tis you, not I, who loves riddles and excels at sums, lad: puzzle it out."

"Twenty-six, Mr. Jameson. Ten plus sixteen. Tis no hard sum. Even for you, sir."

"Enough of your cheek. The *ratio*, lad. Divide your proceeds by four."

"It does not divide evenly, sir. Four goes into twenty-six six and a half times. But what ratio is that?"

"Hmm. I had it dividing evenly. No matter. The ratio? The number of their hands to ours, lad. Five Lamberts with a pair of paws each, four dogs with a quartet of them—an enormous piece of work, is it not, to be carried between the two of us, from here all the way to the Long Wharf?" he asked, surveying the vast canvas, near as tall as a full-length, and twice as wide.

"How will we manage it, sir?"

"Aye, Weston, you are right to wonder. Hire us a cart, then, you little scapegrace, for I shall need more help than yours if we're to get this menagerie back to the circus in one piece."

After a nod and the shallowest of bows, I headed out onto Queen Street to do his bidding.

"Mr. Jameson?" I called from the front hallway some moments later. "Sir? A carter stands at the ready just by the door."

"Aye lad," he yelled from the painting room. "So he does. I can see him from the window. Now just wait there, and soon you shall see the display of levitation you must be expecting."

"Beg pardon, sir?"

"Surely you fancy that this great hulking canvas will soon wrap itself, walk down the stairs, and jump onto the cart," he said, his voice rising in both pace and pitch. "Or else you should *come at once!*"

I sped up the stairs to tender the help he called for. But truly, Lizzie, I was useless, nay, worse. The painting is light enough in subject matter, for Jameson has pinned the family's high spirits, allowing the Lambert pack to make merry in every corner of the composition. But in physical presence, 'tis a weighty thing: a full seven stone, maybe more. Knowing what little my arms can bear, I could only stare, and wonder how I would manage it.

"Don't just stand there, Weston. Grab a tarpaulin and help me wrap the canvas."

I chose the driest and cleanest of our drop cloths.

"Here you are, sir," I said, as I handed it to him.

"Four hands, lad. It takes four hands."

We spread it upon the floor. Then he instructed me to grab the frame at its upper left corner, while he took the upper right.

"Ready to ease her down, lad?" he asked.

I nodded.

"Just so." He said. "Into the sheets we go, on the count of three."

But my side of the bargain thudded loudly to the ground, nearly crushing my hands in the process.

"Weston, confound it, you've nearly wrecked our Rembrandt!" he shouted. "Help me tie the thing up—that, I fancy you can manage. And then bring the carter. He can tote your half down the stairs for you."

Even with the carter's help, 'twas no easy trick to carry that painting down the stairs. I tried to offer what assistance I might—holding wide the door to the painting room, guiding the canvas round the turn of the staircase—but I seemed only to increase the men's burden. Before we reached the front door I had twice crashed into my master. The second time, the canvas pinioned us both in the crook of the landing, and I found myself pressed hard against him by its weight.

"Weston," he sighed, "for God's sake, if you would hold me fast, pray, do not let it be like this."

"Sir?"

"Lad, we need an extra right hand and you bring me three left feet. Heaven above, can you not simply wait by the cart?"

To say the river crossing to the Lamberts' home in Charlestown is not a long one is to exaggerate its breadth considerably. A bridge could span it easily, had Boston the engineers, or the funds, to contemplate such a project. But to Jameson, the Charles might be a great ocean. He refused to board a boat, at any cost, and had arranged to hand off the canvas to Mr. Lambert at a dockside tavern, the Blue Herring. Tis a grubby place, Lizzie, low-ceilinged and soot-blackened, dark even in daylight. At a scant five o'clock—hardly the end of a workingman's day in the summer—men in leather aprons crowded the bar, fortifying their strong words with strong drink. While the carter waited outside, Jameson sat for a mug of cider, and I found a shadowy corner, where I could eavesdrop undisturbed. The talk was of politics, but in a rougher idiom than you would find on the floor of the Assembly, or even at the table of the Red Hens.

"As I reckon it," said one fellow, a cobbler, to judge by the tools hanging at his belt, "the King's farts smell no sweeter than the Guv'nor's."

"Aye, they's all one," another agreed. "London whelped they is. Lobsterbacks, gold-droppers, and affidavit men, with one hand full of court papers and the other in our pockets."

"If it's a hand in my pocket I'm after," said a third, "I know where to find your mother, you great whore's kitling."

In such quarters as these, Lizzie, even so coarse an insult provoked only laughter. And then the thick chorus of banter began again, moving mouth to mouth and table to table around the room.

Twas not long before a gentler voice broke into the mix.

"I spy the infamous Mr. Jameson," Hugh Lambert said with a smile, clapping my master on the back.

"Good to see you, Lambert. But dare I ask: Why infamous?"

"Do I take it you've not read this morning's *Gazette*, then? A Wise Barrister has spread your 'dubious reputation' all around town."

Jameson looked exceedingly alarmed and ventured, in a measured tone: "Nay, Lambert. I've been painting all day, earning my dubious keep."

"Nursing vanity and self-love, no doubt," Lambert said, handing my master a copy of the day's newspaper, and pointing to a letter which I read over his shoulder.

Jameson relaxed as he read.

"Aye, Lambert," he joked. "I'm a lump of vanity and bad taste, to be sure. But your Witless Browbeater needn't bother. I'm a worse critic of my own brush by far. Who the deuce is the fellow?"

"Woebegone Breaches? William Bradstreet, I'd hazard."

"Ah. Of course. Will you still be wanting your portrait, Lambert? Or has the man put you off Art?"

"You can't be serious, can you, Jameson? The man has only stoked my vanity. Rain won't hold off long now, but do you think there's time for a peek at the portrait before we load it onto the boat?"

The three of us went outside. Jameson untied enough of the wrapping to expose the left side of the canvas, where Mrs. Lambert and two younger children disported with one of the dogs.

"Jameson, I am no painting man," Lambert sniffed, his eyes misting, "but you've got a tender heart as well as a keen eye. Indeed, if you can spare the time, I have another commission for you. I cannot pay cash for it. But, as you need cloth, I would be willing to trade fifty yards of soft white duck for a likeness of my sister, Louisa. Her twenty-fifth birthday approaches. She is a great beauty, and I cannot think of a finer gift than a stroke of your brush."

"I would be honored, of course. Where will I find her?"

"Ever since her husband died, she lives with us. And forever more she will, too, if she cannot fetch herself a new one."

"In Charlestown? I'm afraid she'll have to come to me. For I would not brook a boat ride, not even for your enchanting sister."

They chattered on about this Louisa Lambert Beaujardin—"the Widow B.," Jameson took to calling her. And if I understand him half as well as I think I do, he means to court as well as to paint her. Oh Lizzie, surely I will never be courted again, not by any man. And would I want to be? Or would that rob me of my newfound liberties? For all my ciphering, I can scarce reckon the delicate balance between what this Francis Weston has gained, and what has been lost by your,

Fanny Easton.

FROM THE *PENNSYLVANIA HERALD*, MONDAY, AUGUST 20, 1764.

TO BE SOLD,

The Owner having lately suffered a
TURN OF FATE.

Several Concave Mirrors of assorted sizes.

Three reflecting Microscopes, for close inspection of human nature.

A Telescope, with which even the *UNTRAINED* Eye can see distant *GALAXIES.*

Young Gentleman's Arithmetic, for Solving Simple Sums, bound in leather.

Plaster Heads of Shakespeare and Chaucer.

Unused Account Books, Ledgers, and Sundry Mathematical Instruments.

Two Globes, a Pocket Compass, and a Map of Boston.

Inquire at Messrs. *James Stuart and Sons*, Joiners.

CHAPTER 8

The Enlightened Man

Weston, have you ever heard the expression 'turn of fate'?" I asked the lad while we sat to a late supper.

" 'Turn of fate,' sir?"

"Aye."

"Perhaps you mean 'twist of fate'?"

I shook my head, and stared once more at the newspaper Edes had brought by. At last. Thank God. A communication from Alexander. It must be. But what the deuce was I meant to deduce from it?

"Look here, lad," I said, handing the paper to my apprentice. "What do you make of this notice?"

He read it, and asked excitedly, "James Stuart and Sons: Stewart Jameson? A secret message? Meant for you, sir?"

"Just so, lad." I smiled. Puzzling set his beautiful eyes alight almost as much as painting.

"But whatever can it mean?"

"That's what I'm asking you, my clever clogs. You're the expert at riddles."

He studied the paper, avidly.

"Excuse me, sir. But might it not be a looking glass of sorts?"

"A looking glass? You mean the concave mirrors?"

"Not only those, sir. Could not the whole advertisement be a kind of mirror? Held up to you? Meant to . . . mock you, sir? The unused account books, the *Young Gentleman's Arithmetic, for Solving Simple Sums*?"

"I suppose so," I winced. "Not very funny, that."

"No, sir. Of course not. A low blow, I'm sure." He looked down at the paper, trying to hide his grin, and then looked up again.

"Also, sir. Shakespeare and Chaucer: Are they not your favorite writers?"

I rolled my eyes. "I did see *that*, lad, even without the microscope and the telescope that, I take it, are meant to remind me to look carefully, near and far. But all this just means the message is intended for me. What does it *say*?"

"Let's see. Turn of fate, turn of fate, turn of fate. You're right, sir. There's got to be something in it. Tis too unusual a phrase. And marked out, in capitals."

"Aye . . . And so?"

He closed his eyes, and drummed his fingers on the table.

"Confound it, lad. I've not asked you to calculate the compound interest on the Crown's debt. If I'm meant to solve this puzzle, it can't be that difficult. Get on with it."

And still he drummed.

"I've got it!" He cried, tipping his chair over as he stood abruptly. But then his face fell. "Or, no. It doesn't work." He righted the chair, and sat back down.

"What?"

"Turn of fate. I thought it might be an anagram for 'fortunate,' but it has an extra 'f.' "

I laughed, and winked at him. "I have been known to say, lad, that a man can never have too many f 's, if you take my meaning."

Weston blushed.

" 'Fortunate' it must be. Excellent. Come now, what else?"

"Well, sir, I would have thought 'galaxies' and 'untrained' must be anagrams, too, since they are set in just the same type. But I can't puzzle them at a glance; I'd have to work at those for a while."

He closed his eyes, tapped his finger on his forehead, turned to gaze up at the ceiling, and then stared down, once more, at the page.

Suddenly, he opened his eyes wide, and smiled, his face full of mischief.

"What? What do you see?"

But my apprentice had turned coy. He wanted his detection rewarded with details.

"Sir," he said slowly, "who sent this message?"

"A friend," I answered, my smile fading. "This is no time to tease me, lad. What does it say?"

But he failed to observe my impatience, and instead answered my question with another.

"And might you have plans to travel, sir, to meet this friend?"

"To travel? Aye, I do, now. To Philadelphia. You'll have to mind the shop, lad."

"I wouldn't pack your bags just yet, sir. She means—"

"She?" I blinked.

"Your friend, sir."

"There I'm afraid you're wrong, lad. He, Weston. He."

For a moment, Weston's face clouded.

"Excuse me, sir. He. He means to come here instead."

"Yes, yes, yes. To use his compass and map and join me in Boston. I saw that, lad. But, goddammit, I'll not wait here for him any longer, and 'twould be safer, far safer, for me to make the journey."

"Safer, sir?"

"None of your business."

Weston eyed me, wonderingly, and shrugged. My irritation only grew.

"But you are not to go, sir," he insisted. "Your friend knows you well. He has anticipated that you will want to go to him, but he insists that he is to come here instead."

"The bastard," I muttered. And then I demanded, "How can you be so sure?"

Again he hesitated before making his reply. He was enjoying himself. But I was in no mood for it. I had had enough of playing the fish to Weston's hook, and the fool to Alexander's genius. Enough, dear Reader, enough of everything. Enough of worrying, of waiting, of not knowing. Enough of doing nothing.

"Don't trifle with me, lad," I shouted. My voice shook with the force of my grief and frustration, months' worth of both. "Tis a puzzle, but not a game."

"Sir, I—" He shrank from me.

"Sweet Jesus," I thundered, as I stood up, pushed my hair back from my brow, and began to pace the room. "I have lost everything, Weston. God knows, I have lost everything. For nothing. And this friend, this friend. Besides you and Gulliver, lad, he is all that I have in this gob-shitten world. He may mock me, as you say, for he knows my sense of humor, but he is . . . in grave danger. I must know, and at once: Why am I not to go to Philadelphia, this very instant?"

Weston stared at me, for a long minute, as if seeing me for the very first time, as if his astonishment at what he saw as he beheld me had silenced him altogether.

"I'm sorry, sir," he stammered. "I didn't realize how serious, sir—"

I could stand it no longer. I took him by the shoulders and shook him.

"Weston, for Christ's sake! What the deuce does it say? What does the anagram say?"

"Not an another anagram, sir," he answered, his face pale. "An acrostic, hidden in plain sight, and best seen from a distance. Look away, and then look at it again, sir." He handed the paper back to me, and pointed.

Finally, I saw it.

S-T-A-Y—P-U-T.

Damn the man. Am I still to sit and wait?

"But if he is in danger, sir," Weston began, haltingly, "if he was once in danger, sir, he must have been safe when he wrote this. Maybe he has had a turn of fate?"

"Aye, I reckon so. Look, Weston, I thank you for your help, but, truly, 'tis none of your concern. Pray, speak to no one of this." I motioned him to the door. "Now, off to bed, lad, and at once. You will have to rise early to prepare the canvases: we are to visit the Bradstreets tomorrow morning."

Letter VIII.

August the 24th, 1764, midday.

Elizabeth, kind friend,

I wrote to you yesterday evening, as secure of my master, and of my place in his service, as I have yet been. But now, not four-and-twenty hours later, I fear that you were right to worry for me, if wrong about the object of your concern. As was I, Lizzie! As was I! If only you were here, I would fall upon you weeping, and together we should find the dropped stitch that threatens to unravel the fabric of my life, so coarsely knit. And we would pick it up, and work forward with such care that no gap could ever be detected. But alone—so alone am I in this cold, hot world—how can I set things to right?

Last night, after supper, at the end of another long day, during which my mind had been as blank as my brush was busy, my master told me we were to paint the Bradstreets, at their house on Hanover.

"I'm afraid I'm not feeling well, sir," I said, tendering my first excuse.

"You look well enough," he answered, narrowing his eyes. "Aye, you look very well, lad."

"But I'm so clumsy, sir," I protested. "I'm sure to be more of a hindrance than a help."

"Weston, you know as well as I that you're as graceful as a gazelle, except when you've anything to carry. And then, aye, you're worse than useless. But there's nothing for it. With men of Bradstreet's rank, a house call is in order, and I would not be my own cartman. Can you think that Joshua Reynolds totes his own easel? I know him well, and I assure you: the man barely carries his own palette."

"I've no doubt you are the equal of Mr. Reynolds, sir, but I think I had better stay here, and varnish the Hens."

"And I fancied you would tell me I was a demi-Reynolds. No, Weston, flattery suits you ill, and I weary of your excuses." He sighed as he mounted the stairs to his bed-chamber. "It falls to you to do my bidding, lad. We will speak no more of this. Good night."

And so this morning, the pair of us marched west along Queen Street and then north onto Hanover, Jameson striding ahead, his empty hands clasped behind him, while I struggled 'neath the burdens of our trade. I felt like the meanest drayman. But at least the folded easel and the case filled with brushes and colors provided some measure of concealment when the inevitable happened, and my brother passed within three feet of us on the Bradstreets' walkway.

My heart leapt, Lizzie. I wanted at once to hide from him, and to stare into his face, as familiar to me as my own, and yet so changed. He's grown since I last saw him, and he was now costumed in the surplice and cassock of the Church of England. And yet somehow his somber attire seemed only to emphasize his cherry-faced youth, making him look less a man than a gangly boy playing dress-up.

When my master halted, I remained well behind him, and stared at the ground. Once again, the servant's lowly estate proved disguise enough.

"Good morning, Vicar," Jameson offered amiably.

"God's blessing to you, my child," intoned Daniel, putting his hands together, and bowing his head.

My master seemed, for once, at a loss for words. "And back to you, son . . . Father," he fumbled.

After my brother had walked out of earshot, Jameson elbowed me, and whispered, "The Archbishop of Canterbury in a pink silk petti-coat! I thought he might sprinkle holy water on me. Who's the wee pope, and what the deuce is he doing in your Puritan village?"

"'Twas the Reverend Daniel Easton, sir," I answered, unable to suppress a smile. "He serves at King's Chapel."

"Easton? Is he kin to that rod of righteousness? Surely he's stiff enough," Jameson said, winking.

"The Eastons live across the street, sir," I pointed out. "Just next door to the Ushers. But I believe Justice Easton calls himself the Mast of Fidelity, not the Rod of Righteousness. And, yes, that was his son."

"A small world, this Boston. I wonder, what do you call the son of a rod?" he mused, ignoring my correction.

"A staff, sir?"

"Are you blind, lad? He can be no more than two-and-twenty. He's no staff."

"A stick, sir?"

"Not so much as a stout twig. A trembling leaf I might grant you. Ah. Not to fear. I've got it. The son of the Rod of Righteousness can be none other than a splinter. The Splinter of the One True Cross."

I could not help it, Lizzie, I laughed. Jameson has a way of putting me at my ease like no other man I've known. But laughing was my first mistake. For I entered the house with my guard down. And why not? I had survived a trip to the Ushers' house. I had passed an evening in the same room as William and Samuel Bradstreet. And now I had seen my brother, unseen. Surely I might spend a few hours at the Bradstreets', unrecognized. Little could I imagine what awaited me behind that oaken door.

Bradstreet's Cicero, his skin the rich, polished sepia of the chestnut, greeted our knock. He saw to Jameson's coat and then relieved me of my considerable baggage. He is a graceful man, though his gait was awkward—last winter, I'm told, he lost some toes to frostbite. He gave me no more than a glance.

Next appeared William, with his topcoat and cane.

"Mother, your *dauber's* arrived," he called up the stairs, as he headed out the door, without so much as a glance in my direction. My confidence in my disguise grew.

But then, William's sister appeared at the top of the staircase. Here was my second mistake, Lizzie: I had somehow forgotten to consider Patience—Patty—our girlhood friend grown to ripe womanhood under her father's ample roof. As she descended the stairs, her eyes met mine, and I returned her gaze for a second longer than any servant ought.

I fought for breath as the introductions were passed around.

I managed, though just barely, to mumble, "Good day, miss."

* * *

There is, among my acquaintance—and, if you, dear Reader, are equally unfortunate in your circle of friends, you count such a one among yours—a kind of young gentleman who walks with a stick to affect what he is not—aged, and therefore sage—and who, as he advances in society, leans on that stick so heavily that one leg truly grows crooked and frail—and this before the age of five-and-twenty—upon which he becomes in body what he was before only in mind—crippled and weak—having acquired all the aching infirmities of dotage without the wisdom that is so often the reward of long life. Just such a man is William Bradstreet, bent low by feigned dignity. A Wise Barrister, my arse.

It having been agreed that I would enjoy the family's company before beginning my work, Weston and I arrived at the Bradstreets' in time for breakfast. I was relieved to discover that the Wily Bastard would not tarry, pleading a case at court.

But betwixt the Bradstreet brother and sister do seed and egg scatter their traits. Samuel Bradstreet's daughter, Patience, no more than nineteen, is all sweetness and loveliness, artlessness and innocence. When she met us in the hall, my apprentice was so bashful of her that he looked as if he might faint.

✳   ✳   ✳

Oh, Lizzie, I reeled.

"Truly, you look unwell, lad," Jameson whispered to me, gently taking my slender arm with his strong one, and catching me before I could fall.

"I'm afraid my unfortunate apprentice simply cannot bear the heat," he said to Patty, jauntily, in an altogether different voice from the one he used with me. "What mercy he has bound himself to a painter, and not a blacksmith. Would *that* not be infernal?" Twas a kindness, Lizzie. He was covering for me, though he could not ken what ailed me.

"Cicero, take the boy to the kitchen," Patty ordered, languidly. "And give him something cold to drink."

Only reluctantly did I let go of Jameson's arm, but he made sure I was steady, and nudged me forward. "Go rest for a while, lad," he urged, quietly. "I did not realize you were ill else I'd never have dragged you on this outing. I'm sorry I doubted you."

"You could not have known, sir," I whispered.

Cicero led me belowstairs. I stayed behind him lest I reveal that I had known the house's every passage near twenty years. From the hall, I heard the familiar voice of Sarah Bradstreet. Within a moment of meeting my master, Mrs. Bradstreet informed him that Patty was soon to be married—she was warning him off, I take it—to none other than my brother!

"A man of God!" she crowed. "And heaven is not all that my daughter stands to gain in the match. Edward Easton is a great merchant—surely you have heard of him, Jameson?"

"Aye, madam, I was only just speaking of the Mast of Fidelity," Jameson answered, slyly.

"Well, then you know. His trade circles the globe, from the West Indies to the East. We could not have hoped for better, even for such a prize as our Patience."

"Aye," said my master, a familiar, merry tone creeping into his voice. "And they must be celebrating in London and Munich."

"I'm sure I know not. Why?" replied the puzzled Sarah Bradstreet.

"For their marriage shall unite the Houses of Hanover once again!"

As Cicero and I walked out of earshot, Jameson's easy laughter echoed through the house.

✳ ✳ ✳

"Tis my wife, Jameson, who would mark our marriage," said the Honorable Samuel Bradstreet.

What can I tell you of Sarah Morton Bradstreet, Reader? Councilor Usher spoke true: with her large gray eyes and aquiline profile, she looks, at first blush, a great deal like her sister, which is noble indeed. But where Mrs. Lucy Morton Usher is pallid and dignified, Mrs. Bradstreet has an animal intensity, moving quickly, and with fierce determination. She is poised, mind, ever the lady—genteel—but far from gentle.

"She seems a formidable woman, sir. And 'tis a most fitting occasion for a pair of portraits," I replied, as I set up my easel in his parlor. "Let me congratulate you on your anniversary."

"Fie," he said, waving me off. "That's Sarah's charade. I have another purpose in mind for your likenesses."

"What might that be, sir?" I inquired, with no feigned curiosity, for though I was worried about Weston, I found my sitter fascinating. I had liked Bradstreet, immensely, on our first encounter, at the Red Hen Club, a fortnight ago. Indeed, that night, to him, and to him alone, I had confided the story of Ignatius Alexander, altogether omitting my role in it, as Bradstreet had spied in me—and I in him—a sympathetic soul. He is a leader of men, and like all true leaders, he pushes his followers, perhaps farther than they are willing to go. I venture he might earn even Alexander's admiration, and that, I assure you, is no mean feat.

Bradstreet is not a handsome man; indeed, he is rather plain, and indistinct, save for his spectacles, which, being less common here in the provinces than in England, mark him as a man of learning and free from vanity. He wears no wig, unusual for a man of his station, and his thin, scant, brown hair falls, untied, to his slouching shoulders. He is napped in simplicity: a plain brown cloak—of fine cloth if a drab color—and matching knee breeches, white stockings, black shoes, and a linen shirt with ruffled cuffs and neck—ruffled, mind, but not frilly. The only extravagance on his person—the only hint of a taste for luxury—is a pearl-white waistcoat of fine Chinese silk with tiny silver buttons that strain across his ample belly. For so stout a character, he has an uncommonly fine carriage, a nobility borne, strangely, of humility. Yet he is a politician. And like all politicians, he speaks in speeches.

"I have accomplished remarkably little in so long a life, Jameson. No, no, don't interrupt me with protestations to the contrary. Never make the mistake of lying to a man of discernment. I am old. The doctors make an apothecary shop in my stomach, and still I can't piss straight enough to hit the pot. Even with these damned glasses, I can barely see what's in front of me. Yet I see more than most. I have fought for the liberties of these colonies, to be sure, and of that, at least, I am proud. An Englishman's liberty is his birthright, and I would make sure that every colonist preserves that inheritance down the generations."

"A fine sentiment," I offered.

"No, 'tis more than a sentiment, Jameson. 'Tis an argument, one that must be made with Parliament, again and again, till the King's ministers hear it. For if they would steal our birthright, at the tip of a bayonet, we must one day repay them with a declaration of our independence."

"You cannot mean these colonies to be a separate nation, sir."

"I do not wish it. But if it comes to that, yes, I mean it," he said, with neither pomp nor hesitation. "The boycott is but a beginning. We must wean ourselves from the teat of empire."

Reader, I am no Tory. I do not fancy the King's hand in my pocket. But just now, just now I might like to caress the tit of empire. Aye, the mere thought of empire's ample breasts set me to sighing.

Pray, forgive me. I labored mightily to think, instead, about boycotts.

"I can see why these men of Massachusetts have named you their leader in the struggle against the tyranny of Westminster," I replied.

"Perhaps, Jameson," he answered. "But the battlefield lies closer at hand. We must also struggle here, at home, against our baser instincts."

Tis indeed a struggle. I nodded. "Aye, sir. We must always struggle against our baser instincts."

"Yes. And if we would argue for an end to the slavery of taxation without representation, we must follow that argument to its necessary conclusion, and commit ourselves to end slavery of every kind. Else none of us shall be free. Those who barter away other men's liberty must prove poor defenders of their own."

And here he paused, as I moved across the room to open the curtains behind him, showering his head with sunlight.

"I could not agree more, sir, and few men have done as much as you to advance that cause."

"Maybe so. But upon no account do I wish to be remembered as a man who did well enough, and no more. Twould be better to be forgotten, and buried without a headstone. I hope to leave a singular legacy when I go to my grave, and I want this portrait to be part of it. I aim to abolish the slave trade in this colony before I die. It corrupts us all: the master and the merchant, and planter and the ship's captain, even the lady spooning sugar into her tea. But I don't need to tell you this, Jameson. Surely you have read your brother's sermons on the subject?"

"That I have, sir, that I have," I answered, dryly, for I could scarcely work up any enthusiasm for three hundred closely printed pages of Colin's piety, even where I granted his argument.

"Capital, Jameson. I have each and every one of your brother's treatises in my library, you know. Inspiring works. So you understand my line of reasoning. Now you must understand my plan. I have a mind to set the matter to rights. I speak my views on the floor of the Assembly, but my efforts to print them have been thwarted."

"How so, sir? Surely Edes supports you, for I have heard him speak— and passionately—on the importance of a free press to a free people."

"No, Jameson, the printer is not my censor. Edes is a good man. 'Tis Councilor Usher, through the Governor's license, who castrates my text. Full paragraphs of my late treatise were omitted, without remark. Only my fellow Assemblymen have heard my full views on slavery, and those sons of liberty can be sons of bitches."

"But the Red Hens, sir: Are they not of your party?"

"They are not ready to be a party, Jameson. They had rather drink than debate."

"But surely your kinsman, Councilor Usher, is a spirited patriot?"

At this, Bradstreet laughed. "Hiram crows like a cock about American manufactures," he answered, "but he would have slaves toil at his looms."

"You must have hope for some of your compatriots. Newcombe?"

"A good man is doubting Thomas, but no ruffler of feathers. I cannot wait on him or on anyone else. I will, I will, set the matter to rights, if only in my own domain: my house, my estate. If I succeed, maybe one day your portrait of me will hang on a wall at the Town House, bearing the inscription I wish to have as my epitaph: 'Samuel Bradstreet, Esquire. Friend of Liberty, Enemy of Slavery.'"

✳ ✳ ✳

Daniel and Patty, are they not perfect together, Lizzie? Steady in their habits, easy in their stations. How I wish my brother's betrothal were the only news I had discovered in Bradstreet's house. But when I reached the kitchen, still dizzy from meeting Patty, I nearly bumped into yet another ghost from my past, one I had thought removed from this continent, if not this world.

"Cicero, love, set another place when you bring me another mouth to feed." So tender and teasing she sounded, yet a shudder convulsed me. For though I had never heard her voice this unguarded, I recognized it at once: 'twas Hannah, whom I had last seen 'neath my father's roof.

She was Hannah Easton then, I suppose, my father having branded her with his name when he bought her person, her work, and her progeny. Yet now, as then, her face, her bearing, her every gesture, denied her yoke. Her skin—the warm tan of cream toffee—shined with sweat, as if lit from within. To conjure such a color would demand considerable art. I should use a base of Spanish brown, blushing with a pinch of cinnabar, and lightened by a small measures of flake white and yellow ocher. That mixture might mimic the hue, but not yet its glow. To warm the canvas to approximate its model would require the ground gold of orpiment arsenic. Were Tobias to glimpse the object of his wayward passions again, he would find her beauty worn smooth with work, but by no means gone.

Hannah Bradstreet! How can it be? My father told me that he had banished her to the southward. I imagined the Barbados, and pictured sugar taking its cruel revenge, three crops a year, the cane as mighty as the lash. The thought of her suffering haunted me, for hadn't I a hand in it? Instead my father had nudged her barely a hundred yards south of his house. I was at once relieved that she had been spared and terrified of what she should say to me. But where Patience had stared into my eyes, Hannah—who surely has more and bitterer reasons to remember Fanny Easton—barely looked at me before turning to attend the stock-pot and the kettle.

And then a small figure emerged, shyly, one tiny step at a time, from behind her mother's skirts. A girl of about three, just the age of my somewhere-babe, the shadow of a shade.

"Come here, child," Cicero called her.

"Go on, Phebe. It's all right. Your father isn't working every minute. Even he has time to play." Hannah patted the girl's cheek, and then embraced her, almost casually: a fleeting gesture of mother-love, the sort that I am daily denied. Truly, I could almost *see* the warmth pass between them, a muted pink aura that encircled them both, as the last glow of dawn enfolds the horizon when it yields to daylight.

With a nudge of encouragement from her mother, the girl ran to Cicero, her laugh tinkling all the way. He hugged that little girl like a father, and lifted her to him as if she weighed no more than a pillow. But anybody could see that this fair child was not fathered by Cicero, nor by any other African. Her skin, the color of milky tea, was lighter by half than her mother's. When at last she lifted her face from Cicero's shoulder, I thought, for an instant, that I was looking upon my darling sister, Lydia, risen from her too-early grave. For this little sprite looked at me with my father's glittering green eyes.

Oh, Lizzie! Have I become an outcast on an error?

✳ ✳ ✳

While Weston lingered in the kitchen—what the deuce ailed the lad?—Bradstreet's speech became more frantic. He looked about him, wildly, as if fearing to be overheard, though I knew not by whom, for we were entirely alone. And then he offered an extraordinary oration:

"Jameson, though you are all but a stranger, you may be the only man in town I can trust. I was sorely affected by the story of your friend, Doctor Alexander, and what he has suffered, all for the sake of a villain's greedy grasp. I would free Massachusetts from such shackles. In my headier moments, I think I might secure the passage of my bill abolishing the slave trade, but when I am calm, I know it will fail. Nevertheless, I *will* yet set things to right. If my full treatise—*A Modest Inquiry into the Iniquity of Slavery*—is ever to be published, someone else must have its charge. Will you do me this office, Jameson, for I can ask no other? No one in my family knows of it. And you must tell *no one*. Copy it—for my eyes are of no use, and my hand so unsteady I can no longer put pen to inkwell—and send this original to your estimable brother. He must have it printed. He will, I'm sure of it. This is what I ask. Do I ask too much?"

Does he? You may wonder, dear Reader, how this Bradstreet, a man of unlikely confidences, could be a politician. What Parliamentarian ever spoke so frankly, and this to a man he barely knows? Why would Bradstreet discuss with me, an artisan, and a foreigner, a proposal the great majority of his countrymen consider outrageous? Is this how he rallies this town's laboring men behind him, by being no respecter of rank or distinction? Or does his candor go too far? In short: Is the man mad?

Here, I fear, you are wise to inquire, for I have heard not a few men declare, 'neath their breath, that Bradstreet is wholly lunatic. Edes has told me that Bradstreet is by turns silent and loquacious, sullen and animated, and given to a kind of collapse, an entire defeat of his spirits that confines him to bed for days at a time. If I am a poor governor of my temper and a worse governor of my tongue, Bradstreet's governor has long since been deposed.

Yet I accepted his charge. Will I copy the manuscript? I will. And I will even send it to shitten Colin. Will I describe to Hiram Usher the cast of Bradstreet's mind? Certainly not, for I will be no man's spy. Will I paint Samuel Bradstreet a madman? No, Bradstreet has revealed himself to me, as he wishes to be seen. Before a face-painter, every man is his own historian: he looks back upon his life, straining to see himself as he hopes posterity will, for a portrait is a legacy, and a lasting one. I shall paint Samuel Bradstreet just as he asks to be remembered, as a Friend to Liberty, and an Enemy to Slavery.

But just now, I must check on my apprentice. I worry about the lad, Reader. I worry.

※　※　※

You cannot blame me for fainting at the sight of Phebe's eyes, Lizzie. I crumpled, dead away, onto the cool wooden floor. I cannot tell you how long I lay there, only that the sun was considerably advanced when I awoke to find little Phebe holding a cup of water to my lips, her sweet face just inches from mine. The sight of her almost sent me swooning again. Instead, I scrambled to my feet and hastened unsteadily toward the door, just as Hannah carried out the tea.

If only I had escaped Jameson's notice, I planned to slip out. But his eyes found me at once, and he confronted me in the hall.

"Any better, lad?" he asked, softly, taking a step toward me. He put a hand upon my brow. "No fever." He lifted my chin for a closer look at my face, and saw my tears. For a moment, he lingered, caressing my wet check with the very tips of his fingers, moving them down my face, and to my neck, where he pressed them gently to my throat, as if he were taking my pulse. "I am no doctor, Weston," he said, with a wistful smile, "but I know heartsickness when I see it. Sweet Jesus. I suppose it's been a while since one of your perfumed letters arrived. Has she chucked you, then?"

I could not manage an answer, and his tenderness only set me to sobbing.

"God knows, lad, there's nothing worse," he sighed, placing both arms around me, and pulling me close, in an embrace whose warmth and sympathy I have not felt since my mother died.

Still I could not speak.

"She didn't deserve you, Weston."

I did not think to leave his arms, ever, Lizzie, but he stepped back, squared my shoulders, and said to me, firmly: "Go home to Queen Street if you must, lad, but for what ails you, there's no better remedy than painting. I've made good progress on Bradstreet's countenance. Perhaps you could begin the backdrop while our sitter takes his tea."

* * *

I returned to the parlor with my apprentice just as the lady of the house swept back into the room, followed by a Negro maid, carrying tea and biscuits on a tray. Within this servant's skirts, a little girl, of no more than four—a paler and still more striking version of her mama—poked her head out, and stared at us with eyes as green as jade.

"Back so soon, Sarah?" Bradstreet said to his wife, icily. "Thank you, Hannah," he offered to the servant, with a nod. The tiny girl smiled sweetly at the gentleman, who rewarded her with a wink.

"Yes, Hannah. Now you—and the girl, too—leave us," said his wife.

"Pray, just a moment, Phebe," said Bradstreet, as warmly as a grandfather. "I have devised another riddle for you, poppet."

The little girl smiled wide.

"Puzzle me this, my little teacup," said Bradstreet.

> *"Eyes I have, and yet I've none;*
> *I have Joints, yet have no Bone;*
> *I have a Face, but not a Feature,*
> *Yet resemble every Creature;*
> *I'm, in short, just what you please,*
> *Yet am not any one of these."*

"No bones?" Phebe asked.

Bradstreet nodded, and waited.

"Oh, Samuel, will you not send her away?" cried the lady, impatiently, all but rolling her eyes. She resented his fondness for the precocious child, and made no secret of it.

"Just a minute, Sarah," he answered, again, coldly, and then, softly, to the little girl, "Come on, poppet, do you give up?"

Phebe nodded.

"Oh, for goodness' sake, Samuel."

"A looking glass!" laughed Bradstreet. Phebe giggled and took her mother's hand. Each offering a curtsy, they left, Hannah shutting the door behind them.

Mrs. Bradstreet gave a great sigh of exasperation.

"Samuel. You look a fool. She can only answer them from memory. She's but three years old!" I had to agree with Mrs. Bradstreet. Her husband treated Phebe as if she were a toy. Bradstreet ignored his wife, who then turned to address me.

"Jameson, it has been *days* since I've hoped to sit for you—at least since I first saw your excellent portrait of my nephew, Mordecai— oh, you must know, he is my *favorite*—and finally the moment has arrived!"

There followed a half hour of chitchat over tea, prattle with which I would have preferred to dispense, the morning light casting just the right glow, and the paints fresh-mixed on my palette. I took some small comfort that Weston would be able to use the time to begin what Bradstreet had requested by way of backdrop—a window opening to a prospect of a ship in the harbor—and of foreground—a mahogany desk, covered with books and papers. The boy set himself to the task. Sturdy and determined. Excellent.

Meanwhile Mrs. Bradstreet talked of her sorrow at losing Mordecai to Madras, his departure marked for but days hence.

"What *will* we do without him?" she pleaded.

"Now, my dear," said Bradstreet, " 'tis your dear sister's loss and not our own. And, in any case, 'tis all for the good. Mordecai will return a better man."

"How, *better*, my love? Is he not the best of men already?"

"You forget your William, I think," answered Bradstreet, unsmiling, one eyebrow raised above his spectacles.

"Well, of course, dear. They are *both* of them, the best of men."

If Mordecai Usher and William Bradstreet are the best of men, I fear for the race: the first is a rake, the second a rogue. And the lady? I dread painting her. She is full of charm and smiles, and equally full of wiles: a character perfectly fit to perplex mine and, apparently, far more, her husband's. He has little but contempt for her, and she returns the sentiment, though not so transparently.

Reader, had Hiram Usher and Samuel Bradstreet mixed up their brides? For surely the Speaker was better mated to Mrs. Usher than to his own wife, a lady who made me reflect, once again, what a mischief is the mind of a dissembling woman.

"Well, we shall all miss Mordecai, I'm sure," continued Mrs. Bradstreet, as we finished our tea, and she prepared, at last, to leave me to my brush. "Happily, we will send him off in style. You *are* coming to the ball this evening, Jameson, are you not?"

"I assure you, madam, that I would not miss it. But I fear I *shall* miss it if I don't finish your husband's face by midday," I smiled. "For I can't think of putting away my palette without beginning your portrait this afternoon."

"Yes, of course," she answered, doubtless realizing that any further delay might postpone the satisfaction of her vanity. "I'll be going, for I have still more errands to run to make ready for this evening."

✳   ✳   ✳

Jameson spoke true. Painting stilled my spirit. Even when Hannah and her daughter—my half sister!—were in the room, I gathered strength as I put brush to canvas. My master came and stood beside me.

"Good work, lad," he said, with utmost kindness. "Now, when you have finished that rough coat on the furnishings and the drapery, you might try your hand at the ship I have sketched within that window at the right. Work on your *line*, lad; color is not all. Linger on the rigging, as if tying every knot with your slender brush. Give the figurehead a bosom in which you'd fain bury your young head. But save yourself for the bow. Bradstreet means the vessel's name to be clearly legible. It must read H.M.S. *Liberty*. Let the name inspire you. Imagine that its hold contains your freedom, and your fortune."

Yet now I can only wonder whether either lies in the future of the tiny, beautiful, *enslaved* sister of this dazed and bewildered,

Fanny Easton.

CHAPTER 9

In Which You Are Invited

to a Dance

Dear Reader, know this: I am amiable, but ungovernable. I paint well, but I seldom bother to paint as well as I might. My features are pleasing, but they fall short of Grecian splendor. Yet if there is little of which I can boast without equivocation, there is this: I am a generous man.

This evening, while I was sitting at the desk in my bed-chamber, Weston came to the door and cleared his throat. I was surprised to see him. On our return from the Bradstreets' this afternoon, my apprentice had run to his garret and closeted himself for hours. "A painter must paint, lad," I reminded him, when I finally banged on his door. In sullen obedience, he followed me to the painting room, and I put him to his task: a set of exercises in just three colors, a constraint intended to concentrate his attention on form and shadow, and to distract him from his brooding.

"Will you not work at your own easel, sir?" he had asked.

"No, Weston. I find I need a drink."

Thus had I retired to my bed-chamber, where I have had more than a few mugs of ale. I find myself disconcerted, and would keep the lad a room away from me. It seems the best course, for he seizes my imagination, captivates all my tenderheartedness, and I fear his nearness will set loose my passions. When I should be riding to Philadelphia, to find Alexander. When I should be courting Margaret Usher, or Lambert's wealthy, widowed sister. When I should be marrying money. Aye, when I should be doing anything but seducing my innocent apprentice.

That the lad would oblige me I have little doubt. 'Tis a common enough trade between a master and his apprentice, if an unfair one. Weston is my charge, and deserves my fatherly protection, not my amorous attention. Reader, I can only conclude: to be a better master, I will need a lesser apprentice. Weston must leave me, for his prodigious talent demands a wider compass, and it falls to me to set him on his journey. I would have him see Titian and Rafael and Michelangelo and Van Dyck, not on the pages of books but on the walls of galleries. London must be the nursery of his genius.

Aye, when the time comes, I will send him away. But right now, as he is standing at my door, I had best answer him.

"Good evening, my little muttonhead, what brings you?" I asked, as I put down my mug.

"Sir, Mrs. Goddard has left, but she pressed your attire for the ball and bid me give it to you," he answered, placing my suit on the bed.

"Thank you. Feeling better, are you?"

"Yes, sir. Much better."

"Painting helped?"

"Yes, sir. A great deal, thank you. I'd better be getting back to it." He made to leave the room.

"Nay, stay, if you would," I said, rising from my chair and walking toward him. He seemed well enough to bear what I had to say. "There are one or two matters I would discuss with you."

He eyed me nervously, and took a step toward the door. No matter. It must be done, and I have waited too long already.

"Weston," I began sternly, "I suspect you are deceiving me, and you must know I will brook no deception in my house."

He turned pale, so pale I feared he would faint.

"Aye, Weston," I pressed on. "There is a considerable quantity of white lead missing from the cabinet. If you are in want, speak to me, but never steal from me."

I scolded him with as much severity as I could muster, but 'twas no more than my usual bluster. I'm never sure if the lad can see that I am no better a master of men than I am a governor of my passions. ("Give me that man that is not passion's slave, and I will wear him in my heart's core." Alas, Hamlet, I am not that man.) But he seemed—and I say, *seemed*, for, I never know what he *is*, and if you doubt my confusion, discerning Reader, I would ask you to have another look at *The Serving Boy*—he seemed at once surprised, relieved, and afraid.

"I would never—! Sir! How can you think—? I would not, sir, I . . ."

And here, dear Reader, tears began to leak out of his dark eyes, and race down his soft face. 'Twas so affecting I thought he would reduce *me* to weeping.

"Weston, gather yourself up!" I pleaded. Sweet Jesus, I could not endure his tears again. "If it wasn't you, 'twas someone else, and then we will discover him soon enough. That, or he'll next away with Gulliver, and we'll have only to thank him." This cheered him, for he is as fond of the dog as I am, and he gave a faint smile.

"Good," I replied, and hastened to pilot our conversation toward smoother waters. "Now, as for this ball at Bradstreet's this evening, have you ever witnessed one of these country dances, from a kitchen door, perchance, or a street window? Do you know what passes for fashion in this town, by way of dancing?"

"I suppose, sir," he stammered. "I attended . . . a former . . . master at such an event."

"Your venerable father's blasted former master, whose confounded son had a tutor, was it? He dances as well as paints? A talented fellow, lad." I smiled, but Weston looked stricken.

"God above, have you again lost your laughter, lad? She's not worth it, I'm certain of it."

"No, sir. I was just remembering, sir."

"Remembering who stole your laughter?" I asked, as soberly as I could, for I was, I confess, a wee bit drunk.

"I suppose, sir."

"Some things are better forgotten, are they not, lad? Recall for me instead what your father's master's son of a bitch's tutor danced. I know only Scottish airs, and not even those very well. Do they dance 'The Collier's Daughter' here?"

"I have not heard of it, sir."

"Tis my favorite. You must know the music at least."

I have a raspy voice, Reader, but I can keep a tune. I sang the first lines:

> *"The Collier has a daughter,*
> *And, O, she's wond'rous bonny,*
> *A Laird he was that sought her,*
> *Vast rich in land and money.*

"Stirring, is it not?" I asked. But then I saw that the lad was weeping once again. Please, dear God. Not the tears.

"Zounds, Weston, is my singing as bad as that?"

"No, sir. I was just thinking about the collier's daughter. It's in a minor key, sir; it must be a sad story. Does it end badly for her?"

"Have you no notion at all of the Scottish temperament, lad? We are moody bastards. Every Highland air sounds a note of sorrow. But 'The Collier's Daughter' is no dirge."

"Thank goodness, sir."

"And mind: you worry too much about the heroines of books and ballads. Not every story ends with a whipping."

But this only set him to sobbing.

Dear Reader: Mightn't I at least offer him some small comfort? Hold a hand? Lend a shoulder?

I crossed the room, and took him in my arms. In friendship, I swear it.

"Listen," I whispered in his ear, "be my partner, and I'll sing you the rest."

Do not chide me, Reader. He was *weeping*. What was I to do?

I kept him close, and softly and slowly sang:

> *"The Collier has a daughter,*
> *And, O, she's wond'rous bonny,*
> *A Laird he was that sought her,*
> *Vast rich in land and money.*

> *"The tutors watch'd the motion*
> *Of this young honest lover;*

But love is like the ocean:
What can its depths discover!"

By the time I reached the end of the verse, I found we were, both of us, trembling. For we had begun, if only barely, to dance, he taking the female part, and I the lead, as we moved, half-time, in tiny circles, within the center of the room. No formal country reel, in lines, at arm's length, but something between a dance and an embrace. It continued even where my song broke off.

"What can its depths discover, sir?" my apprentice whispered, still swaying in my arms. "You promised me the end. Isn't there another verse?"

"Aye, lad," I said, turning hoarse. "What depths, what depths. Is not love fathomless?"

And then I sang, still more softly—my voice breaking—my lips brushing against his cheek.

"He lov'd beyond expression
The charms that were about her,
And panted for possession,
His life was dull without her.

"After mature resolving,
Close to his breast he held her,
In fastest flames dissolving,
He tenderly thus tell'd her."

We danced on in silence, and he laid down his sweet head upon my shoulder.

"What did he tell her, sir?" he asked, his breath hot upon my neck.
Twas not to be borne.
Hold a hand. Lend a shoulder. No more.
I must turn back to shore, else I drown.
I pulled myself away from him, just a step. Enough.
"Nay, lad. There is no more."

Letter IX.

August the 25th, 1764. Before dawn.

My dear Elizabeth,

How I longed for a letter from you, feeling sure your tender words would quiet my fevered spirit. And when I returned in the wee hours of this morning from the Bradstreets' ball to find an envelope in your hand waiting on the parlor table, my heart leapt, for almost never have I needed a friend's comfort more. But, oh, Lizzie. The notice you enclose from your city's *Weekly Journal* only adds to my confusion after a day, and a night, filled with unsought revelations.

> *ESCAPED . . . one Stewart Jameson, face-painter and libertine, on pain of being confined for debt . . .*

"Proof certain," you call the advertisement, "that your new *Master* is no more a gentleman than the *last* wrongful object of your affections, so easily and liberally bestowed upon painters well practiced in the *arts of deception*."

Tis true, the man described can be none other than my master. But I ask you, which is the more honest likeness: the one his Scottish creditors—nay, predators—paint, or the one I've limned for you myself, line by line? I know I have been a poor judge of men in the past—and haven't I paid the price for my easy credit?—but I cannot think my portrait of Jameson is so flawed. He may be a debtor. He may even be a libertine. But he is a good man, such as I have never yet met with. Trust my eyes, Lizzie. And please—oh, please!—repay my trust in you by honoring the pledge you made when we began this correspondence. You promised to keep my confidences, and surely you know that my master's secrets are mine as well. As collateral, I will increase my debt to you, and tell you of the way my own secrets compound. For if reading your letter has not stilled my turbulent heart, it solaces me to write, and there is no one else to whom I can spill the contents of my heart.

Of the Bradstreets' ball, pray, do not expect an account like those you find in the novels with which you fill your lazy summer afternoons. You have seen enough of candlelight on mirrored girandoles, and eaten enough sweetmeats, and whirled your way through enough hornpipes that you can imagine those parts far better than I can paint them, since I passed most of the evening behind the scenes, with the scullery maids and the footmen. The constant hum of gossip in the kitchen sounded like a bagpipe's drone 'neath the two fiddles and a bass viol that filled the house with lively airs, all keeping time to the rhythmic stamping of fifty pairs of feet. The dancing continued with scant interruption from eight-and-thirty till near midnight.

And then, suddenly, the music stopped, and William Bradstreet entered the kitchen, rapping his silver-tipped cane upon the floor as he commanded the servants to assemble in the hall for an announcement. We followed him into the golden light to find the evening's reigning eminences, three women and two men, arranged as carefully as the players in a *tableau vivant*. Hiram Usher posed stiffly, and no wonder, for his costume was made of a coarse burlap better fit for sails than suits, the material dyed—unevenly—a violent shade of red. Beside him the ailing Lucy, dressed in a pale celadon frock as lovely as her husband's was ridiculous, was allowed a chair.

Just in front of them stood a proud trio: on the left, Sarah Bradstreet, gaudy in vermilion silk and a heavy rope of pearls; beside her—in the center of the grouping, the room, the town—her husband, Samuel, attired in a suit of dove gray that made his skin look wan; and on his right, with his hand open upon Bradstreet's broad back, napped in lace and striped emeraled bombazine, the venerable, the honorable, the *fortunate* Justice Edward Easton, of Easton & Company, West Indies Goods.

The very sight of the man hastened Hannah from the room, to answer some imagined crisis in the kitchen: more punch for the dancers, more claret for the toasts.

Though the theater belonged to Mr. Bradstreet, 'twas my father who directed this next scene. He cleared his throat with intimations of portent that made the noise of the party fall to nothing. And then he spoke, a soliloquy worthy of a player, asking the assembled brilliants to forgive him, for the event they had gathered to celebrate—the Bradstreets' happy union of thirty years—was mere pretext. The true occasion of tonight's merriment, he revealed, was less an old marriage than a new one. Reverend Daniel Easton and Patience Bradstreet would be published in the next *Gazette*, to marry in three weeks' time.

A murmur of surprise vied with a smattering of applause. Samuel Bradstreet seemed to bite his tongue as he answered my father.

"I shall not pretend that you and I have always seen things alike, Edward," he said, smiling ruefully. "But you've raised a fine son. I welcome Daniel into this family, as my Patience has welcomed him into her heart."

At that, my father took Bradstreet's right hand in his, pumping it showily, yet coldly, as if the ballroom were the 'Change, and the wedding of his son to Bradstreet's daughter a mercantile affair.

Nay, a *political* one.

For then, withdrawing his hand from Bradstreet's, Edward Easton clapped. Just twice, a rapid staccato. In an instant, Usher's Pompey materialized at his elbow, dressed for his role in livery of the purest cerulean, accented with gold braid. Truly, he outshone the belles. In his kid-gloved hands Pompey bore aloft a silver tray holding a small white porcelain coffee pot, and two delicate chinaware cups, one of red and the other of blue. He steadied the tray at waist level while my father poured the coffee, lifting the pot high enough to show the hot, brown stream thundering into the cup below.

"Now, if you will indulge me, friend: a toast," my father boomed, addressing the crowd, never Bradstreet. "Champagne is more usual, I admit," he chuckled. "But 'tis coffee, I would argue, that best suits the occasion. Beans from Barbados, water from Boston, cups made in Canton: here you see the silken bonds tying together the four corners of the globe. So Samuel, take your coffee—red, for your Hens!—and toast these fruits of Britain, and the future progeny of the Torch of

Liberty and the Mast of Fidelity. May their little sparks and spars people this land!"

Easton drank deeply, Bradstreet politely. For had he not publicly advocated a boycott on each and every of these imports, from the coffee to the cup? I could only think my father meant to humiliate him, and Bradstreet clearly sensed as much.

But Bradstreet would be made to choke on politics again tonight. Before the men had put down their cups, Hiram Usher strode to the front of the room, carrying a rough clay jug.

"Kinsman, neighbor," he addressed Bradstreet and my father, "let us drink another round, grown closer to home. Allow me to refill your glasses with a measure of *local* cheer."

From the jug, he poured a murky brown liquid into their cups.

"Dandelion wine," he boasted to the assembled guests, who looked more than a little amazed. "I picked the flowers on our own Common ground, and fermented them with the juice of Boston's best beets, the same beets whose skins dyed my suit, of linen spun and wove from local flax, in our very own Manufactory House. Raise your glasses, then," he said, his voice rising, "and let us toast to Daniel and Patience. May their union be sealed in an era of Homespun, Home Brew, and Home Rule!"

Bradstreet's expression showed that the liquid tasted as vile as it looked. My father set his cup down untouched.

Then Usher, still holding his heavy jug, shouted, "Huzzah!" and the violins resumed as down the stairs, hand in hand, came the young betrotheds. All eyes fell upon Patty, virginal in the palest pink, and my brother, who held her hand shyly, and tenderly. Daniel traded a round of kisses with his blushing fiancée's brother, William, and her cousins Mordecai and Margaret. Noticing her father's sour expression, Patty disappeared for a moment and returned with a glass of port.

After offering her father a sip of wine, she kissed his flushed cheek, and returned to Daniel's arms. They stepped to the center of the room to dance a short, chaste *pas de deux*. Then some two dozen couples lined up for the next reel, Daniel and Patience at the head of the line; followed by Mordecai with Justice Finley's daughter, Susannah; William Bradstreet with a girl I did not recognize; and my Jameson with Margaret Usher, who looked up at him adoringly, and held herself far closer to him than the dance required. Nor were her obvious attentions repulsive to him as he partnered her nimbly through a gavotte, a minuet, and a quadrille in rapid succession.

I lingered to watch them, wondering how many kinds of happiness I had forfeited in how few years. Daniel and Patience will be entirely content in their companionship, and I am delighted for them. But I will never have a marriage like theirs. Nor did I want it when 'twas offered, for I would not have wed Billy Bradstreet for all the coffee in Java. I chased something different into the arms of Tobias Cummings— a schoolgirl's fantasy of unfettered passion, an appetite fed by the books I found in my father's library, and never sated. 'Twas naught but pretended passion, mine as much as his, though the cost was real enough. And for what? Surely our embraces were at least as clumsy as his brushwork. If I know not exactly who this serving boy will become, I am glad my likeness isn't titled *Mrs. Cummings*.

But Jameson. He's a different manner of man than ever I have known. He cut one of the most graceful figures in Bradstreet's parlor, as I knew he would, Lizzie, for he and I had danced together in his bed-chamber as he readied for the evening. I say *danced*, but 'twas like no dance that you can picture. And I will not deny it: I relished his embrace, full of ardor, and yet laced with a tenderness I have only ever dreamt of. In his arms, I felt more fully a woman than ever before.

And yet, I am *not* a woman, not to him. What means Jameson's embrace, when given to Francis Weston? Is a boy what he wants? Am I falling in love with a man who would not love a woman? To see him steer Margaret Usher across the dance floor, his hand resting on the small of her back, one long finger trailing lower: 'tis clear her beauty moves him, more than I can stand to see. But unless I'm very far wrong, Weston stirs his passion as well, though I can scarce afford to discover how far, for 'twould cost me my disguise—and my grasp upon my brush.

'Twas then, as I watched Jameson twirling about with Margaret, that Hannah emerged from the kitchen, handed a tray of full glasses to Cicero, and tugged at my elbow.

"Mr. Weston, a word please," she said, and motioned me into the kitchen, where we were entirely, and terrifyingly alone. Before I had time to answer, she began to speak.

"I will not again call you Weston, nor sir, nor even miss," she said. "We have known each other since girlhood. You are Edward Easton's daughter. One of them, I should say."

I stared at her blankly, altogether uncertain how to reply.

"Don't pretend a puzzlement, Fanny. Phebe is your sister. Not that Tobias Cummings wouldn't have taken from me what he could, had your father allowed it."

"I was wrong, Hannah! I was so wrong," I cried.

"Stop your blathering. No apology can answer your actions."

"But what do you want from me, then? Do you mean to reveal me? Please, Hannah, please," I implored, "you cannot send me back to a fallen version of Fanny Easton's life."

"Don't tell me what I may or may not do," she answered coldly. "If I thought revealing your secret would help Phebe, I would find Mr. Edes this moment and bid him print it in Monday's paper. Lucky for you, I do not think so. Not now, anyway. What do I want from you? I hold out some hope that you might help me to secure my daughter's freedom, else I'd never have spoken to you. For we have nothing else to say to each other."

"I would do whatever is in my power to free Phebe. But Hannah," I gasped, my voice choked with sobs, "I had a daughter once, too. Please, I beg you, if you know what happened to my baby, tell me."

Hannah looked puzzled. "She was stillborn."

"So my father told me, but I heard her cries, before the doctor took her away."

"I know nothing of your child."

By now I was shaking. I wept openly.

"Hush," Hannah said. "Save your tears." Then she lowered her voice to a whisper. "But I may one day call upon your sympathy. For I would protect Phebe with my very life. I would kill if I thought it would break her chains."

So vowed the mother of the only sister of this,

Fanny Easton.

CHAPTER 10

In Which Lying Dogs Fail to Sleep

Upon no account would I deceive you, dear Reader, tho' I fear that events begin to outpace my pen. Pray, forgive me, for I have once again neglected to tell you the entirety of my affairs. I am resolved upon a reform and, henceforth, will race to keep up, even as happenings fly by. Let this mark a start.

First, Edes has informed me that a printer in New York, complying with the McGreevys' relentless requests, has run the ad offering a reward for my return in the pages of his newspaper.

"It may have appeared in other towns, too, but this is the first I've seen," he added, when he came to Queen Street to show me the *New York Weekly Journal*. "But Jameson, this notice confounds me. You still haven't told me about this man, Fortune. And I find it difficult to believe you could have lost two thousand pounds at whist, when all you ever do is fold."

Discerning Reader, are my cards so plain upon the table?

Second, although Edes left a letter for my apprentice, the lad remains utterly distracted. He pouts. He dithers. He slithers away. He was to rise early this morning to prepare for our third visit to Bradstreet's, this time to paint, and not to dance, while I lay abed, recovering from our late dissipated night. But when I came down I found him not, and had instead to barge into his third-floor garret, a small affair, with ceilings no more than six foot at best, but exquisite light from its windows. He had not begun to grind the colors, nor fold the easels, yet was busy writing a letter at his rickety trestle table. He looked miserable, and the sight of me made him no happier.

"A pox on you, Weston!" I chided, for where heartbreak is concerned, I find that brusqueness serves better than sympathy. "Do we not all suffer when we drink too much, and what then? I assure you my own skull aches as if it were a well-hammered anvil. And if you failed in your bid to raise the skirts of some serving girl last night, I share your disappointment, for I met with no more success in my efforts to ensnare an heiress, daffy Margaret Usher notwithstanding. But we cannot spend the day writing love-letters. Life must go on. Get *ready*, lad! At once!"

Third—and this I had meant to mention in my last chapter, but had other matters with which to acquaint you—Gulliver is monstrous sick, and his disorder, at least, I cannot blame on either too little love or too much wine. That the dog lies about with his feet in the air I do not count, by way of symptom, since such is his regular habit. But that he is off his food—and his slumber—I report as the chief of his discomforts, if only because these are the most unusual. What does a dog do, else eat and sleep? Hunger is the best sauce, quoth the proverb. But 'tis two days since Gulliver even sniffed at his plate. He begins to froth and tremble. I fear it can only be madness, or what is called the rabies. 'Tis well nigh time to shoot him, but I have instead locked him in the cellar, while I decide what is to be done.

I left him there but a few hours ago, to trudge back, with Weston, to Samuel Bradstreet's house, for a second sitting, only to discover that this gentleman, too, was ill, and confined to his bed.

"What ails your master?" I inquired of Hannah, who met us on her way out.

"I cannot say, sir," she replied, anxiously. "My mistress says 'tis his usual malady, the melancholy, made worse by last night's revelry. But, truly, he is very poorly."

"Zounds! Has the doctor been sent for, lass?"

"Yes, sir. In the small hours, sir. Master had just gone to bed, after the last guests left, when he began to fall short of breath. My Cicero went for Doctor Newcombe, on the bay horse."

"Is the doctor still about?"

"He stays abovestairs, attending my master," said Hannah. "But Mr. Bradstreet improves by the hour, Doctor Newcombe says, and my mistress agrees. They say he will be well enough to go to the Assembly today."

"Well, I'm relieved to hear that the lady is so optimistic. But what will she have us do, Hannah? I do not wish to disturb her at her husband's bedside. Did she leave word? Surely we are to return another day."

"No, sir. I am to run to the apothecary, for calomel. She asks that you set up your easel, as agreed, and she'll be down very soon, and Mr. Bradstreet not long after. In the meanwhile, she says you are to use my Cicero as a sitter—an imposter, I believe she said—to paint my master's clothes."

"Then off with you, lass, and make haste."

We soon found Cicero, a quiet, guarded man, who had already outfitted himself in his master's attire.

"You make an excellent Bradstreet," I declared, clapping him on the back. And 'twas true, for he was the equal of his master in girth, and in bearing.

"Thank you sir, may it please your honor, sir, though I am most unworthy, sir," said he.

"Pray, cease your prosy curtsies, Cicero," I answered. "We are but two laboring men, are we not? I shall not aim to please your honor today, and you shall not aim to please mine. We owe each other only the plain courtesy of common men. Agreed?"

Cicero smiled, but by no means did he let down his guard. "Agreed. But, mind, when milady returns, I'll please-your-honor five times in half as many minutes. Agreed?"

"Agreed," said I.

We set to work in the parlor. Cicero posed, just as Bradstreet had the day before, standing behind a mahogany desk. Wee Phebe played underfoot. For a time, she busied herself folding bleached linens—for her mama, she said—but, truly, she did no more than make a ragged pile of them.

"Lo, you have built an iceberg, Phebe!" I teased. "Now 'tis for you to play Martin Frobisher, and go exploring."

"Pray, who is Fro'sher, sir?" she asked. Whereupon I regaled her with tales of that gentleman's Arctic adventures, and thus we passed a pleasant two hours. Pleasant, that is to say, for me and for the child, but not nearly so for her father, who was about as comfortable in his master's attire as a common tar in a commodore's uniform. Cicero loves the girl, that much is clear, though he cannot be her true father. I could not help but wonder whether Samuel Bradstreet's obvious fondness for the child was evidence of a father's love. Cicero remained restless, however much I tried to put him at his ease. 'Twas a strain to stand so long, especially for a man with a crippled foot, but there was nothing for it; if the lady bid me paint while her husband lay abed, the least I could do was make steady progress.

If Cicero was not still, he was nearly silent; he spoke only to hush the child, when she shrieked as I told her of polar bears. Sensing her terror, Weston began riddling. I was glad to see the color had returned to his cheeks, and his humor had improved. Though the first riddle with which he chose to divert the girl made me wonder whether he, too, was wondering about her parentage.

"Puzzle this, Phebe," my apprentice offered. "'Tis a riddle about a picture of a face, just like the one Mr. Jameson is painting of your master. A man is staring at a portrait and says,

> "*Brothers and sisters I have none*
> *But that man's father is my father's son.*

"Who is in the frame?"

The tiny girl closed her eyes, and pursed her lips as she applied her talents to the puzzle. I looked at Weston, and mouthed, "The man?" But my apprentice only grinned, and shook his head. At last Phebe called out, triumphant, "The son!"

"Ach!" I cried. "It cannot be the sun again, Weston."

"No, sir," Weston smiled. "Phebe's right. 'Tis a portrait of the painter's son." And then he turned to her and asked, "Now how does such a tiny mite as you puzzle that?"

"Master Bradstreet, sir. He's told me that one before."

"And has he taught you any others?"

"I know one, by heart," answered the girl. And then she recited:

> *"Without a bridle or a saddle,*
> *Across a ridge I ride and straddle;*
> *And ev'ry one, by help of me,*
> *Tho' almost blind, is made to see."*

My apprentice pretended to think, at length, tapping his temple with his index finger, before replying. Twas a most captivating performance, I assure you.

"You have stumped me, Phebe," he answered, winking at me. "I give up."

"Spectacles!" she squealed.

For the better part of an hour, Weston and I chatted with Cicero and Phebe. It occurred to me again, as it has before—aye, too many times before—that never am I so happy as when painting with my apprentice at my elbow. While I worked on Bradstreet's draperies, the lad made good progress on the backdrop the lady had requested for her portrait: a curtain pulled back to reveal a small marble statue, a copy of the famed *Diana* of Versailles: the goddess with a stag in one hand, and a full quiver in the other.

At the end of the hour, Hannah, who had returned from the apothecary, descended from the sickroom to gather up Phebe, along with the linens, which no doubt would need laundering once again.

"How fares your master, lass?" I asked.

"He took some tea, sir, but does not look well," she answered, before hastening out of the room.

Just before noon, Mrs. Bradstreet appeared, accompanied by the eminent historian and scholar of physic Doctor Newcombe, a gaunt man, near as tall as I am, with a carbuncle nose. Weston excused himself, to get a refreshment in the kitchen.

"Jameson, how quickly you've progressed," said the lady, as she looked, approvingly, over Weston's work. "Doctor, come here, and see."

"I can take no credit, my lady. Tis my talented apprentice who has painted your draperies."

Newcombe crossed the room, the better to inspect our canvases.

"Fine strokes, Sarah," he said, distractedly. "But now I had best return to my patient."

"In a minute, Thomas," said Mrs. Bradstreet. "You fret too much. Samuel will rest better without us in the room. And I would not wish to waste Mr. Jameson's time."

"Mr. Bradstreet is better then, madam?"

"Much better," she replied and, truly, she seemed entirely at ease on that account.

"I only hope he can get some rest," answered the doctor, who, with a look of resignation, took a seat at the side of the room.

"Is there anything I might do, Doctor, to be of assistance?"

"No, thank you, Jameson. Patience is with her father, and Hannah is at her disposal. I believe we have enough hands on deck. He had spent an evening in dissipation, and was bursting with melancholy humor. I have bled him, twice, and very fully, and have just purged him as well. When he wakes, I may dose him with frog spawn, if he still appears splenetic, but I hazard he will be as well as ever in an hour or two."

"Surely he is not still planning on attending the Assembly meeting then?" I asked.

"I'm afraid he cannot," sighed the lady, "though he is grievously disappointed."

"In twenty-five years, he has never yet missed a meeting," Newcombe mused. "But this summer's work, rallying the legislature against Parliament's nefarious schemes, and the merchants in support of a boycott. Well, the effort has exhausted him."

"That reminds me. Cicero, you must make haste," Mrs. Bradstreet commanded. "Go to Cambridge to inform the Assemblymen that their best member is too ill to join them."

"Cambridge?" I asked. "Are they not meeting at the Town House, then?"

"No, Jameson," the doctor said and shook his head. "Not since the Redcoats arrived, and Bernard permitted the officers to quarter there. Though I venture, in time, the Governor will see the error of his course, and return our Town House to us."

"Just *go*, Cicero. Now."

Relieved to be freed from the role of mannequin, Cicero gave his mistress a nod, and a theatrical bow.

"I will leave as soon as I change out of master's clothes, madam, if it please your ladyship, by your honor."

Mrs. Bradstreet turned to me. "And Jameson, that you shall make the best of the light of midday, I am come to sit for you, as I see you have yet to finish my face."

"Ach, the light of midday. It makes the artist a false friend, madam," I said.

"That's strange, Jameson," Newcombe put in. "A doctor craves strong light, and seldom gets it. Why does the artist shun it? Are we not both anatomists?"

"An interesting question, sir. I have a friend, an esteemed doctor, who has asked me the very same. Strong light produces strong shadows. That's the nub of the problem. 'Tis why foggier climes produce better colorists."

Mrs. Bradstreet's face clouded; she was annoyed, I supposed, that the subject had drifted so far from her for so long.

"I assure you, madam," I hastened to add, " 'twould take more than a sunny August noon to overwhelm your features."

Not long after this, Newcombe, who had been up with his patient much of the night, fell asleep. I at once envied him his nap and regretted it, for I was keen to speak with him; I had far rather converse with this interesting gentleman than with Mrs. Bradstreet, whose countenance was cold, even on this sweltering afternoon. For once I was relieved that my subject was content to sit in silence.

For the next three-quarters of an hour, little but the noise of the doctor snoring disturbed us. Weston returned, and we switched places, he lingering over Mr. Bradstreet's hands—the lad is terrible with hands, and I would give him every chance to improve—while I labored to capture Mrs. Bradstreet's angularity.

All was quiet until upstairs a door slammed. Then we heard a scream, and another. Weston dropped his brush, splashing the floorboards with droplets of deep red paint. The doctor startled awake, and jumped to his feet. Mrs. Bradstreet broke her pose, and her face filled with terror.

The first scream continued, while the second seemed to travel. We heard footsteps on the stairs. Hannah burst into the room, and sputtered, "He's dead! My master is dead!"

Instinct drove me to follow the servant, the doctor, and the lady as they raced to the dead man's bed-chamber. The door opened to reveal Patience pacing the room.

"I was only asleep for a minute!" she sobbed. "I swear it, Mother. I never left him! But look, look . . . he is . . ."

And there, on a high broad bed, below a quilt—even in this heat—her father lay, his face as white as a glacier, his eyes wide and unblinking. A bluish foam trailed from his lips.

"Good Lord!" said Newcombe, rushing to his patient's side. "It's not possible. It's simply not possible. I left him well, just an hour ago."

He bent over the bed, pressed his ear to Bradstreet's chest, and began to shout orders. "Patience, what did he last drink? Hannah, bring me his chamber pot! Jameson, don't let anyone else enter this room."

Hannah pulled the chamber pot from underneath the bed, and carried it gingerly to the doctor. Newcombe sniffed at Bradstreet's last water, and then smelled the secretions from his mouth.

Patience crossed the room and reached for an empty teacup resting on a highboy, but stayed her arm when her mother screamed, "Patty! Don't touch it!"

"Exactly. Patty. Your mother's right. You mustn't touch it," the doctor said, gravely. He turned to his patient—his friend—and gently closed his eyes. Then, quietly, he addressed the dead man's wife. "Sarah, I'm so very sorry. Samuel is dead. And I fear he's been poisoned."

At those words, Mrs. Bradstreet sunk to her knees, grabbing at Hannah's apron, and hitting her, wildly.

"What did you give him?" she shrieked. "You strumpet, you black-faced jade! You *murderer*!"

AT THE SUPERIOR COURT OF JUDICATURE

August 25, 1764

A Coroner's Inquest, conducted at Boston the twenty-fifth day of August in the fifth year of the Reign of His Majesty King George the Third and in the year of our Lord one thousand seven hundred and sixty-four, upon view of the Body of Samuel Bradstreet, Esquire, of Boston, Gentleman.

The Coroner's Jury being Charged and Sworn to Inquire for our said Lord the King, When, and by What means, and how the said Samuel Bradstreet Came to his Death, upon their Oaths do Say that he died on the twenty-fifth day of August by Poison Procured by his Negro woman servant Hannah and given him by the said Hannah and by his Negro man servant Cicero.

In Witness Whereof, as Well I the Coroner, and also the Jurors, do to this Inquest put our hands and Seals.

—THADDEUS MASON, CORONER.

CHAPTER II

Of Prayers and Poppycock

At the graveside of the Honorable Samuel Bradstreet, the Reverend Ethan Cooper, vicar of the church on Brattle Street, said only this: "Samuel the Prophet gave up the Ghost, and all Israel mourned." He took his text from 1 Samuel, verse thirty-five, chapter one. Eleven words. Apt, mind, but curt.

"All Israel mourned, my arse," I whispered, a little too loudly, to Hugh Lambert, who stood at my side, some distance from the grave, as we watched the coffin disappear into the ground. "I like a short homily as much as the next blasphemer, Lambert, but this is too much. Or, rather, too little. Is the parson to offer no tale at all?"

"Nay," replied Lambert, in a tone more hushed than mine, for he was less drunk. Twas near two o'clock in the afternoon, and I had been drinking since dawn. "There ain't to be any preaching, leastways, not till Sabbath."

I have since discovered why.

"There shall be neither prayer nor sermon at funerals, to shun superstition," decreed Cotton Mather, minister to this town's North Church, in his 1726 treatise on the right way to worship, published under the ostentatious title *Ratio Disciplinae Fratrum Nov-Anglorum.* Great God above! Could a bit of well-wishing so easily turn Puritans to papists? Did the pious man fear that a few words spoken over the corpse might raise it from the dead? For this—an "Alas, poor Yorick," mumbled at graveside, or a tearful "God bless ye, my love," uttered by a father shoveling dirt over his stillborn babe—shocking extravagance!—rank superstition!—the minister chides his flock? Well, 'tis wisely said that he who has a mind to beat a dog will easily find a stick.

You will ask, Reader, how I have time for the study of antique religious tracts, what with my bosom friend on the run; my dog on death's door; the McGreevys on my heels; my apprentice run to melancholy and myself in daily danger of seducing him; my best commission interrupted (by *murder*, no less); and Cicero and Hannah, who may well be innocent, imprisoned, along with wee Phebe, who can have committed no crime. Might not I, somehow, *repair* these affairs? Might not I turn this topsy-turvy world back right-side up?

I answer: By the tit of every Salem witch that died under Mather's watch, I would, if only I had the tools, or the talent.

You insist: Might not I at least chisel the bars of the Boston jail?

I answer: No brute instrument can release the poor condemned souls chained to that dungeon's stone walls, as thick as any castle's, for there are stronger fetters that bind them, and faster.

Still, you press on, growing impatient with my excuses: If I have leisure to empty my cups with Lambert, or to sit at my desk reading the disagreeable Doctor Mather (and, aye, the minister carried that title, for he received an honorary degree from the University of Glasgow, the more shame to Scotland), might not I instead fulfill my promise to poor Bradstreet, by copying his pages?

A pox on it! Dear Reader, I beg you: leave off nagging me. I confess: I am useless.

Nay, accept my apology, and pray, read on, for I was sorely vexed before ever you began your pestering.

Let me assure you: I am no black-gowned scholar, engrossed with the arcane. I have tipped a glass or two with Lambert, true, and another three or four with Edes, but by no means have I idled away hour upon hour reading Mather's text. Indeed, I have never even held his book in my hands. Instead I found his remarks on funereal excess excerpted in

Doctor Newcombe's admirable *History of Massachusetts*, a handy volume, in which you will also learn that in the year 1721 this colony's General Assembly passed a law imposing a fine of five-and-twenty pounds on any who would give away black mourning scarves. And more: in 1741 this same Assembly passed "An Act to Retrench the Extraordinary Expenses at Funerals," prohibiting the giving not only of scarves, but also of wine, rum, mugs, and gloves.

Gloves I can live without, but no wine? Such a measure, surely, calls for a drink. Lambert, Edes, another round!

"To Samuel Bradstreet, may thee rest in peace," Lambert toasted, at the Blue Herring, where we had retired after the funeral.

"To the Torch of Liberty, may your light increase!" hollered Edes. ("I would say more," he whispered to me, "but I was hindered by the rhyme.")

This gave me to realize that Edes was near as drunk as I. Just before sagging to the floor, I slurred a final speech: "To Ssamuel Bradstreet, may your troubles ceassse."

Alas, I fear mine are only beginning.

The day of the funeral started dark. It never rained—not a drop—but all the morning it threatened. By noon a patch of blue cut out a corner of the sky. At one o'clock, the sun was shining, and I was already glowing with drink. Weston and I passed Mrs. Goddard, scrubbing the kitchen floor, though she told us she would soon quit for the day to attend the funeral. I grabbed my hat and my flask, and handed the lad his cap. Together we walked to join the crowd assembling on Hanover Street. Weston's skin was pale, his eyes moist, his entire aspect studied and silent.

"A sad day, lad," I sighed, laying an arm across his narrow shoulders, to offer my small comfort. But he shrugged me off.

"Sadder still that you, sir, choose to honor the dead with drink," he scolded, as he squirmed free, and disappeared into the mob.

Know, dear Reader: I would not dishonor Samuel Bradstreet. But my pride forbids me to stay sober and see myself reduced to such helplessness. I was not sorry to see Weston go. Better that I should send him away entirely, and farther still.

Twas then that I bumped into Lambert, and offered him my flask of rum.

"Jameson," said he, "when are you going to paint my excellent sister? Can't you squeeze her in?"

"If she's all you say, Lambert, I can surely squeeze her in," I answered, and truly, I would welcome any diversion from my insolent apprentice.

I took back the flask for another drink.

The bells kept tolling, the sun bore down, and, finally, from Bradstreet's house emerged the Reverend Cooper, followed by the underbearers, six stout Negroes, who carried the coffin on a bier. I saw Pompey among them, but recognized none of the other men. In a ring around them walked the pallbearers, and these I knew, all but the last: William Bradstreet, Amos Quincy, Thomas Newcombe, Hiram and Mordecai Usher, and a younger man who looked so like the last two that he could be none other than Elias Usher. They did not carry the coffin but held, between their fingers, the edges of the black silk pall that covered it. Each of these six gentlemen was dressed in a black cloak and black gloves. All but Elias sported a bright red ring on the smallest finger of their right hands.

"The band of the Red Hen," Lambert whispered, again taking the flask. "Instead of black mourning rings."

Those vermillion bands, set against black gloves, looked to me like nothing so much as blood from a cut, as if each man who wore the ring had severed a finger.

Next came Bradstreet's weeping widow, draped in no less than seven yards of black taffeta—'twould try even Weston's genius with color to paint such a moonless midnight of drapery—and wearing black gloves so rich in glaze they seemed to glitter. In her left hand she carried a black handkerchief; in her right, a black crepe fan. Her daughter Patience, dressed in a modest black frock, held her mother's elbow. Her eyes were dry, her countenance impassive. I would not have expected such reserve of a girl so young and tenderhearted. Behind them trailed a dozen friends and relations, and, next, the most hated man in New-England: Governor Francis Bernard, in an extraordinary wig that fell to his waist, escorted by two dozen red-coated grenadiers. ("God damn those lobsterbacked sons of bitches!" came the call from the crowd.) The Governor was followed by his Council, and some sixty members of the

Assembly—not a few of these gentlemen wearing the same red ring as the pallbearers. Last came we, the rabble, near three thousand strong, parading down Hanover, onto Tremont, and along the Common, where the sight of the soldiers' tents occasioned still more catcalls. The funeral itself was a hurly-burly of lament, with every mourner jostling this way and that, the better to see the Governor, the nearest proxy, in these colonies, to a glimpse of the King himself. And still they cursed him for his calumny in calling for the troops. ("Do you need a corporal to hold your cock while you piss, Guv'nor?")

Lambert had eyes only for Mrs. Bradstreet. "She plays the queen, does she not?" he mused. "Bradstreet shouted down the tyranny of luxury, but his wife, mind, loves her pomp."

I nodded, blearily, and took another pull on the flask.

When the procession halted, we found ourselves just outside the burying ground, our sweaty faces pressed against its cast-iron fence, no more than twenty yards from the Bradstreet family crypt.

"The colony is bankrupt, a quarter of the city lies in ruins, Parliament picks our pockets. Never have we needed Samuel Bradstreet more," said a man whose voice I recognized. I turned to find my friend Edes, his ginger hair blazing in a sea of mourners' black.

Meanwhile, Lambert—who can hold a drink better than you'd think from the look of him—kept eyeing the Widow Bradstreet.

"At least you mourn him, Edes," Lambert observed, passing the printer the flask. "I dare say his wife gives more thought to the gloss on her beads than to her dead husband."

I had to agree. Even as her son William tipped the first spadeful of dirt into the open grave, Sarah Bradstreet busied herself fingering her jewels and stealing glances at the pallbearers.

"Yea, and she won't be a widow for long, mind ye," continued Lambert, with a wry smile. "Though I wonder how well silk and homespun will knit together."

"Shall we place a little wager on when I receive the wedding announcement?" put in Edes.

"Hold, friends," I interjected. "Do I take it poor Bradstreet was mad, murdered, and cuckolded, too?"

"I'll give you two out of three," Edes answered.

"But Usher is not free to marry; his wife is not yet dead," I protested, thinking of the estimable Lucy Usher, too ill to see her brother-in-law buried.

"He may not be free to marry," said Lambert, shaking his head, "but he's free to do as he pleases, so far as Mrs. Bradstreet is concerned. He climbs her rigging, and she salts his cod, if you take my meaning."

"Forget who replaces Bradstreet in his wife's bed!" burst out Edes. "Who will carry his torch in the Assembly?"

"I wager his crooked son will stand for election," answered Lambert.

"The Withered Bastard?" I asked. "But what about Newcombe? Is not he a cock among hens?"

"I'm not yet sure whether Newcombe is cock or capon," mused Edes. "Last year, when the smallpox hit, bolder physicians urged inoculation, but Newcombe was content to tally the dead and dying."

"But he's a man of discernment," I offered, thinking of his illuminating *History*.

"He watches well enough," conceded Lambert. "But Bradstreet meant to call us to action, artisans and merchants alike. I cannot think Newcombe will gather such a flock."

Poor Bradstreet. Half the city has come out to watch him buried, and to see his wife flout the city's sumptuary laws—for she has spent seven hundred pounds on scarves and rings and wine and gray kid gloves, if she has spent a penny. So many of these mourning gloves, each adorned with a ring made of Bradstreet's hair, are passed into the crowd that a pair made its way back even to me. With a fond thought for that fine man, I slipped them into my pocket.

But who mourns for Cicero and Hannah and the blameless little girl, chained and imprisoned? And the deuce of it, the black deuce of it, is: had Bradstreet lived, I daresay he might have found a way to free them, and thousands more.

Hours later, in the Blue Herring, Lambert and Edes pulled me from under a table—not without bumping my sore and surly head—and dragged me back to Queen Street through a driving rain.

"What happened to the sun?" I stammered, my brain a thick ooze, my feet, lumps of clay.

"'Tis past midnight, Jameson," Lambert answered, his speech as clipped as it had been at noon. God, the man can hold his drink. Is there some trick he could teach me?

The cobbles grew slick under our feet. But the soaking began to clear my head. As I climbed the steps to my door, and sent my friends off into the night, I could hear wretched Gulliver, whining. I pledged, not for the first time: if he is no better tomorrow, I will borrow a musket and shoot him.

I barreled into the hall, barely catching myself from hitting the floor. I could see a lantern flickering in the kitchen, and from that direction I heard a sound I did not expect at this unseasonable hour, one that never ceases to make me shudder: the crunch of pestle against mortar.

"Confound it, Weston!" I called, slamming the door behind me. "If you've a mind to grind paints, 'twould be better you did it upstairs in the painting room, lad, for I'd rather not find lead in my porridge. But so long as you're in the kitchen, brew me a pot of tea. Ach, lad, my head is a tempest."

I stumbled into the parlor, slumped into the nearest chair, and closed my eyes.

"Your errand-boy has long since gone to bed, Jamie," said a deep, familiar voice. "Wake up, you great sot. And see a man risen from the dead."

Letter X.

September the 4th, 1764

My dear Elizabeth,

How grateful I am for your letter, and for your promise that the silken bonds of our friendship remain intact. I know I strain those bonds, for I ask so much of you, and give so little in return. I hope it will not always be thus. You tell me you fear your counsel is useless to me, so different have our lives become. But Lizzie, can you not see that you offer me more than advice? It comforts me, more than ever you could know, to take stock of my life upon these pages, and to set those reckonings before your kind eyes, secure that you will keep my secrets close. Only to you, Lizzie, only in these pages, can I be Fanny.

Some of what I must write you may have already read in the papers. Samuel Bradstreet is dead. The Torch of Liberty extinguished! Poisoned, they say, though I can scarce believe it. True, he died suddenly, yet I think he declined more slowly. Memory recolors the mind's eye, but I cannot see him vigorous. Even when we and Patty were girls, he had grown brooding and distracted, older than his years.

But none has time for such a tale of slow-stalking death. *Murder*, Mrs. Bradstreet cried the moment her husband breathed his last. And from every corner of this town the chorus rises to meet her. Within hours, Hannah and her husband had been jailed for the crime. Their guilt is assumed, and the court promises proof certain. For as the gossips cluck, the mere fact of Hannah's and Cicero's slavery gave them motive enough—and means and opportunities to match. Does not every bondsman harbor within his breast an image of a freedom worth killing for? And is not every slave-owner's house, from his toolshed to his hearth to his pantry, an arsenal filled with the weapons of murder?

Yet as I picture Hannah and Cicero bound fast in the cellars of the jailhouse, I think, mostly, of Phebe. You find my fondness for the little girl excessive, and caution that it ill fits my relation to her. But Lizzie, she is my own sister! Imagine that blameless little lamb, as innocent as the babe torn from my womb, punished every hour. I cannot allow her terrible bondage to continue. I will not.

But how do I mean to free her? you will ask. I must answer indirectly.

What I have to tell you now, Lizzie, you can learn nowhere but in my letters. A *Fortune* has landed of a sudden upon our doorstep, not a purse but a man, and he scarcely meets the description in the advertisement you sent me.

If I am to see clearly, as a woman, and not half darkly, as a child, I must begin by giving things their proper names. *Fortune* is a slave name, and a mocking one, for his bondage is the very opposite of luck. I shall call him what he christens himself: Ignatius Alexander. He reads three modern languages and Latin besides; he might be a professor of rhetoric for all his eloquence, and the force of his voice. And he has seen the world of which he would fain be a citizen. He was born of Africans, on their passage into slavery, but by a roll of fate's dice he grew to manhood in freedom—indeed, in luxury—and it shows, despite the terrible turns of fate he has lately suffered.

Doctor Alexander is average in stature, standing a hand higher than I do, and a hand shorter than Jameson. He smelled of soap when I met him, for as soon as he arrived, he had scrubbed himself, burned the clothes he came in, and changed into some of Jameson's, though my master has since bought him better-fitted vestments. The Doctor keeps his head clean-shaven and oiled to a mirror sheen. He holds himself high, and slightly apart, with the bearing of a natural aristocrat. His brow furrows with thought, and his brown eyes shine with his learning. Were I to take his likeness, here would be my recipe for human flesh: I should mix lamp black and cinnabar, in equal parts.

Yet if his mind is deep and his spirit free, his body bears the deep impress of bondage. I have since heard him tell Jameson that his back is all over scarred, a bloody tissue of pain woven as densely as the finest dimity. The letter R brands the back of his right hand, burned into him as if his skin were the hide of an animal. The scar, so newly formed as to remain florid and gruesome, is meant to mark him as a runaway. But he reads it differently.

"In my psalter, Weston," he has told me, "R stands for *revenge*."

When first I met him, I was terrified, despite having recognized his face at once, from the portrait of him I had spied in Jameson's attic. I happened upon him the day of Samuel Bradstreet's funeral. Overwhelmed by grief and sadness, I had slipped away from the mourning crowd, and sat for hours beside the Mill Pond, where you and I so often played as girls. Twas dusk when I made my way home to Queen Street. And there he stood, in the parlor, a shadow within the shadows, pacing and grumbling, his temper as angry as his wounds. I made to scream, but he closed on me in an instant, pressing me against the wall and covering my mouth with his hand.

"Hold your tongue, serving boy," he hissed, taking his hand away from my mouth, moving back a half a step. "I have no business with you, nor will I harm you. I am come for Stewart Jameson, in friendship, and he will own our fraternity, for I have battled my way across the river Styx and into this Hades for that man. He makes a poor Eurydice, I grant, but, mark me, I will play Orpheus and bring him out of here."

"You are his . . . Fortune?" I stammered.

This set him to laughing, a robust laughter, yet edged with anger.

"Is that what Jameson told you? Your master has a fine sense of irony, if an unforgivable weakness for bad puns. For I do not know which of us is the less fortunate man. No, I am not his fortune, nor anyone else's. My name is Ignatius Alexander."

"Ignatius Alexander? . . . Galaxies untrained!"

Doctor Alexander raised an eyebrow.

"You are a better puzzler than your master. Yes, indeed, boy. I am he. But I will tell you no more until you explain yourself to me."

Haltingly I told him my name, and my purpose in this house. The doctor only stared, so intently, that I felt as if his gaze lifted my disguise. I tried to cover myself in words, and began to babble: about the crowds and soldiers at Bradstreet's funeral, and then, of his seeming murder.

"We were there, painting, when he died. Or was killed. When she killed him, I mean. When he died, from the sugar in his tea. Only it wasn't sugar," I said, now almost crying, though whether for Bradstreet, or for Phebe, or for my master, or for myself, I am not sure.

"Ah yes, the Snuffing of the Torch of Liberty," Doctor Alexander replied, a smile curling his lip. "I have read of it in your *Gazette*, for I have spent this afternoon poring over every issue in this house. May I offer my condolences upon your town's loss," he sneered, bowing deeply. "And how *original* are you good Bostonians, to dream up such a novel tale of passion and poison. Do you know that if you would just change the names, you might find the like story reported any year, in any paper, in any port around this vast ocean? I could write it myself. Indeed, your pressman might save himself labor, and precious coins, by printing up a form. *Great Negro Plot Discovered!* he could headline it. Your Edes would have only to fill in the blanks. Was the victim poisoned, or hatcheted, or burned in his bed? Was he pious unto his last breath, or merely kind to his chattel? Was the ungrateful murderer called Caesar, or perhaps it was Cuffee?"

"He was Cicero, sir," I ventured.

"Of course. Mighty Cicero. Shall we attend him next at the stake, or wait to see him rot upon the gibbet? Perhaps a dozen handwritten words, maybe a score, would do the trick. Remember, time is money, as your own Doctor Franklin observed, so pithily. You colonials could use the saved hours to prattle on about your liberties."

He continued, speaking such volumes with such vehemence that I barely digested his meaning.

"If you think them innocent, then someone must solve this terrible crime!"

"What I think, boy, is that neither their innocence, nor its opposite matters one whit. Not to this Bradstreet's human property, surely. For whether they poisoned the man who would call himself their master, or served him faithfully all their days, they will burn, and quickly too, like dry kindling on a winter afternoon. You have seen very little of life if you doubt it."

"And if they did what they are accused of?" For I had not forgotten Hannah's words, *I would kill if I thought that would break her chains.*

"In that case, it is their action—not their certain sentence—that would meet every definition of reason. Sir Thomas More himself would call the death of a barbarian at the hands of the righteous by its just name: of war."

"But this was no war. 'Twas a murder. A good man has died."

"A good, slave-owning man, was he? I only wish my hand had stirred the fatal dose into his tea. Defoe—one of our friend Jameson's favorite writers, though I find him overrated—once explained, 'There is sugar at the bottom of every cup of misery.' "

With that, he raised an imaginary cup to his lips.

" 'The case is as plain as cause and consequence,' Defoe wrote. 'No African trade, no negroes; no negroes, no sugar; no sugar, no islands; no islands, no continent; no continent, no trade.' You see, it is but one chain that spans the globe. Let us call it the great chain of un-being."

"A chain, sir?" I whispered, dizzied by his tale and dazzled by his intellect.

"A chain that holds us all, though it binds us differently. Some feel its shackles daily," he said, revealing to me the freshly bathed scars 'neath his cuffs. "Ah yes, I can see it in your face: my wounds are *indelicate*. They are not pretty, these stigmata of the Indies trade, are they?"

Before I could answer, he ceased his orbit round the parlor, coming to stand before me, his face mere inches from mine.

"Show me your wrists, boy," he demanded, taking my hands in his. "Ah, an artist's hands. Yet you, too, hold the chains, and they you. And though the links of your portion are more lightly borne, they are always, always about you."

"But I don't take sugar in my tea."

"You read, do you not? Take your precious *Gazette*. Do you notice the rewards posted there for runaway slaves, black men and women who have stolen from their owners by stealing themselves? I myself am a man-stealer. My poor master, still reeling from his losses! But he found the hard coin to pay for an advertisement, putting money in the printer's pocket. More links in the chain, Weston."

Here he broke off, poised between rage and reverie. I dared another question.

"Which chains were yours, sir, and how did you break them?"

"What, do you imagine this is Sunday school, and I your soot-blacked preacher, regaling you with tales of my flight from bondage? Is my Virginia to play your Egypt, then, and this—*this?*—my Palestine? Who dares to make a testament of my exodus! I will not speak of it!"

With every sentence the thunder of his voice increased, till he spoke loud enough that I wondered whether the sentry, on his evening watch, might worry for my safety.

Then he banged his fist upon the tea table hard enough to shatter either, or both. Yet the pain seemed not to daunt him.

"Which chains were mine? How did I free myself? It is a tale without heroes. That I will tell you, and four words more. *With my own hands,*" he said, tracing with the fingers of his left hand the branded R that ruined his right. And then he muttered 'neath his breath, " 'What hands are here, what hands are here?' "

"Lady Macbeth, sir?" I inquired, taking his allusion.

But he ignored my question.

"You know not the reddish work these hands have done, boy, and never shall."

We stood in silence, me rooted to the floor, and my interlocutor shifting his gaze from my face to *The Serving Boy*, hanging on the wall.

"An intriguing attempt," he offered, grown suddenly meditative. "At once an ambitious work, and an utter failure."

"Mr. Jameson has worried it overmuch, and lost the likeness."

"Is that what you observe? Then you are as blind as he is."

"This much I do surely see, Doctor Alexander: you must be hungry," I said, eager to break the spell of our strange and sudden intimacy. "Let me bring you some supper while you wait for my master. I expected him hours ago. He cannot be long now."

I brought him a tray, and settled him into the two-room tenement attached to our house, empty since the Goddards left it. And then I climbed the stairs to my garret. But I could hardly sleep, for while I was certain this Alexander was Jameson's long-lost friend, I worried about the violent cast of his mind.

Twas well past midnight when I heard my master's footfalls, lurching and heavy as he came through the front door. A muffled shout and a tipping of chairs told me he had spied his dark Lazarus.

I sneaked down the stairs and peered in at the two men from the obscurity of the hall. They stood in the lantern-lit parlor, entwined in an embrace, a long, tender, manly embrace. Tears streamed down my master's cheeks and the doctor, too, was visibly affected, though more reserved than his friend.

"I failed you, and still you have found me," Jameson said, and reached to take the doctor's hand. But when he felt the violence that had been done to it, he began to weep in earnest. Alexander pulled his branded hand away.

"Jamie, the world is crueler than either of us could have imagined."

"Sander, Sweet Jesus. How have you borne it?"

"I do not think I have borne it, nor could you have done. Neither your sympathy nor my reason offers any bulwark against the barbarity of men."

"What do you mean, you haven't borne it? You're here. You're alive."

"Alive? I am burned and whipped. I am hunted and haunted. And half mad. It took me half the day merely to cleanse my wounds. But yes, I am here. Now pack your bags, and let us find a ship, and escape this Hades."

My master slumped into a chair.

"Sander, I can't. I'm a witness to a murder. I must remain for the trial. And after that . . . the McGreevys . . . I can never go back."

"Do not be absurd, Jamie. I have heard all about this so-called murder, and you know as well as I do, the trial will be a farce."

"But how can you think to run, when you should hide? Given a second chance, Berkeley would . . ."

Once again his voice trailed off, and he dropped his head into his hands. Jameson's misery rent my heart, and, instinct drove me to take a small step toward him. Hearing a noise, the doctor looked up. I cannot be certain he saw me, but I feared it. I retreated farther into the darkness, and inched up the stairs to my garret.

I listened to them talking near through the night, though I could not always make out the sense of it, as I lay awake, wondering what I must do. I could not think how to help either of these men. But I had promised Hannah to do whatever I could to free Phebe, and I meant to make good that pledge.

Dearest Lizzie, I know you will spy the selfishness of my plan. I could hardly bear the thought of Alexander spiriting Jameson away, and I wondered at the depth of the love that lay between the two men. Nor did I relish the prospect of finding another way to exist in this cruel town, when I have begun at last to live. But honestly, my first thought was of my poor sister, that babe held in a dungeon.

At dawn, I went belowstairs to find my master in the kitchen, disheveled and distracted, his unshaven face in every way pained. But he spoke to me softly.

"Morning, Weston. You're just in time to spare me making tea."

"Of course, sir," I answered. He held my gaze.

"I hear that you have met my Fortune."

I nodded, and was about to speak when Doctor Alexander entered the room.

"Good morning, Doctor," I said, keeping as steady a voice as I could, for I was full sensible of the boldness of what I meant to propose.

"Good morning, Weston," said the doctor, coolly.

"I have been thinking, sir," I ventured. "About our conversation last night."

"Conversation?" Jameson asked, surprised. "Sander, you told me you sent the boy to bed."

"Before you came home, sir," I broke in, "Doctor Alexander and I spoke of Mr. Bradstreet's murder, sir, and the injustice of it, and how innocent people might soon be killed by the court, and what men of sympathy and reason might do to avenge that wrong."

"Is that so, Weston?" asked the doctor, giving me a hard and knowing stare. "As I remember our conversation, we were speaking of the doctrine of just war."

"Yes, Doctor," I nodded, daring again to pick up the thread of what I had overheard between the two men. "Of the war of reason against barbarism. Tis no fair fight, you were saying. But I was thinking, sir, that *your* prodigious powers of reason might stand a chance."

Doctor Alexander glared at me, knowing my deception if not yet my intent.

"Confound it, Weston," Jameson said, his irritation growing. "All I asked for was some goddamned tea. What the deuce are you on about?"

"Well, I was thinking, sirs—"

"So you claim," Alexander offered.

"—thinking that we are, all three of us, likely to stay together in this house, for a while at least. The raw wound on the doctor's hand tells the world he is hunted as a runaway. Mr. Jameson, sir, you have so much to keep you in this town. The trial . . . And of course I am bound to your service, sir. And as we were speaking of justice—"

"Weston, for God's sake, spit it out," said Jameson. "And then I could do with the tea, lad."

"What I mean to say, sirs, is that if the trial of Hannah and Cicero is to be a farce, maybe we could yet avert a tragedy."

Jameson looked at me, puzzled. Alexander raised an eyebrow. I soldiered on.

"Mr. Jameson, I have heard you say the doctor is a brilliant scholar, and particularly expert at chemistry and medicine, logic and deduction. If anyone, the world over, could solve Samuel Bradstreet's murder, is not Doctor Alexander that gentleman?"

My master smiled, relieved, amused, and—I dared hope—intrigued.

"The head of John the Baptist on a pewter platter! What can you mean, Weston? We're harboring a fugitive. A runaway slave. We can scarcely appoint him magistrate when 'tis unsafe for him even to leave the house."

"But sir," I protested, "he need never be seen on the streets. You can be his eyes, and I his feet."

"Fascinating," said the doctor, smoothly. "It is not enough that I am whipped and branded. Now I must be both blind and lame."

"Hold on, Sander. Maybe the lad's got something. Tis not a perfect plan, I grant you. But so long as you and I are trapped here, what harm can it do to attempt an investigation? You can sit and cogitate till your prodigious brain aches. And for once, great good could come of it."

"Great good? No, not great good, Jamie. But small good, I might grant you."

"Is small good not sometimes enough, sir?" I pleaded.

"No. Not for me. Weston, understand: if I agree to this masquerade, it is not in order to do your 'small good.' My enemy is not Samuel Bradstreet's murderer. My enemy is slavery, and I will battle that great iniquity unto my death."

"Iniquity . . ." Jameson mused, as if just remembering something. "That's the point of Bradstreet's windy treatise, the one I'm supposed to be saving from the censors."

"What treatise?" the doctor and I asked, in tandem.

"*A Modest Inquiry into the Iniquity of Slavery*, a pithier title than Colin might have chosen."

"And you have the manuscript, here in this house?"

"In my desk."

The doctor paced about the small room. His bearing gave me to hope that he was debating my proposal.

"Did you see the body, Jamie?"

"Aye, and more closely than I had the stomach for, I assure you."

"And Weston, you realize this is dangerous work, and your role in it will be unconventional, to say the least. If I agree to study this matter, you will answer to me, as if I were your master. At my command you must not flinch, not once, not ever, however much your deference to a black man flouts the custom of this country."

I nodded. "That I can promise, sir, without hesitation."

At this, Jameson laughed. "Sander, I cannot think how Weston hopes to honor that pledge, for I'm already his bloody master, and I cannot get so much as a shitten cup of tea."

"Sir. I'll get your tea in just a moment. But Doctor, my reasoning persuades you, then?"

"Hardly, young Weston. No, I have my own reasons," the doctor said. "But I will conduct an investigation. It begins with the dog."

And then he turned from the room and headed to the cellar, without another word to this amazed and determined apprentice-detective,

Fanny Easton.

From the *Boston Gazette*, Thursday, September 6, 1764.

BOSTON.

*T*he Freeholders and Inhabitants of the Town of Boston, qualified as the Law directs, are to meet at Faneuil Hall, Tomorrow at Ten o'Clock in the Forenoon, to choose between Doctor Thomas Newcombe and William Bradstreet, Esquire, as their Representative in the Place of the late Samuel Bradstreet, Esquire, to serve for the remaining Part of the Year.

CAMBRIDGE.

*T*he Public is hereby informed that because news of the untimely death of the Honorable Samuel Bradstreet, Esquire, reached this colony's Assembly before it opened its special session in Cambridge on the twenty-fifth of August last past, the legislation docketed for discussion at that meeting has been postponed, until a new Representative can be elected, and a new Speaker chosen.

To the Editor:

Your readers should be informed of an astonishing feat of Nature. Last week, an ewe in Roxbury gave birth to four lambs. As an increase in our sheep will prevent our importing British wool, we may query whether Governor Bernard will not inform the King of this instance of fecundity, and earnestly recommend another regiment of soldiers being sent, in order to have our rams castrated.

—Bradstreet's Ghost.

CHAPTER 12

In Which the Investigation Begins

"But Sander," I said, full earnest, for truly, I could barely follow the man. "What has my dog to do with murder?"

Aye, Reader, 'tis true: Ignatius Alexander, my long-lost Fortune, has arrived in Boston, at long last. He is not the same man I knew, and loved. But thank God he is here, for there are mysteries afoot that I cannot begin to solve.

"Your dog? Perhaps nothing," he said, inspecting a dish of bluish drool he had collected from poor Gulliver's muzzle. "But a careful investigator overlooks no detail; even the slobber of a demented mastiff can be a clue. In this case, Jamie, it leads me to believe that the animal has been poisoned."

"Poisoned!" exclaimed my apprentice, who knelt beside the dog, gently stroking his fur. "By Samuel Bradstreet's killer?"

"Weston," chided the doctor, pouring a bottle of beer into a bowl for the dog to drink. "Has your master taught you no discipline? Begin with the obvious. A painter's house is filled with toxins. You employ a veritable palette of poisons. Your reds and whites are made of lead, your yellows and greens of orpiment, which is nothing but arsenic sulfide. All of them taste equally sweet to a dog as dumb as this one."

"Will he survive?" I asked, for God help me, Reader, I love the cursed cur.

"If it is lead he has eaten, yes, Jamie. I shall flush it out of him, and he will be well soon. But why did you not keep the paints well away from him?"

"The dog has never gotten into my paints—not unless he's grown a thumb, for I keep the cabinet locked, and the pigment boxes fastened, too," I answered, surly, and still reeling from the shock of finding my most beloved friend within the walls of my own house, looking like a man unhinged, and lecturing me on animal husbandry.

"But sir," ventured Weston. "Remember the missing lead, sir? You said a whole tin of it had vanished."

"Aye, but the tin *itself* is gone. Do you mean to say the dog swallowed the lead, tin and all?"

"Not likely, Jamie, I admit," the doctor agreed. "But who would take the trouble to murder your dog?"

I looked at Weston, who looked at the dog.

"If I may, Doctor Alexander, sir," said the lad, scratching Gulliver behind the ears while the dog lapped up the last of the beer. "I love the animal as much as his master"—Reader, his sloppy syntax made me gasp—"but he is a clumsy, blundering thing, digging up the neighbors' gardens; soiling the street as much as any horse; leaping up on one and all; barking at all hours. Honestly, Doctor, he has naught *but* enemies."

"Sweet Jesus, Sander. What manner of investigation centers on my dog? Wouldn't we do better to list *Bradstreet's* enemies?"

"First things first, Jamie. We need to discover whether the man was even murdered," he commanded, imperiously. "The coroner's report is kept under seal. So I will need to hear from the man himself. Get Mason here, Jamie, the sooner the better."

So it happened, this afternoon, that I found myself in the painting room, face-to-face with Mr. Thaddeus Mason.

"How came you to conclude that Bradstreet had been poisoned, sir?" I pressed the coroner, as he sat for a kit-cat, his tricornered hat but half hiding a slack and ruddy countenance in which stupidity and smugness vied for mastery.

"What cheek, Jameson! How is it any business of yours?"

"None at all, surely, sir," I answered, smoothing his feathers. "'Tis but the idle curiosity of an idle artisan—idle, that is, till you agreed to sit for me today, for which, again, my gratitude"—here, I bowed—"though perhaps you forget, sir, that I was in Bradstreet's house at the moment of the man's death. Were the villainous Negro wench and buck not so swiftly arrested, I might have been a suspect myself."

"Aye, you were there, weren't you," he said, considering. "Maybe you have something to tell the jury at trial, Jameson."

"At trial!" I stuttered, not a little concerned at this turn of the conversation. I had intended to draw out this barber-turned-coroner on the subject of his inquest. Yet here was my first demonstration, if any were needed, that while I know how to pin a man, I cannot catch a criminal. Not a quarter-hour after my interrogation began did my subject turn the tables and begin to question me. I looked across the room at Weston, busying himself applying the varnish to another canvas, but listening, intently. My eyes met his, and, in them, I saw his confidence sinking. I would not alarm the lad. I winked at him. I'll turn Mason to my task yet.

"Truly, sir, if the Attorney General wishes to call me to the witness stand to tell of the angle of sunlight in Bradstreet's parlor that day, or of the number of hairs in my sable brush, or even of the best colors for painting Bradstreet's breeches, I will entertain both bench and bar for the better part of an hour. But as for murder, I fear I observed nothing. 'Twould be as well to ask a carpenter what books were on Bradstreet's library shelves. I have not your astuteness, sir, nor your discernment; I had eyes only for my work."

Mason picked at his ear and shifted in his chair, drawing his vast bulk upward.

"Of course you know nothing of these high matters, Jameson."

Weston offered me a half smile. Mother of Christ, but he melts me. I smiled back, and continued working on Mason's nose, a beak of an alarming angle, fully as triangular as his hat, its hypotenuse blemished by smallpox scars.

"Yet do we not share a set of skills, sir?" I inquired, in the most humble tone I could muster. "Do we not both study the human form? And so: my curiosity. I can see, sir, when I look at you, that you boast prodigious strength and a capacious mind. These I discover in the way your arms fill your sleeves, sir, and in the wrinkle of your strong brow. With my painter's eye, I might even discern something of your history. You keep a cat, sir."

"Who told you about my little Whiskers, Jameson?" he demanded.

"I've not met your wee kitty, sir. Yet my Gulliver has not left off sniffing you, damn him. And I can see from the strands of fur, here and there, upon your cloak, that your Whiskers must be a calico. But how does a coroner look at a dead man, and discover how he died? Forgive me for presuming to inquire after your business, sir, but I am agog: What genius informs your Art?"

Mason grinned—flashing tobacco-stained teeth that reminded me of why I had limned him close-mouthed—took in a deep breath, puffing himself with his pride. Weston watched the coroner closely, and smiled at me once again, his fullest, sweetest smile. And now did the lad wink back at me. Sweet Jesus, how will I keep my mind trained upon my task?

"Aye, Jameson, 'tis a kind of genius, I'll grant ye. And as I like you—you are court painter to the Hens, so I know you keep good company—I'll tell you more than I ought. What I do in a case like this is a bit of deduction, see. The good doctor told me that poor, mad Bradstreet had been poisoned, and that he suspected arsenic. Between you and me, Jameson, this Bradstreet is better off dead. But never mind about that. He died when his heart stopped beating, you know, which was caused by the arsenic, of course. Well, Jameson, there are two places to find arsenic: the gut and the brains. So, I cut open the head, and I cut open the belly. The brain was swelled, and the gut was full of tea and wine—arsenic gives its victim a powerful thirst, and Bradstreet had drunk gallons—it spurted onto me cloak when I poked a hole in his stomach. See here," he said, indicating a stain on his jacket. "But in that sloshing water I found some particles of white powder, not yet dissolved." His face lit up as he nodded his head. "Arsenic, 'twas plain!"

"Sir, this is most fascinating." (Yet, dear Reader, I gagged, my own stomach revolting at his disgusting details.) "Pray, tell me more. How did you discover the powder to be arsenic?"

Mason chuckled. "You are a jackass, Jameson. I *knew* 'twas arsenic, did I not? Newcombe suspected it, *I* looked for it, and *I* found it. Have I not just proven it? *Science*, is what that is."

Weston rolled his eyes at me as he slipped past me and left the room. He has gone to the tenement to make his report to Alexander, of that I'm certain. Though what Mason's testimony proves, except that the man is a dunce, I know not.

*S*cience, is what that is'?" raged Alexander, after Mason left, and the sun had set. "By the light of Galen, Jamie. What manner of place have you led me to? Your coroners are butchers. What are your doctors? Do they still treat men with spiderwebs and bat wings?"

"Frog spawn, as it happens."

"Jamie. Do not trifle with me. This is no joking matter. Let us at least move up into higher regions of Linnaeus's taxonomy."

"Tax what, Sander? And I'm not kidding about the frog spawn."

"Enough Falstaff, Jamie. Can we not progress from amphibians to mammals? Did Samuel Bradstreet have as many enemies as your damned dog?" My friend's eyes turned cold as he paced across the candlelit parlor, rubbing at his wrists.

Dear Reader, ask yourself, if you can bear it, the question that has haunted me: What does it do to a man to be chained and whipped? How does such a one recover?

"Zooks, man!" I yelled, growing exasperated with an inquiry that directed all our attention away from the question that mattered to me most: Will Alexander recover? "Enemies? Bradstreet had a thousand if he had one! Tis true, the artisans loved him, for he watched after their interests as no one else in the Assembly did. But his fellow merchants, while they followed him, feared him, for by forcing the abolition to a vote, he would expose the hypocrisy of their clamoring for liberty."

"All this, any blockhead can learn in the newspaper. Speaking of which, who hides behind the pen-name 'Bradstreet's Ghost'?"

"Aye, who? The whole town talks of it, but none knows the answer—save Edes, I suppose, and he is a man of great discretion. And just as well, for the phantom speaks sedition. But surely he is no murderer."

"There I agree with you, Jamie, though the Ghost interests me. But now, can you tell me nothing of the dead man's private life?"

"Ach, Bradstreet's wife had betrayed him, the heartless peahen, and his son is a wily bastard. Half the townsmen thought their prophet Samuel had gone stark mad, and that confounded muddlehead, Mason, proposed to build an asylum just for him. However ingenious you may be, Sander, listing Bradstreet's enemies makes a bad beginning. Better to name his friends, for they were few enough."

Alexander left off rubbing his wrists, and began tracing the line of the R branded into his right hand.

"Jamie, calm down," he said softly, slowing his pacing for a moment, trying, in vain, to calm *himself*, though he could not manage to stand still. "You think I am as mad as Bradstreet's enemies thought him"—his voice broke. "Do you think I cannot see what I am become in your eyes, even in this dim light?"

"Weston, fetch some tea," I ordered, for the lad had been sitting at the table with me, and I would not have him witness this.

"You are right, Jamie," my friend began, when my apprentice had gone. He spoke erratically, now loud, now soft; this a holler, that a whisper. And still he walked up and down the room, at a frantic clip. "I have lost my mind. I have been made into a monster. I have been nursed, groomed, tutored, beaten into this monster." Here he stopped, at the corner of the room, and pressed his forehead against the wall, next *The Serving Boy*. He sighed, turned, and looked at me. "What mind in bondage is not lost?"

"Sander—"

"No, let me speak it. Some minutes, Jamie, I think I would kill you, I would take up this candlestick"—here, picking it up from the table— "and smash your head in." He took up the lantern, in his other hand. "I would burn this house down. If I thought it would free a single soul from his shackles, I would see all Boston—nay more—all of New York burning."

He held both lights above my face, and stared down at me, his eyes fierce. "For I see in your countenance the color of my former master. And were Woodward—that bastard, that Procrustean fiend—were he here, Jamie, I swear: I would rip his entrails from his belly and tie them about his neck. And still I would not have slaked my thirst for vengeance."

And then he placed both candlestick and lantern down on the table, slumped into a chair beside me, and held his head in his hands. The bell in the Old Brick Church tolled midnight.

I took his right hand, that branded hand, in my own. He flinched, and made to pull it back, but I held it firm.

"Sander, you will not kill me with a candlestick. My skull's too thick."

He smiled, wanly, a tired, defeated, heartbreaking smile.

"O, Jamie, how I have missed you," he sighed. "But it will take more than your dull wit to cure this madness."

Letter XI.

September the 11th, 1764

Dear Elizabeth,

A week has passed since last I wrote to acquaint you with our house-hold's sudden turn of fate. I have scarcely had time to put pen to paper, for I am now embarked upon an entirely different sort of work than Fanny or even Weston has been accustomed to: no more a lady, nor merely a painter's apprentice, but a criminal investigator, such as Mr. Fielding might feature in his reports on the detective work of London's Bow Street Runners. Doctor Alexander, like that famous magistrate, directs my attention to the murkier recesses of human nature.

I speak of the jail, Lizzie, the cellars of a dark and leaky stone build-ing on Queen Street just below its juncture with King, hard by the Town House. Though I have lived quite near it all my life—my father's house but a short walk from it, and Jameson's quarters nigher still—I have never before seen behind its doors. Tis a shocking and loathsome place, full of horrors not compassed in the most spine-chilling gothic. Men of honor would not keep their pigs thus.

I began yesterday in sunnier quarters. I rose at dawn to resume an ex-ercise my master had commended to me. I would sketch the same object, a cup of clear glass, again each half hour, as the light advanced. I had be-gun to lose myself in the work when Mr. Jameson's voice interrupted me.

"Weston, come at once!" he shouted. As I descended from the painting room, I heard knocking at the front door. In the parlor, I found Jameson and Doctor Alexander head-to-head over a game of whist. Since his friend arrived a fortnight ago, the two men have been inseparable. Though their conversation is not always easy, I envy them their intimacy, and even their arguments.

"What do you wish me to do for you, master?" I asked, bowing deeply enough to mock that good man gently.

"Aye, what *do* I want from you, lad?" he asked, wistfully, letting the question linger a moment too long. Even with his friend at his side, he still stares hard at me, Lizzie, for all he wills himself not to. "What do I want from you? That you should play the bloody servant for once, if your genius would give us a moment's rest."

"How may I serve thee, your grace?" I asked, dropping to one knee.

"Just answer the damned door, would you, before that knocking deprives me of my wits!"

I opened the door to find the tall, craggy figure of the Sheriff, George Kettrell. His left hand clutched a scroll of parchment, and his right held a stout staff nearly two yards high, topped with the emblem of this colony: the figure of a poor benighted Indian, naked but for a girdle of leaves, speaking the words, *Come over and help us.* I had scarcely a moment to ponder the sort of "help" our forefathers had brought, when the Sheriff pounded the staff hard upon the doorstep and cried,

"*Hear ye, hear ye.* In the name of His Majesty, George the Third, and his commonwealth in Massachusetts, and the Superior Court of Judicature thereof, I deliver unto you a summons." He handed me the scroll, nodded curtly, and was gone.

"Zounds!" Jameson thundered when he had cracked the seal upon the paper and scanned its contents. "'Tis not enough that we watch this travesty of justice unfold. Now we are told to add our voices to the choir of rogues and fools."

"*We*, sir?" I asked, trembling at the thought, for my alias alone would perjure me.

"*I*, Weston. His Majesty calls me to testify," he sighed, passing me the scroll.

> To Stewart Jameson, Face–Painter, Queen Street.
>
> The Sheriff of this County summons you to appear before the Superior Court of Judicature held at the Town House

the eighteenth of September at nine of the Clock before noon, to
give Evidence in our Behalf against Cicero a Negro man &
Hannah a Negro woman both of Boston aforesaid.

Signed and Sealed this tenth day of September.
William Bradstreet, Esquire,
Council for the Crown.

"I am so sorry, sir," I sympathized. "Truly this is an insult heaped upon a world of injury."

"It is every bit of that," Doctor Alexander said, his voice measured, and his hands more steady than I had yet seen them. "Yet I hear within the good Sheriff's knock the faint tap of opportunity. Weston, hasten to the jail, and find the man on duty. If he is cast according to type he will be a low man, the sort who supplements his meager income as eagerly as he slakes his thirst for rum and corruption. Bow humbly before this ill-natured fellow, and mind: with no trace of your usual sauciness. Tell him your master shall answer his summons promptly on the morrow. Then slip him a shilling and a dram or two, and beg a few minutes' conversation with Mistress Hannah."

How good it felt to be of use, at last, and to earn the opportunity to see poor Phebe. I felt the crispness of the day through my jacket as I made my way, a coin held fast in my hand and a bottle tucked 'neath my arm. The lanes were thick with carters, and the air filled with the cries of peddlers hawking plums, apples, and pears, the last fruits of summer and the first of autumn, heralding a change of seasons invisible to the prisoners held fast within a crumbling stone fortress.

I found the jailer. To my considerable surprise, I recognized not only the type but the man: Enoch Goddard, late of Mr. Jameson's service.

"Weston, in'it," Goddard sneered before I had the chance to present myself. "O, I remember *you*, boy. Did you think I shouldn't? Your services to that molly Scot ended mine. Can't say as I blame Master Jameson," he said, licking his lips. "As your small hands and soft mouth possess those shipboard talents I never 'ad occasion to learn. I'm sure you serve 'im on yer knees, you little saucebox. Martha an' me, we 'ave more honest work: we do the biddin' of prisoners, not painters. Though it comes with its own comforts, if you catch me. That black wench yonder. She's a luscious piece."

With a sickening leer, he nodded toward the far corner of the dungeon, a small cell carved out of a corner of the room that held male prisoners of all sorts, awaiting their trials. As my eyes adjusted to the darkness, I could make out Hannah against the slimy wall, with but a chink in the stonework high above her for light. A small form huddled in the filthy straw in front of her. It rent me to know that it was Phebe.

"Mr. Goddard," I said, extending my hand with the coin plainly visible. "My master sends his greetings, and asks that you convey to the Sheriff his eager compliance with the summons."

"I take yer message, boy, and yer coin, and glad you didn't try to give me no paper money!" he said, greedily palming the silver piece as there issued from his noisome mouth a loathsome laugh. "And is there aught else you wish offer in trade?"

"Yes, sir, in fact, there is," I said, catching the rhythm of the bargain. "Mr. Jameson feared you might thirst as it came on toward noon."

I passed him the bottle. He seized it with untamed want.

"My thanks to yer *Master*," Goddard said. "And what will he be asking to answer his thoughtfulness?"

"Nothing at all, sir. But I wonder if I hear your missus calling to you. Might you be needed for a few moments abovestairs? For I would fancy a short interview with your choicest prisoner. My master knows her, you see. And he would have me urge her to confess, to spare herself the stake, and poor Boston the needless spectacle of a trial."

"Spare your master 'is turn before the bar, is more like," Goddard rejoined. "Three minutes and not a second more," he continued, taking a sharp pull upon the bottle. "Were I a youngster like yourself, that'd give me plenty of time to finish my business. Aye, twice over," he snickered. And with that he unlocked the iron-barred door and withdrew, clomping halfway up the stairs, out of sight if barely past earshot.

I returned home in the bright light of midday to find my gentlemen in a perfect frenzy of eagerness to find out what I had learned.

"How fare Hannah and Cicero, lad? And did you see wee Phebe?" Jameson asked, placing a hand on my shoulder.

"I bought but three minutes, sirs," I said, "barely enough time to discover anything."

"Leave the discovery to me, Weston," Doctor Alexander urged. "Concern yourself instead with the raw materials. Tell us what you saw and heard, and omit nothing. But this is no still life: do not compose the details. Leave their arrangement to me."

I followed his instructions as best as I could, sparing little of what I had witnessed.

Hannah was hungry and sick, chained against the wall, made to endure God knows what at Goddard's hands, and in plain sight of her poor darling babe, whose state appeared even worse than her mother's.

"But I brought Phebe a little poppet, sir," I explained.

"A poppet? A doll?" asked the doctor, incredulous. "Surely you jest. I did not imagine a child, in peril of her life, might have the inclination to play upon the prison floor. And when, precisely, did you make this masterpiece?"

"Twas nothing, sir. No more than the work of a moment. Just some scraps of canvas bound at the top and tied round to make arms and legs. I drew a sweet little face upon her, though. I thought it might cheer the little girl," I said, holding back tears, and I could see Jameson struggling, mightily, against the great sadness that was seizing him.

"God but you sentimental sots deserve each other," the doctor near shouted. "Are we done with the damned doll?"

Jameson cleared his throat and handed me a handkerchief as I resumed my narrative.

"Hannah, you must try, try to save yourself," I pleaded. "Did you kill him? You must tell me. For if we know the truth, at least we are in some ways armed. Perhaps we can rescue your babe, even if you and Cicero have placed yourselves beyond hope."

She stared at me, her eyes liquid with tears that she withheld from her cheeks through sheer force of will. A full minute of my fast-fleeting time lapsed before she answered me.

"I did not want him dead," she said, her voice but a hoarse whisper. "There is no hope, not for me or Cicero. I only pray that he freed Phebe in his Will, for didn't he promise me, often enough?"

"Hannah," I said with a heavy sadness that could not begin to match her own, "Samuel Bradstreet left no Will."

She was sobbing openly when Goddard came for me. As he led me through the cesspit that held rabble of every sort, I passed Cicero, chained to the floor. When he spied me, he lifted his neck, and called to me, weakly.

"Weston, tell everyone you know: Hannah had nothing to do with this business." He could utter nothing else before another prisoner clouted him hard in the mouth.

Thus ended my report. Again, I apologized for its deficiencies.

"You see, sirs, truly I have learned nothing. I believe Hannah innocent, but only her words endorse that belief, and I cannot think how her words might save her."

"Young Weston," Doctor Alexander declared, "you have done well."

"Aye, lad, and you were braver than I could have been," Jameson said, squeezing my hand.

"Goes without saying, Jamie," Alexander laughed. "With your great heart, you would still be there, playing with the little girl and her ridiculous poppet upon the jailhouse floor."

And then the doctor turned to me once more.

"You are sure Hannah said nothing more to you?" he asked, narrowing his eyes.

"Quite sure, doctor."

Nothing, that is, but to call me by the name of,

Fanny Easton.

From the *Boston Gazette*, Thursday, September 13, 1764.

BOSTON.

*L*ast week, *Doctor Thomas Newcombe was* elected to the General Assembly in place of Samuel Bradstreet, Esquire, deceased, in time for the meeting of the Assembly on Saturday next, to be held in its emergency quarters at Cambridge, during which the consequences pursuant to the Currency Act, are to be discussed.

At the same meeting, the Assembly will be asked to give its Assent to enacting the following Bill, *viz.*:

An Act for Further Retrenchment of the Extraordinary Expenses at Funerals.

To the Editor:

The Currency Act to take effect next month, and the language of this Act being difficult to task, your readers may welcome this useful translation:

The paper in your wallet is hereby rendered as cheap as the one you are now reading.

—Bradstreet's Ghost.

CHAPTER 13

Of Emptied Chests

I must have them! I must have them today!" Alexander hollered, after breakfast, as he stormed about the kitchen. Unless I've missed it, he has not slept in the last three days. In the tenement, he has set up a laboratory of vessels and crucibles, powders and potions, where he secrets himself day and night, though only Kingston, the chemist's young man—Jamaican-born, but tawny, and, I hazard, more Indian than African—is admitted often. He brings whatever the doctor requires: alum, camphor, brimstone, lancets, blood stones, Turk's Island salt; good God, a complete set of pocket instruments, in pouches tipped with silver—all bought on my credit. And now my friend asks for more.

"Jamie, get me those portraits, or I swear, I shall get them myself, and damn the consequences."

"Nimrod's ghost in the Tower of Babel! Speak sense! You know you cannot step out from under this roof. With that brand on your hand, you'd be taken for a runaway before you reached the corner. Would you be whipped at the post in front of the Town House? Would you be sent back to Virginia, in chains, to be tortured by a fiend who takes pleasure in your pain?"

"I would, of course, burn the Town House first. But you forget: not every Bostonian of my complexion is a slave. Some were born into freedom; others were manumitted by their masters. And though our numbers are small, we move about this town with a certain degree of liberty. No, do not gainsay me, Jamie. I will leave this house when I wish. I am a free man. That cursed planter bought a property that could not be sold. For, as far as the law is concerned, if anyone owns me"—here a sneer—"it is you."

"But Sander, you can't have forgotten . . ."

"I promise you, I have forgotten nothing. Nothing. I do not forget warnings, for instance."

"Dear God, Sander . . . I'm sorry. I cocked up everything. What more can I say?"

"Could you really have been so gullible, Jamie, as to think Berkeley would let you free me? Could you not see that his trap was set as much for you as for me?"

"I had forgotten about the Earl's harpy daughter. Twas near a decade ago . . . I made her no promises, nor—"

"Do not dare to speak to me of your ill-advised affairs."

"Fine. God knows I had rather not utter another word about any of this. Is it not punishment enough to live with what I cost you? But Sander, you cannot leave this house with that brand on your hand."

Alexander laughed, bitterly.

"I am to hide beneath your roof the rest of my life? Do you forget that I hold three doctorates? Believe me, I can forge papers convincing enough to take me anywhere in this world—save, perhaps, Virginia, and no loss, that, I assure you. But I am perfectly safe on the streets of Boston, especially with a knife in my pocket."

"Mother of Christ. You really are mad. Free people are kidnapped into slavery every day. Papers can be stolen and destroyed."

"It is you, Jamie, not I, who should have known that paper makes flimsy armor, a lesson you learned a little too late."

His words struck me like so many blows. Yet I would not cede the argument.

"Aye, but I won't lose you again. Mark me, Sander: I will tie you to this chair before I let you out that door."

"Alrighty den, massa. I been tied befo'!" he shrieked, his voice a cruel mimicry. "Which means you shall secure the paintings yourself."

"Confound it! Am I to waltz into Mrs. Bradstreet's house, its windows still shrouded with mourning, and simply demand them? What am I to say? 'Madam, my sympathy for your loss, jolly bad luck, but now I have come to repossess my property'?"

"I do not care one whit what you say," he answered, slamming his fist on the table. "I do not care if you break a window and steal the portraits. The trial draws nigh. Bradstreet is buried. Hannah tells Weston that Bradstreet left a Will, which is now mysteriously missing. What good does any of this do us?"

"But why the portraits?"

"Must I disclose to you my every intention? I need Bradstreet! I would dig up his corpse and give it a proper dissection, but you tell me I am not to desecrate the dead, not even to discover a murderer. I have examined his mind through his text; Bradstreet's *Modest Inquiry* reveals an author more bold than mad. I must know him better. If I cannot see the man, I will see his likeness. I know your art, Jamie. I can read it. I will see in your portraits of Bradstreet—and his wife—more than you imagine."

O, sweet God of humility, grant me patience.

"Aye, your logic is flawless, Professor," I hollered. "But you are the fool if you fancy I will run this fool's errand."

"Excuse me, Mr. Jameson, Doctor Alexander, sirs," said Weston, entering the kitchen, like a constable come to break up a cockfight. "But, if I may, I heard this morning, when I was out marketing, that Mr. Bradstreet's estate is being probated today. I wonder, sirs, whether this might not, in truth, be a propitious hour to visit. Mayhap Mrs. Bradstreet would rather have the pictures removed before the probaters arrive. The portraits, since they are not yet paid for, count as a debt, do they not? And however wealthy she may be, the lady would fain have as few debts as possible."

"Truly lad," I smiled, "you have missed your calling. You might have been a merchant."

"What, sir?" he asked, his lovely face falling. "Have I no prospects as a painter?"

"Weston, you have no worries—not on that account. I will be sure you realize your promise as an artist."

And lo, I meant it, Reader. For my resolve to send my apprentice to train in London grows by the day.

"We've no time to talk of art; we need to see it," Alexander said, as if reading my mind. "Your Weston has scripted for you the speech you need make to the widow. Will you go now, you confounded sap-skull?"

"I will go, Sander, but only if you promise to sleep in my absence," I said, rising. "Do you not have some powders in that laboratory of yours to make a man sleep? Take Gulliver into the room with you. That dog's snoring will lull anyone into slumber."

Weston followed me into the hall, and made to grab his coat. I stayed his hand.

"Nay, lad," I insisted. "Go upstairs and varnish Mason's kit-cat. I would have you deliver it, for we could use the fee. And be sure Doctor Alexander keeps his half of the bargain."

"But sir, won't you need help to carry the portraits?"

"I remember your help with the Lamberts' canvas well enough, Weston. I can manage without you."

At least I mean to try, dear Reader. Though I do not relish becoming Alexander's errand-boy, at least the doctor accomplishes this much: his presence in the house, and the tasks he sets us to, mean that I have not spent more than five minutes alone with Weston in a fortnight. I miss the lad, and sorely. But 'tis for the best.

I grabbed my great coat from a peg by the door, for the weather has turned brisk. I found in its pockets the gray kid gloves that had been handed out at Bradstreet's funeral. I tried them on, but they fit me ill. I set them down on the stand in the hall and made my way to Hanover Street.

I arrived at the Bradstreets' house just after noon. As the front door lay wide open, I let myself into the hall and wandered, undeterred, through the first floor. The place looked a tempest. Bureaus, chests, desks, boxes, cupboards, drawers, all had been opened and emptied. China, silver, and plate were littered across tables, and even over blankets spread upon the floor. The inventorying of such a bottomless clutter is no mean feat. At least six clerks undertook the labor, moving from room to room, some flying this way and some that, carrying, counting, stacking, tallying, tallying, tallying. Thus do bankers take the measure of a man.

In the library, I found William, the Wily Bastard himself, hunched over his father's desk. He was so wholly occupied—busily rummaging through a stack of papers—that he did not notice me till I spoke.

"Bradstreet. My condolences for your loss, sir."

He tapped his cane on the floor, at a swift tattoo.

"Jameson? My father died weeks ago."

"I meant your more recent loss. At the polls, sir."

Twas vicious, dear Reader, and pray, forgive me, but the man is a blackguard.

He stopped tapping. I had hit my mark.

"What are you doing here, dauber?"

"I have come to see your mother, sir. Do you know where I might find her?"

I need not have inquired. For Sarah Bradstreet had silently entered the room, behind me, her face as pale as the chinaware the probaters were counting in the next room.

"Billy," she said. "Patty is in my chamber, and begs your assistance with that locked chest."

"Of course, Mother." With a baleful glance in my direction, Wilted Breeches made his exit.

The black widow turned to me.

"Mr. Jameson, it seems you have a remarkable talent for turning up in my darkest hours. Why must you disturb me in my season of mourning, and on this day of calamity?"

"Begging your pardon, Mrs. Bradstreet," I said with a bow. "And please accept my sympathy. Your husband was a great man, my lady, and will be sorely missed even by those, like myself, who knew him but lately. Still, I wondered whether you would prefer me to remove your portraits to my house, where I might finish them."

"Good gracious, could this not wait?"

"Aye, my lady, it could, and I'll leave without them this instant if you like, for I should never wish to discompose you, madam." I paused, and looked her squarely in the eye. "Then again, madam, the removal of the pictures would have one happy effect: your husband had not yet paid me, and if they remain in this house, they will be counted as a debt against his estate."

This gave her to reconsider.

A pair of probaters entered the room, and unburdened the desk of its contents. Methodically, they began to pore over every letter book and ledger, each piece of parchment, not overlooking a single scrap of paper. Surely if there were a Will hidden in this house, these silverfish would discover it.

"Come to think of it, Jameson," said Mrs. Bradstreet, surveying the derangement of the room, "nothing would please me more than to have your portrait of my husband finished, that I might better remember him. Indeed, when you are done, I should like a miniature, to wear in a locket round my neck," she said, fingering the jet beads. "My dear Samuel." She sighed, dabbing her dry eyes with a black silk handkerchief. "You will find both pictures in the parlor, where you last left them. Take them and then, please, go."

"Thank you, my lady," I said, nodding as I stepped past her, and out the door, leaving behind a room papered in paper.

Two silver teapots, a quid and six, each," I heard one of the commissioners say to another, as I walked through the dining room. "Six silver teaspoons, one shilling per . . ."

In the parlor I met another member of the family, or one who would belong to it very soon, though he had about him the droopy air of a dejected swain.

"Reverend Easton." I bowed to the boyish, emerald-eyed vicar, who had been staring at my canvases. He blinked at me. "I have you at a disadvantage, sir," I continued. "I don't believe we have been properly introduced. Stewart Jameson, sir. I've come to collect my paintings."

"Ah. I've just been admiring them. Magnificent." He nodded at the painting of Mrs. Bradstreet. "So like my dear sister Fanny's art. The same delicate mottling of colors."

"I have not met many female painters, sir, and you make me regret that I have not yet had the pleasure of your sister's acquaintance."

"She was fond of mocking the poet Samuel Johnson on that subject."

"I confess I do not follow you, sir. On what subject?"

"On the subject of female painters. Johnson fancies portrait-painting a most improper employment for a woman. 'Public practice of any art, and staring in men's faces, is very indelicate in a female,' he once wrote."

"Did he?" I asked, cocking an eyebrow. "I suppose I see what he was getting at, for a sitter is naked before a portraitist. Would you, sir, wish to expose yourself to a female artist's discerning gaze?"

The vicar blushed deep crimson. But Reader, as I conjured the image, I came to the conclusion that Johnson—a bit of a driveler, even at his best—was most certainly in error. For the thought of sitting naked before a woman painter stirred me to distraction. Suffice to say: a finer way to pass an afternoon I can scarce fathom. Except, if *she* also were naked, her gifts of Nature unadorned, and I had an easel of my own with which to capture her while she captured me . . .

I cleared my throat, and inquired, for I was intensely curious, "And how did your sister answer Johnson's riposte?"

"Fanny liked to say that since surveying women's landscapes was every man's chief employment, the least she could do, on occasion, was to survey the acreage of her surveyors."

Delightful girl. "If she has half as much Art as she has wit, Reverend, your sister must have a very great talent indeed."

"O, she had that, and more," said Easton. "And beauty, and sweetness, and a touch much like yours, if this canvas is any sample. I should like to see more of your work."

"Of course, sir. I'd be honored to have you call at my rooms. Perhaps you might like to sit for me? And might I invite you to bring your accomplished sister? I shudder to anticipate her opinion of my Art, but I like to have my critics near to hand!"

"No, no," he said, his voice turning tremulous. "My Fanny is gone . . . abroad, with our aunt. To tour the Continent."

"Ah. My loss, then."

"O, lost!" He sighed, seized with utmost despondency. "Lost! Lost! As lost as Samuel Bradstreet's fortune. I must relinquish every thought of happiness!"

The greater the vicar's distraction, the greater my perplexity. Best to persuade him to enlarge upon this topic. "But Reverend, that Bradstreet died without a Will doesn't mean he died a pauper, surely."

"No, of course not," he answered. "But his fortune had lately become a fiction. He forfeited everything—he who was once richer even than my father! His ships mortgaged, his shares auctioned, his lands sold, his accounts pillaged. Where his money went, we are, all of us, left to wonder."

"I can only think you must be mistaken, sir. For how can such a man fall so far, so fast?"

"He did not fall. Nor was he pushed. He jumped. If he were mad, there was a method to his madness: he chipped away at his fortune, bit by bit, week by week, like a miner hacking ore with a pick. He was the architect of his own impoverishment and, by it, of the ruin of his heirs. O! My father will never let me marry her now. My Patience, Mrs. Bradstreet, even William: they are, all of them, penniless."

Letter XII.

September the 14th, 1764

Dearest Lizzie,

Nigh unto midnight and my mind races round in circles. Quill in hand, I seek quiet, and find none, for letters are a maiden's form, and remember, my sweet, innocent, friend, that I am no maiden. I scarcely know how to reveal what I must write; I fear you will find it scandalous—more scandalous, even, than you have found my last letters. *Have you reduced yourself so far, that you are now become the servant of a black man?* you write. I assure you, Lizzie, the work I do for the estimable Doctor Alexander is noble and virtuous. I pray you can put aside your doubts, for I cling to our friendship, as tightly as I clutch at the fraying threads of my disguise.

All this day I busied myself about the painting room. By myself. For Doctor Alexander never fails to dispatch my master and me in opposite directions. Truly, I have not spent more than five minutes alone with Jameson in a fortnight. I miss his instruction, and yes, I confess I miss *him*. Am I to be my own master, then? I have dreamt of such an independency. Why does its prospect disappoint me?

Mr. Jameson yet gives me orders. Late this morning, ere he set off on his errand to Hanover Street, he bade me clear the painting room of portraits.

"Make way, make way! Fold the easels, bare the walls, clean the palettes, soap the brushes, neaten the cabinet of colors. You've heard Doctor Alexander, lad: we're to train our attention upon the Bradstreets. Though if you would, take a moment to check on the doctor, and make sure he keeps his promise to get some sleep."

I set to tackling the clutter. The unfinished likenesses I stacked in a corner and covered with cloth, that their ghostly half-countenances would not distract us from our forensic labors. Mason's kit-cat I varnished and set behind the house to dry in the sun, lest the coroner find the surface still tacky when I delivered it later.

As I passed through the hallway, I noticed Doctor Alexander, sitting in the parlor, writing.

"Doctor, you promised Mr. Jameson you would rest."

"Ah, yes. But neither of us is always honest with your master, eh, Weston?"

"I do not take your meaning, sir. I'm sure I've done what I pledged: I cleaned the painting room, as best I could, and I covered all the portraits there."

"But you miss the work of Art that distracts him most," he said, holding my gaze for a moment before indicating *The Serving Boy* with his chin. "He loves you, the poor bastard."

His words set my heart to racing.

"But the portrait is not the sitter, sir," I protested.

"Do not lecture me about appearances, Weston. I will not have some serving boy impede my investigation. Take it away."

With that curt command, he retired to his rooms.

I surveyed *The Serving Boy* a long time ere I took it from the wall. Had the doctor spoken truly? That Jameson is capable of love I do not doubt. He is a man of great heart. But what stirs his passion: a mask or a man? A man or a woman? I stared at the canvas as if it might contain the answers. Yet I scarcely knew whether I looked upon my likeness, or my rival.

About this much, the doctor was surely correct: 'twas a powerful distraction. I had never seen my master pass the picture without pausing, and more than once I swear I've heard him speak to it, in a whisper, and wished he would give those soft words to me. I took the painting from the wall, and wrapped it with care. I brought the package to the cellar, relieved to closet my boyish self.

❧

Near dusk I was interrupted at my work in the painting room by Jameson bellowing from the front door.

"Weston, come at once!" he cried.

He staggered under the burden of two three-quarter-length canvases, unfinished and unframed. There were poor Mr. Bradstreet and his elegant consort, tied front to front and nestled in sheeting—an embrace, I dare say, they had seldom shared in life.

He set the canvases down in the entryway and cut loose their bonds. Then together we carried each one up to the painting room, where Doctor Alexander soon joined us.

"Face the lady toward the wall for now, that we may look, undistracted, upon the dead man," the doctor directed. And so we set Samuel Bradstreet's likeness upon the easel, eager to learn whatever clues lay concealed therein. The doctor paced and muttered, taking in this angle and that, focusing especially on the flesh tones we had worked so hard to achieve, but which looked flat and lacking in the waning light.

"Sander, cease your cogitating for a minute," said Jameson. "I've made a discovery, a first in your bloody investigation. The man was bankrupt. Perhaps he left no Will because he had nothing to give away."

"He had nothing?" I asked, incredulous. "You must be mistaken, sir. He was the richest man in this colony—save, perhaps for one—"

"Enough!" the doctor shouted. "Neither of you says a word I did not know already. Get out, both of you. I need to spend some time alone with the man."

We headed down the stairs.

"Will you take some tea, sir?" I asked, as we stopped in the darkening hall.

"Aye, but I can make my own, Weston. This might be a good time for you to deliver Mason's kit-cat. And take the dog, will you? The streets in the coroner's neighborhood are dead at night."

I smiled, but he appeared not to have caught his own pun.

"Sir," I ventured, looking up at him by the somber light, "has someone stolen your laughter?"

He appeared altogether taken aback.

"My laughter? No," he answered, quietly, as he took my cap from its peg and set it on my head. "But have you ever noticed, Weston, that just when you find one thing, you lose another?" He put his hands on my shoulders, and nudged me toward the door. "Now: go."

"Please, sir. Might I not tarry here with you?" I asked, turning to face him again. "I should like to hear of your visit to the Bradstreets."

"No, lad. I'd sooner have Mason's fee than his face. You know what I always say: When 'tis done, 'tis done, and I am done with it."

This was indeed his usual banter. Yet his tone was wistful. Does he mean he is done with me, then?

"Please, lad. Go." He sighed, seeming to answer my unasked question.

Lizzie, what could I do? I took the kit-cat, and the dog, and I made my way to the coroner's house, south of Milk Street, hard by the rope-walks near the Battery. Soldiers and strumpets strolled the alleys, with nary a second look for me. I knocked on Mason's door, and the coroner took the painting with a grunt, passing it from hand to hand as if it were a slab of mutton, and he checking that the butcher hadn't cozened him.

"Aye, a beauty," he muttered, hastily scribbling a note of hand for me to convey to my master in payment. "Now leave me in peace, boy. I've got but a few days to ready myself for the trial. There's hanging work to be done, eh? And I don't mean picture hanging!" And he laughed, as if the weight of two lives troubled him no more than a feather.

Upon what fine balance perches this sorry world? So many Masons and Goddards, so few decent souls. Oh, the perfidy of men—has it not colored all of my days? And yet, as I walked back toward the center of town, 'twas neither rancor nor vengeance that filled my heart, but longing.

Night had dropped its velvet curtain by the time I reached home. I found my master sitting in the parlor alone, his long legs stretched before him on a stool. He stared into the fire, his great blue eyes hooded with weariness.

"Have you been waiting up for me, sir?" I asked, hopeful of the answer.

He unfolded himself from his chair and strode toward me.

"Aye, I've been waiting, Weston," he said, his voice taut. "What have you done with it?"

"Done with what, sir?"

"Damn your eyes, lad, you know my meaning, and too well. Where have you stashed *The Serving Boy*? If you would deny me the comfort I take from that picture, I swear I shall wring your scrawny neck."

The doctor is right, then. Half right. My master loves a portrait of a sitter who doesn't exist.

"But sir. Did you not say, when 'tis done, 'tis done, and you are done with it?"

"You know very well how I feel about that likeness, lad. Tis *not* done."

"I'm sorry, sir. I put it away," I said, holding his gaze. "Your *Boy* is wrapped neat and safe in the cellar, leaning against the far wall, just behind the stairs."

He heaved a sigh of relief and pushed the hair back from his brow. Tis a habit of his, Lizzie, an unthinking gesture he makes twenty times a day, and yet each time it moves me, as if he were sweeping away a mask. His face softened.

"And my boy?" he asked, more tenderly. "You've been a while, lad. I had begun to worry."

"I was walking with the dog, sir. And wondering."

"Tell me, lad: What fired a painter's imagination out there, 'neath the canopy of stars, on a September evening?"

"It will sound grand, sir. But I was thinking about the abundance of melancholy in this world, and the scarcity of its remedy."

"And did you find a bit of that curing nostrum, Weston?"

"Some, sir."

"Better than naught, lad. Better than naught." He placed his hand ever so lightly upon my shoulder as he urged me out of the room, just ahead of him. "And now, off to bed with you, my little philosopher."

"Good night, sir." And with that I mounted the stairs to my garret, to spill my thoughts upon these pages.

Not a quarter of an hour had passed when I heard his familiar cry, this time oddly muffled.

"Weston, *please* come at once!"

Hastily I buttoned my waistcoat over my shift and bounded down the two flights that separated the landing outside my garret from the front hallway. Following the sound of his voice, I opened the door to the cellar. There he was, halfway up the narrow stairs, inching side-long, trapped by perils of his own devising.

Picture his predicament: in one hand he held *The Serving Boy*, tucked flat against his chest; the other gripped his candle. The flame he kept at arm's length, lest it catch the sheeting wrapping the portrait. Be-hind him was the cellar's rough brick wall, and he pressed himself against it, mindful of the vacant space before him, a drop of six feet or more, with no railing to slow his fall. Warmed by the candle's flicker-ing light, his face looked more beautiful than anything Caravaggio ever painted. Every part of me ached to touch him, to take his face in my hands and feel his lips on mine.

"Weston, 'tis a mission of mercy: you have rescued me, lad," he said, more than a little sheepishly. "The door blew shut, and as you see my *Boy* has me pinned here, quite helpless."

"And your boy, sir?"

I descended toward him, closing the door behind me.

"Surely 'tis the flame that gives you trouble, sir," I said. "You can-not mean to risk the canvas for the candle."

Yet I would risk more.

I took the taper from him, holding his eyes for just a moment be-fore I blew it out. There we stood, face-to-face in darkness, upon a single step not two feet across: a small, secret space, full of unspoken permission.

"O, Weston," he sighed. "Do not think it would be so easy to snuff this fire. Would that it were, lad. Would that it were."

"And if I would stoke the embers, sir? What then?"

"'Tis dangerous hot already," he murmured. "Leave it be. Only a cruel master steals a boy's innocence. I would not be that manner of man."

I advanced toward him, closing inch by inch the tiny distance be-tween us, until I swear I could hear his heart beat.

"And if I were not an innocent . . . boy, sir?"

I placed a hand upon his thigh, just below the edge of the painting, and let my fingers trail down, tracing the muscle of his leg. Barely did I breathe.

"I have dreamed you," I whispered, "and wished I would not wake."

As he searched for words, I kissed him, reaching up to take his sweet face in my hands, my body flush against his, with nothing more than the canvas between us. Only by bracing myself against it did I keep to my feet, for the wave of pleasure all but knocked me over.

And then he kissed me back, fiercely, and with a manly ardor compared to which the most carnal of my dreams was chaste. The stubble of his beard at day's end. The softness of his lips. The taste of ale on his tongue. The hunger of it all, mine as well as his: Lizzie, I was undone.

A minute passed. I prayed this kiss would never end.

Two. I thought it might not.

Three. He broke from me.

"Weston, dear God," he gasped. "You know not where your child's play will lead. My lust would spoil us both."

"*Your* lust?" I could not bear it. My passion turned to fury. "Bugger your *Serving Boy!*" I shouted. "And answer me this: What manner of man puts aside earthly pleasure in three dimensions for a fantasy wrought in two?"

With that I took the taper and ran off to my garret, leaving them there—the man and his phantom—to ponder their fate in the dark, far from this flesh-and-blood,

Fanny Easton.

September 15, 1764

Mister Joshua Reynolds,
No. 47, Leicester Fields,
West End,
London.

Dear Sir,

I doubt not that this missive finds dame Fortune smiling upon your brush, as alluringly as e're she was wont to do.

I send you greetings from Boston. As you make your way down through the City to survey the Thames—that pulsing artery of Culture and Commerce, whose circulation nourishes the globe—you can only imagine this little port, perched between the far side of the vast and furious Atlantic and the sluggish river Charles—to be remote and uncivilized, a wasteland. Having for several months employed my brush here, I can tell you truly: you are right, sir. But though this New-England has lately been the seat of war and desolation, I cherish hope—was I not ever a hopeful man, Reynolds?—that it shall one day become a school of the fine arts, a worthy rival to Bath, if never to London. Have not the labors of Venus, that goddess of beauty, traveled westward so fast and so surely from her birthplace in Rome, that they must one day reach even this Country?

Thus I commend to you a young man who may prove to be Venus's guide on her journey to these shores. Since my arrival in this port I have been blessed with the assistance of an apprentice of promising genius, one Francis Weston. His training has been haphazard at best. And though I have strived with him—truly have I strived—he remains quite deficient in the basic matters of Art. He barely condescends to still life, nor will he study the gradations of light and shadow. His figure drawing lurches between penetrating insight and an almost maidenly reticence. Yet his line work is consistently superb, his sense of color profound, his eye for beauty—and more so, for ugliness—unerring. Perhaps (I can hear you thinking), it is not the apprentice but rather the master who is lacking. About this, too, you are surely right.

And so, it is my intention to deliver him into your expert care. You can expect Weston to wash up on the Strand before year-end, bearing a portfolio of drawings rendered in his hand. In my next letter, I shall enclose a bill of exchange, sufficient to cover the cost of his keep for a year. (You may think the sum excessive, but I assure you: the lad eats a good deal more than his slight form suggests.) Among this Weston's many assets, he also possesses a fine hand, and a decent competence at ciphering. He might keep your accounts, and draft the correspondence for your Society of Artists, releasing you from those burdens.

I pray you will take him under your capacious wing, sir, for I cannot tell you how it pleases me to imagine him grinding your colors, and stretching taut your canvases, as he now grinds and stretches mine. I would have you show him those fair examples of Art that have so long stood the admiration of all the world, and whose close contemplation must, I am sure, animate his pencil, and enable him to acquire that bold, free, and graceful style which comes to him much slower upon these shores, where the mere dictates of Nature, coupled with my own meager example, are fated to remain his best—aye, his only—instructors.

If I am right in my estimation of his talents, I expect to hear one day that Francis Weston follows his countryman, Mister Benjamin West, toward the summit of that Mighty Mountain where the Everlasting Laurels grow to adorn the brows of Illustrious Artists. And if I am wrong, sir? Then you shall have gained a most artistic amanuensis, and at scanty cost.

I await your verdict on the matter. In the meantime, permit me, sir, to conclude by wishing you and, equally, your charming sister, every health and happiness.

> Your most obedient humble servant,
> Stewart Jameson.

BOSTON.

*T*he Trial of Cicero and Hannah, Negroes, *accused* of Poisoning the Honorable Samuel Bradstreet, Esquire, begins tomorrow before the Superior Judicial Court, the Honorable Benjamin Finley, Esquire, presiding. For the duration of the trial, His Majesty's officers billeted in the Town House will evacuate that building's second floor, to allow the Court to use its usual room, and to accommodate the anticipated crowd of spectators.

CAMBRIDGE.

*A*t a meeting of the Assembly held at the College on Saturday last, an Act for Further Retrenchment of the Extraordinary Expenses at Funerals was passed, by a large margin. The said Act dictates that "widows and widowers should stop wearing the costly mourning clothes fashionable at the time and desist from handing out fancy gloves and scarves to other mourners at funerals."

To the Editor:

Our legislators, meeting on the other side of the river, seem to have forgotten that this colony suffers burdensome taxes at the hands of Parliament, under the guns of the King's Army. Have the Assemblymen not passed by the Common lately? Have they not seen British soldiers amassing there, ready to fire their arms on those who would refuse to pay? With all due respect to our glovers, kerchief-vendors, and cloth-sellers, I wonder whether the Assembly will ever again take up more momentous matters, such as the tyranny of a standing army in the midst of a free people.

—BRADSTREET'S GHOST.

CHAPTER 14

Of Trials and Tribulation

Dust off your periwig, dear Reader, for, hear ye, hear ye, court is in session!

We have but steps to go. The Town House is just blocks away, smack in the middle of King Street. Tis a three-story brick building, with a gilded sundial on its east gable and covered, on all sides, with white-trimmed windows of twelve-over-twelve, as if it were decorated with so many bigtoothed grins amidst red-brick lips. A house of false smiles: fitting home for politicians. Bostonians call it the Town House, for the town owns it, though the Governor makes use of it when he sees fit. The ground floor houses the Merchants Exchange. The second story holds the Council Chamber where the Governor meets with his placemen; the Assembly Room, where the legislature would hold its debates, had not this room been seized by His Majesty's Army; and the courtroom, my dreaded destination. Upon its roof perch bronze statues of the English lion and the Scottish unicorn—the latter chained, of course, for 'tis a dangerous beast. A handsome two-tiered cupola stretches toward the sky. The audacity of this cupola: it rivals the height of the town's church spires. Thus does the Crown vie with the Lord.

At eight o'clock, a bell ringer stationed by the whipping post rang the first warning call of the court, an hour before Justice Finley would raise his gavel. Half of Boston had come out of doors—the lazy leaning out of windows—to watch the spectacle: Cicero and Hannah carted from prison to court in a creaky wagon steered by the jail-keeper and deputy-sheriff, my one-time manservant, Enoch Goddard, who spat at the ground and whipped his gray horse at every clop.

"Burn 'em!" cried the crowd. "Murderers!"

"Confess ye devils! Confess!" shouted a minister in a frock.

"Spare yerself trial, ye black bastards!" answered one of his flock.

Barefoot boys raced alongside the cart, rattling sticks on its wooden sides, as if driving cattle to slaughter. Hannah, kneeling, chained, bumped along the road, her dress but tatters, her face hidden in her hands. Cicero, in filthy breeches, stained shirt, and torn coat, with a beard grown full on his chin, stood over her, moving to spare her the worst of the blows from all manner of matter hurled at them: old meat, apple cores, sharp rocks, small cobbles. Phebe was lucky to have remained behind, even in the loathsome jail. As I stood in the crowd, sheltering Weston at my side, I fancied that Hannah lifted her head, and turned, briefly, toward us but, if so, she just as quickly turned away. Neath my arm, the lad shivered. I offered my small comfort—and I will stop at comfort, Reader; I will stop at comfort—a squeeze of his hand, at once glad of the excuse to hold him near and sorry for its occasion. We walked, pressed on by the throng, toward the Town House, amid the clamor, without a word to each other. These last four days, we have exchanged little more than nods, and all manner of awkwardness.

Reader, I will not tell you of the taste of Weston's lips—like heather and honey—though the thought of it consumes me. Nay, it—he—is best put aside. For now, and maybe forever, and, O, very, very far.

The crowd swelled and lurched, the door to the Town House as narrow as the neck to a bottle. We could scarcely get within yards of the building, no closer than the whipping post, and yet I must answer my summons.

"Weston, make your way back to Queen Street," I urged. "There is aught to do here, and you have seen enough."

"But Doctor Alexander bade me to get a space in the gallery, and report back to him at noontime," he pleaded.

"I can report as well as you," I answered. "And you can be of more use painting. Now go, I insist."

He could argue the point no longer, and edged away, swallowed by the crowd. It will be my fate, Reader, to watch him leave me more than once.

"Jameson!" called a sharp voice. I turned around, and looked down, to discover Hiram Usher in his homespun habit. "What the devil are you doing here?"

"I am called to testify, sir."

"Indeed, I have some questions for you myself, painter. When can I count on you for dinner? I'm sure Margaret would like to entertain you as well. Yes. Yes. Remember, Jameson, we have favors to offer each other."

I was spared the discourtesy of refusing this Trojan horse, for suddenly, the Sheriff opened the door, and shouted over the mob.

"We have room for no more of you gawkers! And too bad, for 'twill be a sight like no other. But I come for those summoned to court today. Oyez! Oyez! Answer to your names, and save your fines!"

He proceeded to call the names of we summoned few, the King's witnesses:

"Thomas Newcombe!"

"Here," grumbled the patriot-doctor, who shuffled through the throng.

"Thaddeus Mason!"

"Move aside!" called out the coroner, his tricornered hat today festooned with a red feather, as he pushed his way from the south side of the building.

"Stewart Jameson!"

"Aye," I sighed, just as the bell tolled the half-hour warning.

G ood to see you, Doctor," I offered, as I took a seat next Newcombe. "Yes, if under doleful circumstances," he rejoined.

"Cannot such an event interest you, sir, as a historian?" I was fishing, I confess. I could not guess what he made of this travesty.

"Hardly. Though I still can't puzzle Bradstreet's death. Maybe we'll find some answers here."

"I confess I had rather have boycotted the entire affair," I ventured.

"O, Jameson. With Samuel dead, I'm too weary to talk of boycotts."

Dear Reader, a courthouse is a temple of justice, is it not? At its pulpit, in front of a full-length portrait of the King, sat three high priests of the law: in the middle of the bench, the bent and decrepit Chief Justice, Benjamin Finley; on either side of him, the two associate judges, Edward Easton and Chambers Cotton. Easton makes an imposing figure. A man of less than fifty, with an erect and regal bearing and a well-brushed wig of rain-cloud gray with nary a hair out of place. His countenance—striking green eyes, set deep 'neath a strong, jutting brow—bespoke a similar composure. Truly, he might have been carved out of marble. Cotton, by contrast, had an air of panic about him. He is a scrawny sort, and young. When the Sheriff called the room to rise, as the judges entered, Cotton nearly tripped over his robes while climbing the three steps to the bench.

"The Governor's dullard son-in-law. Just appointed. Doesn't know a writ from his rod," Newcombe muttered to me. "And Finley is older than my grandmother, and even deafer," he added.

"What about Easton?" I asked.

"Ah, the Mast of Fidelity. He'll take Finley's place, and soon enough. Benjamin can't last out the year—his heart's weak, and even copious dosings with pigeon's blood have done him no good. Easton's half as old, and twice as clever, if a rank Tory: he serves the King and damns the people. Mark me: the Crown will make him Governor yet."

"So you are of Bradstreet's party, then?"

"I wouldn't call the Hens a party, Jameson. And I abhor the rancor of faction. No, I might not go as far as Samuel. Nor as fast. Let us see whether the duties are as onerous as some fear, and the soldiers' presence as worrisome."

In front of us sat the Attorney General, Amos Quincy, whose face I had already had the occasion to study, at length, from behind my easel. I was satisfied to find that he looked like his likeness, his weak chin and wrinkled cheeks all but swallowed by his barrister's gown, giving him rather the appearance of a shrunken apple-headed doll. At his elbow, his deputy—none other than the wily bastard William Bradstreet—perched attentively. From the amount of time young Bradstreet spent whispering in Quincy's ear, you would be forgiven if you were to conclude that 'twas the deputy who directed the prosecution—I had not failed to notice that 'twas he who had signed my summons—though he attended, ostensibly, as an observer, for he was an interested party in the case.

Across the aisle sat Cicero and Hannah, facing the bench. I could see them only in three-quarters profile, and perhaps I wished, rather than observed, that Cicero looked resolved and Hannah determined. Nowhere did I see either Patience Bradstreet or her mother—they may have been there, in the back, or in the galleries above, outside my view. Certainly there were no other women in court, which is no fit place for the fairer sex.

At the west end of the room stood a jury box, built of mahogany and containing twelve jurors: yeomen, merchants, tradesmen. I did not envy them their task.

Finley banged his gavel, calling the case of *His Majesty the King versus Cicero and Hannah, Negroes*. Quincy rose. Now was the courtroom no more a temple, but a stage. Quincy carried himself better than ever did David Garrick at Drury Lane.

"What're you doing, Jameson?" asked Mason, who sat to my left. With a fat finger, he pointed to my sketchbook, where I was recording the scene, as much to distract myself as to share it with Alexander later.

"Trifling, sir, merely trifling," I answered, as I traced with my pencil the crabbed hand of Quincy, resting on the stack of books and papers on the table before him, for I do love to draw hands.

"May it please Your Honors, and you, Gentlemen of the Jury," Quincy began as he moved in front of the table, to address the bench and box, turning, not infrequently, to embrace the spectators, too. His timbre is a deep and smooth baritone, as much the instrument of his craft as any actor's voice.

"Gentlemen, you will hear today of a mystery of iniquity. You will hear, from the mouths of our witnesses, that these two Negroes, Hannah and Cicero, did poison their master, Samuel Bradstreet, did murder him in his bed, did watch that kind and august man die in agony. And for what? For a chimera, gentlemen. *For their dream of liberty!*"

"Was he that gave him that dream," Mason muttered. "Mad old cluck, reaped what he sowed."

"And Gentlemen, think not that their scheme, however preposterous, however presumptuous, was *merely murder*—as if such a crime were not black enough. Twas the wickedness known in the common law as *petit treason*. When a subject kills the King, that is treason. And when a wife murders her husband, when a child takes the life of its father, when a servant kills his master: these, Gentlemen, are *petit treason*. A gruesome villainy, the worst kind of usurpation."

Here Quincy paused, with a grim countenance, and then pointed to me and my companions, as he continued to address the judges and jurors.

"Gentlemen, it will appear to you, by the coroner's inquest and by the testimony of eye-witnesses (as we shall, in the course of our evidence for the King, show you), that, in prosecution of such an abominable crime, these two beasts, Cicero and Hannah, did procure poison and did administer it to Samuel Bradstreet, villainously, voluntarily, feloniously, and maliciously."

He approached the jury box, and clasped its wooden rail as he leaned toward the jurors.

"Gentlemen, in you, the people of this commonwealth place their hopes and expectations of future security and repose, that they may sit safely in their houses, and sleep quietly in their beds. I do not doubt, Gentlemen, that when you have heard the evidence against these fiends you will, for your own sakes, your oaths' sakes, and for the sake of your country, find these two Negroes guilty."

O, judicious Reader. What can I add to the tragedy before me? Would you know what happened next? We three King's witnesses took the stand in turn, and did the attorney's bidding, for what else could we do? He was poisoned, said Newcombe. Twas arsenic, added Mason. Aye, I answered, Hannah went to the apothecary that morning.

We played our roles, and exited the stage.

And what then?

I could recount for you all the details of that day: every lisp of bench and bar; the elevated diction of so many wigged heads; every twitch of twenty countenances; the tip-tip of birds pecking at the glass, the hisses and huzzahs from the gallery, the torpor of the room, which grew more stifling by the hour. But as this eighteenth of September in the fifth year of this King's reign was among the sorriest of my days, I would prefer not to catalogue its wretchedness.

Lo, such was the taste in town, such was the desire of these Bostonians to savor the bringing to justice of these murderers, that Edes set a narrative of the trial in type. I have that pamphlet near to hand. Thus you may be assured, meticulous Reader, of the accuracy of the following transcription. But I urge you to consult the original if you would fill your belly. I will feed you only the lean meat of the matter. And if you share my queasiness, take small bites. Of the case's merit, may you be the judge.

The Attorney General, having concluded the examination of his first three witnesses, turned to what these colonials call "Negro Evidence": the testimony of slaves. Tis only by a special dispensation that such men are allowed to speak in court—only in cases like this, where they might indict one another.

Quincy began by calling Kingston, for his master is Charles Cabot, the apothecary. This Kingston is a lively fellow, and quick, and I hazard he is no dissembler.

"How long have you served Mr. Cabot?" asked Quincy.

"Five years now," answered Kingston. "He schooling me as his apprentice."

"What duties do you perform in his shop?"

"I wrapping the powders, and pouring the mixtures into their bottles, and such like. And I keeping his books, for he teaching me to write and cipher."

Quincy grew impatient.

"Enough of your schooling, boy. When have you attended the prisoners?"

"Regular, at least fortnightly, maybe more. Their masters sending them to us—Cicero, mostly, Hannah betimes as well—to fetch remedies and powders and such like, for all the household, sure, but Mr. Bradstreet, he sick, always."

At this, William Bradstreet nudged Quincy, who reminded his witness, "Boy, restrict your answers to the matter at hand. This proceeding is not about medicines, but murder."

Kingston nodded.

Quincy continued: "Did you supply them with poisons too, then?"

"The rich folks in they fine houses, the poor folks in they huts: they all the same to rats, eh? Even this court having rats in the summer. Whole town flooding with them. But the Bradstreets, they fighting the rats all year round. Week in, week out, Cicero coming for ratsbane. Coming regular, like a clock. His mistress not abiding 'em in her cellars. She having the servants whipped when she smells a rat. Whipped hard. I selling the poultices for they scars too."

This prompted an interjection from the bench. Finley spoke, in a high thin voice: "You are not asked about Mrs. Bradstreet, boy, but about the prisoners."

Again did Kingston nod.

"Thank you, Your Honor." Quincy returned to his witness.

"Doctor Newcombe has testified that he dispatched Cicero to you the very morning of Mr. Bradstreet's murder. What gave you him on that day?"

"Doctor knowing as well as me," answered Kingston, with a look at the doctor, "was Hannah that morning. Sir. I giving her two papers, folded and tied round with string. And a receipt for her master's accounts."

"What contained the packages?"

"White powders, both of them. One holding calomel. Doctor ordering it up for Mr. Bradstreet, and plenty to purge him proper. The other ratsbane, two orders' worth, for Cicero missing the order of the seven night before."

"Enough poison to kill a man?"

Kingston paused. "Well, the calomel making him *feel* like he dying, sure. That much ratsbane? Could take down three men as big, and half the rats in this town, too. But I label them packages neat. And Hannah reading better than me."

Quincy smiled, and asked a final question: "Did ever Bradstreet's servants mention a plot to kill their masters?"

"No, sir. Only they rats, sir."

Kingston stepped down, and Quincy called Hannah, whose face I could see at last. On her countenance, every muscle taut, I spied defiance, more than was wise.

"How long have you served your present masters?" the Attorney General began.

"My master is the same as yours, sir," answered Hannah, looking her questioner in the eye, "the great God above, and none before Him."

"I'll not be lectured on religion, wench. Who owns you?"

"Samuel Bradstreet took me in, near five years ago. He brought me out from bondage under Justice Edward Easton."

Easton was not happy to have his name brought into evidence. He spoke brusquely.

"The prisoner shall confine her remarks to answering the questions put to her about the murder of Samuel Bradstreet. And the Attorney General would do well to direct his own interrogation, for his willful deputy seems to behave rather impulsively."

Quincy resumed. "Who nursed Samuel Bradstreet on the last day of his life?"

"Why, his wife, of course!" answered Hannah—again, mark me, Reader, she spoke with too little deference, and even with disdain. Could the girl not see the danger in which she placed herself? But she blundered on.

"Mrs. Bradstreet attended him every minute, from first he sickened, not the morning he died but late the night before, after the ball. Seemed like exhaustion more than illness then, except he could not catch his breath, nor bear his weight. Cicero could barely move the great man to undress him. All the rest of that night Miss Patience stayed by her father's bedside, along with Doctor Newcombe, who was sent for right away. After dawn, Mrs. Bradstreet never left that chamber but that her daughter stayed, holding her father's hand."

"In the morning, what orders did the doctor give you?"

"He bid me go to Cabot's. I ran as fast as I could, on a fool's errand."

Quincy stepped out of character. "Enough of your insolence!" he boomed. Just as quickly as he lost his composure, he regained it, and continued: "What purchases did you bring home from Cabot's?"

"Two packages, just as Kingston described them. Mr. Cabot made up the doctor's order, and another one stood waiting for us, both wrapped in fat envelopes tied up with twine, each labeled in block capitals so clear they might have been printed. Twas not Kingston who gave me the packages, though. Mr. Cabot called him to the storeroom shortly after I arrived. Kingston left Councilor Usher's man, Pompey, at the counter, where he had come to fetch a tincture of opium to stanch his mistress's pain. Pompey grabbed the bottle that held the syrup, and passed me the papers marked 'Bradstreet.' I flew back to Hanover Street."

"And when you returned, what did you with your fatal cargo of physic and poison?"

"Both packages I brought to the pantry, taking care to set the ratsbane in its usual place, upon the highest shelf, behind a blue jug, well out of the reach of my little girl."

Again Quincy erupted. "What did you with the calomel?"

"I mixed it well, as the doctor instructed, adding three parts water and shaking the contents in a glass vial until the liquid came clear. Then I emptied the vial into a cup of tea and carried it up to Mr. Bradstreet's chamber on a tray. A wicker tray. Round in shape. You would like to know its color, perhaps?"

Cotton now took a turn at exercising his slender authority. "Know your place, wench!" he stammered from the bench. "Or I'll have you whipped for contempt!"

"I'm to fear a whipping when you mean to roast me?" Hannah laughed, bitterly, but I nearly cried.

Quincy grinned at the men in the jury box. "We don't need to know the shape of the tray, do we Gentlemen? I have nothing further, Your Honors."

While the bailiff took Hannah to her seat, the crowd hissed, loud and long, and Finley had to call the court to order again. Next Cicero limped to the witness stand, looking wearier and less resolute than he had atop the cart.

"How long have you served your present master?" Quincy asked.

"Long as I can remember, sir," said Cicero. "My mother was owned by the Mortons, Mrs. Bradstreet's people. I went with her to Mr. Bradstreet's household when she was married."

"And how old are you now?"

"About five-and-thirty."

"Have you ever purchased arsenic from Kingston?"

"Yes, sir. Many times, like Kingston said."

"And what did you do with this arsenic?"

"Put it in the cellar, to kill the rats."

"Did you ever give any arsenic to Hannah, for her use?"

"No, sir. I kept charge of the cellar."

Quincy paused, and spoke slyly. "But you have just heard Hannah say she had the poison on the day Mr. Bradstreet died."

Cicero, who had been thus far quick in his replies, now paused. "Yes, sir," he answered more deliberately, "she put it on the pantry shelf for me. Only I ever use it; I put it out for the rats, belowstairs. Rats go low, you see. Can't have it near any food; we just keep it in the pantry, on the high shelf, out of reach of our little girl."

"But Hannah *could* have used the arsenic?" Quincy pressed.

"I don't see how, sir. She was nervous of it, and never touched it unless she had to, like when she brought it back from Cabot's."

"But both you and Hannah could have used the arsenic at any time?" Quincy's voice grew more insistent. "'Twas always there, on that shelf."

"Unless we run out, which was pretty often. But Hannah would never—"

"Now, boy, we don't need your opinions, just the facts. Was your master good to you?"

"Yes, sir. Very good, sir."

"How?"

"Well, he spoke to me kindly. And he meant to free Hannah and our child."

Murmurs rose from the audience.

Quincy, who had been pacing across the floor, in the direction of the jury, now turned on his heel and faced Cicero again. I saw William Bradstreet half rise from his seat in front of me, and sit down again, on a motion from Quincy.

"You believed your master had freed you in his Will?"

"Them. Not me, sir, though I reckon he would have, if it lay within his power. Every man in this town knows Samuel Bradstreet was no friend of slavery."

"Pray, I would understand you better," said Quincy, with a sudden feigned gentleness. "You believed that if Samuel Bradstreet died, you would be free?"

Cicero hesitated but finally answered: "No, sir. He wished it, I know he did. But I belonged to Sarah Morton before she wed, and she owns me still. It's her would have to free me."

Quincy looked to his junior barrister, William Bradstreet, who nodded. Then the Attorney General approached the justices at their bench. The four men conferred so quietly I could not hear them, but then Finley addressed young Bradstreet.

"Mr. Bradstreet, did your father leave a Will?"

"No, Your Honor, by no means," answered William. "In his last years, Your Honor, his mind had become disordered—the ill effects of old age—and he failed to tend to this essential business."

"Thank you, Mr. Bradstreet," said Finley. "Mr. Attorney General, pray, continue."

Quincy recalled Hannah to the stand—to still more hissing.

"Did you believe that your master had freed you in his Will?"

"He had freed me, yes, and my little girl, too—"

Quincy turned to the jury. "Was this not a perfect motive for murder?" he thundered. "Thank you, Hannah, for making an eloquent argument against masters who speak to slaves of liberty."

Hannah rose from her seat.

"Samuel Bradstreet is the finest white man that ever I met," she declared. "He promised us liberty. I saw it written in his Will, as plain as the labels on Cabot's nostrums."

Quincy laughed. "Samuel Bradstreet left no Will. These are more of your lies."

"He did write one, and I did read it. And I can tell you this: if I *had* killed him, that Will is the *first* thing you would have found."

"Ah, but we have not found it, have we?" smiled Quincy. "If what you say is true—if indeed you know the meaning of truth—tell this court, where is that Will now?"

"Would you have me foreswear myself? I know not where the Will is, only that he wrote one. Perhaps his wife or his son can answer better than I."

At this William Bradstreet whispered urgently to Quincy, who abruptly changed tack.

"Did you think you would get away with it, Hannah?"

"I am not the one getting away with something."

"Answer what you are asked!" Quincy thundered.

"Then ask me a better question: *Who killed Samuel Bradstreet?*"

Justice Easton interrupted, but this time addressed himself only to the Attorney General. "If you cannot control your witness, Mr. Attorney General, I would have you ask her to step down."

Quincy obliged, sending Hannah back to the dock. He next called Pompey, surely the most extravagantly attired of all these Negro witnesses, in his brown velvet coat, tan waistcoat, black breeches, polished shoes, and fine black wig.

"Are you a slave or a free man?" the Attorney General inquired.

"A bondsman. Mr. Hiram Usher is my master." Pompey spoke evenly, and with a well-studied courtesy. Quincy treated him gently, with none of the belligerence that had earlier characterized his performance.

"How long have you been his servant?"

"I served Mrs. Usher when she was Lucy Morton, and I went with her to Mr. Usher's house when she married."

"Do you know the prisoners?"

"I've known Cicero all my life. We grew up together. I know less of Hannah."

"Have you ever heard Cicero talk about his master?"

"Yes, sir."

"And what have you heard him say?"

"That Mr. Bradstreet was a good man, sir, and that he had freed the woman and the girl in his Will."

"Did he tell you anything else?"

"Yes sir, it just so happens he did. He told me that Mrs. Bradstreet wanted to sell him. Ever since his foot froze last winter, he can't walk right, and she wanted a whole man in his stead."

Murmurs came from the gallery.

"Silence in the court!" demanded Finley.

Quincy resumed: "When did you hear Cicero say this?"

"At the Bradstreets' ball, sir."

The Attorney General leaned in toward his witness. "Now, I know, that was near a month ago. Try to remember, Pompey: What exactly did he say?"

The courtroom quieted with anticipation. Pompey seemed to relish his place upon the stage, drawing out his words with great care.

"Cicero said, before he was sold away from Hannah and the child, he would get them their freedom."

"Black son of a bitch!" muttered Mason, to my right.

"Burn the bastard!" came the shouts from the gallery.

"O, but this is a dark day for liberty," sighed Newcombe.

Finley gaveled for silence.

When it came, Quincy spread his arms, palms upward, and spoke to the jury: "My examinations are ended, Gentlemen."

N eed I add, weary Reader, that Cicero and Hannah did not mount a defense? Twould have been but a farce to share the bill with the tragedy. Edes's printed transcript notes only this:

> *The Prisoners being asked, what they had to give in their Defense; they offered nothing but peremptory Denials of what had been testified against them, and Protestations of their Innocence.*

Twas near noon when court resumed. How I longed to be home, at my easel if not at my ease. But before I could leave I must watch Quincy close the second act. In his hour-long summation, he revisited each piece of testimony, in tedious detail. At last, he concluded.

"May it please Your Honors, and you, Gentlemen of the Jury, I have distinguished the several points of evidence against the prisoners, and have repeated the substance of what each witness, white and black, has said. I have endeavored to lay no more weight upon any part of the evidence than it will bear. I shall leave it to you to determine whether the accused are guilty or not.

"Gentlemen, these prisoners have been indulged with the kindest of care by the most benevolent of masters. Yet even *he* they have conspired to murder. I cannot but observe that Samuel Bradstreet was generous to a fault; he pitied these Africans held in Boston; nay, he even urged our Assembly to end the traffic in slaves. And his generosity was repaid with treachery. The prisoners believed their master had freed them in his Will. Now, we know that Samuel Bradstreet died without a Will—his son is here, and confirms this—but maybe he meant to free them. Maybe he did. This is not our concern. Our concern is with what his slaves supposed, and what actions those suppositions prompted. To what use did they put their belief in his munificence? Did they wait, patiently, in Christian submission, for the day of their liberation? Did they bow before him in gratitude? No! They together conspired to kill him, with arsenic procured from Cabot's shop, and the wench Hannah put it in his tea. Samuel Bradstreet learned too late that trust is wasted on the sable race."

Calls of "Hear! Hear!" rose from the crowd, till Finley restored order.

"I fear, gentlemen, that we shall never be quite safe, till that wicked race are under more restraint. This, then, is a signal case, whose light might teach the rest of our slaves the penalties to be paid by those who would commit *petit treason*. Bear in mind the consequences of your verdict, and I have no doubt that you will decide to rid this country of some of the vilest creatures in it."

Quincy having worked the good men of Boston into a froth, it took Finley a full ten minutes to calm the courtroom. And then, with brief instructions from the justices that served only to echo the Attorney General's oration, the jury was charged, and withdrew to decide the prisoners' fate.

Letter XIII.

September the 18th, 1764

Dearest Elizabeth,

I have not yet received your reply to my letter of the fourteenth of this month, and I confess that I fear its delivery, for I know you will chide me for my forwardness. Now I write in haste, for in your last, you begged me for an account of the trial. I shall give you one, though I know you cannot glory in the horror of it.

"They are lost," Jameson said, closing our door upon the crowds that stretched from the Town House all the way to Queen Street. He looked entirely defeated, his face a mute witness to all he had heard, and what role the law had required him to play.

"The sentence is pronounced, then?" Doctor Alexander asked, from his seat by the table in the parlor.

"Not yet. The jury yet deliberates, but there will be more of dining than of debate. There can be no doubt about their verdict."

With that my master took a seat next his friend, opened a cloth-covered volume about the size of this letter book, and read to us from his notes upon the trial. He sketched the scene with such minute exactness, I could not think he had missed a single detail. When he read to us his recollection of the Negro evidence, Doctor Alexander appeared, for once, to lack for words.

"That is the crux of it, then," Jameson said, closing his little book. "Twould be easy enough to write the next scene."

He looked at the floor, and I thought he might weep. For he is a gentleman and a gentle man in a world where few can claim to be either. He has known sorrow, sure as I have. But he hungers for joy, and he finds it. He wrings laughter from the least likely places, much as plants in the Arctic steal enough of the summer sun to nap them in green for a few short weeks. So when I write that I have never seen his countenance cloudier than at that moment, you will know the darkness of this time.

The three of us sat quiet for some minutes. I spoke into the silence.

"Will you have some dinner, sir, before you return to wait upon the court?" I asked, color rising to my face when my master met my gaze. "A morsel or two might do you good."

"Aye, it might indeed, lad. But I cannot stomach a single bite. Nor one more word of the King's *justice*. Sander, I place myself in your service. Give me orders to help you, here, somehow. But sweet Jesus, don't send me back there."

The doctor rose and placed his hand upon his friend's shoulder.

"As it happens, friend, I do have a chore for you. *Skin*. I find myself in need of fine white skin, yards of it, spread out before me as if peeled entire from a living body."

"And this will settle my stomach exactly how, Sander?"

"I need a painter, not a butcher. While you played your part in the theater of justice, your painting room is become a theater of dissection. I am the professor, and Weston assists me with a lesson in anatomy. Today we are studying the human *dermis*. I must have Samuel Bradstreet's skin."

"I've used your secret recipes, sir, but I have not revealed them," I offered.

"Well done, lad." He managed a small smile.

The doctor pressed on.

"The likeness you began in the days before Bradstreet died told me a good deal, but not enough," the doctor explained. "So I asked Weston to cover an entire kit-cat with the image of Bradstreet's cheek. He made a good start of it. But now I need your hand, for it is your particular genius to see the true color of a man."

"And what will your task be?"

"I shall leave the anatomical work in your capable hands and return to my laboratory. Your notes from the trial contain much of poison and less of logic, and I would try to precipitate out the nonsense."

"And I, Doctor? Have you orders for me as well?" I asked.

"Alas, I do. In the name of decency, if not of science, one of us must hear the sentence read and I am afraid the short straw falls to you, Weston."

"Sander, you cannot mean to send this child into the belly of that beast. I can go back," my master sighed, and, wearily, raised himself from his chair.

"No, sir," I insisted. "The doctor needs you here, and sir: I am no child."

Before he could protest further, I had grabbed my coat, and was gone.

Twas near two o'clock when I began to force my way through a crowd that seemed to breathe as one. I advanced yard by yard. I could not imagine how I should reach the courtroom.

Then I spied Enoch Goddard, standing near the rear door of the Town House, a pipe clamped hard within his teeth.

"Deputy Goddard," I called across the mob, "my master must presume upon your generosity once again!"

"Make way, make way," Goddard boomed, the authority of even his petty officialdom opening a tiny rent in the human fabric before him, just large enough for me to slip through.

"Thank you, sir," I said, bowing, breathless, as I reached his side. "Mr. Jameson commands me to hear the verdict read, sir, and to protect his good name at all costs."

"His good name, is it? Aye, ye little by-blow, let us talk of costs. Have you a coin or two about you, lad? I fancy it ain't too early to start up a fund for little orphan Phebe."

"No, sir, I'm afraid I haven't," I replied, my heart sinking. "The hazard of pickpockets seemed too great. I brought no purse into the fray, and no drink, either, for I did not think I should chance to meet with such a savior as you, Deputy."

At that he gave a snarl that would have sent Gulliver cowering.

"Mock me as you will, you scurvy bunter. But I hold the key to that door. And ere I turn it, you'll make me a trade."

"But I have nothing to trade, sir."

"Ah, but there yer wrong. Ye carry naught but yer own warm body. That'll do."

I looked at him in horror, suddenly doubting I was man enough to execute my orders.

"Turn yer back to me, lad, and make not a sound. You begged a full three minutes with that wench from me, and I'll have but one from you: A fine bargain, i'n'it? Ah, yes, yes, lad. Yes, there 'tis, yes. Stay still now."

He breathed roughly, and fast, as he slipped one filthy paw from his trousers into the back of mine. My face toward the crowd, I blushed with nausea and shame, thanking God 'twas only his hand I felt upon my bottom.

"I knew it were a soft bun that Jameson buttered," Goddard wheezed, removing his hand from my trousers and reaching into his own while he pressed his machine against my back, a feeling no less distasteful to me for having known it before. Not ten seconds later, I felt him spasm as he palmed his bribe.

"Now, be a good boy, won't you, and thank your *master* for me." He sneered as he wiped his hand on my trousers. "Tell 'im 'is gift'll keep me warm through many a winter's night."

And with that, he shoved me through the open door into the Town House.

"Has the jury reached a verdict?" the presiding justice asked Josiah Whitmore, the foreman. The morning had exhausted old Finley, so it fell to the second justice to take up the gavel after the adjournment. Edward Easton. Yes Lizzie, my father. The sight of him filled me with horror, less for myself than for Hannah, whose fate was thus once again placed in her ravisher's hands. Yet I could not take my eyes from him, and found myself wishing I were safe behind my easel, brush in hand, capturing his likeness.

"We have, Your Honor," said Whitmore, a shoemaker pleased with his important office. "In the matter of our Lord the King versus Cicero, a Negro man, and Hannah, a Negro woman, both of Boston, we find the defendants *guilty* of *petit treason* in the wanton murder of Mr. Samuel Bradstreet, their said master, by the deadly poison called arsenic."

"So say you all?"

"Aye, milord. So say we all."

With a curt bow, Whitmore took his seat. He would sleep well tonight.

"The witnesses have testified, and this court has listened," my father intoned. "The people have had their say. It remains only for the law to sentence these felons to the reward they have called upon themselves. Hannah and Cicero, you have heard the jury's verdict. Now shall you stand to meet your fate."

Each of them shackled at the wrists and ankles, the prisoners rose on trembling legs.

"You are, both of you, worse than murderers," my father declared. "You are traitors, rebels against every principle of fidelity and godly order. Defilers of the liberties of Englishmen! You would chip away at that solid foundation upon which the King's justice is built, would gnaw upon the body politic from within, much as your cursed poisons fed upon your master's vitals until it consumed his very life."

Then my father turned, with a gesture both practiced and familiar to me. He kept his back straight, barely moving even his neck, but adjusting the angle of his chin only, and by that small incline, shifting the entire burden of his power to the spectators, as if already consigning the prisoners to utter darkness.

"Mark it, mark it well, gentlemen," he said. "You have heard today of the most terrible of crimes. Does not every one of us in this chamber feel something of Samuel Bradstreet's death agonies? Do we not each endure the blows that Cicero and Hannah have leveled against the integrity of this realm? It is for that reason that the law reserves its most awful majesty—its most righteous, cleansing fury—for the punishment of the crime of treason."

He kept his gaze trained upon the crowd as he pronounced the dreadful sentence: "Hannah and Cicero, you shall be drawn from the jail to the Neck, there to be tied to a stake and burned, on the last Thursday of this month, between the hours of noon and four in the afternoon. All the servants of this town shall be encouraged by their masters to attend the proceedings, that any who might follow your examples may witness your fate."

The courtroom erupted with a sickening chorus of gasps and cheers. My dinner rose in my throat.

My father continued, his green eyes taking in the prisoners, the spectators, the gallery. I shuddered, almost thinking I felt his gaze upon me, though I knew that, at such distance, he could not possibly pick me out from the rest of the rabble.

"Samuel Bradstreet's death bought you nothing, *nothing*," he told Hannah and Cicero, his voice rising now. "But *your* deaths will serve this town very well indeed. Your final agonies shall remind us all of the vengeance of the Lord, which none of us escapes.

"Murderers! You will find no mercy, but only fairness from this court. I urge you: repent, repent yourselves this moment! Confess your crimes before God and these witnesses, lest the fire that will soon destroy you both serve as but a foretaste of your eternal punishment."

Hannah swooned. Cicero gazed down at her and his eyes flooded. And then he trained his stare upon my father, and began to speak, quietly at first, and then with more mettle.

"I confess it, then: I did, I killed him. Sirs. Fed him poison. Stuffed him with ratsbane. I dumped it in his tea by the spoonful."

Onlookers gasped.

"Yes, but 'twas me, and me alone. Hannah had no part of it. She never touched the powder, not even for the rats. No, she never knew my plan, not even by a whisper."

"No!" Hannah shouted. "No! Cicero, no! It will not help."

"Oyez! Oyez!" My father gaveled the crowd. "Murderer! Traitor! Perjurer! You are already proven a liar. Why should this court believe you now? What motive had you to slay a master whom you yourself called *good* not three hours ago?"

"Samuel Bradstreet *was* a good man," Cicero said. "No, 'twas not my master I hated. Twas his wife. *She-devil!* Pompey spoke true: she meant to sell me away from my wife and child, and he could not have stopped her from parting with her own property, though I believe he tried. At least, if Mr. Bradstreet were dead, my family might go free. I know you mean to send me after him. And I go willingly. But not Hannah. Hear me! She had no hand in it!"

The judges could see as clearly as I could: there had been no rehearsal. They seemed to take Hannah's look of horror as a sign, much as people in days of old believed a murderer's touch would bring the blood to the skin of his victim.

"The court will take a brief recess," Chambers Cotton said, at last given a speaking part in this charade. "You may remain in your seats, gentlemen, but we will have silence. And the bailiff will please return the prisoners to the dock."

The pair of hanging judges inclined their heads toward each other till their wigs took on the aspect of a single puffed cloud hovering over the dark and lowering skies of their robes. The minutes ticked on while they continued their conference. The spectators sat in silence, breathless for the last act to begin.

Finally, my father banged the gavel.

"This court has scrutinized Cicero's confession, which we find to be earnest and heartfelt, made in the full sight of God and this colony. Because he would die penitent, his sentence shall be commuted to hanging at the place and time aforesaid."

A rumble of disapproval rose from the floor.

"Order!" Cotton shouted.

My father continued. "You have heard Cicero's claim that he acted alone. This point is murkier. In the opinion of this bench there is no longer proof sufficient to convict Hannah of a capital crime. Yet her conduct before this court casts doubt, if not upon her innocence, then certainly upon her fitness to serve the people of this town. Her sentence we hereby commute to transportation to the West Indies, and the child with her, after both of them have watched Cicero die."

I gasped. Slavery in the cane fields spelled certain death for a little girl. Hannah might last a year or two, but Phebe would not be so lucky. Had my father not an ounce of feeling for this tiny, blameless child—his own daughter? Yet the crowd considered even this slight solicitude too generous. The balcony erupted in a frenzy of stomping and shouting.

"What, have ye grown soft?"

"Burn 'em both!"

"Hang 'er too, ye bleedin' cowards!"

And then, from the rear corner of the first floor, came a voice I knew well. My brother rose from his seat and walked slowly down the center aisle toward the bench. How my heart filled with my love for him as he spoke with a courage and conviction that my knowledge of the boy did not predict for the man.

"God have mercy on us all!" he cried. "What justice is this for an innocent child? Father, I beseech you: Have you so far forgot your testament? The Lord sayeth, fathers shall not be put to death for the children, and neither shall the children be put to death for the fathers, but every man judged for his own sin. What sin has that small girl committed, beyond the inconvenient fact of her birth? And certainly that is no crime."

"Reverend Easton," my father chided, "would you dare presume upon our relation to speak before this court? You have no business before us. Still, if my associate will allow me, I shall offer a moment's fatherly instruction."

Cotton, plainly stunned by this turn in the proceedings, nodded uncertainly.

"Vicar: you use the Bible as your cudgel against this Bar. What, would you have us lop off the King's head as well? Behold the solemn majesty of Charles II, there in his portrait upon the wall behind me, and remember the fate of his father. These are not Puritan times, my son, and I thank God for it. We are no zealots, no regicides, but men of moderation, and of liberal learning, as I raised you to be. Even you, Vicar, must acknowledge that the Bible does not always give us clear rule."

"'Tis true, generally speaking, but in this case—"

"Yea, and on this delicate matter, Daniel, I might sooner take my counsel from an Englishman, from our Shakespeare. Do you remember the lines from *The Merchant of Venice*—Launcelot's speech, near the end of the third act? 'Look you,' he says, 'the sins of the father are to be laid upon the children . . . There is but one hope in it that can do you any good; and that is but a kind of bastard hope.' Look *you*, my son, before you go raising bastard hopes where they ill belong."

"Father, you cannot mean to prefer the theater to the church!" Daniel cried, newly valiant in the face of this formidable adversary. "I admire your learning. But I cannot think this child bears her father's sins, any more than I do mine. She was not born free. But are we not all, all alike, born innocent? *Neither shall the children die for the fathers*: 'tis written not only in Deuteronomy, but in Chronicles too. And surely 'tis the very marrow of the Gospels."

"Daniel. Son," my father said, seeming now to soften, "your pastoral concern for this child's soul is commendable, and I would expect no less from you. If my brethren will consent to it, I would heed your call to temper justice with mercy."

Chambers Cotton nodded vacantly.

"So be it." Justice Easton lowered his gavel for the last time. "The child will be spared the fate of her mother. Let the girl be sold at the auction of Samuel Bradstreet's property, along with his other goods and chattel. And that our good example be remembered, let us dedicate the proceeds of her sale to the Manufactory House."

Yes, the Manufactory House that was late the home of,

Fanny Easton.

FROM THE *BOSTON GAZETTE*, THURSDAY, SEPTEMBER 20, 1764.

BOSTON.

*Y*esterday morning died Mrs. Lucy Usher, beloved and esteemed wife of the Honorable Hiram Usher, Member of the Governor's Council, after an extended illness. She is to be buried today at King's Chapel. In accordance with the late regulations governing funerals, she is to be buried without pomp. Mourners will receive homespun handkerchiefs.

CHAPTER 15

In Which Our Characters Find
Themselves Face-to-Face

You will do yourself a kindness, dear Reader, and me a favor, to join me in my painting room: I have much to say, indeed, I fear I may prattle on a while, and would welcome your company, for my loneliness chills me, assaulting me in great gusts, like a gale tossing a ship this way and that, with Gulliver once again my only shipmate. Was ever a man blown so far off course?

Day in and out, and mornings most of all, I am all plague and perplexity, wondering how I have come to this, I, who have searched for a bride, on two continents, for lo these last five years, though halfheartedly, I admit. I have found Alexander—or he me—and must soon lose Weston—or loose him. And now does Louisa Beaujardin, *née* Lambert, step into the scene.

By chance, I met her only yesterday, when I happened upon Lambert walking with her along King Street. She is everything her brother promised: nature has formed her into a gentle and lovely woman, amiable and worthy. But would she be my *better* part? Tis Weston whose company I find most agreeable; his conversation that best engages me; his wit that ever teases mine. Would this Louisa share my passions? Would she *see* my Art? Yet I have eyes only for *The Serving Boy*. And when that canvas is not before me, 'tis Weston's soft face—with eyes so dark and lips so sweet—that my mind's eye is always painting. "Mine eye my heart thy picture's sight would bar, My heart mine eye the freedom of that right." Bloody Shakespeare. Aye, and my mind paints not only his face. I have said before, Reader, that I enjoy working with him at my side. But I confess I should as well stand behind him.

Enough of his lips, much less his arse! you rage. And while it pains me, I must agree with you, and heartily.

I will do my duty by him. Certain: I will.

But.

Might I not steal a kiss, just one small caress?

How else am I to get by?

You will censure my self-pity, Sir, and you are right to do so. Surely there are men more ill-fated in love. Were I Cicero, to be sold away from Hannah, I would have killed Bradstreet, too. Alexander disagrees, but I say Cicero did the deed, as sure as night follows day.

You ask, Madam, as you must: How can I even think of Weston with such grave matters at hand?

I answer only with the mystery of human nature: 'tis some men's fate, and decidedly mine, to crave love and affection most ardently in times of death and despair.

I was still abed, engaged in such like reflections, when Alexander broke into my bed-chamber.

"Jamie, wake up, you lazy sot!" he said to me, tugging my covers off. "Enough of your drowsy dreaming. Get dressed! You must *paint*, Jamie, you must paint better, and faster, than ever you have done!"

Reader, there is nothing for it. I cast off my tented shift and with it, my morning thoughts of Weston, to do the doctor's bidding. If the courtroom offers no prospect of justice in this topsy-turvy town, where men who clamor for liberty yet relish slavery, we must discover our own. Come, then, to the painting room.

Letter XIV.

September the 21st, 1764

Dearest Elizabeth,

I gather from your last letter, that you might agree with the words Doctor Alexander spoke to me this morning, at dawn: "Weston! Rouse yourself and not your master for once!"

Just so abruptly did the doctor shake me from my bed this morning, making no apologies for the intrusion or the hour.

"There is no time for breakfast," he declaimed, some minutes later, when Jameson and I had assembled in the painting room. "I have waited near two hours while the pair of you languished in the arms of Morpheus. Cicero is lost, or will soon be. But Hannah and Phebe may yet be saved, and I mean you to fight for their fates. *Paint* is not the most dangerous ammunition in our arsenal, nor your stiff brush the finest piece to fire it, Jamie. But brushwork, by God, is what you have to contribute, and I mean to use every stroke."

"Sir, forgive my confusion," I stammered, addressing the doctor. "I know you would have us finish the Bradstreet commissions. But I cannot think quite how, much less why."

"That lately you cannot *think*, I have noticed, young Weston, and much else besides, I assure you," Doctor Alexander replied, with a sharpness I had not heard in his voice since first we met. "Like your master, yea, like many youth of your sex—and the opposite—you allow your heart to outrun your head. Fear not, ye painter-poets, for I am heartless enough for all three of us."

"Sander, you have denied us breakfast. Can you not spare one soft word?"

"No, Jamie. The time for softness has passed. I must warn you: things will get harder from here. I fear you will find me fierce, and worse, and I wish I could afford to be otherwise. But what I have for you are instructions."

He stood before the fire and rubbed his hands.

"I need two things from these canvases. First, I must see into the hearts of these *gentlefolks*, Mr. and Mrs. Bradstreet. Make human nature thy study, friends. Expose for me their *characters*. Make them *breathe*, Jamie, as ever they did in life. Make them *yearn*, Weston, as ardently as you do. You have shown me Samuel Bradstreet's skin—half convincingly. That is, you have convinced me of the powers of your mind's eye. Yet you have undermined, even without knowing it, the testimony you heard. If I am to believe your colors, the man on that canvas was dying ere he was murdered."

"I'd credit Weston's brush over anything I heard in that courtroom."

"So be it," the doctor continued. "Samuel Bradstreet took his time dying. But not of natural causes. For if his skin bears not the color of health, neither has it the cast of gout, or drink, or snuff, or whores, or any of the other ills of rich men. It is the color of poison, I venture. But not of *arsenic*. One job of your brush, then, is to show me what other compounds I might consider, and which rule out. I have begun to wonder, in particular, about the man's *hair*. That he would be represented without his wig is a godsend to us, for it discloses something of his character, and of his health. Jamie, I would have you pass the morning staring at Bradstreet's head. Bring me a lock of his hair."

With a cry of "Great Scot!" Jameson dashed from the room and down the stairs to the hall. In another instant, he returned, carrying a pair of gray gloves.

"I just remembered, Sander. You're in luck. Incredible luck."

"How so?"

"These gloves, mourning gloves from the funeral, they come with a ring made from Bradstreet's hair. See?" And he pulled from one of the gloves, a band, no thicker than ten strands of hair, fastened with a tiny bow of red thread.

"Excellent, excellent," said the doctor, pocketing the ring and putting on the gloves. He seemed to take comfort in wearing them.

"Zounds, Sander. They fit your hands like proverbial gloves." Indeed, my master took to calling them "the Proverbial Gloves."

"Yes, yes. Very droll. But truly, Jamie, there is much to be learned from a few strands of hair. Meanwhile, the portraits."

"Sir," I interjected. "You said two things. What is the other aspect you mean to discern from these canvases?"

"Ah, Weston, your memory is excellent, and you count better than your master. The second thing I need from these canvases concerns not what I would see in them, but what I would see in others who observe them. First they must be evidence. And then they shall be bait."

✳   ✳   ✳

We set up our easels, back-to-back, between the fire and the windows, for while we needed the light, the painting room was cold, and, as we had no sitters to stare at, we would stare at our canvases.

"Good morning, Mr. Bradstreet, sirrah!" I said to my subject, with a foppish bow and a dainty flourish such as a courtier might give a king.

"And good morning, milady," said Weston to his canvas, with a mocking curtsy.

We peeked around our easels, to exchange a smile.

I had the easier job, for 'twas more particular. Sander had instructed me to enlarge the parchment Bradstreet held in his hand, and to give it an official seal at the bottom. He means it to be Bradstreet's missing Will, though what words the doctor would have me paint upon it, none of us can know. ("We must find that Will!" he muttered to himself, as he stormed back to his rooms.) For the present, this folio sheet is but a blank page, clasped in Bradstreet's left hand, which rests on a desk of the finest mahogany, waxed till it shines like glass. This, and indeed the whole of the man's surround speaks of luxury: he stands beside an exquisitely crafted armchair made of cherry, inlaid with tiger maple, its seat cushion covered in a lavish red damask. With his right hand, Bradstreet draws back a red velvet curtain, as if revealing himself to the world. In the background, a framed window opens to a prospect of the harbor, where a three-masted ship is anchored. Weston has done his line work well: even so far in the distance, the name on the prow, *Liberty*, is easily read.

Alexander is right: Bradstreet's corpulence cannot hide his sickliness. His glistening eyes are a little *too* wet—not my mistake, mark you, for I captured him as he was, misty-eyed—and his skin has a grayish tinge—this I can see even without the magnification of Weston's canvas of flesh. Yet his face is full enough, his jowls earned by a life of prosperity only lately tempered by austerity. All this I have already exposed. But as I recall the man, I can see I need to reveal more. I raise his left eyebrow, just above the round silver spectacles. Aye, he had a quizzical aspect. And let me add a hint of a smile, thin-lipped, and not a little sour. A wry smile, a dare: I am more than I appear. Guess my secrets.

For three-quarters of an hour, Weston and I painted in silence. At last, I grew restless, and eager for diversion.

"I daresay you have drawn the short straw again, my lad," I said to my apprentice lightly. "For we had twice as much time to work on Bradstreet before he died. His portrait was already nearly finished while the lady . . . well, lad, let us simply say: she was quite undone. When you tire of her, I would gladly trade with you. God knows, I've all but forgotten how to bring color to a woman's face, and I'd rather enjoy caressing her breasts with my brush."

"Beg pardon, sir," the lad rejoined, with a maddening flutter of his heavy-fringed eyes. "I know you are a man of the world, who has seen and done far more than I. Yet I did not imagine you a connoisseur of décolletage. I should like to watch you give the lady a flourish, sir."

"You mock me, puppy." I winked. "But you don't know me as well as you think."

"You must admit, sir. Tis not for lack of trying."

* * *

To peer into the character of Sarah Bradstreet is to see—what? The more I labored to bring her face to life 'neath my brush, the more a blankness returned my gaze. Cicero's words ring in my ears. "She-devil," he called her. Yet I fail to see even the passion of great evil animating her countenance. I painted no turmoil behind her eyes, only a casual gray cruelty.

Having met with indifferent success in her face, I next devoted my attention to her dress. I covered her red gown with a mixture of lamp black and Sander's blue, for she must foreswear her scarlet finery and don her widow's weeds. Yet even upon her mourning gown, bows and flounces anoint the neck and sleeves. I preserved as well the tight-fitted bodice that would force a woman's form, long since grown matronly, into the shape of a girl who had yet to know love.

My master and I worked on, in companionable silence, as the room warmed with the sun.

"Shall I dampen the fire, or open the windows?" I asked.

"Perhaps you might remove your jacket, lad?"

I did as he asked, throwing the coat over the chair behind me, and standing before Mrs. Bradstreet in my vest and shirtsleeves.

"I confess, the mistress is a puzzlement to me, sir," I said. "I see her form clear enough. But Doctor Alexander would penetrate her character, and she eludes me. Perhaps I am a mere drapery painter after all."

"That I will not hear, lad. Not a word of it. Tease me as you like—play your game of fox and hound—but I cannot permit you to gainsay your talent. I am still alleged the master, am I not?"

And with that, he walked round his canvas for a look at mine.

"Aye, I see," he said, stroking his chin. "Come here, Weston, and look through my eyes. Maybe I have something to teach you yet."

He motioned me nearer. I stood just in front of him and stared at the lady.

"Not her face, lad. Look lower." He nudged my head down with a press of his chin. "The problem is not in her eyes, but in her *other* orbs."

He passed his right arm around me to point at the canvas.

"Are those exquisite eyes of yours blind?" he asked, his lips near my ear, his voice full of longing. "Or have you yet seen nothing of women? Those are the firm, ripe plums of one-and-twenty. We need the wasting prunes of five-and-fifty."

He was right. Bursting high and proud from Sarah Bradstreet's mourning silks, I had painted my own breasts.

✳　✳　✳

I stood behind Weston, hands on his slim shoulders, while we together studied the preternaturally pert Mrs. Bradstreet. He was so close, inches away. I watched his shoulders rise and fall with his breath. I surveyed his back, slender and straight—aye, so straight that he could barely keep his trousers about his waist. At the nether edge of his vest, his shirt bunched so, revealing a half inch of bare skin, so smooth, so pale . . . I would have him closer. I would touch that skin.

Halt, Jameson! You command. What happened to your pledge, uttered not so many pages ago? Leave the boy be!

I cannot, I will not. I made no vow of chastity, Sir. I promised merely that I would strive to offer my caresses only where true affection takes them. And does it not lead me here, to this little patch of sunlight in a world of darkness?

I put my hands on his narrow hips—dear God, my hands reached two-thirds of the way around him. I let my thumb stray across that patch of skin, tugging his shirt out of his trousers as I moved my fingers across his back.

Virtuous Reader, judge me as you will, but if you would censor me, now is the hour for you to leave my painting room. Go, but hurry, Sir. I cannot wait. And shut the door behind you.

I pressed myself against him, closed my eyes, bent my head, and kissed the downy nape of his neck. His buckled hair, grown soft since he first came to my door—as shorn as a sheep in spring—is not yet long enough to tie. Its loose curls brushed against my face.

I kissed his neck, my lips against the soft down.

Again and again I kissed him, for he seemed to melt into my embrace. And no, dear Reader, not as a child nests against a parent, but knowingly, full conscious of the pleasures his body might give, and take; full sensible—how could he not be?—of the force of my ardor.

I heard him sigh. Nay, surely 'twas a moan. I made to move my hands down his front, yet he stayed me, covering them with his own, and holding them firmly at his hips.

I leaned into the boy's slender form, bracing myself against him as a wave of feeling overtook me. I was swept overboard, and into the undertow.

If you are still here, dear Reader, pray do not mistake my metaphor. This is no shipboard grappling, Sir, but a passion perhaps more familiar to you, Madam, the reader of romances. Tis not just that I would have the boy—though Sweet Jesus, I think I shall die unless I do—I am besotted with him. Surely this is the *falling* of love.

"Weston, dearest Weston," I murmured into his ear, my voice unsteady. "Are you so blind you cannot see that *you* are the master? The greater artist, for certain, and, more, the master of my heart?"

I began to turn him to me, a turn from which there could be no turning back. For I would cover his face with my kisses, and fill his seashell ears with protestations of my love.

But my fall was broken, as Gulliver hurled himself at the door, and then through it, with a deafening crash.

✳   ✳   ✳

What did I feel as I was falling—no, plummeting—into the boundless depths of Jamie's embrace? I felt the urgent force of his manhood, pressing against me. I felt full prepared to open myself to him, in whatever direction he wanted, Easton or Weston. Long enough had I admired his gentlemanly restraint toward his apprentice, even as I regretted it, and cursed myself for placing both of us in such straits. At this moment, I hoped that his command of his passions would fail him. For if I lacked the courage to reveal myself to him, I prayed he would bring the affair to a head, and at once.

But then that great, galloping hound burst into the room.

Light-headed with passion, I struggled to recover my thoughts. Damn the dog: he had stolen my seduction, ruined my ruination! Curse the cur: he had stepped upon my palette, which had fallen to the ground, paint-side up. And yet some still, small voice at the back of my head told me I ought to rejoice in my rescuer. For part of me was glad to have preserved my disguise, and with it, my hard-won freedom, no matter the cost.

But then, as I bestowed some measure of silent credit upon the wretched Gulliver, I saw what he held in his slobbering mouth. Between his paws trailed the menstrual cloth I had stashed 'neath my bedding this morning, when the doctor waked me so suddenly.

It had been years, *years*, since I bled—longer indeed than my monthlies were full upon me. I was but sixteen when my babe began to grow within me. And after her birth I was too fevered, too starved, too ruined, my virtue too far lost, to have blood to spare. I had given myself, more than once, to vicious men who would take me in, in exchange for what I had to offer, and never did I conceive. Nor bleed. How many moons waxed and waned without the return of my courses? I knew my womb was long since dead, as barren as my heart.

Why now, this week? For here was the evidence of my womanhood. A white muslin banner, near two feet long, streaked all over crimson: Fanny's standard, a battle flag. I made to grab the red rag before Jamie saw it for what it was, but too late. Twas Gulliver's prize, and he would brook no detour before presenting it to his master.

With a bark of triumph, he dropped the thing at his master's feet.

There, he seemed to say, with a dog's gormless grin. *Stop what you are doing and see what I have brought you, and then reward me with a good hard scratch behind the ears.*

Would I lose my place, my work, and my love? I blushed with shame and worry, blushed redder than my rags.

I readied myself to speak as Jameson stared at the sanguinary offering.

But then we were interrupted, once again, as the doctor, quick on Gulliver's heels, cleared his throat.

"Dammit, Jamie, will that beast of yours permit me no dignity? He has stolen one of the dressings I use to bind up the scars upon my back." And then he looked at me, squarely in the eyes, and added, "They weep yet, especially when the moon is full, almost monthly, it seems." Thus did the doctor rescue this breathless, bleeding,

Fanny Easton.

From the *Boston Gazette*, Monday, September 24, 1764.

PUBLIC AUCTION.

To be Sold two weeks hence, on MONDAY the eighth of OCTOBER. A Great Variety of Household Furniture, belonging to the Estate of the Honorable *Samuel Bradstreet*, Esquire; deceased—the Sale to be at his Mansion House on Hanover Street—consisting of Mahogany Tables, Chairs, Cases of Drawers, Desks, Looking Glasses, Feather Beds, Bedsteads and Bedding, one Negro girl, three Horses, suitable either for Saddle or Chaise, a Sled, a Sleigh and runners, two Eight-Day Clocks, Tea Chest with Canisters, sundry valuable Pieces of Plate made in London, Pewter, Brass, Delph and Stone ware, China and Glass Ware, &c &c &c. Likewise a Coach, a four-wheel Chaise, a two-wheel ditto, with Harnessing complete; a Library of more than Four Hundred Volumes, with other Articles too many to be enumerated. The Sale to begin at Ten o'Clock, A.M.

Persons indebted to said Estate are notified to pay their Balances immediately, to aid this once-prosperous family, now reduced to the most penurious circumstances at the hands of Parliament's usurious taxation, which have bankrupted so many in our once-prosperous town.

—H. Usher.

N.B. A *Catalogue of Mr. Bradstreet's Library* is available for purchase at the Printer's, for two shillings, sixpence.

—B. T. Edes.

CHAPTER 16

Wherein Our Author Meets with Danger and Debauchery

I owe to the Laird of Firth a letter, *viz.*:

Dear Sir:

Be so good as to recall that twelvemonth since, you paid me for a kit-cat with a new-weaned pup—a weakling and a runt—thinking to keep close both your portrait and your purse. Twas no fair trade, sir—the cur was but a burden to me—and I have ever since awaited, in vain, payment of your fee in pounds sterling, and this in times when ready money is hard to come by, and the more dear to a laboring man.

Know now, sir, that the scrawny pup has grown into a fine hound— aye, he is growing still, and doubtless would have been the pride of your kennel, and the amour of your best bitch, had he stayed in Scotland. He is better bred, I daresay, than many a gentleman. That he has vexed me often, I cannot deny; as recently as yesterday he broke in upon an intimate scene of no small importance to me, though 'twas a kindness, in the end. And just

last night he did me a considerable service. So, herewith, I forgive your
debt. We are on even terms at last.

>*Be assured that you will hear nothing more from,*
>>*Your humble servant,*
>>*Stewart Jameson.*

Fortitude, fortitude! Who knew the dog had fortitude? 'Twas halfway between midnight and dawn, when I was awakened by his barking. A fury! I am mortified to report that I roused myself only to scold and silence him, though perhaps, if you live with a dog yourself—especially if yours is a prodigiously dumb one—you will not blame me for supposing that he barked at naught so much as *naught*—a spider, a mouse, a shoe.

"Damn your blood, Gulliver!" I hollered from the landing outside my bed-chamber, for the clatter came from belowstairs. "Give a man a chance for rest in this weary world!"

But he would not cease.

"Sir?" Weston asked, as he emerged from his garret above, we both carrying candles, in nothing more than stocking feet and nightshirts, each of us hastily pulling up our pants as we headed down the stairs. The sight of the lad, hair tousled, buttoning his trousers, took my breath away. His painter's hands are too nimble. Must he close his buttons so fast?

"Sir, what can be the matter?" he asked, jarring me from my thoughts of the last time the dog interrupted us.

"The matter, lad? The *dog* is the matter—again!" I cried over my shoulder. "I'll soon be the one feeding him lead for his supper. Days in this Bedlam are a torment enough! Cannot a man sleep? Gulliver, you bitch's bastard, you blight of nature! God above, he's louder than that three-headed beast that guards the gates of Hell! What the deuce is its bloody name?"

"You mean Cerberus, sir?"

"No, I mean Gulliver. *Gulliver!*"

We found him in the parlor, and no sign of spider, mouse, or shoe. Picture the scene illuminated by the scant light of our two candles. Alexander stood at the center of the room, wearing his Proverbial Gloves, which I swear he has not removed since first he put them on. In one hand he held a taper, in the other, a knife. Gulliver, every muscle taut, straddled a whimpering man, splayed 'neath him on the floor. The great dog's front paws pressed on this interloper's shoulders. Added to the menace was the timbre of what now came from Gulliver's mouth, lips drawn back, in—what would it be, Reader?—a *Cerberusian* sneer: a low, sinister snarl, as chilled my blood.

"Zooks! Zounds! What in heaven or hell is this?"

"O, massa, sir," answered my friend, in that horrible, minstrel falsetto. "I tink dat dog's done caught 'im a big ol' thief."

"Weston, light a lamp," I commanded, as I approached Gulliver's prey.

By the better light we three stood over the dog, and looked into the face of terror.

"Why, 'tis William Bradstreet, sir!" said Weston, with a cry of astonishment.

"Aye, the Wily Bastard. What the deuce are you doing here, Bradstreet?"

"Call this monster off," Bradstreet croaked. When I hesitated he sputtered, *"Please!"*

It required more than a little coaxing, and the lure of a marrow bone from the pantry, to convince Gulliver to yield up his catch. At last, Bradstreet found his cane, pulled himself to standing, and dusted himself off.

"Tell your man to sheathe his weapon, Jameson! Would you have your Negro assault the Deputy Attorney General? I will see him whipped on every corner of this city," he said, nodding nervously at Alexander, who, truly, looked as if he would as soon cut Bradstreet's throat as slice open a sealed letter.

"I'm afraid I cannot, sir. Not till I have some answers. I ask again, what brings you to my parlor floor?"

"I don't answer to you," he said, drawing himself up more fully, and thrusting the silver tip of his walking stick into my chest.

"Of course." I pushed his stick aside. "You can answer to the magistrates instead. Weston, run to the Town House, and fetch the constable, or, better yet, a soldier, from the sentry box."

"Wait!" Bradstreet said, frantically, as Weston made to leave the room. "There's no need for that, Jameson. We are men of sense. You are right to demand an answer from me, and I will give it."

"I am all anticipation, sir," I offered dryly.

"Well, yes. I had been out walking. I couldn't sleep. I, er . . . I found myself on Queen Street and I knew this for your house when I saw the painter's arms. And, well, you see, Jameson, I have suffered such a great loss, and so many setbacks, and my grief is profound. My venerable father, poisoned, villainously murdered, in what should have been his sedate old age. My beloved, long-suffering aunt, dead and buried. My mother reduced to penury, my sister fated to die an old maid—"

"Aye, Bradstreet, we know all this. Tis a sad affair, worthy of Richardson's purple pen. But I weary of it, and I can't answer for my temper at this hour of the night. Abridge your tale of woe. I crave the climax. Why, sir, are you *here*?"

He sniffed, and dabbed an eye with a homespun handkerchief drawn from his waistcoat pocket.

"I miss my father, Jameson. I miss him so very much, and I yearned for his likeness. Jameson, with your genius, I knew you would have captured him."

"Aye, you Witless Barrister, I read the papers, so I know how you measure my merit. I notice you've not come to have your portrait taken with the rest of the Hens."

"Have you no heart, Jameson? Are you not some father's son?" he simpered. "I only wished to gaze upon my father's venerable countenance, to consult his wisdom. *I simply wanted to see his face!*"

Maybe I am heartless. But this Bradstreet is no tragedian, no Garrick upon the stage. I laughed, and looked at my apprentice.

"Say, Weston, this bastard reminds me of that shitten riddle. What was it again? 'Brothers and sisters, I have none, but this man's father is my father's son'?"

"Sir?"

"The painter, was it? Or the painter's son?"

"The son, sir." He smiled.

"I still can't see it, Weston. But if we're to have some sleep, you'd best fetch the constable."

"No, no, I forbid it!" cried Bradstreet.

Weston made a show of grabbing his cloak, while the barrister squirmed. Alexander caught my eye.

"Massa," he implored. "Remember dat pot in de kitchen? It be boilin' ovuh, sir. We bests attend to it."

"What?"

"In de *kitchen*, suh?"

"Ach. Aye. The kitchen. Of course. Weston, guard the housebreaker. I have business in the kitchen."

When we had walked out of hearing, Alexander leaned close, and spoke in my ear as I gently took the knife from him and laid it on the kitchen table.

"Jamie, you must know that only your dog saved me from killing that man," he explained. "I was sitting in the dark, deep in contemplation, when he came through the parlor window. I had my knife to his throat before Gulliver knocked both my victim and the weapon from my grasp."

"Sweet Jesus, Sander, would you have us all hanged?" I cried, incredulous. "You tried to kill this colony's *prosecutor*? You are madder than I thought, man."

"Would that Reason, not your damned dog, had stayed my hand. But Jamie. Old friend. *Consider*: Why have yon Bradstreet's night wanderings brought him to Queen Street?"

"He has not told us, Sander. You heard the man. Fury and terror tie his tongue twice over. Not an honest word escapes him."

"Indeed. But your mind runs backward, Jamie," Sander said. "It is what he imagines *we* shall give *him*. The man is desperate. He pleads in court for the proceeds of Phebe's sale, lest even that small sum go to the Manufactory House, instead of into his own empty pockets. He ties up the settlement of the estate, and fortunate for us that he does."

"So the Wily Bastard has turned Weasely Burglar? The more pity him. Only a fool would look for money in my quarters."

"True enough. But you miss my meaning. Your burglar and I scout the same quarry: he needs his father's Will. If Samuel Bradstreet bragged of his dispensation to his slaves, you can bet he boasted of it to his heir twice as often. Imagine poor Billy's plight: he hoped the testament contained his rescue, yet feared it sealed his ruin. He searched the mansion top to bottom, two steps ahead of the probate commissioners. And he found: nothing. Not a tittle or a jot. But at least the thing was gone. And perhaps it never did exist."

"Thank you, Professor, but your lecture falls something short of placing that bampot by my hearth."

"You saw it yourself: the trial ended young Bradstreet's repose. Before those hanging-judges, Hannah said it: there was a Will, and it had freed her. Withered William has hunted it ever since, hunted it as if his life depended on it. Which it may, yes, it may."

"Are we getting nearer my hearth, Sander?"

"Faster if you would cease interrupting. Just when he had ransacked every drawer, and taken a glass to every one of his father's papers, again and again, for the hundredth time, Billy remembered: Samuel Bradstreet—strangely enough—admired *you*. And he had seen you carry those canvases from his father's house. Might the Will have been with them? Tucked in the stretcher of a painting, or secreted in a letter upon your person? Young Bradstreet thinks you may have it, and he means to get it back. *That* is what brings him here. Q.E.D."

"Full marks, Professor. But I have nothing of his father's, beyond the portrait, and the *Modest Inquiry*. No clues are concealed in either—that is, beyond whatever you would have me paint into the likeness. So the Weeping Blister can gain nothing from me. And truly, Sander, what shall we gain from him? Do you think he will pour out his tale like Chaucer's parson?"

"Just ask him about the Will. For certain, Bradstreet will tell us nothing. But I would see his countenance, and read his answer there."

I sighed, nodded my assent, and we returned to the parlor, where Gulliver continued to circle his wary prey.

"Worried Breeches, answer me this," I said, as I strode toward him. "What do you know of your father's Will?"

His face, which had almost recovered its composure, now turned, again, to terror, eyes wide, mouth agape, cheeks near as pale as white lead.

"What! Tis none of your business, Jameson. But as you know—you were at the trial, were you not?—he had no Will. Do you dare to mock my family's misfortunes? *He had no Will!*"

"Merely curious, Bradstreet. Now, tell me why I should not have my apprentice fetch the sentry."

"Because if you do," he spat out, "I will have your man here arrested, and flogged, or worse. Can you spare this buck? I daresay you have a tender spot for skin as dark as his. You shared that flaw with my father, who was murdered for his misjudgment, as you may be, too. Indeed, having been in your house, I await with eager anticipation the news that this black fiend has slit your throat."

In a flash, Alexander was upon him, his gray-gloved hands encircling Bradstreet's bony neck. "Red work," Alexander whispered. "These hands have known red work."

"Conquer the Rock of Gibraltar, man! Get hold of yourself!" I shouted, pulling him off. "Weston, get him out of here!"

Bradstreet was visibly pleased by this turn of events. And why not? Alexander's rashness had left me little with which to bargain. I made my best bid.

"Let us make a treaty, then, Bradstreet. I will neither fetch the sentry, nor chronicle for Edes your illustrious career as a burglar, if you pledge to keep an equal silence on the subject of my servant. He was defending my house. He overstepped, and grossly, but 'tis *my* duty, nay, my *pleasure* to correct him."

At this last, the intruder smiled.

"Tis a bad bargain, Jameson, but I would hate to deny any man the right of correcting his slave. You have my word, as a man of honor."

In vain did I try to return to sleep that night, tossing in my bedsheets, haunted by visions of Weston in his shift, and of Alexander with his fingers laced around Bradstreet's neck. Finally, at the cock's first crowing, I dressed.

I wondered, once again, whether Alexander had slept in all this last fortnight, for I had seen no evidence of it. And no man can keep his sanity, much less restore it, without sleep.

I found Weston working by the half-light in the painting room. Gulliver dozed near the hearth, and I was glad my apprentice had made a good fire, for 'twas the coldest day I had yet met with in America. The lad labored, clumsily, on a little study I had assigned him, a bowl of autumn apples and pears. I stepped behind him to look over his shoulder, careful to leave a foot of distance between us.

Disappointing stuff. Twas evident that his mind had not been on his work.

"Tis meant to be *still*, lad, not lifeless. Start again."

"Can *we* not start again, sir?" he said, stepping back and leaning into me. "Without the dog this time . . ."

Struggling against every baser instinct, I forced myself to move away.

"Nay, lad. And I'm sorry I forgot myself. I owe it to you to be a better governor of my passions."

"But what of my passions, sir?" he pleaded, turning to face me.

"You are sixteen, Weston; you are naught but passion: find a worthier object for it. We shall speak of it no more. Now: Have you seen the doctor?"

His face fell, and he paused before answering.

"I haven't sir. Not since last night."

Without another word, I went belowstairs to seek Alexander. I opened the door to his rooms, soundlessly, and stepped inside. The abundance of beakers and flasks, filled with a rainbow of colored liquids, all remained as I had last seen them. At the far end of the laboratory a small door opened into his bed-chamber. I walked toward it, padding as silently as an Indian. Peering through the door, I was relieved to spy my friend on his bed, in a profound sleep. I threw a blanket over him, and another, for his rooms were colder than the rest of the house.

Alas, now Weston and I were left alone. Best to keep busy, Reader.

"We must find that Will," I said, as we breakfasted. "And all I can think is that we should begin with Hannah, for she's the only one who admits that she saw it. And she yet lingers in prison, still unsold—and thank God, as Sander says. So I'm afraid you must retrace your steps to the jail, lad. Plainly she trusts you best."

Weston looked down at his plate and began to tremble.

I put my hand over his, and resisted the temptation to close my eyes at the lurch of desire even so slight a touch stirred in me. I shook it off. "What is it, lad?"

"Please, sir," he said in a quavering voice. "Might not you undertake that errand?"

"I suppose I might, Weston. But you would have more success, and I must paint Mrs. Beaujardin's half-length, and some Red Hen kit-cats, and at a clip! We must think not of Cicero's death but of a life that might yet be spared. Phebe is to be auctioned less than two weeks hence, and we have scarce a shilling to our names."

"But how can we want for money, sir? We've had so many sitters, and no more expenses than usual, at least none that I can see. Shall I get the ledger?"

"Ach, you can't count those chickens, lad. Only some of the Hens have paid for their kit-cats, few of them in full, and too many of them in paper. I can't claim to make much of Parliament's mumbo jumbo, but with your head for ciphers, you must know that the Currency Act costs us dear."

"But still, sir. Unless my books are terribly far off, the balance is far in our favor."

He was right, of course, Reader. For I am not quite so bad at sums as I would lead him to think. But I will not pretend with you. If I owe you nothing else, I have pledged you this: a full accounting of my affairs.

Before ever I heard about the auction, I spent all the money I had. Twas an error, I suppose, on reflection. Will it be ever my misfortune to miscalculate? Pray, know: I acted with the best of intentions.

The morning after I had kissed my apprentice in the painting room—and I would have done more if not for the dog, Sweet Jesus, so much more, beginning by bending him over, for is not kissing but the prologue to the play?—I filled a small wooden box with all the coin I had to my name, in all the minted tender that washes up on these shores: a handful of the province's native pine-tree shillings, three Spanish pieces of eight, a German ducat and a Dutch daalder, a few Portuguese piasters, two English silver sovereigns, and a bright golden guinea, marked by the tiny pachyderm invoking the African mines whence its ore came. Then I sought out Mordecai Usher, haunting the Crown coffeehouse. Released by the death of his mother to pursue his glorious Indian destiny, he would sail at last for London, where he planned to spend some weeks boning up his dubious skill in the arts of rogering, ere he makes his way to Madras. ("Ah, Jameson, I shall leave a trail of broken hearts spanning two continents!" he told me.) Truly, he is as windy a fool as any I've encountered upon these blustery shores. Yet he's harmless enough, and I trusted him as far as I needed. I gave him my motley pile of metal, and he made out a bill of exchange, the only kind of paper that can carry funds across that great ocean.

Do you think I mean to end my exile, Reader? Would that I could. Would that I could. Nay, I had him make out the bill to Joshua Reynolds, as payment, in advance, for my apprentice's tuition and keep. Surely 'twould be enough to fund his training in London. And hadn't Weston earned it as well as I? And now, even if my resolve should weaken, there can be no turning back, for I directed Usher to carry the bill to Reynolds's apartments in the West End. ("Leicester Fields. I know it well," he said, licking his lips.

"Home of a golden-haired tart with a heart-shaped face who knows how to . . .") He sailed Monday, so that even now, my letter draws nearer its destination—so bloody far away—mile by nauseous nautical mile.

Unfortunately, only after Usher's ship had left Boston did I read in Edes's *Gazette* of Bradstreet's auction. And imagine, dear Reader, my distress at realizing I no longer held the coin needed to buy the girl. But I had rather not explain myself to Weston.

"Then your books must be off, lad," I insisted. "Or perhaps I've been careless at cards. In any case, the drawer is empty. We'll have to rake in some custom. How much will they ask for her, do you think?"

"Fifty pounds, at least, sir," he said and groaned.

"'Tis no trivial sum," I agreed.

"So we must paint, sir!" he said, brightening. "Truly, why should I go to the jail to ask Hannah about a Will that may not exist? Let us stay in the house, all this day, and paint together, paint our way to Phebe's price."

How enchanting his plan. But dear Reader, I did not think my new-found resolve should survive the day alone with him.

"No, Weston. We must hunt the Will, *and* fill our till. Fifty pounds is but two clubmen, paid in full, or a fat deposit on a slender widow. Short work, lad! Still, I will take your task, and visit Hannah if you so vastly prefer. Meanwhile, you knock on the door of every Hen house you can find, and get a pullet here by noon. Book no more than a two-hour sitting. My Widow B. comes at three."

I grabbed my hat and coat, and headed for the front door, eager to be on my way. But Weston came running after me.

"Wait, sir, do you have any coins upon you?"

"Aye, lad, one or two farthings," I said, fingering the depleted purse in my waistcoat pocket. "What do you want so urgently?"

"Nothing, sir," he said vaguely. "But you might need them at the jail."

I f you have never visited a prison, happy Reader, do not begin your tour in Boston. The rank, the rot, the filth. The sighs of suffering and moans of misery. The wretchedness. Hogarth might spy a fit subject here—Sweet Jesus, but the man has an eye for squalor—but I find only my old queasiness. I will spare you further description of the place. Even I was nearly spared its sight. Or, rather, *denied* it.

Enoch Goddard greeted me at the prison door and barred my way, dangling a set of keys from his belt.

"*Mister* Jameson, in'it. Fine mornin' to you, sir," he said, doffing his greasy cap and offering an oily grin.

I would not tip my hat to such a man for all the ore in the Andes.

"Goddard, I am come to pray with the prisoner," I said, for this was all the flimsy pretext I could conjure. "Let me in."

"I never knew you to be a prayin' man, sir," he said. "I thought you let yer Weston do yer kneelin' for you."

And he leered at me.

"My apprentice has nothing to do with it, Goddard," I answered, archly. "Now let me in."

"There yer wrong, sir. I have somethin' you want," he said, jangling his keys. "And you have somethin' I want," now stroking his codpiece. "Yer boy is yer ticket through this door. Bring him 'ere, sir, and I'll take care of 'im while you pray with that black wench, who ain't no soul, no ways. Take yer time with her, sir, and I'll take mine with the boy, for the last time I had 'im—ah, and 'e's a luscious morsel, sir, I envy you, I don't mind sayin'—it ended a little too quick."

My blood near boiled. I grabbed him by his coat, and threw him against the wall of the building.

"Think what you say, Goddard. And tell me no more of your vicious lies."

His ruddy face grew ruddier, but he only grinned wider.

"How do you think the boy got in 'ere before, you daft brush? And into the trial, what with a hundred men in line before 'im. Though none so pretty, eh? Did you think I just *let* 'im in? More's the fool, you, sir. I got my price. And I'll have it again."

"Not while I breathe, you won't," I said, and then I hit him full on the jaw with my right hand. As he fell, my fist crashed against the stone wall behind him, bearing the force of my entire weight, and all of my fury. The jail-keeper's pipe spurted from his lips as he slumped to the ground, with a terrible cry, though I hazard my cry was the louder of the two.

This is what it has come to, at last. Alexander was right; I am distracted, *blinded* by my own affections, and place in danger everyone around me, for I have exposed poor Weston to this fiend, this crapulous claw-baw. (Though I wondered, at the same time, whether the lad had tried mightily enough to avoid him.) My hand throbbed, a searing, jagged pain, and bled near as much as Goddard's face. With my good hand, I grabbed the ring from his waist and let myself in the prison door.

I found Hannah sitting in a dirt-floored cell in a dark, damp, cold corner, looking like a phantom, and with no Phebe at her feet, for the girl had been removed to the Manufactory House. No longer defiant, Hannah was mute and lost in the distraction of her grief. I begged and beseeched her as I fell to my knees and hugged my hand to my chest.

"Speak quickly, Hannah! Where is Bradstreet's Will, lass? You must tell me, and not a minute to lose, for I've bashed the jail-keeper to get in here, and may have to clout him again to get out. I won't have it be for naught."

"I don't know, Mr. Jameson. I don't know!" Barely did she look at me. Indeed, she seemed as if she no longer knew even where she was. She felt about the floor. "I must find Phebe's doll. I'll get it to her. She won't sleep without it."

"Think, lass! Forget the doll. Did you ever see the Will? It may save the child, Hannah. Think!"

She held my gaze, at last, and but briefly, lucid. "No."

"At the trial, you said he showed it to you."

"I lied."

This is what I expected, and still I sighed. "There is no Will, then?"

"No, there is a Will. He told me of it."

"And then, lass, what did he say? What? Hurry!" I thought I could hear Goddard's groans growing louder.

"Only that he hid it in a book. He promised me he kept it safe, in a book."

"Heaven to mercy, lass. *What* book?"

"I don't know. Mr. Jameson, I don't know!" And then she mumbled, "Where, oh where is Phebe's doll?"

Letter XV.

September the 26th, 1764

Elizabeth,

You censure my behavior, as I knew you must, though for different reasons than I censure myself. You urge me to ponder whether Stewart Jameson is any better a man than Enoch Goddard. My master, I fear, wonders the same. Where can I find the resolve to end this masquerade, grown so cruel to the man I love best in all the world? Whatever the cost, I must tell him, and pray that he judges me less harshly than you do.

Noon. He promised to return by noon, ready to paint. I had done my part, traversing the town, knocking at the doors of portrait-hungry Hensmen till I found one at the ready. Mr. Thomas Gallagher, hard at work in the grocery adjoining his home on Ann Street, had asked for a likeness weeks ago. Begged for it, truly, but my master could only promise to do his best.

"Aye, Gallagher," Jamie had told him. "We can accommodate you, by November, but I doubt much sooner, for a long queue of upstanding cocks comes before you."

"But 'tis August, Jameson."

"A man can only do so much, sir."

So the grocer was pleased indeed when he learned that his number had come up this very day.

"Mr. Jameson has available an appointment for your sitting, sir," I told him. "Might you join him from noon until two?"

Twas near an insult, such late notice, and an undesirable interval as well. Merchants hold the block for their daily trading on the 'Change; goodwives keep it sacred for the family meal; nor do painters fancy it much, for the light is harsh, and hungry subjects hard to capture. But Gallagher did not hesitate. In an eye-blink, he had closed his cash drawer, put away his ledger, and donned a sash of deep crimson velvet, perhaps four inches wide, with a single feather embroidered upon it in silken gold threads. He hummed merrily to himself as we made our way to Queen Street, rounding the corner just as the bell atop the Old Brick rang the change for eleven-and-thirty. We hurried past the jail, and I said a silent prayer for Hannah, poor lost Cicero, and little innocent Phebe.

I directed Gallagher to the painting room, where I thought to find Jameson readying his brushes before the kit-cat I had stretched and primed. But the room was empty, the fire gone cold.

"My master returns soon, sir. I am sure of it," I told our sitter, who paced the room with a concerned look upon his face. "And we shall not lose this time. He has tasked me to block out the composition. If you would, please take a seat behind that great oak table."

Gallagher proved as compliant a subject as ever I had sketched, asking no more of me than the bowls of fruit Jameson assigns for study pictures. I marked the regions of the portrait with charcoal: the oval of his head, his sloped shoulders, the plane of the table and the angle of his blunt hands crossed upon it. When that work was done I began to mix the colors my master would need. The sash proved difficult, as the claret I saw before me turned a tawny port on my palette.

"Might I borrow the ribbon a moment, sir, lest I fail to catch the red?"

He handed over his prize as if giving good weight on a pumpkin.

"I see it now, sir. It needs carmine. I had guessed vermillion. Reds are tricky, sir, you see."

He nodded agreeably enough, and began to chatter of red cabbages and purple beets as I laid down a base for the flesh tones. The minutes dragged.

Noon, the bells announced. And a quarter, and another.

By the twelve-and-thirty, I had wearied of hearing about onions.

Twelve-and-forty-five, and I began to fret in earnest.

And when the bell tolled one, the placid Gallagher lost his composure.

"Half my sitting is gone, boy. Are *you* to take my likeness, then? I'm sure the master teaches you well. But I should like my brother Hens to see upon my wall a *Jameson*, not a Weston."

"Of course, sir. I cannot think what has happened," I replied—and I meant it, too. "Mr. Jameson intended noon, and though he is not the most predictable of gentlemen, never is he late."

"I am used to being kept waiting," Gallagher said and sighed, resigned. "But that does not make me like it any better. I shall tarry a quarter-hour more, and then I had best answer those who wait upon me."

Twas plain he could hardly bear to make good the threat. But at one-and-thirty, more disappointed than angry, he gathered up his things and trudged back to his store.

"You have forgot your sash, sir," I called after him, too late, for he had already turned onto Corn-hill.

An hour passed before at last I heard Jameson's footsteps in the front hall. By then, my rose-colored worry had ripened into a purple frenzy. His appearance did nothing to quiet my mood, for he looked near as white as canvas when he entered the painting room.

"Jamie, what kept you? Have you forgotten your own instructions, then?" I said, waving the scarlet sash. "Mr. Gallagher has come and gone, and twelve pounds sterling with him. Would you disappoint us both?"

"Jamie?" he replied, his voice dull with sadness. "*Jamie,* is it? Weston, surely 'tis you who forgets himself. Let us pretend that I am the master, shall we? Though perhaps you own many masters. Or, rather, many own you."

His eyes grew narrow, though I could not fathom the balance of anger and heartache in them.

"What happened at the jail, sir? Did you see Hannah?"

"Aye, I saw plenty, and heard more, lad. But I will not talk of it now. Clear out. Madame Beaujardin arrives at three, and before I attend her I would ready the room, and gather my wits."

Twas then that I noticed his right hand—his painting hand—crudely bandaged about the knuckles with a paint-spattered rag.

"Your hand, sir! What have you done to your hand?"

"Ach, my hand, Weston," he said, and only now could I see that he was wincing not only with anger and heartache, but also with pain. "I wondered when your painter's eye might detect the wound. Tis a sad tale: I have smashed it against your honor, a craggy surface indeed."

I feared I knew his meaning, yet I worried more for him than for myself.

"Sir, please, you cannot paint today! After I have fetched Doctor Alexander, I will take your apologies to Mrs. Beaujardin."

"Nay, I forbid it, Weston. Let the doctor sleep, and leave the Widow be. Take yourself downstairs, or up, I care not which. But away with you. For I would fain attend to my wound, and then to the lady, without you fussing about, to my distraction."

Why do you continue to press yourself upon your master? you ask. *What future can you have with him?* But Lizzie, my question is the opposite. What future can he have with Fanny Easton, who stands no higher for having fallen from a lofty, well-feathered perch? Maybe I had best not reveal myself to him after all, for am I not more use to him as Weston? Truly, I cannot see the path before me. I have spent so much time looking backward, gazing upon the sorrows of my past, that I glimpse the future only dimly, in half-light, and bound all around, as if through a peephole.

Tis no fanciful conceit, for I find myself spying through such an opening this very moment.

Cut into the stairway leading from the first floor to the second, just past where the landing makes its tight turn, hangs a small cabinet. Tis no fine joiner's craft, but the landlord's rough carpentry: a bit of painted planking nailed over a hole in the plaster lathe above the wainscot, with a few shelves tacked on to hide the indifferent work Ayers made of the repair. We store some powdered pigments there, where the light does not threaten their brilliance. As I returned the carmine and vermillion to their accustomed places, I noticed in the back board a knothole, no larger than a coin: a tiny, crude telescope into the painting room. Banished from that sanctuary, I press myself against its outer wall like some thieving scullery maid spying upon her master.

My peephole frames a pretty little picture, smaller and livelier than even the most delicate miniature. In front of Jameson's easel, on the Turkey-work chair before the fire, sits Louisa Lambert Beaujardin. She wears a gown of salmon-colored lutestring, its glow subtler and finer than satin. Nary a ruffle distracts the eye from the mantua maker's expertise, tailoring precise to the last tuck and button. (Easily three dozen buttons, plump and cloth-covered, delineate the arc of her spine.) Her neckline is not modest, certainly. But neither does it strain to achieve its effect. Trim and square, it shows a waxing quarter-moon of flesh on each side of her breastbone. Her waist—which has known neither the thickening of age, nor that of childbed—she adorns with a velvet sash of soft gray-blue, a masculine hue that only accentuates the femaleness of her form. Yet there is an honesty about her costume, a rare arrow in the coquette's quiver. One day, one day, Fanny Easton might have grown into such a dress.

Marriage, not birth, bought Miss Louisa Lambert her elegance. She wed young, and well. Her husband, late of Paris, was both wealthy and worldly. *Marcel Beaujardin et Cie* supplied half this colony with wine before his ship was lost on a crossing from the Canaries, and Monsieur B. along with it, not quite a year ago. *Très triste.*

All this she tells Jameson while he paints. As the firelight and the afternoon sun play upon the golden curls piled atop her head, she looks near as lovely as her name. Her conversation—no tears or titters—does nothing to detract from her appearance. If she lacks brilliance, she also wants for guile. I can see in his demeanor, in his very posture, in the cock of his head, in the sway of his walk, how much my master admires her.

But I see, too, the tremor in his arm when he stands behind the easel, hidden from his sitter. He steadies his bandaged right wrist with his mahlstick while he paints, bracing himself against the pain. "A mere trifle!" he told Louisa when she asked about the bandage. "The dog nicked me when I stole my shoe back from his jaws." Yet he sweats with the strain of hiding his distress.

"*Mais vous êtes trop charmant, monsieur.*"

Jamie smiles, but when he turns toward this wall, his countenance is a picture of grief, so crestfallen that I cannot bear to see his suffering, and almost look away, except that here I spy, as I have nowhere so clearly glimpsed before, the difference between the face he puts before the world and the one he wears in private. Oh, Lizzie! Would that I had the courage to rush through the door, steal his brush away, and cover his hand with kisses.

Yet I am stayed, if no other force stays me, by his tender regard for his sitter. And why should he not admire her? There is a genuine sheen about the Widow, like some gem whose soft polish does not dazzle, yet disguises no flaws.

The Lamberts look after her now, the young *madame* explains. They board her patiently enough, yet her brother worries that she will languish, forever a widow, 'neath their roof in Charlestown. Next week she turns five-and-twenty: a quarter-centurion, a crone! Can she not bestir herself to captivate the town's eligibles? Lambert coaxes her. Ah, would he have her parade her wares like a fruit-seller? She smiles at the very thought, confidently but not brashly, like one who knows the value of her own currency and makes no motion either to inflate or to depreciate it.

And my Jamie? Despite his pain, he cannot tear his eyes away from the fruit. He speaks of it, distractedly, as if to hide his attention to her assets.

"Fruit, aye, fruit. I shall leave a blank space upon the tea table. My lad can fill it later on, with a basket of blushing peaches, perhaps, whose ripeness can mirror your own."

Unblushing, Madame Beaujardin parries the compliment with a jest about the proximity of ripeness to rot.

"Ah, but fruit is sweetest when just past its peak, is it not?" Jamie rejoins. "Would that every Methuselah of your advanced years enchanted the canvas so, *vielle madame*."

His accent is flawless, and as she nods a silent compliment, he cannot conceal the pride he takes in his continental manners. He gives her his most handsome smile.

"Beaujardin. *Beautiful Garden*." Then he turns the French over once more, rolling it about on his tongue. "Your married name suits you, *madame. Vous êtes vraiment une belle fleur, n'est-ce pas? Très belle, oui, très belle*."

She colors slightly, and Jamie laughs, instantly melting this pretense of courtliness into the thing itself. Of this I can no longer harbor the least doubt: he can be as fond of a woman as any man living.

He bows his head, doffing, with his good hand, an invisible cap to the lady. She nods in return, ever so slightly, serene in her acknowledgment of a compliment richly deserved, from a man worthy of delivering it.

The painter continues the easy patter that brings his subjects to life. A trade skill, I know, but this afternoon 'tis more.

"I tell you, *madame*, I only wish that every ancient crone possessed a still-older brother as thoughtful and generous as your own, who would pay to mark the passing of her one-score-and-five with a half-length from this humble brush, for I am quite enjoying the work."

That he speaks true, even a woman half blinded by love can see through a knothole.

"*Oui*, just there, *madame*. Look past me, out that window beyond. I would fain capture your eyes by indirection. Seen full-on, their blue might overwhelm the composition."

My face grows hot with jealousy.

She takes his instruction without demurring, and surveys the yard with a gaze that is neither acute, nor imperious, but simply gracious. Tranquil. He in turn surveys her landscape with a practiced eye, checking the angles, the shadows, the light, the play of colors and textures. He stares at the likeness emerging from the canvas, and paces a bit, not quite satisfied.

"Idle hands, *madame*. Hands are tricky, and even such a lovely pair as yours will look lifeless without something nestled between 'em. Needlework would not do for you, I think, much less a fan, for you are no mere dame of fashion. Nor is a book just the thing; you are no bluestocking lady."

He has got her to rights, she agrees, and the two of them cast about for a prop, settling at last upon the cameo pinned at her neck, an oval scrimshaw with a small blue herring painted upon it. She undoes the gilt filigree pin with her right hand, and takes the jewel in her left.

"*Oui, c'est absolument parfait*." Jamie nods. "You may caress it just a bit, but don't *fuss* with it, lass. *Madame*. And no need to present it to me. The window: your thoughts are elsewhere, across the sea."

Still the composition misses; I sense it as well as he does. Jamie rests his brush upon his palette, and rubs his chin.

"Ach, I see it now. The pearls, *madame*. Their glow must not be allowed to rival your own. But don't lose the pose. Might I remove them? I promise to treat your treasures with due care."

She assents, and he walks toward her. Gingerly, the long, tapered fingers of his left hand find the gold clasp at the nape of her neck. With practiced agility, he releases the catch in a thrice, and holds each end of the strand, allowing the cool beads to descend—ever so briefly—till they rest upon her bosom. Then he lifts the necklace away with a small flourish, and drapes it around her left wrist.

"Splendid," he says. "Just so." And then, God help me, he winks at her.

How can he? I cover a shout with a cough. Is it the same wink he offers Weston? There is less heat in it, perhaps, but near as much kindness.

He busies himself with his work, still bracing his bad hand with his good, and still wincing, but now in that state of almost trancelike absorption with which he works when he is pleased with his Art. Not six feet away, I see unseen, choked by lust and envy and rage, three of the deadliest sins, the worse for their combination. For I can well imagine how she looks to him. And I can see him, as if through her round blue eyes. He looks very fine indeed.

"Weston, come at once!"

I near jumped out of my skin when I heard that familiar command, grown suddenly cold. The words came from Doctor Alexander, who stood but two steps below me, watching my watching, ready to call me to account before my master.

"I am weighing it," he whispered. "This boy Weston hangs in the balance. I could drag him by the ear into that room, and expose his deceptions. Yea, every one of them, as you well know. But I shall not. For I confess I prefer the sneak to the flirt. Though in either guise, you steal his dignity."

"But doctor, he has hurt his hand! You must go in and help him."

"If he needed me, he would have found me. I shall not deny him his privacy."

"But—"

"Peep till your blood boils, my dear deluded girl. But do not lie, not to yourself any longer. *You* are what ails him. Look hard, and see exactly what you take from him. And then ask yourself, if you dare: No matter your sex, what would you give him in return?"

With that, the doctor left me to my thoughts.

What would I give him in return?

Beyond the pleasure of a moment, he can have no more use for a boy than I do. And of a woman, he expects—yea, deserves—far more than I can offer. What, would we live upon love?

Louisa Beaujardin is a better woman than I shall ever be.

There, I have written it, and I cannot strike it through. How to fault her? She is no wit, true. But neither is she prim or silly. She is knowing, and known. A faint patina burnishes her beauty, yet she remains unspoiled. She has her honor *and* her fortune; I have neither.

What could I possibly give him?

My talent? Tis no gift at all. Jamie mocks his Art, says he paints for bread. Can I claim even that much? Surely not—not yet, not ever. I can scarce name a single artist of my sex, not even one I have learned of in books. If this Louisa is a jewel, I am a millstone. A *dependent*, near-chattel. A cost, when he must have gains.

Oh, Lizzie, can't you see? Tis not the master but the apprentice who is unworthy. I cannot reveal myself to him. But perhaps the time has come to listen to you at last. How often have you begged me to send word to my father, and to enlist his aid?

You are right. The moment has arrived.

And so I turn my pen from pride to profit:

Mr. Edward Easton,

 You know my hand, and my shame, Father.

 I also know yours. I cannot allow you to preside over the ruin of another of your daughters. I mean to have my bride-price, and to spend it as I wish.

 Fifty gold pieces, let us call it. Hard currency, sir, for I do not credit your word, your honor, or your Fidelity.

 Carry the money with you to the execution tomorrow. There I shall make myself known: to you alone if you comply with this request, to all the town if you do not.

 Think well before you refuse me.

       —F.E.

Just the briefest of notes, scant ink swirled upon the tiniest of pages, small enough to tie around a rock that I hurl through the window of his library, to land on the polished mahogany table beside which I sat with him, so long ago, when I was a richer,

      Fanny Easton.

CHAPTER 17

Of Eye- and Ear-Witnesses to Particular
Crimes Against Nature

R eader, have you ever seen a man hanged?

You can scarce have avoided such a scene in this cruel and vex-atious world, unless you have cloistered yourself in a hut in some ob-scure wood, and lived like a hermit. Here in Boston, as in London, and alike in Edinburgh, and in every hinterland in between, we hang mur-derers. We hang pirates. We hang rebels, rogues, rapists, and robbers. No town lacks for a gallows, or wants for a crowd to watch it do its work.

But O, kindhearted Sir, tender Madam, I hazard you have not rel-ished the sight, for I consider you an enlightened soul, and not only that, but a creature of modest taste and, on the whole, more private pursuits, for who but such a one would have the patience to pore over my pages? You and I take our pleasures elsewhere than in other men's suffering. In-deed, so far do I trust in the power of your sympathy—and so far do I imagine us alike in our wish for the liberty to pursue a happy, prosper-ous, virtuous life of domestic contentment and public esteem—that I picture you, at your leisure, in a cushioned chair, by a warm fire, with a cup of tea perched on a table by your side, upon which sits a candlestick of three tapers—ample light for reading, but not overmuch, lest you fail to lose yourself in my book, and stare too much at *your* world, nearer to hand.

From just such a seat I must ask you now to transport yourself to a place both brighter and darker. Tis the glaring sun of high noon. Not hot—for autumn is full upon us, and a chilling breeze blows from the northeast—but as starkly lit as the tropics.

There is a kind of clear-skied fall day here in this New-England, so crisp that everything out of doors appears as if outlined in India ink, as if the Almighty Himself were a provincial painter, a little too reliant on line. The twenty-seventh of September was just such a day. I had rather it had been as dark and damp and dismal as a January afternoon on the Isle of Skye. I had rather the town had been assaulted by an unseasonable blizzard, blanketing everything in white. Or: I had rather it had rained, a thousand thunderstorms, turning all to black. In short, I wish either that we had jumped from the twenty-sixth of September, straight to the twenty-eighth, or that I could spill that pot of God's ink, and blot out the day.

Would you object, Reader, if I were to insert, just here, a blank white page, or a black one, and beseech you to skip over this chapter and proceed to the next?

To be sure, there are arguments both for and against such an omission. On the one hand: I fancy you would be glad of the abridgement, and so would I be grateful for the opportunity to put down my pen, for I am forced to write with my left hand, a trick I taught myself as a schoolboy, but I find it less diverting now, and more laborious, than I did then. On the other hand: I pledged to Alexander that I would watch Cicero die. But that is three hands in one paragraph, more than any man needs.

"Have you never read Dodd's *Reflections on Death*, Jamie?" the doctor asked me this morning, when I protested that I had rather not attend the execution.

"Dodd on death? Just the thing to cheer me, I'm sure. But alas, I have missed it."

"Unfortunate, but hardly surprising. Your literary taste runs to lower fare, does it not? 'Nothing teacheth like death,' Dodd writes."

"Tis as I pictured, then. Just the thing."

The doctor merely shook his head.

"And please, Jamie, do not tell me you have never read the *Theory of Moral Sentiments* by your fellow Scotsman, Adam Smith, chair of Moral Philosophy at Glasgow?"

"Aye, I know the man, for haven't I painted him, and twice? But alas, of his treatise, I am as ignorant as a newborn babe. Pray, enlighten me."

"Let me furnish you with a specimen of his discourse. Smith reminds us that the sight of a dying martyr will 'animate anew the deformed and mangled carcass of the slain.'"

"Sweet Jesus, Sander. This sentimental Smith is worse than your doleful Dodd!"

He eyed me soberly.

"You must bear witness to Cicero's death, Jamie; your sympathy will be a monument to his suffering; in its way, it brings him back to life."

This seemed preposterous, superstitious cant, but as I have yet to prevail over Alexander on a point of debate—he must always be on the right side of the hedge, as the saying goes—I scarcely countered.

Suffice to say: I attended the execution. And I may as well report it to you, discerning Reader, for Edes's paper will turn it all to politics, and that is not half the truth.

Enough doddering. There is no answer for it. I must to the gallows.

Still, I would put off the dreaded task just a little longer.

Let us begin, not at high noon, but at dawn. I am in no rush to speak of death. Let Cicero breakfast, if he can. Let him breathe his last hours in peace.

The sun has risen. The cock has just crowed, and I have tossed off my bedclothes, only to find that my hand, which Alexander had covered in a poultice and wrapped in linen before I retired, not only aches and throbs but has swelled still more, despite the doctor's best efforts.

"Jamie, why did you not tell me about this when it happened?" he had scolded, severely, for he saw my inexpert bandage only as we sat to a dimly lit dinner. (The days have grown shorter, and we hoard our tallow for painting.) "How could you fail to seek my help? For God's sake, man, have you used it all afternoon? What, were you in a trance from the shock?—the swelling is considerable—there is not much to be done now. Not so late in the day when there is scarce enough light for me to inspect the injury and clean the wound."

I answered sheepishly. "You were asleep when I came home from the jail. Did you think I would wake you for such a trifle? Surely 'tis not as bad as you say. And 'tis nothing compared to your whip-scars, which weep with the moon like some bloody Spanish Christ."

"I will say no more until I inspect the wound by morning's light. For now, answer me this: How did it happen? What did you do, Jamie, punch a man?"

"Me?" I laughed, maybe too heartily. "'Twas my usual clumsiness, and no more. On the walk back from the prison I tripped on a paving stone that had come dislodged from the street, and smashed into a shop front, nearly breaking a windowpane. A cobbler's. It made good sport for the urchins on the sidewalk, who found much merriment in my fall. Come to think of it, maybe the cobbler had set such a trap, to ruin the shoes of passersby. An enterprising tradesman. I wonder: Should we replace the shop sign that hangs in the front of this house with a looking glass?"

Alexander was not amused. He bade me soak the hand, after which he strapped it with a muck made of mustard powder and alum, and sent me to bed, though I will not say to sleep. Even if Gulliver hadn't tried to lick the plaster in the night, the smell alone would have kept me awake.

And so, again: dawn. The cock has crowed. With no small difficulty I had just taken off my nightshirt and tugged on my breeches, when Alexander barged in, without so much as the courtesy of a knock. Behind him, across the hall, I could see Weston in the painting room, sketching the rooflines from our window, which exercise I had recommended to improve his use of shadow.

"Doctor Alexander," I began, merrily and, as it happened, far too jauntily. "We shared lodgings for two years, and yet I must confess, I don't recollect this habit of storming into my bed-chamber when I am bare-chested and but half dressed. I begin to suspect you of being in love with me, sir."

"Maybe once, Jamie," he answered, soberly, yet he spoke evenly, and without rancor. "But you cured me of that affliction."

"Are you cured, then, Sander?" I asked, quietly.

"Of course. Entirely, and long since." I could even hear fondness in his voice. "Now let me see that hand."

From that moment, there was, between us, a newfound easiness. 'Twas not to last. But while it lasted, I relished it.

He motioned me to stand before the window, while he pulled back its curtain of white muslin. He unwrapped the bandages, and cleaned the pulped mess of flesh in a basin of warm water. He turned my hand over, with utmost tenderness, and inspected my knuckles minutely.

"I am afraid I will have to amputate," he concluded, with mock gravity.

"Aye, and I'll have to break my other hand hitting *you* in the face," I answered. "But honestly, Sander. It does ache something fierce. How long before it will be mended?"

"So you admit you were dunderheaded enough to hit a man." He shook his head. But he rightly perceived, from my stare, that I would tell him no more of the affair.

"Are you going to slap on the frog spawn, or do I have to listen to more of your horse shite?"

"Well, the lacerations have bled profusely, but they are superficial. Yet you have fractured two of your proximal phalanges, and the others are badly contused."

"Once again?"

"I believe you have broken two of your fingers, you great sot. I have no way to tell for certain except by palpation and I fear that might do more harm than good. This is the one that hurts the most, is it not?"

And when he touched my ring finger, ever so lightly, I cried out, despite my best efforts to remain stoic. You know, by now, sympathetic Reader, that my courage is not of the physical sort. At the sound of my distress, Weston ran into the room, just as the doctor was delivering his prescription.

"There is nothing for it. I will tape the last three fingers together, so that the bones may set. There will be no painting for you, my friend, not for at least two weeks, and it would be better if you could wait two more."

"Two weeks? Impossible."

"You will have to let young Weston earn his keep, and do the painting for you."

"But we need fifty pounds. Who will pay a boy to do a man's work?"

"A question worth pondering, I am sure. But first answer me this: What, pray, have you done with your money now?"

Dear, calculating Reader: in front of Weston, I waved away the doctor's question—"You know there are holes in my pockets; try as I might, I can't stitch them up"—though I have since told him the truth and, mind, he was only too pleased to hear that Weston will soon sail for London.)

"Whatever else needs mending, friend, you have two mangled fingers, and you must rest your right hand."

"There must be some better remedy. Can you not instead give me a draft for the pain and get me back to my easel?"

"I might, but I shall not. Instead, I prescribe copious amounts of rum and ale to dull the agony, for you have never been able to paint while drunk. If I were to relieve your suffering with a better nostrum, you would paint. And if you did, the bone would set improperly, and you would spend the rest of your life painting houses, not portraits. So you will have to endure two weeks without painting. Possibly a day or two less, if you can manage to hold a brush with a splint on your hand, for your index finger is the only one not much hurt, which is most fortuitous. But ten days' rest at the least. Truly, Jamie, I forbid it. We all three of us will be out on the street if you ruin your instrument."

Weston, who had been looking on with a countenance exhibiting every sign of concern, attempted to interject.

"Mr. Jameson," he stammered, staring at my hand, as Alexander set to wrapping it. "Mr. Jameson, I can finish Mr. Gallagher's portrait, I'm sure of it, in your style, and no one would be the wiser. If you would but pretend to work on it while he returns for another sitting, I could finish it after he'd left. Give me the chance, sir, please. And the Widow: 'tis only the props and drapery that are left. Please. I must be allowed to earn my keep. You must not risk your hand, sir. You must not!"

His eyes brimmed with tears. How my heart flooded, once again, with love for him. I cannot bear to be the cause of his distress, and again I faulted myself for putting him in the path of a rogue such as Goddard.

I answered, with as much cheer as I could feign, "You're right, lad. The time has come to let your talents soar. But I won't hide your work behind my name. We'll offer Gallagher a 'Weston,' at a discount. Get to work, then. At once!"

Alexander set my arm in a sling, to keep my hand still, and then took the basin and headed back down the stairs to the kitchen. Weston smiled, wiped his face with his sleeve, and made for the painting room. I grabbed my shirt and tugged it over my head. But Weston had taken not five steps when he turned back.

"Except, sir, 'tis the day of the execution, and I must go out, a little before noon. I will be quick, sir."

"To the gallows?" I replied, surprised. I pulled up my stockings, and stepped into my shoes. "Not for the world, lad. You will stay here and paint, and be glad to be spared the memory of your neighbors salivating at the sight of a man suffocating to death."

"But I feel I ought to be there, sir, somehow. What if the murderer is there, or a clue to be discovered, a missing piece to the puzzle Doctor Alexander is striving to solve? We cannot miss it!"

"Please, lad, help me with these buttons," I said, as I struggled with my shirt. He stepped forward, and fastened them—aye, and more expeditiously than I had hoped. Could he not linger, just a little? Still, his hair brushed against my chin, a small thing, you will think, but it near set me aflame.

"Thank you," I said, attempting to collect myself. "You are right, Weston. One of us ought to be there, but it must be I. There is little else I can accomplish, one-handed. Although, I must admit, there is the One Thing."

Dear Reader, I beg your indulgence. For lo, I have once again stumbled into chicanery—another tired, lascivious pun. 'Tis a hard habit to break. But I was so buoyed by Alexander's cure and Weston's touch that I could not help myself: I winked at the lad. I wish I had not.

"Aye, there is that One Thing, which I might manage with my left hand. But I'm afraid I can't possibly shave. Pray, run to the cistern and fill up the basin again, and you can do the honors."

He looked doubtful at this proposition but nodded, picked up the basin, and was back shortly. On the small table by the window, I found the soap and shaving brush, and lathered myself as best I could. I pulled a chair toward the basin, and sat down.

"Get to work, then, lad," I said, handing him the straight razor. He eyed the gleaming blade.

"Sir, I've never shaved a man before. What if I cut you?"

"Then I'll bleed, you little cur. So don't."

He set about the task, gingerly. With one hand he lifted my chin; with the other he started at my throat, and drew the blade upward. His nearness was no small pleasure but he minded his task a little too cautiously. Again and again he drew the razor across my face, slowly, a whisker at a time.

"Weston, mark me: I would be shaved before the sun sets."

"The more haste the worse speed, sir, as you so oft tell me," he answered, biting his lip.

"True, true, Weston. They stumble that run fast," I answered, suppressing a smile, for grinning seemed a dangerous thing to do. "Still, a wee bit more alacrity will do no harm, I'm sure."

He continued, only a little less glacially. When he was nearly finished, he paused and asked, "Sir, can I not come along with you to the execution?"

"Zounds, Weston! No, no, and no again. You have work to do here. And even if you did not, 'twould be dangerous. Every drunkard, rogue, and pickpocket in the city will be on the streets today. I have let you out of my sight, and into the path of danger, one too many times. And I am unhappy enough with my task without having to watch your backside all day."

Looking altogether glum, he began a final pass with the razor.

"I must meet someone there, sir. I cannot say more. Please, sir, I cannot fail him."

So startled was I that I flinched, and the blade caught my ear. Twas only a trifle, a tiny nick, but his words, from which I could draw nothing but an overhasty conclusion, made me feel as though the blood had been let from my veins by a thousand leeches. For an instant, and another, I was left speechless. When at last I stood and spoke, I thundered.

"Great God, Weston, have you no shame? An assignation at an execution? Just how far have I misjudged you? The cock and pullet, my ass. And to think that I have whiled away hours worrying about your innocence. I will not have you leave this house!"

Wiping my face with a towel as I strode into the hall, I called down the stairwell to the doctor below. "Alexander, see that Weston stays here till I return. And don't make him any speeches about *Moral Sentiments*, for he has none. Lecture him on betrayal, if you like. But keep him here. If I see his contemptible countenance at the gallows, I will not answer for my actions: I'll string him up myself."

There are not as many places in Boston to get a drink just past dawn as I would wish for, but, on such occasions, one is enough. Blessed

Mary, but my hand hurt. As I knew the Blue Herring would be closed, I started off in the opposite direction. I wandered up Hanover Street, turning onto Prince, with Gulliver at my heel. The lanes were full of cartmen and carriages, ringing out the clatter of hooves and wheels. But not a single tavern had yet opened its doors. At Gee's shipyard I found a flurry of activity, for sailors and stevedores work all hours. Still I didn't find what I wanted, and I grew chilled. I stuffed both hands in the pockets of my coat, not without wincing.

After an hour of rambling, I stopped to buy an apple from a vendor on the wharf. Then the dog and I walked along the water to Hudson's Point, where Gulliver chased gulls while I sat on a pier for many minutes, looking across the river toward Charlestown, where the Lamberts lived. How must the lovely Louisa be spending her morning? Not ducking out for a dalliance—"Just a moment, dear brother, I must dash to an execution to meet a man, whom I best not disappoint!"—of that much I could be sure. Would she be reading to her nieces and nephews? Taking tea in the parlor?

And I wondered, not for the first time: What would it be like to share a house with a woman like that, so prudent, so self-possessed, so even-tempered? It could only be what she is, above all: serene.

One day soon I will elect serenity.

I will.

Today I elect intoxication.

After nearly an hour watching the ferry make its journey across the Charles—if I marry Louisa we will have to live in town, for I would not rely on a boat to leave my neighborhood—I resumed my wandering and found myself at the Green Grapes just as the tavern-keeper was opening its door.

"Surprised to see anyone 'ere just now," said the publican, as he served me a flagon of beer, and put a bowl of water on the floor for the dog.

"It's never too early to ale what ails you," I answered.

He looked at me blankly.

"Of course, sir, of course. I only meant, everyone has headed to the Neck, for the Negro's hangin' is set for noon."

"Aye, but it cannot be close to noon yet."

"Well, sir, the sun is very high indeed."

I have all but worn a hole in the soles of my shoes wasting the morning away, and now I am to miss the execution after all?

"If I leave now, by foot, will I reach the hanging place in time?"

"I doubt it, sir. But you could get a ride easily enough," he answered, pointing out the tavern window. There, in the street, I saw what I can only call a stampede, such as I, who am no country boy, have rarely seen before. Twas no ordinary traffic, for everyone, whether by foot, by cart, or by carriage, was traveling in the same direction: toward the Neck.

I left the Green Grapes and, just as its proprietor had predicted, I encountered little difficulty in securing passage, for a shilling, on an ox-cart. Its driver spoke not a word, but urged on his animal with his whip. I sat in the cart, with my back to the man. Gulliver trotted along beside us, easily outpacing the ox. We made our way along the harbor, from Ship Street to Fish, and then south, through the center of town, past the Town House, out Marlborough and Newbury, all the way to the Neck. Tributaries of traffic merged into a river of travelers. I'd have been wiser to wait on my liquor, for by now the streets were lined with pushcarts ladling rum and gin. Such were the refreshments for the day's entertainment. When we came within sight of the gallows, I hopped off the oxcart, steadying myself with my good hand.

"Don't understand why they're not burning 'im," my oxcart man said to me as I tendered my shilling. "None deserves it as much as a slave what killed his master."

"Aye, but he confessed," I countered. "And the judge had to reduce the sentence."

"No *had to* about it, guv'nor," he answered. "Burn 'im, I say. Look what they did to those rebels in Antigua, sir. Ripped their bodies to pieces before they burned 'em. Turned 'em on the wheel, they did, and starved 'em on the gibbet. Hanging's too good for 'em, I say."

I left him shaking his head, regretting his magistrates' moderation. I gave Gulliver a whistle, and passed through the city gates on foot, downing a dram or two—or was it five?—along the way.

There were, perhaps, four thousand spectators: the face of Boston. Men and women, the old and the young. White and black, for many masters—*most*—had commanded their slaves to attend. Certainly there was more mass of humanity at Cicero's hanging than had paraded through the streets for Bradstreet's funeral. It sank my spirits when they were already low.

Sunk, too, were my shoes, for the Neck is little better than a salt marsh. Tis but a quarter mile wide, with the river on one side and the harbor on the other, bisected by a single, lonely road, rows of wheel-grooves carved into a pasture of mud. Across its narrowest point stretches the high fortification wall that Bostonians trust for their defense against enemies. Just beyond the wall—beyond the pale, they would have it—lies a clay pond, much frequented by the brickmakers who would put a new face on this wooden town. And just beyond the clay pit, on a little rising spot of ground, stands the gallows.

I have gotten this far—have I not?—though I have labored mightily to blur my vision with drink. But if you would have a more sober view—for which you must possess a stouter heart, or at least a stronger stomach—then I would direct you to train your gaze upon the west side of the road. There you would see, beside the gallows, an iron gibbet, for Cicero was not only to be hanged, but caged, displayed to every ship that sailed by, his corpse pecked by gulls and gnawed by maggots till it be wholly consumed.

The crowd grew restless for the arrival of the condemned man.

I distracted myself with the thought of a prospect I might paint from this spot, looking back at the town, or toward the islands in the harbor. I am not a landscape man, neither by trade, nor by inclination. Human nature fascinates me more than any other of God's creations. But this would be a fine study for Weston, one day. The light, from the east, a particular challenge.

No, I will not think of him. Not here, not now. He can learn landscape in London.

As I struggled to rein in my thoughts, Gulliver set to barking, not ten yards away, at a tall man in a black surtout.

"Get him off of me! Get this monster off of me!" I heard William Bradstreet screech, as Gulliver near knocked him down. How the hound had sniffed out his worst enemy in such a mob, I cannot say, for I never trained him to hunt.

"Gulliver, down!" I cried, and was amazed to find that he was, for once, obedient.

I expected Bradstreet to be enraged, but as I grabbed the dog by the collar, the lawyer smiled at me.

"Jameson, so glad to have met you here," he said, sneering. "An auspicious day, is it not? My father's murder, at last avenged."

"If you find comfort in it, sir," I said.

"O, I do, Jameson. I do. Men find comfort in the strangest places, do they not? The most *unnatural* places."

"I miss your meaning, sir."

"I think not, Jameson. I think you know exactly what I mean. Enoch Goddard has told me all about you and that debauched apprentice of yours. The deputy came to inform me that you had assaulted him"—he stared at my sling, and smiled—"though I see you fared the worse for the battle. But I convinced him to let that matter rest, for though he is a constable, the penalty for battery is merely a fine, and I would have a tighter leash around you."

"You cannot mean to credit a word this Goddard says."

"O, I can. And I do. It wounded Deputy Goddard's virtue to speak of it, but I persuaded him to share with me his shocking tale. Finding you and that boy together, stuck together, I might say. Both he and his wife have been so good as to sign depositions, as eye-witnesses to the crime"—here he reached into the pocket of his cloak, and pulled out the documents, which he pretended to peruse—"and I have drawn up warrants for your arrest which I could have Amos Quincy sign this afternoon, if I chose. Do you know, Jameson, that sodomy is a hanging offense in Massachusetts?"

So caught off guard was I that I could do nothing more than stare, though I listed a little, for I was feeling my liquor more by the minute. Gulliver was more eloquent: he growled, adding a snarl for good measure.

"O yes," the Wily Bastard continued. "Hanging is the punishment for 'the detestable and abominable sin of buggery, which is contrary to the very light of nature,' as the statute says. And our forefathers were wise enough to append a bit of scripture to the law, quoting from Leviticus: 'If a man lies with a man as one lies with a woman, both of them have done what is detestable. They must be put to death; their blood will be on their own head.' In short, Jameson, we might as well keep the gallows up for a while, don't you agree? You painters are all libertines, of the worst kind."

I meant to tread carefully, Reader, for while I thought he was bluffing, like many a sharp at cards, I could not be sure, and he had threatened grave peril. But as you have already had occasion to observe, I am but a poor governor of my tongue, and far too amused by my own wit, vices that worsen with drink.

"Bradstreet, Bradstreet," I began. "Surely you know the saying, 'One swallow does not a summer make'? Do not deduce the generality from the specific, sir. Call me a libertine, if you will, but do not judge all artists by my behavior."

He stared back at me, dumbfounded.

"One swallow, Bradstreet?" I winked. "Does not a summer—"

"How comes it that we are speaking of birds, you idiot?" he fumed.

The joke had failed, and just as well, for this was no joking matter. I strived to sober myself.

"How right you are, sir. Birds are neither here nor there," I resumed. "Sodomy is our topic, is it not? I'm afraid I must heartily dispute your claim that it offends nature."

"Then you admit it, you sodomite!"

"I do and I don't, sir. As to your particular charge, against my conduct with my innocent apprentice, I'm afraid I must disappoint you."

"I am hardly disappointed, dauber. For I credit the word of the estimable Deputy Goddard over your own."

"You don't swallow my tale, then? Ach, and I thought it would go down easily. Still, my late chastity—unwanted, I assure you—offers defense enough against this mischief. I've lain with no man, boy, woman, or beast—not a one, sir—since I washed up on these rocky shores. Aye, you might mistake my lodgings for a monastery."

"A bedlam, is more like it."

"Maybe so. Still, what matters my bed to you, sir? Have your courts so little urgent business? It's been more than a century since you hanged a man for sodomy in these parts, has it not? Would you have a man killed for love?"

"*Love*, is it?" he laughed. "Jameson, you amuse me. And you amuse the gentry of this town, and especially we stalwart men of the Red Hen. We—some of us, anyway—have a use for a face-painter here in New-England, and few enough to choose from. So I will spare you, *for now*." He returned the papers to his pocket. "But if you cross me, know this: I will have you and your little darling brought up on charges, and no court in the land will grant you mercy."

While I considered my reply—I leaned toward letting Gulliver get away from me, accidentally, mind—we were interrupted by the cacophony of the crowd at the arrival of Sheriff Kettrell and the cart carrying not only Cicero, but Hannah and Phebe, who were meant—and would be forced—to watch. They passed not twenty yards from where Bradstreet and I stood as they made their way to the gallows, where the holy trinity of justice awaited them: the triune person of Benjamin Finley, Edward Easton, and Chambers Cotton. Whether the law requires them to see their orders carried out, or whether they gathered for the sport of it, I cannot say.

The vile Goddard—now more than ever the object of my detestation—steered the cart, horsewhip and reins in one hand, pipe in the other. Hannah carried Phebe in her arms, as if she would never let her go. The girl, who had been furloughed from the Manufactory House to witness this dreadful spectacle, hugged her mother with a desperation the sight of which set me to aching. Cicero was chained, hand and foot, his entire aspect grim and determined. As they passed, the crowd grew still louder. Twas a reprise of the ride to the Town House the day of their trial, only with many more in attendance, and the mood more boisterous, even jubilant.

Bradstreet scurried away, found his mother and sister, and joined arms with them to follow the cart. With no more ceremony than a kick to the prisoner's back, Kettrell and Goddard dragged Cicero up the steps to the gallows. Hannah collapsed into the cart, Phebe near tumbling from her arms. But Goddard climbed on board with them, and hauled Hannah up to standing. He yanked Phebe's head by the hair, and turned her so that she had no choice but to see where Cicero walked. I thought, again, about what Alexander had said to me: "It is nothing more than judicial murder, Jamie. He goes to his death to save Hannah, and all that remains is for us to insure that he does not die in vain."

Behind the Sheriff and Cicero, Jabez Appleton, vicar of King's Chapel, and Daniel Easton, his young associate, hovered close at hand. The public executioner, a beefy man dressed in black from his boots to his gruesome hood, mounted the platform. (I have painted the face 'neath that mask. I know I have. It can be none other than the coroner, Thaddeus Mason, a man who must relish death, for he surely profits by it; he'll have earned two fees from Samuel Bradstreet's murder.) He and Kettrell bolted Cicero into the gibbet, an iron cage that enclosed him from head to toe. Before making fast the bars, the executioner placed the noose over Cicero's head, throwing the other end of the rope over the gallows arm.

Reader, have you had occasion to look upon Hogarth's *Idle Prentice Executed at Tyburn*? The pickpockets and the biscuit hawkers. The sham preachers, the bloodthirstiness, the weeping mother. The clamor. But Hogarth's is a picture of public order compared to the grotesque scene at Boston Neck on this dark day. I ask you, Sir: Whither Reason when Justice places a man in a cage?

Reverend Appleton, a dapper old man in a neat white wig, stepped to the front of the platform. He raised two spindly hands to hush the crowd. Yet out of this meager form arose a booming tenor. When he spoke, I found I was close enough to hear him—aye, better than I wanted.

"I preach today from Job, chapter fifteen, verse twenty-one: *A dreadful Sound is in his Ears*. And who is it that has the dreadful sound in his ears? Tis the wicked man, who travaileth in pain all his days. Yea, the pain of a wicked man is worse than the pain of a woman in travail. For when she is delivered, she remembereth her anguish no more. But the pain of a wicked man hath no end at all. And who is the wicked man? Tis the man who would corrupt the order of the world: the child who rebels against its father, the wife who rebels against her husband, the subject who rebels against his king. *The slave who rebels against his master*."

He continued with this, his dreadful sermon, for more minutes than I cared to count. Behind him, I could see young Easton pleading with Cicero; praying for him, Bible in hand; begging him to confess not just to his crime but to his sins, so that the gates of Heaven might yet open to him. Cicero shook his head, and said not a word. While Easton continued his ministrations, Cicero looked away, casting his stoic glance from face to face, through the crowd. Finally, he found me, and it seemed, truly, it seemed, as if he wanted to say something. He looked to

Hannah and Phebe, and once again back at me. Thrice more he made this motion. I could scarcely be sure of his meaning, but I hazard this was his last request: *Save them*. I nodded, and made sure he saw it.

If you ask me for more of this scene, Reader, I cannot oblige you. Remember, I had rather left this page blank, or spilled my pot of ink upon it. Suffice to say: the executioner did his work. Hannah let out one short shriek of agony, followed by a longer wail, and the little girl sobbed, and hid her face in her mother's embrace as best she could. The poor man's body twitched for a full minute, inside that iron cage, and then the whole monstrous apparatus swung, buffeted by a chill wind from across the sea.

Alas, that was hardly the end of the spectacle whose principal aim was to terrorize the slaves of this city. After Cicero had gasped his last breath, the executioner, helped by the Sheriff, hooked the gibbet to an iron rod fastened to the gallows arm, while Appleton spoke again.

"To all those slaves here today: take warning from the fate of your unhappy brother, who will hang on this spot till his flesh shall rot and his bones crumble. There is, in many of you, a fondness for freedom. But in punishment for the sin of Ham, God has marked his descendants—your portion of mankind—for bondage. He entrusts ours with your care. And think, bondsmen, what should your liberty gain you? If you were free, you would not live near so comfortably as you do, yoked in an easy servitude. Let Cicero stand as a monument unto you, of the error of your ways."

To this, "Huzzah!" was the ear-splitting answer, from four thousand mouths, a still more terrible echo of the squawks of gulls. I turned from the scene and made my way through the crowd, back to the road, where I spilled my vomit into the muck. I could stop neither my gullet nor my ears. I picked up my pace, my shoes squelching through the mud, Gulliver tight to my heel. But all that long walk back to town, I was beset—hounded and dogged—by that awful, dreadful sound.

Letter XVI.

September the 27th, 1764

Elizabeth,

I wrote you only yesterday, and I dare not overwhelm you with my news, especially when your sympathy with my pursuits grows thin. But I know you will be eager to learn of my father's answer to my plea, and of the terrible trials of my tiny sister Phebe, and of the fate of the man she knew as her father. Hers is a greater sorrow than either you or I will ever face. Oh, Lizzie. Weep no more for fallen Fanny; save your tears for the true tragedies of this miserable world.

A day full of rage and pain and murder, a day passed 'neath clear azure skies that concealed the tears God must have wept: truly, it has been a day fit for a requiem. Ever the high church man in a low church town, my father loved the old Latin Mass set to music that matched its bloody baroque character. Scarlatti's *Missa pro defunctis*: he had heard it sung in his youth, while on the Grand Tour in Rome, and often mused on the beauties of its D-minor harmonies. To hear a daughter dutifully plunk away at it on the spinet was but a pale imitation, he said. Ah, Father, you were right. Those ponderous chords! Had Boston a score of glorious bassos, and were I their choirmaster, I should ask them to bow their heads as they sang to you the haunting strains of the *Dias irae*: day of wrath, day of woe, day of the dead.

My master forbade me to attend Cicero's execution. "I will not have you leave this house," he thundered, the last notes of a crescendo of contempt. I watched him leave upon his grim errand, my cheeks hot with anger, my fists balled at my sides, a scream barely stifled in my throat. After I saw him turn the corner, I paced the floor of the painting room for several minutes more, trying to compose myself for the next round of pleading. If Jameson would not allow me my errand, I must entreat his dearest friend. I reasoned that Doctor Alexander, having known the barbarism of close confinement, would see fit to release me from mine. When I heard his footsteps upon the stairs, thoughts of rescue quieted my heart.

"Weston, how long would you wait to make your case?" he asked, preempting my supplication with his own wry smile. "For you cannot tarry if you are to grab the gold and get back to your easel before your master trudges home from the hanging."

"Gold, Doctor? What can you mean?" I stammered. "You imagine a different purpose for my errand than Mr. Jameson does, but surely 'tis just as fanciful."

"Save your fibs, Weston," the doctor ordered, his tone barely heated above the temperature of indifference. "Hoard them up like a treasure—like fifty pieces of gold, you might say. For there are those whose very lives depend upon your role-play. But I assure you, there is no need to squander that capital upon me, nor any chance I would credit it. You cannot doubt it: I know full well who you are, and have for some time."

A minute passed before I found my voice.

"Sir, yes. I do, I realize, sir, that you discovered last week the secret of my sex, an unhappy accident for which I curse the dog. And I thank you, sir, for keeping that knowledge close. Truly, I am grateful for a kindness I can scarce understand."

"Indeed. But you have misheard me. I did not say I know *what* you are, but rather *who*: you are a woman of parts, fallen hard and far. From the heights, *ut ita dicam*, as it were. Perhaps, my dear, the time has come for me to call you *Miss Fanny Easton*?"

I began to tremble.

"Steady, Miss Easton. You shall not swoon your way out from under the truth."

"But . . . but . . . who can have told you, Doctor?"

"Why, you did, of course. I have read the copies of your correspondence that you keep in that precious letter book of yours, a transgression for which I hope you will one day forgive me."

My legs wobbled, and I crumpled into the chair where Louisa Beaujardin had lately sat, swanlike and imperturbable. Alexander's eyes held mine fast.

"Tut, tut: no fainting, Miss Easton. You make a poor Clarissa, and we have no time for histrionics that ill become you."

"I should think you might feel some shame in rifling the intimate effects of a person who trusted you," I said, regaining my voice.

"There you are wrong, Miss Easton. You have never trusted me. Nor I you."

"But Doctor, are we not bound by our shared purpose? We are both investigating Bradstreet's murder. How do you advance our cause by purloining my letters?"

"*Our* cause, Miss Easton? We have different causes, and different stratagems. You would save your sister. She is your *Aitia monotate*. Your sole cause."

"And what is your purpose, then?"

"I, too, would like to see Phebe freed, of course, if it proves possible. But I am about a great work, trying to solve the mystery of iniquity, and I will take my clues where I find them."

"But . . . in my letters?"

"Yes, even there. Yours is a sad story, though not near so woeful as you suppose. You have lost a great deal, some of it plundered from you. But more of your happiness you have willfully cast away, through your pride and your prejudice. You misplace your affections."

"Do you speak of Mr. Cummings, then, or is it your design to warn me off Jamie?" I asked.

"I mean neither your first painting master, nor your second, who deserves the small honor of having his apprentice call him by his proper name. No, I refer to your father, green-eyed as envy, though cooler in humor. I am heartened to read that your friend Miss Partridge has helped you to find the mettle to seek your birthright. Bravo, Miss Easton."

He clapped, his gloved hands meeting softly, a gesture that betrayed some small trace of admiration.

"But I wonder: How do you mean to claim your prize from Justice Easton, today of all days?"

Taking a deep breath, I drew myself up.

"I have planned it to the last detail, Doctor. I will dress as a gentlewoman should, borrowing some of the vestments Mr. Jameson keeps in the closet, for his female sitters. Then I shall make my way to the Neck, where I'll spy my father readily enough, standing in some place high enough to reflect his station. I will approach him, lift my veil, and force him to regard me, and he will hand over the purse before I relate to his fellow justices the story of my shame—and his. That is how I mean to claim my prize, a prize I shall deliver up for Phebe's redemption. Does this stratagem meet with your approval, Professor?"

"Do not be smug, Miss Easton. You have devised a plan, and a thorough one—thoroughly wrongheaded. You heard your master: the streets are full of rogues and pickpockets, each of them drunk with equal parts of gin and bloodlust: no place for a female Quixote to gambol about, tilting after windmills."

"I wonder at your concern, Doctor. How can I think of my own comfort when the very lives of Hannah and Phebe depend upon our actions?"

"Correct, and a clever girl you are to point it out: you are not the subject of this particular chapter in the book of Fate. The danger to your person may haunt poor love-mad Jameson. He would keep us both here, locked up, to spare us the bruising world. That will not do. No, my concerns lie several rounds ahead in what we might imagine as a game of whist. Do you play?"

"Only a little, sir. Tis not thought a polite game for young women."

"Ah, yes. Not ladylike. Still, you know the fundamentals well enough to follow my conceit. In this game, lives hang in the balance. Our hand is spotty, and we cannot know our opponents' cards. Thus we must hold back our ace—our *queen*, if you will—till we have played more tricks. I trust you take my meaning."

"Not entirely, sir."

"Let me speak plainer, then," he condescended. "You have two hidden assets, Miss Easton: your sex, and your rank. Hold on to those cards. Where Jameson is concerned, I will give you some latitude, for I would fain keep myself at a distance from your master's amorous affairs. But as for your father, just now, he must not see you."

"What then, Doctor? Would you keep me captive here, you, who have known chains?"

"Do not *dare* compare your captivity to mine! Your shackles are largely of your own manufacture, and you shall know no other kind, no matter how far down you manage to drag yourself." His contempt hardened into fury, and I half feared he would wheel around toward the hearth and seize the poker. But with a deep indraw of breath, the doctor reclaimed the madman.

"No, Miss Easton, I would merely suggest a different plan. Today's errand into the wilderness is far better suited to Francis Weston. Do not pretty yourself, my lady; take the opposite tack. Wear your filthiest clothes. Pull a greasy cap low upon your brow. Disappear into the streets. No, not the streets: take the Common. Thread your way through the soldiers' camp. Fall in behind the cowherds, slinking eastward through paths and the haymows, and only at the last moment turning toward the place of execution."

"And then, Sir? Can you think my own father would not recognize me, speaking to him at close range in the light of noon? Do you fancy a mere cap will prove disguise enough? As you know from reading my letter book, when he last set eyes on me, months ago, I could have passed for an anatomist's skeleton. But I am more myself with every day that passes."

Tis true, Lizzie, though I fancy I look less like the girl you once knew, than like the mother I lost.

"Of course he should know you. Which is why you shall not speak to him. Find an apprentice to do your work, as you have done so much of Jameson's. There should be plenty of desperate souls to choose from in the crowd. Pick one who resembles the urchin you were when my friend dragged you in from the cobbles. No, select one younger still. But above all, find a hungry boy. Promise him a bright gold guinea in return for the kind of cozening he does every day. And do it *now*, for Cicero's life will soon be ended."

With that he led me down the stairs, set a cap upon my head, and pushed me out the door.

"Weston, wait," the doctor called before I had ventured more than a few steps. "Your face," he said, a note of kindness softening his voice. Scraping a handful of dirt from the dooryard, he gently begrimed my cheeks and chin.

The traffic was thick along Queen Street, but when I reached the Common, I left the great mass of that human herd behind. The army's encampment, canvas tents pitched in neat rows, was near deserted, cookfires gone cold. Past the camp, cows and sheep outnumbered the thrill-seekers straggling toward the hanging place, and I found pockets of space through which I could sprint. I rejoined Orange Street a little north of the milestone marking the distance from the Town House. Just beyond lay the city wall, its heavy doors flung open to the crowd. By the time the gallows came into view, rivulets of sweat had mingled with the dirt upon my face.

I spied neither Jamie nor his great Gulliver in the crush, and I thanked God for our distance just then. But the three justices, a daub of black behind a stripe of redcoats, were visible enough.

As I struggled to read my father's countenance, I felt a hand graze my backside. I spun around in a rage, visions of Enoch Goddard flooding my senses. I seized the offending arm, only to discover that 'twas stick-thin, and belonged to a ragged boy of no more than six. He stared at me through a fringe of matted black hair, his round, dark eyes made larger by hunger.

"Please, mum," he whispered. "I just wanted to nab a coin, for me brothers. Three of 'em, littler than me, and not enough food to go round. No money since the war what killed my da, you see. Ma sews, but t'ain't hardly enough. Anna, me wee sister, she died of the hunger last winter. Can you help us? If you will or if you won't, either way, I beg ye, you canna call the sentry. He'd throw us all in the Manufactory House, for sure, and we'd starve there, we would."

"Sir, little one. Call me sir. And fear not, I'll not summon the watchman. Perhaps I can help you avoid the Manufactory House, for I would not wish it upon a dog."

He stared at me, his terror turning to puzzlement.

"Look there, child . . . what did you say your name was?"

"Ben, mum. Uh, sir."

"Ben, do you see those black-robed men standing over there, 'neath the gallows?" I said, indicating the justices by the direction of my chin.

"Them three what looks like crows, you mean?" he asked.

I laughed.

"Vultures, I thought. But yes, you're right, Ben: lesser birds of prey. Crows they are, three black birds. The one on the right—don't trouble yourself with his name—has something of mine. He brought it here, but he wants to make a game of giving it to me."

"What sort of game, mum?" Ben asked, uncertain.

"Sir, Ben, sir. Do you know your letters?"

"Yes'm. I can even read, a little."

"Well, the game goes like this. You must sneak up to the man, just as you tried to do with me. But don't pick his pocket! No, you shall surprise him with the rhyme that is our password—I'll teach it to you. And then he'll hand you the treasure, and you'll slip back to me, quick as a wink, your pathway hidden by the crowd."

"Pardon me, mum. Er, sir. But them black crows looks hungry. And I'd have to get past them bloody-backs. What if they catch me up?"

"You're too fast, Ben. Trust me, they've all got bigger prey on their minds. The rhyme's the key, I tell you. And then, when you return, you shall have two golden guineas to set before your mother and your brothers."

"Two *guineas*, mum?"

"Sir! Yes, Ben. Your mother will sweep her little hero up in her arms, and your brothers will sleep well, on full bellies. I promise."

"What's the rhyme, then, sir?" he asked.

"Tis simple, Ben. One line. *F.E. must have her fee.* Can you repeat it?"

"Effie will have 'er fee?"

"Slower, Ben. Two alphabet letters, not a name: F and E."

"F and E," he repeated. "F., E. . . . F.E. must have 'er fee. F.E. must have 'er fee!" he said, clearly this time, and proudly.

"Wonderful, Ben. No need to shout. Just speak your rhyme slowly and distinctly, right past the soldiers, and the great green-eyed crow will play his part."

"Are you sure, mum? Tis all over boys down there, it is. Why me?"

"Sir! And yes, Ben. I'm sure. He shall play with you, and you alone, because *you're* the only one who knows the rhyme. Say it but once, and only to the rightmost crow. Then fast back here with the prize."

It took little Ben not thirty seconds to reach the platform. I next glimpsed him when he sprang, as if from nowhere, through the tiny space separating the grenadiers standing before my father. My father startled, but soon resumed his pose. Staring straight ahead, he made for his pocket with the smallest of motions. And then Ben disappeared again. My father scanned the crowd but he knew not where to look.

"I got it, mum! Effie's fee!" Ben panted as he popped up before me once again. He handed me a soft suede pouch, about the size and weight of a pear.

"Ben, what a perfect job you've done," I said, not bothering to correct his insistence upon my gender as I mussed his dirty mop of hair. "Now you must have *your* fee, my young accomplice."

I reached into the soft leather purse and handed him his well-earned commission. When he saw the glint of gold, he dropped to one knee in thanks, a gesture that nearly made me weep.

"Ben, I would do more to help you if I could. I live on Queen Street, in the little brick house just across from Cabot's apothecary, 'neath the sign of the painter's arms. If you should need me, look for me there, under the name of Weston."

"Thank you, mum, uh, sir," he mumbled, looking now at his own bare feet. And then he vanished.

Purse in hand, I effected my own disappearance. Barely had I regained the Common when the bells began to clang from every steeple for miles around the town, a proper New-England version of the *Dies irae*, all Puritan rectitude and no redemption. They tolled in time with the last beats of Cicero's heart, as the crowd's pitiless roar soon reminded me. The ringing continues yet, in the ears of,

Fanny Easton.

CHAPTER 18

Of Hard-Won Gains and Immeasurable Losses

Why do I bother scraping my shoes when Gulliver gambols through the door with paws as grubby as pig's feet? I grabbed him by the collar, pulled him outside, and turned back into the hall, glad to be in from the cold. I stepped into the kitchen to warm myself by the fire without even waiting to take off my coat, only to be stopped in my muddy tracks by the sight of Alexander and Weston, standing at the kitchen table, counting coins.

With growing distress, I inspected the scene. Every detail of my apprentice's appearance told a story. The same story. The story toward which my late suspicion tended. His shoes were as muddy as mine, spoiled, no doubt, with the muck of the Neck. His clothing was in disarray: his waistcoat half buttoned, his shirttails trailing from his breeches. His small hand held a purse from which he had just emptied a glittering pile of sovereigns, a king's treasure. His face was filthy and flushed, his smooth pale cheeks patched with pink that shone through the smudges.

I made no effort to hide my rage, nor could I, had I tried.

"Didn't even bother to tuck in your shirt, eh, Weston? Your lover made quick work of you, then. I hope you were paid for the task, and not the time. A boy's tight arse, here in pious Boston, must command near a bride-price."

He gave me a look of stunned fury. Alexander stepped toward me, blocking my path to the lad.

"Jamie, leave off," he began.

"Leave off, Sander? Leave *off*? I told you to keep him here, so don't vex me more by denying my right to my rage."

Behind him, Weston, trembling, started to weep, hot angry tears, without a trace of sorrow in them.

I neared the table, picked up a pile of coins, and fingered them with my left hand.

"O, but this *is* good news: we might survive the Currency Act yet, what with the value of Weston's backside. Tis a clever kind of alchemy, isn't it, Doctor, turning flesh into gold? We'll surely prosper, friends, in these hard times. That is, unless Parliament contemplates banning the exchange of filthy lucre. Already there are laws against sodomy—capital laws, as I was reminded just this morning, by none other than the Deputy Attorney General. But perhaps you know that statute, young Weston?"

Alexander grabbed my arm—"Jamie, I mean it, *stop*, man"—but I shook him off.

"Sander, 'tis no business of yours."

I took another step to reach Weston, who spoke not a word, but cried like a child caught red-handed, and still too proud to apologize.

"My God, lad," I spat out, as I stood over him. "Who have you sold yourself to now?"

I waited, but his only answer was more tears. I pounded my fist—my *right* fist—on the table. My instant regret of this action you will readily imagine. I doubled over, hugging my hand to my chest, and screamed at the pain. At all of that long day's agony.

When I straightened myself and spoke again, I near seethed with wrath.

"Weston, I won't have you in my house. Your indenture spells it out in black and white: no fornication, you ha'penny bumfuck. Pack your things, and get out of here. At once!"

With a parting look at Alexander, the lad ran from the room and fled up the stairs, choking with sobs.

"You will have to go after him, you fool," Alexander said. "Those coins cost the boy, Jamie, they cost him more than you know, but they did not cost him what you think, and they will buy a child's freedom. You are so far wrong about him that I cannot consider your blindness anything less than willful. Remember, friend: 'If love be blind, love cannot hit the mark.'"

"What the deuce do you know about love, you mad Mercutio?"

"I know this, you half-wit Hamlet: you are wrong about Weston. I had rather stay well out of whatever lies between the two of you. But I can assure you, of what you suspect, he is blameless."

I reeled at his words.

"Tell me this much, at least: Are you certain the lad has not bartered his innocence?"

"Can you still believe in innocence, Jamie? Would that it were so simple."

How long can it take to climb three stories? Too long. I took the steps to the garret two at a time. The door was open, but I hesitated at the threshold, suddenly shy, overcome with remorse for all I'd said, and unable to imagine how to unsay it. I leaned against the low doorframe, bending my neck to make room for my head. For a minute, I could not speak. The room was cold, a solitary log lit in the fire. A single caned chair sat before a rickety trestle table covered with charcoal sketches. By the far wall, in front of a narrow bedstead, my apprentice stood with his back to me, stuffing his small satchel with his scant belongings, a few bits of clothing and a leather-bound book—a letter book, I supposed. He shivered. There was between us only the sound of breath.

"I'm sorry, Weston," I offered at last. "Sander insists that I am wrong about you, and I cannot but believe him. There's no need for you to go, lad."

"Yes, there is," he replied, his back still to me. "There's every reason."

"Please. Don't make me beg you. But for God's sake, tell me how you came by those coins."

"I cannot, sir. Your rage proves that I should not . . . I had thought to tell you, but now—"

"Why not? Dear God, what am I to think?" I demanded. "Disabuse me of drawing lewd conclusions, for once. Who *are* you, Francis Weston? You turn up at my door half starved, a dusty, desperate, spindle-shanked orphan, your hands thick with calluses. And yet you have been fine-schooled. Sweet Jesus, you hold your own with Sander. You get letters from ladies with elegant penmanship. And your brush, lad, ah, your brush. I have lived near twice as long as you, and traveled far wider, and never have I seen more natural genius. Untutored, or tutored badly—no doubt by your master's father's tutor's son of a bitch—for it falls to me to unteach you all his errors."

I took a step toward him, only to pause at the table, where my face stared back at me from pages and pages of sketches. I ran my fingers over them. Sweet Jesus, but my apprentice knows how to pin a man. At least this man, dear Reader. At least this miserable wreck of a man.

I cleared my throat.

"Your talent was ill directed by this first imposter, and remains undisciplined. You take up faces when you have yet to master fruit, and paints when you have yet to conquer crayons. And yet your pen and your brush, even these nubs of charcoal, near burst with promise—aye, Weston, with genuine *eminence*—though you might be more careful"—I looked up from the papers, so near to the hearth, and our eyes met—"to keep such things a little farther from the flame."

He began to speak, but I cut him off.

"Aye, lad, your brush is full of promise, and not for the lowly work of a portrait painter. I want worthier subjects for you—history, allegory—and canvases as wide as your talent. My pride will admit that I am an improvement over your first instructor—a vast improvement, lad—"

"Then maybe I could stay, sir?"

"Good. Unpack your bag. But you cannot stay forever. The time has come to tell you: I have decided to send you to London, to the Society of Artists. I have already written to Joshua Reynolds, and he expects you."

"To train with Reynolds? When do we sail, sir?" he asked, eyes wide.

"Not 'we,' Weston. You. Alone. In six weeks' time, on the *Flying Squirrel*."

"But, sir! I cannot leave you!" he said, his eyes welling with tears. "I have so much left to learn from you."

I was all exasperation. "What, you would let me toss you out onto the street, to live by your wits, or worse, but you will not allow me send you to London, to live in comfort—on my purse, no less? You have much to learn, lad, that I grant, but I have nothing left to teach you."

"I don't want to go. Please, sir." His tears now flowed freely, and he sat on the edge of the bed and put his head in his hands.

"What you *want* does not come into it, Weston," I said, raising my voice. "You are indented as my apprentice for more than four years still, and where I send you, you will go. If you refuse, and leave now, I will pay Edes to advertise you a runaway, and get you back by hook or by crook."

"And would you brand me with an R then?"

Reader, know: I despise sarcasm. How could I answer this? I have said it before: I am no master of men. My threats are ever idle. Except that I *will* send this lad far from here. Far from me.

I sat down beside him and slipped my right arm around his narrow shoulders.

Comfort, comfort, Reader; I will stop at comfort.

He leaned into me—and God help me—I kissed his brow.

"Weston, Weston, my love," I said, gentle, passionate. "How did you come by those coins?"

"I cannot say, sir. I cannot," he answered quietly and with an aching sadness. "And what does it matter? Whether I tell you or not, you will turn me out, alone, either upon these streets or onto the gangplank of some London-bound schooner."

"I will. I swear it. I will," I whispered, as much to myself as to him.

Comfort, comfort. I would stop at comfort.

But I could not.

I lifted his face in my hands, and covered his cheeks with kisses. O, Reader, his cheeks, salty with tears, and soft as silk.

And still, even as I kissed him, I insisted, "Weston, I must know who gave you that money, for I fear for you." Aye, and I love you, lad. Too much.

He put his hand to my mouth and brushed my lips with his fingertips, stopping at once both my kisses and my questions.

"Please, Jamie, oh, Jamie," he sighed. "You are right that I have fallen far, for I was bred to a gentle station. And 'tis true that I gave up my very last piece of pride to get those coins, though I would do it again, in an instant, to save that little girl. But I promise you—oh, please believe me—that I did not pay the price a villain such as Goddard would have demanded. I will die before I live that life again."

"O, Weston," I moaned, pulling him to me with an embrace meant, truly, to comfort him. I swear it. "And I, who ought to have offered you sanctuary, have proved only another seducer, another portrait in your rogues' gallery. Can't you see? This is why you must go away. You love me as a child does, and I would have you be a man. You must realize your promise, and far away from me, for I fear my love—aye, and my desire—would consume you, as it now consumes me. If I were to take you into my bed"—my voice broke—"I would never let you go. Between us lies—I can only think it must be—*too much* passion. I would lose myself in you, and you in me, as in a vast and furious ocean. I would draw you down—how I would draw you down, even this instant—when you must stand up."

Any who have loved deeply will understand that speaking these words was an agony. For does not love multiply desire as interest compounds debt? God knows, I would have drawn him down. Only with the greatest exertion did I stop myself from throwing him back on the bed and succumbing to the sweet fury that possessed me.

"*I am no child,*" he answered, angrily, "and this"—he placed a hand on my thigh and moved it expertly toward its all too obvious object—"is no child's play."

Dear Reader, if you have not already left this once-cold garret, pray, open the window. I want for breath.

He reached into my breeches, where his fingers discovered the swell and commotion within, and set me into an uproar such as nothing could still.

But just as abruptly as he began, he withdrew his hand, and rose from the bed.

Sweet Jesus of Bethlehem and Nazareth! I did not think I could survive such cruelty!

"If you command it, *sir*, I will stand up. I'm sorry to do it, but I would have you know what it means to be cut off. And I'll beg you to be honest with yourself, if not with me. Your generosity is boundless, of that I could not be more constantly aware, and ever grateful. Yet 'tis not for my sake that you would banish me to London, but for your own. When I'm gone, you will marry your rich widow, and enter her beautiful garden, and till her acres merrily."

I rose, grabbed his arm, roughly, and pulled him toward me, still more fiercely. Reader, I know not whether I more wished to strike or to fuck him.

"I may, Weston. I just may make Louisa my wife, if she'll have me. I won't have you speak of her that way."

He shook himself loose of my grasp.

"She is worthy of you, sir," he said, his voice filled at once with ardor and defeat. "And I will pledge myself to silence on that score."

"I shall hold you to that, lad."

"And I promise, further, sir, to call you, henceforth, by your rightful name, *master*," he continued. "But you must agree to this in return: never again take the liberty to speak to me of *your* love and *your* desire, *Mr. Jameson*, *sir*, when I am consumed, every day, every hour, every minute, by the tyranny of my own, for you."

FROM THE *BOSTON GAZETTE*, MONDAY, OCTOBER 1, 1764.

To the Editor:

Long shall the people of this town remember the lessons we learned at noon last Thursday, when Samuel Bradstreet's murderer met his just deserts. It is rare indeed that we hear a case of *petit treason*—the colonies have witnessed barely a handful in this century—and we dare not fail to see the portent in this one. For surely the perfidy of this Cicero was nourished by the temper of his times, as much as the foulness of his own black heart. Our nurseries raise up patricides; our hatcheries breed regicides.

Gaze upon the gibbet, ye chicken-hearted Bostonians, and behold the fate of one who would cast off his assigned place in the great family of man! Honor thy father! The King rewards our fealty with his protection. We leave that shelter at our peril, and the door slams shut behind us.

—THE MAST OF FIDELITY.

From the *Boston Gazette*, Thursday, October 4, 1764

To the Editor:

The Mast of Fidelity, *so called*, would have us believe that there is no other kind of loyalty except abject devotion to arbitrary authority. Yet I ask you, sir: Can a free people not both love their King, and question his laws? Nay, is it not the *duty* of Englishmen to speak against tyranny? The King's grasp upon his staff cannot be so limp that mere words threaten to pry loose his hand.

The late execution of my man Cicero, for allegedly murdering me, is taken by the Mast of Fidelity as a cautionary tale. But how can a solitary crime speak to the passions of a people? Guilty or no, Cicero was but one man. The champions of liberty are a nation of voices. Who will hear our plea? *Remember me!*

—Bradstreet's Ghost.

October the 7th, 1764

Elizabeth,

How can it be? So much I have confided to you, and yet you still defend my father. *He must want you back, Fanny! I know he has forgiven you!* Can you truly believe the silliness that spills from your pen, Lizzie? Tis true, he paid the price I demanded. But can't you see that he did so to protect his name, and not out of love for me, much less any concern for his other daughter, my dear sweet Phebe. *How he must have suffered*, you write, *not knowing whether you live or die!* Perhaps. But I only see the suffering he inflicts upon others.

More than a week has passed since Cicero's life was ended, taken from him in the name of justice, in the King's name, in the name of the people of this colony. In the days since the execution, the doctor has grown near as agitated as he was when first he came to us. Our investigation has stalled, as we await the auction of Bradstreet's books—and dear Phebe. The doctor closets himself in his laboratory while my master holes up in his bed-chamber. Unable to grasp his brush for his broken hand, unable to regard me for his broken heart, he lies abed, sleeping away the daylight that reminds him that he cannot paint. When darkness falls, he walks the streets with Gulliver, haunting the taverns to staunch his sorrows and his pain with drink. Our lodgings are a clutter and a chaos: Jameson has fired Mrs. Goddard—"I will not have that suckbribe's slip-slop wife in my house!"—and he will not stir himself to find a replacement.

Every dawn, he staggers home, drags himself up the stairs, and collapses on his bed. When I'm certain he's asleep, I sneak into his bedchamber to remove his shoes, even his great coat, if I can manage it, rolling him one way, and then the other, careful with the sling the doctor has fashioned for him. I am become more gentleman's gentleman than painter's apprentice. Not once has my master woken during my ministrations. When he rouses himself, at dusk, he offers me no more than a nod as he heads, once again, for the door. Truly, he has said not ten words to me in as many days.

I miss him, Lizzie, more ardently than I would have thought possible. You tell me you have never known such a passion, and I'm not sure whether I would wish it upon you. Tis a torment to love so fiercely. I yearn even to watch him sleep, wishing he would wake, and smile, and offer me the joy of his company, and once again teach me the Art and Mystery of love and laughter. I sit upon the edge of his bed and stare, full sensible of the virtues of his well-turned limbs, his broad square shoulders, in short, a perfect system of manliness. I have extracted from him a pledge that he never again speak to me of his desire. He is good to his word, but his silence has scarcely quieted my heart.

He slumbers so deeply he barely stirs when I unbutton his waistcoat. Every day, I dare a little more. I rest a hand on his chest, 'neath his shirt, and feel the beat of his great heart. I stroke his face, trace the cleft of his chin, the rough stubble of his beard softening with each day's growth. And still he does not wake.

Belowstairs the doctor rages, his volume growing with each day of unseasonable heat.

"Must the sun shine every day upon the gibbet? Must his blood boil ere his body rots? I cannot abide it, I tell you!" He charged up the stairs to his friend's room.

"Stewart Jameson!" I heard him shout. "Get out of bed, get washed, and get dressed. Your life is no more a tragedy than it is a farce. Drink what you must, but you shall not cradle your empty head upon your useless hand while a man's vitals are eaten out by crows. Tonight the moon will be almost full, and we can see, unseen. I would cut Cicero down and bury him decently. If you and your serving boy do not see fit to help, mark me: I shall break the lock upon his cage and drown myself while I bury him at sea."

Not half an hour later, my master came down to the kitchen, a stumbling shambles, newly washed and yet unshaven, and plainly unable to bear the sight of me.

"All right, Sander. You've dragged me out of bed, though I've barely slept myself sober, and I'm still but half a man." He held up his sling. "I can't see what use I'll be to you, much less to poor Cicero."

"True enough, friend. And I dare say the colored men and women of this town would rather look after their own. Our own. But much as I regret it, we need you, *massa*. For if we are caught, a white man will have to make our excuses to the constable."

With that, the doctor unfolded his plan. He would cut down the body with his own knife—on that point he was terribly clear—but we would also need a hammer to smash the lock upon the gibbet, clean sheeting to wrap the body, and a spade to dig a proper grave. Since the man who leases us our quarters is a cooper, the tools would be easy enough to find in the cellar. But I lost heart when the doctor said we needed a skiff at the ready.

"What, Weston, did you think we could shoulder him to the burying place? No, we will ferry him. After the last bell rings at midnight, we shall slip south, on foot, to the fortification wall. Kingston and a boatman will greet us there. I have made all the arrangements."

"Will five of us manage Cicero's corpse, sir?" I asked.

"Not five, Weston. Three. Three only. I promise you, I am not blinded by color, but I shall allow neither you nor Jameson to touch him."

While I waited for nightfall, I closed myself in the painting room and worked on the basket of peaches Jameson had instructed me to place on the table before Louisa Beaujardin. I quit when I felt a temptation to paint a worm gnawing at the juiciest of the bunch. Instead, I began to varnish Gallagher's kit-cat, dragging out the task to fill the time.

"I see you have taken quite a *shine* to the grocer," Jameson remarked, the faintest trace of a smile brightening his face as he passed the doorway of the painting room.

"Not your best pun, sir. But Gallagher was a decent enough sort, sir."

"I can see that, lad. And 'tis far more than a decent likeness. But if you could leave off and take yourself to Lambert's shop, I would have another ten yards of sailcloth, for I venture we shall soon be back in business."

"Your hand feels some better, then?"

"Aye, lad. Sander says I might remove the sling tomorrow. At least that injury improves."

"That injury? What else ails you, sir?"

He stared at me.

"I am not at liberty to speak of it, lad, as you well know. Pray, remind Lambert that I look forward to supper with his family tomorrow evening."

By the time I returned from this errand, 'twas nigh on dusk. We took our supper separately—the doctor in his laboratory, Jameson in the parlor, and me in my garret—while the bells tolled the hours. Seven, then eight. From my window I could see the harvest moon, fat and yellow, hanging low in the sky like some great pumpkin. Nine, ten. I sketched the rooflines bathed in that eerie lunar light. When the watchman rang midnight, the moon was high overhead. The men waited for me in the hall, the tools for the evening's work wrapped in a spattered tarpaulin. Doctor Alexander shouldered the parcel. And then, without so much as a candle to call attention to our mission, nor a word to name it, we filed through the door into the still-warm night.

By unspoken agreement I led our small band of warriors, like some Indian scout whose knowledge of every bush and blade speeds his silent progress through the forest. I steered us toward the far end of the Common, beyond the camp, where our progress might be less easily seen. Where we could, we stayed 'neath the ancient trees that punctuate the pastureland. Soon meadow gave way to marsh as we scrabbled down the hillside to the mudflats that line the banks of the Charles.

It took us perhaps half an hour of quiet, careful progress to reach the western edge of the fortification wall. A torch shone brightly in the sentry box. We halted, watching the watchman. Assured, after some minutes, that he snored soundly, we inched around the wall, hugging the tideline as we advanced toward the gallows.

By then our eyes had grown so accustomed to the world of shadows that we easily picked out the dark forms of Kingston and another man—"Mr. Jacob Freeman, our boatman," the doctor explained—huddled in a rowboat some yards offshore. Kingston whistled to us, three notes of a nightingale's song. The doctor answered in kind, showing his fluency in yet another language, a night-music he must have used before. Freeman's oars split the water as easily as a knife cuts butter, and with nearly as little sound. Minutes later the five of us pulled the boat onto the flats.

I can scarce describe what awaited us upon the gallows. I whispered a prayer of thanks to the night for dropping a veil over the minutest details of Cicero's destruction. But nothing on this earth could cover the stench of what had been done to him.

"Hand me my knife, Jamie. And stand back; your stomach will not take it. Watch the watchman instead. And remember," the doctor whispered to both of us, "neither of you shall touch him." I returned to the boat, looking on in terror as Alexander climbed to the top of the gallows, knife in hand. Freeman, a wiry older man, opened the trapdoor, and Kingston waited under the platform with the tools, ready to free poor Cicero's mortal remains when the iron cage plummeted to earth. Upon the yardarm, Alexander cut the rope that held the gibbet, strand by strand.

The thud of that dreadful device upon the soft clay was as sickening a sound as any I have heard. Jameson knelt and vomited at the river's edge. He was still retching when Kingston and Freeman emerged, each holding one end of a bundle wrapped in a winding white sheet. I was struck by the smallness of the package, for Cicero had been a large man.

Twas Doctor Alexander who carried the greater burden as he tugged the gibbet to the water.

"No time, man!" Kingston said. "Leave the cage. It's not hurting him now."

"I cannot," Alexander said, weeping, a sight that shocked me near as much as any other on this awful night. "I would drown this instrument of barbarism."

It took the doctor some minutes to drag that heavy cage into the water. Then he returned to Kingston, and the two of them carried

Cicero's shroud to the boat. Freeman readied his oars as Jameson and I nudged the skiff into the river.

"Room for one more," Freeman said. "One only. But which, Doctor? The painter can't breathe for puking, and his apprentice can't heft no more than a girl."

Before Alexander could answer, Jameson, splashing his face with water, choked out a reply.

"I can do."

"No, Jamie," the doctor said. "You are useless on a boat. We shall take your apprentice."

"Nay, Weston. Go home," my master insisted. "I'll manage."

"Sorry, friend," the doctor said. "But for this journey, I would rather have Weston."

And then, for the first time in days, Jamie touched me, offering me his arm as I climbed aboard.

The moon glinted upon the water, which shone black and smooth as obsidian. Freeman hugged the shoreline, steering past West Hill, past Barton's Point, skirting the Mill Dam to stay clear of the shipyards. The whole of our way, while Freeman rowed and Alexander stared gravely ahead, Kingston sang. Softly, yet urgently, a funeral song of his native Jamacia, I suppose. Twas no ordinary dirge, but a gentle, lulling hymn. I could picture Cicero's spirit buoyed upon those notes.

Black upon black, we floated, wrapped in Kingston's song, lost in time. Finally, Freeman piloted the boat toward a lonely stretch of land near Hudson's Point, just below the burying ground. Nothing—nothing in all my years in this town—prepared me for what awaited there.

"We have help," Freeman said. "See there."

No sooner had he spoken than two—or was it three?—pairs of strong hands reached out to pull us ashore. And then I saw in the moonlight dozens of brown faces—nay, hundreds—packed close together, four or five deep, men and women, girls and boys, all silently waiting to walk beside their brother on the final yards of his earthly journey. I could scarce believe Boston held so many colored people. I knew them only in ones and twos, sometimes in small families, hidden even within the homes they serve. Here they stood as a people.

One by one, in quiet voices, in perhaps a dozen languages, they took up Kingston's offer of song. With each of his calls, the chorus of their responses grew more melodious and complex. From the wharves beyond the Point I could hear halyards twanging their accompaniment, like some otherworldly harp.

To my utter astonishment it seemed that Alexander was known, somehow, to all of the assembly. Twas he who led the procession. Behind him followed Kingston and Freeman, bearing Cicero's remains up the steep path to Copp's Hill. From a distance, it almost appeared as if Cicero himself was guiding them, pointing now west, now east, nodding toward every door. After the body came the men, and then the women and children, all, every one of them, softly singing.

When we reached the very back of the burying place, I was met by another surprise. Beneath the graceful canopy of a hickory tree whose leaves had just begun to fall yawned a fresh-dug grave, its corners cut as sharp and sure as any building's, its foot pointing east, toward Africa. At its west end was placed a carefully folded cloth, to cradle Cicero's head for all eternity.

The mourners gathered round in a circle, while Kingston and his fellows gently lowered their fallen countryman to his resting place. Then, one by one, while the singing continued, mourners stepped forward to deposit small offerings, turning that unmarked grave into a tomb worthy of an Egyptian king. The moon peeking through the branches picked out beads, shards of pottery, bits of cloth, a pipe, and a small looking glass. But mostly there were shells, an ocean of them, covering the corpse. Kingston and Freeman each set a coin upon the place where Cicero's eyes might have been. Last came the doctor. His offering fairly gleamed. Lengthwise upon the shrouded body of Phebe's father, he set his knife.

When the grave had filled, earth upon treasures, the song dissolved, voice by voice, as the mourners melted back into the night. Kingston and Freeman returned to the boat. Finally, only Alexander and I were left.

"Come, Miss Easton," he said, relieving me of the bundle of tools I was carrying. Side by side, with wandering steps and slow, we took our solitary way toward home.

"How is it that the whole town knows you, Doctor?" I ventured, quietly, as we neared Queen Street.

Alexander extended his arm to me, and escorted me past the path from the street to our front door, and on around to the lane that leads to the little alley next the tenement. Upon this, his doorstep, he turned to answer me.

"How am I known to the black people of this town, Miss Easton? Welcome to the surgery of Doctor Ignatius Alexander," he said, with a grim pride. "I serve any who would cross this threshold."

"Are there many, then?"

"You have just seen their numbers, have you not?"

I had seen them, Lizzie, as if for the very first time. This night, the doctor's apartment was revealed to me as a house within a house, a city within a city, a Boston never before known to this long-blind,

Fanny Easton.

Post Script.

My master must have reached home hours before us. I spied his boots in the hall, and two empty jugs of Adams's ale upon the kitchen table. As I climbed the stairs to my garret, I looked through the open door into his bed-chamber. The chill of the night, and its dark and heartbreaking scenes of grief, made me ache more than ever for Jameson's company, even if only for the presence of his sleeping form. Was it the specter of death that made my longing for life, for comfort, for love, and yes, for *pleasure*, so ungovernable? Was there not some gift I might give him?

He lay sprawled on his back in a deep sleep, still in his shirt and breeches, one arm trailing toward the floor and the other wrapped in its sling. I tiptoed toward the bed, thinking to cover him with the counterpane.

I leaned over him, pushed a lock of hair from his brow, and tucked it back behind his ear. And then I kissed him, almost chastely. I meant only to brush my lips against his, just for an instant. But I must have waked him, for suddenly, he cupped the back of my head, pulling me closer. He captured me with a kiss by turns fierce and gentle, a kiss with a beginning, a middle, and an end—an end that came too soon. Flush with pleasure, stirred beyond enduring, I could scarcely breathe.

"Weston," he sighed, sleepily, as his head fell back upon his pillow. "This dream grows more real each time."

"Do you have it often, sir?"

"Every night, lad. Every night. And I would fain not wake."

"'Tis a good dream, then?"

I kissed his chin.

"Aye," he mumbled. "Too good. Leave me to it."

I kissed his neck.

He shifted, slightly, as if to settle himself back to sleep—indeed, for all the force of his kiss, he was scarcely awake—but he took my hand in his, played with my fingers, lazily entwining them in his own. He brought my hand to his lips, kissed it, then hugged it to his chest as he closed his eyes, rolled onto his side, and seemed to descend, again, into slumber.

"It gets better, sir," I murmured into his ear. For I had not the least intention of leaving him to it.

I nudged him again onto his back, unbuttoned his shirt and tugged it open, cursing the darkness that denied me the sight of him. I kissed his chest, moving, so slowly, kiss after kiss, down his front. He arched his back and moaned.

"I have pledged, I have pledged," he stammered sleepily, "but dear God, you are making it very . . . hard, lad. Not to mention, difficult."

"Hush, sir. You are drunk, and dreaming. I will look after your pledge."

I returned to my fevered trail of kisses, following the line of fine, dark hair leading to his breeches. He reached for me, but I took his good hand, and tucked it behind his head.

"Weston—"

"Remember your pledge, sir. You have promised not to touch your apprentice. And you shall not. In this dream, you keep your hands to yourself."

I tucked a finger under his waistband, and drew it across his front, to find his buttons, near bursting from the swell of his desire. Through the soft cloth, I ran my hand along the length of his instrument, but could find no end to it.

He drew in his breath, sharply, and protested once more, though 'twas halfhearted, for he smiled, drowsily. "Sweet Jesus, Weston. Would you take advantage of me?"

"I would, sir."

"And you will not cut me off again?" he begged, his voice hoarse.

"No, sir. Not tonight, I shall not. I will take your cock and pull it."

"But who will look after your ass, lad?" He began to laugh, but panting stole his laughter as I last unbuttoned his overstretched breeches. My own smile turned into a gasp of astonishment at what awaited me: an organ of such prodigious proportion for which no study of ancient sculpture could have prepared me.

"So beautiful, sir. And so . . ."

I slipped my other hand inside my trousers.

His breathing was labored, and yet, even so far inflamed, his voice was laced with mirth. "Have you never noticed the size of my hands?"

I stroked his wondrous, velvet-skinned instrument, brushing it with the very tips of my fingertips, each caress its own dance. Moved by his pleasure, and my own, I grasped it more firmly.

"Dear God," he moaned. "Don't let me wake."

I stilled my hand, striving to retard the advance of his ardor.

"But don't *stop*, lad." He placed his hand upon the back of my head.

"Your pledge, sir," I reminded him firmly, pinning his arm to his side.

"All right, lad. No hands."

"Just so, sir," I whispered.

Then I took his cock in my mouth, hungrily, greedily, drinking in the musk of him, and letting my tongue taste what I had longed for.

Now I found I could take my time, deliciously slow, studying—and mastering—the Art and Mystery of what most pleasured him. A most intimate kiss, with a beginning, a middle, and an end. When at last he raised his hips, cried out, and collapsed, I shuddered with the accomplishment of my own bliss. For a moment, I lay my head on his belly, catching my breath. He raked his fingers through my hair.

"Weston, you are a marvel. You cannot be real, my love," he murmured, pulling me to him.

"No, sir," I answered as I gathered myself up. "That's a different dream."

I kissed his lips, one last kiss, tucked a blanket round him, and dashed from the room. I shut his door, and raced to my garret, to still my spirit.

And to write this postscript. But I cannot possibly send it to the dear, sweet, virginal companion of my girlhood. If I am honest, I must admit that I write to a woman I no longer know, and she to one who no longer exists. Lizzie is a trusting and loyal friend, but 'tis no kindness—not to either of us—for me to seek her approval for a life so far beyond her compass. I dare not sever the chain of ink and paper that binds us, for friends in this cruel world are few enough. But from now on, I will send Miss Elizabeth Partridge only the polite and decorous letters she wishes for. Scented notes, in a dainty hand. I will paint for her my surfaces, and nothing more.

Only in the waste pages of this letter book will I spill the contents of my heart.

CHAPTER 19

Of Bidding Fair and Bargains Foul

"Our Samuel Bradstreet was a rather indiscriminate book buyer," said Alexander, disapprovingly, and more to himself than to me, as he sat at the kitchen table, poring over the catalogue of that gentleman's library, while I sat soaking my hand in a basin of warm water. "Heavy on law, politics, and *belles lettres* . . . Addison, Blackstone, Coke, Milton, Pope, Purchas, Richardson, Smith, Sterne, Swift, Trenchard, and Gordon . . . Ah! Malcolm's *Treatise of Musick, Speculative, Practical, and Historical*! A rare volume on this side of the ocean. How I would love to hold it in my hands."

The thought of *hands* perhaps reminding him of me, he pointed to the basin.

"That is long enough. Dry it off. Pray, Jamie, did Bradstreet play an instrument?"

"I think he may have fiddled," I answered, wiping my hand with a rag. "But not much, else he'd have asked me to put a sign of it in his portrait."

He took my hand in his, and inspected it closely.

"Most fortuitous," he murmured, before he let go my hand and picked up the catalogue again, stopping to lick his index finger before turning a page.

"Aren't you going to bandage it again?"

He did not look up.

"Sander—my hand—"

"No, Jamie. You can wrap it yourself. Just not too tightly. And do not bother with the sling. You are a fortunate man, Stewart Jameson. Your hand is healing well."

He furrowed his brow and muttered to himself. "Precious little Boyle and Newton, and few other scientific works . . . a disappointment, a disappointment."

"Look, Sander," I exclaimed, as I used my left hand, awkwardly, to wrap my right with gauze, "I hate to intrude on your reveries, but we're not shopping for books that might alight your fancy. We're looking for books in which Bradstreet might have hidden his Will. The auction begins in an hour. I will not purchase a pig in a poke. Goddammit, man, make me a list: What am I to buy?"

"Ah, the ancient orators," he said to himself, ignoring my question entirely. "Lysias, Isocrates, Isaeus, Demosthenes, Thucydides. A very fine collection. Very fine, indeed."

"Sander," I cried hotly, after tying the gauze, badly, and tearing off the excess with my teeth. "You remember what happened the last time I was supposed to go to an auction—"

"I can hardly forget, friend."

"Aye. And this time, I will heed your instructions, if only you would give them to me. *What am I to buy?*"

At last he looked up, and smiled.

"Do you know what Cicero once said?" he asked.

"That we must save Hannah and the wee girl? Aye. That's why I'm leaving for this goddamned auction with my small savings and Weston's hard-earned, how-earned coins *in half an hour!*"

"No, Jamie. Not that Cicero. The Roman orator."

I sighed, and rolled my eyes. "Alas, no, Professor, you have caught me, once again, in a thicket of ignorance. What did the ancient Cicero say, five thousand bloody years ago?"

"Eighteen hundred and eight years ago," he corrected me. "In his *Laelius de Amicitia*, 44 B.C."

"God above, Sander! What, pray, did he say?"

Here Alexander took my good hand, squeezed it, and smiled. "He said, 'Friendship can only exist between good men.'"

Reader, Sir, Madam, *Friend*, as you undoubtedly know, only too well, nothing except browsing the stalls of a bookstore excites a capacious reader so much as a list of books. Not since Alexander returned to our lodgings in Edinburgh, having won a disputation with a professor of chemistry—something to do with fixed alkali, if I rightly recall—had I seen my friend so wholly contented. In his element.

"Sander, you are dear to me, too, even if you are a pompous son of a bitch," I answered, returning his fond squeeze. "But I beg you, man. Stop panting over Bradstreet's library like some monk in a whorehouse, and start choosing. I'm going upstairs to give Weston his instructions for the day. When I come down, have a list for me, will you?"

I climbed the stairs with a weary heart. Nosy Reader, if you must know, it has come to this: I can hardly bear to look my apprentice in the eye. I am by turns furious at him, and aching to gather him into my arms. I cannot lay my head on my pillow but that I dream of him. How does the sonnet go? "Lo! thus, by day my limbs, by night my mind, For thee, and for myself no quiet find." Sodding Shakespeare. Could he not have added a line or two of advice? Good God, what am I to do? I will count the days. He sails on November fifth. *November fifth*. Four weeks from now. Sweet Jesus. I will tick the minutes.

"Weston?" I called, when I reached the painting room, for my apprentice was nowhere in sight.

"Yes, sir?" he answered, popping up from behind the table by the window.

"What are you doing on the floor, lad?"

"I'm sorry, sir. I tipped over the bowl of fruit, and everything rolled this way, for the floor is sagged," he apologized, holding up a bruised peach.

"Ah," I answered. A ripe opportunity for a pun, you must admit. But I find myself at a loss for words. Tis a strange feeling, and an empty one.

Weston put the peach back in its bowl and advanced toward me, smiling happily. He pointed to my arm.

"Free of your sling, sir?"

"Aye, lad. Resting has been . . . restorative."

I paused, uncertain whether to say more.

"You've been sleeping well, sir?" he inquired, sweetly.

"Weston, you didn't . . . ? I dreamt that . . ."

He looked at me blankly.

"No, no, of course not," I mumbled. "But yes, my hand . . ."

"No hands, sir." I swear he said it. And he winked at me.

"*What*, Weston?"

"Nothing, sir."

I found I was more confused than when I started. I looked past the lad, fixing my gaze, instead, at the likeness of Louisa Beaujardin. I cleared my throat.

"Weston. I'm just leaving for the auction, and I've come to give you instructions. Finish the Widow's fruit, and lacquer her before noon. She'll need to be dry by the end of the day, for I'm to deliver her to the Lamberts' tonight."

"You're crossing to Charlestown, sir?"

"Aye. Don't remind me. Spend your afternoon on Gallagher. The red of his sash is grievously wrong. But as he's so carelessly left it here, you shall have no difficulty fixing the color."

"Yes, sir." Weston nodded, stepping toward me, and placing a hand on my sleeve, willing me to face him. "Sir?"

"*What*, Weston?" I said. With a defeated sigh, I returned his gaze. "What will you have of me now? Dear God, what have you had of me already? 'Tis difficult enough, lad. Just let me be."

"I would never add to your pain, sir," he said, quietly. "It's only that—"

"Aye, Weston. You wouldn't mean to. But you're too young to know what hurts and what heals."

"No? You do not know me as well as you think, sir."

"Perhaps not. Perhaps not. But I dare not get to know you any better, lad."

"Sir, I meant to ask you something different. Please, sir: You won't come back without Phebe, will you?"

This I had not anticipated. I answered him gently.

"I promise. I won't come back without Phebe."

I f Samuel Bradstreet was a promiscuous buyer of books, I have vowed to be more judicious. Alexander having at last given me a list—twenty-two treatises on law, the complete works of Cicero (in eight volumes), eleven tracts on slavery, four narratives of travel in Africa, and three dozen titles on politics—I headed to Bradstreet's house, Weston's suede purse tied to my belt, under my coat. I turned up my collar against the wind as I made my way to Hanover Street. Twas a very cool day indeed. And a puzzling one, for near every house I passed was shrouded in mourning, its windows draped with black bunting.

"Edes!" I called, as I spied a familiar face among the scores of Bostonians gathered outside Bradstreet's house.

"Dark day, Jameson," he answered, shaking his head.

"But Bradstreet's burial was six weeks ago. Why the drapes?"

"Where the deuce have you been, Jameson? Have you not even read my paper? Tis Black Monday."

"Black Monday? Some shitten Puritan day of woe?"

"No, you horse-buggerer. The Death of Liberty, man!"

"What, does 'Bradstreet's Ghost' walk the moors and shake his chains?"

"I shouldn't be surprised. For the accursed acts went into effect this morning. We are becomes slaves. Every free man mourns."

"Not *every* free man," I observed, pointing to Edward Easton's house, where there was not a stitch of black cloth in sight. "His Honor Mr. Fidelity over there isn't at half-mast."

"Filthy Tory," Edes grumbled. "Can't see past his own pocket."

I lost track of the printer as we entered the mansion's large parlor, which had been cleared of its furniture, just as on the night of the ball. But now all the chairs from everywhere else in the house had been gathered in this one room, aligned in rows, facing the fireplace. I placed my coat on a seat near the front, and approached Homespun Hiram Usher, who stood in his signature suit, near the desk he would soon use as an auction block.

"Councilor Usher, sir," I said, with a bow.

"Eh? What are you doing here, Jameson? Would you glut yourself at poor Bradstreet's empty table when you refuse *my* hospitality?"

"My apologies for forestalling your most kind invitation to dinner, sir, but I did not wish to intrude upon your mourning. Let me say how sorry I was to learn of your loss. Your wife was a formidable woman, sir."

He waved aside my earnest condolences.

"What do you want, painter?"

"As it happens, my housekeeper could use a helper, and I've come to bid on the Negro girl, sir."

"Have you?" he answered, surprised. "*You*, kin to the famous Reverend Jameson?"

"Surely now is not the time to chart my pedigree, sir." I smiled, trying to dodge his question. "Truly, I come for the girl."

"Then you've come too late. She is already sold."

My heart sank.

"Impossible! The auction has yet to start!"

"Yes, Jameson, but a buyer came not half an hour ago, offered four times the girl's asking price, took his booty, and left. Two hundred pounds! I could scarcely say no to such agreeable terms, not when even the mere threat of these ruinous duties has bankrupted such once-prosperous families as the Bradstreets."

"Who was it, Usher?" I near growled at him.

"Why 'twas Parliament! Who else could have cleaned out Samuel Bradstreet's coffers?"

"No, sir. I mean, who bought the girl?"

"So sorry. I cannot *recall*. You gave me little enough information, painter, when I asked for it. Now, find your seat. 'Tis nearly time to begin."

If you are a thrifty man, dear Reader, never send me to do your marketing. I am far from profligate, but I am woefully impulsive, the tragic results of which you have already had occasion to observe. I had barely regained my seat when I was gripped by a decision. I stood up and approached Usher again.

"Councilor Usher, sir. How much do you ask for the whole of Bradstreet's library?"

"Every volume, Jameson? There are more than four hundred books! What would an artisan do with such a library?"

"Pray, sir. How much? Let me hasten the bargain, for I know you are anxious to open the bidding on the furnishings. Would you take fifty guineas for the lot?"

Usher rubbed his chin.

"Gentlemen have come from all over New-England to bid on those books. Edes sent his catalogue far and wide."

"True, sir. But how many of those men can pay in coin?" I asked, jingling the purse at my belt. "And think what they will spend on the rest of Bradstreet's goods if his books are no longer for sale. They have come to bleed money, have they not? And surely they will, on one thing or the other."

"Perhaps."

"Indeed, sir," I pressed on. "And auctioning title by title could take days. Are you not a busy man, Councilor, with better things to do than this clerk's work? Had you not rather spend your time lobbying for the Manufactory House?"

He considered, for no more than another half minute.

"All right, Jameson. I will take the library off the table for seventy-five sovereigns."

"That much I don't have, sir. But I might sweeten the pot with a likeness of your beautiful daughter. I should be delighted to paint Margaret."

"The hell you will, libertine." He grinned, wholly pleased with himself. "Now seems a most propitious time to warn you: news has reached my ears that I would be wise to never let you be alone with her, not to mention that only a fool extends you credit. Your friends—the MacGuffins, is it?—haven't had much luck on that score, if I'm to believe what my agents in New York tell me."

O, dear Reader, I am caught at last, and by this bantam blackguard. I could not yet tell how he meant to play the card he held. But I must do what I came to do. There was nothing for it but to bluster on.

"I can do more, sir, if it will buy the books and preserve my reputation. You are one of only two Hens to have eluded my brush, and I'd be delighted to offer a painting of you, sir. Make it a full-length," I offered.

"Pshaw. A man of business has no time for Art. And were you to offer me—what did the MacDonalds lose?—*two thousand* such portraits, I hazard we could not call it even."

Tis a dishonorable, loathsome arrangement, a bribe, and I bridled at it. But, Reader, in these straits, I could scarce afford to hold myself above it. What could I do but answer his unctuousness with servility?

"Sir: Might I purchase the library—and your discretion—by throwing in a kit-cat of your son, Elias? Your wife had told me she particularly desired to have me capture his likeness."

"You are a rank swindler, debtor. That would hardly bridge the distance between your offer and my price."

"As you have discovered, sir, I have naught to barter but my brush. Do you not also have a married daughter, sir, who lives nearby?"

"In Rhode Island."

"Rhode Island. How long is the boat ride?"

"You don't need to take a boat to get to Rhode Island, you idiot. But why the deuce are we talking of boats, except for the one that will carry you back to Scotland in irons?"

"Well, sir. I would give you my guineas, a full-length of yourself, a kit-cat of Elias, and a family grouping of your married daughter, for the whole of the library—and with it, my privacy, sir."

"You beg what you do not deserve, Jameson. But I will counter: I will take your purse and your portraits, and for now—*for now*—one thing more. Paint the Governor—he will fit you in on Thursday next—I shall arrange it—and while you're daubing, find out how much rope he means to extend to those on his Council who are signatories to the boycott agreement. I will have more such errands for you soon enough. Perhaps two thousand of them. O, and Jameson? Take the damned books. But if you disappoint me, I'll see that you have plenty of time to read them. In debtor's prison."

Thus did we seal this dreadful deal, this devil's bargain, this vile skulduggery.

I recovered my coat and left the house, intending to hire a cart. Outside, Usher's Pompey headed a staff of servants boxing up my books. As I neared them, a familiar figure approached me. What, on this Black Monday, am I next to bump into Beelzebub?

"Jameson, you bloody sodomite. What are you doing here?" said William Bradstreet, as he pressed the tip of his cane to my chest.

"Come to spend some money, Bradstreet," I said, pushing the cane aside. "I had thought to buy the little girl, if you are so frightfully curious."

He gave me a gruesome smile.

"Missed out on her, eh? Easton's beat you to it."

"Reverend Easton?"

"No, Justice Easton."

The news relieved me. Thank God she hadn't been shipped to Virginia, or worse. At least wee Phebe was safe, and nearby, till we could find the Will.

"You know, Jameson," Bradstreet continued, "I've a mind to call the constable this instant."

"We made a deal, sir." God knows, I have had enough of deals and bribes and pledges and promises, but this one, at least, fell in my favor, and I meant to hold him to it.

"I hazard the deal is off, Jameson, after the events of Saturday night."

"Saturday night?" I was shaken, and spoke quickly. "What happened Saturday night? I'm sure I slept soundly, sir."

In truth, dear Reader, I was not so very sure. My dreams have become rather extraordinary. But how the deuce could *he* know?

"You know very well what happened. A band of black villains undid the justice this colony's courts meted out."

Ah. Of course. Of course.

Bradstreet continued. "I would not be far wrong, would I, in suspecting that the monster you shelter in your lodgings had something to do with it?"

"What can you mean, Your Honor?" I protested, counterfeiting innocence. "My Gulliver was with me all that night."

"You know exactly what I mean. Your . . . Sancho, was it?"

"How can you know what my servants do at night?"

Bradstreet snickered and, with a nod at Pompey, replied, "I know plenty. I will have justice against this town's black rabble, Jameson. I may just begin by questioning your Sancho."

With that, he stepped past me, and into the house.

As I stood, wondering whether I preferred the Wily Bastard to Half-assed Homespun—and how I could escape either of them—I felt a jostle, barely more than a breeze. I wheeled around, just in time to grab the collar of a small boy's threadbare coat. He couldn't have been more than six, and was almost as pitiful a sight as poor Weston had been, when he first knocked on my door. He made quite a fuss. He squirmed and he wriggled, and he kicked, hard.

"Lemme go! Lemme go!"

"Why should I let you go, you little thief?" I asked, as sternly as I could, for he needs daunting before he picks the pocket of a less forgiving gentleman.

"I ain't taken aught from you, sir. I ain't taken aught!"

"True, lad, but not for lack of trying. I've just spent my last farthing, else surely you'd have pocketed it."

"I wouldn't 'ave, neither!" he cried, tears now streaming down his tiny, dirty face.

"Maybe not, for you make a clumsy ruffian. Your touch is a trifle too heavy."

I let my tone grow kinder, but still he struggled.

"Listen, lad. I'm just about to hire a cartman, and could do with the help of a strong young fellow like you. Three large crates will I bring home, and full of books. If you help me get my boxes to my lodgings, I'll give you a meal when we get there. Agreed?"

He considered for a minute and, at last, nodded. But when I let him go, he sprung away, and made his escape.

"Farewell, little lad," I said to myself as he disappeared down an alley. "I wish I had feet as fleet as yours."

Letter XVIII.

October the 8th, 1764

On the floor of my garret I have found a loose board, covering a hollow just deep enough to secret this letter book. For if I can no longer reveal my heart's true colors to dear Lizzie, neither will the doctor pry his way into that chamber. These pages are become my own archive.

Yet what do I have to chronicle, save my sorrows and my failures, and my misspent passions? Truly, I am thankless, a daughter sharper than a serpent's tooth, as my father was wont to remind me. For this is, by all accounts, a delicious morning: cool but not freezing, sunny but not blinding—a perfect day for painting. Should I not be grateful for the order to stay at my easel, a safe remove from Hanover Street, where the auction of Samuel Bradstreet's property proceeds apace this very moment? Surely I do not envy my master, who must be watching even now as Hiram Usher gavels down the future of little Phebe, pricing my poor sister by the pound. My eyes fill at the very thought that some other bidder might prevail. No, I shall not allow myself to think it! Edward Easton's gold shall win her.

But if 'tis something of a relief not to watch the sale, neither am I happy to be left behind. For I have spent the last hour face-to-face with my worthier rival, Louisa Beaujardin, striving to add a layer of luster to her already considerable loveliness. I have bedewed the peaches Jameson bid me to set upon the tea table before her, though her ripeness hardly needs the allegory; the tones of her flesh—he painted it well—tell that story true enough.

As I leaned the likeness against the wall to dry, I noticed a flat, hinged cherrywood box, oval-shaped, sitting upon the table that holds Jameson's palette and brushes. Heedless of my rightful place—I am an ingrate, I have already confessed it—I opened it. Nestled in velvet the color of the night sky lay a miniature version of the portrait of Mrs. Beaujardin, the face only, rendered in watercolor upon ivory. The medium suits her honest beauty. Surface and essence marry. Whether my master managed the feat with his left hand, or risked the healing of his right, I cannot say. But unless this Louisa's heart itself be made of ivory, the gift is bound to stir her passions. Indeed, if she plays her part in the exchange, she will return it to its maker, a lover's token, a promise sealed.

Jameson returned from the auction this afternoon just before two. From my garret, where I sat writing, I heard cart wheels come to a stop upon our walkway, and the front door open. As I bounded down the stairs the doctor's voice thundered upward.

"Three hulking crates filled with books—fully five times as many as I asked for. And where is the girl? Goddammit, Jamie, did you cock up? You cannot have failed again. God knows, she had no chance to get away on her own."

"Where is she?" I cried. "Sir, you promised!"

"We never had a chance," he mumbled, his face a picture of defeat. "I cannot think what else I could have done."

"How can it be?" I shouted. "By what accounting? Do you value your honor above that poor child's life? Else you should have pledged beyond what I put in your purse, if you had to hawk your every brush to buy her!"

"Never ask Jameson for a careful accounting, Weston. If you had known him as long as I have, you might find yourself twice as disappointed, but not half as surprised."

"Stop it, both of you. Aye, Sander, I've heard it before. Haven't I been prodigal and profligate all of my days? But not this one. Not this one. Weston, I'm sorry. Before the auction began, Usher sold her for two hundred quid."

"Two hundred pounds!" Alexander said, astonished. "Who would pay such a price for a child, and what godforsaken hell has he shipped her to?"

"Usher seemed near as stunned as you do by what she fetched. But at least she has not gone far. Justice Easton bought her."

"It cannot be!" I shouted.

"No, Weston," said the doctor, a bit too brightly for the circumstances, which he knew far more fully than Jameson did. "That means we shall find her readily with our good news. For in this great haystack of books—Jamie, did you buy the entire library then?—we will surely find the key that picks the lock upon her chains."

"Aye, it took every penny in that purse, and a good deal more, more than I have to give, goddammit. But I have bought Bradstreet's cutrate Bodleian. The Will had better be in it."

What could I do but set to the work? I had rather rush to my father's house this very instant and rescue poor Phebe from her bondage. But surely the doctor was right: we must find the Will that would guarantee her liberty, save her mother, and solve the crime.

The next hours passed quickly, as Jameson and I unpacked the library to Alexander's instructions. We emptied the three crates, heaping their contents higgledy-piggledy in the center of the parlor floor, while Gulliver patrolled round the mountains like some demented canine sentry, licking, now and then, at a speck of printer's glue.

"Goddammit, Jamie, tie up the dog, will you?" Alexander ordered. "I will not have his slobber upon the books!"

The books, the books, the books: the doctor would talk of nothing else. He guessed there were six hundred titles or more, including numerous small volumes of too little value to have been listed in the catalogue. There was, it seemed, no order in the makeup of the boxes, much less in the great piles we made as we unpacked the crates. I began to snatch up random titles, shaking each by its spine, until Alexander stayed my hand.

"Not so fast, Weston," he said. "Unless we proceed by system, our work will only multiply."

The books, the books, the books: we should line them up there in the parlor, he said (though the sinuous play of his fingers over their spines made it clear he would as soon have them in his rooms, where he could caress his leather-bound friends at his leisure). Our search for the Will would proceed more efficiently, the doctor reasoned, if we arranged the books by size.

"It will be in a folio or a quarto," he mused, passing a hand over his head. "Of that I am certain. Bradstreet would not have folded the parchment overmuch, lest its thickness make it vulnerable to detection. Thus did he choose a volume large enough to take the sheets entire, or with one crease only. A quarto at least: Q.E.D."

"Q.E.D.: Quantum ego, Doctor?"

"Droll, Jamie. Very clever. Just line up the folios against the wall, and set the quartos beside them."

We made quick work of the folios, for though each of these massive books—some of them stand over two feet tall—taxed my strength, 'twas easy to spot them in the chaos. I noted a two-volume treatise on law; testaments in Greek, Latin, and English; and a complete edition of the works of Alexander Pope, handsomely bound in red kid. I gasped when I saw a collection of Hogarth's engravings and made to take a short peek.

"Weston," said the doctor, gently, "well do I know your hunger. But you cannot sate it now. There will be plenty of time for gluttony once that Will is found, and the girl and her mother freed. Then shall the books have their way with us." His eyes played over the great long spines, as if making mental notes of where first to search.

Next came the quartos, modest beside their giant cousins, but still nearly a foot tall. Of these books—desk-sized volumes of the sort Jameson often puts in men's pictures—Bradstreet had owned fully a hundred. My master pulled them from our makeshift piles, handing them to me as he spied them. As I arranged them along the wall according to their authors' last names, 'twas hard not to speculate about which contained the prize.

"Perhaps 'tis here," I said, "in Colin Jameson's *Religious and Moral Considerations upon Philosophical Reflections on—*"

"Genesis to Revelation, Weston!" Jamie broke in. "Stop while you yet have breath! There are hundreds more words in the title alone!"

"Just shelve the books," Alexander replied, flatly. "We need a system. This is not some flighty thing that proceeds by intuition."

All the same, he picked up the Reverend Jameson's treatise and rifled through it, his brow furrowing in disappointment.

The Old Brick's bell tolled four before I had finished the quartos.

"Weston, your alphabetical scheme is a good one," Alexander said as he again surveyed the wall that had become our library. "But you must set it aside if you are to finish the octavos and duodecimos before midnight. Those you can pile along the opposite wall, a dozen in a stack. The chances of a prize concealed in any one of them diminishes in direct proportion to its size."

"And these littlest ones, sir, what do you call these?" I asked, holding aloft a tiny chapbook, barely three inches square.

"That, I would venture, is a sexagesimo-quarto," he answered, rolling the Latin over his tongue as if it were sweeter than Canary wine. "The printer folds his parchment so that each printed page reveals only one-sixty-fourth of the original, one hundred and twenty-eight leaves to the sheet, if you count both sides. And here you see the sexagesimo's bigger brother," he said, cradling another of the littlest books in his hands. "This is a quadragesimo-octavo, a standard size for a primer. The trigesimo-secundo is next, at thirty-two pages the sheet, good for a lady's pocketbook on pretty subjects, like the language of flowers. Then comes the vigesimo-quarto, then the octodecimo—unusual in the English-speaking world, but common on the Continent—followed by the sextodecimo, and then your octavos, Weston. Schoolbooks and novels, that sort of piffle."

Jameson cleared his throat.

"Professor, I am agog. But you've left out the what-the-deuce-ecimos. You know them: wee pamphlets filled with endlessly boring and useless shite about the size of books? Goddammit: enough! I must ready for supper with the Lamberts. Weston, if the doctor releases you from his flapping jaws for even one moment, you might wrap Madame Beaujardin's canvas for me."

I could hear my master humming in his chamber just above the parlor as I continued to stack books, my arms grown weary with the effort. Perhaps twenty minutes had passed when I heard the familiar request: "Weston, come at once!"

I hurried up the stairs, thinking—was I hoping?—that he might ask for help with his buttons, for still his right hand was bandaged, though he insisted 'twas much improved. But I found him neatly dressed and cleanly shaven, in the painting room.

"The canvas is dry, sir," I said, after testing it with my fingertip. "I shall wrap it in a thrice."

He watched me work. But ere I had tied the last knot, he spoke again.

"Thank you, lad. But I called you here for another reason as well," he said, softly but sternly, fixing me in his lovely stare. "Stand before me, and speak the truth."

I could not bring that night before the light of day.

"The truth, sir? Twas naught but a dream . . ."

His face colored, a blush the hue of a Tudor rose, and he brushed his hair back from his brow. He fingered the case that held his miniature portrait.

"No, Weston. What I mean to ask is, have you been nosing about my things? Tis a small enough house we share, with big enough feelings. I will not have you plunder my goods as well as my heart."

About this, I would not be coy.

"Yes, sir. I looked at the miniature. A sweet thing, worthy of its subject."

"Thank you, Weston. I had but my left hand, and I worked hard to capture her."

"And she you, sir? Tis an intimate gift," I ventured. "I cannot help wondering: Do you mean to announce an engagement upon your return tonight?"

He sighed. "I do not know quite what I mean. Nor can I allow you to concern yourself with the twists and turns my path will take after the fifth of November, lad, for you shall sail, Weston. You shall sail. Though of your journey—to greatness, I hazard—I will think often."

He spoke with extreme tenderness. He spoke, indeed, as if I were already gone.

I made to answer, but I found my words would not out, and I busied myself in wrapping the canvas and holding back my tears. Surely my master's eyes glistened, too.

He pocketed the cherry box carefully. In silence, I followed him down the stairs with the canvas. As he donned his topcoat and his hat, Alexander chucked him on the shoulder.

"Keep at it, friends," Jameson said, giving us both a smile as he stepped out the door.

"I would wish you good luck," Alexander called after him, "but you scarcely need it, for no woman has ever been able to resist you."

Now did my tears spill.

"No tears, Miss Easton," Alexander said, after Jameson had gone. "I will keep your secret, but I cannot allow you to be sorry for his chance at fortune. Take yourself upstairs, and make peace with your woman's heart. I shall attend to the books."

My secret? My burden.

In my garret, I loosed my bindings and folded my costume, putting on the muslin shift in which I sleep. I lit a candle and tried to write, but no words came, nor could I sketch.

And then, as I regarded my reflection in the windowpane, I found my resolve at last, and saw what I must do. *My woman's heart.* I cannot cut it out and bury it 'neath a floorboard. I cannot make Jamie's own heart bleed. Come what may, he must know my woman's heart.

Resolved to speak the truth to him, I took up my pen to write him a letter, but the medium was wrong. An artist learns in color. I hastened to the painting room, and primed a small canvas. But when I repaired to the cabinet in the hallway for some pigments, I chanced upon a better support for my portrait: a sliver of whale ivory, a rectangle barely two inches long, sanded so smooth and so thin that it had become nearly translucent. Had Jamie favored the thicker oval for his miniature portrait because it mimicked his Louisa's solidity? Then this one should capture my fluid nature.

With that object in mind I headed back to the painting room. I mixed a small palette of watercolors, marveling at how few shades I would need. White and pink and gray, nothing more. I took my candle to the window, relying on the reflection in the panes to play my subject back at me. A woman's heart.

Ivory is made for skin. The effects came quickly: youth and sup-
pleness, pallor and buoyancy. The watercolors dried instantly, making
it easy to stipple layer upon gossamer layer. I grew passionate and not
a little flushed as I gazed full upon myself, now in the moonlit window,
now in its tiny mirror—this little portrait—cradled in my hand. Ere the
bell rang ten, 'twas done. I nestled it in Gallagher's red velvet sash, and
placed it upon my Jamie's pillow, with a note:

> *Here is beauty revealed, and your blindfold removed.*
> *Please, darling, come at once. F.E.*

Then I headed back upstairs to wait.

But he did not come at once. An hour passed, Jamie-less, and my ecstasy yielded to gravity. Another hour slipped forever through the glass,
and my gravity has turned to grief.

I have lost him, then.

I can see it in my mind's eye: a family supper at the Lamberts' cot-
tage has resolved into a midnight tryst. She holds him in her knowing
hands, and his soft lips rain kisses upon hers. Her heart welcomes him
home.

Oh, Jamie, I stand here, looking out my window, swaying like a
peach tree bending under the weight of its fruit, alone, in an empty or-
chard.

Tis a fair riddle, my love:

> *What lies exposed and yet unseen,*
> *Ripe but yet unplucked,*
> *Who has dared something full obscene,*
> *And still remains unfucked?*

Surely 'tis none but,

> *Fanny Easton.*

CHAPTER 20

Great Scot!

'Twas past midnight when my odyssey ended.

By the time I reached my door, my gut had finally recovered from the ferry ride, though not my hide. I was chilled to the bone. I was shivering, wet both from the damp wind on the water and from my aimless wandering through the city streets by the light of the full moon, for I had left the Lamberts, my thoughts adrift, long before the last bell tolled.

I found Alexander just where I had left him: in the parlor, buried in books, Gulliver at his feet. I put another log on the fire; in the fervor of his searching for the Will, he had neglected the hearth.

"You haven't found it yet?" I asked, as I stood by the fire, rubbing my sore hand, and trying, in vain, to warm myself.

"No, else I would be asleep by now, would I not?" he answered, full of irritation. I was desperate to talk to him about Louisa, but now was by no means an auspicious moment. I've seen Sander this way before. He's best left alone.

"Has Weston gone to bed?" I traced a finger along the spine of a folio on the top of a tall pile—Shakespeare's tragedies.

"How would I know? I do not follow him as closely as you do," he snapped.

"Good night, then," I said, beset by weariness.

"Yes, yes, my fine Hamlet. Good night, sweet prince," he muttered, rifling another volume.

I carried a taper up to my room and set it on the table. I unbuttoned my waistcoat, tossed it onto the chair, and sat on the edge of my bed to take off my stockings and shoes. But the candle's flicker caught a flash of red on my pillow. Dear Reader, if I gasped at what I saw, know this: 'twould not be my last gasp of the night.

On a piece of parchment little bigger than a calling card, a note:

Here is beauty revealed, and your blindfold removed.
Please, darling, come at once. F.E.

F.E. Who the deuce was F.E.? But the hand was familiar enough: Weston. Neath his note, wrapped in forgetful Thomas Gallagher's red sash, was a miniature, not more than two inches by three, painted in watercolor on ivory, a portrait such as neither you nor I, Sir, nor even you, Madam, have ever seen. A shocking thing. A scandalous thing. A beautiful thing. Nay, the strangest, loveliest, littlest painting I have ever set my eyes upon.

What? What is it? you ask. You grow impatient, but I find it hard to describe.

Pray, give me a moment to catch my breath.

If you can, picture this: a soft, pale, round, exquisite, perfect bosom, that mansion of bliss, a woman's bare breasts, framed with a painted simulacrum of the most delicate white tulle. No more. No head, no belly, no arms. Not even a neck. The breasts, alone: alluring, seductive, impatient, impertinent, presented to me as if on a platter.

I stood inspecting the tiny piece of ivory for a minute, maybe more, by the light of my candle, the red sash still dangling from my hand. Weston, by God. This goes too far. This mocks me too much. I will thrash him.

With no more thought than this—for what could I say?—I stepped out, barefoot, into the obscurity of the hall and ascended the stairs to his garret, the ivory and its velvet wrapping clutched in my left hand while, with my bandaged right, I fumbled for the rail. My fury drove me forward through the darkness. I found the door and turned its handle.

By the bright light of the moon, streaming in through Weston's uncovered windows, I could make out the lad's small form, huddled 'neath his bedclothes. I could even see his soft face against the pillow, framed in curls, silent in repose. A wave of tenderness came over me, but even this only added to my rage.

"Weston, wake up, you heartless bastard!" I yelled, as I yanked the covers off.

Letter XIX.

October the 9th, 1764

Hours I watched for his approach, tacking between my window and my door. The fire—in the hearth if not in my heart—grew cold. Exhaustion at last overwhelmed me. I know neither when I fell asleep, nor how long I languished in the arms of Morpheus ere I heard the door thrown open, and made out his tall, shadowy form, standing above me. He seemed to shiver, but I did not think it to be with cold.

"Weston, wake up, you heartless bastard!" he shouted, pulling back the bedclothes.

"Jamie?" I said, waking with a start.

"Jamie, is it?" he shouted. "Weston, by God, what am I to make of you? You address me as a friend—aye, and more," he said, shaking what I knew in an instant to be my note. "But you are cruel, lad. Cruel to the marrow of your bones, if you would mock that woman. You know nothing of goodness, neither hers, nor mine."

"*Hers*, Jamie? What have I done?" I asked, not yet making sense of his rant.

"What have you done, you son of a bitch? *This!*" he spat, tossing my miniature onto the bed, in a rumpled pool of its scarlet wrapping. "You have done this—this wet dream of what you fancy must lie within Mrs. Beaujardin's bodice. Tell me, Weston: Do you paint your longing, or my own? Nay, it does not matter. You debase us all."

"No, no, you have mistaken my meaning," I whispered, on the edge of tears. "Let me explain."

I rose on one elbow.

"Ach, lad," he said, softening slightly. "That is the beauty of Art, is it not? It brooks no explanation."

*   *   *

O, Reader, if you are bashful, pray, leave. Leave now. Fly out this garret window. And Godspeed.

At the sight of young Weston in his shift, his face caressed by the moonlight as he sat up in bed and rubbed his dark eyes, I was overborne by desire. This is the barbarity of my fate: fury drove me to his bedside, where longing felled me. My knees buckled 'neath me—'twas their will, I swear it, not mine—and sat me upon the edge of his bed.

"Are you even now so blind to me?" he demanded, through his own rising anger, and a countenance covered with tears.

"Blind to you, lad? I only begin to fathom the depths of your cruelty."

At that, he started to speak, and stopped himself. Instead, he caught hold of the velvet sash I had dropped on the bed. Pulling himself up to his knees, he placed the sash over my eyes, and, gently inclining my head with his trembling hand, tied it at the back. When he spoke, his voice was inflamed.

"Then I would put your blindfold back on, sir, to make you see at last."

*   *   *

And now was he blinded, though bathed in moonlight, which made the white of his shirt glow like fine porcelain, and deepened the red velvet of his blindfold to the same midnight black as his wavy locks. My mind filled with pictures I had glimpsed in my youth, on the pages of books written in French and decorously bound in blue covers, books my father had sought to conceal from my prying eyes. Those *demoiselles* I would become for you, Jamie, no longer a boy, but a courtesan, a woman of pleasure. And not in the fabric of a dream.

I rose from the bed and wheeled round to stand before him.

"Shall we play a game, then, sir?" I asked.

He breathed deeply before he spoke.

"I am undone by your games, Weston. Can we not just declare you the winner?"

And truly, he was undone, as a glance at his breeches revealed. How I wanted to fall upon him, but I willed myself to wait.

"But I would honor your teaching, sir. We cannot race ahead, colors before form, the whole before the part. Must not every painter master anatomy? And does not an apprentice oft prove an excellent model?"

Not waiting for his answer, I placed his unbandaged hand upon my arm.

"Name it," I said. "And then tell me how you should paint it."

"I am blindfolded, not brainless, lad. Tis your arm, your right."

He moved his fingers along its length, inching up my sleeve from my wrist to my shoulder. I gasped when he reached around to my armpit, brushing his fingertips lightly, so lightly, over the fine hairs therein.

"Were I to paint it," he said, his words a tumble now, "I should show its softness, no manliness yet upon it, but for these few hairs. Have I won my prize, lad?"

"Not by half," I insisted. "Have another turn."

I moved his hand to my left leg, bent at the knee, my foot resting upon the bed beside him.

"Your leg, Weston. Your left."

Again, he caressed me, toes to knee, enflaming me with his touch till the noise of my breathing threatened to overwhelm his. As his fingers pressed upward along my thigh, I gently moved his hand back to the mattress. Though every fiber in him tensed against this false bondage, he allowed me another turn.

"Describe the canvas, sir," I instructed, all feigned firmness.

"I should lavish light upon the sinews behind your knees," he continued, almost inaudibly. "I feel something of the colt about you just there, 'neath the softness . . ."

His voice trailed away.

"Would *softness* be your theme, then?" I asked, silently unbuttoning my shift and letting it fall to the floor, to proffer at last in flesh what I had tried before to realize in watercolor. Slowly, I carried his hand to my breast, pricked with goose bumps as much from my passion as from the cold.

"And this part, sir: Does it fit the composition?"

* * *

I was stirred beyond bearing, and not a little confused. Weston . . . Weston? To what manner of half-pint hermaphrodite had I lost my heart?

As I felt his—her?—breasts rise and fall 'neath my touch, I choked for air, tongue-tied with astonishment. I tore off my blindfold. Weston stood before me, Nature's Art displayed, her beauty revealed, altogether exposed, her pale skin lit by the moon. I stared, speechless, breathless, at the swell of her breasts, their perfect, wondrous, impossible loveliness barely captured by her self-portrait. A grown woman. No man, no boy, no cock. How the devil could I have been so blind, and for so long? "Thou blind fool, Love, what dost thou to mine eyes, That they behold and see not what they see?" Bloody Shakespeare. My mind raced. I was overcome with rage.

"Judas Iscariot on a flaming red chariot!" I cried as I leapt to my feet. "What manner of betrayal is this?"

"Jamie, I . . ."

Reader, dear Reader, consider: In such straits, so sorely vexed, so tormented, what would you have done? As a great gust of wrath assaulted me from one direction, waves of lust crashed over me from another. Suffice to say: my ship of restraint, a leaky tub in the calmest waters, was overturned.

Ardently, fiercely, even brutally, I reached for her, pulled her to me, and silenced her with a violent kiss, as my hands searched out every part of her.

"Turn around," I ordered.

But before she could do as I commanded, I turned her myself. I ran a hand down her back, and over her backside. Her hips were narrow, to be sure, but how this surpassingly beautiful ass had passed for a boy's scrawny bottom is a question that will keep me awake for many a night. Damn her. I have said before that I am no governor of men, but just at this moment, Reader, I found myself wishing that I had a schoolmaster's paddle close at hand.

"You are a fiend, Weston," I murmured, as I bit her neck. "Why did you deceive me? You are a right Shamela, a damned, impudent, cursed, confounded jade, and I have a great mind to kick your arse. How could you have so wholly betrayed me?"

"Not now, Jamie, not now," she gasped.

She tugged loose my breeches, frantic with impatience.

"You make a fine argument, lass," I conceded.

Twas indeed, Reader, you will admit, an unseasonable hour for an inquiry. A candid explanation could wait. Weston could not. Nor could I, Reader. Nor could I.

I unbuttoned my shirt, and cast off the last of my clothes. I threw her on the bed, fell upon her, furiously, and covered her with a storm of kisses.

"Oh! Oh! Great Scot!" she cried, as I entered her, as slowly, as gently, as I could stand, for her each and every motion, her every sigh and moan, gave me to conclude that despite the force of her desire, and the artfulness of her seduction, here was a woman who had never known love. I do not say that she was a maid, nor even that she was given to maidenly reticence. No, indeed. Yet if she had great expectations for pleasure, she had had an altogether narrow experience of it.

I would widen her world.

"Weston, you lying, disobedient scoundrel, do not come at once," I whispered in her ear.

"But master," she pleaded, panting, "how can I possibly honor that command?"

"Indulge me, lass. Play the apprentice, just this last time, and allow me to show you something of the learning in my brush."

Just this once, she did as I asked, as I offered her a course of lessons in the Art and Mystery of pleasure. And ere the night was through, she turned master, and I, her most obedient pupil.

Aye, and then round again.

Reader, O, Reader. I was borne away into the vast and furious ocean, with neither the capacity nor the least inclination to make it back to shore.

✳   ✳   ✳

Tis a puzzle, if not quite a riddle: Which is sweetest, the longing, or the having, or the having had?

As I watch him sleep, dawn breaking just rosy enough to light my page, I am tempted to choose the third. Is not the laughing and the holding as powerful as the heaving, and even the trembling? To me it is, if only because I was, till this night, a virgin at after-play. This, I had only ever dreamt of.

"Did you doubt me, then, Weston?" Jamie teased, as I lay enfolded in his arms, my hair damp upon my brow, the flush of pleasure lingering upon my chest and neck.

"No, for I have long admired your instrument." I smiled. "And your hands. Though I forbid myself to imagine the numbers that have passed 'neath them."

"A long apprenticeship, lass, but never—"

"Hush. I did not ask you for an accounting. Nor have you demanded one of me."

"Aye, and just as well. For I am no accountant. And in this balance, at least, the numbers matter not," he said and laughed. "Nor much your sex, I confess. Think not that I love you more as a woman, Weston. Or, not *much* more."

"Not much more?" I asked, raising myself upon my elbows.

He lifted his head and, with utmost tenderness, kissed one breast, and then the other.

"Ach, aye. Perhaps only *twice* as much." He sighed, drowsily laying his head back upon the pillow. "But did I not love you well enough before? Your *age*, lass, 'twas your age that was my chief obstacle, for a boy I did not fancy."

"Nor I, Jamie. I would have a man."

"Of that you have made me most acutely aware, lass. And haven't I strived mightily to oblige you?"

"That you have, my love," I agreed. "Never have I felt more a woman."

"Aye. Of course." He smiled, abundantly pleased with himself. "But how old is this woman-Weston? As a lad you were not yet three-quarters grown, a mere kit-cat, but as a lass you are a full-length, are you not?"

"I have long since left childhood behind, Jamie!" I protested. "I am nearly one-and-twenty. But you want to know more than my age, darling, do you not? For your Weston is but a fiction."

"Aye, you are elderly, and all but decrepit," he said, sleepily. "Though I'm relieved to learn I'm scarce nine years your senior, and not near twice your age. But, pray, forgive me. Fiction or no, if I am to know you more deeply than I have, my Kit-cat, let it wait until the morning."

And with that, his whisper faded to a murmur, and then his murmur to a sigh, as he drifted off to sleep while I lay in his arms, finally and forever his,

Fanny Easton.

HANDBILL

Printed under the Governor's Seal.

For public posting at every tavern and way station, and to be read aloud by the Town Crier on the Boston Common, and by every master to his slaves.

October 9, 1764.

At a special session yesterday, the Council of this colony considered the insurrectionary actions of certain Slaves and others of this town, in destroying under stealth of night the gibbet that lately stood upon the Neck, and purloining the body held within it, both to have served as symbols of His Majesty's justice. To punish said crimes, and to prevent their like in the future, and mindful of the great insolence that these people are grown to, the Council have passed by unanimous consent the following ACTS for the Further Regulating of Slaves in Boston and Vicinity:

BE IT HEREBY RESOLVED,

* That any Slaves who shall die within this Town be buried by Daylight.

* That for the Prevention of Great Numbers of Slaves Assembling & Meeting together at their Funerals, under pretext whereof they have great Opportunities of Plotting and Confederating to do Mischief, be it ordained that not above twelve Slaves Shall Assemble or meet together at the funeral of any Slave.

* That if any person or persons whatsoever shall be found guilty of harboring or concealing any Slave, or assisting to the Conveying of them away, if such Slave shall thereupon be lost, dead, or otherwise destroyed, such person or persons shall be liable to pay the value of such Slave to the Master or Mistress.

CHAPTER 21

In Which Dawn Begins to Break

I woke, flat on my back, to a close inspection by a female gaze. Weston, quill in hand, propped an open book against my hip as she scribbled, occasionally lifting her eyes over the top of her page to stare at me. Our covers had half fallen away, for we were warmed, in our nakedness, by each other, and by the sun's slanted autumn rays.

"Weston, my love," I said sleepily, my voice—nay, all of me—speaking my desire. I grabbed the book and pen, cast them to the floor, and reached for her. "As your lord and master, I relieve you of your book-keeping duties for the day, lass."

"I thought I had felled you, Jamie," she said and smiled. "I'm glad to see you're back at your post."

We could neither of us suppress a gasp as she pulled herself on top of me.

"You're a fine horsewoman, lass." And truly, Reader, she had seized my reins.

"Only when mounted upon such a stallion, sir." She laughed, before she leaned down to kiss me, as she rode on.

Was ever a man so blessed?

I fear that even you would lose patience, dear Reader, were I to fill my pages with a minute description of my Weston, to make you full sensible of the virtues of her feminine form—for what words can capture her crop of chestnut curls, those dark eyes, her lips, the astonishingly exquisite taper that directs my hands toward the small of her back, just here—how could it be more beautiful?—the nape of her neck, her softness, the fiery touch of her fingers, her seat of pleasure, her delightful wantonness: a perfection of womanliness. I could write a sonnet about the soles of her feet, and I can scarce imagine more sublime contentment than spending a day painting them. Except, come to think of it, were I to spend that day painting her breasts. Have I mentioned her breasts? Do not get me started. Suffice to say: I am besotted beyond measure.

But fear not: I shall give you neither poems nor portraits. You may be surprised to hear it, but I do have some sense of decorum. More, I would not have you love her as I do. No one, no one, could love her as I do. I had fallen for a lad, 'tis true. And some part of me—grant it, not the larger part of me, just at the moment—mourned the loss of the pleasures I had imagined finding in his arms, aye, and elsewhere. But for once, do not my gains outnumber my losses? For is not my love both sexes in twain, the spirit of a man within the form of a woman? Is she not, in short, my perfect mate?

"Oh, Jamie," she sighed, when she collapsed upon me, and we at last regained our breath.

"Aye, Kit-cat," I answered, caressing her face with my bandaged hand. "And think what I could do if I weren't one-handed, lass."

At this, she hit me over the head with the pillow, and tried to push me out of her narrow bed.

"You are, as your friend says, but a great sot, Stewart Jameson." She laughed, as I held her fast.

"A great *sot*, is it, Weston? What happened to 'O! O! Great Scot!'?" I answered, mimicking her late high-pitched exclamations of delight.

"Great Scot has spent his greatness for the moment, I think, my love," she said, tracing with her finger a line down my front.

"Aye, too true, lass," I said, taking her hand, and pulling her down to rest on top of me, her head tucked into my neck, our chests rising and falling together, our limbs heavy with spent passion. And I would have allowed myself to fall back to sleep, just so, the morning light streaming in upon us, but she sat up again, held my face in her hands, and gave me a sober, critical look.

"Jamie, do you not want to know who I am?"

"Aye, I do, of course, of course," I answered, halfheartedly, closing my eyes. "I will not rest till I know your story, lass. Not for a moment . . ."

Do not imagine, dear Reader, that I feel toward her now anything but the most passionate love, the tenderest sentiment, the fiercest ardor, embittered only with the consciousness that my blindness and her deceit—how am I to account for either, let alone the combination of them?—had cost us so much time. But I feared that my questions, and her answers, would anger us both. And I confess it: I didn't want this moment, so delicious, so precious, so long—so foolishly—delayed, to end. For the present—aye, for as long as the present might be suspended here, in this trance of pleasure—her woman's form was all the knowledge I desired.

"You don't!" she protested. "About the *what* of me you are passionate enough. I can *see* that," she said, with a teasing flick of her fingers, as more than my chest began to rise again. "But about the *who*, you can't bring yourself to care."

"I do. I do. I want to know everything about you." I sighed, as much with exhaustion as with exasperation for, truly, 'twas a struggle to keep awake. "But must I know *now*? Cannot this bliss last, just as it is, a little longer?"

Before she could answer, there came a loud knock at the door.

"Weston?" Alexander called.

"What is it, Sander?" I called back, for there was little prospect of keeping our affairs secret in so small a house, and our unmistakable noise—or, at least, hers—would have carried belowstairs long before this.

"Far be it from me to interrupt your *artistic collaboration*, Jamie," he answered, quietly, his usual sonorous baritone laced with sarcasm, "but there is a spectacularly filthy and immature specimen of humanity here to see your scandalous apprentice."

Weston furrowed her brow and pursed her lips. How I love her expression of puzzlement. After a moment's pause, her face cleared.

"Ben!" she said to herself, and louder, toward the door, "I'll be down in a thrice, Doctor. Thank you."

We heard Alexander's footfalls as he headed back down the stairs.

And then she broke the electrical fluid running between us. Just like that. She bolted up, colt that she is, and began to dress.

"Zounds, Weston," I complained, dangling my left hand over the edge of the bed in a failed effort to catch hold of her. "Must you? And who is this dirty little Ben?"

She answered with a scowl, as she pulled on her trousers.

"*These* are your questions? Not, 'What is your name, darling?' Not, 'Why do you pretend to be a boy, and how did you think to manage it?' Not, 'How came you to be so wholly debauched?' Not, 'Why did you finally expose yourself to me?' "

Reader, are these your questions, too? Truly, they are not mine.

She was working up a full fury now, as she continued what I took to be her usual morning toilet, in the trance of daily habit. From her small trunk she unfolded a long strip of linen, and began wrapping it tightly—severely, and what looked to be painfully—about her beautiful breasts.

"Weston, please, don't. Tis violence to the Art of you."

She paused, as if she had to think about what I meant, and then looked down at her breasts, imprisoned in their bindings.

"What would you have me do?" she cried.

"I'm sure I don't know, lass," I answered, my own temper rising as I sat up. And Reader, whence *her* anger? Hadn't I more reason than she to be aggrieved? "Do you not own a dress? I could fetch you one from the closet of costumes in the painting room. But please, I beg you, don't hide yourself anymore. Tis time—aye, and just the nick of time, too—to put an end to your playacting."

"My *playacting*? Jamie, I donned these rags to save my life," she shouted, her countenance a picture of anguish. And still she wrapped the cloth, round and round. "I let it go on too long, I concede. I wanted to tell you. I just couldn't. I couldn't puzzle the consequences. But 'twas never a game, Jamie. Never."

"Then tell me just what it was, Fanny Easton."

This stopped her.

"But you . . . ? How . . . When did you . . . ?"

"Mark me, lass: I love to play the fool, but I can solve a riddle when I want to. You did leave me a note signed 'F.E.,' after all, and your brother had already told me about his lost sister Fanny, the brilliant woman painter who would challenge Samuel Johnson."

"Tis a detection worthy of Doctor Alexander, I'm sure. And when, precisely, did you stumble upon my name?"

"Last night. Well, actually, sometime this morning, I hazard. I don't think I slept as well as you did, between the hard torture of your tiny bed, and its soft counterpart in the sight of your sleeping form. O, the Art of you, Weston . . ."

"And so my name—which you will not even use—tells you how to fathom me? Then you are not as different from my father as I supposed, Stewart Jameson."

"Your father. Twas he who gave you the coins, at the execution?"

She nodded. "To buy my silence."

"For he had thrown you out on the street, to starve? After some heartless son of a bitch—your bastard-hack of a master's son's fucking painting tutor, I presume—ravished you?"

"A lifetime ago. His name was Tobias Cummings. But I was a full partner in that seduction, I assure you."

"You were naught but a child, Weston. I would wring this Cummings's neck to avenge you, lass. Still, I could wring your pretty neck, too. To deceive me, so cruelly, and for so long. Had I not given you enough reason to trust me? You must have known what pain you were causing me, what agony. Good God, think of what might have been denied us: I nearly proposed to Louisa!"

"You mean you didn't?" she whispered, tears spilling down her face.

"Mary Magdalene in a kilt and sporran!" I hollered, my temper now fully unleashed. "Nay, I didn't. Else I'd hardly have spent the night with you, would I? I told her that I loved another. What do you take me for? Am I both knave and rogue? Not all of us are as capable of betrayal as you."

I was vexed, Reader, and knackered. Slowly, and in a terrible silence, she unwrapped the bindings and carefully returned them to the trunk. She took out a linen shirt, unruffled, but with a placket down the front, and her snug brown waistcoat. Holding the shirt in her left hand and the waistcoat in her right, she turned to me, bare-breasted, and spoke, without tears, but from a place of profound sorrow.

"Francis Weston was not born in betrayal. At first, he was a way to escape. Then he was a way to paint. Then he became a way to be with you, and I could not risk losing that. I wasn't certain you would forgive me, nor that you wouldn't rather I was a boy. I suppose I wasn't entirely sure I didn't prefer it that way myself, for I have discovered that even a half-grown man has more liberty than a full-grown woman. And if you had thrown me out, if you were, even now, to throw me out . . . I would not survive it."

As she spoke, she pulled the shirt over her head, leaving it full open at the neck—indeed, she turned its collar inside over, and tugged at its edges to make of it a square, trim, and alluring neckline. Then she pulled on the close-fitted waistcoat, though she could only fasten its bottom few buttons for the press of her breasts, whose shapeliness was only shown off by this arrangement of her attire, the waistcoat serving as a makeshift set of corset stays.

"O, Kit-cat," I began, softly, and stirred, but she cut me off.

"Twas never a game, Jamie. *He* was never a game. And I never meant to cause you pain, please, believe me. Never did I mean to hurt you, even when I could hardly see your pain for my own. But we have, together, killed Francis Weston, and a soft sweet death it was, too . . ."

With a glance at the floor, she bent down to grab the red velvet sash that I had cast there the night before. She picked up that blindfold, threaded it through her belt loops, hitched her trousers up from her slender hips, where they usually hung, to her narrow waist, where she cinched and tied it in a plain, square knot. She stepped over to me, kissed me chastely on the cheek, and whispered, "Please forgive me." And without waiting for my reply, she left the garret.

I did not rush down the stairs after her. I fell back upon her bed and dozed off—just for a moment. Just for a moment. Startling awake, I went to my room, washed, shaved, and dressed. Twas half an hour before I went down to the parlor, where I found Alexander, still thumbing through pages, his mood even worse than before.

"Still no Will?" I asked, though his face, ashen and hollow, told the answer.

He glared back at me.

"No Will. And I swear I have been through every volume in this library, three times over, while you lay abed rogering your apprentice."

"Sander—" I began, but he blustered on.

"I did discover something, however."

He held up a pair of round silver spectacles. I recognized them at once, for I had painted them.

"Bradstreet's glasses. Where did you find them?"

"In a spectacle case, built into Doctor Gregory's *Elements of Optics*. An octavo, published in London, in 1735. Not an obvious place. I had hoped to find the Will there."

"Why there?"

"Phebe's riddle. You must remember, for you told it to me:

> *Without a bridle or a saddle,*
> *Across a ridge I ride and straddle;*
> *And ev'ry one, by help of me,*
> *Tho' almost blind, is made to see.*

"She said it was his favorite, did she not? I hoped he might have taught it to her for a reason. It would have taken some doing to train a three-year-old to recite four lines of verse."

"But all you found were the damned glasses? Well, do they help you to see where to go from here?"

"Alas, they do not. I might next need to start tearing the pages from the bindings." He winced. "For I suppose he may have hidden the Will behind an endpaper."

There would be no living with my friend if he had to ruin his library.

"Have you seen Weston?"

"Yes, Jamie. I have seen her."

"Her?"

"Yes, Jamie. Her. Your Weston is a woman. I am all astonishment."

"And?"

"And: I bade her good morning. Now leave me be."

What accounts for the man? Either he was genuinely astonished, but too proud to admit it, or else he learned nothing new, which disclosure I could scarce fathom. Reader, haven't I had enough of betrayal? I crossed the hall to the kitchen, for, while I had rather not speak to Weston just this minute, I was ravenously hungry. I had forgotten all about her young visitor.

"So it's you, you thieving guttersnipe," I said, surprised to see at my table the small boy who had tried only the day before to pick my pocket.

He scrambled to his feet, clutched his cap, and made to flee. With considerable agility, Weston beat him to the door, and blocked it.

"No, Ben." She smiled down at him as she held his shoulders. "'Tis only Mr. Jameson. He won't hurt you."

"Aye, that I won't, you little cur," I agreed. "Indeed, I would have given you the meal I promised you yesterday, except that I see my apprentice has already fed you."

I nodded toward the empty bowls on the table, as I served myself some cornmeal mush from the pot hanging over the hearth. The boy stared back at me, eyes still full of fear. I sat down on the bench and picked up my spoon.

"Tell me, lad. Who ate more, you or Weston?"

"Miss Weston, sir. Tweren't no contest," he answered, breaking into a grin. "She eats like a sailor."

How good it felt to laugh, and to see Weston blush.

"*Miss* Weston, is it to be, then?" I asked, skeptically. "I'm afraid I can't manage it, lass."

"No, I suppose not." She sighed, with a bashful smile, just for me, as she sat down on the bench, taking the boy in her lap, and snuggling him, at which closeness they both beamed. "We will have to do something about that. But, you know"—she looked up at me—"I was very hungry."

"You were at that, Kit-cat," I said, quietly, for I took her meaning. It pained me to remember how thin and desperate she had been when she first turned up at my door. "You were indeed. I can scarcely blame you for that, lass."

She buried her face in the boy's hair, and closed her eyes. I could see she was striving, mightily, to hold back tears.

"Miss Weston?" Ben said, his voice concerned.

She lifted her face, and wiped it with the back of her hand. She cleared her throat.

"I nearly forgot, Ben. Mr. Jameson: Ben here did me a service on the day of the execution. And I paid him, two gold coins, but his mama has ordered him to bring them back, minus only six shillings, for she frets that he came by them dishonestly."

"You're a good lad to bring the money back, Ben," I offered.

"But his mother wonders if she might earn some wages, if we have the work, for she's a widow with many mouths to feed."

"Ach, a very bad situation," I answered, not sure what Weston was hinting at.

"And I thought, sir, as Mrs. Goddard has left your service . . ."

"I see," I answered, at last catching her meaning. "Ben, bring your mother back, today or tomorrow. Weston is right: we have a need for some housekeeping. I would fain speak to her about it."

"Aye, sir! I'll fetch her right away!" he shouted, and ran for the door. Again Weston halted him.

"Just a minute, Ben. I have a present for you." She walked to the hearth, and from the top of the mantel took down a book. A very small book, no more than three inches by four, stitched between papers, without a spine. One of Bradstreet's books. Weston must have set it aside yesterday, while Sander prattled on about bibliomancy.

"A book of your own, Ben," she said, kneeling down to offer it to him.

He took it, and held it with reverence, as if he dared not spoil it.

"'Tis a book of rhymes and riddles. See? *The Child's New Play-Thing*. I had the very same one when I was your age, for 'twas printed here in Boston, and my mother bought it for me on my fifth birthday."

Gingerly, he turned back its cover.

"*A is for American*," he read, haltingly. "*B is for . . .* O, I've broke it, mum!" he cried.

For as he opened the book, a single, folded page fluttered to the floor.

THE WILL OF SAMUEL BRADSTREET, ESQUIRE

I, Samuel Bradstreet, Speaker of the General Assembly of the colony of Massachusetts in New-England, do make and declare my last Will and Testament. It is my earnest desire to leave behind nothing but the following:

To my son, William, I give my spectacles, that he may improve his vision.

To my wife, Sarah, I give a widow's portion. May it usher her to the altar.

To my daughter, Patience, I give a tract of eight thousand acres of land in Berkshire County, long since deeded in her name, to her heirs and assigns forever.

To My Negro Woman Hannah I give five Pounds lawful Money. And I hereby testify that I gave said Hannah her Freedom when she arrived in my household, in March of 1761, heavy with Child by her injudicious master. Hannah's child, Phebe, born that June, of a free mother, was by the laws of this colony born free.

It remains my earnest if vain wish that my wife, Sarah Bradstreet, will free her slave, Cicero, at my death.

I hereby nominate and appoint Stewart Jameson, Face-Painter in Boston, late of Edinburgh, to be the executor of this my last Will and Testament.

I revoke all former Wills by me made, declaring this only to be my last.

In witness whereof, I have hereunto set my hand and seal, this twenty-fourth day of August, in the year of our Lord, one thousand seven hundred and sixty-four.

> *S. Bradstreet*
> *Signed, sealed, published, and*
> *declared before God alone.*

Copy number 4 of 4.

Letter XX.

October the 9th, 1764

"The Will! The Will!" Ben shouted gleefully. And then, a softer question, in my ear. "What Will is it, ma'am? And has it hurt the book?"

I handed the paper to Jamie, who scanned the signature and then broke off reading, eager to comfort the child.

"Holy Moses stumbling down Mount Sinai, Ben! Tis none other than the Will of God!"

Ben laughed, and I mussed his hair and gave him a hug as Alexander came striding in from the parlor to inspect the prize. He snatched it from Jamie's hand, read it at a glance, and turned the little slip over in his hand, again and again, as if to conjure more words than he saw. For 'twas scarce a half-sheet of foolscap, with writing on one side only: a paltry thing where we had sought a great one.

"What have you done with the rest of it, child? Where are the other pages? The schedules? The codicils?" The doctor spoke sternly, the force of his voice pushing the frightened boy back against me.

"Don't be scared, Ben," I said, smoothing his hair. "This is Doctor Alexander, a friend of Mr. Jameson's."

"Cod and what, mister? I didn't touch aught, I swear it. Miss Weston gave me the book. She'll tell ye she did. And it were just that one page what fell out. I didn't mean to hurt it!"

"Samuel Bradstreet, you mad, dead bastard." Doctor Alexander shook his head, ignoring Ben. "Matters of life and death tucked into *The Child's New Play-Thing*."

He turned to me. "Well, Miss Easton, I seem to have led us into an error: I was mistaken about the size of the Will and the manner of book in which Bradstreet would have secreted it. You delayed us by taking this *Play-Thing* from the pile, and spoiling my system. But it has been found at last—and just as you were about to give it away!"

"Don't blame Weston, Sander," Jamie broke in. "And where was it found? Twas lurking in some what-the-deuce-ecimo, just as I predicted!"

"Yes, yes. I confess some small disappointment—the document gives us less than I had hoped."

"Less than you had hoped, Doctor? How so?" I asked. "Tis everything *I* had hoped for, and more: a fairy tale! Writ in black and white, it says that Hannah has been free for more than three years already, and that Phebe was *born* free. *Disappointment*, you would name it? Ecstasy, I would sooner say."

"Yes, yes," the doctor sneered. "All the night long the walls have heard you cry 'ecstasy.' And now, wrapped round in morning's glow—or whatever that costume in which you have bedecked yourself—you bring your powers of illumination to this document. I am not surprised that an artist should paint such a pretty picture of Bradstreet's testament. But it is not so simple. This Will is a beginning, but only that. A long road lies ahead of us. And whatever garden path Jamie has been showing you, this one will not be strewn with primrose petals."

"Sander, I'll caution you only once: take a kinder tone with her," Jamie warned, and severely, though Alexander seemed hardly to hear him. "And truly, I can't fathom your reserve. I'm the executor; let me go to the probate judges at once, and have done with this foul business."

"You shall stay put," Alexander insisted. "And if you would dispatch that urchin, Jamie, I can tell you why."

I placed the riddle book in Ben's hand and sent him back to his mother. "Bring her round on the morrow, little friend," I called after him as he walked down Queen Street.

Doctor Alexander would conduct his tutorial in the parlor, where the books were stacked so high along the walls that he could fancy himself lecturing in a proper library.

"Be seated, both of you," he commanded. "Now tell me, Jamie, what you have learned from Samuel Bradstreet's last Will and Testament. Start with the most urgent matters, and proceed to the least."

"Tis just as Weston said, is it not? The Will is short enough already, but I can abridge it. Six words: Hannah and Phebe are free."

"Jamie, darling, that's five words."

"Thanks, Kit-cat." He winked at me.

"Dear God. Is this what my life is to become?" the doctor asked. "Enough, you two! Proceed, Jamie."

"Aye. Well, he proves what Edes and Lambert say about Mrs. Bradstreet and Hiram Usher. At least, that's how I read, 'to *usher* her to the altar.' Nice touch, that."

"Very good. And our dear friend William's inheritance?"

"Spectacles to see . . . what a spectacle the Wily Bastard's mother has made of herself, perhaps?"

"No, Jamie," I burst in. "The spectacles shall let him see clearly the deception that has been practiced upon him: the lie that is his parentage."

"Exactly so," said the doctor approvingly. "Bradstreet labels himself a cuckold, his wife a whore, and his son a bastard—all in just thirty words. Not so few as six, Jamie. But economically done, indeed," Alexander said, raising an imaginary glass to the ghost of Samuel Bradstreet, and then extending the toast to me. "And nice reasoning, Miss Easton, unexpected from a member of your sex, and on so little sleep as well. Go on, tell us what else you read there."

"Women and men reason just the same, do they not, Doctor? Surely we share a common humanity. Or will you next tell me that black men are different from white below the skin? For I did, in my womanish way, see something else indicated in Bradstreet's Will. If you would but grant one of my fair sex permission to speak it, Professor?"

"I'll not grant your presumption of equality between the sexes, Miss Easton. But yes, you have my permission to speak. Pray, continue."

"Oh, thank you, good sir," I said. "I venture Bradstreet means the slight against his wife's honor to cut deeper still. For there is a cipher in it, is there not? If he has given away everything, then he has nothing left but what he bequeaths Patience and Hannah."

"Aye, just as the probate commissioners said." Jamie nodded.

"Well, a 'widow's portion' means the lifetime use of one-third of a deceased husband's real estate, and free ownership of that much of his movable property. But 'tis a dark joke: one-third of null is null. He has left her with nothing: a cruel legacy, even if she has loved elsewhere."

"Maybe she did more than love elsewhere. Maybe the lady offed her poor Macbeth," Jamie suggested.

"Perhaps. But that is not my concern just now. Do you see nothing else, Miss Easton?" Alexander pressed me. "You speak of parentage and pedigree. What of Phebe's? Hannah came to Bradstreet 'heavy with Child by her injudicious master.' "

"Another pun, to be sure, Doctor," I replied, refusing to let him ruffle me. "Edward Easton, the justice, acted *injudiciously* by getting his Negro woman with child."

"Sweet Jesus, Weston: Phebe is your sister?"

I nodded, but before I could speak, the doctor interjected. "Let us not be distracted from our exegesis. Go on, Miss Easton."

But Jamie rose from his chair and demanded, "Sander, you knew this?"

The doctor sighed with impatience. "Yes. All this, and much more, I assure you, I read in Miss Easton's letter book."

"The letter book you so rudely purloined from me!" I added.

"You read her letters?" Jamie cried. "You *knew* my Weston was this Easton—when? When did you learn it?"

"The day I arrived, my friend, the very day."

"And yet you did not see fit to tell me?"

"Obviously."

"Why the devil not? What manner of friend withholds such a revelation?"

"The manner of friend who has witnessed too many of your intimate entanglements, at close quarters. Your Weston was none of my affair."

"And the two of you?" He turned from the doctor, to me, his fury growing. "Damn your bloods. Did you take tea together while I was out, and cackle over what a bloody fool you'd made of me?"

"Hardly, Jamie," said the doctor, smoothly. "What I found in those letters was not mine to expose. That, I submit, was Miss Easton's job. And we see how well she has managed it."

"Aye, Professor," Jamie agreed. "Your lady logician excels at treachery, but has scant talent for sincerity."

"Please, Jamie," I pleaded, panicked. "I own my deception. And I begged the doctor's silence. But we never conspired against you."

"Rest easy, Miss Easton," the doctor said to me. "Our friend may be a poor governor of his temper but he is a surpassingly generous man. A foolishly generous man. He will forgive you."

"Will I? How am I to trust either of you, ever again?"

"It is past, Jamie," Alexander insisted. "Censure us as you will, and at your leisure, but, for now, let us leave it behind, and return to Bradstreet's legacy. God knows Hannah has lingered in that jail for too long already and Phebe must not remain enslaved a moment longer than necessary. While Reason smiles upon Miss Easton, I would fain have her résumé."

Jamie was by no means mollified, but took his seat again.

"You would be a painter, Miss Easton," the doctor continued. "Then shall you read the negative space. Tell me, what is *not* in Bradstreet's Will?"

This line of questioning found me ill prepared, and my thoughts seemed to take me in five directions at once.

"Well," I began, thinking out loud. "He neglects to tell us why he wrote a new Will the day before he died, though that was the day Jamie painted him from life, and he must have been pondering his legacy. But then why bury the document? For truly, Doctor, Bradstreet nearly took his Will to the grave with him."

"Brava. Indeed, you are a specimen of female ingenuity . . . such as it is. And?"

"God in heaven, Sander, *get on with it!*" Jamie broke in, rising once again from his chair, and pacing the room. "Most of the world lies outside that brief Testament. Are we to inventory all of creation, then? 'Tis nigh on noon, and here we sit, prattling. Before the probate court shuts for the dinner interval, let me present the damned Will and have the girl freed."

"Indeed, we must rescue the girl—and her mother, too. But you overlook our forensic purposes, friend. Bradstreet was murdered, and they did not break his killer's neck upon the Neck. We must catch the criminal, if we can."

"But surely, Sander, there is nothing in Bradstreet's Will to tell us who killed the man. Tis not as if he knew who meant to do him in."

"Correct, friend. About his murderer, he tells us nothing. Or at least nothing we can yet quite read, not in the half-light he has given us. No, the trick is not to probate the Will—not that you would succeed in doing so, in any case. A Will with no witnesses? A murdered man's lost last Testament, full of slanders, suddenly discovered by an executor known to the testator for naught but two weeks? You would be lucky to be drummed out of court."

"Then how are we to help Phebe?" I pleaded.

"A better question, Miss Easton. We have dissected Bradstreet's testament quite fully, I am satisfied. Now the so-called great men of this so-called town must read Samuel Bradstreet's last Will and Testament. Our task will be to watch them read—that is, to observe our murderers disclose themselves to us."

Jamie looked incredulous. "Are we to put a notice in Edes's paper inviting the gentlemen of Boston, and their fine ladies too, to file past our dining table with their magnifying glasses?"

"Sarcasm, Jamie? You surprise me. No. You are to *paint*. You left a space for the Will upon that great maudlin canvas of yours; well, fill it in, or have your apprentice do it, if you would. I care not whose hand holds whose brush. Just paint the goddamned Testament!"

"And then what?"

"*Then* shall you post your notice in the papers."

"Aye, our notice: *Come one, come all! Read Samuel Bradstreet's Will, finely painted upon canvas. Five pence a head*."

"The notice, my friend," Alexander answered, "will announce an Exhibition. You and your mistress will collect every canvas you have painted. Call your cocks and pullets back to the coop, and finish every commission you have left undone. And then shall the good people of this town pay you to spy the murderer among them."

"And where, pray tell, shall we open this blasted gallery, Sander? Boston has no exhibition rooms. No Vauxhall, no Foundling Hospital, no Academy. Would you hang my work in a tavern, then? Or in the sodding Manufactory House?"

"You shall find the proper place, Jamie," the doctor said flatly. "You have a great talent for making friends."

"And how do you picture it, Doctor," I protested. "A man will step from the crowd, prostrate himself before the image of Samuel Bradstreet, and cry, 'Alas, poor Bradstreet! I knew him, Horatio. Why did I kill thee, O Samuel?' No player could deliver those lines with a straight face!"

"Who says our player is a man?" the doctor mused. "Certainly, we have no shortage of suspects, both ladies and gentlemen."

"Do we? Just *who*, Professor, is on your list of suspects?" Jamie asked.

"Must I spell it out for you? The obvious suspects, of course, are everyone with intimate access to the house. Bradstreet's servants, his doctor—"

"*Newcombe?*" Jamie asked.

"He had the opportunity, certainly. And has he not gained the victim's seat in the Assembly? Yes. Bradstreet's doctor, his wife, his son, his daughter."

"Patty?" I exclaimed. "She is the sweetest girl I ever knew!"

"Perhaps, Miss Easton. But arsenic is sweet, is it not? Patience Bradstreet was with her father when he died. And none stood to benefit so greatly as she did. Yet by no means would I single her out for suspicion. Your brother, the Reverend Easton: he was there that day."

"The wee pope? You must be joking."

"Hardly, Jamie. Yes, the vicar, and other officials as well. Bradstreet's political opponents, and, yes, even his allies."

"The foxes *and* the Hens, Sander?"

"The whole Boston barnyard, and more: the Will casts suspicion on still others. Only one of four copies has surfaced. What happened— *who* happened—to the other three? And of course, to this long list I must, as you realize, add you two as well."

"Us? Me and Weston? Noah's blasted Ark, Sander, what about Gulliver? That's half the town. Tell me, Professor: What do you mean to accomplish by parading these suspects before Bradstreet's portrait?"

"Not a parade, but an experiment. I will have reactions, pure chemical reactions. I mean the Exhibition to serve as a laboratory. The paintings, you see, are like so many flames. The esteemed members of the audience: they are my reagents. We place them in our crucible, heat them, and watch them respond. If we control the variables carefully, one of them—maybe more than one—will explode."

"It sounds a dangerous plan, Sander. Shouldn't we leave Weston out of it, from here on?"

"Her role is as crucial as yours, and far more complicated, now that she plays both sexes. For God's sake, do not let your fuck muddle my experiment."

Jamie grabbed Alexander by the collar and pulled him to his feet.

"I will not stand for it, do you hear? Rail at me, if you must. But leave her alone."

Alexander smiled, and when he spoke, I heard hate in his voice.

"Leave her alone? Is that not exactly what I have been trying to do: to leave myself well out of what lies between the two of you? To be candid, I would fain never cast my eye upon her countenance again, and, as I am sure you can imagine, I would rather not be imprisoned in this house with the two of you. Leave her alone? Think what you say, man. Had I the least inclination, if I should so much as to touch the hem of a garment worn by a white woman in this town—even one so far fallen as your Fanny Easton—Cicero's death would be a dainty one compared to mine. Do you suppose I live without a body, devoid of all sentiment, of all desire? You can hardly resent my mocking the two of you."

"Aye, I can, and I do," Jamie answered hotly.

For a full minute the two men locked eyes. At last, Alexander shrugged.

"I yield the case but not the axiom. My rage is warranted, and I defend my right to it. But it is misspent upon you."

With those words, and a shallow bow—he dismissed us to our work, and headed off to the laboratory to attend to his own.

Without so much as a look in my direction, Jamie turned and headed to the hall.

"To the easels, then," he ordered, over his shoulder. And from the tone of his voice, I could not discern whether he would next take me in his arms or tell me to pack my bags. I climbed the stairs behind him, for the apprentice doth always follow in the master's footsteps. But as

I reached the landing, I found that he had halted just before the painting room door.

"Ladies first, lad," he said, with a wink.

I had not lost him, then. I felt a flood of relief wash over me. And next, a wave of desire.

He closed the door behind us. "Weston," he said with counterfeit gravity, "you heard our instructions: we are to stage an Exhibition. We must make haste to display our wares."

As he spoke, he unbuttoned my waistcoat, moving with such frantic speed that I feared the placket should tear.

"But master," I asked, tugging my shirt overhead, "where would you mount me?"

"I would fain exhibit your beauty in every room in the house, lass," he answered, as he lifted me in his arms, carried me to the upholstered chair, and set me down behind it. "But just now, I would bend you over this."

"But sir," I demurred, "I am only the apprentice. Tis for the master to display his genius." I peeled off his breeches.

"O, Weston," my Jamie sighed, pressing himself into my spine as I braced my hands against the back of that great chair. With great delicacy, he took up the loose end of the red velvet sash that held my trousers. "I fear I have trained you poorly, lass. For you never have learnt to tie a canvas fast. Let me unveil this masterpiece."

"Aye, sir," I teased, looking back over my shoulder. "I should welcome your critique of the verso of my likeness, if only you might demonstrate for me another aspect of your Art."

"Kit-cat? What might that be?"

"Well, master, I would have you show me precisely how you meant to deploy your brush upon your serving boy."

"Damn your metaphors, Weston. Do you mean for me to fuck your ass, lass?" he asked, astonished, delighted.

"Have you not dreamt of it, sir?"

"Aye, I fancy you know my dreams, and all too well."

"Then I would have you realize them, sir."

"If I must, lass," he said, with a happy lilt in his voice. "If I must." He took a small bottle of mineral oil from a patch of sunlight on the table that held his palette. "I suppose every master ought to encourage his journeyman to stretch his talents."

How can so much laughter mingle with so much passion? I cannot say how long we remained in that Grecian pose, nor yet in others. Nor shall I describe the warmth of those smooth floorboards, which had spent the morning absorbing the heat of the sun. Only this: one way and another (and another, and another), we did not hear the doctor's footsteps upon the stairs. But his impatient knocking was clear enough. With a sudden burst of modesty, Jamie ushered me into the closet and wrapped a tarp about himself.

"Sweet Jesus, Sander, what now?" he shouted. "Can you not let us work here in peace?"

I peered out from my hiding place, watching Jamie stomp toward the door.

"I can hear that you have been busy with your . . . preparations," the doctor said. "Yet I worry: Have you and your apprentice not forgotten something you shall need if you are to paint Bradstreet's Will with the greatest possible accuracy?"

"What, pray what have we overlooked?" Jamie huffed, as he cracked open the door, clutching his makeshift toga like some dissolute Roman orator.

"O noble Cato!" Sander laughed, and warmly, once he saw him. "The Will, Jamie. I venture that you may need the Will."

Shaking his head, the doctor offered his friend the little slip of paper, which had been briefly forgotten by this altogether distracted,

Fanny Easton.

CHAPTER 22

In Which Our Author Is Rudely Awakened

There is a species of slumber from which a man especially hates to wake. Rise, rise! says the day. Nay, nay, say I. I am with my love, my joy; she is in my arms; we have earned our rest. I have waited all my life for this companion. Lo, for so many years I have trimmed my sails, only to tack back and forth, never gaining against the winds of adversity, stalled by the stillness of solitude, and ever at risk of being shipwrecked, cast away, marooned. Please, dear God: I have only just reached port. Ask me nevermore to hoist my sails and set forth into the wide water.

I lay last night, with my Weston, in my ample bed, our bodies entwined, like two pieces of a puzzle at last fit together. Does she not suit me to perfection? Her wit, her Art, her heart? If we stirred, 'twas only for yet another caress, yet another crisis of pleasure. Or for still more murmurs and whispers and smiles. God above, I cannot begin to give my thanks. Accept this silent supplication from your skeptical, errant son: please don't take her away from me.

Does my prayer come too late?

For when I finally woke, fully woke, she was gone.

"Kit-cat?" I called, bereft, as I ran my hand across the impression of her form on the still-warm sheets. Could she not have tarried with me a little longer? Can she not fathom how long I've had to wake alone, and how dearly I cherish the waking together? Does she not cherish it just as much? I would give up my last chance at fortune to marry her. Aye, dear Reader, I would. You will tell me I should marry for money. You may wonder whether I can trust this Fanny Easton, of fallen virtue and, you will say, of dubious integrity. Know that I have asked myself the same. But have I not told you? I am a poor governor of my passions. And I would marry for love.

As I pulled myself from bed, thinking to call for her from the hall-way, I found, on the table by my bedstead, a note:

Dearest,

> "Mine eye hath play'd the painter, and hath steel'd
> Thy beauty's form in table of my heart;
> My body is the frame wherein 'tis held."

I could not bear to wake you, my love. I have gone on your business and my own. Gulliver comes with me. Look for me after noon.

Forever your,
F.E.

What business? Bugger Billy Shakespeare. She would hold a picture of me in her mind's eye, and yet hop out of my bed? What manner of woman puts aside earthly pleasure in three dimensions for a fantasy wrought in two? It cannot be past seven. What business steals her from me for five hours? How could anything be so urgent, except that we rush to the justice of the peace and become man and wife *at once*?

I shivered as I dressed. The fire had long since gone out. But when I descended, I found the kitchen colder still, and no sign that Alexander had eaten. I fixed a fire and set the kettle to boil. Half an hour later, as I finished my tea and toast in gloomy silence, a knock came at the door. What stillness greeted it. No Gulliver yelping, no Sander complaining, no Weston teasing—"What, sir, did you want me to answer it, sir?"

I dragged myself from the bench and went to the door.

"Please, guv'nor," said a haggard but sweet-faced woman, with a clumsy curtsy. "Mrs. Simmons to see ye, sir." She wore a clean bonnet, a frock of faded green, and a brown linsey-woolsey cloak too thin for the day's chill. Her eyes were clear, and kind, but weary, and cautious.

"Mrs. Simmons . . . ?"

"Yes, sir," she said, with an extra curtsy. "Ben's mum?"

"Ach, aye, of course. A fine lad. Please come in, madam," I answered, backing into the hall and gesturing wide with my arm.

"Thank ye kindly, sir," she said, as she stepped past. She glanced from one corner to the next, giving the kitchen a careful inspection. It occurred to me that I had barely seen the room until I saw it through her eyes. Ashes piled in the hearth. Half-empty sacks of grain against the wall. Dirty trenchers heaped in the basin. A ladle lying in the middle of the floor. Truly, our house was a mess.

"My Ben tells me you could use a piece of service, sir," she offered.

I laughed.

"Your boy doesn't tell you the half of it, does he, Mrs. Simmons? We are drowning in our clutter, are we not?"

She smiled. "Well, sir, 'tis not many a bachelor who can keep house, is it?"

"Truer words never spoken, Mrs. Simmons, though I have reason to hope my bachelorhood will soon be at an end."

"Sir?"

"Not of the moment, dear woman," I said, waving her inquiry aside. "Let me show you the rest of the house."

We climbed the stairs to the garret, and made our way down again, stopping on the second floor for a brief tour of my bed-chamber and the painting room, talking, all the way, of laundry and sweeping, stocking the firebox and stirring stews. When we at last arrived at the parlor, having settled on wages, I proposed to introduce her to my tenant.

"Doctor Ignatius Alexander has two rooms just through this door," I said, as I knocked on it.

There was no answer.

I knocked again. By now 'twas midmorning. He could not possibly still be asleep.

"Sander?" I called, loudly, and knocked again.

"Perhaps he's out, sir?"

"No, no, he can't be . . ." I mumbled. And then hollered, "Sander!"

Still no answer. There was nothing for it. I walked Mrs. Simmons to the front door, pressed a coin into her hand by way of pledge of employment, and bade her return on the morrow. I turned on my heel and headed back through the parlor to Sander's door.

"Sander?" I called again, as I entered his sanctuary. I hadn't been in his rooms in weeks. I walked across his makeshift laboratory and peered into his bed-chamber. Empty. That he was gone I could no longer deny. And without so much as a note, much less a sonnet.

I sat down at his long worktable, covered with books and papers and crucibles. Here was more than a clutter; 'twas a chaos. Just as well that Mrs. Simmons had been spared the sight of it. The glass vessels were blanketed in a film of dirt. What kind of a laboratory gathers dust? By the devil's dung, what has Sander been doing back here if not conducting his forensic inquiry?

My curiosity roused, no faster than my temper rose, I could not help myself: I stole a glance at the papers on the table.

Dear Reader, you know what it is to be nosy. Pray excuse me. Indeed, I excused myself, thus: I pictured Alexander reading Weston's letter book, invading her privacy—and mine—and extracting her secrets, *months ago*. And was I not starved for companionship? Words on a page make laudable companions, as no one knows better than you.

At the top of the pile, I discovered notes in Alexander's own hand, a tiny, tight, furious scrawl, covering page after page of foolscap: scribbled proofs, I took them to be. I rifled a little farther. A page of remarks about Hume's dissertations on logic. Old issues of the *Gazette*, heavily annotated. The manuscript of Bradstreet's *Modest Inquiry*. Several months' worth of *Gentleman's Magazine*, and a scattering of the *Transactions of the Royal Academy of Science*.

And then, an envelope caught my eye. Addressed to Alexander, in my care. I picked it up, and caught my breath. I knew this pen: that flourishing, looping signature was none other than my brother Colin's. My hand beginning to tremble, I took the letter from the opened envelope, and unfolded it.

My dear Ignatius,
 How sublimely relieved was I to receive your most eloquent and loquacious missive, my most venerable and estimable friend. And know,

*precociously learned sir, how earnestly and munificently I pray to the
Almighty Author of Mankind, He whose benevolence and wisdom guideth
us all in times of travail—and never were there days more filled with travail than mine—for your eventual and entire deliverance from Pharaoh
and his minions, notwithstanding the mountain of Satan's perils, traps,
and pernicious obstacles set before every Christian . . .*

I read the whole of this atrocious epistle not once, but twice. Three
times.

There are reasons a gentleman does not read his friend's correspondence.

I wish I had not. I will spare you the remainder of its contents—many
more pages, I assure you—for I would rather not implicate you in my
error. Nor reveal to you, at just this moment, either the depth, or the
cause, of my anger.

What to do, how to keep busy, alone, aggrieved, impatient?
Paint. How I long to paint.

But I could not—or, at least, I ought not. Weston had not finished
limning the words of Bradstreet's Will before we lost the light yesterday
eve, and her sure hand was better suited to the task. If I begin to hope,
at last, that my instrument is not ruined (in truth, Reader, for lo these last
two weeks, I had despaired that I would ever paint again), the fingers of
my right hand remain tender enough to make my brush quaver upon
the canvas. I dare not risk my recovery. And, meanwhile, there is different work to do. I am become my own curator.

I trudged up to the storage room opposite Weston's bed-chamber,
where I had stowed my pictures when first I rented the place. I had
brought near a dozen canvases, copies of my best portraits. In my haste
to leave Edinburgh, I scarce had time to choose among them. Never have
I managed to unpack them, for I would not live in my own gallery. Do
not imagine that I have no taste for my own Art. I take pleasure in my
paintings, true, but only while they stand, wet, *alive*, upon my easel. Except for *The Serving Boy*, I have never been able to keep a canvas in my
house long after I lacquered it. Tis, to me, like looking upon a corpse.

And so. It brought me no joy, I assure you, to unroll those dusty portraits. I selected five: the Laird of Firth, the Earl of Berkeley, and the Duchess of Hampton, all at three-quarter length; a full-length of the doctor, and a half-length of my brother. I carried them down to the painting room, to inspect them by the better light.

Were my choices vicious? They were, Reader, they were. The villain who had saddled me with Gulliver; the nobleman whose vengeance had sent me into exile; the harpy, his daughter, who was the engine of that fury; the so-called friend, who, behind my back, corresponds with my brother, the hypocrite. And so: the laird, the earl, the duchess, the doctor, and the preacher.

A royal flush? My own rogues' gallery.

Vicious. Can I be so vicious?

I can.

I lit a fire in the painting room and spent the next hours tacking each of these canvases onto wooden stretchers, to ready them for framing. Stretch, pound. Stretch, pound.

Where is my Weston?

The work required both concentration and exertion, and proceeded awkwardly enough, as I would coddle my bad hand. But the task rewarded me with distraction, even as the bells tolled noon.

Noon. But still no Weston.

I paused only for a supper of cold mutton and hard cider. I was hammering, nearly done, and sweating, despite the chill, when I heard the door open downstairs. I thought, at first, that Weston must have at last returned, until I heard heavy footfalls that could only be the doctor's.

"Sander?" I called as I stepped out onto the landing.

"Who else, Jamie, who else?" was his irritated answer.

Damn the man.

I descended to find him in the parlor, in something altogether different from his usual attire. He had just taken off his heavy cloak, and wore 'neath it a threadbare shirt and trousers tied with rope.

"Who *else*, Sander? Maybe: Weston? For I've been alone here the whole of this unending day, with no idea where either of you has been."

He gave me a look midway between annoyance and pity.

"I had not been apprised, *massa*, that I needed your permission to leave the house. Have you forgotten that I am a free man? Or do you propose to enforce on me this colony's new legislation for the Further Regulating of Slaves?"

With that, he turned his back, and headed into his rooms. I followed him through his laboratory and into his bed-chamber, and stayed there, while he changed back into his own clothes.

"Where have you been?" I demanded.

"I went to see Hannah," he answered coldly. "You remember Hannah?"

"Do I remember her? Damn your blood."

"*My* blood? Your quarrel is not with me, Jamie. Where is your mistress today? Might a man in search of a bit of comfort find her down by the docks?"

"What?" I could scarce believe my ears.

"She needs a leash even more than your goddamned dog."

"You son of a bitch. What do you mean to say?"

"Four words: she is a whore."

Reader, does he want me to kill him? And yet, and yet. Alexander *shams*. Indeed, he has always been a talented actor, a most polished and performing gentleman. But am I not an able reader of men (although, apparently, not of women dressed as boys)? He was counterfeiting, I was certain. Almost certain. Angling. Baiting. But why?

"Are you next to tell me she murdered Samuel Bradstreet? You can only be preparing for a role upon the stage. Or does the professor suddenly hunger for a bar-room brawl? I'm happy to oblige, mind, and I'd prevail, even with my painting hand tied behind my back."

"Ah, yes. But 'When the hurly-burly's done, When the battle's lost and won,' what then? Maybe I am the murderer. I have laid aside my dagger, Jamie, but I confess, I like to pour a little poison in men's ears."

"If you are the murderer, you truly are a marvel—even more than I knew—for you arrived in town after Bradstreet was dead and buried. Cast me as Hamlet, for I fit the part well enough. But spare me your witches and your Claudius, much less your Moorish Iago. Are there not villains enough in this world without your malice toward my Desdemona?"

"Ask Enoch Goddard about your Desdemona, Sweet Prince. I have seen him today. He flourishes, as ever."

"*That's* what you're on about? Grabcock tells you my Weston is a whore? And did he also tell you he's the Sultan of the Turks? I'm sorry you had truck with the man, but leave Weston out of it."

"As you wish."

"How'd you get past him, anyway?"

"I am, as you know, a master of disguise and dissembling. Do I play upon a stage? Of course. For every black man, Jamie, for every one of us, the whole of this new world is naught but a stage."

The truth of this I could scarce dispute.

"Granted. But Goddard. What'd it cost you?"

"O, massa!" he shrieked, in his furious falsetto. "I jus' gone did it, massa. I jus' walked up to that ole jail-keeper man, and I says, 'I'se here to empty dem nasty tubs, mistah jail-keeper man. Pu-lease, mistah, pu-lease can I clean up dat shit?'"

"Dark humor, Sander, but surely you jest."

"Would that I did, my friend, would that I did. But your vile Grab-cock was all too eager to believe the town had hired a slave to do the worst of his work."

"And you saw her, you saw Hannah?"

"Yes."

"*And?*"

"And. I told her that we had found the Will, begged her to believe that she and her daughter would both soon be free, and I learned something I needed to know."

"What?"

"That I shall keep to myself, Jamie, for you are no longer to be trusted."

"'Tis *I* who's not to be trusted?" I growled.

By now he had finished dressing, and I followed him back into his laboratory. He stopped at a stand by the window, emptied a pitcher of water into a basin, splashed his face, and wiped his hands with a cloth.

"What, have you abandoned the Proverbial Gloves?"

"For the time being. You shall have occasion to see them again."

"Aye. Because the professor needs his hands bare to conduct impor-tant experiments here in this . . . laboratory?"

At this, he appeared more amused than annoyed.

"I see you have spied my ill-used equipment, Jamie, for I observe your fingerprints upon my dust-covered flasks—"

"Aye. I touched your flagons! Flog me! And then tell me: What have you been doing with all the powders you've bought from Cabot's, and at such a cost?"

"Perhaps the time has come to satisfy your curiosity on that account. I cured your cur. I healed my scars. And I made myself a fine sleeping potion. I tinkered with a few powders. But, in the main, I have kept myself busy doctoring the colored people of this town."

" 'Doctoring,' Doctor? Admirable work. But I confess, I cannot quite picture the renowned chemist salving wounds and birthing babies. What, will you be hawking patent medicines next? Frog spawn?"

"That much of my life escapes your notice should hardly surprise me."

"But Sander, surely I know who comes to my own house."

"You most certainly do not, nor is it your business. You would make your house my hideaway. I have treated it as my home."

"Fine. It gladdens me to hear it. But what with all your bloody doctoring, have you abandoned your forensic investigation?"

"There are more kinds of laboratories than the chemist's, Jamie. Mine is a laboratory of logic."

"Isaac Newton's rosy red arse! A laboratory of logic?"

"Yes, yes, I have been thinking. And writing, as clearly you've seen." He cast his eyes over his piles of books and papers. "Truly, Jamie, you are not to be trusted. You are distracted by passion, which is ever the enemy of Reason. And you make a poor trespasser, for you leave more tracks than Gulliver." He held up Colin's letter, which I hadn't bothered to return to its envelope.

I nodded at the letter. "You dare to speak of trespass?"

"I knew you would not approve, but that was no real argument against it," he answered quietly.

"You wrote to Colin, that piety-peddling charlatan, asking him to raise a subscription to get me out of debt! Aye, goddammit. You were right: I would not have approved."

"No. And more is the pity."

"The pity?" I hollered, unbelieving. "The pity is, you went to him on bended knee, in my name, and got nothing. Worse than naught! It's a deuced long letter. Let me sum it up for you, Professor: 'Gladly, noble doctor Africanus, will I redeem my sorry, sodding brother, after he has redeemed his blaspheming soul. Prove to me that he has returned to Christ—by which I mean, I want to see him grovel before me, and lick the shite from my shoes. Once he has done so, I will bring to the Mc-Greevys a bill of exchange for two thousand pounds. I will do more, sir—for I am the best of men, the most generous of men, the most humble of men, and I will see that all the world knows it—I will post to my prodigal brother one hundred pounds further, at once making good his debt, and ending his exile.' "

I was near tears now.

"I did not ask you to meet his preposterous terms, Jamie," he said, gently. "And I would not ask it of you. Ever."

"You won't ask me to kiss the hem of Colin's holy robes? Am I to thank you for your restraint? Dammit, Sander, it's my debt, and I can live with it. I don't need Colin's catechism to rescue me."

"Do you not, Jamie? I will not argue on Colin's behalf, for I entirely agree with you. In this case, at least, the younger brother is indeed the better gentleman," he said, his voice now full of affection and solicitude. "And you are an artist of prodigious talent. But need I remind you how wholly it is squandered in this miserable outpost on the edge of civilization? Painting faces here is about as good a use of your gifts as birthing babies is of mine."

"I'm afraid I don't find this New-England quite as forsaken as you do."

"Do you not? You must admit, these Americans are no lovers of Art. They will underwrite your modest trade with their worthless currency. But you will never earn in surplus such a sum as the McGreevys demand. Is that not why you so earnestly craved to send your Weston to London, to have—to be—what you cannot, what fortune—what Fortune—has denied you? It is you who deserves that eminence, not your apprentice."

"You'll not deprecate her talent."

"No? I shall defer to you on that account, for I have not yet had the occasion to take the true measure of her talent. But do not fool yourself. You will never be able to repay the McGreevys. And until you do, you will never return to Britain. You are as fettered as any beast in the King's menagerie, and Colin holds a key that might open your cage. Can you really imagine spending your life in exile, among Philistines, when safe passage home is so near to hand?"

"Aye, I can," I answered, full of passion. "I can well imagine it. I can picture a life here, with Weston—with our *children*, for the love of God. I can make a trade in face-painting. Unlike you, I don't crave fame; I don't want what you want for me, or for yourself; all I require is a reasonable living. Mark me, Sander: never will I go begging to Colin. He's a fraud, and you know it. His false faith. His sickening sanctimony, his pious parsimony. Never will I forgive him. Never."

"Yet his cause is a good one. Even a noble one."

"Colin, noble? There can never be honor in hypocrisy, Sander. Only after years earning his fortune as a slave-trader did he turn abolitionist—in public, always in public. A prophet of amazing grace! Aye, the gaudy glowworm. He could have raised the funds to purchase your liberty, and better than I."

"Yes. And he can still."

"No. Tis too late. Is it possible that you never deduced it? I went to him before I sought out the money-grubbing McGreevys. I *begged* him. Begged, pleaded, beseeched. *Prayed* with him. Kissed that bloody hem, ate that bloody crow. And did it help, even one whit? 'So sorry, dear deluded Stewart, but your unusual friend is far from a useful specimen of slavery's evil. I like to enflame my parishioners by shaking shackles and talking of whipped flesh. I like to hand around woodcuts of black bodies packed into slave ships. An elegant, learned gentleman-doctor would hardly fit the bill. My congregation takes pleasure in relieving the suffering we can see. No, not now, brother. But remind me of this case after your friend has been reduced somewhat, whipped and branded, maybe, and I'll see what I can do.' I say it again, Sander: never, never will I forgive him."

"Your brother is indeed a contemptible man. But surely men with better motives have done less good. Samuel Bradstreet, for instance. For all his fiery eloquence, he accomplished precious little. His 'Ghost' burns brighter."

"Less good? Less good? Sander, did you not hear me? You were to be put on the auction block, and Colin complained that you had not suffered enough. Now he sees his opportunity, sure, for 'tis a better story. 'Celebrated Reverend Colin Jameson Rescues Martyred Genius Doctor Ignatius Alexander from Barbarous Captivity While Redeeming Wastrel Younger Brother—a Noted Libertine!—from Debtor's Prison and Saving His Soul from Perdition!' I will not have it. And never will I forgive you for begging him on my behalf. Never."

Had I not made my point? And hotly? Ought not the scene to have closed, just here?

But Alexander would not cede the argument.

"I suppose I cannot blame you for having tried." He sighed. "But I had anticipated that you would ask Colin, and that he would enjoy refusing you, and that his refusal would drive you to take still more desperate measures. Which is why I told you, Jamie, to do nothing. Berkeley would never have let me go. And when you indebted yourself to the Mc-Greevys, he achieved his heart's desire: *you paid him to steal your freedom*."

I groaned. "When you put it that way, it sounds even worse than it is."

"I merely call a spade a spade, Jamie. And do not be such a fool as to think you can escape Berkeley's vengeance here. He is an idle nobleman with little else to entertain him save hunting you as he would trap a fox, with the McGreevys his pack of bloodthirsty hounds. No, you cannot escape this debt, but must, one day, repay it."

"I do know that, Sander," I answered, exasperated. God knows, I will not prostitute my honor to Hiram Usher forever.

"Good. You agree that you cannot remain an unredeemed captive. You must see that Colin's money is the nearest and best remedy. I will beg for his lucre again. Indeed, I have already written back to him, pointing out that what he proposes is to set a price for your faith, a particularly calculating blasphemy. I am sure I can convince him to raise the funds without bargaining for your soul."

I rested both my hands on the table, leaned over, and glared at him.

"You will do no such thing. I forbid it. I will not accept his money. 'Tis my debt, and I will shoulder it. I have honor enough left for that."

Alexander pushed his chair back and stood up.

"Know this, Stewart Jameson: you have honor enough for us all. But it is not your debt to shoulder alone. It is as much—no, more—mine. You have bartered your life to buy my liberty. It was foolish, and it was useless, but it is done. You have given up every chance not just of fame but equally of patronage and public regard. For me. With or without the manumission papers Berkeley stole from you, you paid his price. I am free. I am free, but only this far: I am free to be beholden to you."

"I never asked for your gratitude."

"Nor would you. But nonetheless I am chained to you as if by iron fetters. Did you not think I know enough to find my way from Virginia back to Britain? Pray, why do you think I risked my life to make it to bloody Boston? I can assure you, Jamie: I journeyed through Hell to get here, and the Devil charges a toll. I am tied to you, and not merely by the bonds of friendship. I will do whatever it takes to end this bondage. Whatever it takes."

This stopped me. I drew in a full breath, and let it out.

"Why, Doctor, I believe you hate me. How had I not seen it before? By God, will I forever be blind to those I love?"

"I do not hate you, Jamie," he began, with painful tenderness, reaching for my hand. He did not find it because, at just that instant, we both heard Gulliver barking. Without another word, we together walked to the hall, where we found the filthy hound, scratching his ear, alongside Weston, tugging off her mittens.

Twas my fate to be greeted this day—nay, this evening, for the sun had by now begun to set—by another return in disguise. She was dressed, once again, as a boy, her beautiful breasts bound 'neath her waistcoat, her face hidden under the drooping brim of a wool cap. She smelled of wood smoke and cider and the salt of the sea. She lugged behind her a heavy valise. She looked up at me, and smiled wide.

Letter XXI.

October the 10th, 1764

I would happily have lain abed all day, sketching my love while he slept, for I can think of no more beautiful sight the world over. But there was work to be done: my work, Jamie's work, and Alexander's great work of vindicating Hannah and liberating Phebe. My errands demanded that I again shroud my woman's form within the boy Weston's coarse costume. I thought I should chafe at my disguise. Instead, I relished the snugness of my bindings, the freedom of my trousers, the sturdiness of my boots, and the warmth of my cloak and cap. I love this Stewart Jameson, more than I can say. Yet I have nurtured a love for my liberty, too. Would that I might have both. Can I not be Fanny Easton within the walls of his house and Francis Weston on the streets of this city?

"Weston, where in God's name?" Jamie asked, as he confronted me in the hallway, the doctor by his side. "Noon, you said in that note, which said little enough. Tis nigh on four! And upon what business? And what fills that bag? And . . ."

Questions heaped upon questions in a great tumbling pile. Before I could venture an answer to even the first of them, Alexander spoke, softly, to his friend.

"Sweet Prince," he said, placing a hand upon Jamie's shoulder. "You and I have said enough. I shall trouble you no more this night." And then, with only the curtest of nods in my direction, he headed into his rooms.

No sooner had the doctor closed his door than Jamie resumed his interrogation.

"Well, lass . . . ?" he asked, tossing my valise 'neath the hall table, then taking my hands in his. "Grant I would rather shower you with kisses than with questions. But tell me where you've been all this long and troublesome day."

"Was it long for you, Jamie? I'm sorry, love. For me, it passed in an eyeblink."

At this he looked wounded, and I tasked myself to jolly him.

"But fear not, sir," I joked, bowing low enough to win at least the flicker of a smile. "Your apprentice has served you right faithfully, sir! Mr. Mason bid me bring you an invitation to the Red Hens' Carnival dinner, to be held the Friday after this. He insists that both you and I attend, to arrive promptly at seven. You have his permission to display his kit-cat at the Exhibition, and he promises to solicit the rest of the Hensmen on your behalf, provided that we make good his invitation to Carnival."

"A Carnival and an Exhibition. Sounds a mite too public, lass," Jamie said, pulling me toward him. "I should have preferred to repeat the private display you and I held yesterday in the painting room. To waste the whole of the day rounding up stray hens: 'tis a petty larceny, is it not? And I have said it before: I will not have a purloining apprentice."

"And pray, sir," I said, playing my part, "what have I taken from you?"

"Hours, Weston. Hours we might have misspent together. No man can redeem time, but I fancy it falls to us to try."

Here he glanced at the staircase, and gave me his lewdest wink.

"Kit-cat, upstairs with me, and I am sure you shall come at once!"

We had not made it past the landing ere I harvested this promise.

Hours later, having exchanged few words beyond the cries and murmurs of passion, I burrowed my face in his chest, and breathed in his sweet smell. I would soon have drifted off to sleep in Jamie's broad bed, but he shattered my repose.

"My Kit-cat," he whispered, nudging the small of my back, "would you now please tell me the whole of your business this day? I have labored mightily since you returned, and I would have you pay me for my efforts. I hazard I have earned the right to know your comings and goings, lass."

I lifted myself to see his face, lit by a lone candle. His smile disclosed that he meant his words in love, though not entirely in jest. Yet I heard them differently.

"I did not think you meant to enforce the terms of my indenture so closely," I said, shaking loose of his embrace.

He mistook the earnestness of my indignation.

"Aye, but I do, naughty wench," he quipped, giving my rump a pretended smack. "I would have you serve me on your knees, my shameless Shamela."

"Well, *master*," I rejoined, my dander rising, "if I am to account for my every moment, I should begin at sunup, when your dog and I paced round the frost-covered Common, from the burying ground southward to the Writing School, then west toward the cliffs, and then back."

"Is this to be *Gulliver's Travels*, then? I do not mean for that kind of tale, lass."

"You would have me proceed more swiftly, sir? But already I have neglected to account for twenty minutes of this, my first circuit. I paused for a time on the great hill, beside the beacon. Yes, I confess it, sir: I looked out over the harbor—thinking of you, sir, if you must know, and of the fathomless depth of my love for you. Then I made my way down Beacon Street back to Tremont. As I rounded the corner, the change rang in the belfry of the Brattle Street church. An hour, then: you may enter it thus in your ledger, and cancel that portion of my debt. Or better still, direct me to undertake that task when next I reckon your books."

"I'm glad you slowed your steps long enough to think of me, lass," he said, hurt, and bitter. "But did you not stop to pee? Mock my devotion, if you must. Have I not told you, long since, that you are the master and I, the apprentice? Just the same, Kit-cat, I would know where you've been since that bell tolled."

"And I shall tell you. But I would not have you imagine that knowledge to be your right. Tis my gift to you, not some tax you have levied upon me. I have been to see my brother. I'll not apologize for it."

"Lady Lazarus in a woolen waistcoat!" he exclaimed, relieved. "You have seen Daniel, then? Was it a sweet reunion?"

Yes, I told him, there had been sweetness in it. But not only that, or even mostly.

I thought to find my brother at King's Chapel. Twas midmorning when Gulliver and I passed 'neath the shadow its steeple cast over the corner of School and Tremont streets. I had grown up with that great gray edifice, built of Quincy granite. As I tied Gulliver to the hitching post beside its small burying ground, my mind filled with one of my earliest memories, of the raw April morning the masons laid the chapel's cornerstone.

I was just shy of six. My father—proud pillar of the Anglican faith since first its light was permitted to penetrate the darkness of this Puritan wilderness—gathered his family round him to witness the ceremony. There were speeches and prayers, dozens, it seemed, as one eminence after another added his bluster to an already windy day. The small, proud tribe of Eastons huddled together against the cold: me; then Daniel, not yet eight; my precious Lydia, but two years old; and baby Henry. I can see my mother wrapping her shawl tightly about the babe, anxious that the chill would carry him off. My father, of course, would hear nothing of her fears, every mother's nightmares, and realized often enough.

She worried rightly, but too soon. Little Henry had grown into a robust schoolboy of five, maybe six, when he entered the at-last completed church, resplendent with gilt and gloss and redolent of incense, upon its dedication day. He looked proud unto bursting as he took his place between Daniel and my father, there in the front-most pew, while my mother, Lydia, and I lingered, silent and decorous, on the distaff side.

Oh, Jamie, would that you had captured my family's long-lost joy! But all portraits of children are death-haunted, are they not? Certainly this pretty picture did not last. Two years more and we happy six were halved by the dread smallpox. And then, not five years afterward, my own babe was taken. And now? Just a decade after that golden cross first shined in the nave of this great church, what wretched remnant remains of that once-happy family.

I walked into the rectory, where I found my brother hunkered over a desk, a hinged Bible open on a stand before him, his quill scratching away at what I took to be his Sunday homily. To see his deep green eyes look back at me: 'twas overwhelming. I could barely croak his name as I stumbled toward him.

"Daniel . . ."

"Who calls me by my familiar name? Do I know you, child?" he said, resting his quill and squinting through the dust motes suspended in the shafts of sunlight streaming through the window high above his desk.

"Tis your own sister, Daniel," I answered, taking another step.

"My sisters both are lost!" he exclaimed as he rose to his feet.

"You have two sisters yet living, and I am one of them. Tis I, Fanny."

"Fanny?" he stammered, astonished, confused. "How can it be? You . . ."

He walked toward me, and gently removed my cap, holding it gingerly, as if its humble cloth were distasteful to him. For a full minute, maybe more, he searched my face. Then finally, wordlessly, he laid his soft hands upon my cheeks, as my tears spilled. I sunk to my knees, receiving the benediction of his touch more greedily than ever I had sought any sacrament.

When I recovered my feet, I took his hands in mine as I told him my glad tidings: that I had endured my trials. That my companions and I had discovered Samuel Bradstreet's lost Will, and meant to see it done. That Phebe—free-born Phebe—was our half sister, and awaited our rescue. That Mr. Bradstreet, who cast off all his worldly possessions to pass through the gates of Heaven, had nonetheless provided amply for Patience.

"You will marry your true love, Daniel! Our father shall not keep her from you."

All this he heard from me gratefully—indeed, tearfully, especially when I spoke of his beloved Patty. But for my own circumstances, he had little of patience, and less of charity.

"O, dear Fanny! But *you* are ruined!" he cried, looking me up and down, his tender expression of fraternity congealing into a preacher's mask of practiced concern.

"None is ruined if she loves truly," I ventured.

But as I told him of my situation, he shook his head, doubtful of my redemption. His lips tightened, and his aspect of concern hardened further, into censure.

"You must leave that house of sin at once, my child, and seek God's forgiveness here, in His house."

My child, is it? Must every man place himself in some vertical relation to me? Oh, Father! Oh, Daniel! Oh, my Jamie! Does your sex have no other way of knowing mine?

Leave that house of sin at once, my child, and seek God's forgiveness: counsel both empty and wrong, for I have never known a house *less* sinful than Jamie's. But Daniel knew no other advice. How he strained to think of ways to help me. His ladies of charity would provide me with alms. Perhaps—just maybe—he could find me a situation as a governess, far enough from the orbit of Boston that the gossips should not hound me. Whence news of my shameful, stubborn survival would not dog him, I think he meant.

These offers of assistance I waved away. I needed no grand rescue, for hadn't I effected my own? Instead, I asked two small favors. First, that he hurry to Hanover Street to give Phebe another doll I had made her, a token to sustain her until the joyful day of our reunion. He looked uncomfortable enough, but did not contradict me when I referred to her as our sister. Second, that he steal up to my girlhood bedchamber to pack me a small bag of my clothes, if any were still there.

Daniel complied, and quickly, though I could not tell whether he was more eager to render what aid I would accept, or to rid his study of my stain.

"Twas neither of those, lass." Jamie smiled, running his index finger along my spine. "Twas fear: he dared not breach the contract you set before him. For a penniless painter's apprentice, Kit-cat, you drive a hard bargain."

In the darkness, he could not see my tears.

"I thank you, young Weston," he continued, mock-courteously. "Tis at long last a very full accounting you've given me, of a very full day. But how much longer can I hold you to your indenture?"

"Not a day, my love, for Francis Weston does not exist."

"Aye, but I would hold you, lass. I would hold you. So I had best place you under another sort of contract, as soon as possible. Let us speak to Edes on the morrow, and publish our intentions in his very next issue."

"*This* is your proposal?" I cried, rising from the bed and gathering a sheet about me. Tis true, I had dreamed of spending my life with this man, whose love I scarcely deserved. I should have been grateful, beyond measure. But his words wounded me. He spoke in jest when I wished him earnest. I would have him cherish me, not govern me. "Do you think it a promotion, to climb your ladder, from apprentice to wife?" I demanded. "Can I not be my own master?"

I did not wait for his reply, but ran up the stairs and slammed the door to my garret, wondering if I were doomed to remain forever the colony of some man.

Held fast by bonds of silk with the strength of irons, I am this Massachusetts, this America, this,

Fanny Easton.

From the *Boston Gazette*, Thursday, October 11, 1764.

BOSTON.

To the Editor:

Not yet one week has passed since that Black Day upon which this town's bells rang the mournful toll of the Death of Liberty. What an appearance does Boston now make: everywhere our windows draped in black, and our streets flashing red. The King's soldiers make their camp upon our Common, parade through our streets, and quarter themselves in the chamber of our Assembly. They place their main guard in our Merchants Exchange, and mount their cannon before it. Once filled with gentlemen transacting their business, and legislators deliberating, the Town House now teems with redcoats, and our ears ring with the music of the drum and fife. One of the first commercial towns in America has now almost stopped its trade.

Was a Governor ever so heartless as our B*****d? For who else would curry favor with a distant and unfeeling King whose people starve and bleed beneath his royal nose?

> *To make us all slaves, now you've lost, sir, the Hope.*
> *You've but to go hang yourself. We'll find the Rope.*
> —BRADSTREET'S GHOST.

CHAPTER 23

A Sentimental Journey

The mare's name was Muck. Inauspicious, was it not? Styfe, the liveryman who rented me both the horse and the cart to which she was harnessed, had little to say on the subject, though 'twas nevertheless more than I wanted to hear.

"Pray, good man: Whence her name?" I inquired, my breath billowing like a cloud in the early-morning cold.

He shrugged.

" 'Er color, sir. Looks like shite, dinnit?"

I say it again, dear Reader: 'Twas inauspicious, was it not?

But the horse was stout enough, and cheap. Eight shillings for the day.

"Money makes the mare go," I said to myself as I tendered the coins. I climbed onto the bench—nothing more than a pine plank—and urged her on with a flick of the reins.

"Onward, my Lady Muck. Let us make our way, for a long road stretches before us."

"If ye park 'er for a bit, blanket 'er, won't ye?" Styfe called after me as I rode from the Corn-hill stable, Gulliver racing alongside.

I was anxious to get started toward Cambridge, but I had first to stop at Queen Street. Twas not yet seven o'clock when I hitched Muck to the post near my door, for I had walked to the stable long before first light, so restless had I been without Weston, so furious. She would be her own master, would she? In what world, pray, is any woman her own master? Sweet Jesus.

I found Sander in the kitchen and asked him to join me in the painting room, to help me pack. For I am Hiram Usher's puppet: he pulls my strings; I paint the Governor. And so, I must bring my canvas and paints to Bernard's mansion, on the other side of the river. I would need an assistant, but I hadn't seen Weston since she left me last night, and I had vowed not to fetch her. Know this, Reader: I have made up my mind to marry her, but I will not be reduced to begging.

"I would be glad to accompany you to Cambridge," said Sander. "Yet I will go only so far as the College. I am done playing the servant. Visiting Hannah in that noxious prison was my last act of imposture. I will be this man again," he said, pointing to my portrait of him.

Leaning against the wall, dwarfing the other four portraits I had placed there the day before, stood the likeness of my old friend, posed as the gentleman-scholar in his study, wearing a rich wine-colored cloak with gleaming brass buttons, silk stockings, and a white wig, before a wall of bookshelves and next a table upon which stood a crucible, a set of scalpels, and a skull. Neath that skull, I had painted the perfect simulacrum of a scrap of parchment, bearing the legend: *A man may imagine things that are false, but he can only understand things that are true. —Isaac Newton.*

"Zounds, Sander!" I exclaimed. "Tis a pretty picture, one of my best. But play the professor tomorrow, will you? The Governor has granted me but one sitting. I can't mix my paints and clean my brushes and find enough time in between to pin the man."

"Of course, of course. So: bring your serving boy."

I shook my head.

"Ah. The lovers' quarrel." He sighed. "An unbearably dull species of argument. Do not speak of it, Jamie, for I am bored before you begin. No, I will go to the College, and no farther."

"But—" Here I broke off, for Weston walked into the room, and tied my tongue. Nay, she did not *walk* into the room. She swept into it, upon cream-colored peau de soie slippers. She wore a gown of the palest blue, a fine, striped silk taffeta, with an ivory front, trimmed at cuffs and neck with white lace, tailored just so, by a seamstress who knew how lavishly her wares would be displayed on so elegant a feminine form, its beauty revealed, or just barely concealed, by a low, curved neckline.

Twas a familiar battle: my desire against my temper. By now you surely know never to wager on the latter.

"Good morning, gentlemen," she said, with a small curtsy, and a shy smile.

Still I could not find my voice.

"Miss Easton, you are a picture of loveliness," Alexander said, with a stiff bow. "But again you threaten to play our best card too soon. Do not squander the Queen of Hearts. Save it for your next trick."

With that, he left the room, calling out as he closed the door behind him: "Jamie, I am ready as soon as you are . . . finished."

"Kit-cat," I began, hoarsely, as I moved toward her. "Do you mean to ravish me with your beauty, or to torture me?"

She took my hands, and kissed me.

"Never to torture you, Jamie. Never . . ."

"I missed you last night, lass," I whispered, as I made to unbutton her bodice.

"And I you, love," she answered, as she threw my coat to the floor.

I confess it: I am a man who loves a petticoat and stays. What gentleman does not? I had rather lingered over them, yet I could not keep the Governor waiting. But if I had scant time to spare, neither could I govern my temptation to steal a few moments—a selfish few moments, I admit—to take my pleasure.

I pressed her against the wall and lifted her skirts. I unbuttoned my breeches, and had my way with her.

Minutes passed.

Not many.

"So quickly, Jamie?" Weston asked, not a little miffed, and still heaving. Scarcely could I blame her.

"Aye, lass, and I'm sorry for it, certain," I apologized, and sincerely, as I hastily tucked my shirt back in. "Mark me: I'll make it up to you tonight if you would but stay in my bed, instead of hopping out in a bad humor, as if my proposal of marriage were an insult. But at this very moment I must ride to Cambridge. Have you not forgotten that I am to paint the great Francis Bernard? Tis not every day a painter has a chance to pin the most hated man in America."

"Oh, Jamie! But I have made other plans. I mean to see Phebe today!"

"Phebe? How?" I asked, absently, as I finished tying the huge canvas in its tarpaulin, for the Governor had requested a full-length.

"I had thought to ask Daniel to bring her to the Mill Pond. But the bliss of that reunion will have to wait, if you need me at the Governor's."

"I do and I don't, lass," I mused, my resentment of our late argument beginning to surface. "I don't need Fanny Easton there. But I could do with young Weston's help. Yet perhaps your spirit of independence won't allow it. You won't condescend to be my wife; how can you remain my apprentice? Tis too lowly a station for Justice Easton's daughter. After all, I am but a poor artisan, unworthy of her hand."

Weston had by now noticed the portraits leaning against the wall and, as I spoke, she had begun inspecting them.

"A mere artisan? Nay, Jamie. Nor is that what holds me back. Such faces . . . though I should confess to you that I have looked upon them before. I found them in the attic. Long have I wondered about them."

She toured my rogues' gallery. "The doctor, of course, in his finery. And this can only be your brother, although he is but a pale imitation of you. But who is this gentleman with a dog that makes our Gulliver look a Lilliputian? And this lady, Jamie: Was she dear to you? I have my own questions, my love. But I would first have you understand why I—"

I cut her off.

"Aye, I would fain understand you, Weston," I said, not a little icily, as I fastened the buckles on the straps that bound the paint case. "And I can introduce you to those painted ladies and gentlemen when we return—for I'm glad you answer my concern with your history with some slight curiosity about mine. We will have time enough to discuss what halts your progress to the altar on the ride to Cambridge, if you would be so good as to don your trousers, and meet me outside."

As I steered the horse toward Marlbrough Street, the wrapped canvas tilting in the cart-bed like a sail leaning into the wind, Alexander called, from the back, "Where are you going, man? Are we not headed to the wharf?"

"Of course not," I answered, irritably, slowing to a stop as I strained to hear him over a herd of cows then crossing the road.

"Have you not looked at a map, you great sot? By water, the journey to Cambridge is no more than four miles and takes a scant half-hour. By road, it is twice as far and, pulling a burdened cart, will take us more than four times as long!"

"Aye, aye, Lord of the Admiralty. But you know I'll not brook a boat ride."

"In that case, I shall meet you later," said the doctor, as he jumped off the back of the cart, and headed toward the docks. "Find me in the College Yard, at dusk, and I will ride back with you when our different business is done."

Muck hardly needed minding, but I steered her toward the Neck, through the city gates, past the gallows, still standing, bereft of its burden, and on across the tidal marshland, where seagulls soared and swooped. Thence we headed west through the Roxbury Flats, a gentle, lonely terrain, and flecked with color. Reader, know: 'tis no Scottish moor of thistle and heather, that perfect harmony of wildness and tameness. And aye, the gorse. Sweet Jesus, but I miss it.

"Do you know the saying about gorse, lass?" I asked Weston, breaking our silence. She shook her head. "When the gorse is out of bloom, kissing is out of season."

"And might the gorse be blooming in Scotland just now?" she asked, with a sweet smile. "For you've a faraway look in your eyes, my love."

I leaned over to kiss her, and with great passion. For, confound it, this Weston's trousers stir me near as much as Miss Easton's petticoats.

"That's the beauty of gorse, lass." I smiled. "It blooms the whole year round."

If this New-England countryside is no Highland moor, it boasts a painter's autumn, a palette of crimsons and oranges, yellows and umbers, glinting with spatters of sunlight against the blue sky. We passed, at a trot, through a pretty scene of plowed fields and golden meadows, dotted with woods.

"Your America has its charms, Weston," I conceded.

"'Tis beautiful, isn't it?" she agreed, her tone wistful. "Well do I remember riding this road in my father's chaise. My mother and I each with a little one in our lap, and Daniel up top with the coachman."

"Little ones? Where are the rest of the Eastons, my Weston?"

"All gone," she sighed. "My darling sister Lydia, my baby brother Henry, our beloved mother: the smallpox stole them from us, all in a single month."

I put my arm around her narrow shoulders.

"A bitter cup, lass, a bitter cup."

"They were not to be my last loss," she replied, her voice catching.

"Hush," I whispered.

"No, Jamie. I have been silent for too long. I was not long motherless ere I became a mother myself. Cummings's babe grew within me. I was barely sixteen."

"The son-of-a-bitch tutor. Did your father threaten to kill the scoundrel?"

"You do not know Edward Easton, my love. My father's blood runs colder than yours. He bribed Cummings to marry me."

"Isaac and Abraham on a blasted billy-goat! As if it weren't dreadful enough that your father would sacrifice you, Kit-cat. How could this vile seducer refuse such a prize?"

"No, 'twas I who refused him. And then he fled. For I thought that he had betrayed me already, and with my own slave. With Hannah."

"You've lost me, lass. Hannah was your father's mistress, was she not?"

"Yes, but at the time, at the time . . . I thought Tobias . . ."

"And your father did naught to disabuse you of your suspicion? Aye, you have convinced me: he is heartless. But did not Daniel counsel you?"

"He was away at College. I was so alone. Or not quite alone, for the babe grew. When the time of my travail came, my father would not even call in my mother's kindhearted midwife, but brought me instead a pretended doctor, a nameless mountebank, from so far away that I did not know him, and never could I find him. But I looked, oh, Jamie! I looked."

"But Kit-cat, I cannot follow you. Why would you seek this pissprophet? Did he harm you, lass?"

"He was naught but a filthy butcher, with his gruesome instruments. He left me bleeding, delirious with fever. But oh, Jamie, I fear he did much worse than that."

By now her tears had begun to fall. I steered the mare off the road, and halted 'neath a copse, just south of the Muddy Brook, that I might hold my Weston in my arms. She pressed on, for though her sorrows choked her, she would finish her story.

"My father told me my child was born dead. But I heard my baby's cries, I know I did! And they never let me see her, not even a glimpse."

"O, Kit-cat, my love," I whispered, kissing her wet cheeks. "Twas a great cruelty to bear, and so young."

"So young and more foolish," she said, while she wept. "For I fled the protection my father's home still afforded, in the faint hope of finding my babe. But how? Near twenty thousand souls live in this town, half of them children. I was mad to try."

"My love, my love, I would have done the same. Did you find her?"

"Oh, I looked. I wandered in a daze, for months, starving and alone, limping from town to town—staring at every babe I met, for every foundling was a fantasy. No, I did not find her. Nor that devil-doctor. I only lost more. The last of my Reason succumbed to the force of my grief until I prayed for death—for I expected nothing of life but to share the fate of all the fallen women in every novel I had ever read."

I stepped down from the cart and pulled her from the seat. I folded her into my arms and carried her to the shade of a maple tree, its leaves the brightest, purest red. I sat down between its magnificent roots, in a pile of crinkly leaves, and cradled her, rocking her like a baby, as a mother's grief overtook her.

"O, Fanny, Fanny. Did not anyone try to save you? Your father, your brother, your friends: they must have looked for you."

"No one looked for me," she said grimly. "My father told everyone I had sailed across the ocean, to care for an aged aunt."

"What manner of man values his good name over his daughter's life?"

"My father, surely. But let me finish, for there is little enough left to tell. One day, as winter came on, a kindhearted stage-driver came upon me, beside a road much like this. He put me on his coach, carried me back to Boston, and left me on the footsteps of King's Chapel. But I would not enter, for I did not believe that even God would shelter such a wretched sinner."

"I would shelter you, lass. I would shelter you from this pain." I pulled her closer. "I would spare you. Do not tell me what followed."

"Oh, Jamie. I would spare us both. I will say only this. Alone in the cold, cold city that winter, so wholly deprived of my senses, I suffered more than one night of vice in exchange for lodging, until a constable dragged me to the Manufactory House, and locked its doors behind me. I endured there—I will not call it living—for near three years. And then I found you, and you took me in, and for the first time in all that while, I allowed myself to think about Art and beauty, and about life, and about love. I was so hungry, Jamie. So hungry for all of it."

"O, my Kit-cat," I whispered. "I wish I had found you sooner. For know this, Fanny Easton: I was searching for no one but you all those years. Searching for my love, my joy, my other, my *better* part. But Dame Fortune has granted each of us another spin of the Wheel, has she not? We can be together, as man and wife, and share a life of Art and beauty and passion. And children, Fanny. You shall be a mother yet. Truly, lass, we have not been mindful of the consequences of our pleasures. We must marry—and at once—for there are bastards enough in this world, and I would not be the author of another."

She stayed where she was, nestling in my lap, and clinging to me, but I could feel her stiffen.

"But what do I have to offer you, you who deserve so much? I have no virtue, and no fortune. And there is yet another thing I can never give you, Jamie: I can never give you children. God has seen fit to punish me. Whether 'twas that sham-surgeon who tore my womb, or the fever that ravaged me, or the nights of vice, or the months—the years—of misery that followed, I am left a wasteland. You think I scorn your offer. A mere artisan! You slander yourself. You boast a greatness, Stewart Jameson, and a nobility of soul, that I will never have. You have my love, and always will. But what else can I give you?"

"Your love is no paltry thing, Fanny. And I would return it, compounded. You have no fortune, 'tis true, but I have less, for I have naught but debts. Considerable debts, I should warn you. Aye, we shall be poor in purse, lass, that I grant you. But we shall be rich in passion."

"So rich, Jamie," she said, her face briefly brightening, as she kissed my hand. "But if I am not ready for the life you promise me? I've come in from the cold to find that I want the world. I long to stand on my own two feet, yet I crave to lean on you. Truly, I am a muddle. I ought to have left your blindfold on, that you might marry Louisa, a woman of modesty and sensibility, of virtue and fortune: everything I lack."

"I may have been blind, but are you deaf, lass? I can live without a fortune, and I do not love Louisa! She has not half your wit, less of your passion, and none of your Art."

"My Art, Jamie? And what of it? When I was a boy, you wanted to send me to London . . . you spoke of promise, even of eminence. Does Easton forfeit Weston's future?"

"Aye, you have a talent, my Kit-cat. You have no discipline, and you don't mind your master, and you are *difficult*, lass, most difficult," I smiled, and she at last smiled wide, and wiped her tears. "But you are an artist, Fanny Easton, in pants or in skirts. And I'm not half as convinced as you are that you will not yet be a mother. Truly, mark me: I will do my best on that account. Picture yourself beside our hearth, a charcoal in your hand, teaching our children to draw."

Here I caressed her, and made to kiss her, for this picture swelled my heart. But she straightened herself, sat up, and spoke rapidly, no longer tearful, but newly resolved.

"No, I would only disappoint you. I could not forgive myself that. Maybe sending me away remains the best course. Maybe I ought still to sail. If I have a talent, I might yet seize it. Maybe my life was spared for that. And then I could leave you to find your fortune and make your family with another, with a woman more worthy of you."

"With *another*? Do you think I would forget you ere the ship disappeared over the horizon? O, the fickleness of youth!"

I tousled her hair and kissed her cheek.

"Where on God's green earth would I find another Fanny Easton? Aye, you are tempestuous; don't think it has escaped my attention. But if you are ruined, then so am I, and all the more reason that we belong together. Believe me, lass, you are an original, and I foreswear copies; they are inferior things."

Muck, who all this while had been contentedly eating grass, began to stir. I looked at the sky, to judge the hour. I grabbed Weston's hand, and pulled both of us up to standing. She was more than steady enough to travel.

"Alas, my love, time flies, and the Governor expects us before noon. Would that we had the leisure for a dalliance, here 'neath this crimson canopy, for I have not forgotten that I owe you a flourish, lass," I winked.

She dusted herself off and grinned at me, once again her mischievous self.

"No time for a fuck on Muck, then, master?"

"Out of luck, Puck," I answered, and with a laugh, picked her up, threw her over my shoulder, and planted her beside me on the plank bench.

We journeyed north for another half an hour before turning east at a great salt meadow, where we rode along a causeway toward the river Charles, reaching the stream at its narrowest point. A short wooden bridge spanned the banks. Not so much as a ferry ride, then. My stomach offered a silent prayer of thanks. Truly, a bridge is a fine thing under the sun.

A pleasant village, scant and scattered, waited on the other side. This town of Cambridge boasts little trade, save the traffic in diplomas, which the brightest sons of New-England earn by years of papery toil. The College is a monument to the noblest aspirations of these American colonies. And in these parts, it passes for ancient, for 'twas founded in the year 1636. But, compared to the centuries-old stone spires of Edinburgh, 'tis not much to look at: five brick buildings, surrounding a Yard, enclosed by a low wall. Students in black gowns and square hats walked briskly across the lawn. The freshmen, and only the freshmen, went bareheaded, and bowed at ten paces before every upperclassman they encountered. We traveled past four large brick halls, the most imposing of which was but half built, before passing a small stone chapel.

"Mr. Smibert sculpted that pediment," Weston said, directing my gaze to a baroque cartouche on the chapel's western gable.

"Did he? Old Smib? Tis rather fine, don't you think?"

"I do. A trifle fussy. But fine. And there," she pointed out, "there rises a new Harvard Hall from the ashes of the old."

"It cannot have burned so long ago," I observed. "The neighboring building is yet black with soot."

"Just this January. The whole of the library—five thousand volumes!—was lost, and all of the College's scientific instruments destroyed."

"God above, Sander will faint when he hears of it."

I steered Muck across the Common, dodging sheep and keeping clear of a horse race. From there we followed the road running parallel to the river, along which stood the town's most opulent homes, huge brick and clapboard piles, walled by privet hedges.

The Governor's house was the fifth of these grand estates. Three stories, painted pale gray, with blue cornice blocks, and vast chimneys standing guard at either gable of its hipped roof.

"Ach aye, we have arrived, Weston," I announced, clapping her on the back, for I found I had to will myself to think of her as my apprentice again. "Behold, this colony's summit of power." And Reader, 'twas a summit of sorts, to be sure, but equally, my rock bottom, for though 'twould burnish my reputation to paint the Governor, I could scarce forget that I was here on Usher's errand, as much as my own.

I tied Muck to a post and tossed Styfe's blanket over her while Weston unloaded the paint box and easel and loosened the ropes holding the canvas. But we had hardly begun to wrestle with it when three members of the Governor's staff came running down the walkway to assist us.

An hour later—following a meal of quail with currants, and apple-cranberry pie, in the kitchen—we had yet to see a hair on the Governor's head. We had set up the easel in his library, next a pair of windows that stretched from ceiling to floor, overlooking the gardens. The room was rich with ornament. Walls of mahogany shelves, a desk covered with maps, a hulking leather globe set upon a brass stand.

After the great man kept us waiting still another half an hour, he entered, and with little ado.

"Jameson," he called, offering a hand. "Delighted."

Sir Francis Bernard is a man of middling stature, with a Saxon's round, flat face. His nose is fleshy but falls short of bulbous. He is thin-lipped, yet boasts an honest, open appearance—hardly the evil dastard that "Bradstreet's Ghost" taunts. He had dressed for the occasion in a purple velvet cloak with dainty, silk-covered buttons. Yet his head was bare and he carried, rather than wore, an enormous curled wig, such as you might see at the Old Bailey, and which must have weighed ten pounds if it weighed an ounce. Despite his costume, he was more plain than I expected.

I gave him my best bow. "I am honored, Your Excellency."

I introduced Weston, who had finished priming the canvas, and we set to work.

The Governor proved unusually obliging. He was happy to be posed where I placed him—standing beside his desk—and pleased to rest his hand on the globe, his thumb over New-England, and his littlest finger touching London.

"You've got this town under your thumb, then, have you?" I joked.

Not the faintest trace of a smile graced his face.

"It should be under my thumb, Jameson, for I am the King's man, and this was still, the last time I looked, the King's realm. But if you think the people of Boston revere me, you must not read the papers. 'Bradstreet's Ghost,' indeed! I'll see the phantom hanged for sedition."

And truly, Reader, what the Ghost said of the Governor in the public prints verged on treason.

"Have you discovered the Ghost's identity, then?"

"Not yet, Jameson. But we shall discover him, and whoever's behind him. And we shall stop them."

"Aye, but do you think this rebellion will be so easily crushed?"

"You Scots do love a good rebellion, I know. Still, Councilor Usher assures me that you are no rebel, and that you have a penetrating gaze. Mark well what you see in this colony, then, Jameson, for you are an eye-witness to an abuse of legislative authority that threatens, every day, to cast us into anarchy. These Massachusetts Assemblymen—Bradstreet, God save his soul, was the worst of them—and now this Ghost, and these hens and chicks, or I know not what they call themselves. A pox upon all patriot-poultry! The genius of the English constitution is its mixture. It balances liberty against its abuse by power, through the three estates of man. The King, the nobles, and the people: none flourish unless all thrive. Yet these colonials would gainsay Parliament! They would topple the bulwark of our liberty!"

"If you would raise your chin a little, sir?"

"Yes, yes."

"Thank you, sir. But, Your Excellency, I wonder, do you serve the King's cause well by quartering troops in the whole of the Town House, even in the Merchants Exchange?"

"Neither well nor poorly, but duly. They are the King's troops, and they enforce the King's right to collect what is owed to him."

"I am no lawyer, sir, much less a parliamentarian. But this measure is a trifle harsh, is it not? And unnecessarily so? As I oft tell my apprentice,"

I said, with a private wink at Weston, "he governs best who uses his rod most tenderly."

"You do say that, master," Weston offered, smiling at me, daringly, as she adjusted the great mass of curls upon the Governor's head. "But do you not also say, 'the more haste, the worse speed,' sir?"

Cock-teasing coquette. Would that it were time for a pause wherein Bernard might stretch his legs, or take his tea, and I might take Weston to another room, drop her trousers, and give her a lesson in good government. I strived, how I strived, to return my attention to my sitter.

"Your apprentice puts me in mind of an important point, Jameson. Mayhap I have acted too hastily, and too strictly, in calling troops to town. I confess I have begun to ponder whether the best way to woo these boycotters isn't to give them their Exchange back, for some of these merchants—Usher among them—are good and loyal men. When you consider the matter carefully, such a gesture would save their faces more than mine, would it not?"

"A brilliant stratagem, sir," I agreed.

"After all," he continued, "the boycott is the height of silliness. What can they mean: that a few middling merchants should starve a great empire? They are but a pack of beggarly boys throwing stones at a castle. They make nary a dent, and I would save them from themselves, before the King's cavalry stomps them underfoot."

"Indeed. Yours is a most calculating genius, sir. For you plainly realize that such a move would repay you twice over with public esteem. Not only would you earn the merchants' gratitude, but also that of the Assemblymen, to whom you would return their chambers."

"Just so. I mean to do it directly, for I would enjoy a renewal of popular support. I lost my best ally in this town when Finley died. You have heard the Chief Justice is dead, Jameson?"

"Aye, sir. A great loss, sir."

"Undoubtedly. But his successor is an even more loyal man."

"Sir?"

"Edward Easton. Have you painted him? I have only recently appointed him. Yes, he will make a fine Chief Justice. And he would make a fine sitter, Jameson, a very fine sitter."

Weston dropped the silver comb she had been holding. It clinked as it hit the floor.

At this interruption, the Governor roused himself, pulled off his wig, and draped it over the globe.

"I hope you've gotten what you need, Jameson. I can spare no more time for you today."

"Of course, sir. More than I needed. You are generous to have sat so long. Please accept my humble thanks, Your Excellency."

He answered my deep bow with a slight nod and, with a parting glance at Weston, he left the room.

D o you know with whom I drank today?" asked Alexander, as he stumbled onto the back of the cart, carrying a small, dark bundle under his arm. He did not sit, but lay down flat, alongside the base of the wrapped canvas.

"Whoever it was, he poured you a few too many cups," I observed, surprised, for I had never before seen my friend drunk.

"Jamie: guess. Who?"

"President Holyoke?" I asked.

"No."

"Sander: tell me. Who?"

"Titus."

"The Roman emperor?" interjected Weston, who was sitting beside me on the plank.

"No, Miss Wessssss-easston. Titus. Holyoke's slave. A very old and worthy gentleman."

"Ah. And was this venerable and elderly Titus a pleasant companion?" I asked.

"Verrry," laughed Sander. "Do you know, Jamie, that this College is to have a new laboratory? On the second floor of that half-finished hall." He pointed to the new building just behind us.

"Aye, I had heard of it, Sander, for the Governor—you remember the Governor, friend?—is its architect."

"Yess, yess. Well, Titus showed it to me. It will be a fine laboratory, and this Titus is a fine fellow. He was also good enough to procure for me this cap and gown," he said, pointing to the bundle he was now putting to use as a pillow. "Though he is still more adept at procuring rum from the college steward. Rum, rum, dum-de-dum . . ."

"Doctor, are you quite well?" Weston inquired.

"Well, Miss Easton? No, I am not. Or at least, I was not, till I fortified myself. Now I am. Well. Jamie, do you know what the undergraduates are preparing to argue at their next public debate?"

"Nay, Sander. Pray: What?"

He took a breath before answering, to collect himself.

" 'Is an Absolute and Arbitrary Monarchy Contrary to Right Reason?' One Elias Usher, a promising lad, is slated to argue the affirmative."

"Funny, Sander. I've been discussing the very same subject with the Governor. A provocative topic, is it not?"

"It is, Jamie. It is at that," he mused, a familiar glint in his eye.

"Sander, did you happen to meet Mr. Elias Usher today?" I asked, for I have never known my friend to miss an occasion for debate.

"I did. In a tavern by the river, where he was dining with his companions."

"You must be brave, Sander, for I know you're not foolish."

"There was no danger, Jamie. They are mere boys."

"And these boys, then. Did you manage to lure them into debate on the assigned topic?"

"I did. For they all fancy themselves hot patriots and I have always been a Tory, as you know."

"Aye, blast you. And you bested this Elias Usher?"

"Need you ask? Of course I bested him, though I confess his ingenuity took me by surprise. He is a gentleman of great virtue and not a little wit. Yet he keeps poor company. Do you know what his friends do when they are not studying?"

"Race horses on the Cambridge Common?"

"No doubt. But they also like to wager on how many bumpers it will take to get Holyoke's Titus drunk enough to pass out. It is a game with them."

"A cruel one," I agreed.

"Indeed. A careless scholar named Hancock once near killed one of the college slaves that way. Poor old Titus by now so anxiously craves liquor, every hour of the day, that he gladly plays along."

Now 'twas my turn to be alarmed.

"Tell me, Sander, is this how you came to be drunk? Did you seek to avenge Titus by turning the tables and drinking his tormentors under the table?"

"I did. And I succeeded, naturally. Still, I came to admire this Elias, who is the least loutish of his companions. When he stands a bit taller, he will be a credit to the colony. Ah, it was a fine day, my Jamie, Jamie, Jamie. My good Jameson. A fine day, for I do love a college town."

With that, he drifted off to sleep, and Weston covered him with the blanket. He made not one sound more, the whole of the long and weary ride back to Boston, under darkening skies.

BOSTON.

To the Editor:

The Governor has apparently had a *Change of Heart*. Saturday last, in the forenoon, the King's officers, billeted in the Town House, summarily vacated the premises and removed to Castle William. In thanks, the people of Boston have taken down their mourning drapes. Is our loyalty to be so cheaply purchased, as if with worthless paper bills bearing Governor B*****d's own likeness? Let us not forget that our town itself is yet a perfect garrison.

—BRADSTREET'S GHOST.

October the 19th, 1764

"Tell me, Kit-cat: Since those dark days when first an artist made the walls of some cave his canvas, has ever a painter suffered a lazier apprentice?"

With a theatrical sigh, Jamie lifted his head from the painting-room floor, where we lay side by side, 'neath a spattered tarpaulin, upon the worn carpet, before a crackling fire, as the squares of sky outside our windows slowly faded. Some minutes before—or was it hours?—I had drifted into a sleep from which he now labored to rouse me, first with a tickle, then a nudge, and finally a hard poke of his elbow between my ribs.

"Ouch!" I cried. But when I tried to marshal a pout, I found only a smile. Jamie parried my grin with a pretended frown.

"Am I not beset like holy Job, lass?"

"And what do you suffer, my love?"

"God plagues me with lust, and you with sloth, when we must, both of us, make haste, make haste," he cried, as he drew himself up to standing. "Mason's invitation was most particular: the Hens take their supper at seven. Aye, and the six o'clock bell rang long since. As your master, I command you: rise and ready yourself to turn this little world upside down. But first, tell me: How does one costume for a New-England Carnival?"

"'Tis a rite of reversal, is it not? Perhaps you should don my dress, and I your breeches," I offered, as I sat up and picked through the pile of clothes beside me.

Jamie laughed as he held my small dimity frock up to his own broad chest.

"Not bloody well likely, lass. A kilt, I might grant you. But not this. Still, as the invitation requests the attendance of Mr. Francis Weston, Esquire, and his humble apprentice Jameson, we neither of us can turn up in skirts."

"Oh, Jamie. I would fain be done with disguises. Cannot we plead another engagement? If we were to stay home, master, I assure you, I would gladly don my trousers for you, sir, if only you would promise to strip them off again."

"Aye, and I should like nothing better than to oblige you, Kit-cat, but I cannot do. I must court these Hens if we're to secure a venue for the Exhibition. Can we not make the best of it, and enjoy a final masquerade?"

And so we agreed: I would wear Jamie's finest suit, of a deep navy serge—though it drooped off my shoulders—his whitest stockings, his frilliest cravat, a silvery wig from the closet of props, and his cocked hat. He would wear his roughest trousers—the ones he dons when he mixes paints—and his plainest shirt, a coarse checkered waistcoat, topping it all with a simple felt cap.

No sooner had I bound my breasts, and fastened his stockings round my calves with his garters, than he placed the wig atop my head and stayed my hand.

"O, Fanny," he whispered. "Don't add another stitch. Let me first demonstrate my loyalty to the Crown."

"To the Crown?"

"Aye, Kit-cat. Every commoner must kneel before a noble member of the Order of the Garter."

And so he did, dropping to his knees and pressing his face into my sex with the ardor of a true acolyte. I braced myself against the wall lest I should faint with pleasure at the attainment of my bliss, which swept over me soon enough.

"Oh, good my loyal servant," I sighed when at last he rose to his feet. "I commend your devotions. I fancy I saw the King!"

What with one thing leading to another, the bell rang seven ere we made it down the stairs.

"Places men! Our guests of dishonor have arrived!"

Thaddeus Mason, his voice thick with drink, shouted to the assembly of Hensmen, and Hensmen's men, who had gathered at table well before we knocked upon their door, under the sign of the plow. The president of the Hens, the town coroner, had swapped his red-crested black velvet tricorn for a tattered straw hat, and his black bombazine suit for coveralls of blue sacking.

"Lazy servant!" Mason slurred, turning from me to Jamie, who followed three steps behind my coattails, ever the obedient apprentice. "Can't you see that you've made your man late!"

"Your invitation said seven, good sir," Jamie rejoined, with a courtly bow.

"I dunno what you're clucking about," Mason chuckled. "But that clock says it's nigh eight, Jameson. We've been brooding for hours. Your cock shall flog ye, and smartly, if you do not mend your ways, you scurvy pullet!"

"Aye, lad," I winked at Jamie, for I meant to honor my pledge: to bluster my way through the evening. "You had best come at once! The roses upon Mr. Mason's cheeks show that we are far, far behind in our cups, for I do not think that they signify that he is a member of the Order of the Garter. We have missed much of the dissipation. Hurry, my lead-footed little snipe, lest we miss the disputation as well!"

"'Tis plain your man serves you ill, sir," Mason nodded at me.

"Though he does serve me, sir, I assure you," I insisted. "And on his knees."

"No doubt. But there will be no disputation this evening, sir. At Carnival, we hatch new eggs and reveal to them the secrets of the roost."

With that, he motioned us into the darkened dining room. Great swathes of velvet, deep cherry in color, had been tacked up round the room, covering even the windows. Everywhere, torches blazed: in sconces along the walls, in buckets of sand set upon the long table round which the merry Hensmen stood, trays in hand, attending their servants, who sat drinking and feasting as they imagined gentlemen should. I spied Amos Quincy, the Attorney General, in shirtsleeves and a leather apron; before him sat Christian Ibitzer, a joiner's apprentice, in a suit of emerald satin. Beside Ibitzer, David Dennie, a poor Irish starveling bewigged and black-robed like a barrister, shifted uncomfortably in his seat, and no wonder; William Bradstreet stood behind him, resplendent in a costume of tattered rags so neatly arranged that I supposed it bespoke for the occasion. Next to Dennie sat Sears Harding, Mason's man, gnawing on a joint of beef, while the club president knelt to offer him a bumper of punch. Thomas Gallagher's clerk wore the grocer's gray coat. Too young to command a servant of his own, the shopkeeper Samuel Clough waited upon his younger brother. And on it went, up and down the table. Every Hensman deferred to his clerk or his journeyman, to his son or his coachman. Finally, positioned behind the head of the table, stood Hiram Usher, tricked out in red livery.

"Only at Carnival would I wear imported cloth," I heard the Councilor explain sheepishly.

But Pompey did not sport his master's homespun. Instead, Usher's slave sat before him, swaddled in a crimson damask banyan, his head wrapped in a golden turban worthy of some Oriental sultan.

Twas meant as comedy, this upside-down dinner. But I had seen enough of rising, and too much of falling, to enjoy it. Jamie felt the same, I could see. There was sadness in his eyes as I moved toward the place Mason indicated, the empty chair between Pompey and Bradstreet's young David.

"Yes, yes. That one, sir," Bradstreet grimaced, his voice taut as he pulled out my chair with his cane, and moved Jamie into place behind me. "Yes, yours is a seat of dishonor, *master*. As you shall see, soon enough. Now, boy—sir," he continued, a note of urgency creeping into his voice as he addressed his cowering stable hand, "you may begin the proceedings."

Then, silence.

"*Now!*" Bradstreet snarled.

"I . . . I cannot remember my lines, sir," the boy sputtered, pushing back from the table and looking about the room in a panic. "I must away to the horse, sir," he said, and he tipped over his chair and fled into the night. A flash of red tumbled from his lap and clattered onto the floor, but Pompey snatched it up before I could discern its shape.

"Allow me to take Dennie's part, for truly, Mr. Bradstreet, I was born to play the judge!" Pompey laughed, sounding haughtier even than Bradstreet himself. "Hear ye, hear ye," he continued, pulling from the folds of his red robe a judge's gavel, painted a scarlet so deep and shiny that it appeared slicked with blood. He rapped three times upon the table. Bang, bang, bang: so many pistol shots. I flinched at each one.

"Order!" he commanded. "I shall have order! Behold, the Dark Lord of Misrule! Bow down before me, as I call this Carnival Court to order. Is the chick in his nest?"

"O, *indeed*," Bradstreet said. "But this is no fuzzy newborn. There are plenty of pin-feathers upon him. Tis clear enough which is the cock, and which the pullet, even on this topsy-turvy night."

"Then let us have him assume his customary pose," Pompey continued.

"I'm guessin' that'd be front to back, sir," Mason snickered.

"So we hear. So we hear," Bradstreet answered, speaking in something between a laugh and a leer. He gave a small nod, at which, he and Mason closed upon Jamie.

"Move closer to your *master*, apprentice," Bradstreet said, nudging him forward. "Just a couple of paces."

I felt a prickle of fear. But I looked over my shoulder and found reassurance, for Jamie appeared more annoyed than frightened. The front of his form met the back of my chair.

"A'right, then, clap them in irons," Pompey commanded. Another crash of his gavel rent the air like thunder.

Bradstreet and Mason converged upon us, each holding a coil of rope painted the Hens' fiery red. Burly Mason pushed Jamie to his knees, and held him there. Bradstreet grabbed his hands, pulling them crosswise round my waist before roping them fast to the back of my chair. This trussing had the effect of binding my arms and hands as well, for I could barely move them inside of Jamie's forced embrace. In a thrice, Mason had knotted the second rope at my ankles, and threaded it through the chair legs, where he fastened it around Jamie's thighs.

My heart raced; I thought I would explode with fear. I clawed at the ropes, desperate to escape. The room rang with drunken laughter, but I was seized with terror, for I had seen it before: disordered by rum, emboldened by gin, even a gentle man will do what he would not otherwise dare, and a dozen inebriates together will attempt still greater cruelty.

I screamed, plainly a woman's scream. Were they too drunk to hear it? By now, several of the Hensmen were not so much standing as weaving. Or perhaps my shriek fed their fantasy of a boy on the edge of manhood rudely, suddenly unmanned? None responded. None but my Jamie.

"Tis naught but a prank," he whispered through the chair back. "An ugly one, aye. But they'll not hurt you. I swear it. Sit tight, lass."

His voice steadied me, but only so far. I tried, I strived, to keep still, as he asked, but it took all my strength, and yet more. And I could not halt my tears.

"I can't see you've noticed," Thomas Gallagher said, "but the apprentice ain't laughing. Haven't we gone a mite too far?"

"More punch for Gallagher!" Mason shouted, waving away the grocer's worry.

"Are your chickens trussed, boy?" Pompey asked Bradstreet.

"They're trussed well enough. But I warn you, Pompey. I'll not stand for you calling me *boy*."

"Noted," Lord Pompey replied, pretending to enter the complaint into an imaginary docket book. "Now, gentlemen. What shall this Dishonorable Court misname the initiates?" He surveyed his fellow servants for answers. But those mock-gentlemen only looked at their feet, while behind them their pretended vassals called out recommendations.

"They are painters: perhaps Michelangelo and David?" Quincy suggested.

"Better you call me a constable and yourself a surgeon, for that is what we will require if you fail to untie us," Jamie cautioned, barely controlling his anger. "Can you not see how far your witless prank has frightened the lad?"

Jamie's warning went unanswered.

"What about Fame and Fortune?" Griggs, the tooth-puller, offered. "For this Jameson must make a pretty penny by his brush. No wait, 'tis Carnival: Infamy and Misfortune, it should be, then?"

"Clever, John, clever," agreed Usher. "But my mind runs to the work of the loom. Let us call them Warp and Weft!"

"Good, Councilor. Good, good," Bradstreet answered. "Cluck, cluck."

"Cluck, cluck," the Hensmen gabbled in response, till the room filled with their squawks.

"Good, yes, Hiram. But I think I've got better," Bradstreet resumed, stroking his chin as if deep in thought, when 'twas clear he had rehearsed his suggestion well. "We shall soon hear tell of a midsummer night's dream. Thus shall we call them: Puck and Bottom!"

"Hear, hear! To Puck and Bottom!" Pompey toasted, raising high his glass.

"To Puck and Bottom! Huzzah!" the standing Hensmen echoed, one by one.

Then came a voice from the kitchen, coarse and gruff.

"I'd say *fuck 'is bottom 's*'more like it, guv'nor."

Into the room stumbled Enoch Goddard.

"Order! Order!" Pompey bellowed, rapping his gavel once again. "Let the witness take his place in the dock!"

Mason pulled out a chair for Goddard, positioning it directly across the table from me and Jamie. The jail-keeper sank into his seat, and gratefully, for so far gone with drink was he that his legs could barely support him.

"Let the mistrial of Puck for gross indecency against this poor Bottom begin."

The servants sat in uneasy silence while the Hensmen cackled—all but Bradstreet.

"Pray continue, Pompey, *milord*," he urged.

"Witness! I would have you place your left hand upon a book of jests, and swear by the Devil that you shall tell naught but lies," Pompey instructed Goddard.

"Nossir!" the jailer slurred. "Tis God's own truth I tell you's all! Last summer, I served in their house of sin. And I saw 'em—and more than once, hear—that painter goin' at 'is boy, hard at 'im, if you take my meaning. Down in the buttery, they were. And 'e buttered that smooth little bun, laid it on right thick, 'e did. Not that the boy seemed to mind . . ."

Goddard flushed, rubbing furtively at his crotch.

The Hensmen laughed, as much at their witness as at his testimony.

"Tis a lie!" I shouted, choking back tears. "He—"

But Jamie drowned out my voice with his own.

"You dim-witted grabcock," he thundered, "we don't even have a buttery!" and to Mason, "I'll not hear one more word from that great grubby grog-blossom."

"Then hear from me, *Puck*," Bradstreet hissed. "I've seen the two of you—in broad daylight—as I looked up at the window of your second-story room, the one that faces the street. About ten days ago, at half after two, in the afternoon. I made a note of it. For I thought I might be called to testify . . . in another court. Would you await the indictment in town, then? Or mightn't it be high time for you to turn itinerant. Take your brushes, and your boy, on the road. Take the back door, and the low road, dauber."

"No, no, William," countered Usher, with still more menace in his voice. "I should like to keep this painter close to hand, under our thumb. For surely he is in our debt, and means to repay us."

"Enough, the both of you. Enough!" Jamie shouted. "Release us at once, Wily Bastard. Or maybe your father ought to usher us out of here," he said, looking from Bradstreet to the Councilor till he was sure both men took his meaning.

"My father? What, would you call upon a ghost?" Bradstreet stammered, as he loosed the knots.

Jamie stood and brought me to my feet. I could feel him trembling with rage.

"Damn your bloods, you chickenhearted sons of bitches. Have you nothing better to attend to than the pants of other men? And someone had better drag that drunkard out of here before I break my hand on his ugly mug again."

Usher approached, and spoke to Jamie, so low I could make out only a handful of words. Something about the Governor, and the Exchange. What could he mean?

I had little enough time to consider this question for Gallagher rose and escorted Goddard out of the room—"Come on, Enoch. Time to go, now. Leave through the kitchen, so the boy can give you a bottle"—just as Mason approached us.

"For chrissakes, Jameson, calm down," Mason urged. "Twas no more than a prank, and a mark of fellowship, of our esteem, even. We mean to make you a Hen. None joins our society but we haze him a bit first, you see. Really, Jameson. You can't think we care where you dip your brush."

"A prank, Mason? A prank? Are you so blind drunk you cannot see the state to which your 'prank' has reduced this boy?"

As Mason gathered his wits to respond, the door to the tavern opened, causing the torches to gutter as Doctor Thomas Newcombe strode into the room.

"What's this?" he asked Mason, his eyes moving from the makeshift curtains, to the servants at table, to the red ropes yet wrapped round my chair, to my tear-stained face. Mason colored, as scarlet as the Hens' glass mascot.

"We missed you, Thomas," he said. "And worse yet, I fear you have missed the Carnival."

"We were to start at nine. William told me so himself, earlier today. I'm sure I did not mistake the time."

"Doctor Newcombe," Jamie said, "I can only think you were meant to miss out on the fun. For your cocks and pullets have been asses."

"Twas nothing, Thomas. Nothing," Bradstreet insisted. "Jameson's tenderhearted boy took our clucking a mite too seriously. We performed a little morality play, a sketch about subjection and domination—about Britain and these colonies, by implication. To show that we will not be made the slaves of empire!"

"Enough, Billy," Newcombe answered. "I would hear from the painter. Jameson?"

"The Hens meant no harm, Mason tells me. In fact, Doctor, he says that they meant to offer me a mark of fellowship. Is that true?"

"Yes, Jameson. We would see you sport the scarlet ring, if you're willing."

"I am grateful for your custom, Doctor. Tis a badge of distinction in this town, to have painted the Hens. But I would not join your brood, nor any other faction." Here Jamie looked daggers at Usher, and added, "I do my best to stay above the political fray, sir."

"I understand," Newcombe demurred. "But I would welcome the

chance to convince you otherwise. I fear we are but at the beginning of a long struggle, and will need men like you, men of stout heart and keen eye. I'll not press you now, for I can see these Hens have ruffled your feathers. And accept my sincere apologies, young man," he said to me, more than kindly.

Then he turned to the assembly.

"I have just received word, friends, of startling news. Parliament, so far from responding to our legislators' remonstrance—submitted last July in the eloquent and inspiring words of your father, Billy—by repealing the taxes under which we now suffer, has instead proceeded with the dreaded Stamp Act." Newcombe shook his head, while the room fell silent with shock at these grim tidings. And then the doctor's voice rose with the tone and spirit of oration, as he continued. "Yes, gentlemen, the Torch of Liberty spoke true: the time to wait and watch is over. The time to drink is done."

"Damn their stamps. But a dram or two never hurt a man, Thomas," Mason interrupted.

"There you're wrong, Thaddeus," Doctor Newcombe continued. "We drown ourselves in rum while the Crown taxes our sugar! We act as if Carnivals can turn our paper into gold! We kiss the Governor's ermine robes for the favor of removing the King's bloody-backs from our own Town House. Are we poultry, or patriots?"

A murmur went round the room.

"Cluck?" Mason offered.

Newcombe scowled.

"Can you not just squawk with us a bit, Thomas?" Quincy asked. "Twas all harmless mischief."

"Yes, Amos. I know you were joking. Most of you," Newcombe said, with a glance at Bradstreet. "But the Crown is no clown. There's a fox in the henhouse, gentlemen, and he steals our eggs. We ignore him at grave peril. For the King will not rest ere he deprives us of every liberty. Would you be English gentlemen? Not without English liberties. For too long the Red Hen has been but a gentleman's club, a place of drinking and ribaldry. The time for secret rites and schoolyard pranks has passed. We must dedicate ourselves to fighting tyranny. I would have us make our purposes plain. Let us, to the last man, cast off our disguises. Let us be Red Hens no more. Henceforth, let us call our-selves . . . the Hens of Liberty!"

This announcement met with an awkward silence. Jamie cleared his throat, and spoke politely.

"The Hens of Liberty, Doctor? I wonder, sir: Might you not coin a phrase that smacks a little less of the barnyard?"

Gallagher piped up. "I've got it! The Eggs of Liberty!"

Jamie raised an eyebrow.

"I know! The Sons of Liberty!" called out Griggs.

"Shut up, tooth-puller," snapped Usher. "That makes us sound like little boys."

Shouting, for one name, or against another, soon came from every corner of the room.

"Friends, friends!" hollered Newcombe, calling for order.

"Wait, that's it!" I cried, seized with an inspiration, and bold enough to speak it. "Not the Hens of Liberty, Doctor, but the Friends of Liberty!"

"By George—or, I mean, Damn George!—the lad's got something!" said Newcombe. "No more the Red Hens. Nor yet the Hens of Liberty. Henceforth, we shall be . . ."

He lifted from the center of the table the club's mascot, a life-sized glass chicken sporting a black tricorn. He caressed the tiny hat, twirling it round the tip of his index finger before tucking it in his pocket.

". . . we shall be . . . Gentlemen, I give you . . . the Friends of Liberty!"

With that he dashed the statue to the floor, which action was greeted by a chorus of huzzahs. Nearly universal. But for one.

"I take your point, Thomas, about the King and all that," Mason mumbled under his breath. "But did you have to go and slaughter Henny Penny?"

As the Friends of Liberty set to work making plans to rally the men of the town, Doctor Newcombe turned to Jamie and me.

"Now tell me, Jameson, is there nothing I can do to smooth your feathers?"

"Pray, Doctor. Let us talk no more of birds." He smiled. "And thank you, for there is one favor I might ask of you. Now that the Governor has conceded that the Town House belongs to the town and not the Crown, might not you and your brethren in the Assembly agree to lease me their great chamber therein? For I should like to exhibit the whole gallery of Hens . . . er, Friends, that all of Boston can gaze upon the faces of independency, painted in an Art whose candor and directness mirrors your own. You, Doctor, speak with common sense, and I should like to think I paint as plain."

"You do, Jameson. An Exhibition is a capital idea, all but unknown in these parts. Your brush shall put Boston on the map. And what an excellent opportunity for this town's . . . Friends of Liberty to step into public view. Art is no luxury in these troubled times. Yes, Jameson. I'm sure I speak for my fellow Assemblymen when I say, you may line our chamber with our faces."

"Thank you, Doctor. I'll not disappoint," Jamie said, sealing his promise with the shallowest of bows, and extending an arm to this friend of liberty,

Fanny Easton.

BOSTON.

AN EXHIBITION

Of upward of twenty original Portraits of eminent Characters in New-England and Britain, painted in oil in the latest London fashion by the ingenious STEWART JAMESON, will be held on Thursday next, at the Assembly Hall in the Town House, newly liberated from His Majesty's Army. In this collection are inimitable likenesses of Governor Francis Bernard; Samuel Bradstreet, Esquire; Doctor Thomas New-combe; and many more notable merchants, ladies, red-letter gentlemen, and particular Friends of Liberty. The doors to open at six o'clock. Admittance one shilling. Tickets to be had, *in advance only*, at the Printing Office. The entertainment to conclude, at Eight o'Clock, with an illuminated PUBLIC LEC-TURE by the celebrated African genius, Doctor Ignatius Alexander, late of Edinburgh, and well known to readers of the *Spectator* and *Gentleman's Magazine*, for his Experiments in the Logic of Deduction.

CHAPTER 24

In Which (Nearly) All Is Revealed

I f you are a patron of the Arts, good Reader, as I have reason to hope you must be—you and I having traveled so many pages together— you may ask yourself whether my paintings have ever been placed before the Public Eye. They have, but just the once.

Twas four years ago, in London, when the Society of Artists, founded for the Encouragement of Arts, Manufactures, and Commerce, held its first exhibition, having successfully petitioned the governors of the Foundling Hospital in Holborn for permission to use that institution's great room, and to invite the rabble to gaze upon landscapes and allegories, histories and faces. I—having only lately attained some small measure of fame, if not of fortune—was solicited to contribute. I offered a youthful self-portrait, which won a prize, and my election to the Society. It hangs in the hospital still, a bequest of mine—though whether this was on my part an act of true charity not a few unfortunate orphans must wonder as they stare at that vain, selfish, ambitious youth, for I had painted it before I was twenty. I suppose you may visit that portrait even today, though I would advise against it. Reader, I was not at my best. Were you at that age? Is anyone?

If you would kindly recall that I prefer never to cast my eye over a canvas I have completed—aye, save *The Serving Boy*, my sweet, sweet *Serving Boy*—you will understand how little I have relished the anticipation of the grand Exhibition here in Boston. I confess it: were it not for my surpassing joy on this, the happiest day of my life—for reasons I have yet to relate—I would be feeling woozier still.

I have done my small part. I paid Edes to run a notice announcing not only the Exhibition, but also a lecture.

"Ignatius Alexander," Edes mulled over the name. "A friend of yours?"

"Aye, Edes. A good friend, a very good friend."

"An African genius, eh?"

"Aye," I agreed, "as he'd be the first to tell you."

Edes smiled.

"Well, this town is chockablock with men who regard themselves highly. I'm sure he'll fit right in."

"Truly, Edes? For I wonder what Bostonian besides 'Bradstreet's Ghost' would suffer a black man to lecture him."

"We've had black preachers come to town before, though they preach only to their own, I suppose."

"Alexander's no preacher. And he doesn't peddle pap. If I know the doctor, his words will be . . . unsparing. Even of the most eminent gentry in attendance."

The printer raised an eyebrow.

"He may even unmask a murderer," I ventured, tentatively.

"Your friend sits upon a powder keg, Jameson. But as I should like to hear what he has to say, I can make sure no one lights the match. He'll leave the Town House in one piece."

"The Herrings?" I asked.

Edes nodded. "You'll see a whole school of them."

This was the last of my tasks. Alexander, trusting no one to do the work as well as he could, had insisted on taking charge of all the preparations.

"I will mount this Exhibition, Jamie. It is more my performance than yours."

I took umbrage at this—and showed it—but was nonetheless delighted to defer to my friend with regard to the installation, and left him to it, for five full days. I spent the time instructing my one-time apprentice in figure drawing, or suffice to say, in looking carefully at the life models closest to hand. And, as I had always observed—but have occasion to be newly gratified by—she brought to the drawing board more natural talent than ever I had seen. She strives, she strives, to sketch every part of me, while I have passed hours painting the soles of her feet. O Reader, in my Weston, I have found my every passion matched, my every fantasy realized, and all at once.

On the morning of the Exhibition, just before Alexander left the house, he offered his parting instructions as we three stood in the hall.

"Find me at the Town House at five, friends."

He turned to Fanny as he made to pull the latch.

"Pray, do not forget, Miss Easton: the time has finally come to play the Queen of Hearts. Wear a gown cut as immodestly as your character."

Twas for the best that the door closed behind him ere I had a chance to reply, for I have had more than enough of his sneering. What barbs he offers me, I can abide—and repay in kind—but I would defend my Fanny against his slings and arrows. Alas, that must wait. As must you, patient Reader, to hear of how my love and I spent that day. For now you need know only this: the afternoon came cold and clear, though the night before had brought the fall's first frost, a glistening glimpse of the winter that would be hard upon us all too soon. The sun set early, by half past four. Before we made the short walk to King Street, we ate a small meal of goose with dried figs and squash, prepared by the admirable Mrs. Simmons.

Her Ben met us at the Town House door.

"G'day, sir, miss," he said, with a grin and a bow, extraordinarily pleased with his role as doorkeeper. "The doctor says ye're to go right upstairs."

I had not entered this edifice since the trial. Could it have been less than six weeks ago? A lifetime ago. We passed through the 'Change on our way to the stairs. I saw a few gentlemen of my acquaintance, occupied with their trading. I offered them no more and no less than a courteous nod. Yet they all, to a man, turned a head at Fanny, on my arm, who looked, truly, more ravishingly beautiful than ever—in every way soft, graceful, and elegant, her glossy auburn curls flawlessly framing her delicate face—so far from the hard, hollow, half-starved foundling I had first met that I began to forgive myself my long blindness, which I had heretofore only cursed.

"I find I had rather walk through these halls with you as Weston, Kit-cat, for I would not have your beauty displayed to one and all," I said, and smiled, though, betwixt you and me, Reader, I was stricken by jealousy. I had adored having her to myself; it pained me to share her with society.

"'Tis revealed only to you, love," she answered, squeezing my arm. "Only to you. Only for you."

Alexander met us on the stairs. He was at his most magisterial, dressed in the scholar's black gown, which he'd borrowed from the College, and the wig, which he'd borrowed from the prop closet.

"Friends! Welcome!" he boomed. "The experiment begins!" He clapped his hands.

"I see you've donned the Proverbial Gloves once again, Professor. And the wig. A nice touch. Do you expect to see the King?"

Fanny laughed, and poked me in the ribs. (Earlier in the day, dear Reader, I had given her occasion to see the whole royal family.) But Sander looked grave.

"No, not the King, Jamie. But yes, the gloves do have their part to play, as does every element in this laboratory."

Sweet Jesus. What the deuce-ecimo was he up to? I wondered, not for the first time, whether conflating the Exhibition of Art with the Display of Deduction was a sound strategy. But there was nothing for it now.

"Sander, tell me this, man: Will we know the name of the murderer before the night is out?"

"We will," he answered, gravely. "We will. The trap is set at last. Phebe and her mother have waited long enough."

"Can we not know now, Doctor?" Fanny pressed him. "Can you not give us a preview?"

"No, my Queen," he rejoined. "I yet require one final piece of proof. But friends: come. Let me take you on a tour of our galleries!"

At the top of the stairs, he ushered us into the Council Chamber, a grand room tricked out in royal purple: the walls painted violet, a purple serge cloth covering the table, around which sat twelve walnut chairs cushioned with plum-colored damask, upon a carpet threaded with purples, golds, and greens. The full-length portraits lining the walls—near a dozen of them—turned this lavishly furnished chamber into a genealogical gallery of the crowned heads of England.

"Kit-cat, I *do* see the King," I whispered.

"Hush," she chided, as Alexander began a lecture.

"Every one of these likenesses was a gift from an arriving governor," Alexander explained. "Bernard brought Mad George," he said, pointing to a tawdry George III, hanging to the right of a door that opened onto a balcony, from which the Governor must often cast his gaze down to the Long Wharf, across the water, and, in these troubled times, yearn for England.

"And here's the Governor himself," said the doctor. Above a massive claw-foot mahogany desk, Alexander and his assistants—Ben, Kingston, and Jacob Freeman, hired for the week—had hung my full-length of Bernard, newly framed in gilt.

"I think he may be a decent man," I ventured.

"And 'tis better than a decent likeness, my love," Fanny said. "You've captured him entirely."

"But I wonder, Miss Easton," offered Alexander, "whether Chief Justice Easton will sit behind the Governor's desk next. And if that time comes, how will your lover pin your father?"

For an instant, Fanny's fair countenance betrayed signs of distress. I couldn't fathom why my friend exerted himself so far toward ruffling her—truly, he did not let pass a single opportunity—but she appeared determined not to satisfy him.

"Doctor," she replied, "I hate to disappoint you. But if you mean to disconcert me at the prospect of my father sitting for Jamie, your parry misses its mark."

Alexander's smile vanished, and he beckoned us across the hall and through a high doorway that opened onto a room near twice the size of the Council Chamber. Twas a study in red: red drapes, red walls, red cushions on the chairs—more than a hundred of them—arranged in rows upon a red-and-gold carpet. At the far end, a fire blazed in a hearth taller than a man, surrounded by a mantel of carved cherry, above which hung a large map—some six feet high by eight feet wide—of the Atlantic and the lands along either edge of it.

"You must have passed through this Assembly Room on your way to the trial," Alexander said.

"Aye, but the walls were bare then, save for that map," I recalled.

"*Terra cognita*: the known world, friends," said Alexander.

To the map's left hung my three-quarter-length of Samuel Bradstreet, gazing out upon us with his secretive stare. I took a step toward it.

"Wait," Alexander ordered. "You are not to begin with Bradstreet. The catalogue dictates that the viewer turn left upon entering the room, and proceed clockwise, first acquainting himself with the painter's lesser subjects."

He indicated the wall where he had hung near two dozen faces. We studied, first, my half-length of Mordecai Usher. Next came the Red Hen kit-cats: Clough and Gallagher (a portrait Fanny had signed as *F. Weston*), Mason and Quincy, and on and on, till we reached Thomas Newcombe, the last of the line.

We turned, passing the likeness of Bradstreet, in front of which stood a dark oak pulpit called the Speaker's desk, where Bradstreet had, for so many years, held forth. We walked under the map, and past the half-length of my brother, Colin.

Turning yet again, we came to the gallery's last wall. Here were my full-length of Alexander, the half-length *Serving Boy*—my love, my joy—and what remained of my rogues' gallery: the Earl of Berkeley, the Laird of Firth, and the Duchess of Hampton.

Finis. I was glad 'twas over. I stood, staring at *The Serving Boy*, transfixed, until Fanny broke the silence.

"Yours is to be not only an illuminated but an *illustrated* lecture, then, Doctor?" she asked, as Kingston lit the last of no fewer than five hundred candles—candles burning in sconces, candles in chandeliers, candles in stands along the walls—a fortune in tallow.

"Indeed, Miss Easton. Indeed. Go on."

"Well, you have arranged an allegory, have you not? It reminds me of the papists, with their stations of the cross. Or if you prefer a Puritan theme, 'tis more like *Pilgrim's Progress*. We begin in Wit's infancy, with a chick not yet initiated into the Hens, foppish young Usher over there, and rise, not in age, nor in wealth and rank, but in wisdom and honor, along the first wall, with the rest of the brood, so that we arrive, at the end, at Doctor Newcombe, a man of virtue and public distinction, unmatched except for that of Samuel Bradstreet. But wise Bradstreet has fled the coop; he stands on his own wall, a temple of fame, alone but for Jamie's brother."

"What bloody temple of fame has Colin in it?" I interrupted.

"Tis a metaphor, darling," she continued, stroking my cheek. "I gather this triptych—Bradstreet, the map, and your brother—tells the story of the late Speaker's opposition to the trade in slaves, which commitment he shared with Colin. They would rule over the sea that separates them, and block every slave ship that strives to pass. Doesn't the *Liberty* in Bradstreet's painting look as if it were set to sail into the map?"

"Such wonderful line work on the bow, Kit-cat." I sighed. "Do you remember the day our easels stood back-to-back—"

"Enough, you great lovesick sot," the doctor snapped. "Let her finish."

"Thank you, Doctor. Well, the *Liberty* looks as if it might be the first in a fleet that would form a blockade against the slave trade. Yet there is a geography lesson here, too."

"Promise me, Kit-cat, that geography will be the last of it. For I begin to worry that you will next get us to bookkeeping."

"Nearly done, Jamie. To the west, the doctor shows us America and the Hens—I mean, the Friends of Liberty. To the east, across the ocean, England and its lords and ladies. Though I am at a loss to explain why Alexander has placed me—*The Serving Boy*—alongside them. Don't I belong on this side of the ocean?"

"Aye, lass."

"Perhaps, Miss Easton," Alexander nodded. "And good work. You have deduced a great deal of my plan. But remember, it is not only an allegory; it is also a chemical operation. The reagents—our audience—must be heated very slowly to catalyze the solution. The experiment begins soon. We have but fifteen minutes before the doors open." He pointed to the great clock in the corner.

"But Professor," I asked, "where is my painting of Sarah Bradstreet? Everyone who read Edes's ad will be expecting it, not least the lady herself."

"Ah, yes. We shall soon learn whether Nature does indeed abhor a vacuum," was his elliptical answer.

"Doctor, I am intrigued. You have made a painting out of paintings, with its own negative space," Fanny observed. "But does my own work not figure in the story?"

"Aye, Sander," I added. "Where the deuce are Fanny's sketches and watercolors? I gave you plenty of them. Can she not display her Genius?"

"Indeed, friend," Alexander said, his tone as mild and as sweet as June butter. "Mr. Freeman hanged her efforts very nicely, in their own little gallery." He walked with us into the dimly lit landing. "Just there, on the left. A place of honor, for these will be the first works our art-lovers see, upon entering the Exhibition."

"In the hallway? Oh yes, what an honor, Doctor," Fanny said, her voice growing fierce. "But how greedy of me, to keep the deepest shadows to myself. Have I no role in this elaborate pageant, then?"

"To the contrary: your role is crucial, Miss Easton, your face as important as any of those hung upon the walls. I would have you exhibit your own loveliness."

"Am I to be Art, and not an artist?"

"For tonight, yes."

"So you consign me to a woman's customary role? I expected a more original script from you, Doctor. Yet mine will be a speaking part, and you have not given me my lines. Many here will recognize me. When they ask me who I am, what would you have me tell them?"

"Speak the truth, of course. Tell them you are Fanny Easton."

Letter XXIII.

October the 25th, 1764

"I'm afraid I cannot call myself by that name, Doctor. Not any longer."

Alexander looked at me in perfect astonishment.

"Miss Easton, Miss Easton," he replied, shaking his head as if I were a sullen sophomore in his seminar. "We have been over this, and more than once. You would have cast off your disguise weeks ago, but that I told you to keep it. Well, the time has finally come to play your hand. No more bluffs, madam. Tonight *you* shall be the trick. Certainly you have dressed the part," he said, raising an approving eyebrow as he surveyed my form.

Of my costume, he spoke truly enough. I had arrived for the Exhibition in a gown Mrs. Simmons had sewn for me, working from a drawing I had clipped from a ladies' magazine. The skirt and bodice she fashioned from velvet of a deep teal, the color the midsummer sky assumes just before night overtakes it. For the stomacher, petticoats, and cuffs, I bought her a silk moiré taffeta of the palest peach, dawn vying against the bodice's dusk. Every stitch of this creation she tailored to my form, pinning and snipping and basting and tucking till the gown fitted me as neatly as my own skin. Of that skin she urged me to flaunt plenty, with not a scrap of lace to veil the intent.

"Yer not yet one-and-twenty, missus," she said, when I asked her to raise the neckline by a hair. "When yer double that—as I am—with the juice all sucked out of ye, you'll wish you'd worn such a dress every day of yer youth. Don't hide 'em away, mum. All things fall, and sooner'n ye expect."

The doctor was right: I looked womanly enough to be this Fanny Easton. But that name had lately become a lie.

Reader, I married him.

I had pushed away his proposal, many times, and 'twas no mere coquetry. I had sworn I would never become the vassal of another king. But my reluctance had more behind it, as Jamie knew, and better than I did. I could not imagine myself a fit subject—much less a helpmeet—to such a noble man.

Jamie convinced me otherwise. After the disaster of that chicken-coop Carnival, he would hear of nothing but making me his wife.

"Never again, Fanny. Not while there is breath in my body will you fear another man. I will not stifle you, Kit-cat. I will not still your brush. But I would cover you, and cherish you till the end of your days, if only you would let me."

All last week, he murmured to me of love and devotion, of Art and Beauty. And when I felt him near, felt the warmth of his sighs, the heat of his caresses, the joy of his laughter, I melted. I marshaled what arguments I could against his proposal, speaking of my unworthiness, my barrenness, my ruin. He cut me off. I told him I must put Phebe's happiness above my own, for she was my family now.

"Keep trying, Kit-cat," he said last night. "But 'tis only common sense that we should wed. Like one of Sander's proofs in logic: irrefutable. And on this point I plan to be as bullheaded as he is."

I began to speak into his speech, but he stilled my lips with his finger.

"Nay, lass. I'll not talk of whether, only of when."

So this morning, after Alexander had left for the Town House, I answered Jamie's question with one of my own.

"When?"

"Five o'clock, Kit-cat," he answered absently, as he worked on a sketch by the window. "You heard Sander. We had best not be late."

"No, love, you mishear me. I mean to ask you: *When?* You remember the riddle:

> *"One thing, kind Sir, of you I crave,*
> *Tis that which you can never have,*
> *Nor ever had in ages past,*
> *Nor ever will while time shall last;*
> *Yet if you love me, as you say,*
> *You'll give it me without delay."*

He stared at me a moment, blinking back tears. And then he put down his sketchbook, swept me into his arms, and spun me around in the brilliant sun that floods the painting room at midmorning. We were, together, overborne by joy.

"*At once*, Kit-cat," he said, his eyes wet, his voice barely a whisper. "Right now. We must find your brother this very second. For I'll not give you a moment to change your mind."

Hand in hand, we near flew the two blocks to King's Chapel.

Daniel was only too happy to solemnize our union, for he would not have us live another day in sin. Marriage was an honorable estate, and 'twas high time we entered it. No, we need not declaim our intentions in church for a month of Sundays; no, the town crier need not publish our bans; no, we need not exchange tokens of our fidelity. Words alone were enough, a bare half dozen of them:

I will.

I will.

I pronounce.

And then, with the Right Reverend Daniel Easton speaking in the name of the Father, the Son, and the Holy Ghost, 'twas done. Amen.

All this I told the doctor, sparing him an account of the afternoon spent transforming my garret into our wedding bower, where we harvested such a wealth of pleasures that Jamie neither envied the noblest duke, nor I the finest duchess.

"So you see, Ignatius," I said, using his familiar name as a marker of our new relation, "I cannot tell them I am Fanny Easton. For I am Fanny Jameson."

The doctor looked stricken, if hardly surprised.

"Congratulations," he said, kissing me on the cheek as the great clock in the Assembly Room chimed six. And then he spoke to us both, with utmost sincerity. "You are fortunate, indeed, to have found each other, and I wish you every happiness. But we will have to celebrate on another occasion. To your places, for the curtain is about to rise. The portrait's the thing wherein we will catch the conscience of the King!"

✳   ✳   ✳

When I reached the great oak doors that opened onto the street, I nodded at Kingston, who stood at the ready. The boy and I fell in behind him. Ben's arms were filled with copies of the Exhibition catalogue, his whole pint-sized person bursting with pride.

"Let 'em in, man!" I called to Kingston, and added, under my breath, to Ben, "The Philistines are at the gate, lad."

And truly, the Public was upon us in a thrice. First came the Blue Herrings: scores of artisans of every sort. Wheelwrights, cobblers, coopers, and smiths: Edes's army.

And then: the Hens, the Hens, the Hens. They might now be Friends, yet they strutted in, frocked in their full avian regalia, red sashes, red bands, a red feather in every tricorn. Though I gave each a greeting—"Welcome, sir!"—I soon wearied of the work.

How to make the time pass? In between clapping stout Clough on the back and shaking Quincy's bony hand, I took a moment to lean down and whisper to Ben,

> *"Hickety, pickety, my red hen,*
> *She lays eggs for gentlemen."*

He giggled, and whispered back,

> *"Gent'men come ev'ry day*
> *To see wot my red 'en doth lay . . . sir."*

I passed a catalogue to Thomas Gallagher, the subject of the only Weston in the gallery.

Next, I greeted Margaret and Elias Usher, arm in arm. I was glad to make the acquaintance of the latter, for he reminded me, altogether, of his excellent mother. Behind them came Homespun Hiram in his burlap hair shirt.

"Councilor," I said tightly.

"Debtor," he sneered.

In came another clutch. Bow, bow, doff, doff, cluck, cluck. I wondered what Fanny was doing. Predictable of Sander to have separated us. How soon could I abandon my post? Not yet.

I whispered to Ben, "Sometimes nine and sometimes ten."

And he grinned and said as softly as he could, "Hickety-pickety, my red 'en . . . sir."

Zounds, we had run out of verses. Now what?

"Did you know I married Miss Weston today, wee Ben?" I asked him, merrily.

Kind Reader, I wonder, have I neglected you? I have oft warned you, have I not, that events, on occasion, outpace my pen? Let me make amends: *Reader, she married me.* My love, my joy, my life.

"I'm glad of it, sir," Ben said, brimming with what looked to be almost as much glee at hearing this news as I felt at sharing it. Then he added, conspiratorially: "But please, sir. I told me mum ye already 'ad, sir, long since, else she'd never 'ave served in yer 'ouse. I told 'er 'twas a secret, that 'er family was against you, but she married ye all the same, sir."

"Clever lad," I laughed. "I won't say a word to your virtuous mother, Ben. Not a word."

And so passed the better part of an hour—bow, bow, doff, doff—before I had the great displeasure of welcoming William and Sarah Bradstreet. I say welcoming, though neither of them deigned to do more than nod in my direction.

"I daresay this is a vulgar arrangement," Bradstreet scoffed to his mother, as they ascended from the 'Change floor to the makeshift galleries. "In what Republic does Art sit above Commerce and within the halls of Government?"

I did not hear the lady's answer, for by then her daughter Patience had made her way to me, leaning on the arm of Fanny's brother. Having resolved to marry, come what may, they looked as happy as two so contented and simple souls could be.

"Stewart," said Daniel, taking my hand. "Good evening, brother."

I was glad of his friendship, truly.

"Miss Bradstreet," I said, turning to Patience, "if I may be so bold, I venture your father would be glad to have you gaze upon his likeness, for he esteemed you very highly, and wanted the world to know it." I spoke true, yet I worried about how she might react to her father's Will. Although that testament treated her generously, she could hardly delight in its contempt for her brother and mother. "And Daniel, pray, do not miss your sister's Art," I said to the vicar.

"Excellent!" he exclaimed, and together he and his love dashed away. Behind them followed Benjamin Edes. He tipped his hat to me.

"Evenin', Jameson," he said smiling.

"Good evening, Edes," I answered cheerfully. "Glad you could make it."

"Wouldn't miss it," he answered. "And I trust my men are in place?"

"Aye, they are. And I cannot thank you enough."

"Thank me? Your friend's lecture promises to be the most exciting news in town since Bernard pulled the troops out. And your paintings, Jameson. I should warn you: I intend to publish a review."

"I hope the critics in these parts aren't as savage as the politicians."

"Ah, well, Jameson. That depends on the Art. But I have a fat purse for you: I sold over five hundred tickets, at a shilling apiece."

"That makes—"

"More than twenty-five pounds."

"I'm sure I'll lose it to you at the card table. In any case, I have another notice for you."

"I've waited for it a long time, Jameson."

"Truly?"

"Aye. 'One Giant Scurvy Dog. Eight shillings to any resident of Boston. Free to anyone from afar.'"

"Nay, I'll not give Gulliver away, Edes." I smiled. "No, what I have is a notice for your vital records."

"What? He's sired pups?"

"Leave off the dog, man! The notice begins like this: 'Married last Thursday by the Reverend Daniel Easton . . .'"

"There's a Mrs. Jameson at last? Who?"

"I'll say no more, except that you'll find my wife upstairs, and you know her well."

Edes tore up to the gallery, eager to fill his nose with the news.

Not long after came Thomas Newcombe through the door.

"Doctor," I began, bowing, "I am delighted you have given me the occasion to express my gratitude, once again, for your generous patronage. Thank you, sir, for the use of the Assembly Room."

He waved me off.

"I told you, Jameson. The hall belongs to the people," he said. "In any case, 'twas the least I could do under the circumstances. How's that boy of yours?"

"Much improved." I smiled. "You will be surprised at just how much. See for yourself, upstairs."

"Good, good," he answered absently, and then turned intent. "Look here," he continued. "Where have you put us? You've not hung the Friends next the Governor, have you? For I would not have Liberty rub shoulders with Tyranny."

I nudged Ben to hand the doctor a catalogue.

"The Hens, er, Friends, are in the Assembly Room, sir, and the Governor in his Council Chamber. I hope you will be gratified by the installation."

"I knew you would do well, Jameson."

As Newcombe headed up the stairs, there was a commotion in the doorway.

"Single file, please!" said Kingston, as the entire Lambert household—save the spaniels—tumbled into the Town House.

"Mr. and Mrs. Lambert! Mrs. Beaujardin!" I cried. "I had not expected to see you, friends. I'm so sorry that your likenesses proved too difficult to transport back into Boston. How generous of you to bring your noble selves instead!"

Mrs. Lambert hurried past, chasing her children up the stairs. Lambert shook my hand, warmly, and then dashed after her. Louisa lingered.

"Mr. Jameson, congratulations," she offered.

How the deuce could she know of my nuptials? She spied my confusion.

"An Exhibition in the seat of government is a mark of distinction, is it not?"

Ah.

"'Tis, indeed, *madame*, though I hazard I am unworthy of the honor," I answered, with a deep bow, for I had rather not meet her azure stare.

"*Et toi? Tu vas bien?*" she asked, quietly, and very intimately, stepping toward me and tilting her head to see into my eyes, for she would not allow me to hide from her gaze.

"*Oui, madame*," I answered gently, and more formally. "*Et vous?*"

She drew back a half step.

"*Je suis très contente, merci. Et je vois que vous êtes encore amoureux, monsieur. N'est-ce-pas?*"

"*Oui, madame*," I said, swept away by shyness, and near swooning at the thought of my bride. "*Vraiment.*"

"*Ah, l'apprentissage de l'amour*," she sighed. "I am glad for you. I only hope your beloved deserves your devotion." She gave me a sweet smile and a small curtsy. "*Félicitations.*"

"*Merci, madame*," I answered, after she could no longer hear me. "*Adieu.*"

✳ ✳ ✳

If Ignatius is a brilliant dramatist, he makes a poor stage manager. For he had not told me where I was to mount the *tableau vivant* he had devised for me. I thought at first to compose myself before the portrait of Samuel Bradstreet, the better to eavesdrop upon this town's lovers of Art as they read his Will for the first time. But surely, the doctor would have posted me there had that been his intent. Then I remembered Jamie's words: Be what you are, wear what you wear. My proper place became clear at once: I would stand 'neath *The Serving Boy*.

Shortly after six o'clock, the room began to fill with the vain, the curious, and the guilty, though I could scarcely tell which was which. Groups of Hensmen gabbled together along the route Alexander had plotted. Most tarried longest before their own likenesses.

Benjamin Edes entered the room and stopped to talk to a fellow artisan while he scanned the crowd. His eyes met mine as if he had been searching me out. He strode straight across the floor.

"Mrs. Jameson, I take it?" he asked with a grin. "Your husband told me I would know you, but he did not tell me the half of it, did he . . . Weston?"

I smiled back, and said, coyly, "Perhaps you don't know every jot of news in this town after all, Mr. Edes."

"O, I'll get the story soon enough. And I shall look forward to it. Very much."

Thomas Newcombe entered the gallery as the clock struck seven. He strolled briskly down the wall of Friends, nodding curtly to each, as if surveying patients in a fever ward. Not until he reached the portrait of Samuel Bradstreet did he break stride. There he loitered, staying long enough to read the Will. His face registered both surprise and sadness. He shook his head—ruefully, I supposed—as he continued around the room, as if drawn inexorably toward *The Serving Boy*. When he reached it, he looked up at the canvas, then down upon me, then up, and down again.

"Miss Fanny Easton! My God, but you look like your mother," he exclaimed. "You are a chameleon, and an adventuress. The spirited girl I once knew glows within the beautiful woman you have become. I am all astonishment at what you have dared, but not that you are the one to have dared it!"

I answered the compliment with an honest blush.

"Such promise you showed as a child, my dear," he continued. "Such boldness, even then! A talent bigger than this town, though your father could hardly see it. I heard he had you stashed away someplace, all these years, to protect you from those who would seek your hand, and your fortune, before he was ready to award those prizes."

"I have indeed been on a long journey, Doctor," I said, flushed with pleasure at renewing my acquaintance with this good man, for I cherished his esteem. "And I am glad to be back. But the beaux will have to salve their hurts, for I am a married woman now. I am Mrs. Fanny Jameson."

"Congratulations, Mrs. Jameson," he said, warmly. "Your husband is as fortunate as he is talented."

With those kind words, he moved back to admire the portrait of Doctor Alexander, in contemplation of which he spent a lengthy interval before assuming, at last, a seat in the front row, just before the Speaker's desk. From there he studied all who passed by Bradstreet's portrait.

By the time the clock chimed seven-and-thirty the room was so densely packed that it had become hard to pick out individual faces, much less voices. But even amid the crush, William Bradstreet's entrance was unmistakable. Though he sported a Hensman's sash, he showed no interest in the portraits of those gentlemen. His mother was on his arm, and he had eyes and ears only for her.

Sarah Bradstreet sashayed into the chamber, parting the picture-viewers like a storm cloud scudding across a clear sky. Her widow's weeds shimmered darkly in the candlelight. As she scanned the walls, and then the printed program, she turned agitated, and whispered something to her son. William cupped his ear, indicating he could not make her out. She repeated herself, this time loudly enough that her words cut through the dense thicket of murmuring.

"What I said, William, was where am I?" she asked, her tone one of outrage rather than confusion. *"Where am I?"*

Then she took her hand from William's elbow and walked, graceful as a queen, down the wall of kit-cats, never stopping, till she stood, face-to-face, with her late lamented husband.

A likeness can offer such comfort, can it not? A fine portrait reaches from beyond the grave, promising a kind of unearthly embrace. When my mother died, I had rather be in my father's study, before the picture Mr. Smibert had painted of her—abloom and ablaze, the very picture of womanliness—than anywhere else. So many hours did I pass gazing upon her image that Daniel—dear pious Daniel—began to worry after my immortal soul, fearing that I worshipped a graven idol.

Did Mrs. Samuel Bradstreet dissolve in tears as she looked into her late husband's eyes? She did not. She ignored his visage entirely. She would see only the Will—precisely as Alexander intended, for he had mounted a sconce upon the wall beside it, to illuminate that section of the canvas more brightly than any other. The painted parchment in Bradstreet's hand shone as if lit by the force of the writer's ideals.

From across the room I watched as first Sarah, and then William, parsed that short text. From the movements of their eyes—left to right, left to right, in quick, tight loops—and their chins—top of the page to the bottom and back—I would guess that each of them read it at least twice.

William's face remained impassive, a statue placed before a portrait, but Sarah Bradstreet made a cut-rate Lady Macbeth, for she was formed of weaker stuff. She swooned. If I had wished more evidence of her guilt, I needed it no longer. Where was Doctor Alexander when he should be witnessing this scene, wherein the culprit revealed herself?

Twas Doctor Newcombe who finally took her in hand, steadying her with his arm, and leading her to a seat next his in the front row. He waved the onlookers away, and spoke softly to her, his face radiating compassion. Twas not until I had watched her for some minutes that I realized her son was nowhere to be seen.

But soon Sarah Bradstreet would have other family around her. As the clock chimed seven-and-forty-five, Hiram Usher came to sit beside her, just as my brother entered the gallery, with Patience Bradstreet upon his arm. This evening marked the first time they had ventured out together in public since the ball. I ran to greet them, my brother and my soon-to-be sister. I brought them to the portrait of Samuel Bradstreet. Patty gazed long and lovingly upon her father, her eyes filling with tears. She embraced Daniel and walked, with poise becoming a vicar's wife, over to her mother.

Sarah Bradstreet sat stiffly beside Doctor Newcombe as the chairs behind them rapidly filled. Mr. Usher moved over, so that Patience could sit next her mother, who laid her head upon her daughter's shoulder so pitifully that a stranger might mistake the mother for the child.

* * *

Where, where in God's name, was Sander? I had not seen him since the doors opened. At a quarter before eight, I mounted the stairs.

"Remember what Alexander ordered," I called to Kingston. "Lock the doors when the clock strikes the hour."

This assumed, of course, that the murderer was still in the building. By my guess, five hundred people had come in, and half as many had already left. In neither stream of traffic had I spied the doctor. Where the deuce was he?

I entered the Assembly Room, and found Fanny, standing 'neath *The Serving Boy*. I took my wife's arm and escorted her to a pair of seats in the front row, in the corner farthest from the Speaker's desk.

"How did you fare, Kit-cat?" I asked, as I took her hand in mine. "Have you solved the puzzle? Has the murderer outed himself like the damned spot he is?"

"Surely not a him, but a her, my love: Tis Mrs. Bradstreet, is it not?"

No sooner had my wife spoken that woman's name than did she appear in front of me, the skirts of her mourning dress blocking my view like a total eclipse.

"I will see you in court, Stewart Jameson," she said, icily. "My son—who is the Deputy Attorney General of this colony, in case you have forgotten—left this charade. This very instant, he is drawing up papers to charge you with slander."

"Is there no one in your family who would not see me in irons, madam?" I exclaimed, hotly. "Slander? I thought your bastard wanted me for sodomy."

Alas, Reader, I had lost the government of my temper, suddenly and entirely. But if my wife was right, and Sarah Bradstreet was a murderess, then the time for courtesy had passed.

Before Mrs. Bradstreet could answer, the clock chimed. The room fell silent. The widow found her seat. All heads turned to the back of the gallery.

Alexander strode down the right side of the room, pausing briefly 'neath his own portrait. Dressed head to toe in borrowed finery, he looked more himself—a gentleman and a scholar—than I'd seen him since the fateful day of his last public performance, in Edinburgh. To the gown, my wig, and his Proverbial Gloves, he had added Bradstreet's spectacles, riding low on his nose. Under his arm, he had tucked a parchment scroll sealed with red wax.

When he reached the Speaker's desk, he set down his scroll, offered a bow to Samuel Bradstreet's likeness, and turned back to face the gape-mouthed audience.

"Good evening, ladies and gentlemen," he orated, in his deepest baritone. "I am gratified by your attendance at this evening's disquisition. I would begin with—"

From a few rows behind us I heard Thaddeus Mason whisper, none too quietly, to Samuel Clough, "What, a talking monkey? Maybe the ticket was worth the price after all."

"I would begin with—" Again Alexander did not reach the end of his sentence, for now Hiram Usher stood up, turned his back to Alexander, and addressed the audience.

"I came here this evening to see if Edes's *Gazette* could have been in error when it advertised a lecture by 'an African genius,' for surely there is no such animal. My curiosity satisfied, I am leaving, and I encourage all you men of the Red Hen, all you Friends of Liberty, to follow my lead."

There was movement at the back of the hall. Turning, I saw a company of Edes's army mass by the door. In the front of the room, Newcombe stood up.

"With all due respect to the esteemed Councilor," he began, "I must urge you all to stay. For I can credit that the man at the podium, if he really is Ignatius Alexander, is a learned gentleman acclaimed across the farthest reaches of the empire. I have read his work. He warrants our attention."

"A learned gentleman?" scoffed Usher. "A circus act, and no more."

"Yea, Father, a learned gentleman," insisted Usher's clear-eyed son Elias, who now rose from a seat in the middle of the room. "I, too, can attest that this Alexander is an accomplished scholar, for I have witnessed him debate; nay, I have been bested by him, sir."

It took more than a little courage to face down Homespun Hiram—as none knew better than I—and a great deal of honor to admit, publicly, to such a defeat. Elias's father looked as if he might gobsmack the boy.

Now did a third man rise from the back of the room. ("Reverend Holyoke," Fanny whispered, "the president of the College.")

"Yes," Reverend Holyoke began, "the worthy Doctor Newcombe is a credit to the colony, and Master Elias Usher, a credit to the College. Ignatius Alexander is a celebrated scholar, and, were the portrait that hangs in this room not sufficient evidence, I am here to certify that the gentleman at the podium is, indeed, that man. I examined him not a week ago, when he visited me in Cambridge, and he gave me abundant proofs of his identity." With no more than this solemn and determinative pronouncement, Holyoke sat down.

Dear Reader, lo, here was I, again playing checkers, while Alexander played chess. I had arranged for strongmen to block the door, while Alexander had packed the hall with eminences to vouchsafe his genius.

"Thank you, sirs," Alexander said. He stared daggers at Usher until the Councilor, not without a huff and a sneer, finally took his seat.

"I would begin with an argument from evidence. You notice, ladies and gentlemen, that I speak without notes. But I will refer to several documents—several *texts*—within your view, here in this very room. My method is the exegesis of these texts; my language, common sense. As a philosopher,

I make human nature the object of my study, aided by all the discernment of both the Sciences and the Arts. The eminent David Hume, chair of logic at Edinburgh, wrote in his *Enquiry Concerning Human Understanding*, that the Arts and Letters 'are nothing but pictures of human life and inspire us with different sentiments, of praise or blame, admiration or ridicule, according to the qualities of the object, which they set before us.' "

Here he paused and gestured wide toward the portraits hung round the hall.

"Ladies and gentlemen, you have had before you 'pictures of human life': this exhibition of faces, by Mr. Stewart Jameson, whose great talent graces this small city. Indeed, Hume might have been thinking of his friend Jameson when he wrote: 'The artist must possess an accurate knowledge of the internal fabric, the operations of the understanding, the workings of the passions, and the various species of sentiment which discriminate vice and virtue.' Do we not see before us, this very evening, how Jameson's Art makes such discriminations?"

Here Alexander paused again, and eyed his audience carefully.

"Hume went further with this metaphor, ladies and gentlemen. He compared the penetrating artist to another discerning character: the anatomist."

Now did the doctor rest his gaze first on Newcombe, and then on Mason.

"Professor Hume contended that the anatomist 'presents to the eye the most hideous and disagreeable objects; but his science is useful to the painter,' for while the painter 'employs all the richest colors of his art, and gives his figures the most graceful and engaging airs,' the anatomist teaches him 'the inward structure of the human body and the use and figure of every part or organ.' My argument from evidence requires both the Arts and the Sciences, the talents of both the painter and the coroner, if you will."

I shifted in my seat.

"Good grief, but Hume is as humorless as ever," I whispered to Fanny. "When he sat for me, 'twas all I could do to stay awake. Pinch me, love, ere he lulls me to sleep again."

"Jamie, *hush*." From the rapt look on her face, I could tell that so far as I had lost Sander's meaning, just so far had she followed it.

"In short, ladies and gentlemen, in vain would we discredit either the artist or the anatomist. For we will need the talents of both to answer my inquiry this evening: Who murdered Samuel Bradstreet?"

＊　＊　＊

"What species of nonsense is this!" Amos Quincy spat, rising to his feet. "We *know* the answer to that question. Cicero *confessed* to the crime!"

"What, would ye have us flog a dead horse, boy?" Mason laughed. "Bradstreet's murderer is already trapped, snapped, and skinned, and I for one, sleep better knowing the King's justice was done. Cluck, cluck, Hens."

A few Hensmen cackled back, but they failed to ruffle Alexander.

"Yes, yes, I saw how your so-called justice stole the life of that noble man," he said, calmly. "But mighty Cicero lied to you. His confession was his greatest oration, a fiction he dreamt up to save his wife and her daughter. He died in slavery that they might live in liberty. I will never be as eloquent as he was, that day, when he stood in the dock, wrapped in virtue; nor yet so eloquent as he was when he mounted the gallows, going silent to his death. But by God I shall try."

"Jameson, you charlatan! This is all your doing!" Sarah Bradstreet cried, standing and wheeling toward my husband. "My family has endured enough at your hands. Are we now to relive the horrors of the trial?"

"Dub me 'charlatan' again, madam, and I'll sue *you* for slander," Jamie warned.

"'Tis a horror to revisit Samuel's last hours, Sarah," interrupted Newcombe, who then turned around to face the audience. "But I'm afraid we must. For we have all—each and every one of us—rushed to judgment once. Let us not make the like mistake again. If we have executed an innocent man, 'tis a blot upon this colony, and we must right it. For free people do not govern with the rod of vengeance, but rather with the staff of law. Pray continue, Doctor Alexander."

"Ladies and gentlemen," said our lecturer, resuming his address as the audience quieted. "The judgment shall be yours. To help you reach an answer, I shall offer not only an argument in logic, but also the raw materials of my proof, that you may follow the matter as well as the marrow of my deduction."

His tone made no concession to Quincy's continued grumbling.

"The first text I examine—Mr. Jameson's portrait of Samuel Bradstreet—you have already seen. Or, shall I say, you have *read*, for the artist—at my direction—has punctuated the likeness with words, powerful words, the very last words Samuel Bradstreet wrote, the few short lines of his Will."

"There was no Will!" Sarah Bradstreet cried. "'Twas proven in Court!"

"Hush, Sarah," said Hiram Usher, sharply.

"Mrs. Bradstreet," Doctor Alexander resumed, now more softly, gently, as he pushed his spectacles up on his nose. "My condolences to you, madam. For this audience surely understands what your husband said of you there. It is another grave loss to you, I know: first your fortune, then your husband, and tonight, your good name. All vanished, expired. Forever. I am a man of Science, madam. I cannot bring back the dead."

"Now 'tis my turn to issue a warning, Doctor Alexander," Newcombe put in. "I will defend to my death your freedom to speak in public, for 'tis the very root of all our cherished English liberties. But I'll not be a party to defamation."

"If you would bear with me but a few moments more, my good doctor, I think you shall see: it is no easy thing to slander Mrs. Bradstreet. Pray, I beg to resume: Samuel Bradstreet left a Will. This Will"—here he pointed at the painting—"written the day before his murder. Bradstreet took care to leave a copy well hidden, lest the ones he gave to each member of his family should somehow, shall we say, disappear."

To *each* member of his family? Did this mean Patience had read the Will? I could understand her eagerness to protect her family's name, but at the cost of Phebe's freedom? If so, 'twas unforgivable.

The doctor then held up Ben's riddle book, and pulled from it the tiny folded paper.

"This last copy he secreted within the least likely of his many books, *The Child's New Play-Thing*."

"So that's why you bought his library!" burst out Hiram Usher, pointing a finger at Jamie.

"Indeed, Councilor Usher, and on my orders. And where are the other copies of Bradstreet's Will? Three others, he tells us. Since burned or drowned or otherwise destroyed by those who knew the shame written so economically therein, and would not have it published. No, Mrs. Bradstreet. Do not shake your head, for your son—I say *your* son, madam, for he is surely none of your husband's, as the Will testifies—has confessed the thing."

Alexander took up the scroll he had placed on the desk before him. Sarah Bradstreet covered her face with her hands, as if to make the scroll disappear. But Daniel, Patience, Newcombe: all sat upon the very edge of their seats, wide-eyed with amazement.

"Here, ladies and gentlemen, is my second text, the ink upon it barely dry. It is an order signed, moments ago, in your very parlor, Mrs. Bradstreet—or, rather, your creditors' parlor—by the Deputy Attorney General of this colony. This paper cannot bring Cicero back to life. But at first light tomorrow, his wife shall be released from the filthy dungeon where she is held. You notice I do not say *freed*. From the bonds of slavery Hannah is free already, and has been, for some years. Her daughter, Phebe, was born into liberty, and shall receive that happy news tomorrow, from her mother's own lips."

Tears of joy began to flow from my eyes as I contemplated the reunion of dear Phebe with her mother—and with me.

"You would turn a murderer loose on the streets!" cried Mrs. Bradstreet. "Hiram, fetch your son this instant! We will soon see into the bottom of this mischief."

Usher turned gray, and visibly shrank from her. "Mrs. Bradstreet, whatever can you mean? Mordecai is in Madras. But indeed, I should like to sit with Elias." And with that, he removed to a seat next his youngest son.

The doctor, with just the hint of a smile, continued.

"I promised you a murderer," he said, his voice rising ominously, "and so far have given you but a miscarriage of justice, though a grievous one that has taken an innocent man's life and kept a woman and child in false chains. Allow me, then, to open another text, of a very different sort. The anatomist, like the artist, reads much besides what lies upon a page."

He pulled from behind the podium a small, unframed canvas. For a long, lingering interval—a minute? maybe two—he regarded it himself, with the distracted gaze of a man deep in contemplation. When he turned it round, to face the audience, I recognized the very oddest of our paintings, the one Ignatius himself had commissioned, of Samuel Bradstreet's skin.

"What cheek that man had, Kit-cat," Jamie whispered. Again I hushed him, sure that Doctor Alexander was about to name the murderer.

"Do you recognize the likeness, Mrs. Bradstreet? Or perhaps your daughter is more apt to know it. Here is no white peach, nor clotted cream, but the hue of Samuel Bradstreet's flesh, as it appeared the day before he died. Doctor Newcombe, please contradict me if you think me in error: this is not the complexion of a *well* man."

Newcombe nodded. "Indeed, 'tis a ghastly pallor. And can you see the gray that lurks 'neath the surface? Samuel often had that cast of late."

"When you say 'of late,' Doctor," Sander asked, "do you mean in the hours before his death?"

"To the contrary," Newcombe answered, "the morning of his death found him more highly colored than I'd seen him in months—perhaps in years. You are right. He had not looked well in many a moon. His age, I suspect."

"There I must disagree, Doctor. No, it was not his age—at least not only that. I would point instead to his diet, a diet regularly leavened by that sweetest of poisons, powdered lead."

"Lead!" Newcombe shouted, and then paused. "Of course. Why did I not see it? Doctor Franklin of Philadelphia has written on the ill effects of lead in just such a case. This metal fits perfectly the inventory of Bradstreet's many symptoms: his headaches, his lassitude, his fretful sleep. Would that I had fitted the pieces of the puzzle together!"

"But what didn't batty Bradstreet complain of?" Mason thundered. "Next I suppose this great ape will tell us that lead accounts for his madness!"

"Bravo, Mr. Mason!" Alexander said, his voice oily with counterfeit approval. "You are that rare coroner, who boasts the eye of a trained anatomist. It is exactly so! As lead builds up in the body, headaches give way to delusions, even a seeming madness. You meant to build him his own asylum, did you not? Then perhaps you might name it after his poisoners."

"You see," Sarah Bradstreet cried, her voice breaking. "That black jade *did* poison him—I knew it, I tell you! The very minute my husband breathed his last! And you would free her!"

"Ah, but there I must disagree with you, Mrs. Bradstreet, although I have, of course, anticipated your response," Alexander rejoined. "As I remind you, I cannot free her, nor can you, nor anyone else, for she is free already. And no, as you yourself realize, Hannah was not the poisoner, nor even *one* of the poisoners. (Mark that I say 'the poisoners,' not yet 'the murderer.') The effects of lead are far more pronounced upon children than upon women and men. Had Hannah handled that substance regularly, we should have seen its signs upon her babe, whom it would render dim and slow. No one who has spent so much as an instant with Phebe could think her leaden. She is the opposite; she is quicksilver."

I smiled at the thought of her.

"But about this much you are right, Mrs. Bradstreet," Alexander said, doffing an imaginary cap in her direction. "The poisoners must indeed have lived with your husband, upon close—indeed, *intimate* terms—to have laced his food day in, day out, over months. If you review your household accounts, I have no doubt but that the poisoners' identities must come clear to you. If still your glass remains cloudy, Kingston, Cabot's man—he let you in the door this evening and stands at the ready, even now—can prod your memory. For he keeps careful records of purchases at the apothecary's. It was a vast quantity of lead you ordered. More than enough to make the plaster for Cicero's bad foot. You might have salved the frostbite of the King's Twenty-ninth Regiment, madam. And even that much lead was not enough. No, your son kept that rabble Enoch Goddard on the lookout for other sources, to spread your trade around. You are a woman of sentiment, Mrs. Bradstreet. Thus it will pain you to learn that Mrs. Goddard's foraging for painter's lead almost killed a noble beast."

"That murderess almost put an end to my Gulliver's travels!" called out Jamie.

"Not a murderess, my friend. For the slow application of lead will dull a man, but it will not kill him, not for years."

✳ ✳ ✳

So I was right! Twas the arsenic that killed him!" sputtered the coroner, from just behind me.

Truly, this Mason puts the arse in arsenic. But, dear Reader, I had to agree with him. Do you? And are you, by any chance, a gambling man? I'd still place my money on Bastard Billy, who could easily have dosed his father, with or without his mother's knowledge. Why the deuce had Sander let him get away? And, Sweet Jesus, when will the doctor unmask the murderer? The clock ticks, the audience grumbles. This is dangerous talk.

"No, Mr. Mason," Alexander answered. "I am afraid there is no evidence of arsenic whatsoever."

"No evidence? No bloody evidence?" Mason screamed, his face ruddy with rage at the insult to his work. "What about my report? I'll not stand for this mumbo jumbo one minute more."

Mason stood up, grabbed his cloak, and made for the door, but Amos Quincy rose and commanded in his high, thin voice, "Thaddeus, you will stay. You are all witnesses to this travesty, which may well become a matter at law. This Alexander is already coated in tar. If he means us to dust him in feathers, let us urge him on. Not a man leaves but that I direct it. For I would have all hands ready."

Reader, 'twas just as I had feared. I searched the room for Edes, but, though his men yet blocked the door, he was nowhere to be seen. I willed myself to be calm.

Muttering Mason retook his seat.

Now came Newcombe's turn to speak.

"Come, Alexander. How not arsenic?"

"I am surprised you did not deduce it yourself, Doctor," Alexander answered smoothly. "The indictment charged that Hannah had dropped powdered arsenic into Bradstreet's morning tea."

"Not just the indictment, boy, but the conviction," scoffed Quincy. "The court proved that indictment, to the jury's satisfaction if not to yours."

"Proved it mistakenly, Mr. Quincy. The facts cannot bear that charge."

"Confound it, Professor!" said Newcombe. "Why not?"

(Hear, hear, I said to myself. Why not?)

"Because arsenic takes some hours to kill a man. Twelve at a minimum. Twenty-four more often. Commonly as many as thirty-six. Bradstreet died at noon. If he had taken arsenic in his morning tea, he would not have died of it in a mere three hours. No, it could not have acted on his circulation so expeditiously, even if that system were already taxed by the chronic application of lead."

"But Doctor Alexander. Perhaps you do not realize that I was called to the gentleman's bedside in the wee hours—midway, I should guess, between midnight and sunup. Already he ailed frightfully—though I guessed, when first I saw him, that he had merely overindulged at the ball."

"As he had, sir," Alexander mused. "Doctor, can you remind us of your patient's symptoms when first you attended him that morning?"

"Certainly," Newcombe answered. "For truly, they made a strange combination. Bradstreet staggered and vomited, and grew flushed, like many a man disordered by drink."

Here Mason snickered.

"And what else?" Alexander asked.

"His breathing came fast, but shallow."

"Like a man winded by exertion?"

"No. That is the strange thing in it. For his skin was hot and dry—and arsenic, much like effort, raises a sweat."

"Just so, Doctor. Just so. As I said, ladies and gentlemen, arsenic did not kill Samuel Bradstreet, nor was the dose administered on the morning of his death. He had already drunk his fatal cup, during the ball, where he met with another poisoner, and another poison."

* * *

"Where is he going, Kit-cat?" Jamie whispered in my ear. "Where is he taking us?"

Truly, if Sarah Bradstreet were not the murderer, I could see the road ahead no more clearly than my husband could. But I knew, at least, where Alexander had been.

"He has not given us an answer yet, love," I replied. "But he forces us, at the very least, to frame a better question. The constables, the coroner, the court: they asked, all of them, *Who dosed the dead man with arsenic?* Ignatius would have us ponder, instead, *What poison killed him?*"

"Allow me, ladies and gentlemen, to shift the substance of my disquisition, very briefly, from Science back to Art," Alexander continued, his gaze now fixed upon a point in the back of the room. "I turn, more particularly, to drama—to tragedy. It is as Macbeth says:

> *"We still have judgment here; that we but teach*
> *Bloody instructions, which, being taught, return*
> *To plague the inventor: This even-handed justice*
> *Commends the ingredients of our poison'd chalice*
> *To our own lips."*

"And now the ebony parrot squawks Shakespeare at us!" Usher hissed. "'Remember me!': perhaps *he* is Bradstreet's treasonous 'Ghost'!"

"I know you cannot rest satisfied, Councilor Usher," said Alexander, "until I disclose to you the contents of that poisoned chalice, along with the identity of those even hands that proffered the cup to your late lamented brother-in-law. But you transpose your tragedies, sir. I was quoting from *Macbeth*, not *Hamlet*. And in any case, it is not Shakespeare who is our next author, nor even 'Bradstreet's Ghost,' but the estimable Samuel Bradstreet himself."

Alexander pulled from a pocket in his gown a small, thick volume, bound in red calf.

"Bradstreet called this treatise *A Modest Inquiry into the Iniquity of Slavery*. He charged Stewart Jameson to send a copy of the manuscript to Edinburgh, where it will be printed by the Society for the Abolition of Slavery. Bradstreet was unable to have the work published here—as you well know, Councilor. For you used the power of your office to censor passages on the same subject, from his earlier pamphlet."

Usher again looked ashen, but had no time to formulate a reply. For at just that moment, Benjamin Edes, his face flush, spoke from the doorway at the back of the room.

"I would set the record straight, here in public. What this gentleman says is true. While I was setting the type for Bradstreet's treatise on the rights of these colonies, Councilor Usher came to my shop and ordered me to castrate it. A printer who answers to the Governor's placemen is a poor printer indeed. If our heartless Governor can geld our books, what freedoms will he not slash from us? Censorship cuts deeper than any other form of tyranny."

"Well said, Mr. Edes," answered Alexander, with a soft clap. "You shall have, at the very least, the chance to sell this pamphlet. For in some months, copies will wash up at your little bookstall. But I would give you a preview this evening."

Alexander opened the manuscript to a marked page, and fiddled with his spectacles. "Mr. Bradstreet's penmanship leaves a little to be desired. His mind was clear but his hand trembled—another effect of lead, as many a painter learns in later years; forgive me if I use his spectacles to help me see more clearly . . ."

He then held the volume up, and read as follows: "'The iniquity of slavery is the basest evil under the sun. It redounds to good men to enact its eradication, as much in their private affairs as in their public ones. Any man who has profited by the trade, in howsoever a manner, must purge his estate of those gains. That my own conduct may serve as a model, I now relate the steps by which I have divested myself of every penny of this filthy lucre. I first redeemed from the state of slavery any souls I had ever owned, and sold away. I next redeemed their descendants, though it took me many months to trace them. In all, I manumitted eight-and-sixty men, women, and children. Twelve more had died before I could save them . . .'"

The doctor read on, at some length, detailing the careful leeching of Samuel Bradstreet's great fortune, soul by soul, pound by pound, lot by lot, over a period of several years, till nearly every drop of blood money was borne back into the great ocean that had brought it hence. He sold his stake in slave ships, and used the money to buy land for his emancipated slaves. He sold his shares in the Royal African Company; his plantations in Jamaica, in Barbados, in the Carolinas; and on and on. Though his recitation sounded like so many pages of an account book, this portion of Alexander's lecture seemed to affect the audience more variously than any other.

"Madness," Mason muttered. "I don't care whether someone dosed him with lead, or whether his brain was boiled in chicken broth. He was mad, one way or another."

Hiram Usher merely shook his head, amazed; Patience listened with an expression of perfect resignation.

And Sarah Bradstreet? She cried her first honest tears, as if this deliberate impoverishment, long concealed, lately pondered, finally explained, and forever to be endured, were the greatest tragedy, the true iniquity.

"But why?" she sobbed, looking now plaintively at the lecturer she had earlier dismissed.

"Because his wealth was plundered, madam, a fortune built upon a piracy: upon the wages of slavery," Alexander said.

He removed Bradstreet's spectacles, and held them in the air.

"But I am here to tell you, ladies and gentlemen: the wages of slavery can never be fully paid. Samuel Bradstreet saw that, as few others do. This was not insanity; this was *acuity*."

✳ ✳ ✳

The doctor set down Samuel Bradstreet's spectacles upon the podium.

"I have yet two more texts for you to peruse with your own eyes," my friend continued, and here his tone changed. He grew less imperious, and more impassioned.

I confess it, Reader: I worried. I was glad Edes had reappeared, yet I readied myself to act, should the need arise. If Edes's men could take care of the crowd, I knew where to hide Alexander, and how to get him out of the building. Wee Ben had done me a great service. "Picked a few pockets here, lad?" I had asked him. " 'Fraid so, sir," he confessed, entertaining me with tales of his narrow escapes during our many idle moments at the door. "Hid out in the cupola, I did," he told me. "Till I climbed out by the Guv'nor's balcony."

"The first of these two texts you have already had opportunity to examine," the doctor said, pointing to my portrait of him on the far wall. "Here I am a free man, and a learned one, raised from infancy as a trial of the idea that informed Bradstreet's vision: that we are, all of us, black and white, born equal. Stewart Jameson shares Bradstreet's unusual acuity. He saw me, and rendered my humanity. Truly, the painter pinned me."

Here he smiled at me fondly.

"My final text has thus far remained hidden, but the time has come to unveil it."

He held up his gloved hands—first displaying the palms to the audience, and then the backs—the gesture of a Covent Garden showman who would convince his onlookers that he kept nothing up his sleeve. Then slowly, he loosened the right glove, one finger at a time.

"Samuel Bradstreet's flesh has already served as a text in this evening's disquisition. Now it is my turn."

Having loosened the last finger of the glove, he pulled it off, all at once, cast it to the floor, and held up, before the crowd, his hand, cruelly branded with that florid R.

"Behold the mark of slavery!" he roared, with a force that near shook the walls.

"We mighta guessed as much," laughed Mason, nervously. "This 'genius' is just another runaway!"

But no one else joined in his laughter.

Alexander thundered on.

"This mark can never be erased. I will not strip off my shirt for you, ladies and gentlemen. But know that my back bears whip-scars lashed so deep that they will never heal. Am I not a man, and a brother?" he shouted, shaking his terrifying fist. "And are you, then, a people wholly devoid of reason?" he asked, his tone once again that of the lecture room. "For you claim to enslave me—my people—because you deem us less than fully human. But precisely by enslaving us do you steal our humanity. And then you use that theft—that dreadful usurpation—to justify our bondage. It is a perversion of logic—indeed, it is the rankest sophistry. Alone among you, ladies and gentlemen, Samuel Bradstreet saw this flaw in your protests for liberty."

He turned to Bradstreet's likeness and offered a shallow bow. Facing the audience again, he picked up the calfskin volume.

"Let me offer you one final passage, this from a text you rightly admire: Samuel Bradstreet's *Rights of the British Colonies Demonstrated.* I will read a paragraph that, as you have heard earlier this evening, your Governor's Council saw fit to expurgate. But Bradstreet would not be silenced."

"Huzzah!" Edes interjected.

"Just so, Mr. Edes," the doctor continued. "Bradstreet repeated the statement in his *Modest Inquiry,* that his words might at last reach the public through that route. I read them to you now: 'We American colonists are by the law of nature freeborn, as indeed are all men, white or black. If we would argue for an end to the slavery of taxation without representation, we must follow our argument to its necessary conclusion, and commit ourselves to end slavery of every kind. Can it be right to enslave a man because he is black? Will short curled hair like wool, instead of what is called Christian hair, help the argument? Can any logical inference in favor of slavery be drawn from a flat nose, a long or a short face? Nothing can be said in favor of a trade that is the most shocking violation of the law of nature, has a direct tendency to diminish the inestimable value of liberty, and makes every dealer in it a tyrant, from the director of an African company, to the petty chapman peddling needles and pins on the Guinea coast, to the printer who advertises for runaways. It is a clear truth

that those who every day barter away other men's liberty will soon care little for their own.'

"Citizens of Boston, of Massachusetts, of New-England, of America," Alexander boomed, his voice rising to a crescendo. He pointed, first,
at Bradstreet's likeness. "I have given you sufficient proofs of how blindly
you followed your prejudices into judicial *murder*, in the hanging of Cicero. I have explicated Samuel Bradstreet's argument for an end to the
trade in slaves." He waved the calf-bound book. "Now I beseech you to
see with Samuel Bradstreet's clarity"—here he raised the folded spectacles—"to hear the words he would have spoken from this very desk"—
he thumped at that pulpit—"*that those who every day barter away other
men's liberty will soon care little for their own. I beg you: do not allow
Samuel Bradstreet to have died in vain!"

A hush came over the room. Then Newcombe stood, and applauded.
Edes joined, and many of the artisans along with him. Other men and
their wives shifted in their seats, and began taking up their coats. The
burly tradesmen at the back door stood down from their posts, the danger averted.

Had Sander concluded? It appeared he had, for he began gathering
his materials, making ready to exit.

"But Doctor!" I called out, across the silence, for I could govern my
impatience no longer. "You have not told us, unless I missed it: Who
killed Samuel Bradstreet?"

He met my gaze and shook his head gravely.

"You have not missed it, my friend. Samuel Bradstreet's murder was
a tragedy. But the greater crime, the greater crime, by far, is the crime of
slavery."

"But what of the murderer?" Newcombe called out. "Does he walk
free? Name the fiend, or none of us is safe!"

Again, Alexander shook his head.

"I shall not. The name of Samuel Bradstreet's murderer is unspeakable."

A murmur passed through the crowd, and Fanny turned, following
the doctor's hard stare to the back of the room, though I could not tell
what either of them saw there.

"Yes," my friend concluded. "His name is unmentionable. He is beyond the reach of justice. His reach *is* justice. He is justice himself."

Letter XXIV.

October the 25th, 1764

From the first part of this night—my last happy hours—I shall always hold fast a few impressions of sight and sound. A room full of faces, variously illuminated: faces along the walls, set aglow by Jamie's brush. Faces in the crowd, lit by candle and by drink, by intellect and conviction, by kindness and cruelty, by honor and shame. A symphony of voices, rising and falling. A concerto of logic, performed with dazzling virtuosity. And then, as the clock struck nine, the doctor's astonishing *coup de grace*: "*He is beyond the reach of justice. His reach* is *justice. He is justice himself.*"

After an hour of speaking so precisely, never resorting to euphemism or indirection, to end with a statement of such opacity. Why? Jamie shook his head in puzzlement. Did any in the audience take the doctor's meaning? Even I might not have, had I not followed the line of the doctor's icy stare to the far corner of the room. There, in the shadows, I discerned the barest stirring—a coat pulled on, a door opened just wide enough for a man to slip through, his back receding. Just a flicker of black upon gray, like a raven alighting from a bare branch at midnight. But I recognized his bearing in an instant. I had studied it all of my days.

I did not wait, not even a heartbeat, not even for my husband. I knew what I must do, and that I must do it alone. I offered no word, no womanly cry, when I leapt from my seat and bolted from that room as if a life depended upon it. As indeed it did.

For more than two weeks I had allowed poor, dear Phebe to languish in my father's house, in the home of a man, who, for all that he had done to me, had done worse to Hannah, had ravished her. My husband, his friend, even my brother: they had each insisted, all that long fortnight, that Phebe was safe, and that her rescue would come soon enough, if only I would cultivate the patience to wait. Wait for Sander, Jamie urged. Wait for the Exhibition, Alexander commanded. Wait for God, Daniel prayed. And so I waited.

But if my father were a *murderer*? My tiny sister would not spend two minutes more there, not while I had breath in my body.

I sped down the stairs of the Town House. On the landing below, I found Ben kneeling upon the floor, frantically gathering a stack of programs that lay scattered all around him.

"He knocked me down, 'e did," said the boy, full of anger. "'Twas that crow, mum. But I've got 'im back, 'aven't I—I've picked 'is fat pocket!"

I rushed past him into the night. The moon was new, the stars covered by clouds, the darkness complete. The temperature had fallen— autumn become winter—but I had left my cloak behind. The cold seared my chest. Behind the Town House, puddles of muck had frozen, stiff and jagged, into a million little hillocks as sharp as broken glass. Weston's boots might easily have taken the terrain in stride, but to my silk slippers, these were the peaks of the Andes. Truly, a pretty gentle-woman is not costumed to run. I slipped and stumbled, falling to my knees twice ere I turned onto Corn-hill, where I kicked my worthless shoes into the gutter.

As soon as I crossed Brattle Street, I left the road, making my way to Hanover along secret routes remembered from my girlhood, through back lots, around woodpiles and cisterns, tearing my skirt on a picket as I hopped the low fence before my father's property. I avoided the grand front entrance, instead stealing around the back of the house, into the kitchen door.

I found the room silent and dark, save for embers still glowing in the hearth, the very hearth where Hannah had cooked, long ago, before my father tapped her to serve his own needs. I had thought to find my dear Phebe there, on the same sort of pallet where her mother once had slept, near the worktable. But I did not—nor did I find any of the other ser-vants—for it had long been my father's habit to reserve Thursday as the staff's night off. At least the sweet girl was spared the sight of me; I must have looked the very picture of a madwoman—my feet frozen and filthy, my skirts shredded and caked with mud, my hair tumbling wild about my face. Yet I had never felt more resolve, or greater clarity.

From the kitchen I made my way past the China room, where my father displayed the porcelains that his fleet ferried from the Orient. I crossed the hallway, my bloodied feet sullying its thick, brilliantly patterned carpet, the gift of a merchant in the Levantine branch of his trade.

At last I stood in the doorway of the library.

A fire burned brightly in the hearth, its glow reflected in the tall windows on either side of the chimney. Upon the marble mantelpiece, a profligacy of candles glimmered, lighting my mother's portrait. I was taken aback to see a specimen of my own Art—my schoolgirl sampler—propped in a small frame just below it.

> *This needlework of mine can tell*
> *That I a child was learned well . . .*

Before the fire, in a high-backed leather chair, my father had settled himself in his customary pose, facing my mother's likeness, that he might imagine her there with him. He was bareheaded, his wig placed carefully on a low oval table before him, alongside a lantern, a crystal decanter, and a small leather globe. A blanket lay across his lap. He held a folio, open midway, his finger moving along as he read.

I stole through the doorway quietly, so quietly, my bare feet making no sound. I pressed myself against the high bookshelves at the rear of the room, stifling my breath, though my chest heaved. For perhaps half a minute, I regarded him from behind, marveling at his composure. He had burst through these doors moments before me—had he not?—having fled a large public gathering where he had been named— all but named—as a killer. Yet his posture betrayed no haste, much less worry. Barely did I move while I watched him, for I imagined that surprise would somehow privilege me in the contest that awaited.

He was not surprised.

"Fanny, I presume?" he asked, his voice flat. He scarcely glanced up from his book. "I've been expecting your homecoming. There was your note, of course. And then Daniel promised I would see you soon. He asked me to pray for you. But what a cold night, and so late! Tis a strange choice, even for one as used to walking the streets as fallen Fanny Easton."

Smoothing my skirts and striding with as much confidence as I could muster, I approached him. The distance from where I stood to that hearth cannot be twenty paces, yet it felt to me like a long and lonely march through the canyons of my girlhood. How many times had my father called me to attend him as he sat in that very spot? Twas from this room that I had fled his so-called care, still bleeding from childbed, still sweating with fever, still leaking the milk my babe would never have the chance to suck. And now I stood before him, the fire at my back, a grown woman, but—in my heart—a girl of eight.

He smiled when he saw me, a twisted, off-kilter smile without a trace of fatherly love in it, nor any warmth, of any kind. His eyes glittered, their pale green giving off the frozen glow that I imagined must lie at the center of a great berg of ice.

"Ah, just look at you," he said. "The picture of elegance, she is, my child, my 'sometime daughter'! How proud you have made your dear old father, Fanny. Truly, my heart brims. Why, 'tis just as Lear's fool says—I've been reading *Lear* tonight, such a comforting play, I find—do you remember it?—in the fourth scene of the first act." He pointed to the page before him, cleared his throat, and declaimed:

> *"A fox when one has caught her,*
> *And such a daughter,*
> *Should sure to the slaughter."*

And then he laughed, a hearty stage laugh, much rehearsed. My blood ran cold at the sound.

"Excuse the digression, Fanny. Brilliant, just brilliant, this play. Do you read still? I do hope you've kept up your learning, dear daughter, for you were always such a clever, quick-witted girl. Too forward, of course, though that proved to be the least of your faults."

"Sir," I said, for I gagged upon the name of "Father," and spoke more quietly than I meant to. "I will leave this house, finally and forever, as soon as you give me my sister."

"Speak up, child! Did that governess of yours never teach you to enunciate? Clear, soft words are a maiden's glory. For a moment, I thought you said 'your sister.' But my Fanny is not mad! She knows her sister is dead, dead and buried, as rotten and worm-eaten as her own well-gnawed virtue."

"*Phebe* is my sister!" I shouted through my tears. "She is your child! And I mean to take her from this house of horrors, this very night, and make a proper home for her. Tell me where she is, else I will search from room to room and never stop until I have found her."

"A home? A 'proper home,' is it!" He shook his head, all pretended amazement. "What *home*, Fanny—the doorway of some dram shop by the wharf? O yes, I have heard men talk of your talents, daughter. Your pallet in the Manufactory House? What, did you think you were invisible to me there? Fanny, Fanny, my dear, darling Fanny: you could not protect a kitten, much less your kin. But you've proven that already, have you not? My daughter is no mother. Ah, but why should I fumble for words when I have the Bard before me! Do you remember how I used to read to my children? Indulge me, darling, would you—just a moment?—while I share with you some lines from *Lear*.

> "*Hear, Nature, hear! dear goddess, hear!*
> *Suspend thy purpose, if thou didst intend*
> *To make this creature fruitful!*
> *Into her womb convey sterility!*
> *Dry up in her the organs of increase;*
> *And from her derogate body never spring*
> *A babe to honour her! If she must teem,*
> *Create her child of spleen; that it may live,*
> *And be a thwart disnatur'd torment to her!*
> *Let it stamp wrinkles in her brow of youth;*
> *With cadent tears fret channels in her cheeks;*
> *Turn all her mother's pains and benefits*
> *To laughter and contempt; that she may feel*
> *How sharper than a serpent's tooth it is*
> *To have a thankless child! Away, away!*"

Just then, when I thought I should faint from rage and shame, I heard the kitchen door slam, and footfalls approaching from the hallway.

"Aye, she will away, away, and soon enough." Flushed with equal measures of cold and fury, Jamie burst into the room, Alexander close behind him, yet in his wig and gown. My husband stopped at my side, and slipped an arm about my waist. "We'll have the child first, though. And mind, I'll not suffer you to speak so to my wife."

"Your *wife*, is it?" At this my father laughed, a full-throated laugh. "O, that's rich. Only a face-painter could put such a rosy glow upon a poxy strumpet. You come from afar, so perhaps you haven't heard: my sweet Fanny, she marries thrice daily. You need settle no portion upon her; a shilling or two buys a few moments' wedded bliss."

Jamie let me go and took a step toward my father, uttering the growl of a furious bear. Alexander struggled to restrain him.

"Where is the little girl, Justice Easton?" the doctor asked, his hand tight on Jamie's arm, his voice as impassive as my father's. "I assured my friends that you have taken excellent care of her."

"Phebe is fast asleep, I should think," my father said, a note of gentleness melting his menace. "Or at least I hope she sleeps, if this rabble hasn't waked her already. Poor little lamb. She's been through so much. She has terrible dreams, dreams from which she wakes screaming. Tis enough to break a father's heart."

"Fuck your fatherhood, Easton," Jamie hollered. "We'll wake her from this nightmare soon enough. In what room does she sleep, you heartless son of a bitch?"

"The mouth on him, Fanny. My gracious. Where does Phebe sleep? Where I can comfort her, and keep her safe, from the monsters that haunt her sleep, and from pestilence and poison, and from housebreakers and runaways and whores and other bogeys who prowl the streets at night. Perhaps I should I call for the constable . . . ?"

"*Where?*" Jamie thundered.

"Why, in my bed-chamber, of course."

"In your bed-chamber?" Jamie said, stunned.

"You need not follow your wife into the gutter, face-painter," my father rejoined. "You'll find nothing but fidelity in this house. My Phebe has her own little pallet, in a trundle, 'neath my great bedstead."

But Jamie was not quieted, not in the least. He turned back to me.

"Where, Fanny? Where is his room? Tis no small house in which to find a tiny child," he said, his voice urgent and strained.

I told him where my father's chamber lay, just above the one where we stood. I pictured Phebe slumbering there, by the bay of windows looking north across the gardens, to take in the Mill Pond, and the Charles beyond it.

Jamie flew up the wide, sweeping stairway.

The doctor held out an arm to steady me, as he had done the night of Cicero's funeral. But I did not—could not—take it. I was frozen, stock-still, a tree whose roots fastened me to the floor. I would have leaned upon my husband's bosom friend—if only I could have imagined how I should move, even an inch.

"Justice Easton," the doctor said, smoothly, "so far have you identified yourself with the powers that govern this colony that you may well lie beyond the force of law. But just the same, I cannot think you mean to test the proposition. Though you and I both are learned men, we may yet underestimate the people of this place. You are indeed a wolf, sir, but they are no sheep. Free men will rail against injustice. And one can never be sure how or when the people will use their power. Your neighbor Samuel Bradstreet must have taught you that; if you learned nothing else from him."

"O, I learned *plenty* from the tiresome Book of Samuel—a lifetime's worth, I assure you," my father drawled, narrowing his eyes as he regarded the donnish Alexander. "But they were not, I must say, the lessons he intended. Poor Samuel: he modeled himself after the prophet who was his namesake. He fancied he would lead the Israelites against the Philistines! But his mind grew disordered—from lead, as you informed me, in your *fascinating* lecture. Administered by his own wife— truly, 'tis *too* rich. Thus he joined the wrong side of the battle. He fought alongside the Philistines, you see—in fact, he marshaled them, *inflamed* them, with his mighty 'Torch of Liberty'! Daily they multiplied around him, his mongrel minions, so many catching his fire that the joke ceased to amuse me. Here is what Samuel taught me: he taught me that rebellion leads to anarchy. That it matters not whether the mutiny occurs in a legislative chamber, or under one's own roof. Or yet whether the like misfortune transpires upon some Virginia plantation, eh, *Professor*? Yes, yes, our Samuel was a prophet indeed, for he reminded me of that great animating principle of the universe: the necessity of order, a moral I have always known, for my father, my King, and my God taught it me, from the days of my youth, unto this."

"You dare to speak of *morals!*" I stammered, for my rage choked me yet. But my father did not answer me. He saved his words for Alexander.

"You see, Doctor, what comes when one neglects the principle of order? I have failed, all too obviously, to instruct my Goneril here. But I bought myself another chance, have I not, when I purchased Bradstreet's little remainder? I keep her close, as I have said. And I assure you, I will spare no pains to teach dear Phebe the virtues of a moral life. Temperance, patience, prudence. And, of course, chastity. Chastity: Twould make an auspicious name for a daughter, would it not?"

I screamed, but neither man looked at me. They stared, instead, at each other, unblinking, for what felt like minutes. I listened for Jamie upstairs. Finally, Alexander's voice, calm and steady, cut the silence.

"Justice Easton, let not this woman's wailing break our concentration upon matters of politics. Truly, I am grateful to you, sir," he said, offering—amazingly—a hint of a bow. "For I now see why you hated Samuel Bradstreet—hated him even unto murder."

"Hated him?" my father interrupted. "To the contrary: I pitied him. Do you know what that great fool once said to me? He said, 'I seldom look upon sugar, Easton, without fancying it covered with spots of human blood.' Can you imagine? That madman would have destroyed the empire!"

"By threatening slavery? Surely Bradstreet's bill would never have passed."

"Of course not."

"The boycott then, Justice?"

"A child's tantrum, and no more," my father said, with a look in my direction. "Signatures on paper will not keep the people from buying what we want to sell them. The fabric of trade is not half as flimsy as Hiram Usher's ridiculous homespun rags. No, what made Bradstreet dangerous was his seditious speech. He gainsaid Parliament, and would convince the people he had a right to do so. With that madman muffled, it will be a decade before these colonials get up the gumption to consider independence again."

"Just so, Justice Easton. Just so. Yes, I see *why* you poisoned him. And I had deduced, sometime ago, *when* you did it. It was at the very moment you extolled the union of your families, was it not? You marked the cups—yours blue, his red, for the Hens, so you said. But the colors held a different sort of portent, ensuring you would not mix them inadvertently. Clever, very clever. I cannot imagine your factors ever get the best of you, sir."

"Thank you, my man." And unless the firelight deceived me, a blush of pride rose to my father's chalky cheek. "I did take some pains on that score, yes. I could hardly risk a mistake, you see."

"Indeed, indeed," Alexander continued. "It is just so in the laboratory. The chemicals must be carefully marked. But forgive me, sir—can you stand just one more question, from an abashed admirer? Abashed, sir, because I must confess: I have not yet deduced *how* you did it. What was your weapon, sir? What powder did you place inside that bitter cup?"

The shadow of a smile—a proud, demented smile—crossed his lips. I began to realize what manner of performance was unfolding before me. Alexander would be Jamie in the painting room, setting a most reluctant sitter—yea, a dangerous one—at his ease. It seemed he might soon pin his man.

"O, Doctor, you shall enjoy it," my father chuckled. "For you proved this evening that you are a poet as well as a philosopher, and I dare say there is some poetry in my selection. I used the fruit of a vine from your native land."

"My native land is England, sir," Alexander replied, his voice growing cold.

"From the African jungles whence your people sprung, then. A vine that bears long spindly pods, which conceal dark shiny beans. They look something like the roasted bean of the coffee plant. And as it happens, coffee was the one slave-made solace with which even poor Samuel could not bear to part. He would give up his servants, his lands, his rum. O yes. And he would have my son marry the daughter he had all but bankrupted, but no matter—let them bleed away *my* fortune so he may wrap himself in virtue's brightest robes. But still, noble Samuel must have his coffee. Forgive me, Professor. I digress. The Calabar bean, they call it, and a potent thing it is, too. *One* seed, ground to a powder, is enough to kill a man, if the thing does not need to be done instantly. And why rush it, I say? Why not linger a bit? I chose it for the name, in large measure. It hearkens after Shakespeare's Caliban, that New World savage, a half-witted ape whom only a Bradstreet could have loved. And who could resist the symbol? He would ram his bloody Africa down my throat, would he? Well, let him choke on it."

"The Calabar plant, yes. I have read of it, in the Royal Society's minutes. *Physostigma venenosum*," Alexander mused. "It is much like strychnine, is it not?"

"There you are wrong, Doctor," my father instructed. "And I confess, I am more than a little pleased to have bested you! No, the Calabar is the very opposite of strychnine. That poison dulls the consciousness. But the victim of the Calabar *knows* precisely what he suffers, as his heart slows and his lungs fill and he drowns in his own drool. Or so I am told."

"Fascinating," Alexander replied. "But it must be terribly rare, sir. How did you come by the stuff?"

"O, o, this is the beauty part, Professor, for 'tis a topsy-turvy story. *Slaves* delivered it into my hands—indirectly, at least. Hiram Usher was given a pouch of the beans by one of his captains, a good man who risks his life daily upon the Guinea trade. This captain got it from his cargo, in another tale of turnabout: they had tried to poison the crew with it, thinking to take over the ship—poor bastards— alas, they could not swim. Usher keeps the pouch in a little canister in his cabinet of curios. Pompey showed it to me, and I saw its possibilities at once. Who better to swallow such a chalice than a slave-lover like Samuel Bradstreet? Not that Cicero or Hannah *wouldn't* have dosed him with arsenic. I just beat them to the punch—or, to the coffee, as it were."

My father looked as if he would fairly burst with pride. Still, Alexander retained his calm.

"As a man of Science, sir, it would intrigue me to study the substance. Have you any left upon which I might conduct a course of experiments?"

"One bean, yes," my father said, his voice growing vague. But before he could finish his thought, the sound of Jamie's feet upon the stairs broke the spell that bound the two men. Soon my love appeared in the doorway, with the dear sleeping babe cradled in his arms.

"A pox on Newton and Boyle," Jamie whispered, keeping his voice low lest he wake Phebe. "This is no time for a chemistry lesson, Sander. Bring me my great coat, would you? I could find naught to bundle her in but her thin blanket. And let us wrap Fanny in her cloak and away, away from this dreadful place at once."

"Yes, Jamie. Yes, yes. But let me beg one more minute of your patience. An eminence has just confessed to murder. It would be hard to find a jury to convict the colony's Chief Justice. But he must pay some price, must he not? Fanny, I should think you might receive the whole of your inheritance now, if you would but name your portion."

My father looked at Alexander in wonder, stunned that pawn and king had suddenly switched places.

"I want not a farthing of his blood money," I whispered. "But I would have him settle enough upon Phebe that neither she nor Hannah should ever again know want."

"You needn't worry about Phebe," my father said. "When I die, Daniel will have his portion, and Phebe shall inherit the balance of my estate. For I am blessed, as long-suffering Lear, to have at last one dutiful daughter."

"Fanny, are you sure you will not accept his money, for we could press him. Here, now. Tonight," the doctor urged.

I shook my head. "Never. Only for Phebe."

"Very well," he replied. "Then, Justice Easton, with regard to Phebe's inheritance, might we have your intentions in writing?"

"O, 'tis written, Doctor. Right here." He patted a sealed envelope tucked into his book. "I'm not such a fool as Bradstreet."

"Might I see—" the doctor began.

"Sander, let us *away*!" Jamie thundered.

"Hush, hush," I whispered, to all of them, for I would not have the sleeping babe awakened. "Oh, Phebe, my Phebe. I swear I shall protect you all my days. Never will you come to harm, now that you're in our care."

"What, would you be a mother, then?" my father asked. "Poor Fanny, I wonder if some sailor gave you a goodly dose of the French pox, which has traveled at last to your brain! And now the bawd imagines herself a Madonna bathed in God's own light. Is it not a species of madness, Doctor? Could you diagnose this dementia for us?"

My father laughed a mad, rueful laugh. And though he addressed his remarks to Alexander, he had trained his emerald stare upon Jamie, as if daring him to drop the babe and rush to my side. But my husband would not take this poisoned bait.

"Come, Kit-cat," he said, in a tone of utmost gentleness. "Even Gulliver knows better than to bite a mad dog. We have your sister; let us hurry home. Help her, Sander. I shall carry Phebe."

The doctor took my elbow, and made to steer me toward my husband and our babe. But I hardly needed his aid, for Jamie's unwavering love had released me. I regained my legs, and I moved, one step, and then another, and another, till I had nearly reached the doorway. Jamie and Phebe and all the future beckoned.

But then, like Lot's wife, I looked back. I would not let my father have the last word ever spoken between us. I walked back into the library and stood squarely before him. I gathered my wits, and my words.

"You shall see, Father, what kind of mother I will be!" I said, my voice cracking despite my efforts. "I will be a mother like my own. If she lived—oh, if she lived—I could make her proud yet! I know I would!"

"O, Fanny, Fanny," my father said, his face aglow in the firelight, his eyes dancing. "You would be Hogarth, I know. But your poor venereal mind has confused the narratives, darling! Tis Bunyan's book, *The Pilgrim's Progress*, wherein our virtuous Christiana carries her babes to the Celestial City. Hogarth's *Harlot's Progress* offers a different ending: Moll's death, her pitiful death, pox-ravaged, in some gin lane. You are Moll, sweet Fanny, not Christiana. And I'll not hear your mother's name upon your lips. It dishonors her enough that her features are painted on your face!"

By now my father did not so much speak as spit, his eyes wild with rage, yet his form strangely still in his chair.

"Sander, for fuck's sake," Jamie said, with as much urgency as a whisper could convey. "Let us get her away from this monster!"

Mightily did he and Alexander strive to lead me from the hearth. But I made myself deaf to them. For I had grown rigid with a lifetime of injustice. And heaven help me, I could not think to leave a room where my mother was being spoken of—yea, where I could see her face upon the wall.

"O, my poor, poor Charlotte," my father continued, his eyes misting, as he addressed that portrait. "I fetched what help I could, darling! But that half-witted Newcombe couldn't save you, or our babes."

Then he turned his liquid eyes upon me.

"Ah, Fanny, Fanny. Did I not feel her loss more keenly than any of you? Such a terrible loneliness, Fanny—you cannot begin to compass it. I thought I would die from the solitude."

He closed his eyes as he shook his head from side to side, and tears seeped soundlessly down his cheeks.

"And what did my Fanny—the plucky sprite who had contrived, I knew not how, to become my only daughter—do to ease her poor father's pain? Why, the little slattern heaped more agony upon me! You *dare* to speak of pride, Fanny Easton? Into this wreckage you brought only more ruin, shame heaped upon loss."

He shook his head at the memory.

"You gave yourself to that stupid hack, Cummings, here in my house, in this very room, 'neath your dead mother's portrait. Great with child, and still you would not take his name! No, not Fanny Easton, not proud Fanny Easton. She would make a whore's kitling my granddaughter. To have you ruin my name, my career—all I had left to me? I could not stand it! No, I would not let your baby's cries pierce the sacred silence of my tomb. I had to put an end to your shame, Fanny. You left me no choice."

"Her cries?" I screamed. "You heard her cries? But you told me she was born dead. More of your lies! What have you done with my baby?"

"*My baby! My baby!*" my father cried, his voice thinned to a mincing mockery of my own. "'Twas no *baby*, Fanny. Your cunt spat out a little bit of whore-spawn. I did with it what I would have done with any barn cat's whelp: I bagged it in burlap and drowned it. Would you visit its grave, my sentimental daughter? You need look no farther than my bedroom window, for thar she lies, at the bottom of the Mill Pond."

His soliloquy finished, my father coughed, and struggled to regain his placid mien. But I could see his breathing, fast and shallow, as he waited to discover whether his arrows had found their mark.

I did not collapse. To the contrary. I felt a strength far beyond my own. I grabbed the poker that leaned before the fireplace, and I wheeled upon him without a word. My first blow found the table beside him, and reduced it to splinters. The decanter shattered. Knocked from its stand, the globe fell to the floor and rolled into the fire. And yet my father showed no fear.

"What, would you kill me, then? Think of it, child: both the great oak and the fallen acorn, murderers, alike. Your painter could glimpse at last our family resemblance. And I would be proud, dear daughter, to have you succeed at least at one thing."

And then he laughed, which sound only enraged me more.

"No!" Jamie cried, as I raised my hands to level a second strike, knowing I should not miss my target again. But just as I brought the poker to the very top of its fateful arc, Alexander stepped before me, placing himself between father and daughter.

"Mrs. Jameson," he said, his voice steady and grave. "This choice is yours, not mine. But hear this: my hands have done terrible vengeance. And its memory—trust me—its memory is not sweet. You have your love. And you have saved Hannah's child. Do not lose them both."

I stared into his brown eyes, stared long enough to see the sense in what he said. The poker fell to the floor with a clatter. Phebe, who had waked, began to cry. I ran to her, and Jamie had the great generosity to place her in my arms, rather than sweeping me into his. A moment of rocking settled the babe back into her slumber. Then my husband placed his strong arm round the two of us, and murmured his love, again and again.

"You are safe, Kit-cat. He cannot hurt you, my love. Let us away, away."

But Alexander did not whisper. He spoke clear—not loud, but level—as his eyes bored into my father's.

"Edward Easton. I see I am to be your judge and jury after all. You are spared the gallows, sir, but your sentence is a painful one, is it not? For you live with the knowledge that your eldest daughter's mercy has triumphed over your cruelty. A victory indeed."

A sentenced witnessed by that daughter, who will never again be the same,

Fanny Jameson.

CHAPTER 25

On the Impotence of Sympathy

Why write? Truly, Reader, I am at a loss to justify it. Have I not said it before? I had rather not chronicle horror. I would not paint for you this pain, for you can neither relieve it nor share it, and so, what use? Why should I give to you a simulacrum of my sorrow, or anyone else's? Might I not spare you its exposure, and myself its revelation?

As Alexander and I sat by the fire in the parlor, counting the hours till first light, when we could at last fetch Hannah from the jail, my friend spoke to me once again of Adam Smith's *Theory of Moral Sentiments*.

"Smith tells us that sympathy is the greatest of human virtues," he insisted.

"Aye, but no man can know what another feels," I protested. "And so surely sympathy is the most impotent of human virtues. How am I to help my wife, who cannot accept my comfort and has wept herself to sleep, clutching a slumbering child who has endured we know not what?"

"You cannot feel what your wife feels," he admitted. "Nor can you know my feelings, or anyone else's, Jamie. As Smith wrote, 'Though our brother is upon the rack, as long as we ourselves are at our ease, our senses will never inform us of what he suffers. They never did, and never can, carry us beyond our own person.' "

"Is this your lesson, then? That sympathy is inadequate? Haven't you taught me as much already? What can I, who am free, know of what it feels like to be reduced to a state of slavery, to be whipped, to be burned? I have not endured your wounds. I can hardly look at them. How am I to fathom what you have suffered? How can my sympathy salve your sorrows?"

He looked at me, tenderly.

"You have been my friend, Jamie, and I suppose that is all that any man dares to hope for."

"And your friendship has sustained me through hard times, Sander," I said, though I found I could not look him in the eye at just that moment. "Yet you will not even speak to me of how you ended up in Virginia, and how you escaped. You keep your story to yourself. Surely that belies your faith in the power of sympathy, or in the power of mine, at least."

He rubbed his hands before the fire, and silence filled the space between us. At last he spoke.

"I will not be turned into a tale, to be hawked between two covers by men like your brother."

"Zounds, Sander. Is this what you think of me? That I would sell your story to Colin?" I asked, astonished. "I do not mean to leaf through your pages, friend. Just the last chapter: Can you not at least tell me how you managed to get away?"

"O, but you are so easily seduced by plot. How many times have you asked me, 'Who is the murderer? Who is the murderer?' I am. I slaughtered my way out of bondage. With my bare hands. I am as much a murderer as Edward Easton."

I took his hands in mine and, for the first time, forced myself to trace with my finger the path of the R that was his deepest scar.

"But you had no choice."

"Did I not? I might have chosen death. My father found his freedom that way, by throwing himself over the gunwales of the slave ship where I was born. I chose life and liberty. *My* life, and *my* liberty, though I stole both from the men I killed."

"God above, are you hunted as a murderer?"

"No, Jamie. I covered my tracks well. Yet no sophistry, no pedantry, not even the light of philosophy can make what I did any less a crime. I am a murderer. I could scarcely allow your wife to kill her father for deeds no worse than mine."

"No worse? Do not compare yourself to that fiend. His crimes are worse, far worse."

"So you choose to believe, and maybe one day I will convince myself of the same. Enough. You now have the bare facts of my tale. You will never hear any more."

"But might it not unburden you to speak of it?"

"Are not our bookstalls already well stocked with captivity narratives? I will not be hackneyed. I am not a character. I am a man. In this, indeed, I share your wife's most passionate conviction. She refuses to follow the fate of the doomed heroine of a sentimental novel. I can well see why you love her, Jamie," he said and smiled. "For I have never before met a woman who could plot her own story."

I could contain my despair no longer. For I love Fanny's defiance, too, even when it vexes me. I have never known its like. And now? My head fell into my hands. My wife, my wife. How am I to help her? On this—our wedding night—I dare not even enter the room in which she sleeps. Alexander held me in his arms as I cried, held me tightly, gently. For many moments we shared this embrace, I full sensible of his gift, and its cost. At last he stood up, squeezed my shoulder, and, tender as a breeze, kissed my crown as he walked by, and headed into his rooms. A minute later, he returned with a book, Bradstreet's copy of Smith's *Moral Sentiments*.

"If you sleep, I will wake you when it is time," he announced, clearing his throat, and resuming his usual imperiousness. "For I will not have Hannah spend one more minute than she must in that prison. If you cannot sleep, read."

I could not sleep, and so I did read, though, for many minutes, I could not parse the text for the terrible scenes that played before my mind. Edward Easton, cackling with the madness of his rage and grief. Wee Phebe, tucked into a trundle 'neath the great bedstead of the Chief Justice of the colony's highest court. Fanny raising a poker over her head, poised to strike, while her father, with grotesque countenance, laughed and wept in twain.

We had stumbled out of that house, Fanny carrying the sleeping child wrapped in my coat. As we stepped onto the street, and into the winter's first flurries of snow, I reached to take Phebe from my wife's arms, yet she recoiled, and even made to run from me, staggering under her burden and more, from the sting of the icy cobbles 'neath her bare feet. I chased her, leaving Alexander behind. She ran fast as a colt. At the corner of Tremont Street, I overtook her, and clutched her sleeve.

"Fanny, Fanny," I pleaded. "Let Sander carry the girl, for you can hardly walk. I will carry you, lass. I will carry you."

She pulled free of my grasp with such strength that I nearly lost my balance.

"I can walk," she insisted, her voice as smooth as ice, her eyes as fierce as a storm. "I can walk. Do not dare take my babe from me."

I shivered, less from the bitterness of the wind cutting through my shirtsleeves than from the coldness of her countenance. I had expected to find her weeping, collapsing, gasping. Instead, she was a glacier, all ice and granite.

"Then I will carry you both," I declared, determined.

And I bent to gather them up together, for we had not more than three blocks to go, and I knew I could shoulder their weight that far. I would spare her this. I would spare her this, at least.

"No!" she shrieked, as she slithered from my embrace, and raced ahead. Where I had braced myself to bear her weight, her absence left me staggering, and I fell to my knees. Alexander caught up with me, and helped me to my feet.

"Leave her. Jamie, she cannot . . ." he began, but I heard not how he ended, for I sped ahead once again. How could I leave her? Please, God, I would spare her this pain.

Again, why write? Why chronicle such sorrow? Reader, I have read my Smith, and, while he was a bore as a sitter, his pages gain my admiration. Yet they remind me that you can never know what I feel, nor I what you do. Nor can I know my wife's agony. We are, all of us, in the end, alone. Alone. Hear Professor Smith on the subject, if I cannot convince you. "When we condole with our friends in their afflictions," he writes, "how little do we feel, in comparison of what they feel? We sit down by them, we look at them, and while they relate to us the circumstances of their misfortune, we listen to them with gravity and attention. But how far are the languid emotions of our hearts from keeping time to the transports of theirs? Nature, it seems, when she loaded us with our own sorrows, thought that they were enough, and therefore did not command us to take any further share in those of others, than what was necessary to prompt us to relieve them."

And how to relieve them? What good is writing?

You may protest, Reader, that I write to activate your imagination. You may even go so far as to propose that I write to exercise your sympathy. Is that not reason enough? But I would answer your question with another. Are you not a creature of my own imagination? Did I not say, long ago, that you are unfathomable to me? And so, we have come full circle, have we not? I imagine you so that you can imagine me.

That is how love works, surely. But I had not, before this instant, known that a writer's affair with his reader was so passionate an acquaintance. I had thought it more like my seduction of my sitters. A harmless bit of playacting. A pleasant trifling. A meeting of surfaces. Yet 'tis something different, deeper, and darker. And I begin to weary of it.

Do not misunderstand me. For your patience and for your compassion, I am grateful. Eternally, in your debt. So there is yet this reason to write: I would not run out on you, you I would not fail, for you are no mean-spirited, mincing McGreevy, and I mean to repay you, if only with my pages. Let us race together toward The End, tender Reader, that I might put down my pen at last, for writing this causes me a world of pain.

I did not catch her again, though I passed Gulliver wandering in the street. By the time I reached the house, she had already crashed through the door and climbed the stairs to her garret.

I found her in her own narrow bed, huddled so tightly against her sister as if to stir would take the last life out of her. She would not turn over, not even to look at me. She flinched when I touched her.

"Leave me."

So cold and fierce were these words I could do nothing but what she requested, though I first made a good fire, for she could hardly think to sleep with the child in so cold a room, on such a night as this. And yet I tarried so long in the garret—with not a word from my wife—that Sander had to pull me away, and drag me down the stairs, to sit with him in the parlor by a fire he had built, for I had set to shivering, a violent shaking, finally feeling the cold that had seized me, outside and in.

He woke me before dawn. I insisted on checking on Fanny and the girl before we left. They had not moved, Fanny's body tucked up next the child's in a mother's embrace.

Alexander and I donned our coats and hats and set out into the white-and-silver streets. The flurries had stopped, having left nothing more than a dusting, though it were beautiful.

"Jamie, I must speak to you of something that will cause you more pain," my friend said while we walked, our boots leaving wet gray footprints in the snow-dust.

"Mother of Christ, is there not enough pain already?"

"There will be more. You must take the child from your wife."

I felt my stomach sink, but I confess it, I was not surprised by what he said.

"Fanny clings to the girl too tightly. She is Hannah's child, and none of her own."

"Aye, I see it. But Fanny has lost so much. And Phebe *is* her sister."

"Phebe has no sister, not that she knows of. Fanny is a stranger to her. Your wife has lost a great deal, but she may not take Phebe as her recompense. She may have been Samuel Bradstreet's pet, but the child is no bauble. Would you tell her that Cicero was not her father—that she is Edward Easton's daughter? Is it not enough for Fanny to live with that knowledge? The sooner you take the child from your wife, the better. You know it, Jamie. I can see that you know it. She clutches the child as if Phebe were the babe she lost. No good can come of that kind of love. No good to either of them."

My tongue was tied. What could I say? Each word he spoke was true.

By now we had reached the prison. We banged on the door for a quarter of an hour before Enoch Goddard roused himself from his drunken slumber. He scowled at me through half-lidded eyes.

"Eh? What d'ye want, buggerer?"

Alexander stayed my hand and made my answer for me, as he handed Goddard William Bradstreet's sealed decree.

"Mr. Jameson comes to carry one of your prisoners away. Here is an order signed by the Deputy Attorney General himself."

The jail-keeper broke the seal and scanned the paper, though I knew he could not read.

"That's the Guv'nor's seal, a'right," he muttered. "Bradstreet told me to expect ye. Come to take that black wench, and he says I'm to give 'er to ye."

Shaking his head, he took his ring of keys from their hook and let us into the dungeon.

We found Hannah sleeping in a corner. Alexander roused her, and helped her to her feet.

"Hannah, it is I, Ignatius. I have returned for you, as I promised. Come, come," he said to her, as tenderly as I had ever seen him speak to any woman. He took off his great coat and wrapped it around her meager form. Her clothes were by now all but rags, and she was covered in filth. Alexander, who shied from every kind of grubbiness, did not balk, nor shrink, but gripped her firmly, as if bestowing upon her, with his grasp, her full humanity.

"My daughter, my daughter, where is she?" Hannah blinked at the daylight as we walked outside, where I was surprised to discover that Jacob Freeman awaited us, with a horse and cart. Alexander took Hannah by the waist, lifted her up, and placed her next his friend Freeman on the cart bench.

"Phebe is safe, at Jameson's lodgings. He and I will go to fetch her now. I did not think you would want her to see you like this. Jacob will take you home, and his wife will care for you. A warm bath, clean clothes, and a hot meal await you there. By the time you are dressed, Hannah, I promise you, I will deliver your Phebe into your arms."

Hannah wept, and reached for Alexander's hand.

"Ignatius, how can I ever repay you? Thank you, good sir. Thank you."

He bowed, gallantly, and stepped back to make way for the cart to roll. "Onward, Jacob!"

As Freeman drove away, I turned to my friend.

"How long ago did you make these arrangements, Sander?"

"Some time ago," he answered, vaguely, as he strode ahead. "I hope you see the wisdom of this course."

"Aye, I do," I answered, grimly, for while I was, at this moment, more full of admiration for him than I had ever been before, for the nobility of his mind, the clarity of his vision, and the goodness of his heart, I dreaded the role that now fell to me.

"You will do what is needed, Jamie?"

"Is there no other way?"

"Of course there are other ways. Yet this is the kindest to the child and to her mother, who deserve our first attention. You will do it."

"Ach," I sighed. "It will feel to Fanny as if I tear a suckling babe from her breast, and she will not easily forgive me. But I will do it. Pray, do not enter the house. Wait for me outside."

He nodded, and not another word passed between us.

My wife and the child must have waked just moments before I entered the garret. And when I saw them together, my resolve grew, for the girl looked confused, and not a little afraid. She sat on the bed, silent and sleepy-eyed, while Fanny sat beside her, very close, brushing her hair. What could such a mite make of this unfamiliar house, this strange companion?

"Phebe," I said, as I kneeled before the bed. "Do you remember me?"

She bit her lip and gave me a puzzled stare. Fanny made to speak but I held up my hand, begging her to wait.

"Martin Fro'sher?" she asked.

I smiled. "Nay, I am not Martin Frobisher, but I told you the story of his Arctic adventures, lass. When I came to Mr. Bradstreet's house to paint him, and your papa wore your master's clothes while you built an iceberg out of your mama's clean laundry?"

She smiled back, ever so shyly.

"You are the painter, sir?"

"Aye, lass. I am the painter. I've come to take you to your mother, who waits for you at the house of a friend. Pray, don't be frightened. 'Tis but a short walk, through a city blanketed in snow. You can pretend you are on Frobisher's ship, sailing across the ice!"

I reached for the girl as swiftly as I could, even as Fanny grabbed and clawed at my arm and began to scream, "No! No! You cannot take her!"

I did not tarry to answer, but gathered Phebe in my arms and dashed from the room and down those three short flights. Sander waited just outside the front door. In a series of motions so swift they might have been as one, I passed Phebe to him, pulled the door shut, and barred it with my body. When my wife reached the hall, she all but threw herself at me, trying to get to the door. I held her by the wrists and strived to still her.

"What have you done? You child-stealer! You slave-catcher! What have you done with her?"

Her frenzy was a fury, and she screamed so loudly she could hardly hear my reply.

"Fanny, listen to me. Listen to me. Sander has already brought Hannah to Freeman's, and now brings Phebe there. To be with her mother. Where she belongs. Where she needs to be, and at once. Tis for the best."

At first she fought to get free of me. When she found she could not—for all her unnatural strength of the night before now began to seep away from her—she berated me for my betrayal. Then she argued with me. She would not hear my explanation.

"But Jamie, she could be here with us, and with Hannah. She is my kin. I would keep her close to my breast, and love her all my days."

"You are a stranger to her, Fanny. How would you explain yourself? All Phebe knew was Weston—though she hardly knew him—and you saw how she could barely recollect me. If you revealed yourself as her sister, what then? Would you deny the child the memory of Cicero, the father who loved her so far that he gave his life for her liberty? And what of Hannah, who was once your slave? How could she live with us now? What future of domestic happiness does such an arrangement make? Nay, Phebe will live with her mother, and you may visit her, I'm sure, and befriend her, if Hannah sees fit."

I pleaded, and I argued, and she began to be persuaded. She calmed, if slightly. And then I carried the argument further than she was ready to follow me.

"Fanny, I marvel at the love you have for the little girl—for you have so much love to give, Kit-cat—and yet I cannot fathom it. For if you are a stranger to her, she is nearly as much a stranger to you. Do you not think it possible that Phebe has served as a blank page upon which you write your longing for your own child, the bairn so cruelly taken from you?"

She stopped struggling, and I released her wrists. She stumbled backward across the hall and near fell onto the stairs, holding the railing to steady herself until she collapsed on the bottom step.

"So cruelly taken from me?" she cried, looking up at me through her tears. "As cruelly as you have taken Phebe?" She wept, violently, hugging her knees and rocking herself, not ten paces away from me, yet a world apart. I ached to close the distance between us, and yet I knew that were I to move but an inch, she would dash up the stairs. I did not think I could bear to watch her run from me again.

You may wonder, Reader: Was I so willful at twenty, so fiercely fighting for my independence? I was, and a hazard to everyone around me, not least myself. Tis the memory of that rash age that counsels my patience, and makes a further claim on my affection—for don't I admire her spirit, and love her for it? Not to mention: my misery at the spectacle of her suffering is nothing compared to hers in enduring it. And I had rather watch her push me away a thousand times than to see her, for even one minute, reduced to the helplessness of mourning for a bairn all but torn from her own flesh when she herself was yet a motherless girl.

When her wailing muffled to sobbing, I spoke.

"Fanny, you cannot truly mean to compare me to your father," I said, as steadily as I could, though I could not keep my voice from breaking with anguish.

"But you snatched my babe from me!"

"Not your baby, Fanny. Hannah's child. I gave Phebe to Sander to bring her to her mother. *To her mother.*"

"But I could be her mother! I could be a mother . . ." she pleaded, her voice trailing off, as if her sorrows had become confused.

"Kit-cat, you are Phebe's sister."

And now she placed her hands over her belly. At first she looked past me, as if into a faraway place, and then she trained her eyes upon my face, though she seemed scarcely to recognize me.

"But my baby . . . Where is my baby?"

I sat down beside her, careful not to touch her, while I whispered what I must.

"Fanny, my love. Your baby is dead."

I laid my hand on her back. But 'twas as I feared: she flinched at my touch. She pressed her brow against the stair rail, her hands clutching the balusters. And then slowly, painfully, she drew herself to standing, and trudged up the stairs, her torn skirts trailing behind her. She turned back to look at me, just once.

"Please, Jamie, let me go."

How passionately I yearned to gather her up, and carry her, and comfort her, I will leave you to reckon, dear Reader. Yet Professor Smith reminds me that you cannot reckon it, for you and I, we cannot fathom each other. And still we are both of us spared the worst kind of pain, the horror that must haunt Fanny's entire imagination, the sound of her babe's final, lonely distress. "What are the pangs of a mother, when she hears the moanings of her infant?" Smith asked, and gave this answer: "In her idea of what it suffers, she joins, to its real helplessness, her own consciousness of that helplessness, and her own; and out of all these, forms, for her own sorrow, the most complete image of misery and distress."

There is no worse.

I waited the rest of the morning. I waited past noon. Finally, I could wait no longer. I tiptoed to the door of the garret room, and listened, but I heard not a thing. Not a cry, not a sigh. Not a rustle of a sheet, nor even the popping and spitting of a fire in the hearth.

Alexander did not return.

I spent my time in the painting room, fussing over a miniature. Then I went to my bed-chamber, to write by a warm fire.

I looked out the window at the snow-covered roofs. I worried about the fire in the garret. Unless she had tended it well, it must have gone out by now. It must be so cold up there, Reader. So cold. I would just add a log, and pump the bellows. No more.

I was relieved to find the door unbolted. Thank God I had not been so far shut out. Twas, as I feared, terribly cold. But before I could attend to the hearth, I froze where I stood. For on the bed, uncovered, lay my wife. Her dark eyes were wide open, and yet she saw nothing. I ran to her side and tried to rouse her, calling her name. I could feel her breath; in the cold, I could even see it. But I tell you, Reader, my thoughts were morbid. As I shook her, I felt as if I were pulling her from her own grave, as if I had become a resurrection man.

I wrapped her in blankets, and carried her down to my bed-chamber. To our bed. I tucked her in. I rubbed her hands. I put a glass of brandy to her lips. I covered her face with kisses. Then I lay alongside her, and warmed her body with my own.

"Please, Fanny. Please, Fanny, my love. Kit-cat. Come back!"

Only after many moments did she at last blink.

"Jamie?" she whispered, her voice rasping like a muller against marble.

"Thank God, thank God." I held her tighter.

She stared at me through vacant eyes.

"You are right, Jamie," she said, in that same eerie voice.

"Hush, love, hush."

"You are right; I was wrong—grievously wrong—to compare you to my father. Had I searched the world over, I could not have found a man more entirely the opposite of Edward Easton. He would destroy everyone around him. You would save us all, my love. Maybe you and Sander have saved Phebe. Yes, I suppose you must have."

Her words fell away. But after a moment she began again.

"I do see that, Jamie, truly. Even if it was from me that you had to save her. And I? I can save no one, not even a newborn, not even so tiny and helpless a soul can I protect from a world of unspeakable horrors."

"But Kit-cat," I began. "I can—"

"No, Jamie," she said softly, miserably, as she brushed the tips of her fingers over my lips, pleading for my silence. "I do not want to be saved."

B O S T O N.

*A*ny who doubt the progress of the higher branches of knowledge upon these humble shores had occasion to visit the Town House last Thursday evening, where unfolded a most unusual display of fine Art and forensic Science. Of the latter demonstration, much has been said already on the streets of this town, to which popular verdict I venture to add nothing further.

But the artistry of Mr. Stewart Jameson, late of Edinburgh, deserves our careful attention. A Duchess, a Laird, and an Earl: these *aristocrats* the artist shows in their true colors, full of ease and negligence. Whence comes their leisure but from the taxes laid upon our labors? The contrast between these lazy nobles and the honest, hard-earned dignity of Boston's men could not be more pronounced. The portrait of Samuel Bradstreet—what fire yet breathes in the Torch of Liberty, so violently extinguished! The canvas the artist titles *The Serving Boy* is, for quality, the first portrait in the room, all the more elevated for the humility of its subject.

Worthy of mention as well is the likeness of Thomas Gallagher, a canvas signed by Jameson's promising apprentice. The grocer's portrait ennobles both subject and artist.

BIRTHS, MARRIAGES, DEATHS

Married at King's Chapel on Thursday last, Mr. Stewart Jameson to Miss Frances Easton, sister of the Reverend Daniel Easton, junior vicar of that parish, who officiated at the ceremony.

Died last week, after a brief illness, in the forty-ninth year of his life, Mr. Edward Easton, Esquire, lately appointed as the Chief Justice of this colony's Superior Court of Judicature.

To the Editor:

Readers may be interested to learn that during last Thursday's Exhibition, moments before the illustrious Doctor Alexander exonerated my so-called murderer, I cut from the picture of Governor Bernard hanging in the Council Chamber a piece of canvas exactly describing the shape of a heart, and left the following note in its place:

> *Surely you have no need for this particular organ,*
> *Which you use seldom enough.*

The foul crimes done in my days of nature now burnt and purged away, I go to my eternal rest at last.
—BRADSTREET'S GHOST.

Letter XXV.

November the 1st, 1764

An ocean of time I drifted in my husband's bed, moored in the safest harbor I have ever known, and yet at sea. Jamie carried me there the day after our wedding, only to watch me sink 'neath waves of grief, ever deeper into myself, until I had become more his babe than his bride. Days he fed me, a diet of broth and bread and brandy and brotherly embraces. Nights he lay beside me, as chastely as two spoons in a drawer. Can I call myself this good man's wife? Hardly do I deserve the name of helpmeet, for I can scarce match the bounteousness of my husband's heart with one so broken as my own.

So broken, so bankrupted, so utterly impoverished: I am naught but loss. At once—and once again—I have lost my baby, my sister, and my father. Of these three cuts the first must ever be the deepest. I might live to the age of three-score-and-ten; and, were I ever to be so blessed, my children, and their children might gather round my feet; and still that wound shall never heal.

Phebe's departure opened that scar again, yet Jamie spoke true when he said that the dear little girl was not mine to forfeit. She cannot long for a sister she cannot name. Phebe has suffered as no child should. But she has her mother. God help me but I envy her that.

And my father? Edward Easton is dead. Had my strength not failed me, had not Ignatius stepped between us, my father might have died by my own hand.

"You could scarcely have killed him, Fanny," the doctor told me, as he stood by my bedside. "For he had already begun to kill himself. Dark prince of Calabar: he ground that last bean and swallowed it, greedily. I venture that he dosed himself as soon as he left the Town House, for the signs were hard upon him by the time we reached him. Whether you had struck him or no, he cannot have lived to see the dawn."

Ignatius discovered the body. That first, terrible morning, after he had delivered Hannah to Jacob Freeman's lodgings, he walked down to Hanover, and crept round the yard of my father's house. He peered through the parlor window, knowing what he should see there: Edward Easton's lifeless form, rigid in its chair. He went to fetch Thomas Newcombe, and returned with that good doctor at his side, revealing to him the earthly remains of the man who was four times a murderer, for he had killed my baby, and Samuel Bradstreet, and Cicero, and finally himself.

"Newcombe understood the dimensions of the plot at once," Ignatius said. "Your father thought to cheat the people of this colony—black and white—of the fullest understanding of their liberties. But he did not manage to silence Samuel Bradstreet, American liberty's greatest prophet. Not entirely. I thwarted him, and you defeated him. You trumped his last trick, Mrs. Jameson. He wanted to goad you into murdering him, to disguise his suicide. What perversity! But you refused to play the hand he dealt you. You were too strong."

"Too weak, you mean," I whispered through my tears.

I wept oceans for my father, more water than I thought a body could hold. Why now? He has been dead to me for years. The man who spat poison at me while he poisoned himself was no longer the father I once knew. Was he? No: he was monstrous, murderous, mad. Can I love him yet? Surely he loved me—once. Did he?

These are no woman's questions, but a child's. And I am an orphan. Who will hear them?

Not Doctor Newcombe, whose nostrums cannot reach my broken spirit. Daily he came to take the measure of my progress.

"She has suffered a terrible shock, Jameson," he told my husband on the third day of my lying in. "She shows scant appetite. Still, she is young, and strong. Her body will recover. Yet I cannot know her heart as you do, sir."

His words offered but cold comfort. Daniel's visit brought more of the same.

"Fret not, sweet Fanny," my brother said, his face full of a gladness he thought I must share. "There was nobody in the house when our poor father died, and Newcombe will keep our confidences. There will be no inquest, no whisper of suicide. He is buried already, in the churchyard beside Mother, precisely as he wished to be, and long ago. Nicholas Partridge rides from New York, even now, to execute the estate, as Father decreed. And Mr. Partridge has assured me that there will be no scandal. We are safe. None will tarnish our name."

Our name? Surely 'tis none of mine.

And my Jamie: Did he ken my tears?

"My Kit-cat, my love," he said, raking his fingers gently, so gently, through my hair. "You're safe. You'll not suffer one word more from your father. He cannot hurt you, ever again. Get up, my love. Come back to your life with me."

Truly he felt my sadness as his own. He would lift it from me, and carry it upon his broad shoulders, if only I would let him.

No, 'twas Lizzie, dearest Lizzie, who surprised me by bringing the most knowing comfort. She turned up yesterday, unannounced, unanticipated, altogether unexpected. She had ridden from New York with her father, and while he attended to my father's estate, she made her way to the sign of the painter's arms on Queen Street, using my letters as her guide. Mrs. Simmons showed this solitary visitor to my room.

How changed was my childhood friend from the last time I had seen her, when she was but fourteen, a scrawny girl, with barely the buds of womanhood. Here she was, in full flower, round and soft as a Botticelli, with the flaxen hair and azure eyes of an angel.

She fell upon me, in tears.

"Oh, Fanny!" she cried. "Why, in your direst hour, did you not reach out to me? Did you think I would not notice when your letters—your deep and honest letters—suddenly turned shallow, latticed with lies? My compass may be narrow, friend, but I am no longer a schoolgirl."

"But Lizzie," I answered, overcome, "our worlds had grown so very far apart. You disapproved of my situation. I thought I had done you a kindness—"

"A kindness? Twas the same kindness you practiced so long ago, when you broke the chain of letters that bound us. You cut me out of your very heart, but I kept you in mine. Do you not know what torture it was, to wonder what had happened to you, all those years? When I might have helped, Fanny. Somehow, I might have helped. I shall not allow you to sever our bonds for a second time."

"I promise you, Lizzie: I thought only to spare you, to release you from the bondage of such a meager friendship as I can offer—"

"To spare me what? The chance to condole with you upon the loss of your father? To celebrate the joyous news of your marriage? Is it that you trust me so little, or did you think I had nothing to offer you? I offer you my heart."

"Oh, Lizzie, I have wronged you. I am no mother and no daughter, no sister and not much of a wife. And you are right—I am still less of a friend."

"You are a better friend than you know, for you have shown me a wider world. And though—you are right—I would fain not follow you there, neither will I stand by while you again cast yourself into ruin."

"But my sorrow runs so deep. I cannot find my way out of it."

"First, Frances Jameson, you must find your way out of bed. And then, I would have you remember what your husband says: a painter must paint."

Hours after Lizzie left, I took her counsel, and rose from my bed. I was wan and weak, still aching with tiredness for all I had slept. Jamie smiled, watching from his desk as I washed my face and combed out my hair.

"You look beautiful, Kit-cat. Can I fetch you some supper?"

"Maybe just some tea. In the painting room. I mean to spend some time at my easel."

"Then I would paint with you," he offered, though truly 'twas more of a plea. "I was to go to the Town House, to patch up poor heartless Bernard. But as the Governor's survived this many days with a hole in his chest, I'm sure he can survive another. I would stay here and paint by your side."

"In time, my love. In time." I placed my hand lightly upon his arm. "But if I am to walk again, I had rather take my first steps alone."

"As you wish, Mrs. Jameson," he answered, wounded. "I would bank the fire for you, if you'll let me do that much."

After stirring the embers and adding a log, he headed down the stairs and left the house, to make our Governor a new heart, while I thought how to repair my own.

A painter must paint. But what? I cannot bear to think of a still life—in all but name, a portrait of death.

A face, then? Many times, when I was yet his apprentice, Jamie urged me—that is, urged Weston—to attempt a self-portrait. When he spoke of sending me to London, he insisted upon it. The "pearl of any portfolio," he called that exercise. But how—and *who*? Surely not *Beauty Revealed*. I have only just learned to see surfaces. I lack the insight to plumb anyone's depths, least of all my own.

If not my face, then another. For some hours I tried to sketch dear Phebe, to make a likeness of her sweet countenance that I might keep near to me, though she were far. I worked with charcoal, moving quickly, as Jamie had taught me: spirited drawing, no mincing curves. My pencil soon produced a convincing little sprite. But I had failed in her particulars, and I soon realized why: I could not see Phebe in my mind's eye, for I did not know—had never known—quite what she looked like. I had coveted Hannah's babe blindly.

At midday, as I labored over the sketch, Ignatius entered the painting room with a tray: a mug of tea, an apple, a plate of cold chicken, and some johnnycake with honey. Mrs. Simmons had tucked a yellow napkin 'neath the trencher, and it made a pretty composition.

"Do you mean for me to paint it?" I joked, as he set the meal down on the workbench. "'Tis colorful enough, but it needs more of texture in it."

"No, Mrs. Jameson. It is a gastronomic exercise only. Your husband would not forgive me if I failed to press food upon you at every opportunity."

"Is Jamie not belowstairs?"

"No. He is at the Town House, repairing his portrait of the Governor. Now: eat."

But I still could not stomach more than a mouthful.

Alexander walked around the easel and surveyed my drawing.

"It is Phebe, then? But her nose is longer, is it not? And her eyes a bit wider spaced. You have her mouth, though, Fanny, and that is the hardest part, for her life resides in her laughter."

I thanked him for his appraisal of the likeness, which rang true enough. And I told him I was glad to hear of the little girl's happiness.

"You might do more than hear of it, Fanny. You might see her for yourself," he urged. "Freeman's place is not a quarter mile from here. Hannah has told me she should like to thank you for all you did for her, and for her daughter. It is no small thing, to owe someone your life."

My heart leapt at the thought of a visit with Phebe, but I stilled myself, lest even in my mind, I steal an ounce of Hannah's joy.

"I would see her. But I might should wait, until I'm a bit stronger," I demurred. He knew at once that I meant something other than the vigor of my body.

"You are stronger than you think. You need not go this afternoon, but you cannot tarry forever. Hannah makes plans to leave this town, and there is something you must bring her."

He handed me the soft leather purse, heavy with coins, which Ben had lifted from my father on the night of the Exhibition. Mrs. Simmons had returned it the very next morning. Ten pieces of eight and a few shillings and pence lay within, undisturbed.

"Hannah must have it," I agreed. "'Tis rightly Phebe's money, along with the rest of my father's estate."

"Have you not guessed it? Your father left her nothing."

What manner of fool had I been, to believe anything my father said? There was a Will; that much was true. Ignatius and Newcombe had found it: a single page.

The last Will and Testament of Edward Easton, hardly of sound mind, bequeathed to his son, Daniel, the sum of five hundred pounds. Twice that he earmarked for the upkeep of the Easton family crypt at King's Chapel. The balance of my father's estate he left to his brothers, one in England, and the other in Jamaica. The testament made no mention of any daughter ever born to him.

"So you see, Fanny," Ignatius said, "that purse holds Phebe's future after all. It would be fitting and proper if you were the one to deliver it."

The rest of the afternoon I passed sketching, and thinking, and writing in this letter book. Soon after the bell in the Old Brick rang five, with darkness already full upon us, I heard Jamie's quick steps upon the stairs. How my heart gladdened at the sound! I rushed to him in the hallway, throwing my arms round his neck. His cheeks were flushed with cold, and he smiled widely as he returned my embrace.

"O, Kit-cat," he said, covering my head with tender kisses. "I have counted the hours till I might come back to you. But you have improved the time, lass. For I can see the strength returning to you. Nay, I can *feel* it."

"Aye, master," I said, with a curtsy. "I have labored mightily in your absence."

"Have you, lass?" Jamie laughed, hugging me closer. "Then I would comment on your etchings, and truly, I would fain show you what I can do with my brush."

He looked toward his bed-chamber with love and longing.

"No, Jamie. Soon love, but not yet." I pulled him into the painting room instead of the destination he had preferred. "I did not mean to tease you. I should love to have the master's eye upon my work."

"What a fine head of Phebe. And object studies. Why Weston, you were ever an insolent apprentice, would you finally take direction?" He looked at me quizzically. "Why now? Why does Mrs. Jameson begin to build her portfolio?"

"'Tis as you always say, darling: a painter must paint. I cannot see whether I have accomplished much. But I found real solace at the easel this day."

For the first time in a week, Jamie, Ignatius, and I took our supper together. Mrs. Simmons was so glad to see me belowstairs that she insisted on staying late to serve us. She heaped our plates high with the last fruits of fall: turnips and onions and potatoes stewed with some kale, and a fat golden hen that she'd roasted upon the spit. My favorite foods of the season, yet I was still so weak that I could take only a little bread soaked in some of the juices.

As we pushed back from the table, my husband gave me a tentative, hopeful look, and indicated the stairway with his chin.

"Shall we to bed, my love?" he asked, with a theatrical yawn. "I must away early in the morning, for I am to paint the Reverend Holyoke in Cambridge."

He gave me a wink, in case I had missed his meaning. I was overcome with tiredness; I would have to demur this invitation. But before I could speak, Ignatius cleared his throat.

"Mr. and Mrs. Jameson," he said, taking up his lecturer's voice, "it is customary, in more civilized households, to read aloud, now and then, of an evening. I thought I might share with you a novel that I have lately discovered among Bradstreet's books. The author is not one you will know, Fanny, for her writings are not much seen on this side of the Atlantic, but for occasional verses in the pages of *Gentleman's Magazine*."

"*Her* writings?" Jamie asked, bemused.

"Yes, Jamie. A Londoner by the name of Charlotte Lennox, though she has had many names, and near as many careers."

"Lennox?" Jamie asked. "I think I may have . . . met her. Was she an actress?"

The doctor raised an eyebrow. "Yes, and a celebrated beauty. She tried the stage before the page, but she found greater success upon the latter, becoming lately a member of Samuel Johnson's circle of *dilettanti*. A circle, of course, that includes many of your acquaintances, Jamie. Reynolds, for one. And his sister, the painter, an especially close friend of Mrs. Lennox's."

"A woman painter?" I asked.

"Aye, love. And a good one, though not half as talented as you, Kit-cat."

"She makes her *living* by painting?" I was astonished.

"Well, she's painted Johnson often enough, no small commission, that. For a time, I believe she lived with this Mrs. Lennox, whose husband was some manner of wastrel."

"Correct, friend," the doctor interjected, raising an eyebrow. "A chronically indebted Scot, who ruined her."

"And now?" I asked.

Ignatius answered. "And now Miss Reynolds paints, and Mrs. Lennox writes. The world is full of possibilities. Indeed, that is the point of the book from which I would read to you this evening."

He took up the small volume.

"*The Female Quixote*, book one, chapter one—"

"*The Female Quixote*?" I interrupted. "It sounds like *The Female Husband*. And I cannot bare another sad story. Forgive me, Ignatius, but I must know: Does it end badly for her?"

"It *begins* badly, Mrs. Jameson. For our heroine has no mother, and all she knows of the world, she has learned from novels that she found in her father's library. But her travels teach her that the story of her life is hers to write. So I suppose you could say that it ends well."

This morning Jamie left soon after breakfast, bound for Cambridge under lowering skies. His Weston gone forever, he took Ben Simmons with him—no apprentice, not yet, but sweet company, and a nimble pair of hands to lift his burdens and clean his brushes.

I went back to my easel, where I had found some peace, and began work on a small painting of a bird's skeleton, an exercise Jamie had pressed upon me some time ago, allowing three colors only—ivory black, chalk, and burnt umber for shadow. Twas the sort of thing an academician practiced often, and if the work was not pleasing, neither did it admit easy mastery. I imagined a studio full of aspiring artists, all busy at the same etude, working to best one another, and themselves, while vying to capture the master's eye. Oh, to paint that scene.

I had mixed my colors and blocked the composition and applied a base coat, a wash of gray—about an hour's work, I venture, for I was lost in it—when Ignatius knocked upon the painting room door.

"It will snow before night falls," he said. "Hannah will not linger much longer in this town."

"You are right, Ignatius. I shall go."

"You will find Freeman's lodgings on Back Street just past the Old Way, opposite the Baptist meetinghouse. A small gray clapboard, with a boatwright's shop on the first floor. It is not a four-minute walk at your pace. But I would have you take a little detour first."

"What, am I become your errand-boy?" I joked.

"Quite the opposite. It is time you went about your own errand. Head down to the Long Wharf before you go to bid goodbye to Hannah and Phebe. The *Flying Squirrel* is at anchor—she came in yesterday. A proud, three-masted schooner. You might have a look. She holds a berth reserved for one Francis Weston."

I could not hide my astonishment.

"You cannot want me to sail, Ignatius."

He was silent.

"Can you?" I asked again.

"Your husband wanted you to go to London, did he not?"

"But that was before, before . . . And the ocean journey would be so difficult for him. I cannot fathom how he crossed in the first place."

He stared at me hard. "No, Fanny. Your husband must not go with you."

"Then I cannot think what you mean. That I should go alone? But we are newly married. If Jamie would have me see London, then he will conquer his seasickness, and we will sail together."

"I do not consider his squeamishness, but another, more dire constraint. I wonder that you have not already deduced it, but I am hardly surprised he has never confided it to you, for he has a prodigious amount of pride. No. He cannot go because he would be thrown in debtor's prison the moment he arrives."

"Imprisoned?" My heart lurched at the thought. I recalled the advertisement Lizzie had sent me so many weeks ago—"much addicted to card playing and horse racing"—and yet still I could scarcely credit it.

"Is it gambling, then?"

"Hardly. No, neither gambling, nor any other vice. Our Stewart Jameson is indebted to his virtue. He borrowed a staggering sum of money to buy my liberty. In Britain, if not in her colonies, he is well known, and his debts widely published. He will not escape his creditors, unsavory men, egged on by a . . . patron, shall I call him? who bears him a particular malice."

"But surely he could paint, and sell enough of his work to satisfy them?"

"Two thousand pounds' worth? From prison? Joshua Reynolds may live like a squire, but if Jameson were thrown into the dark cellars of the Gate House, he would be reduced to copying the portraits of lesser painters for three shillings a head, near as much as it would cost him to pay for the candles to light his canvas. Fanny: it would end him."

"Oh, my poor, poor Jamie! But why, then, do you tell me to visit this sailing vessel?"

"I speak out of love for him, and for you, my dear. Even if he cannot accompany you, even if he cannot say as much, even if he does not know it himself, he wants you to go. No artist can realize his—*her*—promise in a life lived entirely on this side of the ocean. The *Flying Squirrel* sails Monday. You must do as your head and your heart dictate. But I ask you to listen to them carefully."

I stopped at the ship, and looked across the water. So far. Can I travel so far, and so alone? Could Jamie bear it? Could I?

Soon after, I found myself knocking upon Jacob Freeman's door. He gave me a warm smile, and I returned it, remembering his many kindnesses the night of Cicero's burial. He led me up the stairs to his lodgings, two snug rooms on the second floor.

Phebe sprawled upon the smooth wood floor of Freeman's parlor, playing with the doll I had made her. She smiled at me, a touch quizzically. Hannah stood beside her, packing a small trunk. She too smiled when she saw me, and it relieved me to see the warmth in her expression. Forged of the same steel that made Ignatius, she had come back to herself.

"Fanny Easton," she said, her voice level. "I shall never forget you. I might have died in that jail cell, but for you and your friends."

I offered my paltry sympathies for her unspeakable losses, and gave her the purse Ben had liberated, telling her nothing of where it came from, for I would not have her see my father's blood upon those pieces of eight. She took it without protest, explaining that 'twould help her and Phebe a great deal while they looked for a situation in

Philadelphia. They would begin their long journey to Pennsylvania ere week's end.

"Hannah, I wish you well. Before you go, I would tell you that I am sorry for what pain I have caused you. I turned a blind eye to my father's venality. And more than that, I am certain my jealousy made your life harder. I was a poor mistress, and my father a worse master."

"You were but a motherless girl. But remember this: there is no such thing as a good master."

Snow had begun to fall, in great wet heavy flakes that turned the streets the color of the sky, till the world came white all around me. I walked down Back Street, crossing the little wooden bridge over the Mill Creek.

Fifty paces brought me to the edge of the Mill Pond. I made my way along the shore, trudging through sea grasses bent low by the snow and the gathering wind, until I reached the spot directly behind my father's house. I turned my back upon the place of my birth to gaze across the pond, its black surface pocked with white. I cannot say how long I stood there, while the snow fell and the sky dulled. The wind howled, but I scarcely felt the cold. This was my daughter's grave, and I meant to mark it.

The Mill Pond is not deep, yet its shallows seemed bottomless. I pictured her resting there, in the cold and the darkness, a tiny skeleton lying upon the silt. I wept for her, and for my lost family, and my lost years. I wept, but I did not wallow. For what floated to the surface of my mind were not the cruelties of *Lear* but something softer and more magical, a fragment of the spirit Ariel's song, from *The Tempest*:

> *Full fathom five thy father lies;*
> *Of his bones are coral made;*
> *Those are pearls that were his eyes:*
> *Nothing of him that doth fade*
> *But doth suffer a sea-change*
> *Into something rich and strange.*

I had suffered a sea change. But when I felt least worthy of it, a strange richness had stolen into my life: my babe's eyes became pearls; her bones, coral. And now I must see the beauty that mingles with the sadness. And now I must lay to rest the part of me that died with her. Full fathom five.

Her grave could have no stone but the pebbles that line the bottom of the pond. But I would give her, at long last, a name. I thought at first of Hope, a name that spoke of a daughter's future and the joy she might bring to the world around her. But my own hope had just begun to grow, and I had rather nurse than bury it.

Innocence, I will call her.

Innocence: I was not ready to lose you when I did.

Innocence, you are gone from me, never to be regained.

Innocence: there is life beyond you, a brave new world, wide and rich and strange.

I mean to sail until I find it.

From the *Boston Gazette*, Thursday, November 1, 1764.

LONDON.

As Readers in New-England have a particular interest in the fate of the Stamp Act under discussion in Parliament, the Printer takes the liberty of excerpting, below, a report received from the Flying Squirrel, *just arrived from London.*

—B. T. Edes.

Extracts from the Votes of the House of Commons on September 10, 1764.

An Act for applying certain stamp duties in the British colonies and plantations in America, toward further defraying the expenses of defending, protecting, and securing the same, by requiring a stamp for every piece of vellum, or parchment, or paper, which shall be written, or printed upon, to include all legal documents of every type and sort, degrees taken in schools or universities, ecclesiastical decrees, licenses for taverns and all other manner of licenses; as well as every pack of cards, every pair of dice, every pamphlet, and every newspaper. Said Act was debated and received widespread support among Parliamentarians, who propose to take a formal vote on the matter this winter.

BOSTON.

Governor Bernard's picture has been hung up once again at the Town House. Our ingenious limner, Mr. Jameson, by the surprising art of his brush, has re-

stored as *good a heart* as had been taken from it; tho'
upon a near and accurate inspection, it will be found
to be no other than *a false one*. Long may this portrait
remain hanging, to show posterity the true picture of
the man whose weak and wicked Administration is
awakening a whole people to their liberties.

N.B. The Printer takes this Occasion to announce that
a provocative treatise authored by the late Honorable
Samuel Bradstreet, Esquire, *A Modest Inquiry into the
Iniquity of Slavery*, has just been published, and will
be sold at B. T. Edes's shop, printed, stitched, and
bound, for five shillings.

CHAPTER 26

Odds, Bodkins, and an End

The Reverend Holyoke is a jowly man, but no jolly one. Twere just as well, for I was in a foul mood when I painted him. The ride to Cambridge, with only Ben for company, was cold and lonely. Worse, every turn of the cart wheel took me farther from my wife.

"Go, Jamie," she insisted, as she sat up in bed, hugging her knees to her chest, while I dressed. "I will be fine with Mrs. Simmons, and it will do you good to get out, and to paint, love."

The color had returned to her cheeks, and she managed a smile.

"If I must, Mrs. Jameson." I sat down beside her while I buttoned my waistcoat. "But I will miss you."

Did I not miss her already, dear Reader? For the one-week anniversary of our wedding had come and gone, with no embraces but those offered in solace.

She took my meaning.

"I miss you, too, Mr. Jameson." She leaned toward me and kissed me—bashfully, at first, and then hungrily, and, finally, with a passion that matched my own.

"O, Kit-cat," I moaned, as I fell back upon the bed, pulling her on top of me. "I have missed you."

But as I reached 'neath her shift, she stayed my hand.

"No, love," she said firmly, but she smiled, sweetly, and not a little seductively. "Not just yet, for I will not be rushed, and you are in a hurry. You have a long ride ahead of you—"

"Aye, and I would give you a long ride, lass, as long as you like."

She laughed. Sweet Jesus, how I love that sound.

"Later, darling. Later. The President of Harvard does not like to be kept waiting!"

When at last I arrived at the College, he kept *me* waiting, more than three-quarters of an hour. Tick, tick, tock. Damn the man.

"He is meeting with the Fellows," his clerk informed me. "They confer every Thursday."

"Wot fellows?" Ben whispered.

"Gentlemen whose pockets you must not pick, lad," I whispered back, conspiratorially.

Finally the meeting adjourned, and I set up my easel in the President's narrow, book-lined study in Massachusetts Hall. Holyoke sat in a catastrophically complicated, three-legged chair, turned and topped with finials. Twas more medieval than a crenellated turret, a throne better fitted to the castle that looms over Edinburgh.

"Whence the chair, sir?" I asked.

"I can't say, Jameson, I can't say. Came across it here, in one of the college buildings, and I find I quite like it. It communicates a certain sense of office, don't you think, a certain sense of occasion?"

I could not but agree.

Holyoke bade me paint the new Harvard Hall into the background, the prospect of which conveniently appeared through the window just behind him. He was a contemplative sitter, a truly studious man, and I repaid his silence with my own, for my thoughts were elsewhere.

The time passed as sludge through a sieve. After two hours, I could stand it no longer.

"I'm afraid I'll have to trouble you for a second sitting on another day, sir," I apologized. I put down my palette and pointed, with my brush, out the window, where foreboding clouds had gathered. "The light grows dim, and a storm threatens. My wife has been unwell, sir, and I must return to town before I'm snowed in."

"Of course, Jameson, of course," Holyoke muttered, sympathetically. So distracted had I been that 'twas only at this instant that I realized he must know Fanny, and her family, more than passing well, for hadn't Daniel been his student? Tis a small world, this little corner of New-England.

As Holyoke rose from his great throne, he pulled from the pocket of his robe an envelope, sealed in crimson wax.

"Pray, Jameson, deliver this letter to your friend, the African doctor," he commanded, handing it to me. "Tis a commission from the Fellows of the College."

"Certainly, sir," I answered, surprised.

The ride back to Boston was naught but a race against the storm.

"Looks to be a fierce 'un, sir," said Ben, as he scanned the horizon. "I hope the fishermen's come in a'ready."

"Aye, lad, and all the better that we get home before it hits," I answered, flicking the reins.

We reached Queen Street just as snow began to fall, in great clumping flakes. I unloaded the cart, and instructed Ben to drive it back to Styfe's livery. I found Alexander in the parlor, reading by the fire, Gulliver at his feet.

"A letter for you, Sander. Mysterious stuff." I handed it to him.

It took him no more than a moment to break its seal and read what news it held, after which he handed it back to me with a scowl.

"But, Sander, this is wonderful!" I cried when I had gleaned its contents. "Holyoke asks for your services as Librarian at the College. Your heart's desire, is it not?"

He laughed, mordantly.

"My heart's desire? What my heart desires, Jamie, my heart can never have. You fancy your life a farce, and you are wrong. Your wife deems hers a tragedy, and she, too, is wrong. It is my story, Jamie, *my* story, that defies every convention of genre."

"So you tell me. But Holyoke recognizes your genius. He said so, before the whole bloody town."

"He acted well at the Exhibition. But you have misread the letter if you think he means to appoint me Librarian. It is an invitation to an office far lower, halfway between custodian and cataloguer. I am to have rooms in Harvard Hall, and a chance to live among what passes here for men of learning. Were Holyoke to appoint me Chair of Logic, he might make me an offer that matches my qualifications. But he asks me, instead, to scurry in the stacks like a library mouse. Pshaw!"

"You will reject his offer, then?"

"No, I shall not reject it. The President strove mightily, I suspect, to extract as much from the Fellows of the College. I like to think he would have done more, if he had been able, but these American gentlemen are not ready for what I would profess. No, I will accept it. What choice do I have?"

"A devil's bargain, then?"

"A bit better than that. I had rather live at the College than anywhere else on this vast continent. At least I will be able to study, to practice physic, and to use the laboratory, and to enjoy a kind of liberty while you and I are doomed to remain on this side of the ocean."

"Sander, you don't have to stay here for my sake."

"Let us not revisit that argument, friend. We will find a way out of your debt, I promise you."

O Reader, maybe we will. I doubt it. But I tell you—for I would never reveal this to Alexander—I had rather be Edward Holyoke's library mouse than Hiram Usher's shitten spy.

"Yes," Alexander continued, "I choke on the crumbs that Holyoke offers, but I will not spit them back at him."

"I'm sorry that you have not obtained a situation better suited to your genius. But remember, 'twas just months ago that you fled Virginia. Maybe the world is a better place than each of us thinks. And the College may surprise you yet. Mind, I expect you here, once a week, to best me at whist."

"Of course." He smiled. "I will look forward to that."

And then I tensed. The time had come. I had to ask him a question that had been welling within me.

"Sander, tell me. When did you first suspect that Easton had murdered Bradstreet?"

"Quite a while ago," he answered, vaguely, closing his book. "About the time of the trial."

"And how long ago did you decide that Fanny would have to confront him?"

"Ah," he said, standing up, tucking his book under his arm, and walking toward his rooms. At his door, he held the knob and turned back to me. "That, too, I deduced, some weeks back. And I began my preparations not long after. As you observed the day you entered my laboratory, Jamie, I did not conduct my experiments there. I conducted them in this house."

"In this house?"

"Of course. On the two of you."

"What?"

"Come now. You suspected my counterfeit, did you not? Or did you really think I would damn as a whore a woman who had earned your love and my esteem, except that I had a reason?"

"Goddammit. What reason?"

"I needed to be sure that you, and especially your wife, could bear what Easton would say. I needed to steel you to him, and let you cool, as if I were dipping you in molten metal, again and again, adding one layer, and then another. It pained me to do it. For you could hear my words as nothing but cruel, if staged, jealousy. Your Moorish Iago, you dubbed me, and I suppose I fit the role. Yet I had to harden you, so that, at the crucial hour, you would not break."

"Zounds, man. You *knew* what Easton would say? Did you deduce, even, that he had murdered her child? And you placed Fanny in his path. Could you not have caught him, and yet spared her?"

"I could not be certain about the child, of course. Though I had guessed it. And no, I could not have spared her. Nor could you. She was an element—nay, she was the catalyst—and she performed as I predicted. Very well indeed."

"*As you predicted*: This was your plan? That her father would suicide on some shitten African poison no one has ever heard of? That he would try to provoke Fanny into murdering him, and fail? This was your preposterous plan?"

"More or less, my friend. More or less."

"And did you need the new moon? And the ice on the street? Was it important that the Exhibition fell on a Thursday?"

"You mock me. But, yes, all of those things mattered."

"Aye, I mock you. What kind of a plan was that? And at what cost? Have you not an ounce of remorse?"

"Remorse? Remorse would be wasted."

"How? Truly, I can't fathom your calculation, Professor."

"No, you cannot calculate at all, my friend. You reckon in sentiment, and not in sums. Is that not at once your worst vice and your noblest virtue?"

"Tell me, then, in *numbers*. How do you account for yourself?"

"With regard to single acts of justice, as Hume tells us, ' 'tis impossible to separate the good from the bad.' I cannot give you the reckoning you desire."

"If not a reckoning, at least a summary?"

"It is as simple as this: private interests may suffer for public good. A 'momentary ill,' Hume tells us, is 'amply compensated by the steady prosecution of the rule of law.' "

"Private interests? First my wife is an element in your experiment, and now her despair—a grief so great it all but deprived her of her reason—is no more than a *momentary ill*?"

"Frankly, yes. The evil of slavery cannot compare to your need for a passionate marriage. Yes, I would have sacrificed even your domestic felicity to the greater good of Bradstreet's message. You have seen that Edes will now print his *Modest Inquiry*? Five hundred copies of a tract that could change the minds of ten thousand men. That, friend, was my plan. Q.E.D."

"How about S.O.B.? Was it worth it, Sander? Was it worth destroying my wife?"

"She is not destroyed, Jamie. You know that as well as I do."

I thought no more of my rage at him. I looked at him and dared to hope.

"Truly? How can you be so sure?"

"Because I am never wrong."

And with that, he turned the knob, and disappeared into his rooms, closing the door behind him.

Twas by now near dusk. I lit a candle to climb the stairs to my bed-chamber, altogether anxious to see my wife. But I found our bed empty.

"Kit-cat?" I called, confused.

"She left this morning, sir, not long after you did," came the answer from the painting room, where Mrs. Simmons was sweeping.

"She *left*?" I cried.

"Yessir," the good woman answered, shaking her head. "I warned her there was a storm comin', but she said she'd be back afore dinner. There weren't no arguin' with 'er, sir."

I strove to calm myself.

"You best be getting home, Mrs. Simmons. Snow's falling hard now, and your wee Ben'll be waiting."

"Much obliged, sir," she answered, with a curtsy.

I followed her down the stairs, and grabbed my great coat and hat. Gulliver shadowed me out the door, galumphing in the falling snow, chasing at flakes, and skidding over the slippery cobbles.

There was but one place I could think to go. As I ran through the fast-emptying streets, already covered with half a foot of snow, shop-keepers closed their doors and housewives shuttered their windows. The wind blew hard from the harbor. I stumbled across the Bowling Green toward the doleful body of water that was my destination. The Mill Pond.

Upon the water's black surface, sliver-thin floes of ice crashed against one another, cast about by the fierce wind, toward the dam, where they shattered like so much glass. I could barely see through the blizzard. But Gulliver put his nose to the ground, and I followed him. He headed toward the edge of the water, where I could just discern the outlines of a solitary, hooded figure, pale as marble. Still. I might have taken her for a shrouded statue. Gulliver sniffed, wagged his tail, and ran past her, to bark at the ice.

When I reached her, I was breathless, and panting.

"Fanny!" I gasped.

Neath her hood, her face was wet, though whether with tears, or with melted snowflakes, I could not tell.

"Fanny, come," I cried, taking her hands in mine. "Come home, Kit-cat. Quickly. You are frozen."

She stood where she was.

"I had to say good-bye," she said, her voice steady and determined.

I slid my hands 'neath her cloak and drew her to me.

"O, Fanny," I sighed, as I kissed her face. "Dear God, but you are brave."

For many minutes, we stood there, in silence, huddled against the wind, folded into each other. Finally, she spoke again.

"There is one more thing I must do."

I shook my head, creating a small avalanche with the snow that fell from my hat.

"Do not speak of it now. Let us home."

"No, I must, while I have the resolve this haunted place has brought me."

She reached up, and held my face in her hands, to fix my gaze upon her, even as I made to look away.

"On Monday I will sail."

My heart fell. I reeled with dread.

"No! No! You cannot!" I stepped away from her, and beckoned her to follow me. "Come home, Fanny. Come at once."

She took one step toward me, near enough that I could hear her over the wind, though she had to shout.

"Jamie, I must go. You knew as much, for you booked my berth. Six months, my love. And then I will never leave you again. Never. *Never.* But please. Six months."

"More than a month to sail there and nearly two to sail back? You'll have only weeks in London. Three months at best. Can it be worth it?"

"Three months will have to last me a lifetime. I could not bear to be away from you any longer."

"Then I'll come with you," I screamed, though I shuddered to say it, for in my mind's eye I could see aught else but pitch-dark prisons—a ship's hold, a jail cell—with no air to breathe, and no light to paint. "I'll come with you, Kit-cat."

"No, my love," she shook her head. "I must go alone."

"Have we not both had enough of alone, lass? Years of wandering, adrift, yours and mine. We are married, now and forever, moored to each other, even against such storms as these—"

"*You* have had enough of wandering, my love. My world has been but two miles long and half as wide. I was born not a hundred paces from this very spot. From my daughter's icy grave. I need to leave this pond and sail into the wide ocean. Just once. Please, Jamie, don't make me choose between my life and my love."

Dear Reader, what else could I say? When she was Weston, and again when she was Easton, I had sworn that if—when—this time came, I would not hold her back. *You must realize your promise. I will not stifle you. I will not still your brush.* And I would honor that pledge. But God above. So far? And so soon?

"Monday?" I said, striving to swallow my sorrow. "Must you leave in four days' time?"

"The sooner I sail, the sooner I sail back to you, darling," she whispered as she kissed me. "Please, Jamie. Six months. And then I will never leave you again."

Four days. We had barely four days left to us.

So much to do, and so little. I wrote to Reynolds.

Dear Sir,

You are expecting my apprentice, but the bearer of this letter is my wife, more precious to me than my life. Teach her, of Art, all that you would teach a man, for her genius will repay your instruction, as much as ever would have Francis Weston's. Do I go too far to suggest that she might live with you and your sister? Please, sir, apply my bill of exchange to cover her costs, in the most suitable situation possible. I will honor any payment you make in fulfillment of this request. But please, Joshua, in the name of our friendship, I beg you, I beseech you: see that she comes to no harm, and send her back to me, in no more than six months' time. Not a day, not an hour, not a minute more, for I cannot live without her . . .

"You will have to take Gulliver," I told her, waving away her protests of the inconveniences this would heap upon her. "He will keep you safe, and the thought of that great slobbering hound gamboling at your heel as you walk through the streets of London will give me some small peace of mind, and not a little occasion for mirth." (Both of which, dear Reader, are sure to be in short supply during this season of solitude.)

Friday dawned clear after it had snowed all night. Gulliver and I trudged to Edes's shop through waist-high drifts.

"Got your blade on you today, Ghost?" I asked, for I knew very well 'twas he who had knifed the Governor. Reader, was not this specter as plain as print?

"Glad to see you, Jameson." He smiled. "I venture that particular Ghost will haunt us no more. But I thought you might want to challenge me to a duel over what I did to Governor Bastard's portrait. Except," he winked. "I wasn't sure you'd have the *heart* for it."

"God knows, I have naught else, Edes. But, man, did you have to defile my work?"

"Sometimes the sword is mightier than the pen." He grinned.

I shook my head. "Aye, maybe so, Edes." Yet Reader, my thoughts carried his metaphor in another direction: I won't be dipping my quill for quite a while. "In any case, I've come to buy paper and ink for Mrs. Jameson. She sails for London, and I will leave her with no excuse for failing to write to me."

You will write, Kit-cat," I commanded her. "Every day. You will not fail, will you? The minute you reach shore, send a letter back on the swiftest vessel, before you leave the dock, that I may know you have crossed safely."

She offered her assurances, and I said no more. But, Reader, to you I add: Sweet Jesus. At least three weeks there, and more than six weeks back, against the trade winds. It will be more than two months before I hear so much as a word from her. How will I get by?

You may wonder whether during this interlude—on the strip of time between the pond and the ocean, shall we say?—we once again shared the pleasures of the marriage bed, whether, in short, we renewed that species of acquaintance that makes life worth the bother of getting out of bed in the morning. Or staying in. I can answer you in no other way but to say: truly, pursuing such pleasures was, in very large measure, how we spent what time was left to us. Three days, and four nights, snowbound. Bedbound. How else to prepare for half a year of misery but to hoard bliss?

Yet I will not so much as begin to describe that bliss, and not out of concern for your modesty, Madam. I have had enough of that. This is the eighteenth century. The Dark Ages are over! Nay, I will keep the memories of those final scenes close only because I am storing them; they will have to last me a very long time. Despite what Alexander says, I do have some sense of economy. I would save, and not spend, these treasures, for is not love, Sir, the wealth of nations?

"Jamie, I think we must sleep," my wife sighed, contentedly, on Saturday night, her brow and mine drenched with sweat, as she lay on top of me.

"I have six months to sleep, Kit-cat!" I protested, rolling both of us over, still inside her, until I was astride her once again. "Aye, I will sleep on Tuesday, I will rest on Wednesday, I will slumber on Thursday! For haven't you bid me to hibernate all winter long? But no, I will not sleep tonight!"

Yet, I confess it, Reader, I was all but unconscious not a quarter of an hour later. A man can only do so much. The deuce of it is: a man can only do so much.

On Sunday, we hauled buckets of water in from the cistern, and heated them, taking turns bathing each other in a tub we carried into the kitchen. She packed her small wardrobe in my bags. Alexander came back from Cambridge to bid her good-bye, and removed the last of his own belongings from his rooms, taking a ride from Jacob Freeman to his new quarters at the College. He took with him most of Bradstreet's books, but left me a small library of volumes he had chosen for my winter reading. "A course of philosophy, Jamie," he said, and a dreary syllabus it looked to be. He gave to Fanny two books—Mrs. Lennox's *Female Quixote*, and a folio of Hogarth's engravings—gifts she cherished.

Mrs. Simmons made us Sunday dinner, a feast of duck and pumpkin, though my wife ate scarce a morsel. Ben came with his mother, and, while I enjoyed their company, I was eager to hustle them out the door when the meal was through. I would husband these last hours with my wife, alone. And I did. All through the night.

On Monday morning, I prayed that a storm might delay her departure. The *Flying Squirrel* was to sail at noon. But dawn broke with not a cloud in sight. Just after breakfast, I placed her bags in the hands of a cartman, and charged him to bring them to the ship's porter, at the dock.

"We must to the wharf, Mr. Jameson," she said, when 'twas hardly ten, as we sat reading Edes's paper at the kitchen table.

"So soon, Mrs. Jameson?"

"You can't mean me to miss my ship."

"I can do, Kit-cat. I can do. But I won't make it so. Come, then."

I donned my coat and hat and wrapped her into her cloak. Gulliver beat us to the door, which was not hard to do, since I dragged my feet as if they were stuck in muck.

"Jamie, let's *go*," my wife urged.

"Surely we are in no hurry," I answered. "We have nearly two hours to walk five blocks. Do not fret, lass."

"We need to leave a little time for parting, do we not?"

"I suppose," I muttered. "I suppose."

Once we shut the door behind us, we found, to our surprise, that we were met with a press of people, whose noise we had not heard from within the house, still shuttered against the late storm.

"You have so far distracted me, Mr. Jameson," said Fanny, with a wink, "that I forgot. November the fifth. Tis Pope's Day."

"And how do the people of Boston celebrate the preservation of the British Nation from the Popish Plot of Guy Fawkes?"

"Like this." She shrugged. We stood in the doorway watching the revelers pass by, on foot and on carts, spilling tankards of Adams's ale, and firing muskets into the air. "All the apprentices take to the streets, and stage a battle between dueling effigies of the Pope and the Devil."

Reader, let me assure you: 'twas mayhem. Twas Bedlam. To call it a parade, to call it, even, a *chaos*, is to give it an undue sense of orderliness. The crowd moved like a swollen and furious river, crashing against buildings and pouring round them like as so much water sloshing over a broken levy. The Blue Herrings had made this Guy Fawkes Day into a political protest, carrying burlap sacks labeled SUGAR—but packed with snow—and throwing them in every direction. Meanwhile, there fluttered through the air scraps of paper, like so much confetti. I caught one, and handed it to Fanny. Twas the size of a paper note, and printed in the style of the colony's now defunct and valueless currency. It bore, in an oval frame, a woodcut of Governor Bernard, above which read, in bold print, the word WORTHLESS. And next the Governor, this verse:

> *I have no heart but such fair face,*
> *That lures poor men into disgrace.*
> *Never hard and no more tender,*
> *The bane of workingman and lender.*
> *Swear off sugar; bees make honey,*
> *Spread it on your paper money!*
> > *—D. EBTS, Printer.*

"Tis an indifferent anagram for B. T. Edes," she mused, as she read it, "for it lacks the second 'e.' And the rhyme is even worse."

"Aye, lass. Edes is no Shakespeare, I'll grant you."

"But Jamie, the picture looks like your work," she said, eyeing me with surprise. "Did you? Would you . . . ?"

I would, and I did. Governor Bernard may not be the worst of men, but I disagree with him—and heartily—so I had obliged Edes, when he asked me, by doing my wee bit for the patriot cause. Lo, I am become an American after all.

As soon as we stepped out from the shelter of the doorway, the flood carried us off. Gulliver disappeared before we were two steps from the house. I held my wife tightly around her waist and she clutched my coat but a cart jostled us, and we were separated. I lost her.

The length of Queen Street I looked for her. I had no doubt that she would find her way to Long Wharf without me, and quickly, for she was a colt, but I hated to part from her any sooner than I had to. At last, as I neared the Town House, she found me. She had climbed the steps to its western door. She called to me. I cut my way through the swell and finally reached her. I pushed the door open behind her and we stole inside. The floor of the 'Change was altogether empty, silent as a tomb. The merchants, at least, knew better than to travel through town today.

"This is astonishing news. The whole of Boston has staged a snowball fight to send off my beautiful wife. They throw money at you! What next?"

"And I had pictured a somber and tender parting, darling," she said with a smile.

"I had rather be spared that scene, Kit-cat. But this one goes a little too far in the other direction."

The bell in the Old Brick tolled eleven.

I looked up, seized with an inspiration, and grabbed her hand.

"Come, Fanny. We have just enough time."

I led her to the stairs, up to the second story, and down a narrow corridor between the main stairs and the Assembly Room.

"Where are we going?"

"Hush, minx," I answered. "You'll see."

Behind a tapestry, I found it: a wooden door. Twas unlocked, as it had been when Ben had shown it to me, the night of the Exhibition. I had to duck my head to fit 'neath it.

"Where . . . ?"

My only answer was to grasp her hand, and tug her along. The spiral stairs to the cupola's first tier were narrow, and steep. But we did not tarry there.

"Come, love," I insisted, as I opened another, still-smaller door, squeezing through it to mount the final two dozen steps.

Breathless, as much from excitement as from exertion, we reached the top of the cupola. I pushed open a trapdoor and helped Fanny onto the landing. I shut the trap. We stood on a floor no more than six-foot square. The walls of this little room, if I can call it a room, were four arched windows, framing views of the whole of the city.

I took my wife in my arms, and whirled her round to spy out each of the windows, seeing all, and yet unseen. The cobalt ocean. The snow-covered rooftops. A battalion of Pope's Day paraders, burning piles of Edes's worthless money, next the soldiers' camp on the Common. The forest of ships' masts in the harbor. Before us was displayed, in every direction, an exquisite prospect of this world, this small, brave, wondrous, rebellious world.

"Oh Jamie," Fanny sighed, delighted. "'Tis perfect."

"You know, Kit-cat, I do love your wee city."

"I know, love."

"And you will love the vastness of London."

"Truly?"

"Aye. 'Tis as Johnson says, when you are tired of London you are tired of life. You will love it. But not so ardently that you won't be able to leave it," I warned, gently.

And then I adopted a tone of pronouncement as I directed her attention out each window, by turn. "Young Weston. Fanny Easton. Mrs. Jameson. My Female Quixote. Think of me here, waiting for you. Like a sailor's wife, watching the sea."

We stopped, at last, before the window that faced due east, onto the Long Wharf, where rioters were dumping their sacks of spurious sugar into the water.

I stood behind her. She leaned into me.

"One last dance, Mrs. Jameson?" I murmured into her seashell ears, as we began to sway. "For I never did sing you the ending."

"The ending?"

"The ending to 'The Collier's Daughter.' And I skipped a verse in the middle, lass."

And then, as I turned her, slowly, so slowly, about the miniature room, I sang.

> *"The Collier has a daughter,*
> *And O, she's wond'rous bonny,*
> *A Laird he was that sought her,*
> *Vast rich in land and money.*
>
> *"The tutors watch'd the motion*
> *Of this young honest lover;*
> *But love is like the ocean:*
> *What can its depths discover."*

I unbuttoned the back of her gown.

"What depths, love?" she asked, breathless. "What's next?"

I loosed her stays.

"You'll see, lass.

> *"He had the art to please ye,*
> *And was by all respected;*
> *His airs sat round him easy,*
> *Genteel, but unaffected.*
>
> *"The Collier's bonny lassie,*
> *So fair that none could blame ye,*
> *Aye, sweet, and even saucy,*
> *Secur'd the heart of Jamie."*

"It does *not* say 'Jamie' in the song," she protested.

I caressed her breasts.

"You've caught me there, Kit-cat. Twas 'Billy,' and something about a lily. I have taken some liberties. Just a few. And I would fain take more."

I raised her skirts, and placed a hand 'neath them.

"The climax is coming, lass, if you would only have the patience to wait."

I moved my hand inside her, tacking between Easton and Weston.

> *"He lov'd beyond expression*
> *The charms that were about her,*
> *And panted for possession,*
> *His life was dull without her.*
>
> *"After mature resolving,*
> *Close to his breast he held her,*
> *In fastest flames dissolving,*
> *He tenderly thus tell'd her."*

She sighed, and moaned.

"What, what did he tell her?" she begged.

I smiled.

"Still panting, are you lass? It's coming. One last verse.

> *"My Collier's daughter bonny,*
> *Let nothing discompose ye,*
> *Tis not your scanty dowry*
> *Shall ever make me lose ye:*
>
> *"For I have gold in plenty,*
> *And Love says, 'tis my duty*
> *To spend what Heaven's lent me,*
> *Upon your wit and beauty."*

She shuddered, and sank into my arms.

When she had recovered enough to speak, she scolded me.

"Damn your Highland dirges. Neither of us has any gold. What, what would you spend upon my wit and beauty?"

"Would you have me show you what Heaven's lent me, Mrs. Jameson?"

"Great Scot, Mr. Jameson. I think you must, sir."

I turned her toward the window, standing close behind her.

On King Street, just below us, we could see the Red Hens and even hear their muffled calls. "Friends of Liberty! No Sugar in our Tea! No Stamps on our Papers!"

I kissed her neck. Nay, I did more. I bent her over, my hands tight about her waist. I anchored myself inside her. Her hands gripped the rail below the sill, her knuckles white. One last, passionate, perfect embrace. The panes rattled in the wind. I spent all that I had. Her cries mingled with mine. If I could have stopped time, I would have.

It took us some minutes to regain our breath.

"Did you see the King, love?" she teased.

"Nay, Kit-cat, for this is America," I answered, buttoning my breeches. "I saw the People."

M ight I end here? Truly, I am spent, Reader. And I am out of ink. A man can only do so much.

Just a few words more, and I shall close this book.

We left the Town House and walked toward the Long Wharf, while the guns at Castle George saluted the day.

"Even the cannons fire for you, Kit-cat." I winked at her.

But now she could manage no smile, though she yet held back tears.

We squeezed through the crowd and reached the dock, where we found Gulliver waiting for us. The dog has more wits than I give him credit for. 'Twas near noon; we had but moments left to us. I did not need to speak it; Fanny knew I would not board the boat to settle her. I could not.

I pressed into her palm a parting gift. A miniature, watercolor on ivory, of a pair of hands clasped together, hers and mine, set 'neath glass in a silver locket, a red velvet ribbon through a ring at the top. (Not a ribbon, exactly, but poor Gallagher's sash, which I'd cut and sewn to make twin, slender bands; one I used for my gift, the other for hers to me, for I now wore *Beauty Revealed* in an identical case, tied loose round my neck, 'neath my shirt. Next my heart, Reader. Next my heart.)

She cried as she touched it.

"So beautiful, too beautiful," she whispered, for she had all but lost her voice for the choke of her tears.

I cleared my throat.

"'Tis only to remind you that you are a terrible painter of hands, Kit-cat, and I a prodigiously talented one. Try to improve in London, will you?"

And don't forget me, lass. Dear God, don't forget me.

As she faced the boat, I stood behind her and tied the ribbon round her neck. And this was the last time I touched her, dear Reader: the tips of my fingers, next my lips, and then my tears, softly brushing the fine hairs on the nape of her lovely neck. And then only this: I nudged her forward, a little shove with my knee, into the back of hers, and though she staggered on the first step, she walked up the gangplank, sure-footed, motioning the dog to her side, turning back, incapable of speech, and able only to mouth the words, "*Six months.*"

I forced myself to watch her as the sailors loosed the moorings, and raised the anchor. I watched as the wind lofted the sails. Even as the ship inched out into the harbor, I forced myself to watch her. She stood on the stern, leaning against the gunwales, staring back at me. Only when her face became a blur, and I could no longer see her eyes, those dark and lustrous eyes, did I turn on my heel, and put one foot in front of another.

But I had not taken half a dozen steps when, suddenly, a sound made me turn back. A splash, a very loud splash, and urgent calls from the sailors on the boat. "Overboard! Overboard!"

I raced back to the end of the dock and scanned the water, desperately searching the surface for her. I stripped off my coat. No matter that I had not the least idea how to swim. I would dive in. If only I could see where.

And then I saw.

There!

Ach.

Swiftly closing the distance between the ship and the wharf, swam Gulliver. And a fine swimmer he is. He bobs and he twists and he paddles like an otter. The mangy four-footed prodigal son. The cursed cur has come back to me.

For fuck's sake, but that was cruel.

"Come, Gulliver," I snapped, as he shook himself dry on the dock. "Let's go home, you son of a butcher's bitch."

And now, dear Reader, now and at last.

Tis done.

And I am done with it.

THE END.

A WOMAN'S
PROGRESS

The Life, Art, and

Adventures of Fanny Jameson,

Face-Painter

CHAPTER I

The Beginning

You bade me write, dear Reader, dear, beloved Reader, and so I would begin at the beginning.

But who can say upon what wave of pleasure a new life begins? Tis a blind spot, for though it marks us all, we can never see it. Yet I have no doubt that you would try, Sir, given a choice in the matter. You would find that precious moment, and hold it still, within your hands, those beautiful hands, whose touch I miss already, more than I can express.

The beginning? Twas some weeks ago, I venture, though I cannot say precisely when. The middle is yet months off, just as here, now, the shore is far from view.

I stared at that shore, even after the dog had regained it, till I lost sight of you.

And then, I lost my breakfast. Over the gunwales. For though I have always been a hearty sailor, I am more seasick than ever I have seen you, my beloved.

Or, not exactly seasick. Lovesick? Certain. And more. Were I to paint a self-portrait, I would have to title it: *Love Revealed*. Upon this vast and furious ocean, I find that I am not alone after all.

AFTERWORD

Blindspot is a twenty-first century novel in eighteenth-century garb. It plays with the conventions of eighteenth-century novels, newspapers, and histories. Readers often ask us whether anything in *Blindspot* is true. The answer? Yes and no. Novels look for a different kind of truth than history books, and while *Blindspot* is fiction, it relies on our work as historians, on every page. For us, writing this book didn't involve visiting someplace new; it involved thinking differently about a place we've known for a very long time. Because we are professors of early American history and literature, we relied on our combined four decades of researching and teaching to breathe life into the look, feel, and sound of daily life in eighteenth-century Boston.

We relied on documents, too—on everyday traces of the past. Much that happens in the novel is based on actual events and adapted from archival evidence chronicling both ordinary life and extraordinary transformations: the American Revolution; the Enlightenment; the eighteenth century's bawdiness, its anticlericalism, its obsessions with wit and sham and rank and pleasure. A few of *Blindspot*'s characters were inspired by real people; many of its buildings are based on edifices that still stand; its portraits resemble paintings that now hang on the walls of museums. A sizable number of very short passages in the text are taken nearly verbatim from eighteenth-century letters, newspapers, account books, diaries, sermons, novels, poems, riddles, philosophical treatises, and legal records. For example, *Blindspot*'s very first page, a runaway ad from a Scottish newspaper, is a composite of ads from eighteenth-century papers. The ad Jameson places in Edes's Boston *Gazette,* searching for "a likely lad of promising genius," comes from a notice placed in a Boston newspaper in 1723 by Benjamin Franklin's brother, who had to look for a new apprentice after Benjamin ran away. When Fanny tells Lizzie that her schoolmistress hands "would best a needle fit," she is quoting the Puritan poet Anne Bradstreet. The rhyme on Fanny Easton's needlework sampler comes from a sampler that survives. *Blindspot* is a sampler, too, of all that we love best in the museums we have visited, the archives we have frequented, and the old newspapers and novels we have read, for years. We quoted, we borrowed, we took liberties. But we also kept faith with the past.

This Afterword offers a glimpse at some of our sources. It is by no means an exhaustive inventory. But dear Reader, be forewarned: there are spoilers here. Read the book first!

A Rogue's Gallery: The Art Behind Blindspot

Like their countrymen back in England, Scotland, and Ireland, Britons and their descendants living in the North American colonies loved portraits. A likeness taken at marriage, or to commemorate success in trade or in war, marked one's progress through life. More than that, a portrait left tracks in time, serving as a tangible, enduring emblem of ties across oceans and down the generations in an era when life was precarious and photographs didn't yet exist. In a good portrait, the eighteenth-century painter Jonathan Richardson (1665–1745) wrote, "we see the persons and faces of famous men, the originals of which are out of our reach, as being gone down with the stream of time, or in different places: and thus too we see our relations and friends, whether living or dead, as they have been in all the stages of life. In picture we never die, never decay, or grow older."

Yet theorists of art such as the English painter Sir Joshua Reynolds (1723–1792) insisted that portraits were common things: higher on the ladder of genres than still life or needlework or seashell mosaics, but decidedly lower than true Art. Reynolds (just as Jameson says in *Blindspot*) favored history painting in the grand manner of the old Italian and Flemish masters. Portraits, by contrast, smacked of flattery—and of commerce. They were copies of nature, not insightful artistic "performances." They required that an artist possess a good hand but not a noble mind. Reynolds told his students, "An History-painter paints man in general; a Portrait-painter, a particular man, and consequently a defective model." Nonetheless, patrons wanted portraits. Reynolds spent evenings robed in his academic gown, lecturing the young gentlemen of London's Royal Academy of Arts on the glories of mythology and allegory. But he spent his days taking likenesses of gentlemen and gentlewomen, their bratty children, and even their dogs.

Joshua Reynolds stood atop a very large heap of talent; prospective sitters in London had dozens of famous and talented portraitists to choose from. One art critic writing in the early 1780s said that the city was "overrun with painters, as much as with disbanded soldiers, sailors and ministers."

Not so Boston. Provincial New England had more than its fair share of out-of-work soldiers, sailors, and ministers, but artists were notably scarce. On the eve of the Revolution, the colonies could not boast a single school of art to train the hands of young painters, or a single great collection of pictures to train their eyes. Even reproductions in line engraving or mezzotint—virtually all of them imported, as were paints, canvases, brushes, pencils, gilt, and most other manufactured goods— were hard to come by. Nor was a portraitist's work steady enough to provide a dependable income. Most colonial artists were self-taught jacks of several trades. Charlestown-born Joseph Badger (1708–1765) painted houses, signs, coaches, and coats of arms as well as portraits on canvas. Charles Willson Peale (1741–1827) kept a saddler's shop while he built his business as a painter.

For all these reasons, British itinerants dominated the colonial portrait trade. Edinburgh-born John Smibert (1688–1751), the painter of *Blindspot*'s Charlotte Easton, worked in Boston for over a decade before his death. Joseph Blackburn (dates unknown) shuttled between Boston and Newport, returning to England by 1764.

The artistic traffic across the Atlantic went east as well as west. Beginning in the 1760s, ambitious young would-be artists from the colonies journeyed abroad to study and paint and, above all, to see. Some stayed for a season or two; others remained for a lifetime. Benjamin West, Charles Willson Peale, John Trumbull, Mather Brown, Matthew Pratt, Gilbert Stuart, and John Singleton Copley constituted something of an "American School" in London, as Pratt titled a 1765 painting of West's atelier.

Among the artists jockeying for pay and position in British America, Stuart (1755–1828) and Copley (1738–1815) most directly inspired many aspects of *Blindspot*'s main characters, Stewart Jameson and Frances Easton. Like our Stewart Jameson, Gilbert Stuart—the son of a Jacobite Scottish snuff-maker who emigrated to Rhode Island after the Battle of Culloden—was a noted raconteur and a chronic debtor. He was a superb portraitist, known (again like Jameson) for his ability to portray a sitter's inner life on canvas—to "counterfeit the soul," as an admiring younger painter put it.

Stuart mocked Reynolds's high-flown ideas about Art and Genius, calling history paintings "*ten-acre* pictures" crowded with "prophets and apostles." Surely "no man ever painted history if he could obtain employment in portraits," he quipped. Like *Blindspot*'s Jameson, Gilbert Stuart understood himself as a man who worked with his hands, mastering his craft. "I have a family," he told one acolyte. "I paint for bread."

John Singleton Copley, by contrast, was lit by a burning ambition. (Jameson's letter introducing Fanny to Joshua Reynolds borrows extensively from letters Copley penned in the 1760s, in which he yearned for England and for fame in roughly equal measure.) By the early 1760s, the self-taught Copley—the son of a tobacconist—had become the leading portraitist in his native Boston. But like *Blindspot*'s Fanny Easton, he fancied a bigger pond. His rise to international fame began in 1765, when he sent his portrait of his half brother, Henry Pelham, titled *Boy with a Squirrel*, to London to serve as a painted calling card for his talents.

This striking picture, along with Copley's celebration of craft in *Paul*

Revere (1768), inspired *Blindspot*'s canvas entitled *The Serving Boy,* Jameson's portrait of Weston as a boy with a dog. Both of these paintings hang in Boston's Museum of Fine Arts. Visitors to Harvard's Fogg Museum can also see Copley's portrait of *Reverend Edward Holyoke* (ca. 1759–1761), evoked in Jameson's portrait of the Harvard president.

Blindspot's Fanny Easton shares Copley's provincial birth—Boston was "a thousand leagues" from London, Copley lamented—his prodigious talent, and his dauntless ambition. But she is not lucky enough to share his sex. There were very few women painters in the English-speaking world in the eighteenth century. Privileged girls learned to draw, a polite accomplishment like playing the pianoforte and reading a smattering of French. But they were not encouraged to imagine careers at their easels. Only two female artists numbered among the founding members of London's Royal Academy; neither was primarily a portraitist. Sitting for one's portrait was considered an intimate, even erotically charged encounter—a "dangerous employment," as the essayist William Hazlitt wrote. Staring deeply into his subject's eyes, the painter, Hazlitt mused, could soon "slide into the lover." In the eighteenth-century mind, the painter—*the looker*—was male, and the object of his gaze, female. This was why Samuel Johnson found "publick practice of any art . . . and staring in men's faces" to be "very indelicate in a female." Johnson had experienced this "indelicate" situation firsthand, when he sat for a portrait by Fanny Reynolds, the talented, thwarted, spinster sister of Sir Joshua, whose fate Fanny Easton strives mightily to avoid.

By the early nineteenth century, American cities played host to a number of women artists eking out a modest living by sketching likenesses in pastel, or cutting silhouettes, or painting miniatures. An extraordinary object painted by one of them, Sarah Goodridge, served as the model for what may seem the most implausible painting in *Blindspot*. Fanny's gift to Jameson, which she calls *Beauty Revealed,* was inspired by Goodridge's breathtaking 1828 miniature, watercolor on ivory, also titled *Beauty Revealed,* a gift to United States senator, presidential aspirant, and famed orator Daniel Webster, whom we can only assume was her lover. It is part of the Gloria Manney Collection at the Metropolitan Museum of Art.

Blindspot is a love story and a murder mystery, but behind both those plots is the narrative that's usually at the foreground of American history: the coming of the American Revolution. We kept the Revolution in the background because, at least in 1764, that's where it was for most Bostonians. The story of the Sons of Liberty is stirring stuff, but it's a twice-told tale. We wanted to tell the story of ordinary people. Their struggles—against arbitrary authority, against Parliament, and, for many, against African slavery—seized Boston in the 1760s.

The colonial response to Parliament's passage of the 1764 Sugar and Currency acts is the best-known piece of the political history *Blindspot* relates. We have reproduced the text of those laws, and of the colonists' protests against them, making only very minor changes based on the need for clarity and the demands of our plot. As for the actual *Boston Gazette,* the instrument of the resistance movement, it was printed, once a week, by John Gill and Benjamin Edes at their printing office on Queen Street. Our Edes, along with a few other real people whose names we have borrowed, including Edward Holyoke, Francis Bernard, and Joshua Reynolds, is a fiction, although we have leaned heavily on the writings of each of these people in our portrayals of them.

We have in some cases tinkered with time and place. The Sugar and Currency acts actually went into effect on September 24, 1764—known as the Black Day—not, as in our novel, on October 8 of that year. More importantly, Governor Francis Bernard didn't call in troops until 1768, when they not only occupied the Town House and pitched camp on the Common but besieged the Manufactory House, where *Blindspot'*s Fanny toiled in misery. And, while someone really did cut a hole in the shape of a heart out of a portrait of Bernard (painted, of course, not by the fictional Stewart Jameson but by John Singleton Copley), that happened in 1769, and not at the Town House, but in Harvard Hall, in Cambridge. Nearly all the discussion of this event, including our remarks about it in the *Boston Gazette,* is taken from items written by the actual Benjamin Edes, who was known as the "trumpeter of sedition" for his zealous advocacy of the patriot cause. (Edes's masthead really was engraved by Paul Revere.)

Many of Edes's acerbic attacks on Bernard we took from the newspaper. For instance, it was Edes who wrote, "The printer has been informed of an astonishing feat of Nature: an ewe in Roxbury gave birth last week to four lambs. As an increase in our sheep will prevent our importing British wool, we may query whether Governor Bernard will not inform the King of this instance of fecundity, and earnestly recommend another regiment of soldiers being sent, in order to have our rams castrated." When the Stamp Act was passed in 1765, Edes refused to buy stamps, draped his *Gazette* in black mourning ink, and, at John Adams's suggestion, changed the paper's motto to "A free press maintains the majesty of the people." When the British seized Boston in 1775, Edes narrowly escaped, under cover of darkness. He carted his printing press and types to the Charles River, rowed them to Watertown, and, just weeks later, in a makeshift printing shop there, he started printing the *Gazette* again.

Edes was one of Boston's Sons of Liberty, a group formed in 1765 in response to the Stamp Act (not, as in our novel, a year before). We invented the Red Hens, but London's Kit-Cat Club did exist, and similar gentlemen's clubs were a familiar feature of eighteenth-century Anglo-American life, in Boston as anywhere. Most involved secret rites and ceremonies, including toasts, feasting, parades, mock trials, casual sexual banter, pranks that often went too far (one initiation ceremony in Philadelphia famously led to an apprentice's accidental death by burning), and lots and lots of drinking, as is most hilariously chronicled in Dr. Alexander Hamilton's "History of the Ancient and Honorable Tuesday Club," written in 1745. As the colonial resistance intensified, some of these clubs became political organizations.

Meanwhile, slavery was much on the mind of Bostonians in the 1760s. Not only did British colonists complain that Parliament, by taxing them, had made them "slaves," they were also debating, avidly, whether to abolish slavery themselves. That American revolutionaries failed to abolish slavery historians like Edmund Morgan have called "the central paradox of American history." In 1765 a town meeting in Worcester, Massachusetts, instructed its delegates to the legislature to propose a law prohibiting the importation and purchase of slaves by any Massachusetts citizen. On May 26, 1766, just one week after news of Parliament's repeal of the Stamp Act arrived, Boston's town meeting urged its members to consider voting "for the total abolishing of slavery from among us." In 1767, Boston merchant Nathaniel Appleton argued in *Considerations on Slavery*, "The years 1765 and 1766 will be ever memorable for the glorious stand which America has made for her liberties; how much glory will it add . . . if at the same time we are establishing Liberty for ourselves and children, we show the same regard to all mankind that came among us?"

Our murder victim, Samuel Bradstreet, was inspired by the leader of the colonial opposition, the brilliant Boston lawyer and orator James Otis, Jr. (1725–1783), called, by John Adams, "a flame of fire." Otis, who wrote, "Taxation without representation is tyranny," also argued eloquently for an end to the slave trade, a proposal that was the subject of vigorous debate in Boston in the 1760s (though it wasn't brought before the legislature until 1771, when it was vetoed). In spring of 1770, in the days and weeks following the Boston Massacre, the Massachusetts legislature again debated abolishing the slave trade. In a sermon delivered before the legislature in May, the Reverend Samuel Cooke, John Hancock's uncle, warned legislators, "Let not sordid gain, acquired by the merchandize of slaves, and the souls of men, harden our hearts against her piteous moans. When God ariseth, and when he visiteth, what shall we answer!"

James Otis was not murdered, but he did go mad in 1770. After thirteen years of lunacy, he died in 1783 when he was struck by lightning. Bradstreet's *Rights of the British Colonies Demonstrated* as quoted in *Blindspot* is a lightly edited version of Otis's stunning 1764 treatise, *Rights of the British Colonies Asserted and Proved*. Edward Easton's political writings are a composite of Tory sentiment; his letter in the *Boston Gazette*, under the pseudonym "Mast of Fidelity," using Romans 13:7 ("Render therefore to all their dues: tribute to whom tribute . . ."), turns upside down a sermon actually preached by the Bostonian Jonathan Mayhew in 1750, "A Discourse Concerning Unlimited Submission."

Ignatius Alexander may strike some readers as the most implausible character in the book—surely he is too educated, too refined, too modern—but our portrayal of him is very closely based in fact. Several Africans in Europe and America joined the literary and scientific circles of their day. Alexander, had he lived, would have known the African-born poet Phillis Wheatley (1753–1784), who was brought to Boston as a slave in 1761 and began publishing poems six years later; she eventually became an international celebrity. Alexander is more specifically inspired by two black protégés of the Duke of Montague, whom Montague had educated as part of his enlightenment experiments on racial difference: Ignatius Sancho (1729–1780), an African writer and composer who was raised in England and painted by Gainsborough; and Francis Williams (1702–1770), a Jamaican-born poet and mathematician who was educated in England and eventually returned to Jamaica, where he was painted by a local artist. Sancho's letters, including his correspondence with Laurence Sterne, were published in 1782 as *The Letters of the Late Ignatius Sancho, an African*. Sancho's portrait is owned by the National Gallery of Canada; Williams's hangs in London's Victoria and Albert Museum.

The events surrounding the trial of Cicero and Hannah were inspired by the real-life trial of Mark and Phillis, two slaves who were convicted in 1755 of poisoning their master, Captain John Codman, of Charlestown, Massachusetts, with arsenic. Both Mark and Phillis were found guilty, after which Mark was hanged and gibbeted and Phillis was burned at the stake, in Cambridge. Mark's rotting bones were left on display for decades. In 1775, when Paul Revere made his famous ride to tell everyone the British were coming, he made note that he rode past Mark's bones, still hanging. Some of the testimony in our trial of Cicero and Hannah borrows from the trial of Mark and Phillis, while parts of it were inspired by the abundant court records pertaining to the 1741 investigation of the "Great Negro Plot" in New York City, in which that city's slaves allegedly conspired to burn the town and kill their masters. The sermon given by the fictional Jabez Appleton at Cicero's execution is based on Cotton Mather's *Tremenda*, which he delivered on the occasion of another execution of a slave convicted of murder, and which was published in Boston in 1721.

Harvard, too, was caught up both in the early stirrings of the Revolution and also in the debate about slavery. In 1759, the question during the commencement debate really was (as it is in *Blindspot*) "Is an Absolute and Arbitrary Monarchy Contrary to Right Reason?" In 1764, Harvard Hall burned down, and the college's president, Edward Holyoke, raised money to rebuild it by taking out an ad in the *Boston Gazette*. Governor Francis Bernard really did design the new Harvard Hall, although he did not live in Cambridge. In *Blindspot*, Alexander, while in Cambridge, meets Titus, who in our novel is Holyoke's slave.

Titus was actually the name of a slave owned by Harvard's President Benjamin Wadsworth. John Hancock, while a student at Harvard in the 1750s, had been involved in "being most remarkably active in making drunk" a black man "to Such a Degree as greatly indanger'd his Life." In 1765, Elbridge Gerry argued the affirmative in the commencement debate, "Can the new Prohibitory Duties, which make it useless for People to engage in Commerce, be evaded by them as Faithful Subjects?" In 1766, Harvard students staged the famous Butter Rebellion—protesting rancid butter served at commons—in imitation of the Stamp Act protests. In 1773, the Harvard Speaking Club held a debate, "A Forensic Dispute on the Legality of Enslaving the Africans."

Finally, the legal and public records that appear between Jameson's chapters and Fanny's letters are, in most cases, adapted versions of actual documents (generally taken from Boston in the 1760s and involving, of course, real people, whose names we've changed). This includes, for instance, the indenture agreement, runaway ads, the coroner's report, arrest warrants, and the notice of the auction of Bradstreet's goods.

On the Spot: A Tour of Eighteenth-Century Boston

When *Blindspot*'s Stewart Jameson first glimpses the "thicket of steeples" marking the skyline of Boston, the town feels to him a small, prim, provincial port on the far western edge of the English-speaking world.

Small it was. The Puritans' would-be "City on a Hill" occupied a clover-shaped peninsula less than two miles long and at most a mile across. In the mid-eighteenth century, much of the land remained unsettled; the three peaks that dominated the town's west side—Beacon Hill, Pemberton Hill, and Mount Whoredom, the colonists called them—pushed Bostonians toward the eastern half of the isthmus, where they built a maze of streets nearly as crooked and narrow as cow paths. Most buildings were made of wooden clapboard, many of them but one story tall. Fire was a constant threat. Six "Great Fires" leveled whole quarters of the fragile town before 1700. The eighteenth century witnessed sixteen major blazes, including the one whose ruins Jameson spies on Cornhill in 1764 and the one that destroyed Harvard Hall, in Cambridge, that same year. Jameson's Boston housed roughly sixteen thousand people: less than a third of the population of his native Edinburgh and a bare fraction of that of London, which teemed with nearly three quarters of a million souls by the mid-eighteenth century. The first truly urban place in British North America—a dynamic commercial center as far back as the mid-1600s—Boston as Jameson found it had grown economically and demographically stagnant. New York and Philadelphia boomed; Boston's wealth and population stood much where they had a generation before, and much where they would remain a generation later.

Yet in other ways, Boston led the colonies and, indeed, Britain's empire. Most Bostonians, like the people of New England more broadly, were "middling" sorts: neither very rich nor very poor. They owned property more widely, and exercised their voting rights more vigorously, than the denizens of virtually anyplace else in the English-speaking world. They experimented with money and paper credit. And they defended what they understood as "British liberty" with zeal when the King and Parliament threatened to usurp it. In many ways, Boston earned the nickname its denizens gave it: cradle of the American Revolution.

To reconstruct the lanes and byways of eighteenth-century Boston in *Blindspot*, we relied extensively on John Bonner's map, *A New Plan of ye Great Town of Boston in New England in America* (first printed in 1722 and regularly updated thereafter), and Henry Pelham's *Plan of Boston in New England with its Environs, 1775 and 1776*, as well as on other maps, travel narratives, and public records. Some of the buildings in the novel still stand, and many of the sites described in the novel can be visited. The Town House is now called the Old State House and sits on State Street (known as King Street until the Revolution). The Long Wharf, Copp's Hill, the Old South Meeting House, King's Chapel, Boston Common, the Old North Church, the Granary Burying Ground (where James Otis is buried), and Faneuil Hall are all stops on Boston's Freedom Trail.

Jameson's lodgings were inspired by the Pierce/Hichborn House, owned by the Paul Revere Memorial Association and right next door to the Paul Revere House on Boston's North Square, just behind Hanover Street. Edward Easton's house is loosely based on the first Harrison Gray Otis House, on Cambridge Street in Boston, designed by architect Charles Bulfinch and completed in 1795. It is now owned by Historic New England and operated as a museum. Governor Bernard's house was

John Bonner, *A New Plan of ye Great Town of Boston in New England in America* (176•

AMERICA

Bartons Point.

Charles River

Ferry to Charles-Town

Mill Pond.

Eln Mill Dam

HARBOUR

Fort Hill

S. Battery.

Long Wharf

Old Wharf

inspired by the Hooper-Lee-Nichols House on Brattle Street in Cambridge, originally built in the late seventeenth century and greatly enlarged in the mid-eighteenth. The Cambridge Historical Society now owns the house, which is open to the public. Only two of the buildings standing in Harvard Yard in 1764 survive today: Holden Chapel and Massachusetts Hall.

An Ocean of Words: The Literature of Blindspot

The novel as a literary form was invented in the eighteenth century, and it was inextricably bound up with the art of writing history. Early novels, like Daniel Defoe's 1719 *Life and Adventures of Robinson Crusoe* (a fake journal kept by a castaway), borrowed from the conventions of historical writing, even passing themselves off as historical documents—especially journals and letterbooks, the forms we use in *Blindspot*. Many eighteenth-century English and American novels, like Henry Fielding's 1749 *History of Tom Jones, a Foundling*, unabashedly called themselves "histories" and boasted, on their title pages, that they were "Founded in Fact." Defoe even went so far as to insist that he was merely the editor of Crusoe's journal: "The Editor believes the thing to be a just History of Fact; neither is there any Appearance of Fiction in it."

Blindspot both plays with these conventions and takes its narrative sensibility from them. Our novel is two novels—or two sets of fake documents—in one: Jameson's picaresque and Fanny's letterbook. *A Painter's Eye: The Life, Art and Adventures of Stewart Jameson* is much influenced by Laurence Sterne's *The Life and Opinions of Tristram Shandy, Gentleman*, published beginning in 1759. Jameson's rambling digressions (known, in the eighteenth century, as "Shandyisms"), his winks at his reader, and his weakness for bawdy humor: these come from Shandy, as well as from Fielding's comic novels, especially *Joseph Andrews* and *Tom Jones*. Fanny Easton's letterbook has more in common with sentimental novels, often written in the form of letters, like Samuel Richardson's 1748 epistolary novel, *Clarissa*, and the American Susanna Rowson's 1791 *Charlotte Temple*. Fanny has also clearly read Daniel Defoe's novel of a prostitute, *Moll Flanders* (1722), and the erotic novel *Fanny Hill; or, Memoirs of a Woman of Pleasure*, written by John Cleland—from debtor's prison—in 1748. By the end of our story, she has become intrigued with

Charlotte Lennox's *The Female Quixote*, published in 1752, a kind of gender-bending crossover, in which a woman writes a narrative of her life, adventures, and opinions. *Blindspot*, in short, is both a fake eighteenth-century novel and a modern send-up of a long-dead genre.

Blindspot's play with genre is bounded by certain historical constraints. For instance, the work widely considered the first gothic novel, Horace Walpole's *Castle of Otranto*, wasn't published until 1764. Though we tossed some gothic elements into *Blindspot*, we therefore didn't include many. Detective fiction hadn't been invented, either. Eighteenth-century crimes didn't have detectives; they had judges and juries and, above all, confessions. With the exception of Henry Fielding and his brother John, who set up a kind of sleuthing shop in London in the 1750s, criminal investigation is a nineteenth-century development, as is detective fiction, which was born with Edgar Allan Poe's 1841 "Murders in the Rue Morgue." But eighteenth-century novels are riddled with proverbs, puns, and all sorts of wordplay. We put that same stuff in *Blindspot*. Some of it we borrowed; some of it we made up. "The Collier's Daughter" is taken from *The Musical Miscellany*, printed in London in 1729 (though, as Jameson admits, we have altered it a little). Several of the riddles (Spectacle, Sun, Eye, Looking Glass, Husband, The Painter's Son), we took or adapted from two eighteenth-century riddle books: *The Child's New Play-thing*, printed in Boston in 1750, and *The Big Puzzling-cap*, printed in Worcester in 1786. Jameson's love of proverbs is influenced by Benjamin Franklin's *Poor Richard's Almanack*, which Franklin printed in Philadelphia from 1732 to 1758, although Jameson's proverbs are not Poor Richard's.

In *Blindspot*, Jameson reads promiscuously, everything from sentimental novels to Shakespeare. The distinction between highbrow and lowbrow was different in the eighteenth century. Books and newspapers mattered to everyone, to one degree or another. The Enlightenment was, in may ways, a celebration of the printed word, and *Blindspot* is, too. It's chock-a-block with books; we hope readers will be inspired to go dig them out of the library. Where we identify books and authors, we have generally referred to actual texts, including: Henry Fielding's *Female Husband*, 1746; Cicero's oration on friendship from 44 B.C.; John Bunyan's *Pilgrim's Progress*, 1678–1684; Samuel Sewall's *Selling of Joseph*, 1700; Elihu Coleman's *Testimony Against That Anti-Christian Practice of Making*

Slaves of Men, 1733; John Woolman's *Some Considerations on the Keeping of Negroes*, 1754; David Hume's 1748 *Enquiry Concerning Human Understanding* and his 1739–40 *Treatise on Human Nature;* and Adam Smith's 1759 *Theory of Moral Sentiments*. (Smith's *Wealth of Nations* was not published until 1776, though we nod to it anyway.) Where we quote from actual texts, we have done so accurately, with some small exceptions— usually elisions for readability.

Some books mentioned in *Blindspot,* however, are entirely our invention, including Colin Jameson's *Religious and Moral Considerations upon Philosophical Reflections on the Keeping of Negroes* and Thomas Newcombe's *History of New England,* though these are inspired by the writings of John Newton and Thomas Hutchinson. As mentioned above, our political pamphlet, Samuel Bradstreet's *Rights of the British Colonies Demonstrated,* is based on an actual book, written by Speaker of the Massachusetts Assembly James Otis, Jr., and published in Boston in 1764 as *Rights of the British Colonies Asserted and Proved.* Otis's treatise, however, was not expurgated, as our novel suggests. The passages he wrote damning slavery appeared in print in 1764 and not, as in *Blindspot,* in a book we made up, Bradstreet's *Modest Inquiry into the Iniquity of Slavery.*

Filling *Blindspot* with literary allusions is one way we tried to anchor our readers in the eighteenth century's swirling ocean of words, and to hold close to the period's idiom and its spirit. Our characters make frequent references to their favorite books, as when Jameson, a Chaucer lover, asks, "Is the parson to offer no tale at all?" or when Fanny wonders whether she must play Moll Flanders to Lizzie's Pamela. Edes's "Modest Proposal" is in imitation of Jonathan Swift's 1729 satire. When Jameson says to Weston, "You are a right Shamela, a damned, impudent, cursed, confounded Jade, and I have a great mind to kick your arse," he is paraphrasing Henry Fielding's 1741 parody, *Shamela.* We mined eighteenth-century prose for words like "by-blow," "bloody-back," "clawbaw," "fecklaw," "grub-grime," "lathey-made," "scumble," "slip-slop," and "suckbribe." We also quoted liberally from British and American literature to help establish an eighteenth-century idiom. And yet the language of *Blindspot* is not really an eighteenth-century vernacular at all. We've aimed throughout to create a simulacrum of the sound of Revolutionary America and Georgian England that's plausible to the twenty-first century ear and readable by modern-day readers.

We have loved this world, the passion of the Revolution, the brilliance of the Enlightenment, the playfulness of the eighteenth century's prose, and the ambition of its portraits. We wrote *Blindspot* to bring that world to life, on the page. And if, Dear Reader, you should ask again, is *Blindspot* fiction or history, we should answer thusly: Pray, take this book as you please, for your pleasure has ever been the chief concern of your most grateful

—Authors,
Cambridge, 2009

P.S. Alas! One Thing More! We dare not put down our pens without marking in our ledger our obligation to the Muses Adrianna Alty, Elise Broach, Leah Price, Rachel Seidman, and Cindy Spiegel, as well as our incalculable debt to two particular readers . . .

Professor John Demos: To you, Sir, it is owing that this book was ever begun.
Mistress Tina Bennett: To you, Madam, it is owing that it was ever done.

FURTHER READING

A brief bibliography of some helpful introductions to eighteenth-century Anglo-American literary, political, urban, and art history, and a few primary sources, too.

Bailyn, Bernard. *The Ordeal of Thomas Hutchinson.* Cambridge, Mass., 1974.

Berlin, Ira. *Many Thousands Gone: The First Two Centuries of Slavery in North America.* Cambridge, Mass., 1998.

Brewer, John. *The Pleasures of the Imagination: English Culture in the Eighteenth Century.* New York, 1997.

Bridenbaugh, Carl. *Cities in Revolt: Urban Life in America, 1743–1776.* New York, 1955.

Brown, Vincent. *The Reaper's Garden: Death and Power in the World of Atlantic Slavery.* Cambridge, Mass., 2008.

Carretta, Vincent. *Equiano, the African: Biography of a Self-made Man.* Athens, Ga., 2005.

Copley, John Singleton. *Letters & Papers of John Singleton Copley and Henry Pelham, 1739–1776.* New York, 1970.

Craven, Wayne. *Colonial American Portraiture: The Economic, Religious, Social, Cultural, Philosophical, Scientific, and Aesthetic Foundations.* New York, 1986.

Davidson, Cathy N. *Revolution and the Word: The Rise of the Novel in America.* Rev. ed. New York, 2004.

Goodell, Abner Cheney, Jr. *The Trial and Execution for Petit Treason, of Mark and Phillis, Slaves of Capt. John Codman.* Cambridge, Mass., 1883.

Hamilton, Alexander. *Gentleman's Progress; The Itinerarium of Dr. Alexander Hamilton, 1744.* Ed. Carl Bridenbaugh. Chapel Hill, N.C., 1948.

Hochschild, Adam. *Bury the Chains: Prophets and Rebels in the Fight to Free an Empire's Slaves.* Boston, 2005.

Kamensky, Jane. *The Exchange Artist: A Tale of High-flying Speculation and America's First Banking Collapse.* New York, 2008.

Lepore, Jill. "Just the Facts, Ma'am," *The New Yorker,* March 24, 2008.

———. *New York Burning: Liberty, Slavery, and Conspiracy in Eighteenth-Century Manhattan.* New York, 2005.

Lovell, Margaretta M. *Art in a Season of Revolution: Painters, Artisans, and Patrons in Early America.* Philadelphia, 2005.

Miles, Ellen G., et al. *American Paintings of the Eighteenth Century.* Washington, D.C., and New York, 1995.

Morgan, Edmund S., and Helen M. Morgan. *The Stamp Act Crisis: Prologue to Revolution.* Chapel Hill, N.C., 1953.

Nash, Gary B. *The Urban Crucible: The Northern Seaports and the Origins of the American Revolution.* Cambridge, Mass., 1986.

Pointon, Marcia R. *Hanging the Head: Portraiture and Social Formation in Eighteenth-Century England.* New Haven, 1993.

Porter, Roy. *London: A Social History.* London, 1994.

Prown, Jules David. *John Singleton Copley.* 2 vols. Cambridge, Mass., 1966.

Reynolds, Joshua. *Discourses on Art.* Ed. Robert R. Wark. New Haven, 1975.

Sancho, Ignatius. *Letters of the Late Ignatius Sancho, an African.* Ed. Vincent Carretta. New York, 1998.

Uglow, Jenny. *Hogarth: A Life and a World.* London, 1997.

Watt, Ian P. *The Rise of the Novel: Studies in Defoe, Richardson and Fielding.* Berkeley, Ca., 1957.

Whitehill, Walter Muir, and Lawrence W. Kennedy. *Boston: A Topographical History.* Cambridge, Mass., 2000.

Young, Alfred F. *The Shoemaker and the Tea Party: Memory and the American Revolution.* Boston, 1999.

Blindspot

Jane Kamensky and Jill Lepore

A READER'S GUIDE

A Conversation with Jane Kamensky and Jill Lepore

Random House Readers Circle: In eighteenth-century fashion, *Blindspot* is chiefly comprised of letters and chapters written by the two main protagonists, Fanny Easton and Stewart Jameson. Did one of you write Easton's voice and the other Jameson's?

Jill Lepore: There are two of us; we have very different voices; there had to be two narrators. Otherwise, the novel would have been a mish-mash. Not to mention that I really am a witless, blustering Scotsman who curses like a sailor and drinks like a fish. So, yes: I wrote Stewart Jameson's picaresque; Jane wrote Fanny Easton's epistolary. We wrote by turns, in weekly installments, the way people used to read serial fiction. I'd write one of Jameson's chapters, email it to Jane, and wait, frantic with impatience, for Fanny's next letter to show up in my inbox. But then we edited each other and edited the whole thing together, and, in the end, it's his, hers, and ours.

RHRC: What truths did writing a novel allow you to explore that writing a history wouldn't?

Jane Kamensky: *Blindspot* pays more attention to sensory truths than most history writing does. A convincing fictional world needs the truths of the flesh, ear, nose, and eye more than the truths of the archive; what Boston looked, smelled, sounded, and tasted like in the sweltering summer of 1764; how frail bodies experienced the vicissitudes of everyday life as well as the demands of epochal events—those are the humble truths that drive the novel forward.

Writing *Blindspot,* and especially choosing to write it in the first person, also gave us a freer hand with consciousness than we have as historians. Our characters take stock of their world, but they also scrutinize themselves, unsparingly. Few eighteenth-century men, and almost no eighteenth-century women, left documentary evidence of their interior lives. And the farther down the ladder of society one climbs, the scantier that evidence gets.

RHRC: *Blindspot* seems to be partly a hilarious send-up of eighteenth-century novels and partly a very serious and historically accurate rendering of life during that time period. Did you feel any tension between those two aspects of the novel?

JL: I'm a sucker for eighteenth-century fiction. I love its artfulness and its silliness and its bawdiness. I laugh when Fielding wants me to laugh. I cry when Richardson wants me to cry. And when Franklin tells a dirty joke, he's totally got me, no matter how many times I've read it before. I also laugh, always, at Jane's jokes. That's why writing the book was, above all, fun. But we do, of course, have scholarly claims to make about the period. Jane's work on money and exchange, for instance, is all over the book, as is my work on liberty and slavery. Was there a tension between trying to write an entertaining novel and wanting to write fiction with something we might think of as historical honesty? Absolutely. Deciding not to have our convicted murderer burned at the stake—as was the punishment in the actual case on which our murder is based—was a decision we made about what the emotional range of the novel could bear and what it could not. The lives of ordinary people in Boston in the 1760s weren't uniformly a farce or uniformly a tragedy, either. That's why the book's a genre send-up: a mystery, with traces of the gothic; a love story, with an overwrought romantic sensibility;

a picaresque, somewhat overblown. That's all part of *Blindspot*'s gambit, to use the literary forms of the age to tell the story of the coming of the American Revolution.

RHRC: Did you conceive of *Blindspot* as an explicitly feminist project? There's some role-playing with gender, and Fanny is a strong, bold character.

JK: We wanted a set of questions about gender and genre that were true to the way we think about the past but also true to the past. So quite a lot of how Fanny questioned the boundaries of a woman's life could also be found by reading eighteenth-century letters. Masquerade was a key element of eighteenth-century urban culture—for men more than for women—but there were women who dressed as men and fought in the Revolutionary War. And certainly the Enlightenment broadly and the American Revolution particularly opened questions about who gets to be what, questions that remain the unresolved work of American democracy. Fanny's questioning of a woman's place is very much a part of that eighteenth-century project. I think she comes to somewhat bolder answers than most women of the time would have dared.

RHRC: What were the complications of writing, now, about race, then?

JL: If we weren't historians, we might have handled the subject of race differently. We wanted our two narrators to be people of their time and place, but even the most enlightened eighteenth-century Europeans and Americans are hard for modern readers to bear on the subject of race. We couldn't afford, and didn't want, unsympathetic narrators. We decided that, rather than tiptoeing around this problem, we'd brazen through it: we gave Fanny a backstory that, we hoped, made it plausible that she could change her mind about some things, and we made Jameson about as enlightened as he conceivably could have been. Nevertheless, they are, if not unsympathetic narrators, unreliable ones; they barely see Cicero and Hannah and Phebe, whose motives they are helpless to understand and to which they are, despite their protestations to the contrary, indifferent. It was painful to do that, to write that blindness into our narrators. That's why Ignatius Alexander is forever reminding the reader about our narrators' blind spots. "You remember Hannah, Jamie?" Alexander asks, when Jameson has clearly forgotten all about her. Alexander bridles at this sorry task, as he ought, but we wanted him to have his say, and to convince the reader of the inadequacy of eighteenth-century fictional forms to contain the grim and manifold evils of slavery.

RHRC: News clippings and arguments about, say, sugar taxes are interspersed throughout the novel. Did anything surprise you in your research of old pamphlets and papers?

JK: The two of us have been reading and teaching and writing about those old pamphlets and papers for decades. But *Blindspot* asked us to encounter familiar sources in new ways. Take the *Boston Gazette,* from whose pages we freely adapted a number of news items, and into which we inserted letters, editorials, and advertisements of our own devising. As scholars, we tend to read those newspapers in disembodied ways, scanning reels of microfilm for particular names or topics. The digital age has thinned out the experience still further; you input search terms and receive your "hits" in little boxes. For *Blindspot,* we wanted to read the paper the way Stewart Jameson and his friends read the paper: to page through it, to pore over it, to pass it back and forth at the post office and by the fireside. So we printed out the entire run of the *Boston Gazette* for 1764, broadsheet size, and had it bound. Reading it in that format just knocked us out. The proxemics of the past came through so vividly: highfalutin debates over imperial taxation set beside a notice hawking a young Negro boy on the cheap, reports of battles in Europe laid out next to an advertisement seeking a full breast of milk for an infant whose mother has died. The relationship between figure and background came clearer than in any of the times I've read that paper, and others, in bits and pieces of my own devising.

RHRC: Have you used novels in your history courses? Did writing the book give you new perspectives on the relationships between literary writing and other forms of historical evidence?

JK: I've used period fiction as an integral part of courses on early American history and culture. *Charlotte Temple* is the text I've assigned most often, and Fanny Easton's voice—and plight—owes a great deal to Susanna Rowson's woebegone Charlotte. I've sometimes used contemporary novels set in the past as well, especially Brian Moore's *Black Robe,* which is based quite closely on the Jesuit Relations. I ask students to read the seventeenth-century documents alongside the novelist's version and to think about what Moore borrowed, what he changed, and why. I also teach a course on the Salem witch trials, where we look at several centuries of representations of 1692 in various genres and media. Arthur Miller's *Crucible* is a key text in that class. Its concerns are purely contemporary, the zeitgeist of 1953 rather than that of 1692. But the voices are marvelous, an unparalleled example of a modern sensibility let loose on a foreign vernacular. Scholars of visual culture have been, of late, concerned with recovering the "period eye" of a given place and time. Miller speaks to what we might call the period ear. That was one of our goals for the novel: to communicate to a new set of readers something of the music of our work in the archives. Fiction may offer us different avenues—more palpable or visceral paths—for doing that sort of work.

RHRC: What are some common misconceptions about Revolutionary America that you hope *Blindspot* will dispel?

JL: I'm not sure the point of the novel is to dispel misconceptions, but I do worry about our culture's abject reverence for the founding fathers. I hear people say, all the time, "Oh, those leaders were so much more virtuous than ours! Oh, what an age that was!" Yes, the Constitution is altogether brilliant, and sure, I love Franklin. But to imagine that the United States was founded by people wholly unlike ourselves is to let us completely off the hook. To imagine that the founding fathers were gods doesn't demand more of our democracy, it demands less: compared to absurdly inflated founders, we are so hopelessly deficient, so utterly lacking in virtue that, well, why bother working at making anything better, ever? Reverence is the flip side of cynicism. And I find cynicism insidious, so in *Blindspot* there's a great deal of goofy irreverence because, in fact, the Revolution was nothing if not irreverent. The novel's irreverence, though, is also meant to suggest that ordinary people weren't sitting around, worshipping at the feet of John Adams, just because he had made a great speech in the Assembly Hall. They still wanted him to return that ten pounds he had borrowed a fortnight ago; they still wondered if he might be willing to lend them a copy of *Tristram Shandy*. "Surpassingly fine speech, Mr. Adams, sir," Jameson might say. "And now, pray: about that book . . ."

(Parts of this interview originally appeared in an interview by Lauren Porcaro on Newyorker.com.)

Reading Group Questions and Topics
for Discussion

1. Discuss the motifs of blindness and seeing in the novel. Why do you think Jane Kamensky and Jill Lepore chose *Blindspot* as the novel's title? What types of blind spots do the characters in the novel experience?

2. Jameson's and Fanny's narratives are quite different from each other. What are the stylistic differences between them? What aspects of Jameson's and Fanny's roles and experiences account for those differences? Do their styles of writing remind you of other novels you've read?

3. *Blindspot* is meant to be read as if it were written in Boston in 1764. How do the authors signal the language, values, and feel of that place in time? What role do the excerpts from the *Boston Gazette*, many of them loosely adapted from the actual newspaper, play in setting the mood and advancing the story? Why do you think the authors chose to tell the story with both fictional elements and historical documents?

4. Not long after landing in Boston, Jameson points out an irony inherent in the colonists' desire for freedom: "Ably do they see the shackles Parlia-

ment fastens about them, but to the fetters they clasp upon others, they are strangely blind" (p. 26). What do you think of his statement? How does the novel address issues of liberty and slavery?

5.   Jameson often addresses his "dear Reader" directly. Who do Jameson and Fanny assume their respective readers to be? How do their assumptions about their audience affect the ways they tell their stories?

6.   In her letters to her childhood friend Elizabeth, Fanny Easton bemoans the limits placed upon female education and ambition. What constraints shaped Fanny's life as a woman, and does she successfully escape them by posing as Francis Weston? How different were the expectations governing American women's lives in the eighteenth century from those in our own day? What can Jameson do that Fanny can't?

7.   *Blindspot* is rife with riddles, puns, and wordplay. Jameson's speech is filled with bawdy puns, and Fanny enjoys entertaining him with riddles. In fact, the solution to the book's mystery is found in the pages of a book of puzzles. Discuss the role of puzzles in the novel.

8.   Although Jameson is technically Francis Weston's superior, he often feels controlled by his apprentice: "Are you so blind you cannot see that *you* are master?" he implores Francis. Discuss the various master/slave relationships in the novel. How do they develop as the novel progresses? Did Kamensky and Lepore complicate your previous notions of this relationship?

9.   Why do you think the authors chose to make the main characters of *Blindspot* artists? What kinds of connections do the authors draw between Jameson's paintings and the patriot politics of the Friends of Liberty? Is Jameson's art itself revolutionary?

10.   Although the character of Ignatius Alexander—an erudite and refined African who has been educated as an experiment—may seem surprising, Kamensky and Lepore's portrayal of him is actually very closely based in fact. Discuss his function in the novel. How well do Jamie and Fanny understand Sander's world and his vision? Why do you think the authors chose

to tell Sander's story through Jamie's and Fanny's voices, and why does the doctor resist telling his own story?

11.   Jameson seems just as attracted to Francis Weston as he is to Fanny Easton. What do the authors suggest about understandings of sexuality in eighteenth-century America? Do you think our society today is more or less tolerant than the one depicted in the novel?

12.   *Blindspot* is a historical novel, but many of the issues it addresses still feel relevant today. What kinds of similarities did you notice between the political issues addressed in the novel and the ones you think about in your own life?

13.   Did the novel support or upturn your previous sense of Revolutionary America? In which ways was it similar, and in which was it different? Did anything surprise you?

ABOUT THE AUTHORS

JANE KAMENSKY is a professor of American history and chair of the History Department at Brandeis University. Her previous books include *The Exchange Artist,* a finalist for the 2009 George Washington Book Prize, and *Governing the Tongue.* She is co-editor, with Edward G. Gray, of the forthcoming *Oxford Handbook of the American Revolution,* and is working on a book about American artists in London in the late eighteenth century. She lives in Cambridge, Massachusetts, with her husband and their two sons.

JILL LEPORE is the David Woods Kemper '41 Professor of American History at Harvard University, where she is chair of the History and Literature Program. She is also a staff writer at *The New Yorker.* Her books include *New York Burning,* winner of the Anisfield-Wolf Book Award and a finalist for the Pulitzer Prize; *A is for American;* and *The Name of War,* winner of the Bancroft Prize and the Ralph Waldo Emerson Award. She lives in Cambridge with her husband, three sons, two cats, and a very large and formidable dog of entirely mysterious extraction.